# The Raving Eunuch Monks

Thanks for resuscitating me, I guess. I was trying to kill myself.

Flynn

Visit www.amazon.com to order additional copies.

GLYNN E. THOMPSON

# THE RAVING EUNUCH MONKS

# The Raving Eunuch Monks

# TABLE OF CONTENTS

# INTRODUCTION

LUBBOCK, TEXAS
Home of the Texas Tech Red Raiders, Buddy Holly, and Jesus
Christ
December 12, 1970
2:30 A.M.

*Je's gahdamn...muth'fugin' Chris'.*

The mangled words stumbled into the man's semiconsciousness, sloshing knee deep through pools of unprocessed alcohol. A violent shudder rattled his body. He was aware of a soft, muffled crunching and the presence of a dull, white light.

The man attempted to move.

Nothing—he remained a motionless, snow covered blister on the white landscape of the alley, his mind a splatter of rapidly disconnecting half-thoughts generated by a short-circuiting brain frantically attempting to orient itself.

He was blurred. Numb.

Thirst. Agonizing thirst.

Voices.

Something brushed his face then slapped it several times.

More voices.

The man felt a pressure against the back of his head. He was grasped above the elbows then suddenly, sickeningly, pulled into a sitting position.

Mind reeling dizziness.

Two spots of light suspended in a swirling cloud of smoke stabbed his barely opened eyes. He squeezed them shut.

He was propelled upwards. Every struggling thought in his throbbing skull lost its footing.

Voices again.

The pressure under his arms increased as he was set in motion, head bobbing, trailing feet plowing the snow behind him.

The lights faded. His lids parted slightly. The side of a car floated by. A door opened.

A radio—"Teach Your Children Well".

Two strangers, faces hidden in clouds of frozen breath, placed him on the back seat of the car then lifted his snow covered boots onto the floorboard. His arms remained limp. His body slid in the direction of the muffled thud of the door, gaining momentum as it slipped over the vinyl seat cover. He came to rest against the door, head touching the window, eyes shut. A shock wave rolled through his body.

Doors opened. A gentle rocking. Two muffled thuds. The music faded to a murmur.

"Make sure he stays awake," a tired voice ordered.

"Hey!" a second voice from the front seat. "Hey, yew!" accompanied by a rapid, metallic banging on a wire mesh screen separating the front and back seats.

The man in the back seat jerked violently.

"Sit up! Sit all'a way up!"

The command didn't register—the passenger's brain still misfiring. He squinted in the direction of the voice.

"Sit up! Now, dammit! Righ' now!"

The passenger slowly, painfully struggled into an upright position.

"Don'ch ya go ta sleep back there an' ya damn sure better not puke. Un'erstan' me, boy?"

No response.

"Yew un'erstan' whud I'm tellin' ya?" the voice louder, the screen slamming more violent.

The passenger shut his lids tight and nodded.

"Open 'em eyes!"

They opened.


The driver finished arranging some papers on a clip board then looked over his shoulder at the passenger.

"Yew got some ID?"

The passenger sat, quaking violently, concentrating on keeping his eyes open and remaining in an upright position.

The two officers exchanged glances.

"Ya know who we are?" the driver again.

Blank.

"We're the police. Y're in a police car. Un'erstan'? We saved y'ur ass jus' now, so try ta he'p us out here. Okay?"

The passenger squinted. He cocked his head a little, trying desperately to bring the driver into focus.

"Ta hell with this shit," the other policeman snorted.

He began slamming an open hand against the wire mesh.

The passenger recoiled as if he were about to be struck.

"Gimme y'ur damn wallet 'r y're goin' downtown!" the voice. "Gimme y'ur wallet!"

"I got a...wall't in my...a wall'...here...somewhe..."

"Take the wallet out," the driver ordered.

The passenger began clawing at his right hip.

"Ya cain't git ta y'ur pocket," the driver. "Y'ur coat's in'a way."

The passenger leaned forward to pull the coat up. After a short struggle, he freed the wallet then crashed back against the seat, panting in agony.

"Take y'ur driver's license out," the driver continued to coach the man. "I need y'ur driver's license 'r I'll have ta take ya ta jail."

The passenger opened the wallet and dumped a cluster of cards and papers into his lap. He sorted through the stack, straining to remember what he was looking for.

" 'at's the one," the driver. "Y'ur finger's right on it. Pick it up an' pass it through the slot here."

The passenger tried to follow the orders.

"This guy's really screwed up," the other policeman sneered. "Look at him."

"Take y'ur glove off," the driver suggested, trying not to laugh.

The passenger raised his hand to his mouth then held the fingertips of the glove in his teeth. The arm went limp. The hand slipped from the glove. He opened his mouth. The glove fell into his lap.

Picking up the driver's license, he sent it on a meandering course toward the slot in the screen. The first attempt failed. He backed it up a few inches, corrected his aim, and then shot the license through the opening.

The driver snatched it away.

The passenger fell back into the seat. Exhausted. Dizzy. Nauseated.

"Open 'em eyes!" the second officer shouted.

His lids popped apart. He sat, breathing heavily, the constant quaking gradually giving way to an occasional convulsion.

The driver looked over his shoulder at the passenger.

"I thank I know this guy," turning a flashlight on him.

The passenger slammed his eyes shut and threw his head down.

"Gil McNeil," the driver mumbled while examining the figure in the backseat more closely.

The man's features were almost completely obscured by hair. Shocks of wildly knotted curls jumbled out from under a shaggy sheepskin cap. A bushy, tangled beard reached to the collar of a long, furry coat. The beard looked as if a maniac with an air hose had groomed it. A pair of large, shaggy snow boots reached half way to his knees. The melting snow and ice clumps clinging to every inch of him were slowly transforming the man into a matted hairball reeking of beer, urine, cigarette smoke, and stale sweat.

The beast raised his ungloved hand in an attempt to block the light. The hand danced about like a kite in a heavy wind then fell back into his lap with a damp smack. Shivering uncontrollably, he buried his chin in his chest and hunched his shoulders forward. His face disappeared into a churning sea of wet, tangled hair and fur. The ungloved hand was the only visible flesh remaining. He was quivering, continuing to thaw.

"Damn sure didn' recognize him right off, but it's him," the driver. "Went ta high school with him. He was in my Ag class. Future Farmers."

The second officer didn't seem to care.

"It's a Washington state driver's license, but it's got a local address scribbled on it in ink," the driver again.

"Must'a been through this drill b'fore," the second officer.

"It's only a coupl'a blocks from here. We'll take him home," the driver decided.

The snow behind the car glowed red as he hit the brakes and shifted into first gear. He let up on the brake. The fire in the snow extinguished. The squad car inched forward, tires cracking free of the alley's icy grip. The beast's snow angel impression slipped under the hood of the car. The alley darkened behind the car as it crept along, crunching loudly down the frozen strip between the backsides of shanty-like garage utilities, past mauled trashcans, discarded stoves, refrigerators, toilets, sinks, evaporative cooler hulls, and water heaters—everything under a light layer of snow.

"Another ten feet an' yew'd'a nailed him," the second officer.

The car eased from the alley onto the snow covered street then proceeded to the address on the license.

The shivering passenger was in a daze, fogged eyes staring out of the windshield from the back seat. Shadowy forms of houses eerily crept into the headlight's arc then slowly slipped back into darkness as the car made its way through the night. It had a hypnotic effect on the passenger. He cleared his throat loudly.

"I's li'e this...no...li'e we're in a neon kin'a bubble. A tube thing...where...where ever'thing...glowin' whide. *White,* an'...we're mofin' so...slow. So muth'fugin' slow motion...through a...a sea 'r somethin'. *Ing*! I's a sea'a blag ing. E'scuse me...*black...ink*! Know whud I'm sayin'?" head teetering and bobbing. "E'scuse me. I's jus' a thoughd."

The two officers broke up laughing.

The passenger laughed along with the officers then added, "Bu' i's a kin'a funny fugin' thoughd."

"Yeah," the driver. "Real fugin' funny."

The car came to a stop in front of a large, old, two-story house.

"206," the second officer reading the house number. "That utility in'a back'a the driveway's pro'bly B," aiming the flashlight at the small structure.

He turned to the passenger.

"Yew recognize 'at buildin' back there?" pointing at the utility.

"Yeah."

"Ya didn' even look. Look up the driveway an' tell me if ya live there."

"Okay."

"Turn y'ur head an' look at the buildin'!" raising his voice.

"Okay," as the passenger rolled his head in the direction the driver was pointing.

"Yew live there?"

"Yeah."

"Ya sure?"

"Sure."

The driver slipped the passenger's license back through the slot in the cage.

"Take it," the driver ordered.

The passenger obeyed.

The driver pulled on his gloves before exiting the car. He carefully maneuvered his way around to the passenger's door and opened it.

"Put all'a y'ur papers an' things in y'ur coat pocket," sternly.

The passenger's hand wandered between his lap and his side until all the papers and cards were stuffed away.

"Beautiful," as the driver reached inside to help him out of the car. "Yew c'n sort it all out later."

The passenger wobbled to his feet, one hand clutching the officer's coat, the other tightly gripping the top of the open door. The frigid air burned his lungs. He began coughing violently. His knees buckled. The driver kept him from falling.

"Take y'ur time. Take y'ur time," the driver.

"Leave the door open," from inside the car. "Smells like a shithouse in here."

The driver eased the passenger away from the car, pausing to let him regain his legs before advancing toward the utility. With one of the passenger's arms around the officer's neck, they made their way up the driveway.

The officer suddenly halted—the shed door was wide open.

The officer inched his way toward the utility then propped the passenger against the wall next to the door.

"I want ya ta lock y'ur knees, lean against the wall, an' be quiet. Un'erstand?" the officer whispered.

"Sure," and began sliding downward.

"Lock y'ur damn knees," the officer hissed while hoisting the passenger back up.

The passenger nodded. The driver eased his grip. The passenger remained in place, shaking, head down. The officer removed the flashlight from his belt, switched it on, and then cautiously entered the utility.

The door, a single key still in the dead bolt, had been thrown open so violently the doorknob had jammed in the sheet rock wall. Drifting snow had covered the floor around the entrance, piling up against a rumpled throw rug lying about three feet inside the room. The light beam swept the space.

He turned the light off, easing his free hand to the revolver at his side.

Everything remained quiet.

He switched the flashlight back on then pointed the beam at a man lying on his stomach in the middle of the room.

The body was huge, its arms fully extended past the head, legs straight as boards and tightly locked together. It looked like Superman, frozen in flight, had fallen face down to earth.

Watching closely for any signs of movement, the officer edged his way over to the body.

*No sign'a blood.*

He knelt beside the figure's shoulders, removed a glove, and then slid two fingers under its coat collar.

*Good pulse.*

The head was resting on its forehead and nose. A puddle of saliva had collected on the floor around the body's parted lips. The puddle bubbled slightly with every shallow, exhaled breath. Tangled strands of long, black hair covered the floor almost to the elbows of the outstretched arms. The officer stood up, keeping the light beam on a grotesquely disfigured patch of flesh on the back of the head.

*Some kind'a burn. Hell uv a burn.*

The scar, beginning at a jagged line immediately below the crown, ran from ear to ear. It continued down the back of the skull and neck where it disappeared under the collar of a faded, olive drab, military issue field coat.

The officer slowly panned the room with the flashlight. A metal bunk bed with thin, sheet-less, cotton mattresses stood against the wall by the front door. Fully opened, the door barely cleared the end of the bunk. The opposite end of the rack protruded about six inches beyond the frame of a doorway leading to a second room. Worn, disheveled, wool blankets lay on the mattresses.

A softly sputtering gas, floor heater centered along the wall opposite the front door struggled to stay lit in the breeze from the open door. Spent matches, cigarette butts, and ashes littered a rust spotted tray in front of the glowing ceramic grill pieces—one missing, another broken in half. Every inch of space on top of the heater was covered with empty beer bottles, bottle caps, beer cans, more burnt matches, cigarette butts and ashes. The trash overflowed onto the floor. Behind the heater a few butts, matches, and ashes hung suspended in midair, trapped in a dense collection of cobwebs mooring the heater to the wall and baseboard.

A dingy sheet covered a single window located directly across the room from the bunk bed. Thumbtacks meandered around the window frame, loosely holding the sheet in place. A pile of soiled flannel shirts, blue jeans, heavy woolen socks, and long underwear were shoved up against an empty, olive green duffel bag in the corner.

A double window was alongside the front door. The window was dressed in a faded orange shower curtain secured to the top of the frame by several large nails. The curtain reached to just above the sill. The stained, warped, peeling, dust covered ledge was thick with dried fly carcasses.

A light bulb in a chipped porcelain socket dangled from the center of the unpainted, water stained, plywood ceiling. The socket was plugged into an extension cord stapled across the ceiling. The cord ran down the wall behind the bunk bed where it plugged into an uncovered outlet box that had worked its way free of the wall.

The unpainted sheet rock walls of the room were peppered with small holes, thumbtacks, and nails of every size. All the walls were bare with the exception of a child-like sketch tacked above the heater. The drawing, done in black marker on a piece of grocery sack, was of a cow and a bird. The bird was standing on a pile of manure. The bird appeared to be feeding on the dung as the cow looked on. "me" was scribbled on the bird, "them" scribbled on the cow's flank.

Fine strands of cotton clung to everything in the room. They were in the cobwebs infesting the place, on the sheet over the window, the mattresses, and in the hair and on the clothing of the prone giant. Dirt, twigs and dried leaves were strewn all over the floor. The officer stepped to the doorway at the end of the bunk and directed the light beam into the adjoining room. Cockroaches scurried for cover.

The room was smaller than the front room. An old, winged, linoleum topped kitchen table, both flaps down so it could fit into the space, was pushed against one wall. The tabletop, pasty with spilled beer and wine, was a clutter of drained bottles, cans, bread crumbs, cigarette ashes, and empty jars of mustard, mayonnaise, and relish. What was left of a loaf of bread was smashed against the wall by the weight of it all. A beer can had been cut in half and fashioned into two ashtrays. Butts flowed from both halves, some of the butts ending up on the worn, plywood kitchen floor.

The sink and a grungy, makeshift counter extended along the length of the front wall. A few inches of water stood in a porcelain coated, iron sink dotted with rusting chips bleeding dark brown stains. Some plastic spoons, forks, and limp paper plates were locked in a layer of orange grease that had formed on the water's surface.

A doorless closet across from the table contained a disgustingly filthy toilet with a picture of Lyndon Johnson duct taped to the inside of the lid. A rusty, freestanding shower stall was adjacent to the commode. To access the stall a person would have had to step over the commode. To have used the toilet would have required sitting with both feet on the kitchen floor.

An ancient, two-burner stove stood to the right of the officer. A dented tin pan, insides coated with a hardened, brown substance tinged with orange grease, sat on the back burner. Two empty cans of chili sat on the narrow stovetop to the right of the burners. The stovetop, like every other flat surface in the kitchen, was painted in grime and spilled food. Spattered grease had created a shiny arc on the wall above the stove.

*No refrigerator?*

The officer returned to the front room, pausing to glance at the scar before walking out into the fresh air. He took a few deep breaths to clear the stench from his nostrils. The passenger had slid into a squatting position, forehead on his knees, gloved hands by his sides, palms up in the snow. The officer gripped the man's coat, pulled him to his feet, and then dragged the man into the front room. The passenger groaned softly as he was lowered onto the bottom bunk. The officer covered both bodies with a blanket then turned the heater up. He knelt down beside the scarred hulk, gently lifted the skull, rolled it a bit to one side then eased it back to the floor. The body's breathing became less labored. The policeman freed the doorknob from the sheet rock then quietly shut the door.

# CHAPTER ONE
## December 12, 1970
### 9:30 A.M.

A wareness was slowly clubbing me awake. A murky, sloppy, disoriented awareness of grunt-noises emitted by the sturdiest of brain cells, those muscle bound, primeval, cave dwelling cells which, like cockroaches, survive the centuries while everything around them either dies off or evolves. Cells so primitive they are capable of producing only the simplest of signals—the orgasm's howl; the moan of an agonizing hangover.

For thirty minutes I laid near death.

Gradually more sophisticated messages began to sketchily identify specific areas of severe distress—cold sweats, heaving stomach, detonating temples. Certain needs—flaming thirst, bursting bladder, nicotine deprivation—were demanding to be met.

Sandblasted eyeballs peered through tiny, swollen slits into a shimmering room filled with shimmering, out-of-focus objects. I fixed my quivering gaze on Homer's blurry form. He was lying across the room from me in a tight fetal position on top of a pile of clothes. A damp, muddy throw rug covered his head. A dirty, cream-colored Navy issue blanket trailed from the center of the tiny room to between Homer's legs. His breathing was heavy, labored— each slow, wheezing breath raising his shoulder several inches then rapidly falling with a rush of exhaled air.

An eternity passed. I needed aspirin, nicotine, and caffeine. I needed something solid in my stomach. Without them, all of them, I would die. Eyes closed, I struggled into a sitting position and rested my head against the running rail of the top bunk. My fingers clutched the mattress as I spun out of control for a few seconds. A churning stomach lodged itself in a parched, swollen throat. I gagged, on the brink of puking. My breath came in quick, shallow gasps—lungs charred to near uselessness after a drunken night of chain smoking. Another wave of cold sweats.

I pried my lids apart to see if I was perpendicular to the floor. I was.

The room was stifling. I began stripping down. First the gloves then the wool cap followed by an exhausting two or three minute struggle to remove the soggy, heavy fur coat, a sweat shirt, a flannel shirt, and two undershirts. Each peeled layer added more twigs, dried, shredded leaves, dirt, and fine strands of cotton to previous deposits of debris on the mattress and floor.

I sat, panting, nostrils in shock.
*Smell like a rotten corpse.*

I leaned away from the bed, painfully eased myself into a standing position, and then turned sideways to support myself against the top bunk, thighs and calves cramping under the weight. I was trembling. Weak. Faint. Nauseous again.

After a pause, I made my way down the bunk to the kitchen door. Releasing the mattress, I wobbled slowly through the doorway to the commode. The elastic waistband of the bottom pair of long johns stung like salt in a wound as the elastic tore free of a dark red ring around a midriff rubbed raw by sharp bits of twigs and pieces of cotton hulls. Debris fell to the floor as I let the damp, mud caked pants and two pair of grimy long johns drop to my ankles.

Finished, I pulled everything up, carefully resituating the waistbands above the abrasion. I stepped to the sink to search for a butt-free beer can. I found one, filled it with water, and then downed it. I filled it again and began sipping it slowly. After pulling a deformed slice of bread from the loaf on the table, I staggered back into the front room. I fell onto the bunk and worked my way into a sitting position, back against the wall. I took a small bite of bread and began to chew it slowly. Each movement of the jaw set off an explosion in my temples. A mild sweetness began to replace the bitter, ashen taste in my mouth.

*Rich people don't have ta put up with this kind'a crap. They c'n drink all night, then wake up the next mornin' in a bed with clean sheets...in a clean, carpeted room 'at dudn't smell like a sewer. Take a bunch'a vitamins. Down a handful'a prescription pain killers with a bottle'a Pepto. Shower in a clean, roomy, carpeted bathroom. Drink some cold orange juice. Sip coffee while puttin' down a big-ass breakfas...*

Homer sneezed, coughed loudly, stirred, and then wilted.

I pulled my coat onto my lap. The mud tangled fur was damp.

For that matter, everything was damp and muddied—the mattress, the blanket, pants, boots. Even the floor was spotted with evaporating mud puddles.

I searched the right coat pocket for cigarettes. I removed a fistful of moist papers and cards along with a soggy wallet.

*Shit. Must'a dropped it in a toilet somewhere last night. Again.*

I found a smashed pack of cigarettes in the left pocket and shook a bent, water stained cigarette out. After retrieving a dry book of matches from the top of the heater I fell back onto the bunk.

Striking the match was a clumsy chore executed in slow motion with stiff, swollen fingers. It took several attempts. The first deep drag was a coughing, hacking, skull splitting torture. I doubled over, gasping into my lap. Succeeding tugs on the cigarette were no easier.

It had to be done, however, the nicotine requirement outweighing the threat of spitting my lungs up one piece at a time.

Homer moaned. His fetal position tightened then relaxed. Muddy boots crept toward the center of the room as he straightened his legs, slowly rolled from his side onto his back, crossed his arms over his chest, and then went limp.

I forced several more drags off the cigarette. The violence of the hacking fits lessened by small degrees with every draw. Homer reached for the throw rug covering his head. He pulled it away. His bloodshot eyes fixed on the ceiling.

The slits closed.

"Cigarette?" I asked hoarsely, fighting to stifle a cough.

Several seconds passed before one of Homer's arms rose from his chest. The arm hung suspended then fell with a thud to the floor, outstretched in my direction, palm up, fingers forming a V to receive a cigarette. I slid from the bunk to my knees and crawled to the hand. I lit a cigarette and placed it in the V. Homer's hand drifted to his face.

I joined Homer in a barking duet after resituating myself on the bunk. A long period of silence was broken only by the coughing spells. Homer pulled a mutilated pack of cigarettes from his coat pocket, removed one, and then lit it off the first butt. He crushed the butt out on the floor.

I listened to the soft, steady hiss of the Dearborn heater while quietly losing myself in the placidly undulating layers of smoke slowly forming in the room.

After a few minutes, Homer pulled himself into a sitting position, chin falling to his chest. The spellbinding haze swirled wildly, its trance-like effect broken. Homer leaned forward and deposited the cigarette butt in one of the beer bottles on top of the heater. After shifting to his hands and knees, he lumbered off for the kitchen, head down, his long, black hair trailing stiffly over the floor, collecting bits of debris as he went.

I sat on the edge of the bunk, vaguely aware of the sounds coming from the toilet then the kitchen as Homer traced the steps I'd taken earlier. Eventually he staggered from around the end of the bunk, a tortured slice of bread in one hand, a beer can of water in the other, a bent cigarette dangling from his lips. He mumbled something about needing air as he brushed against me on the way to the door.

An Arctic blast.
It felt good. It smelled clean. Fresh. I decided to join him outside.

"Damn," Homer whispered.
"Holy shit," following Homer into a gray, overcast world frozen under Lubbock's first snow of the season.
It was almost comforting. Perfect for a hangover. A giant ice pack. No blinding, happy-ass sun or bouncy, bubbly puffs of cottony clouds playing in a deep blue sky—everything shrieking what a lovely, wonderful fucking morning it is.

"When'd this happen?" more to myself than to Homer.
"Must have been after we left...left the...uh...left wherever it was we left last night. Can't remember."
"Alcoholic," I coughed.
"So, where were we?" Homer, slowly munching his bread.
"Hell, I don't know," hacking painfully.
I let something foul dribble from my mouth onto the snow.

Everything in the backyard of the big house, our front yard, was covered in white. All the trash, beer cans, bottles, car parts, the landlord's secondhand building materials—the whole dump—was under a few inches of snow.

"Looks pretty good around here when you can't see all the crap," I said.

"Yeah," Homer agreed.

We smoked a couple of cigarettes.

"How you feeling?" Homer, flicking the second butt down the driveway.

"Feels like I may'a caught a cold last night. How about you?"

"Feel great," stifling a cough.

"Y're so full of shit," I snorted. "Y're hurtin' as bad as I am."

Homer walked back into the room, ducking so his 6-foot plus frame could clear the top of the doorway. I followed him, too cold for more than two cigarettes. I paused at the threshold and rapidly fanned the door.

"Honest-ta-God," I coughed, "this place smells like a dead body."

The flames in the heater flickered and popped as the gas jets alternately extinguished in the breeze then burst back to life, reignited by an adjoining jet. The gray sheet and orange shower curtain rippled stiffly.

"Do we smell as bad as it does in here?" while sniffing my armpits.

I wrinkled my nose. Homer didn't answer. He sat down on the clothes in the corner and leaned against the wall. I shut the door and eased myself back onto the bunk.

Cigarette smoke slowly filled the little room again.

"I didn't mean to get you fired," Homer.

"I wudn't fired. I quit."

Homer stretched out on the floor.

"Still...I'm sorry. Wasn't thinking."

"Stop worryin' about it. There's better jobs'n 'at in Hell."

I'd met Homer while tromping cotton for a slave driver named Deacon. Deacon's plantation was east of Lubbock on the outskirts of a little place called Idalou. I'd gotten the job while standing around outside of the Texas Employment Commission back in September. This stocky, bearded, greasy looking guy in oily coveralls, a sleeveless blue jean jacket, and a bandanna worn pirate style on his head, had come up to me. The guy'd promised me as much work as I could handle. Paid cash at the end of the day. Sixty-five cents an hour. The Commission didn't have squat, so I'd taken the guy's offer. A week later the same thing had happened to Homer.

Homer'd been out of the service about a year when I'd met him. He was an Oklahoma Indian of some kind. After his discharge from the Marines he'd gone home, but couldn't find steady work. He'd decided to head out for California, but only made it to Lubbock before running out of money. Lubbock's not that far from Oklahoma. The dumbass must of left home with around thirty-five cents to have only made it this far.

*Poor guy...goes an' volunteers f'r the Marines, gets out an' goes back ta Oklahoma ta find work, an' then tries ta make it ta California on thirty-five cents.*

Those are damn good examples of the kind of thinking that make for a successful cotton tromper.

Tromping is hard work. Harder than filling sandbags. A tromper works in a large, wood-floored trailer of chicken wire wrapped around an angle iron frame left open at the top. The trailer looks like a big, flimsy, 10-foot high cage on small rubber tires. A tractor pulls the trailer down the rows of cotton. The tractor is rigged with a machine that strips the cotton from the plant then feeds the cotton into the lower end of an auger. Stripped cotton shoots from the upper end of the auger into the center of the trailer. The upper end of the auger opening is about three feet higher than the top of the cage.

The tromper's job is to scatter the cotton evenly around the inside of the trailer with a pitch fork, packing it tight by stomping around in circles until the sides of the trailer bulge out and the cotton is piled high enough to touch the auger opening. The stripper sucks up the cotton, cotton hulls, twigs, dead leaves, dirt, spiders, field mice, empty beer cans, old tires, abandoned cars, and whatever else that isn't nailed down. The trompers are pelted with a high velocity stream of crap all day long. It works its way under a tromper's clothes where it rubs away at the skin like sandpaper. The dirt and dust turn to mud as they mix with sweat during the heat of the afternoon. Every crack and crevice of a tromper's body festers after the first week. It's filthy, backbreaking work. Cold in the morning, hot as hell in the afternoon. It was, however, character building.

And there weren't any other jobs around.

Gradually, Homer and I'd gotten to know each other pretty well. We'd started taking turns driving out to Idalou. We began hanging out together, getting drunk in the bars around the Texas Tech student ghetto where we lived. It was selfish on my part, but one of the things that drew me to Homer was that he wasn't anymore successful at hitting on the ladies than I was. It gets depressing when you're running with somebody who's always sucking up the goods and you never get past the first slap in the face. After ten weeks, we'd gotten to where we felt fairly comfortable around each other. Homer and I decided to rent a place together so he could save enough cash to continue on to California and I could sock some school money away. I hadn't been able to save squat while living with my brother, Chad.

Chad was raping me on the rent, drinking up the booze I'd bring home, and smoking all my cigarettes, never once offering to pay me back or restock anything. Once Homer and I'd started sharing a place, things began looking up for the both of us. We weren't saving any more money, but it was a little easier to stay drunk or smoked up and one of us always had a pack of cigarettes.

# THE RAVING EUNUCH MONKS

Then things went to crap.

We'd never missed a day in the ten weeks we'd worked for Deacon. We considered ourselves model employees. For some dumbass reason we thought that meant something—like maybe Deacon thought we were special or that he actually appreciated the extra effort we made to keep showing up every day no matter how hung-over we were. At any rate, Homer was already upset because Deacon wasn't going to let him have a few days off to attend his grandfather's funeral back in Oklahoma. Then, to top it off, Deacon goes and tells everybody the trailers had weighed in short all day long so everybody was being docked two hours pay.

The Mexicans and Blacks were pretty calm about it. I guess they were used to that kind of thing. I was cussing right and left as we'd walked back to the turn row where Homer's truck was parked. He hadn't said a thing. When we got to the truck Homer'd continued on up the turn row toward two fully stuffed trailers. Homer'd gone to the back of the tractor still hooked to one of the trailers, removed a GI can of gasoline, climbed onto the mountain of cotton in the trailer then scattered the contents of the can all over the heap. He'd climbed off the mound, pulled a Zippo from his pocket and then held it to a pile of dried leaves and twigs collected in one corner of the trailer. Once the kindling began to burn good, Homer'd headed back to where we were parked. As soon as he'd reached the truck the gas soaked cotton had lit off in a soft whoosh.

He'd climbed into the truck then suggested we leave right away. We took off, not particularly fast, but not particularly slow. It was a cool, Hollywood kind of exit. All the trompers parked along the turn row honked their truck horns, waved, and cheered. It really was a little like the ending of a movie where the losers pull the last trick. Only now we were unemployed and close to broke. They always leave that part out in the movies.

We'd driven to town and gotten real drunk on what money we had left. Judging by the way I felt right now, we must have gotten real, real drunk.

I coughed, cleared my throat, and lit a cigarette.

"When're ya leavin' f'r Oklahoma?" I asked.

"Not going," after a long pause. "No money."

"I've been thinkin' about that. My seabag's still over at Chad's. I've got some money stashed in it. About eighty dollars. Lemme come with ya an' I'll pay the way."

"Can't do that."

"I've never seen an Indian reservation," I argued. "It'd be a learnin' thing. I'll help ya drive."

"There isn't a reservation. Never was."

"Whatever," and struggled to my feet. "I'm goin' over ta Chad's right now an' get it."

"I'll pay you back."

"Nope. I don't loan money. It's y'urs."

"I owe you one, then."

"That won't work either. Too goddamn much trouble over the long run keepin' track'a who owes who what an' how much. We'll use what we need ta use an' f'rget it."

Homer followed me out the door into the gray.

"I'll be back in an hour 'r so," I told him and began carefully negotiating the slippery driveway.

I decided to walk to Chad's place, still too hung-over to mess with deicing the truck and driving.

*The truck!*

I paused at the end of the driveway to look around. No truck parked along the curb anywhere. No truck in the yard.

*Maybe it's in the alley. Screw it. Can't deal with it right now.*

# THE RAVING EUNUCH MONKS

I headed up a bitter cold Ninth Street. Picking up the pace, I hurried past a 3-foot snow erection, testicles and all. A few houses later, across the street, a huge set of tits. The snow sculptures were a student ghetto tradition of sorts. In high school, after a good snow, a bunch of us would pile into a car and go to the student slums adjacent to the east end of the Texas Tech campus. We'd drive around gawking at all the oversized breasts, spread eagled nudes, exaggerated pricks, and copulating, glistening snow couples twisted into every position a sexually frustrated college student could imagine.

None of the monuments lasted long. Within hours of their completion the ghetto Jesus freaks would overrun the neighborhood to conduct a cleansing for Christ—squads of frothing, shrieking, Bible quoting believers performing jackbooted breast reductions, castrations, cockectomies, and committing violent acts of coitus interruptus.

The wind was picking up again. It sent long swishing lines of powdery snow snaking across the ice covered street. Hunkering my shoulders, I tried to protect as much of my face as I could against the biting gusts.

Two bundled figures approached on the other side of the street. They passed a set of enormous snow boobs without stopping to bash them back to prepubescence.
*Fellow heathens.*
One was poised like an ice skater—bent over, hands clasped behind the back. The other figure was pushing the skater over the thin veneer of ice hidden under the snow. When they were directly across from me the skater suddenly lunged forward and crashed to the ground, done in by one of the geologic features of the student ghetto—the convulsing, uplifted sidewalk.

Fifty years of weathering combined with the root systems of trees planted by the affluent, original occupants of the neighborhood had resulted in miles and miles of concrete outcrops and cracked, crumbling trails. Some pieces of sidewalk jutted four inches into the air. A 6-foot length of level walk was a rarity in the old neighborhood. Other sections had deteriorated away to dirt paths. After picking up a few scars, I'd learned to walk in the street when returning home from the bars at night, although the streets weren't much safer than the sidewalks.

The streets were surfaced with red bricks put down during the Depression. The entire road system had become a network of rolling, dipping ripples pockmarked with fist to crater sized cavities. It was brick anarchy—no two brick's surfaces sharing the same plane. As a result, not a single set of aligned tires existed in the ghetto. The gutters looked like a secondhand auto parts store. Black splotches of tar filler dotted the streets, replacing whole sections of brick that had completely disintegrated. It was a losing battle. All the gaps and holes managed to stay ahead of the occasional tar repair, steadily increasing in depth and size, steadily creeping towards each other, year after year, in a conspiracy to form one great pit into which the student ghetto would someday disappear. At least that's what the Baptists in town were praying for—an apocalyptic end to the student ghetto. In their minds, such an event would be right up there with the destruction of Sodom and Gomorrah.

My moustache was frosting over. I was quaking, becoming nauseated again.

*Should'a checked that bread f'r mold 'r somethin'. Need a cigarette. Here I am, damn near dyin' an' I go an' volunteer ta drive Homer half way ta Hell an' back. Christ.*

I trudged through the snow, slipped between two houses, cut down an alley, and then entered an unfenced backyard where a large two-car garage was located at the end of a driveway. The structure, like every other freestanding garage in the ghetto, had been converted into a utility apartment. The driveway ran between a big, dilapidated, two-story wood house and an equally large, run-down, brick house. A small, tarp covered car was parked halfway up the drive.

*Chad's here.*

I walked around the corner of the utility and stepped over to the door. My eyes felt like they'd iced up. I freed the key from my pocket. I was shaking so violently I had to hold the key with both hands while trying to insert it into the lock. I finally succeeded and turned the doorknob. The door gave a little then stopped.

*Deadbolt's tripped.*

"Hey, Chad," leaning heavily against the door. "Chad!" tapping on the glass in the upper half of the door, breath frosting the window. "It's me. Open up."

I could hear hurried footsteps inside. I listened for the metallic clink of the deadbolt being thrown. Long seconds shivered by.

No metallic clink. The shed was silent.

"Chad!" rapping on the glass, louder this time. "Hurry up. It's freezin' out here."

Nothing.

"C'mon, Chad!" pounding on the doorframe. "Open the goddamn door! I know y're in there!"

The corner of a blue velvet curtain covering the window in the door lifted slightly. I caught a quick glimpse of Chad's face before the curtain dropped.

"Hey, goddammit!" hitting the doorframe so hard the shed trembled.

"Come back in ten minutes," Chad shouted.

*Chad's got somethin' in there with him.*

"WHERE THE HELL AM I SUPPOSED TA GO F'R TEN FUCKIN' MINUTES?" Tell the bitch I'll shut my eyes! I'M DYIN' OUT HERE, YA LITTLE BASTA...," breaking into a deep, painful gagging. I slipped to one knee, expecting to puke. I was sweating ice water. Dizzy.

"Give me a minute," Chad.

Remaining on one knee, I rested against the door, fighting to catch my breath. I could hear Chad frantically pleading with someone. A female's voice hissed at Chad.

"No! Not 'til he's gone."

"Please! It's no big deal," Chad begged.

"I don't care! Make him go away first," the female insisted in a harsh whisper.

*She don't care? She don't care that I'm out here dyin' because she dudn't want one more guy ta see her naked ass?*

I stood up and began kicking furiously at the doorframe.

"YOU BETTER CARE YA SORRY LITTLE WHORE! HEAR ME? YOU BETTER FUCKIN' CARE!"

Sheets of snow slid from the steeply angled roof of the shack. Chunks of ice broke free of tree branches, landing in the snow with muted thuds. A dog in the big wooden house up front was barking like mad. The curtain in the door window jerked back. Chad presented himself in the window, his tanned, bony little chest as puffed up as he could puff it, his face a masterpiece of rage. He looked like a rabid capon.

"Watch your language," he squawked. "There's a lady in here," before disappearing behind the curtain again.

I kicked at the door.

"YOU SORRY LITTLE TURD! YA GODDAM...," my voice shattering.

A stabbing coughing fit seized me—deep rattling spasms sending electric shocks into my temples, through my shoulders, and down my spine. I bent over, grabbed my knees, locked my elbows, and leaned my butt against the shed. My stomach was on fire. I gagged, waiting for the heaves to begin. The wave passed. I addressed the door once more.

"I'm givin' ya three minutes," I panted. "If 'at door idn't open in three minutes I'm gunna rip the top off'a that goddamn car'a y'urs an' puke all over the inside of it."

*I think I c'n hold it back f'r three minutes.*

"You don't have a watch," Chad shot back, thinking he'd found a loophole. "How will you know when three minutes are up?"

Still bent over, I spun around and repeatedly smashed my fists against the shed like a boxer striking a punching bag.

"I'LL KNOW, GODDAMMIT! I'LL JUST FUCKIN' KNOW!" followed by more hacking, gagging, and coughing.

I raised my head and looked around for a place to spend the next three minutes. Some place out of the wind. Someone in the wooden house up front was staring out of a window from behind a large American flag. The face disappeared behind the flag as soon as we made eye contact.

*Fuckin' hippies. No concept'a rage. They're pro'bly cleanin' the crap out'a their drawers right now.*

The back door of the house opened. A naked, solid figure with thick, black hair all over his body stepped out onto a small porch.

"Hey! Whu' the shit's y'ur problem, man?" the ape slurred. "Git in here. Y're gunna freeze y'ur ass off 'r them goat ropers nex' door're gunna kick it all over Hell."

The naked body stomped back into the house, mumbling as it went. The voice had a sluggish, sloppy, drugged quality about it. The door was left open. I slammed my fist into the doorframe one last time before stumbling across the yard and up the steps.

I entered a large kitchen. Empty wine bottles, liquor bottles, beer cans, and plastic Budweiser cups were everywhere. A keg floated in a tub of soupy water thick with deteriorating cigarette butts. The hairy guy had put on a pair of stiff, oil stained jeans and a sleeveless olive drab tee shirt that was no cleaner than the pants. A large, black Labrador Retriever was stretched out under the table, head resting on his paws. The dog greeted me with a single tail thump on the floor.

The Doors were playing somewhere in the house.

The man motioned for me to join him at a large, wooden dining table littered with roach clips, rolling papers, and a baggy with about half a lid in it.

"Still trompin' cotton?" the man slurred through a tight-lipped grin.

"How'd ya know I been trompin'?"

" 'cause ya smell like shit an' y're all covered in lint an' crap, man. Yew don't even 'member me, do ya? Texas Employment Commission?" hinting while rolling a joint. "Deacon?" offering a second hint.

I continued to stare at him. He was about my height, maybe five feet nine or ten, but stocky like a caveman. His tanned, rugged, face was covered in a close cropped, black beard. His rumpled hair, entering the early stages of balding, was cut short. Two black dots, jittering in a sea of blood, were scarcely visible through swollen eyelids. His fingers were so thick they approached stubby.

Then I remembered.

"Yeah. Y're that son of a bitch…'at guy who turned me on ta the trompin' job."

" 'at's cool, man. 'at's cool. I know I'm a son uv a bitch," cackling to himself. Suddenly, loudly, "HEY!" Then softly, "Shittin' job's ever'thing I tol' ya it'd be, idn' it? Lots'a money. Good outdoors exercise. Chance ta meet some hot-ass women," followed by a hissing kind of cackle.

"Beat starvin'."

"Yeah. Lots'a shit beats starvin', man. Gotta eat. Guess ya wan'a kick my ass now, don'ch ya?" while lighting the joint. "I'm Jerry," offering me the first drag. "Jerry Chaff, but all my frien's jus' call me Jerry. Git it?"

I sat in the chair, shivering.

"I's a fuckin' joke, man. My name's Jerry, but all my frien's call me Jerry?" repeating the introduction. "Now ya git it?" furrowing his forehead. "Shit, man, lighten up," sounding disappointed.

I took a deep drag and returned the joint.

"Gil," then exhaled.

"Whu'z 'at?" brows raised.

"Gil. My name's Gil McNeil."

"Oh, yeah. Jerry. Jerry Chaff," introducing himself for the third time. "Glad ta meet ya, man."

Jerry took a long, deep pull off the joint, held it, and then exhaled slowly.

"Damn," hissing. "Hate ta run out'a this shit. This...this is... real...real shit, man," lifting his brows and squinting tightly as he closely examined the joint. "Yew spell y'ur name with one L 'r two uv 'em?"

He didn't wait for an answer.

" 'cause I used ta know this guy once 'at spelled it with one L an' he wuz queer as hell. Not tha' bein' queer matters, man. I don't give a shit about queers. I'm lib'ral abou' tha' kind'a shit. I'm real lib'ral about ever'thing but lesbians. Damn. Cain't han'le lesos. Good lookin' stuff's hard enough ta git anymore without a bunch'a lesos hangin' aroun'. Know whud I mean? An' rednecks. Rednecks're fuuucked up, man. I cain't git lib'ral about lesbians an' rednecks. Like 'em sons a bitchin' chicken pluckers nex' door," jerking a thumb in the direction of the brick house on the other side of the drive. "Turds went an' called the cops las' night 'cause my cousin went an' threw a grenade inta their fuckin' party. Not a *real* grenade, man. It wuz a *trainin'* grenade, but...shiiit. No fuckin' sense'a humor. Now I ain' got no more trainin' grenades ta dick aroun' with. Know whud I mean? I mean, whu' the fuck c'n ya do with a live 'un? Blow somebody up? Gittin' a laugh idn't worth goin' ta jail for, man."

Jerry took a drag out of turn before handing the joint back to me. I took a quick drag, intending to back it up, but as soon as the joint cleared my lips he was reaching for it.

The dog under the table whined. I leaned back and looked down at him. The dog sneezed, shook his head, and then stared at me as if expecting something from me.

"Don't min' him," Jerry. " 'at's one fucked up dog, man. Donal's done turned him inta a psycho dog. Wa'sh this."

Jerry tossed an empty beer bottle onto the floor. The dog shot from under the table. He began scooting the bottle all around the kitchen floor, whining, crashing into the walls, the stove, the refrigerator, desperately trying to pick the bottle up in his mouth.

Jerry lit a cigarette.

"This'll *really* crack y'ur ass up, man. HEY, ZERO! LOOK HERE!" and waved the lit cigarette around. "LOOK HERE, BOY!"

The dog froze, ears cocked forward, gaze fixed on the cigarette. Jerry tossed it into the middle of the kitchen floor. Zero lunged at the cigarette. He struggled to pick it up in his mouth, yelped and backed away. Zero, ears perked, head cocked, began to whine, never taking his eyes from the cigarette. Zero tried again with no better luck. He dropped his head, began pawing at the cigarette, and barking frantically.

"Donal' started him out when he'z a pup retrievin' things," Jerry shouted over the dog, "an' now, 'at's all the son uv a bitch c'n think about. Is 'at fucked up 'r whut, man?" Jerry sneered before continuing. "Damn near got killed las' week when a car drivin' by lost a hub cap. POW! There he went, right out in'a traffic, man. Tires screechin'. Horns honkin'. People cussin'. Shiiiit. Thoughd he'z a goner. Tha's one stupidass dog, man."

Jerry rose from his chair. He patted the cigarette out with his bare foot, grabbed Zero by the scruff of the neck, and then threw him back under the table.

"SHUT UP!" Jerry ordered.

The dog shut up.

The table was pushed up against a tall double set of sheet covered windows facing the driveway. I leaned forward, lifted the sheet, and then looked toward Chad's place.

"Yew know Chad?" Jerry, finally offering me the joint again.

"Yeah. I know the squirrelly little bastard," and took a drag. Jerry took the joint back.

"Whut happen, man? Rip ya off on some dope 'r somethin'?"

"Nah. Nothin' like 'at. He's just a squirrelly little bastard."

Jerry turned serious.

"Chad's my bes' frien'. Saved my fuckin' life overseas," and stared me right in the eyes for a few seconds before breaking it off with that hissing cackle.

He opened his eyes wide and raised his brows to the limit.

"Jus' messin' with ya, man!" slamming an open palm on the table. "Chad's a li'l faggot. Owes me about fifty bucks f'r differ'nt shit."

I looked out the window again.

*Is this guy still drunk 'r just out'a his goddamn mind?*

"So, Whu'z the deal, Gil? Chad porkin' y'ur ol' lady in there 'r somethin'?"

"Nah. Gotta get somethin' he's been keepin' for me."

"Well, I guess if y're stupid enough ta be a cotton tromper," back to cackling, "then I guess y're stupid enough ta leave y'ur stereo gear with 'at li'l turd. I mean, don't go takin' 'at wrong 'r anything. I'm jus' talkin' facts, man."

"Chad told ya about my stereo?"

"Tol' me about it? Hell, he wuz gunna sell it ta me. Tol' me he needed the money ta git a wheelchair f'r his brother 'at had his legs blowed off 'r somethin' like 'at. Fuuuck. C'n ya b'lieve 'at shit? Who'd'a ever thoughd he'd'a lied about somethin' like 'at. Tha' boy's evil, man," he sneered.

*Chad, you sorry son of a bitch.*

I checked the utility again. Jerry handed me the roach clip. I sucked the last of the joint to nothing, held it in until I could feel the buzz, and then exhaled slowly.

*Damn. Homer could use some'a this.*

My hangover was letting up. Except the stomach thing.

"Hey!" Jerry shouted then dropped to a whisper, "Yew feelin' aw righ' now?"

I eased back into the chair.

"Yeah. I feel pr'tty good."

*Don't even feel like beatin' the crap out'a Chad anymore. Too much effort. I'll just yell at him. Get my money out'a the seabag an' just yell at him. Then leave. Embarrass him in front of his bitch. 'at's what I'll do.*

"Somebody's comin'," Jerry, looking out the window.

I floated forward and peeked around the sheet. Chad's head poked out of the doorway. He cautiously stepped outside and reconnoitered the area, poised to jump back inside if need be. A sweet young thing was immediately behind him. The glass in the door rattled as Chad pulled it shut.

"Damnation." Jerry whispered. "Look a' tha' shit."

She was a tiny, platinum blond wearing a tight pair of ski pants, knee high moccasins, and a furry, white jacket stopping at a wisp of a waist. She wasn't dressed near as classy as what I was used to seeing Chad with. She looked more like something I'd end up spending too much money on in a bar before dragging her back to the house to have her fake passing out on me.

Her hands clutched the top of the jacket, holding it against her face. Little snips of frozen breath dotted the air as she hurried to the car. She waited with her back to us as Chad removed the tarp from his car. Jerry and I stared out the window at the slut. She was doing a little dance, lightly tramping her feet to stay warm. Her long wavy hair tickled a tight little ass that hinted at a jiggle with every bouncy hop.

"Shiiit," Jerry steamed, his hot breath clouding the window. "No panty line," hurriedly wiping the haze from the pane.

Once the tarp was removed she darted around to the passenger side. Chad unlocked the door and opened it for her. She released her grip on the jacket when she bent over to enter the car. The jacket opened enough to reveal a well-developed set of lungs about to pop out of a low cut, skintight kind of tank top. She had the sweetest little face and cutest little button nose.

Gone—she'd flung herself into the car.

"Damn. I'd'a give good money ta been his peter las' night," Jerry wheezed. "Know whud I mean?"

"How's he do it?" running my hand over my face. "What's he got that makes him such a cuntsman?"

"Other'n a sports car, slick clothes, money, grass, a place off campus, an' y'ur stereo system? I's a real fuckin' mystery, ain' it," cackling.

"Yeah, but look at him. I mean...he's no Robert Redford 'r Paul Newman 'r Steve McQueen. What the hell's his trick?"

"Maybe he's hung like a bull el'phant."

"Nah. It's not that."

"Oh, yeah?" How ya know tha' shit?"

"He's my goddamn brother."

"No shit?" eyebrows lifted as high as they could go, then slamming to a serious squint. "I wouldn't go broadcastin' 'at aroun', man. Short shanks is a inherited thing. Ya run aroun' tellin' ever'body whud a teeny wienie y'ur bubba's got an' ya might as well be tellin' ever'body 'at yew..."

"Gotta go," as I stood and walked to the door. "Gotta catch him b'fore he leaves."

"Hey, man. There's this party right down the street at Eighth an' W t'night. Okay?"

"I'll try ta make it. Thanks f'r the joint," and shook his hand.

"No problem. No problem."

I made my way out to the car. I could here the bitch screaming.

"Would yew hurry up! I'm freezin'!"

"Not so funny when it's y'ur ass freezin' off, is it?" I shouted.

Chad looked up, gasped, and then went into shock. He slammed the trunk shut while maneuvering to keep the car between us. He shook his finger at me angrily.

"Are you happy?" he shouted. "God I hope so! I really hope so! You have completely humiliated my date!"

He was pouring everything into the performance. It sounded as if the little bastard was on the verge of throwing a few punches. His eyes, wide and fearful, gave him away. The bitch, however, couldn't see his eyes. She only heard the noisy bravado.

"Go ta hell, Chad," as I looked him over.

He was wearing a dark brown suede sports coat, a pair of smartly pressed tan slacks, a crisp white dress shirt with French cuffs, and golden cuff links that managed to sparkle even under overcast skies. The top button of the shirt was undone. An expensive, silk, paisley tie was draped about his neck. His styled, fashionably long, peroxide bleached hair and sun lamp tan made him look like one of those male models in some faggot-ass, "My Shit Don't Stink" fashion magazine.

"I need somethin' from inside," I said, beginning to shiver again.

"What? The stereo?" Chad whined. "I mean, the deal was to leave the stereo here since my place is so much safer than yours. You're upset because I didn't drop everything I was doing a minute ago and open the door exactly when you wanted me to. Right? Absolutely no regard for the lady's situation, no..."

"Shut the fuck up."

"All right, go ahead. Take the damn thing. Take it all. Do you think it's been fun trying to pack all your crap into that tiny closet of a house? Do you know what a pain in my butt that stereo has been for me? I've done nothing but worry about a robbery. A robbery you would probably accuse me of having something to do with. Gil, I have had nights I haven't been able to sleep for worrying about it. So, take it all."

It was pure drama.

"That why ya were gunna sell it all ta Jerry?"

It was like I'd hit him in the face with a brick.

"You know Jerry?" he asked nervously.

"We're tighter'n hell."

"He never...never mentioned that," brain frying, frantically cooking up an explanation for the deal he'd tried to cut with Jerry. "Jerry misunderstood me," he insisted quietly. "I would *never* sell your stereo," taking a deep breath and letting it out slowly. "I know how much it means to you. I know what you went through to get it. I'd asked Jerry how much he would be willing to pay for a stereo system like yours. I'd asked several others, for that matter. That's all. Simple inquiries to establish a reasonable value," voice trailing off, head lowering. "I needed the information so I could buy you a theft insurance policy for your Christmas present."

After a long pause I slowly made my way around the car and stood in front of him.

"Chad?" reaching out and gently grasping his shoulders.

He looked up at me and smiled innocently.

"Chad," tightening my grip and pulling him to me, "y're so... so very, *very*...full'a crap."

"The suit! I just had it cleaned!"

"I'VE HAD IT WITH Y'UR BULLSHIT!" yelling in his face then taking a deep breath. "I've had it with y'ur lyin'. I've had it with y'ur lockin' me out'a my own place. I've had it with y'ur borrowin' money from me an' never payin' me back. Startin' right now, things're gunna change. Y're gunna give me fifty dollars'a the money ya owe me an' y're gunna give it ta me b'fore ya pull out'a this driveway."

"This isn't your place anymore," blubbering.

"As long as y're borrowin' from me ta pay the rent, it's my place," letting him go.

Chad backed away and straightened his suit.

"I want fifty dollars," I demanded. "Now."

"Gil, I *swear,* I wish I had…"

"Don't push me asshole! Please. Don't push me," my voice a low growl. "If ya got enough money ta take 'at slut out an' spend what ya had ta spend on her ta get her ta poke ya then ya've got fifty dollars you can give ta me."

"Chad!" from inside the car. "I'm freezin' ta death!"

"Fifty bucks," thrusting my hand out. "Right now."

He reached into his coat pocket and pulled out an expensive looking leather wallet.

"Fifty dollars won't even leave me gas money," he whined. "I don't get another check from home until next week."

"CHAD!" the voice inside the car screeched.

He removed two twenties from the wallet.

"I'll think twice before I ever come to you for anything again," trying to make it sound like a snarl. "I mean it, Gil. *Never* again."

I jerked the bills from his hand.

"Forty'll do f'r now," glad to get that much. "Is the deadbolt unlocked?"

"Of course it's unlocked. How else could I get back in?"

I turned and headed for the shed.

"You don't care one bit about the bind this is going to put me in, do you?" Chad, close to whimpering.

"No," over my shoulder.

Jerry waved from the kitchen window and flashed that weirdass grin. I nodded at him. Chad's Healy started with a roar. He didn't give it any warm up time. The car sputtered out of the driveway, clouding the area as it went. I unlocked the door, gave the knob a twist, and then pushed. The door gave a little then stopped. The dead bolt hung tight. I spun around. Too late. Chad had made his getaway.

# THE RAVING EUNUCH MONKS

*That sorry-ass bastard!*

I frantically pumped the door through a half inch arc—open, close, open, close, open, close, faster and faster, harder and harder, the glass pane vibrating louder and louder in its caulkless stops. Completely drained, I surrendered. I rolled to my back then slid down the wall until I was sitting in the snow.

*Fuck me dead.*

*What are my choices? If I break the glass, there's gunna be all kinds'a complications. But…I gotta get get the money. But…I can't break the window then leave the stereo gear here. Shit! Jus' plain SHIT!*

Moments passed. Long, thoughtless moments. I was rocked by a series of convulsions. My legs, feet, hands, and butt were numb, nose running like a faucet.

The back door to the big wooden house opened. It was a strain to look up.

*Christ. It's the nut case.*

Jerry had a beer bottle in one hand and a cigarette burning in the other. When he reached my side, he looked down and nudged me with his boot.

"Y're a real pain in'a ass, man," Jerry scowled. "Ya got this decision makin' thing goin' righ' now, ain't ya? Ya jus' cain't fig're out whu' the fuck ta do abou' this door, c'n ya?"

Before I could answer him, the bottle slammed against the glass in the door. The pane shattered with a loud crash.

*Awww…dammit.*

I dropped my head between my knees.

*Dammit. Dammit. Dammit.*

"There," Jerry, reaching through the opening, tripping the dead bolt, and then shoving the door open.

I struggled to my feet and made the turn through the doorway into the front room. Jerry stepped around me, glass crunching under his unlaced jungle boots as he moved over to the heater to turn the gas up.

"Worry abou' the door an' shit later," he said before stomping out, closing the door as he went.

I leaned against the wall and looked the room over. The place smelled like grass, incense, perfume, and do-it. The room was large—twice the size of the place I shared with Homer. It had a nice kitchen, a large walk-in closet, and a good sized bathroom with a tub and separate shower. The walls and ceiling in the front room were entirely covered in tie dyed sheets. Dark green shag carpeting ran throughout the house, even the kitchen. A king-sized waterbed took up a third of the front room. The headboard was positioned midway against the wall so the bed stuck out into the room, dividing the room in half. Black, silk sheets were in a pile at the foot of the bed. My stereo gear sat on a set of shelves constructed of bricks and brown stained lengths of board. On the floor, under the bottom shelf, at least fifty record jackets were lined up. My reel-to-reel tapes were alongside them. Two blue beanbags, now covered in broken glass, were pushed up against the wall separating the front room and the kitchen. Six or eight hanging plants were suspended from the ceiling. It gave the place a garden kind of feel.

*What a muff trap. No doubt.*

It sure as hell hadn't looked like this when I was living with him. Almost all of the three hundred dollars I'd lent Chad over the past three months probably went into this place.

*Homer an' me ought'a consider doin' somethin' like this ta our place.*

I staggered over to a walk-in closet and entered. It was about eight feet deep by six feet wide. A small desk was against one wall. Spiral notebooks were scattered all over the desktop. Books were stacked in a wicker chair next to the desk. Clothes hung from every inch of a wood pole running the length of the opposite wall. The pole was supported in several places by pieces of two-by-fours to keep the pole from sagging under the weight of the clothes.

I found my seabag in the far corner, dumped its contents onto the floor and began rummaging through the uniforms, dive gear, small boxes, papers, and junk. I found my left inspection shoe, removed it from a wool sock used to protect the spit shine, and then shoved my fingers into the toe of the shoe. I removed a folded piece of paper.

I owe you $80.00. Thank You.
Your loving brother, Chad.

It took a few seconds to sink in.
Then, I guess I went a little berserk.

I jumped up, grabbed the pole, and then yanked on it as hard as I could. The pole snapped. All the clothes fell to the floor. I stomped up and down the closet, grinding the soles of my boots into the clothes. That wasn't enough. I grabbed an arm full of silk shirts then carried them to the front door where I tossed them through the broken window. I made six or seven trips before throwing the front door open only to be knocked to the floor by Zero. He stood over me with a shirt hanging from his mouth. I pushed him aside, got to my feet, and then stormed out of the shed. I kicked the pile of clothes all over the snowy drive, cussing with every kick. Zero was in dumbass heaven, jumping from one airborne shirt to the next, barking insanely.

Someone came up behind me. I turned around and saw Jerry wearing Chad's velvet bathrobe. He had a beer in one hand, a joint in the other. He nodded then joined in.

"Die, ya sorry son uv a bitch," talking to himself while kicking a stack of pants into the air. "Die," as another pile went flying.

Zero, breathing heavily and frothing at the mouth, trotted over to Jerry. After dropping a sport coat at Jerry's feet, Zero plopped his butt onto the snow.

Jerry held the joint out to me.

"Wan'a drag?" he asked.

Winded, I shuffled through the clothes and took it.

"Ya ought'a do somethin' abou' tha' temper, man," Jerry, seriously. " 'specially b'fore ya git aroun' fordy years ol' 'r somethin' 'cause ya do this shit at fordy, an' drink, an' smoke, an' do dope then y'ur fuckin' heart'll like...BOOM! Blow up. Heart shit ever'where. If a bunch'a kids're aroun' they'll all be scared shitless an' cryin'. Then their mammas'll be kickin' at ya an' callin' ya names f'r scarin' the crap out'a their babies an' shit. Ain' no happy endin' ta tha' story, man."

I returned the joint. Jerry handed me the beer. I took a swig, surveyed the mess, and then sat down on a pile of wet, muddy slacks still clipped at the cuffs to their shiny wooden hangers.

"Well," I mumbled, "I sure as hell don't want my goddamn heart ta blow up an' I damn sure don't wan'a go scarin' any babies."

"Damn straight," and took the beer from me.

A window about eight feet above the ground in the brick house next door flew up. A big guy with a boyish face and broad shoulders filled the opening.

"Y'ALL SHUDUP 'R I'LL KICK Y'ALL'S ASS!" angrily.

Jerry exploded.

Throwing the beer at the house, he charged the open window. The bottle crashed against the brick a few inches above the startled youth, drenching the figure in beer and broken glass. Wide-eyed, the boy jerked his torso from the opening. He slammed the window shut. Jerry smashed into the side of the house, jumping up and down, pounding his palms against the wall.

"WHU'S 'AT MAGGOT? Y'RE GUNNA KICK MY ASS?" while bouncing up and down like a lunatic on a pogo stick. "YA CHICKENSHIT WORM! GIT OUT HERE, YA REDNECK SON UV A BITCHIN' TURD!"

Zero joined in, barking wildly. The kid pulled the shade down. It snapped back up.

Jerry kept on raving.

"GIT OUT HERE, MOUTH! I'M GUNNA KILL YA! HEAR ME? I'M GUNNA FUCKIN' BEA'CH YA TA DEATH!" continuing to assault the house.

The shade came down a second time. It remained down.

Jerry stopped.

He stood beneath the window panting, staring up at the window. He turned around and rolled his shoulders a few times. After pulling Chad's bathrobe closed over his chest he walked back to where he'd been standing before the interruption, used the toe of his boot to push a few shirts into a pile, and then sat down on the shirts.

"Bubba's got good taste," Jerry, fingering a shirt as if nothing had happened. "Bubba don't own a gun 'r anything like 'at does he?" snickering. "He may be wantin' ta shoot y'ur ass off after he sees this mess ya made."

"Jesus," and pulled the furry cap from my head. "What if 'at guy calls the cops? Ya throw a grenade into his house an' now ya threaten ta kill…"

"*Trainin'* grenade. 'at don't count. An' it wuz my cousin threw it, not me. Fuck him anyways," cackling.

I ran my fingers through my hair. Zero curiously sniffed at my cap. He sneezed.

"Look. I gotta get out'a here. I gotta drive a guy ta Oklahoma this afternoon, but now I got all *this* shit ta worry about," pointing at the shed.

"Drivin' ta Oklahoma in this kind'a weather?" raising his brows.

"Yeah. F'r a funeral."

"Who died?"

"This guy's granddad. Lives in Oklahoma somewhere. Met him trompin' cotton."

"This frien'a y'urs. He a big guy with some hair missin'? Mexican lookin'?"

"Indian. Ya got him on with Deacon right after ya got me on."

"Seems I 'member him tellin' me he'z a jarhead," rubbing his chin.

"Yeah. Got out'a the Marines about a year ago."

"When ya plannin' on leavin'?"

"Soon as I can. Won't get out'a here any time soon now," lighting a cigarette.

Jerry scratched his chest.

"I'll take care'v it for ya," he said.

"Ya would?" looking over at him. "I'll pay ya for it."

"It's a fav'r, dumbass. It ain't a fav'r if I git paid f'r it. Tha' makes it a job. B'sides, here ya are hung over as shit, runnin' all over hell the day after a blizzard tryin' ta git hold'a some cash an' ya wan' me ta b'lieve ya got money ta pay me? Shiiit, man. Don't go blowin' smoke up my ass like 'at," taking a few steps toward me. "Ya need somebody ta take care'v it, I'll take care'v it, but don't go pullin' 'at 'I'll pay ya later' shit on me when ya know there ain' no fuckin' way. How stupid do I look, anyways?" crossing his eyes and sucking his cheeks in. "Yew trus' me?" seriously.

*What choice have I got?*

"No reason not to, I guess."

"If ya trus' me then take off. I'll take care'v ever'thing here."

"Ya sure?"

"Damn. Whud I jus' say? Di'n' I jus' say 'don't sweat it'? Ain' 'at whud I jus' said?"

"Where c'n I find ya when I get back?"

"I don' know f'r sure," shaking his head slowly, "but I'm thinkin' 'at ya might git real lucky an' fin' me righ' here where I fuckin' live. 'at's jus' a wild-ass guess, though. I could be wrong as hell. Know whud I mean?"

"Yeah," a little embarrassed. "Thanks f'r helpin' me out," and shook his hand.

"I ain' doin' it f'r yew, man," and walked back to the house.

Zero, a shirt dangling from his mouth, raced after him.

When Jerry reached the steps he stopped and turned.

"Tell 'at Marine buddy'a y'urs I wuz sorry ta hear about his gran'pa."

"I'll do that."

He went up the steps and into the house.

*Damnation. 'at's one strange mother.*

I reentered Chad's, got my seabag, and then headed back to my place. I was feeling better. Tired. A little hungry. I retraced my steps through the backyard, down the alley, the shortcut between the houses, finally arriving back on Ninth Street.

*Must be past noon. Hard ta tell with the clouds as dark as they are.*

I turned up the crumbling driveway leading to our utility. My truck, a semi restored 1935 Ford, was sitting in the drive. Homer's old '52 pickup was parked next to it.

*Where'd they come from?*

I entered the utility. Homer was comatose on the bottom bunk, feet projecting beyond the end of the rack. The air was sweet with the heavy smell of cheap incense.

I stripped down in the kitchen, trying not to make any noise. The telegram Homer'd received from Oklahoma was on the table. All Homer had told me when he'd gotten it was his grandfather had died. I picked it up and read it.

GRANDPA DEAD STOP FUNERAL MONDAY STOP

I placed it back on the table, stepped into the shower and braced myself for the initial, searing pain of water contacting open sores.

Homer'd slept through my shower. I rummaged through the
pile of clothes in the corner trying to find a clean shirt.

*Fuck. Ever'thing reeks.*

I wrapped up in a blanket, slid into my boots, and then stepped
outside, carrying with me the clothes I'd taken off. One by one I
shook as much as I could of the dirt, twigs, leaves, and trash from
the nasty rags. I figured the cold, fresh wind would help air them out
a little. Shivering, I jumped back inside. I put the bare minimum on
then stuffed every piece of clothing in the house into Homer's duffel
bag. I counted the change in my pocket.

*Shit.*

I grabbed the bar of soap from the shower then headed out to
a laundromat a few blocks away.

\*\*\*

"Got some soda money?" Homer, shaking me awake.

I got up from the wooden bench and stretched.

"Got two twenties," I yawned. "Barely had enough change ta
do the wash. Couldn't even afford laundry soap."

I went over to the dryer and checked to see if they were dry
enough to take out.

"Goddammit," I muttered.

The clothes were covered in hair.

"What's wrong?" Homer, stepping up beside me. "Oh," after
looking inside the dryer.

"It's fake fur," I mumbled. "I thought it'd wash."

"What's the coat look like?" Homer, pulling it from the
dryer.

He frowned.

"Put it on," handing it to me. "Maybe that'll help."

I slipped into it while walking to a mirror near the coke
machine.

*Mangy. Looks flat-ass mangy.*

Homer came up behind me.

"It doesn't look too bad," trying to comfort me. "A little skimpy now, but...it's okay. Smells a lot nicer."

"Yeah," sighing. "I suppose."

I returned to the dryer and began shaking what I could of the coat hair from each piece of clothing before stuffing them into the duffel bag.

"Chad gave me forty dollars of the money he owes me," I told Homer. "The little bastard paid me out'a the eighty he stole from my seabag," as I sniffed a yellowing tee shirt.

*Good enough.*

"Did you kill him?" checking under the machines for change.

"Didn't discover it 'til he'd left."

"We could probably make it with forty dollars. We're good for grass."

"Yeah. Guess so," bouncing the seabag on the floor to make room for the last of the clothes. "We could try ta find Chad t'night. He'll be at a party somewhere aroun' here. Shouldn't be hard ta find him."

"Yeah," calling off his unsuccessful stray quarters search. "Not many silver Austin-Healeys in the neighborhood."

I secured the top of the seabag, tossed it to Homer, and then headed for the front door. Two young ladies entered.

*Sweet lookin' little things.*

Homer checked to make sure his bandanna was in place. We smiled warmly and nodded politely as I held the door for them. They smiled and nodded back. We stepped outside.

"I got the impression the tall one wanted me, Homer. It was jus' kind'a in the air. That unspoken 'take me like a sweaty buffalo hunter' kind'a signal. Did ya pick up on 'at, Homer?"

Homer grunted.

"Listen," I said. "Since we can't go ta Oklahoma 'til we find Chad, why don't we spend the rest'a the afternoon sprucin' the place up just in case we meet somethin' t'night? What'a ya think?"

"Yeah. We could do that."

"It's like 'em chicks back there. I mean, what if they'd worked up the nerve ta ask us ta plank 'em while their clothes were washin'? Would ya really wan'a bring 'em ta our place? It's a fuckin' toilet. I swear ta God, if we don't do somethin' about that place it's gunna end up costin' us more leg than lightin' farts in a bar. You should see Chad's place. The devil could get a blowjob off a nun in 'at place. It's got the right atmosphere. It *oozes* orgasm. How about it? Wan'a turn the place inta a snatch trap?"

"Sounds good," not overly enthused.

"I'm serious as a heart beat, Homer. As soon as we get back ta the house, let's clean it up. We got enough time b'fore goin' after Chad. We could even go up ta Buffalo Beano's an' spend a little bit'a this forty on some posters an' one'a those fancy India-Indian bedspreads. One'a those cheap, goofy lookin' dyed ones. Tack it ta the overhead. I'll get my stereo back from Chad."

When we got back to the house we stood in front of the heater and glanced around the room. I walked over to the doorway to the kitchen and looked in. Homer looked over the top of my head.

"Maybe we should work on talking them into taking us to their place," he suggested.

"Yeah," flatly. "That'd pro'bly be best."

Homer showered while I rested on the bunk. We put on our freshly washed clothes, jumped into his truck, and then headed out to eat. It was 3:30 by the radio.

The IHOP was six or seven blocks from the house. It was nearly empty. We hung around another hour or more after eating. I thanked him for retrieving the trucks.

"Where'd ya find 'em?" I asked.

"The bar."

"No shit? Imagine 'at. Our trucks parked outside a bar. Damn, Homer. Which bar?"

"Mother's. And you left your keys in your truck again."

We fell silent for a good while, looking out the window at the snow covered campus across the street. Lounging in a soft, clean booth. Stomachs full. Bodies warm. I could have stayed in that booth forever, sitting, smoking cigarettes, and drinking coffee.

"Work," Homer, breaking the trance. "We've got to find work."

"Yeah," agreeing. "No low payin' shit-job this time. As soon as we get back from Oklahoma we'll start lookin'. It's not much longer 'til school starts an' I c'n use the job locator service on campus. I c'n pull a few openin's f'r you too. How're they gunna know y're not a student?"

Homer liked the idea.

"With the GI Bill," I continued, "I'll only need a part time job. We'll find you somethin' more substantial. Ya thought about goin' ta school next semester? It's almost like free money."

"Nah. I'll probably work a while then try for California again."

"How long ya think it'll take ya ta earn enough?"

"Have to see what kind of job I find."

We sat for a while longer, swapping a few military related California stories before falling silent again.

"Ya ready ta go?" I asked after about ten or fifteen minutes.

Homer slid from the booth without saying anything. I caught the check and we headed back to the house.

It was 5:30 and already dark. What little ice and snow had melted during the day was beginning to freeze again. The clouds had begun to break up. Here and there a cluster of stars popped through. Homer pulled into the drive. A party was shaping up in the big house in front of our utility. Janis Joplin was screaming her lungs out.

"Best park near the front'a the driveway 'r we'll be blocked in again," I told him.

Homer backed up until the rear bumper was over the sidewalk. He adjusted the bandanna on his head before stepping from the cab of the truck into the bright lights flooding the drive. We entered our tiny shack. I climbed onto the top bunk. Homer walked back to the toilet. Neither one of us had bothered turning the light on, both preferring the softly dancing, orange glow of the heater.

Janis gave way to the Stones.

"When ya wan'a go lookin' f'r dipshit?" loud enough for him to hear me in the other room.

"I don't know. Let's hang around here a while."

He returned to the front room, pulled his bandanna off, and then began scratching the scar on his head.

"Itchin' ya again?"

"Yeah. I'm out'a lotion," pulling his coat off and crawling into the bottom bunk. The bunk shook and rattled as he settled in. Homer's Zippo clinked open. The sound of a flint strike followed. The lighter clinked shut. The smell of tobacco smoke drifted up. I must have dozed off.

A loud banging at the door startled me awake. Homer got up and answered it. A long haired kid, silhouetted by the lights from the party house, was standing in the doorway. The boy, cigarette dangling from his mouth, held a bottle of beer in each hand.

"Yew guys're invited ta the party if ya wan'a come," holding the beers out.

Homer, still half asleep, took the beers and turned to hand me one.

"Yeah. at'd be great," as I sat up.

The kid was staring at the back of Homer's head, mouth half open, wincing like somebody'd smacked him with a big stick. Homer turned around in time to catch the kid gawking.

*Goddammit!*

The kid backed up.

"Okay. 'at's... 'at's cool. We'll be, uh...expectin' ya," then turned and hurried away.

Homer slowly eased the door shut, took a few deep, noisy gulps from the bottle, and then turned to me.

"Acted like he'd never seen a Cherokee before," he said.

"Pro'bly hadn't. Least not a real one this close up," sliding from the bunk to the floor. "Let's go lookin' f'r an Austin-Healy," pulling my coat on.

"Sounds good," pushing his long black hair back over the top of his head and carefully tying the bandanna in place before grabbing his coat.

The back yard glittered brightly in the lights from the big house. The party was growing louder. Led Zeppelin was up.

"Mind if we drop by this place on Eighth an' W b'fore we start lookin' f'r Chad?" I asked. "I need ta see if this guy took care'a somethin' for me."

"Sounds good."

I climbed behind the wheel, trying to ignore the faces staring at us from the big house.

It took less than two minutes to find our party. The house was a monstrous, two-story affair. It was a big party. We ended up having to park a block away. Credence Clearwater echoed down the street as we got out of the truck. Half way up the block I stopped at an old Dodge panel van.

## JERRY CHAFF
### I support the local pigs

was sloppily painted in freehand on the side of the door.

"That's the guy I'm lookin' for," pointing at the van.

We moved on to the party.

A narrow, covered porch ran along the front of the house.

Dead, leafless vines dangled from a number of hanging planters. Some of the planters contained crushed beer cans. Homer checked his bandanna as we walked up the steps, crossed the porch, and then entered the house. Other than a few quick glances, nobody paid us much attention.

"SMELL 'AT?" I shouted over "White Rabbit".

"NICE!" Homer.

The place was packed, butt to butt, wall to wall. A few of the females looked pretty nasty—painted up, braless types. Some were in skintight jeans, some in bellbottomed corduroys cut so low at the belt line you could see panty tops. Others were wearing short, tie-dyed tee shirts exposing taut, flat tummies and accenting perky little nipples. There were a few long, brightly colored, loosely laced, settlers' dresses. I looked over at Homer. As usual, he was expressionless, but focused. I had to put my mouth to his ear to speak to him.

"Screw it. Nothin's happenin' here. Let's go," as I turned around.

Homer, without taking his eyes off one of the nastier looking ladies, grabbed my arm. He cupped his hands around his mouth to avoid yelling.

"Let's have a beer or two before we leave."

"Hell. If you insist," I answered.

We worked our way through the crowd, heading for the kitchen at the back of the house. That's where the liquor would be. By the time we got there I was half high from the smoke. As I entered the kitchen I felt somebody behind me poke me in the ribs. I turned around and found Danny Wright, an old high school friend, smiling broadly.

"Holy shit!" smiling back. "How the hell ya doin'?"

"Too early to tell," shaking my hand.

I introduced him to Homer. After they shook hands Homer

headed for a tub filled with iced down beer bottles close to the back door.

"Y're lookin' pr'tty good," I told Danny.

Danny struck a muscle pose then patted a noticeable paunch that had developed since high school.

"You're looking a little thin," as he reached over to pat my stomach. "When'd you get back in town?"

"September."

"That's been a while. Where've you been keeping yourself?"

"Workin' my ass off."

Homer returned and handed me a beer. He exchanged nods with Danny then continued on into the living room.

"Where'd you meet the Jolly Green Giant?" Danny.

"Trompin' cotton."

"No shit? I did some tromping south of Levelland when things got real bad last year. I decided at noon on the first day my finances weren't in that bad'a shape. At the end of the day I quit. If I'd tromped another second I wouldn't have had a brain cell left."

Danny finished his beer in a series of heavy gulps.

"What kind of work did you find after tromping?" he asked.

"Shit," I burped, "that's *all* I've been doin'."

"Since September?" looking at me in disbelief. "That's all you could find?"

I was beginning to feel like an idiot so I changed the subject.

"When'd ya get out?" I asked.

"Well, it's like this. I never went in. I didn't do too well on the physical," somewhat apologetically.

"Ya didn't miss much," I mumbled.

"That's what I've heard," looking down at the floor.

"I finally lost my virginity, though. Twenty 'r thirty times."

Danny looked up and laughed.

"Hey. Remember Doug Pitt?" he asked.

"Hell, yeah. I remember crazy Doug. Always in trouble an' shit."

"He's here at the party somewhere. Got drafted the summer we graduated. If I see him, I'll tell him you're here."

Danny bummed a cigarette and a light from me then asked if I was planning on going back to Tech.

"That's the plan," looking the crowd over, partly for that Jerry guy, partly for some easy butt. "Need ta find a part time job then sit back an' learn ta be a college kind'a guy. Just take it easy."

"What kind of work are you looking for?"

"Anything part time 'at dudn't have anything ta do with cotton."

"Maybe I can help you out. Grab a coupl'a more beers then wait here," before bulldozing his way into the crowded living room.

I did as ordered, returning to the doorway between the living room and the kitchen. Even with almost all the windows open, the overcrowded house was hot and stuffy. I thought about pulling my coat off and tossing it on a growing pile of coats in the kitchen corner next to the beer tub. I decided against it. Although the washer thrashing had thinned it some and left it a little patchy, it was still a pretty cool looking coat. The ladies seemed to love it. I didn't want to risk having it stolen.

I saw Danny round the corner across the room. He waved for me to come over to him. I fought my way to his side.

"You're in luck," Danny announced with a smile and took a beer from me. "Follow me."

We passed by a stairway, then through a large entrance way opening into a room as big as the living room and front room put together. We ended up in the far corner of the room.

A knot of people had gathered around a short, solid figure in a set of pressed khakis. His eyes bulged a little, his deeply tanned, rugged face almost perfectly round. He was smiling broadly, head slightly bobbing. We worked our way through the crowd until we were behind him. The knot was listening intently to a lady speak.

She was stunning—full lips, high cheek bones, large brown eyes, straight brunette hair to her thighs. A waist so small, I swear, I could have gotten my hands around it.

And her breasts!

*My God!*

They looked magnificently out of proportion on that tiny frame. The undersized sweater she was wearing exaggerated the deformation. I was smitten.

*I must wed this fair maiden.*


Danny waved at her. She winked back.

He tapped the man in khakis on the shoulder. The man turned and smiled warmly.

"Hugo, this is Gil, the guy I was telling you about. Gil, this is Hugo Tripp."

Mr. Tripp extended his hand. I kept staring at the lady.

"I'm glad ta meet ya, Gil," in a slow, soft, West Texas drawl. "Danny's jus' told me some nice things about ya."

Danny stabbed me in the side. I looked away from the lady and grasped Mr. Tripp's hand.

"Glad ta meet ya, sir," glancing back at the future Mrs. McNeil.

"Are you inter'sted in the Baha'i Faith?" he asked.

"The what?"

"The Baha'i Faith," as he nodded at the lady. "I noticed ya seemed ta be inter'sted in what Joan's talkin' about."

"Oh. Ye'sir...that. I was just, ya know, listenin' in."

"I understand y're goin' back ta school an' need some part time work."

"Ye'sir," trying to put Joan out of my mind for the moment.

"I've got some serious doubts about hirin' anybody who'd stick with trompin' cotton f'r ten weeks," laughing.

"I've done worse, sir," smiling politely.

"Hugo. Call me Hugo."

"Ye'sir, I mean, Hugo."

"This is no place ta conduct an interview. Why don't ya come out ta the farm sometime this comin' week an' we'll talk it over. Here's my card. Make it b'tween 7:30 an' 8:00 in the mornin'."

"Sure. Thank you. Thank ya very much. Would Thursd'y be all right? I'll be out'a town 'til then."

"Thursd'y'd be fine," nodding.

"Sir, excuse me, Hugo. Could ya use two people? I've got this good friend who's lookin' f'r work too."

"I'm sorry, son, but I don't think so right now. I c'n keep somebody busy f'r about twenty hours a week, but no more'n 'at 'til the spring. This is the slow season f'r land surveyin'."

Hugo sounded like he genuinely felt bad about it.

"No problem. No problem," I told him.

"Is y'ur friend recently out'a the service?"

"Ye'sir. About a year. Marines."

Hugo looked down, furrowed his brow, and thought a minute.

"Tell ya what, Gil," looking up, "lemme call around an' see what I c'n do f'r y'ur friend while y're gone. Gimme a call as soon as y're back in town."

"Thanks, Mr. Tripp," shaking his hand. "Thanks a lot. He'd really appreciate it."

Mr. Tripp nodded then turned his attention back to Mrs. McNeil who was busy answering questions about the Faith thing.

*Joan McNeil. It's like...poetry.*

"See? No sweat," Danny, nudging me.

"Yeah. Damn. I can't b'lieve it. A shittin' job...just like 'at."


We stepped back from the knot a few feet. I positioned myself so I could keep an eye on...

*Joanie. That's what I'll call her. Jo maybe.*

"Where'd ya meet these people?" I asked.

"I've surveyed with Hugo from time to time. Hugo goes to Baha'i meetings sometimes to speak about different religions. Religion and spiritual stuff is a hobby or something for him. He knows some Sufis, crystal freaks, Druids. He even got me to go to some mind control meetings."

"Mind control?"

"Not the kind you're thinking of. It's not brain washing. It's a method of controlling stress, mood, sleep, healing, and some other things like that. About eight months ago he invited me to one of the Baha'i meetings. That's where I met Joan."

"Anybody doin' her?"

"Are you kidding? She's really into this Baha'i thing. It's a part of their religion...no premarital sex."

"Ya sure? Baha'i sounds pr'tty damn hippie ta me," looking back at my one and only love. "How's somebody get invited to a Baha'i thing?"

"You show up. I'll take you if you want, but you're wasting your time if you think you're going to get a piece of ass out of it."

"Maybe I'm goin' ta find some kind'a enlightenment."

"Awful convenient having your search for enlightenment *and* your quest for a piece of ass dovetail so neatly."

"So, when's the next meetin'?" ignoring the comment.

"Every Tuesday night."

"I'll be gone this Tu'sd'y. Let's do it the next week."

"That'll work. I'll pick you up at 6:45."

I gave Danny my address, got his phone number, and then worked my way toward the stairs. Danny was right behind me.

Suddenly, all hell broke loose in the stairwell. A lanky guy with a goatee came charging down the steps, screaming at the top of his lungs.

"OUT'A THE WAY, GODDAMMIT!" clawing his way through the crowd. "MOVE! MOVE!"

A crush of others, all yelling and screaming, were following him. The panicked guy fought his way to the kitchen. Behind the mob a bewildered looking Homer slowly descended the steps. He stopped at the foot of the stairs as we approached. The entire party was spilling out of the kitchen into the backyard.

"What the hell's goin' on?" I asked Homer.

Homer paused before answering, glanced upstairs, and then turned back to me.

"Don't know," with a blank look. "I was upstairs talking to this guy. I pitched a beer can out the window and this damn dog went flying out the window after it," his voice trailing off. "I think it's dead."

"Black Lab?" I asked.

*Fuck. I already know the answer.*

"Yeah. Kind of stupid looking."

"You killed Donald's Lab?" Danny gasped. "Zero?"

"Let's go, Homer," as I took his arm and headed toward the front door. "I'll call ya when I get back," over my shoulder to Danny.

Danny waved, still registering a look of shock over the possibility of the dog's death.

I hurried Homer down the porch steps and across the yard to the sidewalk.

"Can you believe that?" Homer, becoming more upset. "You think he's dead?"

"Hell, no. The snow would'a broken his fall."

*Poor bastard pro'bly died of a heart attack b'fore hittin' the ground.*


"Shit," I muttered as we passed Jerry's van. "I f'rgot about findin' 'at guy."

"Oh yeah," Homer, fumbling in his pocket. "That's the guy I was talking to when...when the dog...," his voice tapering off.

He handed me a roll of money with a rubber band around it.

"The guy said there was four hundred dollars there. He said to tell you he got four twenty-five, but he kept twenty-five for his commission."

"Jerry gave ya this ta give ta me?" confused.

"Yeah, I think that's what his name was. The same guy who got me hired on to tromp cotton. He saw us from upstairs when we first got to the party. I didn't know if you were coming upstairs or not. That's why he gave me the money."

I came to a halt.

"DAMMIT! That shithead went an' sold my goddamn stereo! He fuckin' sold my goddamn stereo," shaking the money in Homer's face. "He said he'd *take care* of it for me, the son of a bitch."

"Guess he did," Homer.

"I ought'a go back an' kick his flaky fuckin' ass," pulling the rubber band from the wad. "The bastard," I grumbled as Homer watched me count the twenties.

"All there?"

"Yeah," counting it again. "All four hun'r'd."

"That's a lot of money."

"Just a little short'a what we made trompin' cotton f'r ten weeks."

"That much?"

"Yeah," looking back at the house. "But," raising my voice again, "he still didn't have the right ta go an' sell the motherfucker like 'at."

"Your right. But it's still a lot of money."

At the truck I worked the rubber band back around the roll. I held the bundle in my hand. It felt big. It felt heavy. It felt good.

*Damn near three months pay in the Navy. With combat pay.*

"Where do we start looking for Chad?" Homer, quickly shifting the truck's gears from reverse to first, back to reverse then first again, finally breaking the tires free of the ice in the gutter.

I gave it a few seconds of serious thought.

"Ta hell with Chad!" I whooped. "We're fuckin' rich! We're goin' ta Oklahoma! We could afford a private jet," holding the roll up.

Homer produced a baggie of rolled joints from his coat pocket.

"Look what else he gave me."

"Let's go home, smoke a few, then hit the rack," I suggested. "That way we'll be fresh f'r the trip."

"Sounds good," Homer nodded.

"If we leave right after the tower wakes us up, will 'at give us enough time ta get ta where we're goin'?"

"Even if the roads are bad it'll only take about eight hours."

"There's the plan then."

The driveway was full of cars when we got back to the house. We had to drive up the alley and park in the backyard. Once inside the utility Homer and I stretched out on the bunks. We shared a joint, took turns counting the money, and then listened to the music from the party. The Animals. Cream. The Beatles' "Rubber Soul" album.

*Good shit ta go ta sleep to.*

"Hope that dog's okay," Homer whispered.

I wandered off with the Moody Blues.

\*\*\*

The scratching and popping of a loudspeaker coming to life woke me. The noise was immediately followed by a screaming choir of at least a million hysterical voices.

> "ONWARD CHRISTIAN SOOOLDIERS,
> MARCHING AS TO WAAAR,
> WITH THE CROSS OF JEEESUS,
> GOING ON BEFOOORE...,"

I rolled onto my stomach and covered my ears.

Sunday morning in the student ghetto.

Every Sunday morning at exactly 7:30, from the largest speakers in the tallest belltower in West Texas, the same battle hymn would pound away. It was the most effective antipagan weapon in the Lubbock First Baptist Church's arsenal. Every dope smoking, pill popping long hair, every hung-over ag major wan'-

a-be cowboy, every newly sacrificed virgin, every Godless art, anthropology or philosophy major living in the ghetto would be blasted from whatever drug or alcohol induced stupor they were lost in. The damn song had three verses. Occasionally someone would snap—loud screams from a front yard or wailed bursts of profanity echoing in an alley.

I remained on my stomach, half awake, remembering a time when Sunday morning meant singing in the choir during the hour-long early morning service, an hour of Sunday school, then a final hour or more attending the late morning service. The Sunday afternoon schedule wasn't any lighter—choir practice, Training Union, and the evening service. Tuesday evenings it was visitation followed by Royal Ambassadors, a Baptist oriented, Nazi styled version of the Boy Scouts. On Wednesdays, it was the church supper and prayer meeting. All that time spent memorizing the recipes to make all the bullshit more or less palatable and the voodoo more or less believable.

*Still be stuck in 'at sorry-ass routine if Bob Dylan an' then the military hadn't come along when they did.*

The final verse of the song ended. The siege guns fell silent. Three minutes had passed. Homer was stirring. A match popped. The pungent odor of high quality grass drifted up from the bottom bunk.

"Breakfas' in bed?" I yawned.

His hand, joint between his fingers, appeared at the edge of the bunk.

"No thanks," turning the offer down.

The hand sank out of sight.

After Homer finished the joint we set about getting ready to go, using his duffel bag for both of our clothes. Within thirty minutes we were pulling out of the backyard. It was a perfectly clear morning. The air froze our breath. Everything smelled fresh and clean.

"We ought'a try this sober thing more often," I commented. "Feels pr'tty nice."

"Sounds good," Homer grunted while fiddling with the heater controls.

The cab filled with a loud clanking noise coming from under the dash. Homer turned the heater off and looked over at me.

"The fans shot," he mumbled. "It might get a little cold."

"What makes ya think 'at?" I growled. "Middle'a the winter with three hun'r'd feet'a snow on the ground an' we're drivin' north. What makes ya think eight fuckin' hours in an icebox is gunna be cold?"

"More like east-northeast. Want to go back for the blankets?" slowing as we approached a corner.

"Nah, but I'll take 'at joint now."

I was hoping Homer would open up and tell me a little about his grandfather, his family, or something during the trip, but he kept the conversation tuned to bullshit. At one point, out of nowhere, Homer asked me if I ever had dreams.

"I don't know if they're dreams 'r not. I wake up an' feel like I was pro'bly havin' a dream. Actually...it feels more like a nightmare. I mean, I feel...uncomf't'rble when I wake up. I don't remember any details 'r anything. I just have a bad feelin'. How about you?"

"It's a little like that," then he paused for a moment. "For a second after I wake up I remember something, but it goes away so fast. I try to remember what it is, but...it's too late."

"Ya know what it's like f'r me? It's like somethin' wakes me up. That's when I get nervous. I'm not sure what it is 'at wakes me up. It's real intense f'r a second 'r two. Almost scary. Then it b'gins ta wear off right away. It's a little like my brain has ta pull ever'thing back t'gether the way y'ur eyes have ta readjust after a flash bulb goes off in y'ur face," as a chill ran down my spine. "I don't know if it's a dream causin' all of it though," lighting a cigarette.

Homer fired one up.

"I guess it's a little like that for me too," Homer, quietly.

"Sometimes, after a dream, it takes a while for me to recognize where I am."

"Why ya askin'?" working my coat further up my neck to trap more body heat.

"My grandpa dreamed a lot. At least he said he did. He said he remembered his dreams."

"Did he dream Indian stuff? Like talkin' ta wolves an' ridin' on a white buffalo?"

"I guess. Mainly it was voices explaining things and telling him to do things."

"Like what?"

"All kinds of things. It doesn't really matter. Nobody ever paid him any attention."

Homer fell silent. I decided that was as far as he wanted that line of conversation to go.

It was a seven hour trip. The snowy landscape began to roll more dramatically the further east we got into Oklahoma. Every nerve in my body had gone numb with cold. From Soper, Oklahoma it took us a final hour of creeping over snow and ice covered dirt roads to reach his uncle's place. The sun was setting as we eased our way into a hand shoveled area in front of a low, wood framed house. Clear plastic sheets were taped over all the windows. Rips in the plastic had been patched with duct tape.

We slid in along side a fairly new Ford pickup truck. Homer honked the horn several times.

"This is it," his breath a cloudy puff. "Uncle Lee's."

"Not much of an Indian name," I frowned, running the back of my coat sleeve under a dripping nose.

"That's his first name. His last name is Screaming Charging Laughing Howling Broken Arrow Eagle Crazy Wolf Elk Bear Beaver White-Eyed-Ass Kicker…"

"All right, all right. I get the picture."

Homer looked into the rear view mirror, adjusted his bandanna, and then looked over at me. I nodded in approval. The front door of the house opened. A tall, stocky, brown-skinned man stepped out. He was waving and smiling. Homer and I slid out of the truck and walked over to the man.

"I am so glad, Homer. So glad," the man smiled. "We didn't know if you were coming or if you had even gotten the telegram."

He grabbed Homer up in a powerful hug. Homer shut his eyes and waited to be released. As soon as his grip loosened, Homer backed away.

"This is Gil," Homer, pointing at me. "Gil, this is my uncle, Lee."

Lee's handshake was like a vice.

"Glad ta meet ya, Mr. Cherokee."

Lee's face instantly darkened. He turned and glared at Homer. Homer looked down at the ground. As quickly as Lee's smile had vanished, it was back.

"I am very glad to meet you," letting my hand go. "You are very welcome here. I didn't mean to be rude, but sometimes," glancing back at Homer, the smile disappearing again, "I get upset at certain things," followed by an uncomfortable moment of silence.

*What the hell'd I say wrong?*

"But not now," Lee declared loudly and hugged Homer again. "I'm not upset anymore."

Homer looked relieved, as if he'd narrowly missed an ass beating.

"Come inside," Lee, motioning toward the door. "It's too cold to be standing around outside. I will catch you up on everybody. You will first get the truth from me before your aunt fills you with her gossip and rumors."

*What an accent. Sound's like what an Indian should sound like. Like the Indians in the movies. Thicker than Homer's.*

I fell in behind Lee. Homer walked over to the corner of the house, stopped, and then looked off into the distance.

Lee stopped.

"Dammit," under his breath.

"I'm going up to Grandpa's," Homer.

It didn't seem to be open for discussion.

"Aren't you tired? Hungry? Come in first and..."

"I want to go now, Uncle Lee. Alone."

Their eyes locked. They glared at each other for a long moment.

Lee's eyes misted over. Homer's face remained stone cold. Emotionless. He turned away when he noticed me staring at him. Lee ran his coat sleeve over his face.

"You will have to walk. The lane is all drifted over," he said.

Homer nodded and disappeared around the corner of the house.

"Won't he need a flashlight?" I asked as we entered the house. "It's gettin' dark."

"No. Not as many times as he has made the trip. He could do it blindfolded."

The low, water spotted ceiling of the house made me feel tall. The house smelled of burning wood. It was warm. I shivered violently, beginning the defrosting process. Photographs in hand carved wood frames covered a narrow table behind a couch draped in a bright red wool blanket. I noticed a few portraits of figures in military uniforms, the kind everybody has made right out of boot camp. Lee took my coat and placed it on the couch.

We entered a large kitchen. He told me to sit down at an old, heavy looking dining room table.

"What do you want to eat?" and smiled.

"I appreciate the offer, but I'm not all 'at hungry. It's nice ta just sit here an' thaw out. Homer's heater wudn't workin'."

"All the way from the Texas panhandle in December without a heater," gently laughing. "That is a Homer plan all right. How about a little Jack Daniels and water? You like it that way?"

"That'd be perfect."

Lee scurried around the kitchen pulling the order together, returned to the table and placed a beer mug sized glass in front of me. He practically fell into the chair opposite mine. We both lit cigarettes. I sipped the drink as he watched.

I couldn't breathe.

"Too stiff?" Lee grinned.

"No...no," gasping for air. "Just right."

*Good God, almighty!*

"It's not really Jack Daniels," he confessed.

*No shit.*

"I make it myself and then put some of it into a Jack bottle. I use the Jack bottle for guests. It makes things feel more special."

"Thank you," I managed after another sip. "Appreciate it."

"Where did you meet Homer?"

I paused, playing with my cigarette, before answering.

"Sir, I, uh...I'm not sure what I should be sayin'. I mean, I feel like I stepped on it outside somehow an' I don't know if I should be tellin' ya things Homer hadn't told ya. No offense 'r anything, but I just don't wan'a say somethin' that's gunna make trouble for him 'r say somethin' I'm not supposed ta."

I studied his face for any signs of anger.

"Are you afraid he will beat you up?" lifting his eyebrows.

"Fuc...hell no! Homer's not like 'at. It's just not somethin' he'd do ta me so I'm not gunna do it ta him. We kind'a trust each other that way. I like it like 'at."

Lee leaned forward and glared at me. It was one of those "I'm in y'ur head" kind of looks you can't turn away from.

"I am glad you are Homer's friend," speaking softly. "Homer has been looking for a friend like this ever since he came back from the military. That's too long to go without a *good* friend."

I was embarrassed. It must have shown. Lee hurried to explain what the problem had been when we'd first arrived.

"What happened outside did not have anything to do with you," swigging his drink then taking a puff on his cigarette. "It's a long story in some places. Do you want to hear some of it? The important parts?"

"Sure," and sipped the drink.

*Christ. No ice cubes ta water it down.*

"I will make it short and with no gossip, or if it is gossip, I will tell you it's gossip. Okay?" raising his brows.

"Okay."

Lee took a drink then began.

"We were all born Whiteman, that is, all of my brothers and sisters...Homer's aunts and uncles. Whiteman wasn't our *real* name, though. Dad had another name before Whiteman. A *real* name. Dad wasn't always well. He heard voices. He said he heard voices because he had powers. The doctors said he had a mental problem. Mother said he drank too much. Before marrying mother, before they even met, he had one of his dreams. He said that in the dream he was told he had to change his name. The reason was because the Cherokee and all the other tribes had not fought hard enough to keep the land. Once they were sent out here to Indian Territory, they forgot the old ways. Because of this, they were no longer like real people, but became more like the whites. Everyone would have to change names because no one was worthy of a real name because real names had Spirit powers. Dad changed his name to Whiteman."

"Damn. Kicked himself pr'tty hard in the ass with 'at one."

"Yes. I think that is what he was trying to do."

"So, Homer's name is Whiteman?"

"His *official* name is," and took a big gulp from his glass. "I don't know what the very first name was, the name before Dad changed it to Whiteman. Dad changed it before he got married so that was a long time ago. It was never talked about. Homer's Dad, Jeb, was killed in a grain elevator accident in Leotta, Kansas when Homer was eight. His mother died two years later. Me and Rolene, she is my wife, we didn't have any kids, so we took Homer and his sisters in. I shouldn't have let Homer spend so much time with Dad because Dad was crazy, but then, I probably couldn't have stopped

Homer from seeing him even if I had tried. Rolene says I should have tried harder to make Homer go to church," pausing to put the cigarette out, "but it wasn't worth the fight to get him to go. He hated church."

I was beginning to feel a buzz.

"Anyway," continuing, "I think Homer spent too much time with his grandpa because Homer finally got a little crazy too. I didn't know *how* crazy Homer was until he changed his name to Cherokee. He thought it would make his grandpa happy if he changed his name like that. It didn't. Dad never spoke to Homer again. Dad didn't know what that did to Homer. Dad was becoming real crazy at the time and it kept becoming worse. Anyway, Homer changing his name got *everybody* upset because it made everybody think about things they didn't want to think about. I was the only one to see him off when he left for Marine training," pausing a moment. "That is what all that was about out front when you first got here. You didn't cause anything. If he didn't tell you about it, how could you know about it?"

"Did y'ur dad ever write ta Homer?"

"Dad couldn't write, but I don't think he would have anyway. That is how mad he was. Dad didn't talk to Homer when he came back on leave or when he would call home from overseas. He didn't say anything when I told him Homer had been wounded. When Homer got out of the Marines and came back...Dad wouldn't even let him in his house."

"Damn. No offense, but tha's pr'tty severe. 'at's damn near mean," and took a gulp from the glass.

"Maybe, but...he was old. He was born around 1880 or '82. Not too far from here. He lost a lot of things early on. Mom died during the Depression. There were seven of us kids. Two died before they were four years old. My other two sisters moved away during World War II. They were young and very good-looking. A lot of things were going on everywhere else during the war. Nothing was going on around here. So, they left. We never heard from them again. One of my brothers was killed in that war. Then Homer's Dad died. I'm all that is left. All of that made Dad do some things that made him look like he was a little mean. Plus, like I told you, Dad was always a little crazy anyway."

*Damn. I'm really feelin' this...this whatever it is. Feelin' good. Loose.*

"Mr. Whiteman..."

"Lee," quickly correcting me. "Call me Lee."

"Excuse me. Lee, ya know, I was kind'a wantin' ta ask ya somethin', but I don't wan'a sound disrespectful 'r make ya mad."

"Ask."

"Well, I was wonderin', ya know...about Indian names. Ya tol' me how y'ur dad felt about names an' I c'n un'erstan' 'at, but...where the hell'd 'Homer' come from. I mean, in the phone book ya'd think he was a hillbilly 'r somethin'. Couldn't y'ur brother at least'a given Homer a cool Indian first name like...Tall Eagle 'r somethin'?"

Lee laughed.

"I was hoping you would help Homer not be crazy, but you are talking like him now," clearing his throat to begin. "Using white names wasn't all my Dad's idea. Back then, the whites would get mad and beat the sand out of you if they heard you speaking the language. Using an Indian name made them even madder. This was going on even before Sequoia. Ever heard of him?"

"No."

"Doesn't matter," and waved it off.

"So how'd y'ur dad come up with Lee an' Jeb f'r names?"

"The Civil War. Most of the tribes in Indian Territory sided with the rebels during the Civil War. We even had a Cherokee general named Wati. He gathered up a bunch of Indians and called them the Cherokee Brave, but other tribes also joined. John Ross was the Chief back then. He didn't like North or South. They were all white to him, but the South promised the Cherokee a free nation if they fought on the Rebel side. When the South lost...we paid for it."

"Damn. On top'a ever'thing else, you guys threw in with the wrong side in the war. Bummer."

"It wouldn't have made any difference if we had sided with the North. Both sides were white. Once the war was over, either side would have acted like they forgot everything they promised us. Whites have as much trouble with remembering things as they do with being honest."

A look of horror crossed his face.

"Not *all* whites!" terribly embarrassed. "I don't want you to think I am saying these things about you!"

"Don't worry about it. I know what y're sayin'. Now-a-days, ever'body knows how bad you guys got screwed an' it was the whites 'at did it to ya. You got a right ta feel the way ya do. The whole thing is…it's so damn…screwed up."

"Yes. Very screwed up, but today you can't take things that happened way back then personal," somberly. "What is done is done. What is gone is gone. Not accepting that is what made Dad crazy," shaking his head. "Anyway, Dad named us after Southern generals."

"Sounds like he was tryin' ta beat up on himself again. Like choosin' Whiteman f'r a last name."

"Could be. Maybe that was what he was thinking," in a low voice.

"So where'd Homer's name come from?"

"Homer's dad named all his kids after towns where something good happened to him. Homer has three sisters…Joy after Joy, Kansas, Lima after Lima, Colorado, and Dallas after Dallas, Texas. Homer is a small place somewhere in Nebraska, I think. Can't remember."

"So what happened in those places 'at was so good?"

"I can only make a guess, and this might be the gossip part. Anyway, from some of the things Jeb would tell me when we were drinking together…I think he had a few girlfriends he was serious about. He was tall and very handsome. I think the names came from the places where he had girlfriends."

We took time out to light up and take a sip.

"Ya know what, Mr. Lee?" really loose. "It's a good thing Homer's dad never got laid in Faggot, Missouri."

Lee looked at the ceiling and rubbed his chin.

"I think I would have talked him out of that one for a name," before breaking into a loud laugh.

"So, where's his sisters at?"

"They are around. One lives in Oklahoma City, one in Denver, and the youngest, Joy, lives about twenty minutes from here. None of them will be at the funeral. None of the girls were very close to Dad. He scared them. Some of the things he would do would embarrass them up at the school. Having a crazy grandpa was harder on the girls than it was on Homer."

"Did Homer's grandpa have a heart attack 'r somethin'?"

Lee looked up, pausing before answering.

"It was the 'or something'," voice saddening. "It wasn't a heart attack. The coroner is trying to call it a…a suicide, but it wasn't like a *real* suicide."

That caught me off guard. I waited as Lee took a drink, almost emptying his glass.

"Dad had a dream around two months ago. He went more crazy than usual. He said a voice from a cloud told him the Cherokee would be allowed to remember everything that was forgotten about the old ways if they would prove they still believed in the Spirits. He preached this all over the county. He would show up outside churches around here. He would dress up in white leathers that he made and would yell at everybody. He would yell at them about his dream. He made a long spear. He would shake it at people," jabbing the air a few times with an imaginary spear. "The sheriff got upset and told me to keep him away from crowds unless Dad agreed not to carry the spear. Then, about ten days ago, Dad came down to the house and told me about another dream he had. In the dream, a big, black horse charged at him. He said he wanted to run from the horse but the Spirits told him not to. They told him to point his spear at the horse. He said that is what he did and the horse turned into dust. At that exact moment in his dream all the people began dancing and chanting all the things they had forgotten. I told Dad he should stay with me a while. Dad got mad and left. He quit coming down to the house. From time-to-time I would see him walking around and around a fire he started to keep burning twenty-four hours a day in a pit in front of his place. When I would go up to see him he would curse at me and go inside his place until I left. Then," Lee's voice dropped as he looked down at the table, "then, Wayne, he's the sheriff, Wayne showed up last Thursday morning. Somebody had found Dad's body up near the railroad tracks. About a mile from here."

Lee got up and walked to the sink. He poured a few shots into the glass and added a dash of water. He turned back to me and leaned against the sink.

"At first, I didn't believe him. Wayne said it was hard to tell who it was right off. He finally figured out it was Dad. Dad was wearing his white leathers. That is how he figured out who it was. I still wouldn't believe him. Wayne and me walked up to Dad's place. He wasn't there. The fire was out cold. His leathers and the spear were gone. That is when I knew Wayne was...that it was Dad."

"Ya hadn't had any time ta tell Homer any'a this yet, have ya?"

"No," looking down at the floor. "And his going up to Dad's before I tell him isn't going to make it any easier to tell him. I am afraid it will make him as crazy as Dad ever was. I am very afraid of that happening."

"Well, when he comes back, I'll go clean up so ya c'n be alone ta tell him," I offered.

"He doesn't need to know I told you all of this. You need to know since you are his friend, but he...he doesn't need to know I told you all of this."

"If he ever brings it up...I'll act su'prised," I managed through a big yawn.

"You are tired," Lee, heading out of the kitchen. "Stretch out on the couch and rest. I will find a pillow and a quilt for you," over his shoulder.

I was worn out. The liquor and the flickering fireplace were making it difficult to keep my eyes open. Lee returned with the pillow and quilt.

"Make your own schedule. Towels are in the hall closet if you want to shower."

***

*Bacon?*

My stomach growled.

I rolled over to face the fireplace. The room was filled with a dull light, the winter's early morning sun muted further by the sheets of plastic over the windows. I was comfortably warm, pulled into a ball under the soft, heavy quilt. Content. Safe. I wanted to go back to sleep and wake up here again.

*Wake up exactly like this, with everything in the room exactly the way it is at this exact moment. Then go back ta sleep ta wake up here again. Over an' over.*

*But with a naked woman beside me.*

My stomach roared.

*Jesus. That really is bacon.*

I reluctantly left the womb, scratched my butt then yawned loudly. After using the bathroom, I entered the kitchen and found an elderly woman busily cooking at the stove. Her back was to me. I cleared my throat to let her know I was there. She turned to flash a smile.

"Sit down," she ordered. "I've got eggs, toast, bacon, and milk. What do you want?"

"Toast, milk, an' some bacon, please. C'n I do anything ta help?"

"You can sit down and eat. More people will be coming and I'll need the table space."

She placed a large plate of scrambled eggs and bacon in front of me.

"You ever had fresh milk?"

"I..."

"Not *store* fresh. *Cow* fresh."

"It's been a while. I've got relatives in east Texas. My gran'ma Ressie still milks a cow b'cause she dudn't like store milk."

"Do *you* like fresh milk?" impatiently.

"Yes, ma'am. It tastes fine."

*With a gallon'a chocolate syrup in it.*

She put a glass of foamy milk on the table next to my plate.

"Thanks," and touched the glass with my index finger.

*Warm. An' no chocolate syrup.*

"I'm Rolene. Lee's wife. Homer's aunt."

"I'm Gil. Homer's fri..."

"Homer's friend from Texas. I know. Lee told me about you. Maybe you can talk Homer into going to the funeral. He's gone crazy. Exactly like his grandpa. The very same kind of crazy," charging about the kitchen.

"He's not goi..."

"Homer's decided he's not going. He told Lee last night. Going up to that shed last night made him as crazy as his grandpa."

Rolene spun around then slammed her fists into her hips, eyes glaring, elbows out as if she were going to fly across the room at me.

I stopped chewing—it somehow seemed inappropriate.

"Do you know *why* he's not going?" she snapped. "He's decided the old coot wouldn't approve of a *Christian* burial," turning back to the stove.

I began chewing again, washing it down with a few polite sips of fresh, warm, foamy milk.

"Lee asked Homer last night, 'Well, Mr. Medicine Man, what kind of funeral do *you* want to have?' as if Lee didn't already know what Homer was going to say. You could have bet on it. Homer wanted to have a 'traditional *Cherokee'* burial. Whatever *that* is," slamming the frying pan onto a burner.

Rolene spun around again.

I stopped chewing again.

"Absolutely *no* consideration for the man's soul," she steamed. "Even though he died a heathen, maybe God would take into consideration that he was at least given a *Christian* burial, but I guess that's too much to expect."

Rolene turned back to the stove and threw some bacon into the pan.

"Can you talk some sense into him?" she asked.

"I guess I could say somethin' to him about it," trying to make it sound like I meant it. "Where's Lee?"

"He left to go to the church. Visiting hours are all morning long, although I wouldn't expect very many people will be dropping in. He'd outlived nearly everybody he knew and everybody else who knew him will probably stay away. Who wants to be seen at a *crazy* man's funeral?" huffing.

"Where's Homer?"

"He's still asleep."

"No I'm not," as he entered the kitchen.

Homer patted my shoulder as he walked over to the chair I'd been sitting in the night before.

"Eggs are here on the stove," Rolene snapped. "Bacon is on the counter. If you want toast you'll have to make it yourself. If you decide to go to the funeral, I'll be leaving in *exactly* two hours," exiting the kitchen, furiously wiping her hands on her apron as she went.

"Nice meetin' ya, ma'am. Thanks f'r..."

"Nice meeting you," still snapping.

Homer got up and went over to the stove.

"Not hard to see who rates with Aunt Rolene."

" 'at's b'cause I'm not crazy an' don't run around upsettin' ever'body."

He filled a plate, poured some milk then returned to the table.

"You know what crazy means around here?" Homer, before shoveling a spoonful of eggs into his mouth.

"It's got somethin' ta do with just about anything an' ever'thing y'ur grandpa ever did. Sounds like he must'a set some kind'a community standard f'r whacko."

"That's close enough. And if *you* don't think he's crazy, then you're crazy too," reaching for his glass of milk.

"That's *fresh* cow milk," I warned.

He gave me a "no shit?" look then took a big gulp.

"Well, it might not be a big deal ta you, but I don't get *real* cow milk all 'at often."

"What do you think about it?" stuffing more eggs into his mouth.

"Tastes like warm hyena pee."

He grinned.

After finishing his breakfast he leaned back in his chair.

"I guess Lee told you about my name and now you think I'm some kind of a liar or fake?"

"Yeah, he tol' me ever'thing, an', yeah, I'm pr'tty upset. I wan'a divorce. Ya know what?"

"What?"

"After I talked ta y'ur uncle a while, ya know what he said?"

"What?"

"Lee thinks I might be a little crazy like y'ur grandpa an' you."

Homer liked that.

"He really said that, huh?"

"Yeah."

"I'll be damned. So, what else did he tell you," a little apprehensive.

"Nothin' much. Mentioned somethin' about that homo phase ya went through in junior high, but he fig'res the Marines beat that out'a ya."

Homer nodded his head and grunted.

"They did, didn't they?" raising my brows.

"Most of it."

After smoking a cigarette in silence, Homer stood up then crushed the butt out on his plate.

"We need to leave before everybody starts getting here," yawning. "They're all coming over for breakfast. I don't want to be here."

"I gotta take a quick shower then I'll be set ta leave. Where we gunna go?" finishing off the last of my eggs.

"Back up to Grandpa's."

"Hang there 'til the funeral?"

"Something like that," under his breath.

"I'll make it fast."

Homer's aunt moved back into the kitchen once we were out. I got cleaned up and went looking for Homer. I found him in a small back room sitting on the end of a bed with an overstuffed mattress on it.

"This used to be me and my sisters' room. Uncle Lee put in bunk beds. He added a room for my sisters on the other side of the house when he felt like they'd gotten too old to be sharing a room with me."

"Smart move."

"They won't be at the funeral," ignoring my remark. "They didn't like him much. Anyway, this became my room. It's a spare bedroom now," and got up from the bed. "Ready?"

I nodded.

After rounding the corner of the house we heard a car revving its way up the snowy road.

"That's the first of them," Homer, picking up the pace through the knee-deep snow. "Did Lee say anything about how Grandpa died?"

"No," keeping my promise to Lee.

Ten struggling minutes later we arrived at his grandfather's shack. It was fairly run down, unpainted wood weathered to a light gray. The roof steeply pitched toward the back. The structure was more of a lean-to than a house. It wasn't much bigger than our place in Lubbock. The front door faced the east. I helped Homer bring some firewood from behind the shack. We started a fire in a shallow pit located a few yards outside the front door. We scooped up some smaller pieces and went inside.

It was one room with a dirt floor. Animal furs had been scattered all around like throw rugs. Two small, hazy windows allowed what little light there was into the dark room. A potbelly stove sat in the far corner of the room. The ceiling was so low Homer had to crouch when crossing the room. I looked around as he started a fire. The walls were insulated with more animal furs, blankets, and a few old, torn quilts. Feathers, strips of leather, and small bundles of different kinds of grasses and dried flowers hung here and there from the ceiling.

A small, narrow bed, not much larger than a cot, was against one wall, a worn, wooden table and chair against another. A set of shelves was nailed to the wall above the table. The shelves were crowded with leather pouches, jars, cups, feathers, bird talons, and small animal skulls and bones. A kerosene lamp, a tin cup, and a metal plate with a scalpel resting in it sat on the table. There was no electricity or plumbing.

It didn't take long for the stove to warm the place up. Homer lit the kerosene lamp, pulled two joints from his pocket, and gave one to me. He then laid back on the bed. I fired mine up and inhaled deeply. Dancing, orange shafts of light escaped from slits in the side of the stove. Combined with the lamp, the whole room took on a soft, warm glow.

"So, what do you think?" Homer.

"It's some good shit," examining the joint.

"Not the grass. I mean, what do you think about Grandpa's house? His tepee? His wigwam?"

I studied the room for a while before answering.

"Instead'a turnin' our place into a snatch trap, let's just cover the walls in pelts. I like the feel."

Homer nodded his approval of the idea.

"The place doesn't make you feel uncomfortable?" he asked. "You don't think all the skulls and bones are spooky?"

"It's differ'nt. But it's a neat kind'a differ'nt. Makes ya feel safe 'r somethin'. It's hard ta say just what it is. I like it though. Feels... cozy."

"My junior year in high school I brought a girlfriend up here to meet Grandpa. We'd been going out about six months. We were thinking about getting serious. I brought her up here and she freaked out. She wouldn't have anything to do with me after that. Couldn't get anyone to go out with me until I was a senior."

"White chick?"

"Mostly. Didn't matter, though. Between this place and Grandpa she was one hundred percent freaked out," more to himself than to me.

"What religion?"

"I think she was Catholic."

I snorted.

"Hard ta b'lieve a few bones an' skulls could freak somebody out who's pro'bly got a bleedin' corpse nailed to a cross hangin' above her bed."

"If I'd taken her to a motel instead of here I probably could have made her. Blew that one, I guess."

"So what," holding a hit. "Y're not the only one 'at's blown a sure thing," as I exhaled loudly. "I ran inta one'a the biggest whores in Monterey High School at a livestock show in Lubbock one night. I was gettin' my sheep ready ta show..."

"You had sheep in high school?" surprised.

"Yeah. In FFA. Future Farmers. I had sheep, chickens, pigs, and an Angus show calf, but lemme tell ya what happened. This girl was drunk as shit. I started hittin' on her. She started droppin' hints 'at she was up ta doin' the dirty deed. You know...sayin' things like, 'Gee, Gil, I sure wish ya'd put y'ur penis in me', an' hints like 'at," holding another deep hit.

"Most guys wouldn't have picked up on that," Homer.

"Yeah, I know, but," exhaling. "Where was I? Oh, yeah. Then we started makin' small talk about showin' sheep an' she decided she wanted ta show one'a mine the next day. That's how fuckin' drunk she was. She got all hung up on the idea. She wanted me ta teach her how ta show sheep right then an' there. She kept brushin' up against me an' gettin' me hotter an' hotter. I was doin' fine, Homer, I mean...it was guaranteed. I was five minutes away from my first piece'a buttocks an' I was only sixteen years old. I started teachin' her all the little tricks ta showin' sheep an' she was eatin' it up. Then I showed her how ya make the sheep tighten up its back muscles f'r the judge by shovin' y'ur finger up the sheep's ass."

Homer shot into a sitting position and looked at me in shock, choking on the hit he'd taken.

"You shove y'ur finger up..."

"Yeah, yeah, but that's not important. What's important's that when I pulled my finger out, she took one look at it an' then puked all over the place. She jumped up an' ran off screamin'. She told *ever'body* about it back at school. That was my junior year. Just b'cause'a her I ended up havin' ta wait 'til I got overseas ta get my first piece'a tail. Anyway, there wudn't *anybody* raisin' sheep who was gunna get any after 'at happened. The whole ag class went ta pig projects an' raisin' chickens 'at next semester."

"You shove your finger up a sheep's *ass* to show it?" Homer, still in shock. "There's *no* other way to show sheep?"

"That's the *best* way, but ya missed the whole point'a the story."

"I don't know which is harder to believe," Homer, falling back on the bed, "that you actually *did* that shit or that you go around *telling* people you did that shit."

"My point is," mind drifting around inside my skull, "y're not the only poor bastard 'at's jacked himself out of a sure, you know...a sex, uh...thing."

"That's...it's unbelievable," Homer moaned softly. "Ungoddamned believable."

"Yeah. Tell me about it," resting my head on the table. "Prick teasin' bitch."

We fell silent, fogged up and floating for a long time. Well over an hour maybe.

A car horn in the distance found us in the mist. Homer got up slowly from the bed and stepped outside. I followed him through the doorway.

"What time is it?" I asked as we stood next to the smoldering embers in the pit.

"Funeral time," somberly.

"You all right?"

"Yeah. I'm fine."

We threw some more wood into the pit then walked back to his uncle's place.

His aunt appeared to be pissed.

"Couldn't you hear the horn? I've been honking for ten minutes. The others have already left," then scurried into the driver's seat and hung her head out the window. "Let's go! Let's go!"

Homer hesitated.

"Ya know, Homer," stepping to his side, "let's take y'ur truck. If ya don't like what's goin' on...we c'n leave."

Homer sighed deeply.

"I'm taking my truck!" he shouted.

Aunt Rolene scowled, threw the car into reverse, and then spun out on the ice. Still backing, she slammed the clanking gears into first then floored it. The spinning tires burned their way through the ice to frozen dirt. Traction. The car bolted forward. Aunt Rolene fishtailed her way down the road.

"She'll be cussing the both of us all the way to the church," Homer.

"Not me," I told him. "She likes me."

The trip to the church took half an hour. There was no parking lot. A few cars were parked along both sides of a rutted, sloshy road. We did our best to make it to the front door without picking up too much mud. Homer brushed his hair back before entering. He looked over at me.

"Looks good," I said. "Y're covered."

We entered a small foyer. I pulled my coat off and tucked it under my arm. Lee was with a group of men standing in the doorway of the auditorium. He rushed over.

"Thank you for changing your mind," Lee, shaking Homer's hand then mine.

Lee returned to the doorway.

I stepped to his side.

"Lee?"

He turned around.

"Thank you for talking Homer into coming," he smiled.

"It was his idea, not mine. Listen, Lee, did ya have a chance last night ta tell Homer about the train?"

"Yes. He didn't take it very well."

"Imagine not. Just wanted ta know," then returned to Homer.

Lee turned and motioned. It was about to begin.

There were two rows of ten pews in the auditorium. A worn, faded blue carpet ran down the aisle separating them. The pews were old and cushionless. A simple pedestal stood at the front of the church. Two floral arrangements, nothing fancy, had been placed to the left of the pedestal. To the right of it, a simple, glossy, wooden casket. The lid was closed.

A photo portrait of Homer's grandfather, one of those old black and white flat mattes touched up with paints, sat on top of the casket. He appeared to be somewhere around fifty. He was wearing a suit, his graying hair parted down the middle and pulled back. The hair might have been in a ponytail. It was hard to tell. If it was, the photographer had put an effort into trying to hide it from the camera's view. The face in the picture was stern, almost fierce. He looked defiant. The photographer couldn't hide that from the camera.

Only three of the pews were occupied. Homer and I slid into one of the back pews. I picked a hymnal from the bookrack on the pew in front of me and glanced through it.

Homer leaned over.

"He wouldn't have wanted it like this at all," he whispered. "This is all wrong."

"Give it a chance," I whispered back.

The service began with a prayer. A few hymns followed. Then the sermon. I honest-to-God thought Homer might lose it. First, the preacher made certain everybody understood Homer's grandfather was burning in Hell. Then the preacher dug up every goddamn thing the old man had ever done and made it into an object lesson. People kept turning around and looking at Homer to see if he was listening. The more the preacher went on, the more nervous I became. Ten minutes into the sermon Homer poked me in the ribs.

"I'm leaving," and got up.

I followed him out of the church then back to the truck.

Homer eased the truck down the slush-slicked road.

"I want to pick a few things up at Grandpa's," mumbling. "Then we'll head back to Lubbock."

"It's one a'clock. That'll put us back inta town pr'tty late."

"I can't stay here another night. I'll drive back. You can sleep."

Homer slid to a stop in front of his uncle's. We practically ran up the lane. He went behind the shack and returned with a plastic milk carton. I followed him into the shed. Homer paused inside the door, glanced around, and then quickly swept through the room, grabbing a rolled up cowhide, a few clusters of feathers bound together at the quills with a strip of leather, and a turtle shell rattle. He gently placed all the items into the plastic container then sat down at the table where he began emptying the shelves, carefully tucking everything into the milk carton.

Homer went outside and placed the carton alongside the pit. He turned to me.

"Help me bring some firewood inside. Stack it in the middle of the room."

"Wait a minute, Homer."

He stopped and looked at me.

"Homer, seriously...can't we talk about this? I mean...if y'ur plannin' on settin' fire..."

"This isn't wrong," flatly.

Homer looked tired, beat up. Stressed. He hurried around the corner, returning with an armload of wood. He dropped the wood inside, came back out and disappeared around the corner again.

*Shit. Double shit.*

"Where's the state penitentiary in Oklahoma?" I asked as I followed him to the rear of the lean-to on his next trip.

He ignored me.

It took the two of us less than five minutes to move the woodpile. Homer made a final trip, returning with a five-gallon gas can marked "Kerosene". He stepped inside. After a few moments a puff of smoke belched through the doorway. Homer hurried out then picked up the plastic carton filled with his grandfather's things. We moved down the lane about thirty yards where we stopped and turned around to watch.

It was cold. Perfectly calm. The smoke rose straight up into a brilliant blue, cloudless sky. Within minutes short bursts of flame began to appear under the eaves of the shack. The roof gave a little, shooting glowing embers into the air. I could smell burning fur.

"They're throwing a body in the ground," Homer, in a low, deep voice. "That's all they're doing. Grandpa would have wanted something like this."

He lit a joint, took a drag and handed it to me. We smoked the joint and watched the flames.

"Grandpa tried to stop a train with a stick," Homer, softly. "Something about a vision he had. He *really* believed he could do it."

"Wan'a be left alone?"

"No."

A wall collapsed, followed immediately by a second. Smoke billowed upward carrying with it a thousand swirling sparks high into the sky.

"Grandpa was a joke to them. They never listened to him. They called him crazy because they didn't understand a word he said or a thing he did or why he was doing it. He pretended like it didn't bother him," pausing a moment. "He always treated me good. He tried to teach me the language. He showed me a lot of things that, at the time, didn't mean anything to me. Things that didn't work for me because I didn't believe in them. I know he made up a lot of the things he showed me and told me. He would say the Spirits were talking to him and telling him about things. It didn't matter if those things did or didn't work or that he was making it all up. That wasn't important," shuddering a bit and taking a deep breath before continuing. "I liked being with Grandpa. I guess those things he talked to me about still don't work for me. And it still doesn't matter if he made it all up. Right now, right this second, all that matters is…is that I miss being around him."

His voice was strong and steady.

The shack collapsed, sending one last swirling blast of sparks and smoke into the sky.

Homer watched the funeral pyre a few more minutes then turned away.

"It's time to go," and started toward his uncle's house.

The walk back to the truck was much slower than the trot to the shed.

"Ya gunna leave a note 'r somethin' ta tell y'ur uncle we left?" when we got to the truck.

"No," glancing at the smoke column. "He'll figure it out."

Homer placed the milk container on the seat between us. We got into the truck and drove away. I looked over at Homer. He looked a lot like a younger version of the man in the picture back at the church.

An announcement about an upcoming job fair in Tulsa aired on the radio.

"Did I tell we might have jobs waitin' for us back in Lubbock?" I asked.

"Doing what?"

"Doin' what? Damn, Homer. If it's not trompin', who *gives* a shit what it is?" straightening up and lighting a cigarette. "Anyway, I didn't ask. I gotta call this Tripp guy an' set up an interview an' find out what he's dug up f'r you. Actually, now that we're rich, we c'n afford ta be a little choosy. Right? I mean, why rush inta another shit job? That's what I did wrong b'fore. I panicked. It was like if I didn't land a job right off after gettin' out then I'd starve ta death 'r somethin'. So I jumped on anything. Now that we're rich, we c'n sit aroun' Mother's an' wait for a brain surgeon 'r a bank president position ta come along. We still got three hun'r'd an' sixty dollars left. This trip was a lot cheaper than we thought it was gunna be."

"I want to be a gynecologist," Homer.

"No problem. An' when they fire ya after a coupl'a weeks, after findin' out ya don't know squat about pussy, no big deal. You could live a whole year on what those bastards make in two weeks. Right?"

"Ten years in Mexico," agreeing. "Probably longer."

I finished the cigarette, hunkered back down and tried to get warm.

"One last thing then I'll leave ya alone," my teeth chattering. "You realize this is twice in just three 'r four days 'at you got bent out'a shape an' burned somethin' ta the ground?" pulling my coat over my ears. "How many girls ya have ta set fire to b'fore ya got one of 'em ta go ta the prom with ya?"

"Just one," he grunted.

It was going on 2:00 in the morning when we pulled into the driveway. Almost all the snow had melted away. The junk in the yard was back again. The utility still smelled like dead skin. Homer crashed with no problem—he'd driven all the way back. I crawled into the rack and fired up a joint. I thought about school starting in a few weeks.

*That'd be the honest-ta-God, f'r real new b'ginnin'. All this other shit like trompin' cotton, bein' broke, not meetin' a lady, an' shit was just a false start.*

*Dead time.*

*Just takin' a little longer than I thought it would f'r things ta shape up.*

*Been to a bunch'a parties lately an' been meetin' all kinds'a women. One of 'em's gotta fall in love with me sooner 'r later...'r at least start puttin' out. For the most' part, though, things're finally b'ginnin' ta shape up.*

*Even have some money ta work with.*

*God, what a diff'r'nce a little money c'n make.*

*Find out why the truck keeps dyin' an' get it fixed. Dress the place up a little. No more stealin' toilet paper from the heads on campus. Get a new toothbrush. After meetin' somebody, I have enough money ta take her out somewhere nice.*

*Joan!*

*That's who I'll take out. Ask her ta dinner when I go ta that Baha'i thing.*

*Damn! It's only Tu'sd'y mornin'.*

*I c'n make it ta the meetin' t'night. I'll call Danny first thing this mornin'.*

*Need ta find out more about this Baha'i thing b'fore t'night's meetin'. Danny could tell me enough f'r me ta fake it a little. Don't wan'a look like I don't know squat about it.*

*Jesus, she's one fine piece'a female.*

*Gotta find Chad. Kick his ass. Get all the money he owes me.*

*Looks like I've got what's pro'bly gunna be a decent-ass job 'at's pro'bly gunna pay pr'tty good.*

*Damn, damn, damn. Things really are comin' t'gether.*

I put the last bit of the joint on my tongue and swallowed it, rolled over, and then dozed off.

*\*\*\**

I'm not sure if I ever went completely to sleep, but I was up at dawn. Homer was out hard, breathing in loud blasts. I wanted to get to the laundromat and call about the job by 7:30. I guessed it was around 6:30, maybe a little later. I cleaned up and left quietly. It was cloudless in the ghetto. Cold enough to frost your breath. A few bundled students were on their way to the campus for early morning finals.

The phone didn't complete a full ring before somebody answered it.

"Hugo's," a low, raspy voice.

"Ye'sir. This is Gil McNeil. Mr. Tripp asked me ta call about an interview for..."

"J'st a minute," the voice interrupted. "HUGO! IT'S F'R YEW! SOME GUY LOOKIN' F'R WORK!"

I heard a phone pick up. Sitar music was playing in the background. The first phone hung up.

"Hello," in a soft drawl.

"Ye'sir. This is Gil McNeil. I met ya Saturd'y night at a party on Eighth Street. Ya asked me ta call ya about a job when I got back from Oklahoma. Well, I'm, uh...back."

"Yes, Gil. I was hopin' you'd call. How was y'ur trip?"

"It was all right. Snow on the ground all the way up. It was pr'tty nice."

" 'scuse me, Gil. I've got ta turn this music down. My hearin' idn't what it use' ta be."

The sitar was silenced. Hugo's voice returned.

"There. 'at's much better. I've been tryin' ta acquire a taste f'r that kind'a shittin' music, but I'm havin' a great deal'a trouble overcomin' a pref'rence f'r Bob Wills. When do ya wan'a start?"

"Don't ya wan'a interview me 'r somethin'?"

"No. Danny, Joan, an' I ended up at the IHOP after leavin' the party. Danny had nothin' but good things ta say about ya, so, when c'n ya start?"

"T'morrow. I c'n start t'morrow," I gushed. "Thanks. Thanks a lot."

"C'mon out around this time t'morrow so you c'n meet ever'body else b'fore they head out."

"Ye'sir. Thanks. Thanks very much."

"Wan'a know how much I'll be payin'?"

"Is it more'n sixty-five cents an hour?"

"I c'n do ya better'n 'at."

"Then I'm happy."

"Ya have any questions about what you'll be doin'?"

"If it idn't trompin' cotton, I don't *care* what it is."

Hugo laughed.

"Y'ur friend, the one who killed Donald's dog, is he still lookin' f'r work?"

*Shit. The son of a bitch did die.*

"Uh...ye'sir, but he didn't mean ta kill 'at dog. It was an accident. Homer didn't know..."

"Oh, hell, I know that. I didn't mean ta make it sound like he did it on purpose. It was only a matter'a time b'fore somethin' like 'at was gunna happen ta that poor bastard. I swear, if 'at dog ends up in Heaven there won't be another soul make it ta Hell. Ever' time Saint Peter tosses somebody inta the pit, Zero'll be draggin' it right back out."

I chuckled politely.

"At any rate, I know somebody who wants ta talk with y'ur friend. An old compadre'a mine. Repairs player pianas an' does some other odd ball things. He's located down in the campus area. Would y'ur friend be inter'sted?"

"Yes. Ye'sir. I know he would."

"Got somethin' ta write with?"

"No, shi...I'm sorry. I'm callin' from a laundromat down from the house."

"You live in the student area across from Tech?"

"Ye'sir."

"Are ya callin' from the laundr'mat on Tenth?"

"Ye'sir."

"T'morrow mornin', have y'ur friend go west in the alley b'hind the laundr'mat. JD's place is in the first block *east* of University. The alley entrance is a big slidin' metal door with 'J.D. Grubb piano deliveries' painted on it. Have y'ur friend bang on the door 'til Grubb answers. It may take a bit. JD has this...this arthritis. It tends ta slow him down from time ta time."

"I'll tell him. He'll be there. He'll really appreciate it. Thanks again. For both of us. I'll see ya t'morrow."

"Do ya know how ta get out here?"

"Uh, no. Not really," feeling a little stupid about not thinking to ask.

"Go south on University to Ninety-Eighth Street. Go west on Ninety-Eighth for half a mile. You'll see a set'a buildin's to the north'a the road. One of 'em's a big red barn. Can't miss it. There's no other buildin's anywhere around. Come up the drive on the north side'a the road. That'll put ya right at the garages. Ya enter the office through the garages. Yell up the staircase when ya get here."

"Got it. Thanks again."

"I'm lookin' for'ard ta havin' ya out here," and hung up.

*I'll be goddamned. Homer'll shit. Absolutely, positively shit. Not even 8:00 an' both of us have jobs.*

I dug around in my pocket for another dime to call the number Danny'd given me. A woman answered.

"Yes, ma'am. My name's Gil McNeil. I'm tryin' ta..."

"Gil McNeil?"

"Yes, ma'am."

"Danny said he'd run into you. This is his mother. I'm so glad you're back all safe and sound," an honest sense of relief in her voice.

"I thought I recognized the phone number Danny gave me," lying.

"How are you doing? Is everything okay?"

"Ever'things goin' real good, Mrs. Wright. Thanks ta Danny I've got a decent job now. Starts t'morrow."

"Oh, congratulations! How wonderful. That Danny," sounding frustrated, "I swear, he seems to be able to find work for everybody except himself."

"Oh?" not sure how to respond. "Well, some're pickier than others about that sort'a thing. Or somethin'," my voice trailing off.

"Maybe so. I'm so glad y're back. Danny missed everybody so much. It really hurt him when he couldn't go into the service when the rest of you went. He's been wanderin' around like a lost soul."

Her voice lowered to a hush.

"I guess Danny told you about Doug being back?"

"Yes, ma'am. He'd mentioned it."

"He hasn't changed much. He's still, how do I put this? He's still...troubled."

"Can't be much more polite about it than that, Mrs. Wright."

"I hope troubled is as serious as it gets. I don't know exactly what happened. He'd been back a week when his parents asked him to leave their house. But enough about Doug. How're y'ur parents doin'?"

"They're fine. They live in Abilene now. I spent Thanksgivin' with 'em."

"I want their address so I can send them a Christmas card."

"I don't have it on me. I'll give it ta Danny."

"Don't stay away. We'll have to have you over for dinner sometime soon. Fatten you up. Danny said you looked all skin an' bones."

"I'll look forward to it, Mrs. Wright. Say hello ta Mr. Wright for me."

"I will. Lemme get Danny. It's so good ta hear from you. Take care."

"Same to you, ma'am."

Telling her I'd spent Thanksgiving in Abilene with my parents was close to the truth. I'd only talked to them on the phone a few times since my discharge. I kept putting off a visit even though it was just a 160 mile drive. It'd been two years since I'd seen them. Dad'd met me at the door and made it pretty clear no hippie was going to set foot in his house or shame him in front of his neighbors. He'd reminded me that, as an ex-corpsman with the Marines, he knew thirty different ways to kill a man with his bare hands. Whatever that was supposed to mean. Dad ordered me to stay away until I'd shaved, gotten a hair cut, changed my whole "goddamned" attitude, and started going back to church.

With enough grass and liquor I think I could've lived with the first three demands.

It was obvious Chad had—accidentally, I'm certain—let some exaggerations slip about my beard, my hair length, my foul mouth, my not going to church, my smoking, all my nasty, drug crazed friends, my fornicating, and on, and on. I was just as certain Chad'd couched it in terms of his concern for my soul. I'd gone back to Lubbock and gotten drunk with Homer Thanksgiving night. We'd done it up right, however, sticking with Wild Turkey.

"Gil!" Danny on the line. "What's up?"

He sounded glad to hear from me.

"Soundin' pr'tty jolly for a starvin' unemployed guy," I told him.

"You've been talking with Mother."

"Yeah. She didn't say anything bad about ya, though. Except the bum part. An' the leech thing. Somethin' else about bein' a lazy bastard. It wudn't anything I didn't already know."

"You got back sooner than you thought," blowing me off.

"Yeah. It dudn't take long ta throw a body in a ditch if ya know what y're doin'."

"Went to Oklahoma for a funeral?"

"Didn't I mention 'at the other night?"

"No. All you said was that you and your friend were going to spend a few days in Oklahoma."

"Oh. Well, Homer's granddad died. I went along ta help him drive. If I'd a known ya wudn't workin', you could'a come along with us."

"Next time."

"Doubt there's gunna be a next time, Danny. I'm pr'tty sure about what dead looks like an' his granddad looked pr'tty much that way."

"I'm guessing you're calling about tonight's Baha'i meeting."

"Hell, no. I was callin' ta see how y're doin'. I was worried about ya. That's all."

"Right. You've been back in town over three months and you never bothered to get in touch."

I hesitated. Danny had me there. Tromping had kept me busy as hell, but I really hadn't made any effort to contact anybody I'd know before going into the service.

"Only kidding," he said seriously. "I'd heard you were back. I figured we'd hook up eventually. Anyway, the meeting begins around 7:00 this evening at a place on Twenty-First or Twenty-Second off University. I'll pick you up at 6:30."

"What should I wear?"

"A sheet and no underwear. Tonight's the annual Feast of Bare-Naked Fondling."

"When's the Feast'a Num'rous Blowjobs?"

"You really are trying to develop your spiritual side."

"Praise the Lord."

"When are you going to call Hugo about the job?"

"Already did. I start t'morrow an' Homer talks ta somebody in the mornin'."

"Well, hell...congratulations! You're going to have to get me drunk this weekend."

"If I'm not bangin' Joan."

"Like I said, you're going to have to get me drunk this weekend."

"We'll see. T'night. 6:30."

"See you then. Congratulations again on the job."

"Thanks for...,"

He'd already hung up.

I hurried to the house to share the good news with Homer. He was still crapped out.

*It can wait. Time f'r a run ta the strip.*

Lubbock was a dry county so package stores were illegal. Lubbock was, however, surrounded by wet counties. It was some kind of an arrangement the Baptists had worked out with God. The "strip", a mile of liquor stores, began right at the county line. Normally it's about an hour round trip from the student ghetto, but this time I'd be picking up more than just beer. Today I'd be doing some intense shopping. I took Homer's keys from his coat pocket and headed out.

It took two hours. Homer was in the shower when I got back. I arranged all the booze on the floor in the front room like a liquor store display. Homer nearly stumbled when he entered the room.

"Damn," his eyes wide.

I launched into an inventory.

"A bottle'a Kahlua, two bottles each'a scotch, bourbon, an' vodka, three cases'a beer, two cases'a Ripple, a sixteen carton box'a cigarettes, a cooler with ice in it, two hamburgers an' fries. All for less 'an a hun'r'd an' fifty dollars."

Homer looked at me like I'd gone nuts.

"This's a good deal, Homer," defending the purchase. "In the long run, we'll come out way ahead. Think about it. We'd spend *ten* times this much if we drank all'a this one drink at a time in a bar. Drinkin' here at the house'll save us a fortune. I figure this ought'a last us at least three months. Maybe longer since I'll pro'bly be studyin' all the time."

Homer opened a bottle of scotch and slowly passed it under his nose. He grinned at me. A big-ass grin. I jumped down from the bunk, opened the cooler, and then removed a bottle of champagne.

"An' this is ta celebrate our new jobs," holding the bottle up.

"*Our* jobs?" screwing the cap back on the scotch.

"*Our* jobs. One for me. One for you. I already called that Hugo guy I was tellin' ya about. Ever'thing's set," easing the cork from the champagne bottle.

"When do we start?"

"T'morrow," as the bottle popped.

The cork pock marked the plywood ceiling. A quarter of the bottle's contents was lost to foam.

"Actually, I'll be startin' t'morrow. You have an interview with this friend'a his. Tunes 'r fixes pianos 'r somethin' like 'at. He's just east'a University somewhere."

"Which way is east?"

"Head down the alley b'hind the laundromat toward the

campus. Can't miss it," and took a gulp from the bottle before passing it to Homer.

"So, I don't have it for sure yet?" and took a swig.

"B'lieve me. You've got it."

"Damn."

"No shit, damn," taking the bottle back.


We sat on the bottom bunk eating our hamburgers and drinking the champagne.

"Got any plans for this evenin'?" I asked between bites.

Homer stopped chewing and looked at me awkwardly.

"Yeah," I said. "I guess 'at was pr'tty dumb. Well, I've got somethin' goin'. I been thinkin', it's time we expanded our horizons. Time ta do somethin' for our intellectual an' spiritual sides. It's time we went to a special kind'a meetin'. A *special* kind'a Do."

"What kind of a *special* 'Do'?" not too excited.

"It's a meetin' about some kind'a new religion Danny told me about. We're gunna go ta this meetin' t'night then wander up ta Mother's an' have a few drinks."

"What about all this?" waving what remained of his hamburger at the booze display.

"Well, we have ta be flexible with this. Occasionally I expect we'll have ta go to a bar. How else we gunna meet anybody? All this is for routine drinkin' an' for when we have the ladies we meet in the bars over."

"That does seem to happen a lot around here," mumbling.

"Well, it's gunna *start* happenin' a lot. Especially once I'm back in school. You'll see."

"If you say so. I guess I better go with you tonight to make sure you don't hook me up with something that falls short of my standards."

"Wait 'til y'ur balls turn a deep shade'a blue. Then we'll see what happens ta y'ur standards."

"What time do we have to be there?"

"Danny'll be comin' over at 6:30."

"Where'd he serve?"

"Didn't. Don't really know the story on 'at. He tried, but got hammered in the physical. He's still a nice guy, though."

Homer finished his burger.

"Food is a good thing," he burped, exaggerating an Indian accent.

"What're ya gunna be doin' this afternoon?" I asked.

"If you'll loan me a few bucks, I'll fix the heater in my truck and take a closer look at your truck. The more I think about it, the more I think it's a short in the wiring that makes it die on you all the time."

"No problem. I'm gunna go over ta the campus an' wander around a while. Maybe go by the bookstore. Unless y're gunna need some help," and counted out a hundred dollars.

"No. I can do it myself."

"Here," holding the money out.

"It's not gunna cost that much."

"Keep it. I still got plenty. Y're gunna need a little cash ta get ya through ta y'ur first pay check."

"Thanks."

I stood up, peeled off my coat and tossed it onto my bunk.

"Won't be needin' this. It's warmin' up real nice outside. Catch ya later," and headed out the door.

I walked down Ninth Street to University Avenue then turned left toward Broadway. Broadway was a major street in Lubbock, stretching from the main entrance of the Texas Tech campus on the west side of town all the way to the poor east side of town. The first block of Broadway across from the campus was a collection of trendy clothing stores with the exception of Broadway Drug. It was located in a two-story building on the corner of University and Broadway. The drug store, dating back to the late 1920's, had a food counter which made the place a popular hangout for students.

The second block off campus was lined on both sides with huge, elegant, well-preserved mansions. This was fraternity row, although a few sorority houses were thrown in. The First Baptist Church of Lubbock's parking lot ate up the entire third block on the south side of Broadway. Beyond the cathedral, a few blocks of well kept homes then a slow descent into the fringes of a deteriorating downtown. East of downtown—old Lubbock. Pre-Texas Tech Lubbock. East Lubbock might as well have been a thousand miles and two hundred years away. Even that was too close according to a lot of citizens occupying Lubbock proper.

I was standing at the corner of Broadway and University, next to the drugstore, waiting to cross the street to the campus when I heard the unmistakable rumbling of approaching Harleys. Two choppers were moving up University at a deliberately slow parade pace, their riders occasionally blasting the engine's deep sputtering idle into a loud roar.

I recognized Jerry as the bikes rolled up to the intersection. He was shirtless, wearing a red bandanna on his head, a blue one tied around his neck, aviator's goggles, and a pair of greasy, filthy blue jeans. The fingers had been cut away from his leather gloves at the second knuckle. Jerry casually pointed at me. At the light change he nonchalantly cut a car off while passing through the intersection. He slid into a parking space in front of the drugstore. The second bike eased in along side Jerry's. They both gunned the bikes until everyone in the area was watching them then turned the bikes off. Jerry swung off his bike. He pushed his flyer's goggles onto his forehead then swaggered over to where I was standing. The second rider executed a distinctly personalized, but equally cool dismount.

People at every corner of the intersection were watching us. It felt like being in a movie. A biker movie. It felt…special.

Jerry pulled a cigarette out and lit up.

" 'at damn injun git ya y'ur money?" he slurred.

*Christ. He's in no better shape than he was three days ago.*

"He swore up an' down 'at he'z y'ur frien', man, an' I saw the two'a ya showin' up at the party t'gether so, I fig'red he wudn' bullshittin', but, fuck, man," taking a hard drag from the cigarette, "yew cain't hardly tell no more. Know whud I mean," glancing around suspiciously, one eye closed to a slit, the other opened wide.

"Yeah. I got all four hun'r'd of it."

"Four hun'r'd? 'at's whud he tol' ya? Shit, man. I give him five."

"What?" playing along.

"Jus' kiddin'. Jus' kiddin'," cackling, raising his eyebrows. "Four hun'r'd an' twen'y-five's whud I got f'r it. Four hun'r'd an' twen'y-five. I kep' twen'y-five uv it. Tha's my fee. Twen'y-five dollars. Tried ta git ya more, but the asshole didn't want any'a y'ur hippie-shit music tapes 'r none'a 'at orchestra shit. I got the tapes in'a back'a my van. Gimme y'ur address an' I'll bring 'em by."

"Ya know where 206 Ninth is?"

"Lemme make a wild-ass guess. I's somewheres 'tween 204 an' 208. On Ninth Street more'n likely. Right? I mean, I could be wrong as shit, but...am I close?"

"Yeah," feeling a little stupid again. "The utility in the back," as I walked over to the bikes, Jerry following.

"Do I know where 206 Ninth Street is?" grumbling to himself. "Shiiit. Whu' kind'a moron ya think I am anyways?" slipping a pair of oval, wire rimmed sunglasses on.

"Nice bike," I told him.

"Yeah. It's all right," dropping his voice. "Shit, man!" suddenly exploding, both eyes blown wide open. "Y'ur buddy nailed 'at damn dog," lowering his voice, relaxing his face, and then leaning toward me. "Did ya hear abou' that? Donal' wuz lookin' f'r y'ur buddy's ass," Jerry sneered. " 'til Donal' foun' out how big the son uv a bitch is. All uv a sudden ol' Zero didn't mean 'at much to him I guess. Hell," rubbing a hand over his face, "I don't know whud he's thinkin', man. I don't git paid f'r 'at kind'a crap. The whole shittin' place's got too much...shit, man...ain' no use ta...," stopping to look around while taking a deep breath. His cheeks ballooned as he exhaled loudly through pursd lips.

*Jesus Christ! He's gone an' wandered right out of his own damn conversation.*

"Too stinkin' busy ta mess with this crap anyways," and paused again for a moment or two before turning to the other rider. "This here's Neil," apparently abandoning his search for the previous line of thought. "Neil's a badass biker," turning to look at him. "Ya didn' see him at the party the other night 'cause he's a Mes'c'n. He could'a come if he wuz a Mexican, but he ain't. He's a Mes'c'n. There's a diff'r'nce. Like the diff'r'nce b'tween bein' a black dude an' bein' a nigger 'r bein' white 'r bein' a white trash redneck. Ain' 'at right, Neil?"

Neil remained motionless, face frozen.

"Neil's a damn homo, man. 'at make ya nervous?" looking back at me. "He's takin' medicine ta git over it, but he's got it bad. I'm like his support person. Ya know whud I mean? I's like when ya try ta quit drinkin' an' the wino guy wants a drink an' he calls his support guy up an' the support guy calls the wino a weak-ass pussy f'r wantin' ta git boozed up an' stuff. 'at's whud I do f'r ol' Neil here, man. Ever' time he gits this urge ta munch a knob, he calls me up. Damn phone never stops ringin'. Tell ol' Gil here whud'a badass, homo biker ya're," turning to Neil again.

Neil shifted his weight from one leg to the other, while looking around to see if any of the passersby had heard Jerry.

"Uh-oh," Jerry, brows up. "I may'a pushed him too far this time, Gil. He's really pissed at me this time. Hey, Neil. I wuz only kiddin'. I'm sorry as shit, man. Really. Ever'thing cool?" then turned to me. "Gil, I wuz only kiddin'. Neil ain't no homo."

Neil barely nodded his head, evidently accepting Jerry's apology.

"But he is one screwed up Mes'c'n," and broke into a loud cackling fit, bending at the waist and tucking his hands into his mid section.

Neil stopped nodding.

Jerry popped into serious.

"Gil...listen, man. Wuz four hun'r'd enough money f'r tha' shit? If it wudn', I mean it, jus' say so. I'll go git it back 'r somethin'. Jus' gimme the money back an' I'll go git it righ' now," snickering. "I'm sure yew ain't spent none uv it."

"Nah. That's fine, Jerry. I need the money more'n a stereo right now. Ya really did me a favor."

"Yeah, I know. 'at's whud I wuz thinkin' when I did it, man. Ya cain't think straight when y're all loaded down with material shit so, I thoughd I'd help ya shed some trash. Ya see, ya gotta go Jesus if ya wan'a pull it t'gether, man. I mean it. Like, if we wuz anywheres near a desert righ' now, 'at's where I'd be righ' this minute. Jus' sittin' in'a desert like Jesus did. Pullin' my shit t'gether. Recomposin'. I'd sell the van, sell the bike, an' hit the desert. Me, Jesus an' a li'l weed. 'at's whud I ought'a be doin' 'stead a hangin' aroun' with this badass Mes'c'n biker," glancing at Neil. "Know whud I'm sayin', Gil?"

"I gettin' y'ur gen'ral drift."

"Yeah, I know ya are 'cause it jus' ain't 'at damn hard ta fig're out once ya take the time it takes ta fig're it out, but...I gotta go. El Badass here's payin' me ta help him find a bike f'r a buddy'a his. Hey, man, yew wan'a bike? I mean, a nice chop with all the papers an' numbers, an' ever'thing?"

"Hell, I'd love it, but there's no way. No money."

"Shit, man, I c'n find ya somethin'. Think about it then lemme know. It's cheap wheels an' the broads'll screw y'ur brains out. 'at's why Neil's thinkin' about gittin' rid'a his bike. He don't like women no more. He's done pussied out."

Neil mumbled a barely audible, "Go to hell," mounted his bike, kicked the engine over, gunned it a few times, and then darted into the traffic.

"Ya don't think it wuz somethin' I said, do ya?" Jerry, snickering while watching Neil swerve to avoid a pickup truck full of cowboy hats. "Whud a turd, man," cackling. "Ol' Neil wants ta be a Bandito, but he ain't got the balls so he runs aroun' town gittin' on ever'body's nerves an' shit. Gives us citizen independents a bad name."

"Banditos? That a local gang?"

"Yeah," looking at me like maybe I was kidding about not knowing. "They think they're a bunch a badasses, but there's meaner floatin' aroun'."

"There's some Hell's Angels in Lubbock?"

Jerry looked at me contemptuously, his face twisted all out of shape.

"I cain't b'lieve y're thinkin' 'at-a-way. Damn. U. S. Marines're the baddest motherfuckers aroun', man. Shiiiit. Hell's Angels? I cain't b'lieve yew went an' said 'at. Why don'ch ya jus' kick me in the nuts 'r somethin'?" wincing as if he was in some kind of ungodly pain.

"Sorry."

"HEY!" snapping straight again. "Talk about mothers! Y'ur brother wuz cryin' all over me this mornin'. He thinks somebody broke inta his place an' took y'ur shit. The stereo stuff an' the tapes. He wuz askin', all nervous like, if I'd seen anything. I thoughd about tellin' him 'bout how I sold the shit, but he wuz so much inta thinkin' it wuz stolt I couldn' see messin' with his head. I fig'red it wuz bes' ta jus' let him keep b'lievin' his own shit an' not cloud him up with whud I knew about it. Know whud I'm sayin'? Who knows? Maybe I wouldn'a 'membered it right. Tha'd'a been the real shits…ta go jackin' his reality up with the wrong story. Know whud I mean? So, anyways, he thinks y'ur shit's done been stolt, man. I gotta go. I'm serious this time."

"Wait a minute. Did Chad say if he was tryin' ta find me?"

"I don't 'member ever'thing, man," mounting his bike. "Like, I wuz a li'l screwed up at the time, but I don't think he's lookin' f'r ya real hard. He wuz scared. He's pro'bly gunna try dodgin' ya f'r a while," sneering.

Jerry hung the sunglasses back on his belt, pulled the goggles down, and then kicked the engine over. The bike roared to life. He coaxed the maximum amount of noise from the engine. Broadway Drug's large display windows shimmered wildly in the sun. Jerry pointed at me while pulling away from the curb then rumbled down the street. He had everybody's attention.

*CUT! That's a take. I LOVE it!*

I decided to look into the bike thing.

I crossed the street and spent the next few hours wandering, reveling in the feeling of having something to look forward to. All the sweet possibilities.

*School. New job. More money.*

*A bike. Maybe.*

*An' there's Joan...Joanie...Jo.*

It was going on five and turning cold by the time I got back to the house. The hood flaps were up on the '35. Wires were dangling all over the inside of the engine compartment. A few were scattered around on the ground. It didn't look encouraging. I stepped into the house and found Homer in the corner, sitting on his pile of clean clothes. He offered me a half-empty bottle of scotch.

"No thanks," and waved it off. "Gotta stay sober for this Do t'night."

"Got some good news...my heater fan's fixed."

"What about the '35?"

"That's the bad news."

I sat down on the bunk and prepared myself for the worst.

"Actually," nodding his head, "it's not all bad news. The *good* bad news is that it isn't the wiring in your truck that's bad. The *bad* bad news is I don't know what the hell the problem is," finishing with a burp.

"Oh, well. I'm considerin' sellin' it anyway. I figure, even if it idn't runnin', it's pro'bly worth at least a thousand b'cause it's an antique an' it's in damn good shape."

"At least a thousand," Homer agreed before taking a swig from the bottle. "Maybe more if I can figure out where all the wires go back in."

"Don't worry about it. I been thinkin' about it all afternoon," and lay back on the bunk. "What'a ya know about Harleys?"

"Harleys? Like Harley motorcycles?"

"Yeah. Choppers."

"Always wanted one."

"I'm thinkin' about sellin' the truck an' buyin' one. Could a thousan' get me a pr'tty decent one?"

"Probably," then, after a few seconds thought. "About as reliable as a Harley chop job can be. My cousin built one. He spent more time working on it than riding it."

"I need somethin' 'at's reliable. Low maintenance."

"His bike was reliable. You could always count on it to break down."

"Remember Jerry?" ignoring what I didn't want to hear. "The cotton trompin' guy? He gave ya the money at the party."

"Yeah."

"I ran into him this afternoon. He said Chad thinks my stereo gear was stolen."

Homer didn't say anything.

"Ya know what pisses me off?" more to myself than to Homer. "He hadn't come over yet ta tell me he thinks it's been stolen. The little bastard. I wonder how he's gunna handle this."

Homer took a tug off the bottle.

"You still plannin' on goin' ta this thing with me an' Danny t'night?" I asked.

"Nope," raising the scotch bottle and shaking it. "Made other plans."

"Okay, but the future Mrs. Cherokee might be comin' t'night."

"The future Mrs. Cherokee won't be hanging out at any church meetings."

"It's not a church meetin'. It's a *spiritual* thing."

I went into the kitchen and got ready, joining Homer outside when I was done.

We were sitting on the tailgate of the '35 smoking a joint when Danny showed up in a mid-sixties Dodge, pop top camper-van. Danny pulled himself from behind the wheel and lumbered up to the truck, hands stuffed into the pockets of his khaki pants.

"Damn, Gil," he whistled. "That is one nice piece of machinery."

"Yeah," as I hopped up from the tailgate to shake his hand. "Too bad it dudn't run."

"This yours?" reaching out to shake Homer's hand.

"Nope. Mine runs," pointing to his truck. "Heater works too."

Homer was pretty wasted.

"What's a truck without a heater," Danny smiled, apparently amused by Homer's condition.

Homer offered Danny the joint.

"No thanks. I'm driving."

"Can I have your hit?" Homer.

"Go ahead."

"Thanks," putting the joint to his lips and inhaling deeply.

"Dressed good enough f'r this thing t'night?" lifting my arms from my sides and turning 360 degrees.

"This is what I'm wearing," holding his arms out and turning around for me.

His khakis were wrinkled, work boots scuffed, and his short sleeve khaki shirt wasn't tucked in.

"Let's go then," I said. "You be good, Homer, an' don't go porkin' the baby-sitter," as we walked toward the van.

Homer waved.

Danny pushed a tape into the eight-track. Woodstock. Country Joe and the Fish.

"Tell me ever'thing ya know about this Baha'i thing, Daniel" as I turned the music down. "I don't wan'a show up dead ignorant about it."

"Well, it goes something like this, but keep in mind, this is how *I* understand it. I could be missing something here and there. A Baha'i believes in a cycle of nine prophets, some more important than others. They believe as man evolves intellectually he can accept more complex truths. You know, more complicated spiritual realities that replace previous, less complex revelations. Anyway, that's what the nine prophets have been up to since the beginning of mankind. These prophets have been gradually revealing more and more about what's really going on. When God feels man is ready, He sends a new prophet down with an update. The prophets in the past are people like Adam, Abraham, Moses, and get this, Buddha, Mohammed, Krishna, and even Jesus. The last prophet in the series, the major, the most important one, the one who pulls it all together, is a guy named Baha'u'llah. He lived back in the late 1800's in the Middle East. If you believe all this, then you're a Baha'i. That's the short of it," pausing before pressing for a reaction. "So, what do you think?"

I lit a cigarette and mulled it over.

"Well...it's no more whacked out than Christians b'lievin' in a zombie."

"Damn, Gil. You're gunna get us hit by lightning."

"If it's a Christian God, I guess it's a possibility. No matter what religion God is, though, He's not takin' me out any time soon. No matter what I do. He's havin' too much fun jackin' with me. You know how it is? It's Saturd'y night in Heaven. God's sittin' aroun' listenin' ta some harp shit on the radio an' poundin' down a few brews. Bored ta tears. Jesus comes up to him an' says, 'Hey, Dad, I don't have nothin' ta do.' God says, *'Anything*...ya don't have *anything* ta do. When's the last time ya jacked with Gil McNeil?' an' Jesus tells God, 'This afternoon. I had Homer pull all the wires out of his '35'."

"Not feeling too persecuted are you?" Danny commented.

I was about to defend myself when he pulled to a stop in front of a run down duplex. Cars were parked bumper-to-bumper on both sides of the street.

"This is it," Danny. "Looks like a good crowd. Promise me you won't say 'hard-on' or 'boner' tonight?"

"Damn, Danny. I'm not gunna go liein' ta somebody at a spiritual thing. Some chick asks me what I've got in my pocket, I'm gunna tell her...'It's a stinkin' boner'."

Danny knocked on the door. He told me about the hosts while we waited.

"This guy's name is Ahmed. He's from Iran. His whole family's in jail over there for pissin' off some kind of Muslim high priest because they're Baha'i. Some of Ahmed's friends have been beat to death over the whole thing. He's married to a lady named Julie. Her father's a big wig in the Baptist church in Amarillo and disowned her after she got married to Ahmed because, according to her father, he's a heathen camel jockey. Ahmed and Julie are both grea...,"

The door flew open.

A short, heavy set, dark skinned man leapt through the doorway.

"Allah'u'Abha! Welcome Mr. Wright! Welcome!" in a heavy Middle Eastern accent. "We have not seen you in several weeks, Mr. Wright," stepping aside and waving us in. "We have missed your wit."

He grabbed Danny's hand and shook it furiously before taking my hand and pumping it just as furiously.

"Allah'u'Abha, my friend. Welcome. My name is Ahmed. JULIE! JULIE!" over his shoulder. "Come quickly! Danny is here!" then turned back to Danny. "She will be so happy to see you," excitedly, as he took our coats. "Joan mentioned you might be coming tonight. Tell me about your friend. Please. Tell me."

"This is Gil McNeil. An old high school buddy. He recently got out of the military."

"Excellent! Excellent! Very pleased to meet you. Danny, I'm helping Julie in the kitchen. Could you introduce Gil to the others? We'll be starting soon, so please make the introductions for me."

Ahmed grabbed my hand again, shook it wildly, and then ran off.

"He's normally not that standoffish," Danny. "He'll warm up to you once he gets to know you."

I scanned the room for Joan.

WHAM!

There she was, in all her braless bounty, sitting in a studio chair, leaning forward tying a shoelace, her long silken hair touching the floor. I felt something crawling around in the pit of my stomach.

Several long-haired guys were gathered around her chair trying to act like they didn't want to rip her tee shirt off and disappear into her cleavage.

"Who're the fairy lookin' guys sweatin' all over her?" as I nodded in Joan's direction.

"You're not the only one looking for religion," Danny answered. "Don't worry. They don't have any more of a chance at her than you do."

"They Baha'i?"

"Don't know. Haven't seen them here before. Let me show you around," leading me into the room.

I grabbed his elbow.

"In'r'duce me ta *her*," accompanied by an exaggerated nod in Joan's direction.

"I was going to save the best for last."

"Ta hell with 'at. I need religion an' I need it *now*," pushing Danny across the room toward Joan.

We stood for a moment outside the circle of goofballs. Joan had straightened up and thrown her shoulders back in what appeared to me to be a carefully rehearsed, intentionally provocative, stretching routine.

*Damnation. That's even nastier than when she was bent over tyin' her shoe.*

She spotted Danny.

"Danny!" and sprang to her feet. She squeezed sideways between two of the jerks. It was a tight fit. Joan bounced over to us, went to her toes, threw her arms around Danny, and then hugged him hard. She released him and stepped back. The freaks were close to tears. They wandered off in defeat.

"I heard Ahmed, but I wasn't sure you were the Danny he was yellin' about," looking over at me and smiling.

"Joan, this is an old friend of mine, Gil McNeil. Gil, this is Joan."

Then the undreamable—she stepped up to me, put her arms around me, forced her breasts into my ribs, and gave me a quick, tight hug. It happened so fast. Her perfume, a sweet lemon scent, stunned me like I'd been darted. I couldn't speak.

I couldn't even manage a nod.

"Gil's an expert on religions," Danny continuing the introduction. "Lately he's been reading everything he can find about the Baha'i Faith."

"Really?" throwing her hands together in delight.

"Yeah, well," glaring at Danny, "it's kind of a hobby. It's really not much more'n 'at. I mean, *more than* that," hurriedly correcting my English.

"What did you think of "Like A Thief in the Night"?" tossing her hair back over her shoulders.

"You know, actually, that's the one I've been havin' trouble gettin' hold of."

"Really?" a surprised look on her face.

*Shit! I'm blowin' it. Dammit, Danny.*

Joan took my arm at the bicep and pulled me to her side. I tensed the arm to give her a shot of muscle.

*Feel 'at Joanie?*

She led me across the room to a set of built-in wall shelves.

"Ahmed keeps loaner copies around," plucking a copy of the book from the shelf and handing it to me. "Here," with a huge, sweet

*Inviting?*

smile.

"Thanks," pretending to study the cover. "This is the one by God."

*Think, dammit! Think!*

"By golly," nervously scratching my sweating forehead.

Ahmed scurried back into the room, frantically clapping his hands as he came.

"Okay! Okay! Let us begin! Sarah, will you open with a prayer, please?"

Joan hurried back to her chair, tossing me a quick wave as she went. Danny eased up beside me.

"Thanks, buddy-fucker," I muttered.

"No problem. You're on your own from now on, though."

Sarah, a large woman in a Mama Cass dress and forty pounds of beads around her chubby, squat neck, launched into a ten minute prayer about God is one, mankind is one, and all religions are one. She petioned for the quick establishment of a universal government and mentioned something about there being more than one path to the top of the mountain. Sarah finally shut up and sat down.

Those of us who didn't have a chair sat on the floor. Ahmed introduced a squirrelly looking guy who went on for a good twenty minutes about a fasting period coming up in January. A feast would follow the fast. It sounded like it was going to be some kind of Baha'i New Year.

I looked around. Twenty or twenty-five bodies were crammed into the front room where I was sitting cross-legged on the floor. Ten or so bodies were in an adjoining dining room. Two of the ladies present were pretty decent looking. Nothing like Joan, but something you wouldn't be ashamed of being seen with in public.

THE RAVING EUNUCH MONKS

*This thing has the same problem the bars have—the guys out number the women three to one.*

Almost everybody looked hippied-up with the exception of a few sets of slacks and sport shirts. An older, balding guy was in a suit.

The speaker finished. His effort earned a polite round of applause. Ahmed announced the location of the next meeting. It was to be a question and answer meeting for the growing number of newer attendees. Everybody was then invited to stick around for snacks and coffee.

Danny and I stood up and stretched.

"This is when the hustling begins," Danny. "Recruiting time."

"Pr'tty high pressure, huh?"

"Not at all, but it's still there. You know the feeling...you're more a prospective convert than somebody they really want to know?"

I went to the bathroom. When I returned Danny was talking about the stock market with the old man in the suit. I looked around for Joan. She wasn't in either room. I checked the kitchen. She wasn't there. I was starting to panic. I walked up to Ahmed and asked if he'd seen Joan.

"Joan had to leave," smiling. "She has a night class."

My disappointment must have shown. Ahmed tensed and eyed me suspiciously, the way a father might eye a young man who'd just asked him if his daughter wore crotchless panties.

"I...she got me this book but didn't tell me how much it cost 'r who ta pay. I was tryin' ta find her ta ask her about it."

Ahmed immediately relaxed and lit up.

"No! No! It is free! Borrow it. Take it. Bring it back when you are finished or give it to some one else to read," suddenly gripping my arm, panning the room, and then lowering his voice as if he was about to share a deep secret with me. "Tell me, honestly, did you enjoy this evening? Did you find it worth your while?"

The look of apprehension on his face was so intense that if I'd hated every minute of the meeting I would have lied to him about it.

"Ahmed," with all the sincerity I could muster, "I loved it. I'll be back. I'm especially lookin' forward ta that question an' answer thing next week. Sounds like a real hoot."

His face went off like he'd had an orgasm.

"Good! Excellent! Excellent! I will see you next week, then."

Poof! He was gone.

*Fuckin' "Alice In Wonderland".*

I went over to Danny.

"Excuse me," interrupting the conversation Danny was having with the suit. I pulled Danny aside.

"Ya ready ta go?" I asked.

"What happened? Get your face slapped trying to cop a feel?"

"Worse. Joan left."

"Talk to somebody else. Your chances of finding spiritual fulfillment are probably better with anybody else in this room than with Joan."

"It's apples and oranges."

"Melons and lemons would be more like it."

"Whatever," irritated. "Let's go up ta the bar an' have a few. I can't get drunk though. Gotta start work t'morrow."

"Okay. Give me a minute to say goodbye."

"I'll be out front havin' a smoke."

Danny emerged from the house as I finished the cigarette.

"Ya don't mind leavin' do ya?" as I crushed the butt under my boot.

"Nah. I'm a little thirsty myself."

"C'n ya b'lieve 'at bitch didn't even say goodnight? An' I'm supposed ta b'lieve 'at she's concerned about my goddamn soul?"

We got into the van and headed to the bar.

"So, when are you going to become a Baha'i?" Danny.

"Soon as they get a bowlin' team up."

"Not too impressed, huh?"

"I don't know, Danny. It sounds good in some ways, but in other ways it's pr'tty much the same ol' shit. I mean…if a person can't buy inta all the separate religions, how c'n he be excited about a religion 'at says it brings 'em all t'gether under one roof. It's like what they're tryin' ta do is ta take a whole bunch'a *little* piles'a crap an' make one *big* pile'a crap. I'll have ta read a little more about it. Joan gave me this book," and held it up.

"How'd you like the people?"

"Friendly enough. Didn't talk ta too many of 'em. I like 'at Ahmed guy. He's wired. An', if worse comes ta worse, I wouldn't mind plankin' a coupl'a the ladies 'at were there. I'll pro'bly go ta a few more meetin's. What the hell. Right?"

"Yeah. What the hell," then, "HOLD ON!" as the van sped up.

Danny cut in front of a car in the lane to our right then whipped into the IHOP parking lot. Eight-track tapes were thrown all over the van.

"Sorry," Danny, pulling into a parking space.

"No problem, I guess," yanking myself upright.

"Dammit. I don't know why I'm doing this," while staring into the rear view mirror.

I turned around and looked out the back window.

"Know who that is?" Danny.

I could see a man wearing white sweatpants and a hooded white sweatshirt. He was carrying a small paper sack and stooping over an outdoor butt can located under the awning of the restaurant's entrance. He picked something from the butt can then placed it in the paper sack.

"No," shaking my head. "Can't say as I do."

"That's Doug Pitt."

"No shit? What's he doin'?"

"Here's the deal. I didn't have time to tell you at the party. Doug's decided he's going to be an urban scavenger and live off the land, so to speak. Live off what everybody else throws away."

Doug moved into the light of the restaurant windows.

"Where's he live?" I asked.

"In a little place in the alley between Fourteenth and Fifteenth off Avenue W. This one-armed, Vietnamese guy took him in."

"Vietnamese?" surprised. "How'd a Vietnamese guy end up in Lubbock?"

"Don't know."

"How'd he loss his arm?"

"He was in the Vietnamese army. I think it was shot off. Land mine. Bomb or something. Real nice guy. Real calm."

"So, Doug's tryin' ta make it off the land?" continuing to watch him.

"Gutters, garbage cans, dumpsters," Danny. "That's his hunting ground."

"Damn. He had ya over f'r dinner yet?"

Danny'd already exited the van. I jumped out and followed him over to Doug.

"Doug!" Danny called out.

Doug looked up.

"Danny!" straightening and spreading his arms wide.

He moved toward Danny, dragging each foot as if his shower shoes were made of lead. Doug was smiling broadly, emitting a wheezing kind of laugh. They shook hands.

"Great to see you, man," Doug. "How long's it been?" furrowing his brow in thought, rubbing his lightly bearded chin. "Three days? Three whole days! You've really grown," all the while smiling and wheeze laughing.

"Do you remember me telling you about running into Gil at the party the other night?" Danny asked.

"You know, Danny, I *do* remember *that,*" speaking slowly, carefully enunciating each word, "but what I *don't* remember...and correct me if I'm mistaken," slowly moving his hands in front of his face in a flowing, circular motion, "what I *don't* remember is...*me* asking *you* to bring *every* person I've ever known by to...watch me pick cigarette butts from the...trash. *That*...that, Daniel, I do...*not* remember at all. That, Daniel...I do *not* at all appreciate. Thank you."

Although still smiling, his eyes were flaring wildly. It was eerie. Danny backed away a few feet, looked at me then returned to the van without saying anything else. Doug shifted his glare to me. It was uncomfortable as hell. Unnerving. I felt like I needed to do something, to say something before breaking it off.

I pointed at the sack in his hand.

"Listen, Doug. I'm out'a work right now, an' I hate ta ask ya, but could I borrow a cigarette 'r two?"

For a few seconds we stood there, staring at each other. I got the feeling he thought I was messing with him, somehow making fun of him. Without changing his expression Doug slowly raised the sack and handed it to me. I took the sack, opened it, and began picking through the butts. I retrieved one and put it between my lips. Doug, still tight-jawed, lit the butt for me. I thanked him for the light and selected a few more butts from the sack. I showed them to Doug.

"These okay ta take? I'll pay ya back as soon as I can."

Doug nodded, his expression unchanged.

"Thanks. Nice seein' ya again, Doug. No kiddin'. Catch ya later."

I returned to the van and hopped in. As we pulled out of the lot I waved to Doug.

He stared back.

Danny was upset. Not mad, just real upset.

"Goddamn' prick," he grumbled. "I keep trying to help him and he keeps freaking out like that. You know what will happen next? I've got his routine down pat. He'll settle down, think about what he did, feel bad about it, and a month'll pass before anybody sees him again. Then he'll resurface and act like nothing ever happened. Give it a while and something else will set him off and he'll cycle through again."

"Drugs?"

"Maybe. At least I hope so. The alternative is scary," pulling into a space directly in front of Mother's.

The place was dead. We stopped at the bar. The bartender, busy washing glasses, looked up and nodded.

"Evenin', Gil. Danny."

"Evenin', Bo," I said.

"Where's Homer?" he asked.

"At the house. He's givin' up drinkin' on Tu'sd'y nights b'tween 8:45 an' 9:00."

"Why're ya all slicked up?" drying his hands on a bar towel. "Almos' didn't recognize ya without all 'at crap all over ya."

"Changin' my image. Even got on underwear t'night."

"Keep it up an' ya may end up gittin' laid out'a here. Ya want the us'al?"

"Nah. Make it a pitcher."

"Somebody die an' leave ya some money?"

"Sold somethin'. Ya mind puttin' 'at Stone's tape on? Flowers? All'a that candy-ass shit ya play f'r the frats sucks."

Danny and I found a table in the back. He was still pretty knotted.

"You'd think the Army would have straightened Doug out a little, but he's as scrambled as he ever was," Danny.

"That's all I remember about him from high school. Always in trouble. Did he make it overseas?"

"To Vietnam?"

"Yeah."

"He was there a year. I don't know what he did exactly. Something to do with communications, I think. We wrote each other a lot, but he never mentioned his job. His letters were typical Doug...long, rambling dissertations on reality, the meaning and purpose of life. God. Existence. None of it ever made any sense. He got pissed as hell when he got back and found out I hadn't saved any of them. He accused me of not reading them. Made a big scene over it." Danny slammed a fist on the table, threw himself back in his chair, and then lurched forward, planting his elbows on the table. "Then, three weeks after he accuses me of *not* reading them, he accuses me of lying about throwing them out. He claimed I was going to publish them and take all the credit for them. That was the next big stink."

Bo brought the pitcher and two frosted mugs to the table.

"Stones comin' up."

"Thanks," I nodded.


"So where else was he stationed?" filling the mugs.

"Two years in Korea and the rest stateside. He learned karate in Korea. Practically lived at one of those karate places off base."

"I thought karate was supposed ta help pull y'ur shit t'gether."

"Not his. The letters from Korea were as screwed up as the other letters. He never wrote when he was stateside, but he'd call about every month or so. That's another tantrum he had," taking a long drink. "I got a telegram from him once. It must have cost two hundred dollars. It went on and on about what a lying hypocrite I was because I claimed I was his friend and he'd been trying to call me for three days and I wasn't home and what kind of friend would do that, blah, blah, blah. It was insane."

"Why didn't ya tell him ta go ta hell?"

"I couldn't do that. Christ, I've known him since grade school.

What's beginning to get on my nerves lately is that he seems to be having more and more trouble staying on the swing."

We quietly listened to the Stones. After a while, Danny broke into a quiet laugh.

"What?" I grinned.

"When Doug got out last August, he didn't tell anybody he was coming home. When he got here, he took a cab from the airport. You know the motorcycle place on the road to the airport?"

"Yeah. Sells mostly dirt bikes?"

"That's the one. Right across the road from that big lumber company. Anyway, as Doug's passing the motorcycle place, he tells the driver to pull in. He sends the cab on its way and begins looking around at all the dirt bikes. He'd gotten off the plane with three hundred and fifty dollars. Doug got the biggest used bike he could buy for three hundred and fifty bucks. Remember, he's still in his uniform. I mean, he'd only been out of the Army six hours at the most. Doug jumps on the bike, winds it up all the way, lets the clutch out, and then blasts out of the lot. The salesman told me Doug was damn near airborne when he shot across both lanes of traffic and thirty feet of berm on the other side of the road. Doug smacked right into the side of the lumber company. He ended up with a cracked elbow and a few broken ribs. And you know whose fault it was? He blamed me because he tried to call me for a ride from the airport, but I wasn't home!" Danny slapped his palms on the table. "His own parents threw him out after two weeks and got a restraining order to keep him away."

"Yeah. Y'ur mom mentioned that."

"It's really a waste. He's a damn good artist. He'll never do a damn thing with it, though."

We finished the pitcher, paid, and then left.

When we arrived at the house I got out and walked around to Danny's side of the van.

"Ya mind pickin' me up f'r next weeks meetin'?"

"Nah. And guess where it's going to be?"

"Joan's?"

"That's right."

"Damn. Maybe I'll have a chance ta steal a pair'a underwear from her bedroom."

"Religious relic?"

"Somethin' like 'at," slapping the side of the door and walking away.

Danny pulled out and drove off, Arlo Guthrie blaring into Los Angeles from over the poles.

\*\*\*

The alarm under my blanket woke me at 5:30. I smacked it then fired up a cigarette. I let a hacking fit pass before sliding to the floor. A little scotch remained in the bottle on the floor near the bunk. I shook the rack to wake Homer.

"How ya like y'ur eggs?"

He rode out a coughing spasm then looked at me through bloodshot eyes.

"You got eggs?" hoarsely.

"No. Just curious," clearing my throat and swallowing hard. "Listen, since y'ur job's just down the street, would ya mind if I took y'ur truck out ta this surveyin' place t'day?"

"Go ahead. Drop me off on the way," rising from the bunk and lighting a cigarette.

Homer began coughing again. Hard coughing. Gagging.

"Damn, Homer. That cough sounds like shit. Ya ought'a switch brands b'fore ya do some real damage," moving to the clothes corner to find a clean set of anything.

"How'd your thing go last night?" Homer.

"Not bad. Learned some shit," picking through the clothes. "Didn't get laid."

"Going back?" as he entered the kitchen.

"Thinkin' about it. Why? Ya wan'a go next time?"

105

The shower spit and sputtered before water began to beat against the metal stall as loudly as hail on a tin roof.

"Yeah," he shouted over the racket. "I spent last night thinking about putting something together!"

"I guess those meetin's would be as good a place as any ta start."

"What?"

"Sounds like a good idea!"

"That's what I was thinking," he shouted back.

Homer finished showering then dried off in front of the heater.

"Ya got any money left from yesterd'y?" I asked. "Enough ta eat on?"

"Got plenty. I'm going to pay you..."

"Homer," cutting him off, "don't do that to me. I'm not a fuckin' bank. Okay?"

"Okay."

"Well?" Homer, after dressing. "What do you think?"

His hair was brushed back, bandanna tied securely in place. He was wearing a clean pair of Levis and a clean flannel shirt. He'd even knocked the mud from his boots and buffed them up a bit.

"I'd hire ya in a heart beat," I told him. "Even better'n 'at. If I was a lady I'd be humpin' y'ur leg right this very minute. No shit."

"I'll go ahead and walk," moving toward the door.

"Ya sure? If ya walk ya might ruin 'at spit shine on 'em boots."

"Yeah. I'll walk," looking down. "I found some shoe polish in your seabag. They haven't looked this good since I got out."

"Remember where the shop's at?"

"Yeah. Down the alley to a metal door that says 'J.D. Grubb Pianos'," repeating it to be sure.

"Okay. See ya this evenin'."

A few minutes later I stepped out into the clear, chilly morning. Last night's freeze had left a thin layer of silvery frost on everything. It didn't do anything to hide all the crap in the yard.

*Ought'a find out where the landlord lives, pile this shit inta the back'a the truck, then dump it all in his goddamn front yard.*

Mr. Tripp's place was about two miles past the last housing area on the south end of town. Ninety-Eighth Street was an unpaved, wash boarded, sorry-ass excuse of an ice choked rut. By mid-afternoon, it would be a sloppy nightmare. The hundred yards of lane running north from Ninety-Eighth to a set of buildings wasn't any better. I pulled into an asphalt parking lot at the end of the lane.

I eased to a stop behind a new, bright orange, Ford pickup. A rusted out, late 50's, Chevy pickup was parked beside it. Both were mud caked. The old Chevy had a big Texas Tech double T decal in the back window. A small, faded Future Farmers of America decal was surrounded by a slew of collegiate rodeo stickers. The old truck's radio antennae sported a plastic pennant with an attacking eagle over "Abilene High 1968". Two bumper stickers were plastered on the tailgate. One read "Better A Sister In A Whorehouse Than A Brother In Canada", the other "Footprint of the American Chicken" followed by a peace sign. The orange truck had a single bumper sticker, "Hippie And Heathen Begin With H".

*Shit.*

I parked next to the Chevy and glanced around. The parking area separated a large, single story, red brick ranch house from a white, neatly kept, miniature barn-looking structure. A four-bay garage was attached to the little white barn without detracting from the barn-like theme of the building. One of the garage doors was up, but I couldn't see inside from where I'd parked. A sign hung over the first door.

## HUGO TRIPP
## LAND SURVEYOR

I stepped out of the truck, lit a cigarette and leaned against the bed. I checked the whole place out.

It was different. It was like a miniranch. A second barn, painted red, was about fifty yards north of the lot. It was a good bit larger than the white one. From what little I'd ever seen of big red barns, this one looked to be in pretty good shape. The whole ranchette, well over 10 or 12 acres of short dry grass, was surrounded by a tidy, four rung, five foot high, white fence. A huge, rugged looking corral occupied the northwest quadrant of the field. The heavily constructed corral butted up against the west door of the red barn. The corral was a good six feet tall with three rungs. The rungs were made of railroad ties. The ties were secured at each end to posts made of what appeared to be three old telephone poles banded together at the top, bottom, and in the middle. Some of the ties were bowed outwards while others, apparently broken, had been banding-spliced back together. All the triple posts leaned outward to varying degrees. The whole thing wobbled its way around the three or so acre enclosure.

At one point the corral split a small metal stock tank in two, half inside the fort, the other half outside of it. The corral half of the tank was dented and crumpled. A thick cloud of steam rose from the tank into the frigid air forming a coat of ice on the ties immediately above it creating long, crystalline icicles that glistened in the morning sun.

An old, beat-to-shit Volkswagen bug sat in the middle of the corral. Every bit of glass, from the brake lights to the windshield, had been knocked out. The front wheels were noticeably cocked in opposite directions. Every square inch of surface on the bug was stove in, mauled, or smashed.

A half dozen, long legged, crippled goats, some ragged ducks, a cat, and two mangy dogs were standing around in the field between the red barn and the parking lot. They appeared to be hanging out. A skinny, pathetic looking steer was walking in a slow, tight circle, bobbing his head up and down. Two rangy peacocks and a goose were huddled in a knot, heads together and low to the ground as if they were telling dirty jokes. Every one of the animals was screwed up in one way or the other. It was a collection of mangled, deformed, moth-eaten Noah's ark rejects. I'd have just as soon shot the poor bastards.

I heard a door open inside the garage.

"Grab a bundle'a flags an' stakes," someone ordered.

A husky, mustached man in jeans, an orange cap, and an orange hunting vest over a bright yellow, flannel shirt, emerged from the garage. He held a wooden box in one hand while steadying a tripod on his shoulder with the other hand. The instant the man saw me he froze.

"Holy shit, Stan!" turning around and yelling into the garage. "Git the gun! The big 'un! We got us another hippie out here!" then turned back to me. "Stay calm, son. Smoke one'a them happy cigarettes 'r shoot somethin' up, but j'st ya relax. Okay?" cautiously walking around me, never breaking eye contact. "Ever'thangs cool, par'ner, I mean, man."

I made a sudden jerk in his direction.

He jumped back, eyes wide.

"Dammit, Stan! Where's 'at gun?"

A tall, hefty young man stepped from the shadow of the garage into the morning light. He was clean shaven and wearing a sweat stained, felt cowboy hat, a sheepskin coat, faded Levis, and a muddy, beat up pair of cowboy boots.

"This ain't no hippie, Roy," the young man declared. "His clothes're too clean."

"I b'lieve y're right, Stan," Roy, sniffing the air. "He does smell washed. God Almighty, mister," as he walked over to the orange truck, "I didn't mean ta go callin' ya a hippie like 'at. The sun was in my eyes an' 'at coat'a y'urs…I'm awful sorry. That is a coat ain't it?"

Roy placed the wooden box in the cab, threw the tripod into the truck bed then came back over to me.

"Yew must be Gil. The new guy," shaking my hand. "I'm Roy an' this here's Stan."

Stan took my hand, gave it one solid pump, and then stepped back.

"Is whudever y'ur coats got catchin'?" Stan, as he examined the coat.

"Only through sex'al contact," trying to be one of the boys.

"Here 'at, Stan? A sense'a humor," Roy. "A surveyor needs a sense'a humor."

"An' a secon' job," Stan snorted.

"Shit to, boy! Don't go listenin' ta him, Gil. Hugo pays 'at retard damn good money. No other surveyor'd pay twenty-five cents an hour f'r a half-wit like Stan."

"There ain' no other surveyor in town," Stan pointed out before tucking some snuff into his lower lip.

"Don't go changin' the subject on me, boy. Git in 'at truck b'fore I fire y'ur lazy ass. Again."

Stan climbed into the passenger side of the truck.

"Nice meetin' ya, Gil," and waved. "Take her easy."

I glanced at the bumper stickers on the trucks.

Roy must have noticed.

"Don't take none'a 'at stuff pers'nal," nodding at the bumpers. "They're good f'r b'ness, but if dumbass here in'a truck gives ya any crap about how weird ya look, yew know, makin' fun'a y'ur beard an' hair an' all…'r 'at coat, j'st yew lemme know an' I'll kick his draft dodgin' butt. Bes' git on inside now. Hugo 's waitin' f'r ya. See ya later."

Roy jumped into the truck and backed out. I could hear them arguing as they pulled out of the lot.

"Yew couldn't kick my ass if I was hog-tied an' passed out drunk," Stan growled.

"That right there goes ta show j'st how damn stupid ya are, Stan...showin' up ta an ass kickin' all hog-tied an' passed out drunk. Damn y're one dum..."

"An' quit tellin' ever'body I'm a damn draft dodger. My number didn't come up in the lottery."

"Ya should'a volunteered out'a patri'tism."

Their voices faded as the truck moved down the lane.

*Yee, fuckin', haw.*

I made my way into the garage. A scratched, dented, dirty, light blue station wagon was parked behind one of the closed garage doors. From the garage, I entered a small, darkened room reeking of ammonia. A big reproduction machine and a large table covered in blue prints filled the space. I opened a door near the end of the machine and stepped into a room so bright it made me squint. Everything was white. Even the linoleum tiled floor was solid white. Two drafting tables with large glaring florescent lamps attached to them intensified the brightness. A steep, narrow staircase was located to the right of a closed front door.

A door at the foot of the staircase swung open. An attractive, young woman, much shorter than me, stepped out of a bathroom. The little pixie smiled at me then announced up the staircase that I was here. She adjusted her shoulder length hair then approached me. She stopped and nodded at the door I was blocking.

"Oh. Pardon me," pushing up against the wall to allow her room to pass.

She smiled again without looking at me then stepped through the doorway. She was cute. Thin face. Button nose. Oriental-like eyes. Light huddle of freckles on each cheek. Sleek, well-defined curves. Average sized boobs, but one *hell* of a nice butt. No beauty queen, but damn cute in her own way.

*I'd do her at the drop of a hat.*

Mr. Tripp's warm, drawling voice invited me upstairs. The creaky, narrow staircase led to a small room with a low ceiling. Mr. Tripp was in an old, high back, leather, office chair. His back was to the lone window in the room. He sat behind a heavy, antique looking desk. He was leaning over a map, studying it closely.

The room was paneled entirely in a dark wood with lots of tiny knotholes. The floor was a different kind of dark wood polished to a high shine. A huge bearskin rug, head and paws still attached, covered almost all of it. Two faded, burgundy colored, felt, smoking chairs, worn with use, pinned the bear to the floor. The chairs sat side by side facing Mr. Tripp's desk.

The walls of the room were thick with aging photographs of cowboys posing with horses and yellowing pictures of frontier dressed people standing on turn-of-the-century ranchhouse porches. There wasn't a tree to be seen in any of the shots. A mounted deer head and a few old, framed maps were mixed in among the photographs.

Three shelves ran the length of the wall opposite the stairs. The shelves were filled with a strange mix of books—stock market, Indians, all kinds of religion and philosophy books, folklore, guns, real estate, veterinary medicine, astrology. Atlases. Several volumes of Ron Hubbard, Kahil Gabran...

*...Neets...Nitz...sche? Screw it.*

An old, portable record player was on the top shelf at the far end.

Mr. Tripp, wearing stiffly starched khakis like the pair he'd been wearing the night of the party, looked up, leaned across the desk, and then shook my hand. His grip was firm, hands thick and rough.

"Have a seat, Gil," nodding at one of the chairs.

His eyes, magnified by thick glasses, appeared to bulge from their sockets. He sat down, the high back chair silhouetted by a halo of golden light from the small window behind him.

Mr. Tripp began describing the business and the work I'd be doing if I wanted it. His voice was soft and quiet. Mellow. His head bobbed slightly, rhythmically, while he spoke. It sounded like good work, pulling a measuring tape or chain or something to measure land boundaries, measuring houses around town for title companies, and doing a few chores around the office. It was outdoor work and the pay was as good as you could expect in this part of the world. Mr. Tripp guaranteed a laid-back work environment, friendly people to work with, and eighty-five cents an hour with a raise after thirty days. I told him I planned to attend Tech in January. He said he'd go ahead and work me full time until I had a class schedule then set my hours up around the schedule. With all the details worked out, Mr. Tripp stood up and welcomed me aboard.

He reached for a dusty felt hat. It wasn't a cowboy cut. It was a worn, 1940's dress hat missing the silk ribbon running around the sweat stained crown.

"I b'lieve I heard ya speakin' with Roy an' Stan?" moving from behind the desk.

"Ye'sir."

"There's a pair ta draw to. Stan's an Animal Science major an' Roy's been an on-again, off-again part time student out at Tech since 1956 'r '57. He's majored in damn near ever'thing from art ta zoology," stopping to adjust his hat.

Mr. Tripp caught me looking at his books. He waved a hand at the shelves.

"Workin' on some answers," he told me.

I followed Mr. Tripp down the stairs.

"I didn't expect ya back from Oklahoma this soon," Hugo. "I don't really have anything lined up for ya t'day. Bernie's here all day on Tu'sd'ys an' Thursd'ys, so ya might be goin' with him t'morrow ta learn how ta measure houses f'r the title companies. Right now I think I'll have Hope show ya some'a the chores you'll be doin' around the place. Did ya meet Hope on the way in?"

"I b'lieve I saw her."

"She's a doll," as we entered the room with the machine in it. "Damn," Mr. Tripp coughed. "Blue line copier. Uses ammonia. One'a the first things you'll be doin' t'morrow is ta fig're out why the hell the vent fan idn't workin' on it anymore."

We passed through the garage then out onto the parking lot. Mr. Tripp stopped suddenly. He dropped his head, slowly shaking it. I spotted Hope in a garden area behind the ranch house. She was standing on her head in the middle of a thick cloth pad. She was wearing a tan colored, skintight leotard. Her legs were fully scissored and parallel to the ground. Her back was to us. She may as well have been naked the way the thin material stretched tightly over every muscle and pulled into every crevice.

*Good God!*

"Yoga," Hugo grumbled. "I've all but begged her not ta do it right there. Twelve goddamned acres an' she claims 'at the best vibrations on the place're smack dab in the middle'a the front door ta my business. I should'a j'st given her a damn Bible instead'a intr'ducin' her ta all 'at other stuff," taking his glasses off with one hand to rub his swollen eyes with the other. "Dammit," still grumbling. "It's gunna take me the rest'a the mornin' ta get my concentration back," blinking, head bobbing. "Hope!"

Hope fell forward and looked in our direction. She grabbed her coat and jeans and clutched them to her chest.

"Turn around!"

"F'r Christ's sake," Mr. Tripp.

We both did as she'd ordered.

"Yew c'n look now," after a few seconds.

I turned and watched her glide across the lot towards us. She floated, taking quick, tiny steps, one foot crossing in front of the other the way strippers walk a runway. Hope slid up alongside Mr. Tripp and wrapped an arm around his waist.

"Sorry," she whispered.

Mr. Tripp placed his hand on the small of her back.

"Hope, this is Gil. Gil, meet Hope."

I stuck out a sweaty palm anticipating the first press of flesh. Hope withdrew slightly and told me in a heavy West Texas accent how pleased she was to meet me.

*God! She's so damn cute!*

"Hope, would you show Gil around. Give him some'a the chores you've got. He'll be workin' full time 'til school b'gins next month. Might as well fill him in on the exercise pen while you're at it."

Hope let go of Mr. Tripp's waist then sexied off into the office.

Mr. Tripp moved closer to me and began explaining Hope's situation.

"She answered an ad f'r a chainman position I was runnin' in the paper about five months ago. She's got days she'll talk y'ur ear off, but sometimes she c'n come across as bein' a little...reserved. She's livin' out here while she's pullin' some things t'gether f'r herself."

Hugo called it a sabbatical. Hope had sworn off everything from cigarettes to men.

*Dammit!*

Hope returned, tossed a set of keys at me, and then slipped through a gate near the end of the little barn. I excused myself before taking off after her, remaining a few paces behind. I watched her tight little butt shift delicately from side to side as she executed that sultry slide of hers. My gaze must have burned a whole in her ass. Hope stopped and turned to allow me to catch up before continuing. She was careful to maintain a good three feet between us.

Hope began rattling on about how she really liked Hugo and the other people who worked here. She especially liked all the animals Hugo collected. They were special since they were all sick, deformed, or abandoned. That's why Hugo'd adopted them.

"Hugo ended up namin' most uv 'em, but he let me name some uv 'em. See 'at 'un?" pointing at the goat closest to us. "She's blind. Her name's Faith. The red 'un next ta her is called Bertran'. He's got mental problems. At least Hugo says he acts 'at'a way. An' see the dog over yonder with some'a his hair missin'. Hugo stolt him from somebody's backyard. Hugo says 'at the owners must'a left him chained up outside in the sun f'r a coupl'a days 'cause his skin wuz comin' off in chunks. Hugo took him ta the vet an' fixed him up. I named him Bill after mah gran'pa Bill. He's dead now."

"Wouldn't Hairy'a made him think a little better of himself?" I joked.

"I don't *thank* so," looking at me like I was some kind of heartless bastard. "He'd thank we's makin' fun uv him."

*Dolly Parton! That's who she sounded like.*

" 'at cat near the barn?" continuing the introductions. "She cain't control herself. She jus' goes aroun'...yew know...goin' on herself. It's kind'a nasty, but it's also kind'a sad. Her name's de Beauvoir. It's hard ta pr'nounce, but it's pr'tty."

"What'a ya call the steer?"

"Hugo named him John Q. An' the one peacock's called Utopia an' the other 'uns called Bliss. The goose 'at's with 'em's called Verneuil. It's French. Hugo named all'a them."

"What's wrong with 'at other dog?" pointing to a scruffy mixed breed. "He seems ta be in pr'tty good shape."

"He...he is. Sort'a. His name's Alamo. Hugo thanks he's a Pit Bull-Chihuahua mix."

*Jesus! That must'a hurt.*

She hesitated before adding, "He's...he's got three...three," face turning red.

"Three ears?" pretending not to know what she meant.

"No."

"Three eyes? Tongues? Toes? What else is there?"

Hope stopped suddenly and spun around.

"Testicles. Alamo's got three testicles," then turned and continued on to the water tank. "See 'at ol' VW over yonder in the corral?"

"Yeah," as I caught up with her.

" 'at's whut we use ta exercise some'a the stock 'at's in the barn. 'at's whut y're gunna be doin' this mornin'...herdin' the stock aroun' inside the corral."

I glanced at the corral then nearly tripped.

"That's a damn boar!"

Hope halted.

"Yeah. 'at's Ayatolla."

"That's the biggest damn boar I b'lieve I've ever seen."

"An' he's j'st as mean as he is big. Ah thank he's crazy. Oh, yeah," and pointed toward the center of the corral at a rooster standing in the middle of a clutch of chickens. "The rooster's name is Pius Nine. 'at's another 'un Hugo named. I wan'a change his name ta Bossy 'cause'a the way he treats the chickens. He's f'rever peckin' at 'em an' ever'thang. 'specially Mary. She's the one with most uv her feathers all gone. She used ta be one'a the pr'ttiest ones b'fore Pius showed up. C'mon. Lemme show ya the fish," and moved on to the bashed up stock tank.

I stepped up beside her and gazed down into the steaming water.

" 'at's Yin an' Yang," introducing me to two goofy looking fish about the size of two fists.

Their long, flowing red, blue, green, and gold tails and back fins glowed iridescent when they swam through the side of the tank beginning to catch the morning sun. Hope told me they were some kind of imported fighting fish. They were Hugo's pride and joy. He'd paid a fortune for them since they were a breeding pair. One of my jobs would be to feed the fish and make sure the water heater was working. The heater was an aluminum cone plugged into six or seven lengths of extension cord running from the red barn. Hope picked up a coffee can, popped the lid, and then sprinkled some rank smelling crud over the surface of the water. She kept her tiny nose wrinkled until the lid was back in place. Hope tossed the can back against the fence then told me to head out to the VW and get it warmed up. She was off to the barn.

The car's doors had been spot welded shut so I had to crawl in through the window on the driver's side. I got it started and turned it in the direction of the barn doors.

*This'll be a hoot. Gettin' paid ta chase a bunch'a sick-ass horses an' cows around in a beat-up ol' VW.*

*Peelin' out. Poppin' wheelies. Slidin' all over the place.*

*Gunna have ta drag Homer out here with me sometime an' let him...*

Hope waved to me then flung the left barn door open. She ran to the fence, and scurried to the top.

Two colossal buffalo trotted into the corral.

*Holy...*

The smallest was twice the size of the fucking VW.

*...shit!*

They headed for the car, picking up steam as they came, tossing their massive heads around, slinging snot and spit into the air, and foaming at the mouth as if they were rabid or something. They were real, honest-to-God, rampaging, killer buffalo...

*...an' they're comin' right at me, an' they're comin' goddamn fast, an'...SHIT! The son of a bitchin' car won't go inta reverse, an'...NO REVERSE! Pop it back inta first an' floor it. Jesus Christ those bastards're big!*

I was throwing two feathers of mud twenty feet into the air as I wheeled about and raced toward the fence in first gear. The engine sounded like it was going to blow up. The fence was coming up fast. Hitting the brakes failed to slow the wreck as it skimmed over the mud into the railroad ties. I hurled myself through the open windshield, leapt to the fence, dug my fingernails in, and then hung on while trying to find some footing. I clawed my way onto the top rung in a panic, not entirely sure they weren't going to plow right on through the barricade after me. I did a belly flop onto the ground. It knocked the wind out of me. Gasping for air, I flipped onto my back, raised up on my elbows and then stared in the direction of the snorting, frothing monsters.

The bigger, meaner, nastier one had stopped right at the fence and lowered his head to glare at me between the ties. It was three feet from me. The rungs and pilings creaked as he pushed his huge, shaggy, horned head against the fence. I back paddled through the mud, increasing the distance between us to about eight or ten feet. We stared at each other. He shook his head and took a few steps backward. He looked at the VW, then back to me. He did this several times.

*The son of a bitch wants me ta get back in the car so he c'n take another stab at tryin' ta convert my ass to a quiverin' blob'a broken bones an' mangled flesh. That's what this jerkoff's tryin' ta tell me.*

The smaller son of a bitch was on the other side of the VW wanting another run at me too. I stood up slowly, cautiously eased my way over to the fence, and then had a word with the bigger one.

"There is *no* fuckin' way in hell I will *ever* step inside that goddamn corral *ever* again. *No* way in hell."

They stared at me, huffing heavily and licking snot from their noses.

A tiny voice in the distance was shouting. It was Hope asking if I was okay.

I began raking the mud from my clothes. I could hear her

giggling as she drew closer. She'd enjoyed the hell out of it. Hope stopped a few feet from me.

"Whud'a ya thank about Criswell an' Manson?" grinning. "They're Hugo's way'a findin' out if yew c'n take a joke."

"Yeah, well, that's pr'tty damn funny all right," continuing to scrape the mud away.

Hope waved in the direction of the little white barn. I looked up. Tripp was standing in the bed of Homer's pickup watching us through a pair of binoculars. He waved. I ignored him.

*Sick bastard.*

"C'mon," Hope, still grinning. "I'll show ya the rest'a y'ur chores."

We entered the red barn where she showed me everything I'd need to take care of the loony zoo. The barn was as neat and orderly as a cowboy museum. Saddles, bridles, ropes, barrels, hay bales, feed sacks, pitchforks—everything a gentleman rancher needed was there and in its place. When we got back to the office-barn it was going on 11:00. Hope stuck her head in the back door, yelled to Mr. Tripp, and then pranced past me on her way to the ranch house, waving goodbye as she went.

"Thanks f'r showin' me around an' damn near killin' me," I shouted.

"Anytime," yelling back. "Sissy!"

*Damn. I think she likes me.*

Hugo came out to the lot and asked me what I thought about the chores.

"Well, sir, I think I'm gunna like it," looking back at the corral. "How often do the buffalo need exercisin'?"

"That's mostly Bernie's 'r Roy's job. You might have ta do it now an' then if they can't, but that won't happen all 'at often. If ya don't have any questions, that should do it f'r t'day."

"Thanks. An' thanks f'r Homer too. He went down ta talk with y'ur friend this mornin'."

"Good. Good. JD's easy ta work with. See ya t'morrow," shaking my hand before walking back into the garage.

I looked around for Hope's slinky little body as I pulled out of the lot. She must have gone inside.

*Hope McNeil. Damnation. The two just b'long t'gether.*

I drove to the piano shop to see if Homer'd nailed the job. The front door was locked so I went around back to the alley where I found Homer and a skinny old fart sitting in the sun shooting Tequila and sucking on lime wedges. Homer'd stripped down to his tee shirt. The sliding metal delivery door to the shop was wide open. The sounds of a fast moving Dixie type piano tune flowed from the shop and flooded the alley. Homer introduced me to his new boss, Mr. J.D. Grubb. Mr. Grubb nearly fell down when he stood to shake my hand, blaming it on his arthritis. Neither one of them seemed to notice that I was caked in dry mud.

Mr. Grubb was one worn out old codger. He really looked bad. Thin wouldn't cut it—he looked bled, emaciated. A ring of uncombed, shoulder length, white hair encircled a bald dome covered in dark splotches and bulging purple veins. Wiry muscles clung to bony arms, his skin wrinkled and dried out. His coveralls, filthy and a little on the stiff side, were about twenty sizes too big. He was shirtless under the coveralls. He had on a pair of old, scuffed up, dark dress shoes with no socks.

Mr. Grubb was drunk as shit.

Homer'd gotten the job, telling me the old man had liked Homer's demeanor and attitude so much he'd hired him on the spot then closed the shop for the day to celebrate Homer's good fortune.

"Mind if I show my friend around?" Homer.

Grubb waved a hand in the direction of the door and burped.

We entered a large room roughly fifty feet wide by about a hundred twenty feet deep. The sounds of a fast moving piano polka followed on the heels of the Dixieland tune. Two dingy skylights overpowered a few scattered, bare light bulbs dangling from the beams above. The interior had been completely gutted over the years. Even the walls had been stripped to the original red brick. No telling what kind of place it had initially been back in the 'teens.

One corner looked like it was trying to be an office area. Several battered pianos had been pushed into place to serve as make-shift room dividers. An army cot, piled with furniture moving blankets, was shoved up against the wall. A roll top desk sat opposite the cot. Stacks of papers covered the desk and a table next to it. Some papers had fallen to the floor. A dozen or so cardboard moving boxes lined another piano wall. The boxes were crammed with what looked like rolled up charts, some brown with age.

An eight-foot high landslide of colored glass scraps and discarded beer, wine and liquor bottles filled the corner opposite the office. Three huge wooden worktables occupied the space between the foot of the scrap heap and the storefront. Plywood sheets ran the length of the glass front, blocking the bottom four feet of the view. The rest of the room was a maze of workbenches, scattered tools, woodworking equipment, piano parts, and upright pianos in various stages of hurt.

The single working upright was honky-tonking its way through "The Yellow Rose of Texas". The piano was in mint condition. I went straight to it. Homer came up beside me. We watched the keys dance up and down.

Homer told me the old man restored players and planned to teach him to fix them. Grubb had told Homer player restoration was becoming a lost art. JD also played around with stained glass, fixing church windows every now and then.

The music stopped. The roll, wrapped about a small brass tube, flapped around and around inside a little compartment above the keys. Homer unplugged the piano. A vacuum cleaner died somewhere inside the player. I told him this was some pretty hot stuff. He agreed.

"So, what's he pay?" I asked.

"Not sure."

"When do ya start?"

"I think I already have. Mind if I put on another roll?"

"Nah. Didn't ya ask him about y'ur chance ta advance, stock options, insurance, retirement? Paid vacations?"

Homer grunted. He plugged the piano back into the extension cord. The piano took a deep breath then began to whir loudly. Homer reached under the key board. The roll began to rewind.

I told him a little about my land surveying job, the buffalo, and Hope as he replaced the player roll.

"Let's go grab a few drinks tonight after work," Homer suggested.

"When's quittin' time?"

"Don't know. Why don't you show up at the bar around 4:00. I'll be there as soon as I can. We have to deliver this piano this afternoon."

"Yeah, right. He's too drunk ta stand an' y're not too far b'hind him."

"He's not drunk," reaching back under the keyboard. "It's his arthritis."

The piano took a long, deep breath then began plinking out "Oklahoma".

Homer walked me back to the alley.

"I'll be there at 4:00," I said.

I said goodbye to Mr. Grubb and drove off down the alley.

Back at the house, I sipped a beer and smoked the last of the Jerry joints while sitting in the cab of Homer's truck listening to the radio.

*Things're lookin' even better t'day than they were yesterd'y. This is so damn much closer ta the original plan. Damn near right on target.*

Homer and I got real drunk at Mother's that night. We didn't mean to. It was an accident. We were planning on having one pitcher of beer and talk a few things over. Once we got started, however, the conversation took on a life of its own, dragging us along with it. Actually, I did the talking. Homer would grunt in agreement or mumble an occasional "damn straight" or "sounds good". The more I talked, and the more Homer grunted, the more convinced we became that, when it came to the way we felt about the really important things in life, the two of us had too damn much in common to let the two of us ever drift apart. At that point, we decided to have one more pitcher to toast the friendship then go home.

We'd be friends forever. It was a fate thing, not simply a coincidence. Our meeting each other was supposed to happen so that's why it did. So, here we were, two foul mouthed, dirty minded guys, glorying in our latest career move and checking out the ladies. We'd have one more pitcher, toast the ladies' tight little butts and then head for the house.

If only these gold digging college sluts could see through our rough exteriors. If they would just, for a second, get to know *us*. The *real* us's. Then they'd realize how much collective potential was sitting at our table and how damn happy we could make them. Superficial bitches. Why couldn't they see that we were *exactly* what they wanted? What they *craved*? Especially the really nasty, sleazy looking ones. We decided to switch to whiskey and offer a final toast to all the nasty, sleazy looking ladies in the bar. Then go home— tonight was *not* the night to tie one on.

We agreed that quitting cotton tromping was one hell of a

bold, intelligent, necessary career move. We assured ourselves that when we'd made that decision, we'd put ourselves into a position where destiny could take over. God helps those who help themselves an', by God, we were damn sure gunna start helpin' ourselves. To *ever'thing*. That was toasted with another round of shots.

By God, we weren't gunna get bogged down in some miserable shittin' rut an' waste our lives on some shithead job jus' b'cause it offered security, money, an' comf'rt. No more shit san'wiches f'r us! From now on, *we* owned the goddamn res'rant so *we* would decide what kind'a shit was gunna be on the goddamn menu.
Whatever 'at was supposed to mean.
Another round, doubles, to toast a future 'at was to be free of takin' any more shit off anybody.

B'sides, it's the frien's ya make along the way, the relationships ya build, personnel integrity, self-respect, not sellin' out, bein' free, havin' control over y'ur own life…it was all'a 'at kind'a shit an' more'a the same 'at really mattered in life. Ta hell with huge-ass bank accounts, fancy cars, an' big houses in the right part'a town. We knew better, by God. We weren't gunna be like *'em*. 'nother roun'a doubles.

We *knew* what life was…a raw adventure filled with unknowns. Takin' chances. Experiencin' life was experiencin' good times 'at felt like emotional orgasms 'r somethin' like 'at. An' life meant survivin' the bad times 'at hurt as much as the good times felt good. We weren't swallowin' this crap about havin' ta prove how goddamn respons'ble an' successful ya are by wastin' y'ur life meetin' all the societal measures'a respons'bil'ty an' success. We already learned *that* lesson. *Fuck* the lyin' pol'ticians, the lyin'-ass gove'ment, an' the mil'tary. *Fuck* society, man. 'nother roun'a doubles since Bo woul'n't give us triples.

We were gunna experience *life*. We were gunna *be* life itself. Sure, we might die with jus' 'nough money ta buy one las' beer, an' we might have ta borrow our las' cig'rette, but, but…by God, if ya lived it right, if ya been true ta y'urself an' uncompr'misin' in y'ur b'liefs, then ya could res' assured tha' there'd be a buddy there with ya in 'at las' moment ta loan ya tha' las' cig'rette an' share 'at final beer with ya. Even Bo agreed with us on 'at 'un when he came over an' tol' us ta tone it down. We ordered one las' roun'a doubles ta toast Bo's intell'gence.

Bo moved us to a table in'a back'a the bar where me an' Homer decided tha' we were damn lucky ta fig're all this out so early in life. Tha's the singular pos'tive thing 'at came out'a all 'at shit overseas. It taught ya ta…ta…HELL, yeah, Homer, it taught ya ta survive, no doubt about tha', but I wuz thinkin' a somethin' else, but I can't 'member it righ' now. Anyway, whud if we hadn't fig'red all this shit out 'til a lot'a years later. Whud if we'd squandered our lives jus' makin' money an' buyin' a bunch'a crap 'stead'a livin', tastin', feelin', smellin', *wallowin'* in life. One more roun'a doubles.

An' ya wan'a know whud else! There's no damn way we'd wan'a have anything ta do with a system where ya *bought* y'ur goddamn frien's, man. We *knew* what frien's was, by God. Frien's bled t'gether, an' fought t'gether, an'…went through some shit t'gether. Gahdamn! We sure fel' sorry f'r 'em draf' dodgin', f'aternity maggots. C'n ya even *imagine* how much shit they gotta eat, an' eat it *all* the damn time, man? *Ever'* damn *day*! An', hell no, by God, we'd never even think'a takin' out a fugin' s'rority bitch. Damn overpriced, amateur whores. Hell, we had more respec' f'r Juarez pros'tutes than we did those muth'fu…

" 'scuse me? Whu's 'at? Well, first off, my frien' here idn' a fugin' Mes'c'n. He's a fugin' In'ian an' if I'd'a wanted y'alls fugin' opinion I'd'a asked f'r it an' if y'ur bitches don't li'e the lan'uage then they c'n jus' kiss my ass. Idn' 'at righ', Homer? HOMER!"

*Holy shi…*

# THE RAVING EUNUCH MONKS

# CHAPTER TWO
## May, 1971

I rolled into the front yard and parked my bike alongside Danny's and Jerry's on the east side of the house, away from the full force of the blowing sand. I ran up the stairs leading to the second floor of the old mansion, threw the door open, and then burst into the kitchen. Jerry was seated at a small kitchen table rolling a joint. Danny was watching, sipping on a soda.

"Is that little bastard here?" out of breath, wind torn, dust stiffened hair porcupining in all directions.

"Nope," Jerry answered, concentrating on the joint.

"Good afternoon to you too," Danny. "What's got your panties twisted? Can't take a little dirt in your beard?"

"Ya know what he did?" I yelled, hurrying to the sink. "His rent check bounced again! That's three times since we moved in. That's three fuckin' times out'a four months I've had ta cover him," holding a nostril closed while blasting the mud out of the other into the sink.

"We could kill him," Jerry suggested, lighting the joint.

I reversed the process to clear the other nostril.

"Castration. That'll teach him," Danny.

Jerry slammed his knees together.

"Damn," grimacing as if in extreme pain. "I don't care whud a man does, I ain't cuttin' his nuts out. Man, 'at's cold," and took a hit before offering the joint to me. "We should jus' kill him. We could do it t'night. We could put a pilla' over his face an' stab him ta death then make it look like one uv his bitches did it."

"Well, no matter what, he's out'a here this time," handing the joint back to Jerry before storming out of the kitchen.

I walked to the end of a long, wide hall, stopping in front of a pad locked door. I kicked it open, splintering the stops. The hasp ripped out of the door leaving three large screw holes. I quickly looked around then attacked. I threw the window open and began emptying the contents of the room into the front yard. Posters, tie-dyed sheets, record albums, throw rugs—everything went out the window where it was immediately carried away by the wind. Heavier objects, like the lava lamp and record player, crashed straight to earth. A few students walking along Tenth Street stopped to watch.

Jerry entered the room.

"Yew damn sure got a thing f'r tossin' bubba's shit out, don'ch ya?"

"What else can I do? I've fuckin' had it. He still owes me two hun'r'd f'r rent from last fall, forty of the eighty dollars he stole from my seabag, an' the four hun'r'd an' fifty he thinks he owes me f'r the goddamn stereo," heading for the closet.

I grabbed an arm load and charged back to the window. Jerry entered the closet to browse through the clothes.

"Look'a this faggot shit," wrinkling his nose.

I reached around him and grabbed another load. Jerry joined in. Within two minutes we'd emptied the closet. The wind had strewn the wardrobe over the entire corner of the block.

"You gunna be here this afternoon?" I asked Jerry as we looked out the window at the mess below.

"Nah. I'll be at Vann's helpin' Doug 'b'come one with his damn bike parts. Doug ain't gunna start puttin' it t'gether 'til he un'erstands the 'spiritual essence' uv ever' damn piece, man. He's drivin' me an' Vann snake shit nuts."

"Ta hell with it," I muttered. "I'll put a note on the front door tellin' Chad he's out'a here."

"Hello, gentlemen," Chad from the far end of the hall. "How is everyone feeling this blustery...MY DOOR!" bolting into his room.

Danny, laughing, went to his room and shut the door. Chad looked out the window. He spun around and began shrieking.

"Who did...?" stepping towards us. "Which one of you...?" fists clenched at his sides. "*You* did it!" and pointed his finger at me. "You did it because of the rent! *Didn't* you?" screaming louder.

"Like that's not a good enough reason?" I yelled back.

"You did this because of a fifty dollar rent check?" What is *wrong* with you?"

"*Fifty* dollars? Fifty dollars my sweet ass. Try eight *hun'r'd*!"

"Eight hundred?" registering a look of shocked disbelief. "I've paid you at least five hun..."

"Bullshit, Chad! Bullshit!"


Jerry leaned out of the window.

"WHU'S 'AT?" looking down into the yard. "YEAH! GO AHEAD! TAKE IT!" cackling. "I don't give a shit," glancing back at Chad. "Ain't like it's my crap, man," he mumbled.

Chad darted to the window in a panic and stuck his head out.

"Goddammit! Put that down or I'll call the police! Don't touch any of that!" charging from the room. "You're going to pay for every broken thing," yelling over his shoulder. "Every stolen piece of clothing! Do you understand, Gil? Wait until mom hears about this!"

We heard him clunking down the steps.


I walked over to Jerry as he was closing the window. We watched the scene below while the window frame rattled in the wind. A car, slowing to asses the booty, saw Chad coming and sped away. Two ladies sorting through some pants looked up as he rounded the corner of the house. Chad practically knocked one of them down while tearing a pair of bellbottom slacks from her grip.

"GET AWAY FROM HERE!" as he stood in the middle of his things. The ladies shot him the bird and walked away. Chad glared up at us.

"The least you could do is help me carry everything back up before it's all stolen!"

"Uh-oh," Jerry, squinting while forcing his eyebrows up as far as they would go. "He ain' gunna like whu's comin', bubba Gil."

I raised the window and stuck my head into the blowing sand.

"Ya sorry son of a bitch! Ya don't stinkin' *live* here anymore! Y're gone! Y're out'a here, ya lazy-ass freeloadin' jerkoff!"

"HIST'RY, MAN!" Jerry added. " 'at's whu' ya're. Damn hist'ry."

"YOU CAN'T DO THIS TO ME!" Chad wailed. "YOU CAN'T DO THIS! I'm the one who found this place! If it wasn't for me, you an' Homer'd still be living in that little dump! You *owe* me for all of this! It was *my* idea for all of us to..."

"I don't owe ya squat!"

"You can't do this! I'm paid up until the end of the month!"

"*I* paid ya up 'til the end'a the month ya stupid turd!"

"I'm coming up and we're going to discuss this like two..."

"Chad, if ya come up those steps...I *will* hit ya. I mean it, Chad. I *will* hit ya. Hard. Ya best b'lieve me, Chad!"

"This isn't fair," whining. "I'm your *brother*, for God's sake. Where am I going to go?"

I shut the window.

Jerry was slowly nodding his head, brows raised.

"Ya know, bubba Gil...he's gotta point," seriously. "I mean... goin' an' kickin' y'ur own flesh an' blood out like 'at."

"What? Just a minute ago you were cheerin' me on. Now I'm some kind'a bastard?"

"Jus' remindin' ya uv the cons'quences," slurring. "Whu' ya done's jus' like 'at guy in the Bible done when he killed his brother so God turned him inta a nigger."

"You have *got* to be shittin' me, Jerry," and looked at him, hoping for a sign that he was jacking around.

Jerry wasn't smiling.

"Yeah," expanding on his interpretation as we walked to the kitchen, " 'at's where niggers come from. This guy whacked his brother, so God, ZAP…turned him black so ever'body'd know whud he done."

I shook my head and rubbed my eyes with the heels of my hands.

"That's the most fucked up thing I've ever heard," taking a seat at the table.

"It ain't fucked up, man," he frowned. "It's the way it is."

"Where the hell do ya come up with this…this…*crap?*"

"It ain't crap. It's in'a Bible. Be y'ur brother's keeper an' shit. Go whackin' on him an' y'ur ass is grass. Tha's jus' the way it is, man."

"Well, I guess I'll just take my chances with pissin' God off. No matter what he does ta me, it can't be worse than havin' ta live with 'at douche bag brother'a mine."

"I cain't b'lieve ya went an' said 'pissin'' an' 'God' all in the same sentence, man. Y're screwin' up. Y're askin' f'r some real heavy shit."

"Let's drop it, Jerry. Okay? If y're worried about my ass, then you c'n mention my name in y'ur prayers."

"I ain't lettin' God know I know yew. Ain't no way 'at's gunna happen."

Jerry sat down. We waited to see if Chad was going to try to come back into the house.

"So," while he began rolling a joint, "yew gunna work full time'r go ta summer school?"

"Work at Hugo's durin' the day an' Dancers three nights a week."

"Dancers? 'at new place? How'd yew git that? Ya gunna be bartendin'?"

"Barbackin'. Washin' glasses an' shit."

"Oh, *hell* yeah. 'at's real smart. 'at's the way ta git laid in a place like 'at. All 'em women'll be dyin' ta have a dumbass dishwasher thump 'em. No shit. I hear 'em talkin' about it all'a time. It's like a sex'al fan'asy with 'em rich bitches," cackling. "That 'un an' doin' the sweaty gardner, an'...an' the swimmin' pool cleanin' guy."

"Gotta take what jobs I c'n get. Don't have much of a choice with those goddamn bike payments I'm makin'," leaning back in the chair.

"Shit to, man. Now ever'thing's all my fault? Listen turd...'at bikes the bes' damn thing 'at's ever happened ta yew. 'specially since ya ain't got pooh-pooh f'r personal'ty. Beats the shit out'a tha' jalopy don't it?"

"You should'a got more'n two hun'r'd dollars f'r that 'jalopy'. It was an antique. A classic."

"I done the bes' I could. Hell, it wudn' even runnin'. Damn wires hangin' out all over the place an' shit. Horn di'n' even honk. Don't go blamin' all 'at crap on me, man. Talk ta tha' dopey-ass injun mechanic'a y'urs."

"No matter what, I've gotta pull in some serious jing b'fore the end'a August 'r I'm gunna be in a world'a hurt. Plus, I need a break from the school routine," as I leaned forward and planted my elbows on the table.

"Yeah, I know whu'ch ya mean. Pullin' a coupl'a D's an' a C c'n take it right out'a ya."

"Eat me."

"Too much partyin', man. If y're gunna go ta school, ya gotta go ta school. It's like a job. Course, if it wuz like a real job, yew'd'a done been fired by now 'cause ya went an' dicked it up so bad."

"Next semester," I yawned.

"I'm thinkin' about goin' back ta work full time myself," lighting a cigarette.

I looked at him doubtfully.

"Shanghaiin' bodies for Deacon again?"

"Ain' no way, man. Look whut happened las' time I did tha' shit. Ended up meetin' yew an' 'at damn scalp hunter. The *las'* damn thing I wuz wantin' ta do when I got out'a the Corps wuz ta come back here an' hook up with another damn jarhead. Shiiit, man," finishing in a low growl.

"So, what'll ya be doin'?"

"Weldin'. My ex-brother-in-law wants me ta do some weldin' an' cuttin' f'r him on a bunch'a bike frames. Wants me ta start Mond'y."

"Ex-brother-in-law?" surprised.

"Yeah. I wuz married once. Got divorced about eight months ago. Even got a kid. A boy. Cain't ever see him though. Bitch put a peace bon' on me jus' 'cause I said I wuz gunna kill her. Only said it once an' I wuz drunk as shit when I said it, but damn...'at didn' matter ta the judge. They decided I wuz a p'tential murderer an' won't lemme see my own damn son."

"I'd'a never guessed it. You married an' a father ta boot."

"Whu's so hard ta b'lieve about it?" mildly agitated. " 'cause I smoke a li'l dope now an' then? 'cause I ride a chop job? 'cause I don't shave ever'day? Ya sound like 'at damn judge, man," scowling.

"No, no. It's not that. I just can't see ya settled down like 'at. It seems like ya have too much fun bein' single. That's all I meant."

"Fun? Ya think I'm havin' fun?" slurring heavily. "Ya think I like the way things are t'day? Ya think I like ballin' strange shit all'a time? Havin' ta waste all 'at rack time trainin' 'em? Time after time, after time?"

"Virgins ever' night?"

"Virgins ain't the problem. It's the ones 'at *think* they know whu' they're doin'. At least a virgin don't argue with ya," muttering. "Ya might git a 'casional *'eeeewww'*, 'r a 'I ain't doin' *'at'*, from a virgin, but they come aroun'.'"

"Y're so full'a y'ur own crap."

Jerry threw his head back, slapped his knee, and then began cackling.

"Yeah. I know. I know." Then, softly, while staring at the ceiling, "I know."

Danny entered the kitchen.

"Who's gunna take Chad's place," opening the refrigerator to get a soda.

He had that "I've been thinkin' " look on his face, brows furrowed, lips pressed tightly together.

"Ya ought'a ask y'ur buddy Doug ta move in," Jerry snickered.

"I don't think so," shaking my head. "There's no tellin' that whatever Doug's got idn't contagious. Why don't you move in, Jerry?"

"Too crowded. Gotta have my privacy. My cousins never at the house so it's like livin' alone now 'at Homer scared Donal' off. Homer still live here? I ain't seen him the last few times I been over."

"He keeps a room here an' pays his share'a the rent," I answered, "but he usually passes out up at the piano shop."

"Here's the deal," Danny, walking across the kitchen and hopping up on the sink. "I ran into Joan last week and she's looking for a place closer to the campus. Close enough to walk to classes. She's been trying to find a roomie because she's afraid to live in the ghetto alone."

"Oh, shit!" Jerry burst out. "Did ya see 'at ?" pointing at me. "Did ya see 'at horny mother lickin' his lips?"

"Bullshit!"

*So what if I did?*

"Bullshit to! Yew wuz lickin' y'ur lips," snorting loudly, eyebrows lifted, face contorted, folding his hands into his stomach, and rocking wildly.

Danny looked down at the floor.

"Forget it. I shouldn't have brought it up."

"No. Wait a minute. It's a *damn* good idea," I told him. "It wouldn't hurt ta ask..."

"It wouldn't work," Danny. "Everybody would have to watch themselves too closely."

Jerry shook his head in agreement. I continued to argue in favor of the idea.

"It wouldn't be any diff'r'nt 'an when she hangs around the bar with us 'r sits around JD's place listenin' to us cussin'. There'd be nothin' said that she hadn't already heard us say."

" 'at's a fact," Jerry, nodding and pointing a finger at me.

"What about the drinking and doping?" Danny.

"I'll share mine with her," as I turned and slapped Jerry on the shoulder.

Jerry snickered.

"Seriously," Danny, "she may not want to put herself in a position to be busted. She may not want to be around it all the time. Especially since she's clean."

"Still can't hurt ta ask," refusing to give up.

"She ain' gunna move inta any hard-on locker, man," Jerry, pulling a baggie from his pocket.

"Dammit. At least we c'n ask her," I persisted.

"At least we c'n ask her," Jerry, imitating me in a high pitched, whiney voice, "An' then we c'n beg her, an' then we c'n promise ta bow down to her all the time, 'an call her Ms., an' bring her ass breakfas' in bed ever' mornin'."

"Eat me, Gerald."

"Jerry ain't short f'r *Gerald*, butt-breath" he snarled. "It's just plain *Jerry*."

"C'mon," turning back to Danny. "We gotta at least *try*."

Danny paused before caving in.

"All right," rubbing his forehead. "Do you want me to be the one to ask her?"

"Bes' not be Gil," Jerry snickered. "If he cain't git her ta go ta dinner with him there ain't no way in hell he's gunna git her ta move in with him."

"Screw you. She was carrin' eighteen hours last semester an' workin'. She didn't have time f'r nothin' else."

"Oh? Is 'at whu' she tol' ya?" Jerry, brows raised. "She seemed ta have plenty'a time f'r 'at freak-ass religion she's inta. An' 'at's somethin' else ta think about, man," putting the joint down and looking seriously, first at Danny, then at me. " 'at shit she's inta, 'at Baha'i crap...they don't b'lieve 'at Jesus is the Son'a God an' they don't b'lieve in'a Bible. If she moves in with ya," squinting one eye, opening the other wide, "yew could end up piss...makin' God mad as hel...all git out. I might have ta fin' some other place ta hang."

I dropped my head to the table.

"Goddammit, Jerry...just plain..."

"I'll ask her," Danny, sliding from the sink then walking over to the table. "But I'm going to make sure she knows what she's getting into when I ask her."

"Yeah," I said. "But be sure ta point out the positive influence she could have on us in the long run. Put it to her like 'at."

"Hear 'at, Danny?" Jerry, cracking up. "Gil wants ya ta put it to her, man."

"She doesn't work Saturdays," Danny, shaking his head. "I'll go see her this afternoon and run it by her."

"Go over ta Will's an' call her now," I suggested.

"Look'a there," Jerry, cackling again and pointing at me. "He's back ta lickin' his lips."

"Did you say somethin', *Gerald?*"

"Knock 'at shit off, man!" he barked.

"I'll go this afternoon," Danny. "I think it'll go over better in person. Did I hear you say you're gunna begin working at that new bar?"

"Yeah. Dancers. Saw it advertised out on campus. Start t'night. Gotta be there at 6:00."

"I've bartended off and on during the past few years. It's not that bad a deal."

"I'll be barbackin'."

"So? Work your way up. How late are you working tonight?"

" 'til 2:00 'r 2:30 'r the mornin'."

"You're gunna be beat. What time did you go to work this morning?"

"I was up at 5:00."

"I'll be comin' up ta visit ya," Jerry. "I'll keep ya awake. Yew c'n slip me a few freebies. Chicks love it when ya go inta a place an' ya know the bartender. They think 'at shits cool. 'at right there's gunna git me laid t'night."

"I gotta grab some sleep," ignoring Jerry.

"All right, bub," Danny.

"See ya t'night," Jerry.

I stepped out of the kitchen and crossed the hall to my room. It was the biggest room, but the noisiest at times since it was so close to the kitchen. Even with a living room down the hallway, the kitchen would end up as the gathering point unless it was a party.

The smallest room off the hall, used as a storage space, was sandwiched between the kitchen and my room. A large bathroom with two sinks and two metal shower stalls was on my side of the hall. Danny's room was on the other side of the bathroom. Next to Danny, a corner room at the end of the hall. Chad's old room. Another corner room was alongside it. The living room was located across the hall from the bathroom and Danny's room. A single window at the far end of the living room looked out onto the front stoop. The hallway itself was about twice the width of a normal hall.

Chad was right—it was a lot better than the dump Homer and I'd been living in. Chad finding this big of a place at fifty bucks a room had allowed Danny to move out of his folks place *and* buy a Sportster.

The few problems that had cropped up were related to Chad's bitching about the comments we'd make when he'd drag some slut home to bone. Chad was constantly complaining about all the "biker trash" that hung around. Especially Jerry. Chad hated Jerry because Jerry would never cut him any slack. Jerry would always be ragging on Chad about whether his check from my parents had arrived or about paying back the money Chad owed me.

*Jerry'll pro'bly end up missin' Chad.*

I was beat. I unlaced my jungle boots and kicked them from my feet. Dust powdered the air as they hit the far wall. I stripped down to my underwear and lay down on the pallet in the middle of the floor.

*Fuck.*

*Seems like all I've done the past five months is work, go ta class, an' study. Party a little on the weekends. Well, party a lot on the weekends an' a little bit durin' the week.*

*At any rate, I don't have shit ta show f'r anything.*

*Bum grades. No money. No lady. In debt.*

*This school shit's a lot more expensive than I thought it was gunna be. What was left'a the stereo money ended up goin' f'r books an' supplies. The hun'r'd an' fifty dollars of booze lasted two weekends.*

*Should'a seen 'at 'un comin'.*

*Twenty-five dollars a month ta Hugo 'til November f'r my share'a the lawyer he got Homer an' me f'r the fight at Mother's.*

*Bringin' home thirty-five ta forty bucks a week at Hugo's f'r thirty hours work. Shit. That barely covers rent, utilities, a minimal amount'a food, an' the bike payment. If it wudn't f'r the GI bill, I'd'a had ta quit smokin' an' drinkin'. Things were shit five months ago, but at least five months ago I wudn't in debt.*

*But then five months ago I didn't have a chopper.*

*What' a machine. A real motherfucker.*

*Could pay it off t'day if Chad'd pay me back.*

*Chad. What a piece'a shit.*

I listened to Jerry and Danny arguing about whether Joan would decide to move in with us.

*I'd shit if she did.*

*Joan. Another waste'a time an' money. And erections. Goin' ta two stinkin' meetin's a month. F'r what?*

*F'r nothin'.*

*Buyin' her sixty million dollars worth'a coffee in the student union. F'r nothin'.*

A yawn. A big one, eyes tearing up.

*Takin' her ridin' on my bike when I should'a been studyin'. F'r nothin'.*

*The whole damn operation adds up ta one big-ass zero.*

I rolled onto my side.

*She must think gas an' coffee're free 'r somethin'. Selfish bitch...*

\*\*\*

Startled, I jerked into a sitting position and looked frantically around the room.

*Smoke. We're burnin'!*

"It's me, Danny." And stepped into the room. "You okay?"

I fell back on the pallet, temples throbbing. Sweating.

"Didn't you have to be at Dancers at 6:00?" Danny, quietly.

"Yeah," shutting my eyes and wiping the sweat from my forehead with the back of my forearm.

"It's a quarter after 5:00. Can I do...can I get you anything?" sounding concerned.

"No. No thanks, Dan. Appreciate the offer. I'm just tired," rubbing my eyes. "Real tired. An' thanks f'r wakin' me up. I guess I dozed off b'fore settin' the alarm."

"I've got to make sure you're up there tonight. I'm out'a money so I can't pay for all the orange juices I'll be putting on my tab for Joan."

"What'd she say about movin' in?" standing up and stepping over to a chest of drawers that should have been shit-canned thirty years ago.

"Here's the deal," taking a deep breath then exhaling loudly. "She wants to talk with you first."

"Me?"

"Just you."

"She say why?"

"Not exactly, but she did say she thinks you're attracted to her and that concerns her."

"No shit? Five months with my nose up her dress an' she *thinks* I'm attracted to her. I've damn near done ever'thing but have 'I wan'a lay ya' tattooed on my damn forehead. For some strange reason I was about ta decide she didn't give a rat's ass."

"She probably doesn't."

"She say anything else about me?" pulling a clean tee shirt and socks from the top drawer.

"No."

"What's she afraid of? She think I'm gunna cop a feel while she's sleepin'?"

"Been kicking the idea around, haven't you?"

"Christ, ya make me sound just like Jerry sometimes."

"No matter. She's going to drop by Dancer's tonight after her mind control meeting. You can catch her on one of your breaks and talk to her then."

"Fine," walking by Danny and heading toward the bathroom. "What time're ya comin' up?"

"If you're going to be at work at 6:00, I'll be there around 6:01. You're going to let me run a tab aren't you?"

"I'll try. Hell, I don't even know how that shit's set up," shutting the bathroom door behind me.

*The way it's shapin' up, ever' son of a bitch I ever met's gunna be at Dancer's t'night. All of 'em tryin' ta drink f'r free.*

I got cleaned up.

Drying my hair was taking more and more time.

*Finally gettin' to a respectable length. Too wavy though. Beard's lookin' good...down ta b'tween the first an' second buttons of my shirt.*

After dressing, I pulled a beer from the refrigerator, lit a cigarette, and then stepped onto the stoop. It was dead calm, the sky as clear as it could be—turning a dark turquoise in the early evening. Sunsets were really nice this time of year. Especially after a sand storm. We'd developed a habit of sitting up on the roof to watch the sun go down or, at night, stare at the stars. Drinking. Smoking. Talking. The roof was a good place to retreat to.

I opened the beer and looked down at the bike. It was a beauty—a black and chrome '57 panhead, 1200cc FLH. Raked. Extended. I thought about walking the two blocks to Dancers. I was probably going to end up pretty drunk tonight. I didn't need to crack the bike up or have the cops stop me. But, then, that possibility never stopped me from riding it drunk before. I decided to take the bike, for show if for no other reason. I finished the beer, grabbed all my riding gear from the bedroom, and then walked down the steps. As I neared the bottom of the stairs I began thinking about the start-up, a meticulously choreographed performance with every movement ritually executed.

I sauntered over to the shiny black beast and straddled it nonchalantly, confident everybody in the neighborhood was probably watching the cool-ass biker prepare to charge down the street. I removed a key from my front pocket and placed it between my lips. I eased a red bandanna from my back pocket and sat down on the bike. Folding the bandanna into a triangle, I pulled it tight across my forehead and then tied it in the back, tucking the free end of the triangle under the knot. I removed the key from my mouth, inserted the key into the ignition, turned the key to the right, reached under the peanut tank to turn the gas on, and then hit the ignition toggle, all in one flowing, graceful movement.

I stood up and pumped the kick start a few times to build up compression, rolled the throttle once or twice, rose into the air, and then came down with all my weight on the kick start. If I was lucky, the engine would thunder to life. This evening I was lucky—it exploded on the first try, blasting the panties off every snot-ass coed in the ghetto; annihilating every redneck, drugstore cowboy; every rich-ass, draft dodging fraternity punk on campus.

*I feel so...so fuckin' bad.*

I pulled it into an upright position and slammed the kickstand into the frame with my left boot heel. Gunning it loudly, repeatedly, I rolled across the lawn to the gravel drive at the foot of the stairs. I paused a moment before roaring out of the driveway and down the street, wondering how many orgasms I was leaving in my wake.

# GLYNN E. THOMPSON

*Oh, hell yeah! It's worth ever' goddamn penny'a the payments.*

I was at Dancers in less than two minutes. Several people were out front—some stylishly dressed guys in bellbottom slacks and two ladies dressed in short skirted French maid's outfits, their slender, panty-hosed legs shinning like polished bronze.

I pulled in behind a Corvette and pushed the bike, rear end first, into the adjoining parking space, occasionally gunning the engine for dramatic affect. I'd developed an unbelievably sharp peripheral vision in the three months I'd had the bike. A biker had to act like he didn't give a shit *who* was watching while, at the same time, confirming for himself that everybody *was* watching. Might as well ride a rice burner if the show didn't matter to a biker. I was receiving my fair share of attention—the ladies smiling, the guys trying their best not to look.

The dismount was as dramatically choreographed as the start up. I gave the engine a few quick guns, slowly reached under the tank to shut off the gas, flicked the toggle, and then removed the key. I stuck it in the front pocket and finally, without looking down, used my left boot heel to push the kickstand into place while leaning the bike into it. I slowly rose from the seat. Straddling the bike, I performed an exaggerated stretch and flex routine—like I'd been jamming the highways on that bad boy all day long.

I caught a glimpse of the ladies out of the corner of my eye. They were watching and whispering. I lit a cigarette then removed my bandanna. I casually stuffed the bandanna into my right back pocket, leaving about half of it to dangle down my butt. I slowly brought my right leg over the rear end of the bike and stepped away. I executed a few shallow knee bends and stamped my feet a few times. As I walked away from the bike I peeled the fingerless gloves from my hands and stuffed them into my left back pocket. At this point I made my first eye contact with the audience—a nod for the ladies; a cold stare for the boys.

*I have 'em right where I want 'em, by God...the females droolin', the males nervous as hell...on the defensive. Damn. Ta hell with James Dean. CUT! That's a take! Print it!*

A loud crash behind me—metal hitting asphalt.

Something clobbered me in the gut.

I froze.

The spectators, mouths and eyes opened wide, were looking in the direction of my bike.

*Jeeesuus Christ...not that. Please, God...not that.*

I slowly turned.

*Fuck me dead.*

The son of a bitching bike had fallen over, barely missing the Corvette.

Shutting off the peripheral vision, I strolled back to the bike, trying to act like this kind of thing happens all the time.

*No big deal. Ever'thing's cool.*

As casually as I could, I attempted to pull it upright. It slid across the parking space, the tires slipping over some loose gravel. I spit the cigarette from my mouth and tried a second time. It took three attempts and 10,000 agonizing years before I managed to right the bike. I maneuvered it back into the middle of the space, reached down and pulled the kickstand into place, this time checking to make sure it was firmly slotted. I pulled the bandanna from my pocket and, without looking up, pretended to be thoroughly absorbed in the task of removing something from my hands while passing by the onlookers. Reaching the door I slammed into it with my shoulder. I bounced back.

A female giggled.

"Ya have ta pull," a dry, male voice from behind me.

I jerked the door open and entered the club.

*Just plain...shit.*

Fuming, crushed, I stomped through a lobby area then into the main part of the club. I walked around and looked it over while pulling myself back together.

A lot of work had been done on the place since last week's interview. About forty or so white cloth covered tables were scattered around a large dance floor. Every table was dimly lit by a flickering candle inside a glowing, red glass globe. The tables were tall enough for bar stools and large enough to accommodate six to eight stools. A boxed-in glass cage atop a four-foot high stage sat against the wall at the far end of the dance floor. Blue, green, lime, and yellow painted figures danced across the black background of the walls. Strategically placed black lights made the figures glow. A set of swinging double doors was located to the left of the main entrance to the room.

I stepped through the doors and passed down a thirty-foot bar then through a gap at the end. I knocked on the door located immediately inside the gap.

"C'mon in," a female's voice.

I entered the club's cramped office. A slender blond sat on a plush, red velvet couch opposite a cluttered desk. Her hair was done in a braid draping over her shoulder and covering her left breast. Her lap was covered in bits of papers and forms.

"Yew know anythang about accountin'?" looking up at me in frustration.

Her eyes were a deep blue, her delicate features classically elegant. This wasn't the painted up old hussy who'd interviewed me before.

"Uh, no. I'm a histo...," catching myself, "pre med student. Don't know much about accountin', but," catching myself again, "I play the stock market all the time. It's a hobby'a mine."

"Dammit," tossing the pile of papers on the couch next to her and jumping to her feet. She was barely five feet four inches tall in high heels. She began wriggling as she tugged and pulled at her skirt until the hem was about midthigh.

"Too short?" holding her hands away from her sides.

"No, not at all. Tall ladies make me nervous."

"I meant the skirt, silly."

"Oh. Sorry. The skirt is perfect."

*Ever'thing about ya's perfect...a goddamn livin', breathin' Vargas drawin'.*

"My name's Sonny," holding her hand out. "I'm the temp'rary manager. Yew gunna start workin' here?"

"Marge hired me last week," while shaking her tiny hand. "I'm Gil McNeil."

"I knew she'd hired some waitresses, barbacks, an' bartenders, but," picking some hand scribbled notes from the desk and sorting through them, "she didn't mention anythang else. She left ever'thang in such a fuckin' mess..."

*Oh, God! She uses the "F" word. Good sign. Damn good sign.*

"...an' I was s'posed ta be the day time manager, sort of an assistant, but now that she's quit I got the whole damn thang ta myself. Yew a barback 'r a bartender?"

*Just how complicated c'n bartendin' be?*

"Bartender."

*I could fake it t'night then have three days ta learn more about it.*

"Got much experience?"

"Part timed it at enlisted men's clubs in the service."

"Were they speed bars like this 'un?"

"Well, uh. They were set up ta handle more people, but pr'tty much the same idea."

*Hot shit! It's workin'.*

"Marge mention if ya were gunna b'gin at the top 'r the bottom'a the scale?"

*This is too easy.*

"Top."

"Full 'r part time?"

"Full time," quickly adding, "until fall. That's when I start back ta scho...med school. Then I'd go ta part time."

"Okay," throwing the notes onto the desktop. "If 'at's the deal she made ya then 'at's the deal I'll stick with."

"I appreciate that, ma'am," pursing my lips and nodding a few times.

"Call me Sonny," smiling. "Don't call me ma'am."

"Okay, Sonny," smiling back at her.

*Wonder what kind'a money a top end bartender makes?*

"I thank we're s'posed ta open at 7:00," Sonny told me. "Marge wanted ta have ever'body come in an hour early ta get acquainted with thangs. Ever'thang b'tween t'night an' the grand openin' next weekend's s'posed ta be like a dry run ta work the bugs out."

"Yeah, I b'lieve 'at's what Marge had discussed with me last week."

Sonny leaned toward me and grabbed my hand.

"Yew could really he'p me out by settin' the bar up an' givin' the ticket books to the girls. Make a list as they come in, all the new people, an' send 'em back one at a time. The head bartender won't be here t'night. Could ya pleeease he'p me out? I gotta do the cash register, the wine idn't here yet, an' the dee jay should'a been here thirty minutes ago. An' the bouncers," anxiously. "Two bouncers'll be comin' in," as she opened the door.

"No problem," dropping her hand and stepping out of the office. "Don't worry about a thing out here."

"Thank yew, thank yew, thank yew," shutting the door.

*Sonny McNeil. Oh, God, yes. Perfect.*

Two guys, both sneering, were standing inside the swinging doors. They'd witnessed the fiasco out front. I walked over.

"Can I help ya?" bracing for any wise-ass comments about my earlier humiliation.

"Pro'bly not," the taller one, tossing his head to flip the hair out of his eyes and giving his buddy a look that said "why am I talking to this *worm?*"

"Gil McNeil," and put my hand out. "I'm the head bartender. If ya don't work here, I'll have ta ask ya ta leave. We won't be openin' 'til 7:00."

They looked at each other in surprise.

"Actually," the taller one again, "we were hired Tu'sd'y as bartenders an' told ta be here t'night. We're lookin' f'r Marge."

I hung my head, cleared my throat then looked at the tall guy.

"Marge...Marge committed suicide on We'n'sd'y."

Danny's face appeared in the porthole of one of the swinging doors. I continued talking to the boys.

"Marge's sudden and unexpected death has slowed the whole start up schedule thing. We won't be needin' as many bartenders as we thought we would."

*Should I...oh, HELL yes! Do it.*

"Listen, I still need a coupl'a janitors. C'n you guys clean shitters an' pissers an' keep the puke up off the head floors?"

They looked at each other in disgust.

"I don't thank so!" the tall one snapped.

They both spun around and stormed through the swinging doors.


I followed them out of the bar area. Danny was standing near the glassed in booth.

"What's up, bub," walking over to me, glancing around the empty room. "Not much of a crowd for a Saturday night."

"Not really open 'til 7:00."

I heard the front doors open and some ladies laughing.

"Danny...listen quick. The manager thinks I'm a bartender an' wants me ta set the bar up an' get the waitresses goin' an' I don't know shit about it, but this a golden opportunity *we* can't let pass. All ya gotta do is go inta the office an' tell the manager y're one'a the new bartenders Marge hired last week. Just work this one night an' then quit if ya want, but I need ya ta teach me some things t'night. Okay?" pushing him toward the swinging doors.


The two bronze legged French maids I'd seen out front earlier entered the dance area.

"Just a minute," waving to them. "Have a seat, please," continuing to shove Danny along.

Danny dug his heels in.

"I can't just walk in an..."

"Do this f'r me an' I'll owe ya f'rever. A barback makes a buck an' a quarter an hour. A bartender pro'bly makes twice 'at much. Maybe more. C'mon, Danny. Help me get through t'night. If you'll be a bartender f'r six 'r eight hours, you c'n have my first daughter the night b'fore her weddin'," begging while steering him through the doors and then down the bar toward the office.

The office door opened. Sonny stepped out and rounded the corner.

*Good God! She looks just as hot at a distance as she does up close.*

"That's her," I hissed. "That's the boss."

Danny stopped resisting.

Sonny swayed up to us.

"Anybody else showed up, Gil?" nervously. "It's a quarter after."

I glanced at Danny. He was smitten. He pulled his arm free of my grip and extended his hand.

"Danny. My name's Danny Wright. I'm a bartender."

"Oh, Danny," taking his hand in both of hers. "Thank God y're here!"

Sonny went to her toes, hiked a foot into the air behind her, gave Danny a quick hug, and then stepped back.

"I wish I had time ta properly intr'duce myself, but...well, Gil c'n explain. Okay?"

"Two waitresses are here," I told her. "When do ya wan'a see 'em?"

"Later. Go ahead an' git 'em started, Gil. Tell 'em whut's goin' on an' apologize for me."

Sonny tilted her head, spun around, and briskly swayed her way back to the office.

Danny was in shock.

"Is she married?" he asked.

"Don't think so."

"It's a transvestite?"

"In *Lubbock?*"

"Lesbian?"

"Doubt it. An' ya know what else? She uses the 'F' word."

"Time to go to work then," Danny declared.

"You take over. Tell me what ta do. An' the waitresses. An' the bouncers."

"Here's the deal, Gil," Danny, scratching his nose and looking down. "I've never really *bartended.*"

"WHAT?"

"Now, wait a minute," looking up to explain. "I've barbacked. I'd help mix the easier drinks when things would get busy. If there's a Boston Bartender's Guide behind the bar…we should be fine."

"Sure. Sure. We'll do fine."

*Maybe. Dammit.*

Danny slapped me on the back.

"I'll take care of the waitresses while you find out where everything is behind the bar…glasses, mugs, liquor, beer, wine, things like that. And check out the storeroom. Try and find something that looks like a small receipt book and grab some pens from the office. I'll be right back," then charged through the doors into the dance hall. "Hello, ladies. How are you this even…," his voice echoing in the dance area then fading as the doors sealed behind him.

I ran to the back of the service line and began to throw cabinet doors open, mentally inventorying their contents.

*This is gunna work, by God. We had this by the balls. No fuckin' problem.*

By 6:55 the glass dee jay cage was manned, the bouncers and waitresses were stationed, and Ray, the other bartender, was in place behind the bar. The Doors were blaring over the speakers. Danny'd thrown it together like he'd done it a thousand times before.

He stepped up to the drink well.

"Ready for a crash course in bartending?" he asked. "I'll teach you everything I know about it and it won't take five minutes."

"How'd ya know how ta do all this?" and nodded at the bar then the double doors.

"Watching. Now you watch."

Twenty minutes later Danny had me convinced that, with the bartender's guide, I was ready for anything. Sonny toured the place then came over to Danny and me.

"Most'a the advertisin's been f'r the grand openin' next weekend," she told us. "We aren't expectin' much ta happen b'tween now an' then. If ya have any problems, lemme know so we c'n fix 'em."

I spent the next two hours reading the Guide and downing every practice drink I mixed.

*Nothin' to it. When next weekend rolls around, I'll have it down pat.*

Danny spent his time wandering around talking with the waitresses, the bouncers, and the other bartender. Eventually Sonny came out of the office. She had me make some fancy drinks to see if I knew what I was doing. I was slow as hell, but she didn't bitch about how they tasted. I guessed I'd pulled it off.

At 10:30 a waitress stuck her head into the bar area and announced the arrival of a group of customers. They sounded rowdy. A few seconds later Jerry poked his head through the swinging doors and gave me a greasy smirk.

"They ain't fired y'ur ass yet? Hey!" continuing without giving me a chance to answer. "I got a complaint, man," snarling as he walked over to the bar. "Me an' my ol' lady been here f'r over two damn minutes an' we still ain't got shit ta drink. Whu's it take ta git some service aroun' here. This ain' the only damn place in town, man. I don't have ta put up with this kind'a treatment."

I pointed to the dance area.

"Sir, please take a seat an' wait f'r someone ta take y'ur order. Unauthorized personnel aren't allowed in the bar area."

"Oh. Well, 'scuse my ass. The las' thing I wan'a do is break the damn rules," then disappeared through the doors, cackling as he went.

I followed him from the bar. Jerry's hand was cupping the butt of a young looking girl. Doug, JD, and all the bar help were seated around two tables pulled together near the dance floor. Sonny had even reeled in the bouncers.

Sonny, damn near as drunk as I was, came over to me.

"Yew make an excellent White Russian," and winked. "If ya wan'a sign out an' be with y'ur friends, go ahead. 'at's whut Danny's gunna do. I told all but one'a the waitresses they could go home if they wanted to."

"Ya sure?"

Sonny glanced around the empty room, looked at her watch and sighed.

"I'm sure," disappointed. "I thought we'd have more walk-ins."

"That crowd'll make up for it. A few more're supposed ta be comin' in later."

"I guess the one real problem is the barback 'at didn't show up."

"Ya got all week ta find a replacement. I might even know somebody."

"Listen, I already told Danny...I really 'preciate whut ever' one did t'night," giving me a tight hug.

I didn't need that. Not after being around those French maid waitresses all night. Sonny let go.

"Let 'em run a tab if ya want," she told me. "Ray's goin' back ta watch the bar. I'll be back in a minute," slowly pendulum-hipping toward the office.

Ray came over.

"Ya positive ya wan'a keep workin'?" I asked. "We could take turns."

"Nah. Go ahead. Yew c'n he'p me carry the first round out, though. One uv 'em bought a pitcher f'r each person. Give me a fifty ta pay f'r it. Tol' me ta keep the change."

Hugo, Joan, and Homer strolled in as Ray and I delivered the last of the pitchers.

It was always the same every time I'd see Joan. Didn't matter if it'd been ten minutes or a week—that figure, those eyes, her face. The long dancing hair. The whole damn package would kick my ass.

Homer followed me back to the bar when I went to get a mug for Hugo and an orange juice for Joan.

"How'd your finals go?" Homer.

"Sucked," and placed my order with Ray.

Homer looked tired.

"Been puttin' in some long hours?" I asked.

"Yeah," and practically laid down on the bar. "When was the last time you were at the shop?" through a loud yawn.

"Tu'sd'y, I guess. I b'lieve it was after my anthro final."

"Come over when you have a chance. JD took in some real old, real fancy church windows yesterday. He's going to fix them up."

"He still plannin' on teachin' ya how ta do that?"

"Yeah. I think so," lifting his head from the bar and looking at me. "Seriously, come over and take a look at them. I put them out in front of the shop so they got a lot of light. The colored glass...damn. You'll have to see it. It's unreal."

"I'll try ta get by t'morrow."

Ray placed the mug and the glass of juice on the bar.

"Thanks, Ray," and picked them up.

Sonny stepped from her office and closed the door behind her. She hurried toward us, her head down as she struggled to tug the hem of her skirt back down her thighs. She'd removed her panty hose. Homer saw her and stood up, quickly checking his bandanna. Sonny was on top of us before she looked up.

"Oh!" she shrieked, backing up a few steps, eyes wide. She placed a hand over her chest, trying to collect herself. "My God," quickly taking stock of Homer's hulking frame. "I'm sorry. I wudn't expectin'...I wudn't payin' attention," she stammered.

"This is Homer. One'a my roommates," sensing something was about to go terribly wrong with me and Sonny's budding love affair. "Homer, this is Sonny. My new boss."

Homer offered her a hand as long as her forearm. Sonny's left hand remained against her chest as they shook.

"I'm so sorry. Yew su'prised me," Sonny, still flustered. "I didn't mean ta..."

"Don't worry about it," Homer, uncomfortably.

"Yew gunna join us at the tables?" gushing sexy.

"In a minute."

"I'll...I'll save ya a place," and teetered off, glancing over her shoulder, big blue eyes twinkling.

Homer shuffled his feet self-consciously.

"Goddamn, Homer," I hissed. "I can't *b'lieve* you. What's *wrong* with you? Huh? She all but came right out an' asked ya ta take her like a...like a sweaty warrior chief an' ya went cold on her! She *wants* ya, Homer, an' I'm not talkin' shit this time."

" 'at's def'nitely the impression I got," Ray.

"Think so?" Homer asked Ray, apparently more impressed with Ray's opinion than mine.

"*Think* so?" as I spun around a few times before throwing myself against the wall. I turned back to Homer.

"Christ, Homer! *I* got a boner watchin' *her* watchin' *you*! What kind'a sign ya waitin' for? She gunna have ta grab ya by the nuts an' drag ya into her office b'fore ya get the message?"

"That would take a lot of the guess work out of it," grunting.

I walked over to the doors.

"Can ya b'lieve 'at shit, Ray?"

Ray grinned. Homer followed me into the dance area.

The party had pulled two more tables over. I gave Hugo a mug and placed the juice in front of Joan. She smiled warmly and patted the seat of a vacant stool between her and Hugo. I slid onto the stool. Sonny was sitting on the other side of Hugo. Joan cocked her head and mouthed a silent thank you. She leaned forward onto her elbows. Her breasts, completely unrestrained by a flimsy tee shirt, came to rest on the table. Sonny, pausing mid-sentence while talking with Hugo, glanced over at Joan. She quickly recovered, continuing the conversation right where she'd stumbled.

"Has ever'body met ever'body else?" I shouted over the music.

That was stupid. Everyone reintroduced themselves, furiously shaking hands across and under the tables, shouting, laughing, and clanking raised mugs and glasses. Joan and Sonny never got around to exchanging greetings with each other. The racket gradually died down.

"Honky Tonk Woman" filled the room. A waitress pulled Doug onto the dance floor. Smiling sheepishly, Doug struggled to imitate his partner's moves. Jerry led his young lady onto the floor. He began gyrating wildly. She swayed from side to side, head back, eyes closed.

Sonny, still engaged in conversation with Hugo, hurriedly, but politely, cut Hugo off. She turned to Homer who was sitting on the other side of her at the table. Sonny whispered something in his ear. Homer shook his head. She tried again, this time lingering at his ear and pressing closer. Christ, I could see the goose bumps on Homer's arms from where I was sitting. Sonny jumped down from the stool then pulled Homer from his. He allowed Sonny to lead him onto the dance floor.

It was close to comical—Goliath fast-dancing with Tinker Bell. Homer looked uncomfortable, nervously checking his bandanna every five seconds, attempting to incorporate the checks into his dance moves. Sonny was doing a fast, high-stepping kind of pony trot that was driving the hem of her skirt up her thighs. No one seemed more focused on Sonny's bouncing display than Joan.

Hugo tapped me on the shoulder and asked me about the hours I'd be working at the bar. Without taking my eyes from the dance floor I told him what I thought my hours would be. He wanted to know if I thought I'd be able to bartend at night and survey full time. I assured him if Roy could play fiddle at The Westerner four nights a week, then I could handle this schedule, continuing to stare at Sonny.

*How far up she gunna let that hem go?*

Poor Homer, towering above her, was missing the whole show.

I felt an elbow in my side. I looked over at Joan.

"I had no idea Homer was such a good dancer," Joan, sarcastically.

"Yeah, to bad he's wastin' his moves on a three-footed dog like Sonny."

Joan picked her glass up and rattled the ice in the bottom.

"More juice?" I asked, trying not to stare at her chest.

She placed her hand behind my neck and pulled my ear to her lips.

"Could ya put a double shot'a vodka in it this time...without anyone knowin'?"

Her warm breath in my ear gave me a chill she couldn't have failed to notice. I asked her to repeat the request for the cheap thrill of it. She obliged.

"Won't take a minute," and hurried back to the bar before she changed her mind.

*Somethin' must'a happened at that mind control meetin'. Maybe they'd hypnotized her an' taken her back to a past life where she'd been a cheap, nymphomaniac slut an' they didn't bring her all the way out of it. That kind'a shit pro'bly happens now an' then. Maybe.*

When I returned, Joan was on the dance floor bouncing to another fast Stones song with Danny. I set the glass down and climbed onto the stool. I was torn between focusing on Sonny's thighs or Joan's quaking chest. Hugo picked the glass of juice up and took a sip.

"Damn," putting the glass down. "She ask f'r that?"

"Well, I'm not supposed ta say, but…yeah."

Hugo looked toward the dance floor.

"Ya sober enough ta understand what's happenin' here?" and pointed to, first Sonny and Homer, then Joan and Danny.

"Hell yeah," not at all sure about what he meant.

"Joan feels a little threatened."

I looked at Sonny and Homer then Joan and Danny. It hit me like I'd been kicked in the crotch.

"Joan wants *Homer*?" panicked.

"My God, son," Hugo laughed quietly. "No wonder y're havin' problems with the ladies," and shook his head.

"I'm not havin' any problems. I just can't get laid."

"You'd think that after four years in the Navy you'd'a learned a little more about the fairer sex."

"What I learned about women when I was overseas was 'at the more open sores they had on their legs the cheaper they were."

Hugo put his hand on my shoulder.

"Ya know, Gil…ever' time I have the pleasur'ble occasion ta chat with a former sailor, I go home afterwards an' drop ta my knees. I'll spend an hour thankin' God f'r allowin' me the good sense as a lad ta have joined the Army."

"How am I s'posed ta take 'at?"

"As a compliment, of course," chuckling. "Without you fell'a's, the spectrum'd be missin' a few shades. Now...back ta Joan an' Sonny," pointing to the dance floor. "Joan's gotten used ta bein' the main attraction. Sonny's come along an' upset what Joan considers ta be the nat'ral order'a things. Sonny, on the other hand, feels compelled ta unseat the queen bee. It's nothin' pers'nal...it's just the way it is. They're both out there fightin' f'r the hive," nodding in the direction of the two flailing, thrashing females. "I do b'lieve Joan enjoys the way y'all break inta a sweat around her. If she ever gets drunk enough ta kiss one'a ya, I swear, you'd spontaneously combust. It might'a dawned on her t'night that you fell'as're gunna start fishin' a different pond if ya don't b'gin ta get some nibbles."

I leaned closer to Hugo.

"She ever said anything ta you about me? Anything, ya know... special?"

"Lord, Gil. I can't share a confidence like 'at. I try ta be a gentleman about those things."

"Well, if she ever asks ya how I feel about her, you c'n tell her 'at she makes me hotter'n shit."

" 'at'll damn sure turn her head!" he nodded.

"Couldn't ya at least tell me if I gotta *chance* with her?"

"God Almighty, son! 'at's all any uv us has got when it comes ta findin' *true* love," and slapped me on the back. "An' I know 'at's what you're lookin' for," giving me a wink. "Idn't it?"

"Hell, yea. So, what'a ya think my chances are with Joan?" I pressed.

"What kind'a chance do ya have'a goin' across the street ta that empty lot, pickin' up a handful'a dirt an' findin' a gold nugget in it?" looking down at his drink.

"Well," I snorted, "those odds pretty much suck ass."

"Yeah," sighing heavily, "that they do. 'at's why most people eventually settle f'r a lot less than gold. They get tired'a bein' alone. They get scared. Lookin' f'r the real thing c'n wear a fell'a thin. Whatever the real thing is," coughing into his hand before continuing. "So...most people end up talkin' 'emselves inta settlin' f'r anything 'at's even the least bit shiny. They convince 'emselves 'at's all they really wanted in the first place," pausing to take a slow sip from his drink. "Any'a that make any sense to ya?"

"I think so," way too distracted by Joan and Sonny to fully concentrate on what he was trying to share with me.

Hugo must have considered the information fairly important. He apparently thought I'd have a better chance of remembering the conversation if he reduced to pill size and dragged it through the gutter.

"Look at it like this," he said, "when it comes ta relationships even a cow patty c'n b'gin ta taste a little like a sweet roll if ya put enough sugar on it, an' the hungrier a person gets f'r a sweet roll, the less sugar it takes," then stood up. "I've gotta lose some'a this beer," and headed toward the restroom.

I watched his slightly stooped figure slowly move away from the table.

"Good Vibrations" cleared the dance floor.

"Cain't dance ta that," Sonny announced after climbing back onto the stool.

She may as well have taken her skirt off. She and Homer began whispering and grinning. Doug sat down between the two waitresses he'd been alternately dancing with and began talking away, his hands painfully shaping each meticulously selected word. Danny escorted Joan back to her stool. Joan remained standing. She reached for her drink, keeping her back to Homer and Sonny. Joan sucked on the straw. Her eyes popped open as the double shot of vodka fried her tongue.

"Can you believe Doug was dancing?" Danny.

"He's even talkin' to 'em," Joan, coughing lightly.

"That could fuc...," I looked at Joan, "mess things up for him. Sorry, Joan."

She winked and kept sucking.

Hugo returned to the group of tables, but joined JD. Joan ordered Danny to take Hugo's place at our table.

"Since neither one of ya's brought it up," she began, "I guess I will. I've been considerin' Danny's offer ta let me move in with you guys an' I've reached a decision."

I glanced up at Danny and held my breath. Danny, elbows on the table, was massaging his temples, eyes shut.

"I won't do it..."

*Shit.*

"...if I'm the only female in the house."

*What?*

"So, I've talked Hope inta movin' in..."

*This idn't happenin'!*

"...if there's room for her."

Danny's eyes and mine collided. I knew I'd heard her right, but it wasn't fully registering.

"Yeah, uh. Well..." Danny stammered.

He'd been caught completely off guard and was, for the first time I could remember, speechless.

"We can work it out," my voice a few octaves higher than usual. " 'at won't be any problem at all. We c'n even assign shower times an' bathroom times an' set some house rules as far as bein' in y'ur underwear an'," rambling on excitedly, "an' have a lights out rule an' noise rules. Whatever it takes, I mean, whatever ya want."

Danny kicked me under the table and glared at me. Joan leaned forward to rest on her elbows, the weight of her breasts dragging the table cloth with her.

"Hope an' I talked it over t'night in class," taking a suck on the straw. "She told me she wouldn't mind b'cause she knows all of you well enough ta know she'd be safe an' she feels like she c'n trust ya, which, by the way, is exactly how I feel."

"Safe?" furrowing my forehead.

Danny kicked me again. Joan held an empty glass up and rattled the ice.

"Want another 'un?" I asked hopefully.

"Yes, please," and winked.
I headed for the bar.

Ray was pouring up more pitchers of beer.
"Need any help?" my mind still reeling over Joan's proposal.
"Hell no. Y'ur friends're tippin' like mad."
I fixed Joan a double in a larger glass and returned to the dance
area.

Danny and Joan were slow dancing to "Paint It Black", not
quite touching each other. Sonny and Homer were also slow dancing,
Sonny's boobs grinding into Homer's midriff, her hands stuffed into
his back pockets. She was nipping at his tee shirt and smiling.
*That's not a nat'ral lookin' smile. That's a nasty-ass smile.*

Within thirty minutes I was making Joan another double. Ray
mentioned something about the tips again and how much everybody
was putting down. I hurried back to the tables. Sonny and Homer
had moved to a table away from the group and were talking. Sonny'd
shifted into cutesy—all giggly and jiggly. Homer looked relaxed.
As I walked past Doug, I caught a little of the conversation he
was attempting with the waitress he'd been dancing with. He was
intently explaining about obviates and the shadow people and how
the obviates have all the power since all the rules are second nature,
obvious, to them and not so obvious to the shadow people.

Jerry was making out with his date. Hugo and JD were
hunkered over their drinks, both leaning forward to avoid having
to shout over the music. The flickering candle in the red glass globe
between them created shadowy highlights on their craggy faces.
They looked like two old cowboys around a campfire.

Joan and Danny were hashing out the details of the living
arrangements as I approached the table. Joan took the drink from
me before I could set it down.

"Got it all worked out?" as I watched Joan ease the straw between those lovely, moist, intoxicated lips.

"No sweat," Danny, taking a deep breath then exhaling slowly. "Here's the deal. Joan can move out of her place on May twenty-seventh. Hope doesn't want to move in until Joan does."

" 'at's next week end," I said.

"Thursd'y," Joan corrected.

"I'll take Thursd'y off an' help ya move," I volunteered excitedly.

"You don't have ta do that," and put her hand on my knee. "Danny c'n move me an' you c'n help Hope when ya get off work at Hugo's Thursd'y evenin'."

"Has anybody mentioned any of this to Homer?" Danny.

We looked over at Homer and Sonny. Sonny's foot, resting on Homer's stool, was sandwiched between his legs. She was slowly moving the foot up and down, rubbing the inside of his thighs. The hem of her skirt was damn near to her waist. Her skimpy white panties glowed under the blacklights.

"Let's wait until tomorrow," Danny recommended.

"Yeah," I agreed. "Looks like somebody's busy workin' on gettin' lucky."

"What's so lucky about catchin' gonorrhea?" Joan snipped.

Danny and I looked at her in surprise.

"Homer's clean," I said. "Sonny won't catch anything from him."

"Ha, ha," Joan.

The three of us spent the next thirty minutes setting a few ground rules for the new living arrangement.

Jerry came over.

"Shit, man," slurring. "This place is all right. Gunna have ta come back. Don't go screwin' up an' gittin' fired," sloppy and slow. Wasted.

"Ya leavin'?" I asked.

"Yeah. Watchin' Homer an' whu's her name's got me all lathered. Gotta go do somethin' about it b'fore I die. Thanks f'r invitin' me," then stumbled to Hugo and JD's table. He shook their hands, gathered up his lady, and then staggered toward the lobby.

Danny and I went back to watching the Sonny and Homer Show. Sonny, her foot still on the stool, had leaned forward and placed her hands on Homer's upper thighs. She was massaging the inside of his legs with her thumbs.

Hugo and JD got up and came over. Hugo's eyes locked on Homer and Sonny.

"My word!" he grinned then placed a hand on Joan's shoulder. "Are ya ready ta go?"

"Yes," glancing at Danny and me. "I think we've got ever'thing worked out. B'sides," looking at the love birds, "I feel like I'm gunna be sick."

Hugo nodded his head at me.

"What'd I tell ya?"

I nodded back.

"Tell him what?" Joan frowned.

"Nothin', nothin,'" patting her shoulder. "We were talkin' about y'ur upcomin' livin' arrangements earlier. That's all."

"Gahdamn commune's whud i's gunna be," JD, the drunkest in the group. "Y're all jus' a bunch'a gahdamn horny li'l sex maniacs. Ain'a one'a ya got no common sense 'r decency. Look at 'em two!" nearly falling down while gesturing in Homer's direction. "She's all but tuggin' him off right here in public, gahdamn sorry..."

"Let's go," as Hugo pulled JD toward the lobby.

Danny and I stood up and walked them to the front door. Joan hugged me, then Danny, and thanked us for the evening.

"Tell cor'pal Stiff I got a gahdamn ride home," JD ordered. "No thanks ta his sorry ass."

As we were returning to the dance area, Sonny whipped around the corner into the lobby. She was tooted—sniffing and trying to hold back a sneeze.

"Gil," grabbing my arm to steady herself. "Could yew lock up f'r me? I'll put a spare set'a keys on the office table. Don't bother cleanin' anythang up. Lock the cash register drawer in the office an' make sure ever'thang's turned off. Okay?"

Then she was gone.

Danny and I walked back to the bar to tell the others. Ray gave me the register drawer and the night's tickets. Danny and I went on to the office. I found the keys under a pile of bills and turned to leave. Danny was standing alongside the couch holding Sonny's panty hose.

"You know," he grumbled, "if it'd been anybody else other than Homer...I'd be real pissed off right now."

I stepped around him and walked through the doorway. Danny followed, easing the door shut.

"What're ya plannin' on doin' with those?" pointing at the pantyhose in Danny's hand.

"Oh...yeah," opening the door and tossing them back into the room.

"Damn, Danny. Y're one sick son uv a bitch."

We entered the dance area. It was silent.

"Where'd everybody go?" Danny yelled.

The dee jay turned the microphone on in his booth. The speakers squealed loudly then died down.

"That b-big guy and Sonny are p-probably b-balling in the parking lot," over the sound system. "I t-think everybody else went t-to get something t-to eat. Want me t-to shut it down? It's m-midnight."

"Yeah, go ahead!" then turned to Danny. "Stutterin' Jonas. Sonny knows him from Dallas 'r somethin'."

Danny and I sat at one of the tables and poured up the last of a pitcher.

The dee jay stopped at the table on his way out.

"Whose '57 p-pan head out front?"

"Mine," I answered nonchalantly and offered him some beer.

"No thanks. You b-build it?"

"Yeah," glancing over at Danny.

He wasn't going to give me away.

"R-ride with anybody?"

"Nah. Independent," I said.

"I just g-got mine up. Maybe we c-can get t-together sometime. Do s-some riding."

"Ya know Jerry?" I asked.

"D-don't know anybody. Just m-moved here from D-Dallas. S-starting school in the fall," and lit a cigarette.

"Why here?" Danny. "I mean, damn. Why not Austin?"

"Went where they'd t-take me. Gotta b-bring the grades up to g-get into T-Texas A and M vet medicine."

Danny and I exchanged glances.

"You're in pre-vet?" Danny.

"I'm g-going to try."

"Damn," Danny whistled. "Pre-vet."

Jonas extended his hand.

"I'm J-Jonas."

"Yeah," as we shook. "Sonny said it was Stutterin' Jonas."

"Some call me that," dropping the smile.

"I'm Gil. This is Danny."

They shook hands.

"B-been in?" Jonas.

"Yeah," I answered.

Danny shook his head no.

"Get out of t-the States?" Jonas, looking at me.

"Brown water Navy. River rat."

"Army. G-ground pounder."

He headed for the exit.

"Jonas," I called after him.

Jonas stopped and turned around.

"I bought the bike the way it is. I didn't build it. Danny here's the Harley expert."

"W-whatever," and started to leave again.

"Hey, Jonas!" Danny called out.

Jonas stopped and looked back.

"What stutter?" Danny asked.

Jonas smiled, waved, and then left.


"Think Doug'll get laid t'night?" I asked. "I mean, it'll kind'a piss me off if 'at maniac gets muffed an' I...*we* don't."

"If he does get something going with her it'll only take him a few days to find a way to screw it up."

"Think he screws things up all the time on purpose f'r some reason?"

"I really don't know. It's hard to say how much control he's got over what he does."

We finished the beers.

"Ya ready ta go home?" as I yawned.

"Sure."

"Thanks for helpin' me out t'night," slapping his back.

"No sweat, bub. I may even keep the job for a while. I'm gettin' a little low on cash. You're not the only one making bike payments."


We turned all the lights out, locked everything up, and then stepped outside. I checked to make sure the front door was secure.

"Ya sure ya feel okay about Joan an' Hope movin' in?" straddling my bike.

"Yeah. And if they don't turn out to be the morally upright individuals they've presented themselves to be, we'll throw them out. Right?"

"Right. I'm not livin' with a pack'a sluts. See ya at the house."

Danny kicked his Sportster over on the first try. It took me three jumps.

\*\*\*

GLYNN E. THOMPSON

## "ONWARD CHRISTIAN SOOOLDIERS, MARCHING AS TO WAAAR, WITH THE CROSS OF JEEESUS…,"

I rolled over and wrapped the pillow around my head. It didn't work.

*There ought'a be a fuckin' law. When we throw parties 'at keep the whole goddamn neighborhood up, we end up meetin' ever' cop in the county. Fuck it.*

I got up and lit a cigarette. Something foul hacked into my mouth. Bitter.

*Damn. Best not swallow this 'un.*

It flew out the window.

I put my pants on then walked down the hall to Chad's old room. I looked out the window to see if his things were gone. They were. I quietly approached Homer's room and peeked in. Empty.

*Guess they went ta her place ta do the rabbit.*

I got a beer from the frig then stepped out onto the small porch. The church racket stopped. I sat down, dropped my feet over the edge, and then rested my arms on the bottom rail. I was only slightly hung over. A pleasant surprise.

*Ever'body pro'bly got laid last night but me an' Danny. This shittin' routine's gettin' old.*

I looked to my right toward Will's place on the corner. It was a huge single level with five bedrooms and a full basement. He lived there with a couple of young hairdressers. I think the girls were from some armpit of a hick town south of Lubbock.

*That's pro'bly where Chad ended up.*

*Pro'bly doin' one of 'em this very second.*

*Bastard.*

I was hungry. It was time to grab a bite to eat.

*Swing by the shop an' grab JD since Homer wudn't gunna be there ta force the ol' fart ta eat somethin'.*

Danny was still snoring. I finished dressing and tromped down the steps, deciding to walk instead of ride the bike.

It was a nice day. Clear and warm. Good day not to have a hangover. Good day to sit in the alley behind the piano shop and have a few beers. Listen to a bunch of piano rolls.

Hanging out in the alley behind JD's shop on Sunday and Saturday afternoons had turned into a regular happening. At first it was only the bunch of us, but right after it got warmer more and more strange faces began showing up. Lately as many as twenty-five or thirty people. Initially the player pianos seemed to be the main draw, but it didn't take long for the gatherings to develop into something like a forum for heavy discussions about religion and the meaning of life. Or lack thereof. Sometimes I'd take the later position if I sensed a chick showing up for the first time might be into shoveling nooky at negative type attitudes. Christ, it was getting to where I'd damn near say anything for a piece of ass.

*Fuck it. I will say anything ta get laid.*

The alley had become quite the place to be seen if you were working at being associated with a certain circle—that biker, artist, potty mouthed, philosopher, dope smoking, long haired, rebel, truth seeking, beer swilling loser circle. Or anything approximating those kinds of attitudes.

The majority of people who would show up were a pretty nice bunch. Jerry'd take care of the exceptions. He'd engage the occasional asshole in conversation, or at least something as close to a conversation as Jerry could manage given the condition he was usually in. He'd then rag on the guy until the jerk was disgraced into leaving. There were several lines that would put Jerry into the attack mode. Among them, "Yeah, I've been thinkin' about buildin' a chopper," to which Jerry would respond with what he considered to be one of his more brilliant thrusts—"If y'ur balls wuz as big as y'ur brain I guess yew'd be on a chop job righ' now, wouldn' ya!" and sneer. The other lines Jerry particularly hated to hear were "Do I look that stupid? I got a student deferment," and "Do I look that stupid? I enlisted in the Air Force." Jerry didn't have a come back for either one of them. He'd simply grab the asshole by the hair, drag him to the end of the alley, and then toss him into University Avenue. Jerry was never going to have ulcers as a result of keeping anything pent up inside for any length of time.

Joan would show up occasionally and whine about how the whole world was starving and she wasn't doing anything about it. She'd bitch about how bad she felt because she couldn't find the courage to quit school and join the Peace Corp or go to Africa and convert everybody to the Faith. Joan had a real problem with the guilt thing. I'd do my damnedest to comfort the poor thing, but, no matter how hard I tried to help her, I guess she didn't consider it helpful enough to do me for it.

Hugo'd join us from time to time and keep everybody's facts straight on the different philosophies and religions. After becoming too wrecked to argue, JD'd stumble around hitting on all the bare bellied artist ladies, some of whom had elevated him to cult status once finding out about his stained glass expertise. JD was probably slapping it to a couple of the uglier ones. The Harley riders would get drunk, act mean, and talk dirty. Everybody would get high. It was an odd mix, but it was always a hoot.

When I got to the shop JD was sitting on a crate, staring down at the ground, a beer in one hand, a cigarette in the other. His dirty, misshapen straw cowboy hat was barely hanging onto the back of his head.

"Have a good time last night?" as I approached.

"Bes' git y'urself in there an' talk ta y'ur boy," he snarled without looking up.

"Homer's here? Is he alon..."

"Git in there an' talk to him," sternly.

I slipped through the narrow opening. It took a few seconds for my eyes to adjust to the darkened shop. When they did, I found Homer lying on his pallet, staring at the ceiling, hands behind his head. I walked over and sat down at his feet.

Five minutes passed. Homer remained motionless. I finally cleared my throat and asked what was wrong. He slowly sat up, pulled the bandanna from his head, and then ran a hand over the scar.

"Right in the middle of it all," and held the bandanna up, "she pulls it off. When she felt the back of my head...she couldn't get away from me fast enough," and lay back down.

Another long pause.

"Fuck her," I said.

"Yeah...fuck her. Fuck her and everybody else like her," throwing himself back into a sitting position. "Fuck all of them. Fuck everybody who sees it and shits."

I looked down into my lap.

"Can you blame them?" he continued. "Ever looked at it close?" dropping his head down and pulling his hair forward.

I gave it a quick glance then turned away.

"She was fine, Gil," flipping his head back to get the hair out of his face. "Really fine. This one, for some reason, hurts bad."

I got up, went over to the cooler and got a beer.

"Want one?"

"No. I'm still half drunk."

I returned mine to the cooler and walked back over to him. I seated myself on a rickety piano stool, lit two cigarettes then handed one to Homer.

"Why didn't ya let the military fix it b'fore ya got out?" I asked quietly.

Homer didn't respond right away. He rubbed the scar and thought a while.

"I wanted out," finally. "I just wanted out."

A period of silence.

"You could still go ta the Veterans Administration," I suggested. "What about the hospital up in Amarilla 'r the one in Dallas?"

Homer fidgeted.

"I could set it up..."

"I don't want shit!" standing up and pacing about his little sleeping area. "I want *her*, Gil! *That's* what I want!"

Homer trudged over to the wall and rested his forehead against it, arms hanging limply at his sides.

"Christ, Homer. F'rget about her. There's plenty'a women who wouldn't give a damn abou..."

"No!" turning to face me. "There haven't *been* plenty of other women and there won't *be* plenty of other women."

"Then become a fuckin' priest," getting pissed.

"Fuck you!" stepping toward me. "How the fuck could you understand? Just how the fuck?"

"Maybe I don't," equally loud. "I got lucky. Ya can't see mine. Ya wan'a know what I don't un'erstand? I don't un'erstand why all of a sudden the only ones who seem ta count are all the jerkoffs who make ya feel bad about it. What about the ones who don't give a shit about it? I don't un'erstand why, all of a sudden, *they* don't fuckin' count."

"They're just being polite and you know it."

"Polite? Fuck you polite! What makes ya think they owe ya that? Huh? They don't owe ya that! Goddammit, Homer," lowering my voice. "It just dudn't matter ta most people," slowly enunciating each word. "It's like ugly chicks...once ya get ta know 'em they usually turn out ta be okay people. After a while, ya don't even notice they're all 'at ugly. Not that much anyway. People like ya b'cause'a the way ya are around 'em. The way ya treat 'em an' shit."

"Quit blowing smoke up my ass."

"Ya know what, Homer? Somethin' just dawned on me. Maybe ya don't wan'a hear it dudn't matter ta some. Hell, as far as I know, ya might even get off ta people noticin' it. Is that what the scar is? Y'ur advertisement that ya've seen some shit so pardon my ass f'r bein' a drunk-ass doper?" regretting the charge the instant I'd leveled it.

"Bullshit!" he shouted.

Homer stormed to the front of the building and looked over the top of the plywood into the street. He didn't move for a long time, several minutes passing before turning around and slowly making his way back to me.

"This...this argument," he said, "it's...wrong. All wrong,"

"I agree. I'm sayin' shit I don't really mean."

Homer walked to the front of the building again. After waiting a few minutes, he returned and stood in front of me.

"I didn't have the head fixed because," and turned away, "because they said fixing it was going to hurt like all hell. I was tired of hurting. Got tired of being in pain all the time. So I left it alone and quit thinking about it."

"Yeah, well, you're doin' a *real* good job with not ever thinkin' about it."

Homer went over to the corner, dug through his duffel bag, and then removed one of the leather pouches he'd taken from his grandfather's place. I came over to him. Homer took a small, rounded, shiny black stone from the pouch.

"Here," handing the stone to me. "I don't know what Grandpa used these things for, but it was his so it means something to me. I want you to have this."

I took the stone and held it tightly in my hand. Homer suddenly grabbed me up in a bear hug and lifted me from the ground. Setting me down, he stepped back, looking a little embarrassed.

Homer lowered his head.

"Last night with Sonny...I've never felt that way about somebody. Never. She's so damn beautiful and...and I got the feeling she sort of liked me."

"Ever'body in the damn bar was gettin' 'at impression f'r some reason."

"I'm serious. This time it's different. It hurts deep."

"I'm sorry," apologizing for the flippancy.

Homer reached under his pallet and pulled out two joints. He gave me one and we lit up.

"Homer?" after finishing the joint.

"What?"

"Homer, I got the answer."

"To what?"

"Y'ur head. Y'ur scar. If it makes ya feel that bad," getting excited, "buy a wig!" serious as a heartbeat. "Just cover the motherfucker up an', POOF! It goes away."

Homer, expressionless, stared at me several seconds before responding.

"I pour my heart out to you," dryly, "and all you can come up with is...I should become a cross-dresser?"

"Lots'a guys wear wigs, Homer. It's no big thing."

"Until Jerry finds out."

"Ta hell with Jerry. Get one'a those expensive kinds. Not the cheap kind. Get a good 'un that really looks real. Nobody'll ever know," completely sold on the idea's merits.

Homer squinted and looked at me, his face one big question mark.

"What color?" as dryly as before.

"Black. That's y'ur nat'ral hair color idn' it?"

"What kind of a hairstyle?"

I thought for a moment.

"Perky. Chicks *looove* perky."

We smoked a cigarette without speaking. I finished mine and got to my feet.

"Let's wander on up to the drug store an' get somethin' ta eat," as I stretched.

"Sunday. It's closed."

"IHOP, then. Califórnya company. They just tell the Baptists ta fuck off. Chow down ten 'r fifteen cheese sandwiches, then come back an' get seriously smoked up. I don't wan'a get drunk, though. It'd be too much of a bitch surveyin' with a hangover in the heat t'morrow."

"What about my wig?"

"That's been decided. We'll ask one'a the hair dressers livin' at Will's ta find ya somethin' perky an' black."

"Watch them show up with a black whore on speed," following me to the door.

I slipped through the narrow slit. Homer had to throw it open two more feet to make it.

"Want anything from the IHOP?" I asked JD.

He looked up at Homer.

"How ya feelin'?" he growled.

"Fine...for an ugly chick," putting his bandanna on.

"Y're still drunk as shit, ain't ya?" JD snorted.

"Just drunk. We're bringing something back for you to eat and you're going to eat it or I'll give it to you rectally," Homer threatened.

"J'st *try* ta touch my ass, ya goddamn faggot," grumbling. "I'll kick y'ur goddamn balls from here ta Hell an' back, by God. Ya ain't makin' me do nothin' if I don't wan'a."

We were gone for over an hour. I told Homer about Hope and Joan moving in. Homer didn't think it would happen, but thought it was okay if it did. He offered to move into the small room between the kitchen and my room since he was hardly ever at the house.

By the time we got back to the alley it was beginning to fill up. I didn't know two thirds of them. We brought two fried bologna sandwiches back for JD. Homer took JD's cigarettes and kept them until JD ate the sandwiches.

Joan never showed.

I ended up drinking two or three bottles of Ripple and doing some hash Jerry had. I don't remember when I passed out, but when I woke up it was pitch black. I found Homer passed out on his pallet and JD passed out on his cot. The alley was empty. I pulled the sliding door to, then slowly walked to the house, staying in the alley so I wouldn't have to worry about tripping on the sidewalk or a brick in the street.

*** 

I got to Hugo's a little late the next morning. No particular reason, just moving kind of slow. I was in more of a mild fog than hung over. I parked the bike in the garage, fed the animals, threw a couple of bales of alfalfa around, and then opened the barn doors so the buffalo could get out. They wandered into the corral. Criswell stopped and looked at the VW. He looked over at me. I shot him the bird. He lowered his head then lumbered off toward the stock tank.

*Sorry-ass motherfucker.*

Roy looked like he'd been up all weekend. Wouldn't have surprised me if he had.

"Ya fed the stock?" he mumbled while arranging a stack of papers on his clipboard.

"Yeah."

"Stan won't be in this week. He wanted a break b'fore summer school starts. Yew'll be with me, an' I don't want ya goin' an' embarrassin' me, goddammit. When we're out drivin' aroun' town an' I tell ya ta duck down, then, by God, ya duck down. I don't need f'r any'a my friend's ta be seein' me with a filthy hippie."

"What're we doin'?" and approached the drafting table.

Roy threw his body over the clipboard.

"I'll tell ya when I feel like ya need ta know," straightening up while holding the clipboard to his chest so I couldn't see it. "Goddamn druggie. Even if I told ya, yew'd f'rgit it in thirty secon's."

"F'rget what?"

Hugo entered the office.

"Good mornin' men," softly. "How is ever'body this mornin'?"

Roy jumped to his feet and confronted Hugo.

"Didn' ya tell me yew was gunna fire this long-haired freak?"

Hugo, chuckling, placed a hand on my shoulder and winked as he passed by me.

"You wouldn't know what ta do without ol' Gil here ta pick on," climbing the stairs. "Could I see ya a second b'fore ya get out'a here, Gil?" without slowing his ascent.

"Ye'sir."

Once Hugo was out of sight, Roy hurried over.

"Whut the hell's 'at all about?" he hissed.

"On Frid'y Hugo gave me the weekend ta think over whether I wanted y'ur job 'r not. Might have someth..."

"Ya lyin' bastard. I'll load the truck while y're kissin' ass upstairs," and left the room.

I walked up the stairs and sat down in one of the old chairs in front of Hugo's desk. Hugo was propping the window open with a stick. He turned around and sat down, locking his fingers together in a large fist in front of him.

"Gil," beginning slowly, his eyes bulging, head bobbing slightly. "I don't want ya ta think I'm tryin' ta stick my nose inta somethin' 'at's pro'bly none'a my business. Okay?"

"Okay," not certain of where this might be going.

"Ya know...Hope's come a long way since she first came here."

Certain now where the conversation was headed.

"She's b'come special ta me. Lord God Almighty, when she first approached me with the idea'a movin' inta town with y'all, I didn't know *what* ta think," pausing, shaking his head slowly. "But...she's over eighteen. She c'n decide f'r herself, I reckon. I decided not ta try an' talk her out'a the idea," looking at me and smiling. "No offense, Gil, but I feel like she's packin' herself off to an asylum 'at's bein' run by the damn patients," raising his brows and breaking into a nervous laugh. "You boys gunna keep an eye on her for me?"

"Hugo, we'll treat her like family," as sincerely as I could manage.

"Any history uv incest in y'ur family?"

"Damn, Hugo. We got our problems, but ya know she'll be safe. Ever'body thinks the world'a her. She's one fine lady."

"An' I'm tickled pink y'all feel 'at way about her, but...she's developed certain...*habits*...while she's been here. A certain way'a doin' some things 'at could easily be misinterpreted," rubbing his chin.

"So she's a little weird. Who's gunna notice in the ghetto?"

"She's not weird in *that* sense. She's developed a...a kind of Scandinavian attitude about some things. Like sunbathin' an'...," his voice trailing off.

"What was 'at?" and leaned forward. "I couldn't hear 'at last part."

Hugo looked up at me. His face was red.

"Nudity," he blurted out. "She likes ta sunbathe naked," swiveling the chair around and staring out the window.

Damn good thing too. Hugo didn't need ta see my reaction.

I regrouped, cleared my throat, and then attempted to assure Hugo it was no big deal.

"Christ, Hugo," fighting for calm. "We've all been overseas."

"That's supposed ta make me feel more secure about things?"

"I guess what I'm tryin' ta say, Hugo, is 'at, well...if ya've seen one tit, hell, ya've just about seen 'em all. More 'r less," immediately realizing I was going to have to do better than that to sound convincing. "I mean, if I was ta run into her sunbathin' on the roof, that's where we sunbathe…I swear, Hugo, I pro'bly wouldn't hardly even notice if she was naked 'r not," feeling like I'd done a little better job that time.

Hugo spun back around and looked at me.

"Ya know, Gil," he chuckled, "you can't lie f'r shit."

I grinned.

"Don't worry, Hugo," dead serious. "Nobody's gunna let anything happen ta Hope."

"I know, I know. An' I don't think any'a you'd ever intentionally hurt anybody. That even goes f'r 'at Jerry fell'a."

"Jerry comes across as bein' kind'a rough, but underneath he's as sensitive as a dry shaved scrotum."

Hugo dropped his head and looked at me from over the top of his glasses.

"I can't tell ya how comforted I am ta hear that about him," raising his head. "But be aware'a this one thing for me. Remember this…*unintentional* does the same amount'a damage as *intentional* when it's all said an' done. Un'erstand?"

"I know, Hugo, but b'lieve me…ya don't have a thing ta worry about."

Hugo thought a moment or two then slowly got to his feet.

"Ya better be gettin' down stairs. Roy'll be chompin' at the bit."

I walked to the head of the stairs then turned around.

"She's gunna be fine, Hugo. You'll see," and proceeded down the stairs.

I meant it, too. Hope'd be safe as hell and treated with all the respect she was due.

*But…still…*

*Nude sunbathin'?*

*Shit. It's just the start'a summer.*

*Nude Yoga!*

*Oh, my God!*

*Should'a thrown Chad out a looong time ago.*

Roy, obviously in pain, was slumped over the wheel. I quietly opened the door and slid onto the front seat.

"Don't go slammin' 'at door," grumbling without looking up.

"Want me ta drive?"

Roy rolled his head on the steering wheel and fixed his hemorrhaging eyeballs on me.

"Whut the hell makes ya thank I cain't drive?" in a deep, gravelly voice.

"Well, I can't imagine what partyin' all weekend must do ta a man y'ur age. I was just tryin' ta help ya out. That's all."

"My age? Is 'at whu'ch ya said?" and started the truck. "An' I wudn' partyin'," he growled as we rolled down the drive. "I was workin'."

"Silly me. How could I'a mistaken playin' fiddle in a bar, drinkin' f'r free, an' porkin' waitresses all weekend long as partyin'?"

"It's hell,"pursing his lips, "but I j'st cain't brang myself ta turn any'a them ladies down."

"Sort of an obligation thing. Right?"

"Yeah."

"Y're a regular white knight, Roy."

"Yeah, I know it. It's my own damn fault. Ever'thang went ta shit the first time I let one uv 'em have an orgasm. I should'a j'st hopped her, got my rocks an' gone my merry way like ever' other son uv a bitch does. Not me though. I had ta go gittin' fancy an' start showin' off. Once the word got out…it was all over. Now ever' lady out there wants a piece'a ol' Roy. Yeah, I'm payin' f'r my arr'gance now, by God."

"I'll swap my problem with y'urs anytime ya want. I can't even get a broad inta bed much less think about givin' her an orgasm."

"At least ya recognize 'at ya gotta problem. 'at's an important step ta' gittin' y'ur first piece'a free stuff."

"What makes ya think I never had free?"

"Now Gil…ya've made a lot'a progress here this mornin', admittin' ya cain't git laid without havin' ta pay f'r it an' all."

"I never said anything like…"

"Don't go backslidin' on me with a lie about all'a the free stuff ya've had. Hell, Homer told me about how ya used ta show sheep an' if…"

"There's nothin' wrong with the way I showed them fuckin' sheep!" I protested loudly. "That's how ya show 'em."

"Settle down, now. I wuz jus' thankin' that if 'at same queer-ass sheepherder 'at told ya how ta show sheep also advised ya on how ta handle women then…"

"What's Homer doin' tellin' ya 'at shit for anyway? That was supposed ta been a private conversation."

"He's worried about ya, Gil. Damn. *All* uv us are. 'specially now 'at this sheep shit's out in'a open."

"Go ta hell," and turned the radio up.

Roy turned the radio down.

"Speakin'a which," having too much fun to let it go, "I heard there's this one part'a Hell where a bunch'a pissed off sheep git ta show former FFA boys. Whud'a ya thank about that?"

I turned the radio up, louder this time.

We stopped and got some coffee and a few doughnuts. Roy removed a jellyroll before tossing the sack to me. He took a bite then wiped his moustache on the back of his sleeve as he pulled into the traffic.

"We'll be workin' in east Lubbock this mornin'," mouth full. "Got any racial issues with 'at?" fishing for a way to jack with me.

East Lubbock was mostly blacks. It was the only part of town that still had some unpaved streets. Even Guadalupe, the Mexican neighborhood north of the campus, had the majority of its streets paved.

I ignored the question.

He filled his mouth again then tried again.

"Ever thank about trimmin' y'ur beard up, cuttin' y'ur hair, an' gittin' a cowboy hat an' a pair'a boots? Ya see, Gil," not waiting for an answer, "y're drillin' f'r water in the Sahar'. The big myth about hippie chicks is 'at they all fuck at the drop uv a hat. It j'st ain't so. Hell, ya should'a already fig'red 'at 'un out by now. Not that yew'd'a gotten any even if they did. The truth is, not that many uv 'em do. They're a bunch'a prick teasers. Runnin' aroun' with no bras 'r panties. Now, cowgirls…cowgirls tend ta fuck like crazy. Ya ever listen ta the words in mos' cowboy songs? Pure pornogr'phy. It's suggestive, real subtle, but it's still porn. A lady sits aroun' drankin' an' listenin' ta 'at shit all night an' somethin' unconscious happens. It's kind'a like a…a mental Spanish fly."

"Sorry, Roy, but most shit kickin' music sucks."

"Too bad. Buck Owens c'n sound pr'tty damn good when y're in the middle'a gittin' a hummer."

Roy pulled up in front of a large, wood framed church. It looked like it hadn't been painted since it was built. Several windows were broken out. He exited the cab.

"Let's do it," through one last mouthful of doughnut.

I pulled the hundred foot metal tape reel out from under the seat. It was called a "chain" because, way back when, surveyors used a hundred feet of links for measuring distances. I guess it must have looked something like a chain. Roy sketched the church's layout. We walked up a dirt path to the front door to begin measuring the outside dimensions.

"Should I knock on the door an' tell God what we're doin'?" I asked.

"Nah. He knows."

We finished the church then drove over to one of the better parts of town. It was west of the Tech campus. Roy drove down a paved *alley*. In Lubbock, if your alley was paved, then you'd reached the top rung of the ladder. Roy eased to a stop alongside a six-foot high redwood fence. Two garbage cans were sitting in a Swiss chalet looking hutch against the fence.

"Me an' Stan got the front'a this place last week then run out'a time," briefing me. "Yew know how 'at clock-watchin' yahoo is. We only need the back measurements. The back gate's locked so y're gunna have ta climb the fence an' measure the place up by y'urself. I'm too old ta be climbin' fences," unwrapping a block of chewing tobacco.

"See what I mean about y'ur age, Roy? Y're slowin' down."

"Maybe so, but slowin' down ta ninety still puts me out front'a yew, by God, an' don'ch ya f'rgit it. Now git y'ur sorry ass out there an' let's git this over with. Climb up on 'at garbage can thang an' jump over. An' don't go stompin' on any flowers."

I took a chaining pin from the toolbox. A chaining pin was a foot long length of metal with a loop at the top. The pin was about half as big around as a pencil and painted with red and white stripes. It was used to mark distances or to fend off asshole dogs.

I climbed onto the little hutch, stuck the pin, loop end first, into my back pocket and then looked around the backyard for any evidence of an asshole dog.

"Hey! Roy!"

"Whut?" sticking his head out of the window and spitting.

"Dog shit's ever'where."

"It's a coupl'a Chihuahuas."

"Don't think so. They look more like elephant size shit piles."

"They're *big* Chihuahuas. Now, goddammit, git y'ur ass over 'at fence."

*Fuck me.*

I slammed the fence a few times, and yelled. Everything remained quiet. I tossed the reel into the back yard and then lowered myself down. After scanning the yard again, I bent over and picked up the reel. I crept toward the back of the house, listening intently for a jangling dog collar or a low, deep growl. Reaching the corner of the house, I ran the pin through the leather loop at the end of the metal tape then shoved the pointed end of the pin into the ground, checking to make sure the '0' on the chain held firmly against the corner. I crept down the side of the house to the front fence, slowly unreeling the chain.

A dense China Berry bush in the corner where the fence met the front corner of the house came to life. I didn't wait to see what it was. I turned and hauled balls, a vicious series of thundering barks right on my heels. I tossed the reel over the fence at a dead run and went over the top after it, collecting two arms full of splinters, taking some skin off my chest, and ripping my tee shirt open in the process. The reel, still unwinding, slid across the truck's hood as I hit the ground. I tumbled into the side of the truck. The beast smashed into the fence, snarling, barking, and clawing away at it.

"Hey, goddammit!" Roy. "Watch out f'r the paint job!"

I got to my knees and stared at the fence. The animal was jumping straight up, head momentarily appearing when it took flight then disappearing as it fell back to earth.

*Dobermans don't get that fuckin' big! Do they? No nat'ral dog does!*

I shot to my feet, threw myself against the passenger door of the truck, and then stuck my head into the cab.

"GODDAMMIT! THAT SON OF A BITCH COULD'A KILLED ME! Is 'at why you an' Stan didn't finish it the other day? Ya figured ya'd feed my ass ta that motherfucker! Goddammit, ya could'a at least fuckin' warned me!"

"Then yew'd'a j'st worried about it all mornin'," mumbling without looking up from his clipboard. "Cain't make some people happy, I guess. Why the hell do I even try?" and continued to scribble some notes on a blue print while slowly shaking his head.

"Fuck you, Roy, goddammit! JUST PLAIN FUCK YOU!" adrenaline still screaming through my body. "*Double* fuck you, motherfucker!" as I began to stomp back and forth along side the truck.

Roy got out of the truck, picked up the reel, and then rewound his way over to the garbage can hutch. He climbed onto the hutch.

The dog went nuts, his shoulders clearing the top of the fence with each leap. Roy smacked his lips loudly.

"Nice puppy. Nice doggie."

He sat down on the hutch, spit, and then lit a cigarette. Roy offered me the pack.

"I got my own," I snapped and reached inside the cab.

Neither one of us spoke until we'd finished our cigarettes.

I put mine out and walked over to Roy.

"That was raw, Roy. *Real* raw. I could'a gotten seriously hurt. It was just plain *wrong*."

Roy looked down at his boots.

"Y're right. I'm sorry," looking up. "I should'a never let Stan talk me inta somethin' like 'at," sounding sincere as hell. "It *was* Stan's idea ya know."

"I don't care whose idea it was. It sucked! There wudn't a goddamn thing funny about it."

"Y're right. I c'n see 'at now. Somehow it *sounded* funny when Stan was twistin' my arm ta do it. That son uv a bitch," under his breath while holding his hand out to me.

I looked at it, debating whether I should go that easy on him.

"C'mon, Gil," he pleaded. "I feel bad enough as it is. I jus' wudn't thankin'. Don't go makin' me carry this thang aroun' inside me f'r the rest'a the week."

I thought about it a little longer before finally shaking his hand.

"I guess I'll get over it."

When we were climbing back into the truck he stopped, one foot in the cab, the other still on the ground. He snapped his fingers and looked over at me.

"Damn. Almost f'rgot. Ya left my chainin' pin in the yard. Would ya min..."

"NO FUCKIN' WAY! I'll buy ya a new one!" slamming the door.

Roy eased in behind the wheel.

" 'at's my fav'rite pin," sadly. "My good luck pin. Had it ever since I first started surveyin'.'"

"You an' Stan c'n come back next week an' get the motherfucker," I snarled.

"Yew ain't never gunna make it as a hippie as long as ya go aroun' harborin' 'at kind'a harshness in y'ur heart," he mumbled.

He tuned the radio to the noon time Paul Harvey show then slowly drove down the alley spitting at telephone poles as he went.

"Where ya wan'a eat?" Roy.

"Ya ought'a be buyin' me a steak after tryin' ta kill me like 'at."

"By thunder, if ya wan'a steak then 'at's whut I'm gittin' ya."

Five minutes later we pulled into a Dairy Queen parking lot.

"Dairy Queen dudn't have steaks," I huffed.

"This 'un might," leaning out the door to clean the plug out of his mouth. "Let's go inside an' see," opening his eyes wide and crossing his fingers.

Steaks weren't on the menu. Wouldn't have mattered—Roy didn't even have enough money to buy me a coke, much less a steak. I washed my mayonnaise sandwich down with water and listened to Roy go on about how the two of us should come up with a plan to get even with Stan for the dog thing.

We spent the rest of the day driving around town measuring houses and talking about Hugo's business. Hugo'd been surveying since the late forties. Roy'd shown up in the mid-fifties, so he knew about everything you'd want to know about Hugo's place. He told me about some of the crackpots Hugo'd hired in the past. Roy said that, at one time or an other, an ex-priest, a retarded guy, and a couple of ex-cons had worked for Hugo.

"Once Hugo even hired a coupl'a reformed prostitutes. At least they'd convinced Hugo 'at they'd reformed. They worked here the same time 'at retarded fell'a worked here. Didn't work out too well, though," taking a chew of tobacco. " 'at's why it kind'a su'prised me when Hugo didn't fire Hope after findin'out about her, but then, she wudn' a real hooker an' she don't really survey. I heard that a boyfriend'a her's would git her drunk at parties an' then let his buddies jump her f'r a coupl'a bucks 'r somethin' like 'at. He'd even take Polaroids uv it. C'n ya b'lieve 'at shit?"

"The guy must'a been a real bastard. Her bein' so damn sweet an' all."

"No doubt. An' don't go tellin' anybody else about it. I didn't mean ta let that slip out. I'm serious as hell. F'rgit I even mentioned it. Anyway, back ta them whores. Leo, the retarded guy, he kept comin' up broke j'st a few days after ever' payday. Hugo looked inta it an' found out these two hookers, Candy an' Jewel, was fuckin' his brains out. At least they was givin' him a discount. Hugo run 'em off. They went up ta Amarilla. Hell, when Leo found out where they'd gone to, he hopped the next bus north ta go lookin' for 'em. Hookers 'at'll give ya a discount're hard ta come by. 'at boy knew a good deal when he saw it. He might'a been retarded, but he wudn' dumb."

"One'a the convicts Hugo'd hired stole the company pick up. Turned up in a ditch in Lou'siana. They never did fin' the fell'a. An' then there wuz this blind guy…"

"A totally blind guy surveyin'?" doubtfully.

"Yeah, I know. Sounds crazy as hell, but he was. Jim was blind as a bat. Lemme tell ya, though…it *damn* near worked. Hugo'd team him up with somebody ta measure houses. Yew'd put Jim at a corner with the dead end'a the chain an' he'd hold the rang right on the corner. Ya don't have ta see ta do that. Right? Whoever else was workin' with him'd read the measurement. When ya was done at a corner, yew'd yell out an' move on ta the next corner. Jim'd feel his way right down the side'a the wall. Hell, he'd follow ya aroun' the buildin' like a dog on a leash. Got ta where Jim could make damn good time aroun' a place."

"What happened to him?"

"Well, Hugo sent Jim out with Bubbles...'at's the nickname we gave the ep'leptic."

"An ep'leptic?"

"No shit. A goddamn ep'leptic. Anyway, Jim an' Bubbles was measurin' aroun' this house. Jim was feelin' his way along the wall ta the next corner when he j'st, all uv a sudden, *plunk*, falls right out'a sight. The son uv a bitch'd stepped inta a goddamn deep-ass hole. Bubbles f'rgot ta tell Jim about the hole, I guess. Anyway, the fall knocked Jim out cold. Bubbles had a seizure when he saw Jim layin' in the bottom'a the hole. I guess they'd a both died if it hadn't been f'r some nosey ol' fart comin' over ta see if Jim an' Bubbles knew anything about who'd bought the house they was measurin'. An' then 'at ol' fart damn near had a heart attack when he was runnin' back ta his house ta git the p'lice f'r Jim an' Bubbles. Bad day f'r ever'body," lighting a cigarette.

"There's been a guy with j'st one leg, an' once he hired a homosex'al. The queer, Abby, might'a worked out 'cept his lover, some guy named Reggie, had a drankin' problem. Ever'time Reggie'd git all liquored up he'd show up at the office cryin' an' shit. Puked on a draftin' table one day. Tha's the last straw f'r Hugo, so he let Abby go. Ya know, 'at wudn't all 'at long ago. Maybe two years. I b'lieve y'ur friend Danny came ta work f'r us f'r the first time right after Abby left."

"I guess Danny was pr'tty much a breath'a fresh air after them others."

"Yeah, it started ta lookin' like a reg'lar b'ness f'r a while. Even Stan feels comft'r'ble aroun' Danny. Ya gotta give Hugo credit, though...he's always tryin' real hard ta he'p people. Even after that con stole his truck, he kept right on hirin' weirdos. In about '61 'r so, he hired this Korean War vet. 'at was one screwed up fell'a. Ended up feelin' pr'tty sorry f'r the guy. He must'a been shell shot 'r somethin'. He was related to a friend'a Hugo's. The ol' boy was havin' a hell uv a time, so Hugo brought him on. Real sad, I mean, ya got the impression this fell'a was really tryin'. He j'st couldn't seem ta pull it off. Couldn't quite fig're it out. Drugs. Did a lot'a drugs. An' he drank a lot."

"What happened to him?"

"Shot himself. Used a Winchester Hugo used ta have on'a wall up in his office. Shot himself out near the big barn. Damn near killed Hugo when he found out about it. Hugo made it ta where all 'em other guns'a his in his office cain't fire anymore."

"Damn."

"Yeah. Didn't stop Hugo. He don't give up on people. He's had a special thang f'r vets ever since 'at fell'a shot himself. Plus Hugo's a vet. He was in 'W' 'W' Two. He ever mention 'at to ya?"

"Nah. He hadn't said anything about it."

"Well," pausing to think it over. "Yew've worked here longer than most'a the wing nut losers he picks out'a the gutter. I don't thank he'll mind my tellin' ya about it. Hugo was with 'at bunch 'at freed some'a the concentration camps in Europe. Janice, his ex-wife tol' me about it. He's never pers'nally said anythang about it ta me. One'a the places was Dachau. 'at's the one she mentioned by name, but there wuz a few others. I guess it made a pr'tty damn big impression on him. Might even be part'a the reason he's always lookin' inta differ'nt religions an' shit. Wudn' 'til after 'at guy went an' shot himself 'at he really started ta change though."

"Change?"

Roy glanced over at me.

"Hell, yew pro'bly ain't even noticed how flat-out strange he c'n get sometimes. Hugo's pro'bly normal as shit ta yew. Hugo used ta hang out at the country club. Live in a big house in town. Entertain a bit. He's completely differ'nt t'day. Hangin' out with weirdos. Listenin' ta weird music. Readin' weird books. Yeah…he ain't the same person he was when I first started workin' f'r him."

We measured up four more houses then took the afternoon break at a gas station. Roy was fading fast. I kept thinking about the girls moving in.

"How late we workin' t'day?" I asked as we pulled out of the station.

"Why?" Roy snapped. "Ya need a fix 'r somethin'? Go lick the battery posts on the truck. 'at'll hold ya over."

"I gotta be at Dancers no later than 7:00 t'night."

" 'at new dance club in the Tech ghetto?"

"Yeah. I started workin' there Saturd'y night. Bartendin'."

"Yew? Bartendin'? Talk about the fox watchin' the damn hen house. I didn't know yew could bartend."

"Can't, but I'm learnin'."

It was a struggle, but Roy managed to work until 5:30. As we were pulling into the drive, I spotted Hope coming out of the red barn.

"I gotta talk ta Hope," I told Roy.

"Keep it in y'ur pants," and smacked my arm.

I thought about what Roy had said as I walked toward Hope. *Somebody should'a shot that bastard f'r doin' 'at ta her.*

We met half way across the field. She was in her leotard and sweating a little. Hope stopped and smiled timidly.

"Doin' y'ur Yoga?" smiling back at her.

"Yeah," softly.

"Well, how're ya feelin' about the big move? Still gunna do it?"

Hope giggled and turned away, pulling the towel around her neck up over her head to cover her face.

"What's wrong?" stepping in front of her and tugging gently at the towel.

"Nothin'," turning away again and pulling the towel tighter against her face.

"Nothin', hell. Somethin's got ya goin'."

Hope stepped away, dropped the towel from her face, turned to look at me, and then cocked her head to one side.

"It's all kind'a...yew know...embarrassin'. We're about ta be *livin'* t'gether an'...it sounds kind'a funny. 'at's all."

"Well, look at it like this then. You'll be livin' with Joan an' it's Joan who's the one 'at's livin' with us guys."

She hit me with the towel.

"Silly," stepping around me and then gliding toward the gate. "It's the same thang. Yew j'st went an' said it differ'nt. I'm *still* gunna be livin' with three men."

I remembered Hugo's concern for Hope. I fell in behind her.

"Don't do it if ya have any doubts about it," staring at her gently swaying hips.

"It ain't that an' yew quit lookin' at mah butt," covering her bottom with the towel. "Git up here b'side me 'r walk up in front'a me," she ordered.

"So you c'n look at my butt? An' I wudn't lookin' at y'ur *butt*. I was tryin' ta read the label on y'ur leotard. I been thinkin' about pickin' up somethin' like 'at f'r my mother f'r her birthday," moving up along side her.

"L'ar."

I turned the conversation back to the living arrangements.

"I mean it. If ya don't feel comf'tr'ble with movin' in, then say so. It won't hurt anybody's feelin's."

"It's j'st 'at it's been so long since I lived with anybody," and glanced around the ranch. "Here don't count. I got the whole far end'a the house ta mahself out here, so it's almos' like livin' alone. An'...I don't wan'a end up bein' a problem f'r anybody."

"Hope, I can't imagine that you could *ever* be a problem ta *anybody*. I mean 'at. I don't think ya know how much ever'body thinks'a ya."

Then, for the first time since I'd met her, Hope touched me. She took my hand. My stomach jumped.

"Don't go gittin' no ideas," as she tugged my hand.

"I won't," and tugged back.

"Jerry tol' me all about yew sailors."

"Like Marines b'have any better?"

"Jerry worked with *preacher* Marines. He wudn' like 'em others."

"He told ya he was a chaplain's aide?"

"Yeah. A chaplain's aide. Yew didn't know that?"

*That lyin' piece'a shit.*

"Yeah, I knew it. He's mentioned it a few times. Didn't think he'd say anything ta you about it, though. He usually talks about it only when he's real drunk. I don't ever remember ya bein' around when he was 'at drunk."

"It was when all'a us went out ta the Cotton Club three 'r so weeks ago. 'member? Joe Ely was playin'."

"Uh...yeah. I remember. Parts of it."

"He didn't seem ta be all 'at drunk. He jus' started talkin' about it while he was tellin' me about how he wants ta be a preacher someday."

*I can't b'lieve 'at low-life son of a bitch!*

"He'll make a good 'un, no doubt," I said. "He's got all the makin's f'r one."

When we reached the gate Hope dropped my hand and ordered me through first.

"Damn," I hissed.

She giggled quietly.

"C'n I come over t'night an' see mah room?"

"Of course. Me an' Danny won't be home, but Joan's gunna drop a few things off an' Homer's gunna be movin' his stuff inta the smaller room. Y're takin' his old room."

"But..."

"No buts, Hope. It was Homer's idea b'cause he's hardly ever at the house. He wanders in an' showers from time ta time, but I can't remember the last time he spent the night. He usually passes out up at the piano shop."

"Ya sure, 'cause I don't..."

"I'm sure. *Real* sure. That'll put you an' Joan right next ta each other."

"If ya say so," giggling again as she did a little skip. "Ya know whut? I might even go back ta school. Would yew an' Danny he'p me git mah GED? Hugo said I gotta git that since I ain't...since I *don't* got a high school diploma. With a GED, he says they might even let me inta Tech someday," excitedly. "Ta be a teacher."

"Hell yeah, we'll help ya. Maybe you could be a cheerleader."

I ducked as she swung the towel at me. Giggling again, Hope pranced off to the house.

*This is gunna work out fine. This is gunna be a hoot.*

\*\*\*

I gave the bike full throttle as I came out of the turn at University and Broadway. I roared past frat row, went left onto W then raced toward Main. As I approached the corner, I saw Chad sitting on Will's front porch with Will's two sluts. The white haired one was busy painting on a large canvas. Chad, smirking, casually waved.

*Bastard. Always lands on his feet.*

I ran the stop sign, slowed at the alley, turned into the gravel drive, rolled across the dead lawn, and then parked under the covered drive next to Danny's bike. I executed a shortened version of the dismount then ran up the stairs into the kitchen.

Danny was sitting at the rickety little table beginning to wolf down the first of two large Lotto Burgers. He'd unwrapped the other one and had added more ketchup to it.

"What's the matter, Fast Daniel?" reaching for the spare. "Burger not gorpy enough?"

Danny's hand shot out and crushed it. Ketchup and mayonnaise oozed out from between the flattened buns. He picked his hand up slowly and looked at the mess in his palm.

"See what happens ta stingy bastards?" I remarked.

Danny wiped the goop from his hand with the smashed burger then tossed it back onto the table.

"Better eat it fast," as he pointed at the sloppy mess. "Don't want to be late for work," then took a giant bite from the one he was holding.

"Yeah, right," I frowned. "Y're willin' ta share now ya've turned it inta barf on a bun."

Danny reached for it. I beat him to it then rushed into the bathroom to shower.

After dressing, I joined Homer and Danny in the living room. I asked Homer if I could borrow his truck to move Hope on Thursday evening.

"Sounds good," he answered. "I'm moving my things into the smaller room tonight."

"Hope'll be droppin' over later on ta check her room out," I told them.

Homer stood up.

"Better get started then," moving toward the doorway.

Danny remained prone on one of the three couches in the room.

"So, what else did Hope have ta say?" Danny yawned.

Homer paused for the report.

"She's still feelin' pr'tty good about the move. I don't think she'll change her mind."

Homer walked into the hall.

"Uh...Homer!" I called out.

Homer stepped back into the room.

"Don't any of ya take this wrong, but Hugo talked ta me this mornin' about Hope movin' in here. Seems like she's b'come sort'a like a...a daughter 'r somethin' ta Hugo. He asked me ta make sure we take real good care of her an' watch out for her. He says he's not worried about us. He's hopin' we'll just keep an eye on her in gen'ral. I told him I'd pass 'at on ta ever'body."

Danny rolled from the couch onto the floor, ending up on all fours.

"No sweat," slowly standing up, groaning throughout the whole process.

Homer looked at me seriously.

"If I hear of anybody messing with her...," pausing. "Well, I don't think anybody's going to mess with her," and left the room.

"Ready to go?" Danny, stretching his arms out and arching his back.

"Walk?"

"Yeah. We've got time."

We yelled goodbye to Homer and left.


Danny headed toward Will's place.

"Let's go this way," as I turned down the alley.

"What's wrong?" Danny, coming up along side me.

"Looks like Chad's moved in with Will. Chad was sittin' out front with a coupl'a those hairdressers when I came home. Just as soon not run inta the little fuck-wad."


We lit up and shuffled our way down the alley, raising a light cloud of dust as we went.

"6:45 and it's still light," Danny commented.

"Yeah. I like the longer days. 'specially when there's no wind."

"Ya know, Gil, I've been wondering...why'd you come back to Lubbock? I mean, of all the places you could have gone, you came back to this shithole. Remember how we used to cuss this place up and down when we were in high school? We couldn't wait to launch out of here."

"Why are you here?" dodging the question.

"Here's the deal." Danny coughed into his fist. "If this son of a bitch in Santa Fe hadn't run off with the company's money, I'd still be out there learning how to make hand painted, kiln fired pool and floor tiles. I ended up back here because I was broke and didn't have anywhere else to go. I've been hanging around because it's...it's comfortable. For now, anyway. Believe me, I'd like to find a way to blast my ass out. So...what brought you back?"

"I came back ta go ta school," flatly.

"You could have gone to school in better places than this."

"I guess havin' friends here had somethin' ta do with comin' back," hoping that might be the end of it.

"Bullshit," Danny snorted. "You didn't even look anybody up when you got back. Besides, you make friends faster than a Brando look-a-like in a leather bar."

"Sometimes."

"Can't you remember the *exact* moment you decided 'By God, I'm gunna go back to Lubbock because...,' " then pointed at me while raising his eyebrows, attempting to coax a response.

"B'cause," and paused to consider how honest my response needed to be, "b'cause it was a decision I didn't have ta put a lot'a thought into at the time I had ta make it," opting for honesty. "I guess 'at's why. I mean, decidin' ta come back here made the whole thing easier. The whole thing about where ta go. What ta do next. I mainly just wanted ta go someplace where I could think some things through. Pull it back togeth...figure some things out," backing away from total honesty. "Lubbock felt like a good idea. I don't regret it. Not yet anyway. I don't mind it here. I've got a good job. I'm meetin' some decent people. I'm in school. If I could find a sweet young thing ta fall in love with me an' fuck me numb three 'r four times a day...I'd be happy as hell."

"It'll change."

"Goddamn hope so. I'm beginnin'' ta think my balls're gunna stay blue f'rever."

"No, I meant the way you feel about Lubbock will change. It'll begin to close in on you. It's really amazing that a place with so much open space...it's really amazing how claustrophobic this place can be."

"Is it me or are you feelin' kind'a down t'night?" glancing over at him.

"It's me. I've been thinking too much today."

"What's botherin' ya?"

"Nothing, Gil. Really. Nothings bothering me. I get an itch now and then and can't figure out where to scratch. I stole that line from Hugo."

"Sounds like a Hugo line."

We crossed the street and approached the front door of the club. I wanted to get the initial contact with Sonny out of the way.

*If I didn't need the job so bad, I'd quit f'r what she'd done ta Homer. Bitch.*

We were greeted by the sound system screaming "Jeremiah Was a Bullfrog" at full volume.

"Holy Christ," I shouted. "That sounds like pure crap!"

"Jonas didn't strike me as being a Three Dog Night kind of guy," Danny shouted back.

"He was pro'bly lyin' about bein' a pre-vet major to," continuing to shout.

We walked into the bar area and knocked on the office door. It flew open. A big dandy looking dork stepped out.

"Sonny here?" I asked.

"Who wants ta know?" the dork snarled.

"It's discourteous to answer a question with a question," Danny smiled. "So, here's the deal...you answer *his* question then it will be yo*ur* turn..."

"They're the ones I was tellin' ya about, Max!" a voice from behind us.

"Y're both fired!" the dork. "Get out'a here!" spinning around, stepping back into the office, and then slamming the door.

Danny and I turned to see who the bastard was who'd, as far as we were concerned, just gotten us canned. The two frat guys I'd sent home on the first night were standing outside the storeroom. One came over to us.

"Whut's the matter?" he sneered. "Lookin' f'r work?"

I had blood on my shirt before I realized Danny'd even thrown a punch. The guy's head popped back then his body collapsed onto the floor. The little shit was out cold, nose gushing red. The second guy jumped into the storeroom and slammed the door shut. I had never seen Danny commit an act of violence before. I was damn near shocked.

"Christ, Danny," and looked down at the bloodied turd.

"Didn't mean to do that," he said somberly. "Let's get out of here."

I followed him out of the club.

Danny stopped as soon as we got outside. I didn't say a thing while he slowly pulled a cigarette from the pack in his khaki shirt pocket then lit up.

Danny tugged at his shirttails.

"You think he would have fired us if I'd had my shirt tail tucked in?"

"Most likely. It's all wrinkled."

"Fuuuck. I honestly did *not* mean to do that."

"The little snot had it comin'."

"No he didn't," he mumbled. "Let's go find a beer," stepping from the curb.

A pale yellow pickup truck screeched up to the stop sign across the street. The driver began honking the horn and flashing the lights as the truck peeled out then flew through the intersection. Danny jumped back onto the curb as the truck slid to a halt in front of us. It was Sonny. She leaned across to the passenger side and threw the door open.

"Y'all hop in!"

Danny obeyed. I hesitated. I didn't really want to have anything to do with her. I didn't have to. Sonny wasn't my boss anymore.

"Come on, Gil!" she begged. "I need ta talk ta ya! Please!"

She was probably feeling bad about the way she'd dumped on Homer.

*Gimme her side'a the story then want me ta say somethin' about how I understood an' then tell her she shouldn't worry about it an' that I didn't think she was a self-centered little whore.*

"C'mon," Danny urged.

I got in without looking at her. The truck cab stank like perfume and burnt rubber.

"I guess ya'll found out about ever'body bein' fired?" Sonny.

"We didn't get the particulars," Danny, in full perfume shock.

"Where y'all headed?" as she slapped it into first and peeled out.

"We were going over to Mother's," Danny again.

"It's *all* my fault," Sonny whined. "I didn't go in on Sund'y ta clean up 'r close the register out. Max came in Mond'y mornin' an' had a shit fit. Max is the gen'ral manager uv all'a Horace's clubs," taking the corner at Broadway without even pausing for the stop sign. She sped off toward University.

"If y'all still want work, I can git *one'a* ya on as a weeknight bartender at the lounge in the Roadway Inn on Fourth. I'll be workin' at the lounge on the weekends. It's a real nice, cozy little place with a tiny little dance floor an' a jukebox an' real fancy booths. It's a real romantic place," turning onto University while continuing to pitch the job.

"It's never all 'at busy, but it's got its reg'lars 'at hang out there almost ever' evenin' after work. Then there's the hotel guests. The tips c'n be good an' the pace is a lot slower than whut it would'a been at Dancers."

Sonny pulled into a parking space in front of Mother's, leaned forward, and then looked over at me.

"What about it?" brows raised, tip of her tongue touching her upper lip.

Danny and I glanced at each other.

"I don't know about Danny, but I'd like a day 'r two ta sleep on it. Okay?"

"Okay," a little disappointed. " 'member, there's only one openin'. I tell ya whut...whichever one'a ya wants it, jus' show up We'n'sd'y night. I'll come over an' intr'duce ya ta the manager an' show ya aroun' the bar. How about that?"

"That'll work," Danny.

"Okay," as I pushed the door open and stepped out of the cab.

"Gil? C'n I talk with ya a minute more?" she asked as Danny slid out. "Please?"

"I'll be inside," Danny.

Sonny patted the seat. I climbed back into the cab.

*Here it comes.*

"Did Homer..."

"He told me ever'thing," pissed.

"I need ta see him."

"I don't know that Homer's all 'at big on apologies," looking over at her. "Why don't ya just pretend it never happened. Pretend like ya were drunk an' don't remember any of it."

"No. You don't un'erstand. I *like* Homer. I wan'a see him again," her voice trembling a bit. "I know I screwed ever'thang up, but I didn't mean ta. It su'prised me. If he'd'a warned me...I wouldn'a cared a bit. Not a *bit*," leaning over to rest her hand on mine. "*Please*, tell him."

"Okay," and looked out the window. "I'll tell him."

She squeezed my hand and thanked me.

"Wan'a come in an' have a beer?" asking her out of pure politeness.

"Cain't. I'm interviewin' at the Westerner t'night. Gotta go git ready."

"Out by Fiftieth?"

"Yeah. Dance band ever' night. Good crowds all through the week. Should be real good f'r tips. If they like me they'll put me on weekends after a while."

"When ya go ta work t'night, go up ta the band an' ask f'r Roy...the fiddle player. Tell him Gil sent ya. He'll put in a good word for ya."

"Friend'a y'urs?"

"We used ta be gay lovers b'fore I went straight. Be sure ta tell him all 'at. Tell him 'at ya met his ex-lover, Gil."

"I'll do that," laughing, visibly relieved by my kidding with her. "Please talk ta Homer as soon as ya c'n," reminding me again. "Tell him I'll be at the Roadway ever' night this week. Okay?"

"I will," and hopped out of the truck.

*Wonder what it feels like ta have somethin' 'at fine, 'at nasty, 'at fuckin' hot cravin' ya as much as she seems ta be cravin' Homer.*

I walked into Mother's.

"Danny swears y're gunna b'have y'urself t'night," Bo told me as I walked passed the bar. "Is 'at right? Yew gunna b'have?"

"What in my present demeanor would indicate otherwise, Bo?"

Since the fight back in December, Bo would ask me and Homer the same damn question whenever we'd come in. The owner'd wanted to ban us from the bar forever, but Bo'd stuck up for us and got it reduced to thirty days.

Danny and I had a few beers then headed for the house. Danny launched into his theory about how an invisible rubber band was tied to his ass, so whenever he tried to leave Lubbock, he'd only make it so far before it would snap him back. I reminded him of a bumper sticker we'd seen once back in high school—"Lubbock Doesn't Blow, It Sucks".

Hope's and Joan's cars were parked in the gravel drive.

My stomach jumped, my groin tingled.

We could hear the radio in Danny's room belting out some Rod Stewart as we passed through the kitchen. I walked to the living room and peeked around the corner. JD was passed out on one of the sofas. An empty pint of apricot brandy rested on his bare chest.

"In here!" Danny called out from Homer's new room.

I walked back to the end of the hall and looked in. Homer was stretched out on the floor. Hope and Joan were sitting cross-legged opposite him. Homer wasn't wearing his bandanna.

"Fired that fast?" Homer.

"Fuc...hell no," catching myself. "We quit. Benefits sucked."

"Seriously," Joan. "What happened?"

"Fired by the owner," I told her. "F'r liein' about our experience," trying to keep it short.

"Oh, well," Homer.

"Yeah," I nodded. "Oh, well."


Homer'd been showing some of his grandfather's things to the girls. Joan gently lifted an eagle's wing from the carpet.

"This was his grandfather's," she informed us. "He was a Cherokee shaman."

Homer tensed and looked at the floor.

"Yeah, I know. Ya should'a seen his place."

Homer relaxed, but still wouldn't look at me.

Hope held up the leather piece with the drawings on it.

"An' this...look at this," awe struck with the seeming authenticity of the artifact. "Yew ever seen anythang like it?" reverently placing it back on the carpet.

"What was it like?" Joan, excitedly as Danny and I joined them on the floor.

I poked Homer with my foot.

"Ya mind me tellin' 'em?"

"Nah. Go ahead."

"Well, it was really neat. It was just one room with animal skins, a wood burnin' stove, an' all kinds'a sacred things layin' around. The door faced east since that's the direction the Spirits'd come from. Homer told me that. What's hard ta describe is the feelin' ya got. Real calm. Protected. Like ya could'a laid down inside an' the whole world would'a left ya alone," looking over at Homer.

He was fidgeting with the pouch.

"Remember in mind control," I asked Joan and Hope, "when they ask ya ta imagine y'urself in the most comf'tr'ble, peaceful place ya've ever been?"

They nodded.

"When I do that now, I put myself in his grandad's place, layin' on this comf'tr'ble lookin' cot covered in thick quilts with the fire in the pot belly stove goin' an' the wind blowin' snow outside."

"I wish I could see it," Joan, reaching over and touching Homer's leg. "C'n we go see it sometime?" eyes wide.

"Can't," Homer snapped.

Joan looked surprised. Hurt.

"Can't," I jumped in, "b'cause…b'cause they had ta set fire to it as part'a the burial ceremony. A shaman's place has ta be burned. It's a Cherokee thing."

That sounded reasonable to the girls.

"Homer was tellin' us about Sahdahk an' Tohkahm," Hope, "but I guess yew already know about it."

"A little bit."

*Tohkahm? Sahdahk?*

"It's so beautiful," Joan. "I wish I had some kind'a connection to a spiritual tradition like that."

"Got the Bahai's," I reminded her.

"It's…it's not the same. I b'lieve in Baha'u'llah, but it's not like bein' born into an' raised around a purely natural, spiritual interpretation'a the universe. Like Indians have."

"Did have," Homer.

Joan missed his comment.

"Don't ya think bein' religious an' bein' spiritual're two completely different things?" Joan.

"Religious people can't be spiritual?" Danny.

"I didn't mean that. What I'm sayin' is…in *practicin'* a religion it seems like a lot'a people lose sight'a the spiritual side of it. They think the rituals and beliefs of their religion are all there is to being spiritual. That's why I think religion c'n prevent spiritual growth in some cases."

"I think the majority of religious people don't care about the spiritual," I huffed. "All they want is ta sleep at night an' not sweat burnin' in Hell f'r anything they do wrong."

"Bein' religious is easy," Homer. "Bein' *spiritual* is a bitch."

Everyone agreed.

"It's hell puttin' it inta words, idn't it?" yawning while I stared at Joan's breasts.

"I b'lieve in Jesus, but I don't go ta church," Hope. "So, am I religious 'r spiritu'l?"

"It's what you do with your belief in Jesus that decides that," Homer. "If your belief causes you to do things and feel things that help you grow spiritually then you are adding to your Tohkahm. Anything you do or feel that doesn't allow your Tohkahm to grow is considered Sahdahk."

"Good versus bad," I mumbled.

"No," Homer. "Good and bad are about judging. Tohkahm and Sahdahk aren't about judging. They're about becoming more spiritual or not becoming more spiritual."

"How come there's so many differ'nt religions but there's s'posed ta be j'st one God?" Hope. "Seems ta me like only one uv 'em could be tellin' the truth." Hope.

"Unless they're all lyin'," Danny.

"Faith," I said. "If somebody *really* wants somethin' ta be the truth, the guy *makes* it true just by b'lievin' it's the truth. He has *faith* that it's the truth. Faith is the divine abracadabra."

"But that don't make it true f'r ever'body else does it?" Hope.

Joan started to answer.

"It's…"

"It's bedtime," I yawned again.

"Yeah, that's a question that could take a while," Danny.


"So, Hope, whud'a ya think'a the place?" as I stood up.

"I thank it's real nice," smiling generously. "I thank I'm gunna like it here."

"It's filthy dirty!" Joan squealed. "This weekend everybody's gunna stick around an' help clean it up."

*What the hell is this?*

Homer, Danny, and I exchanged glances.

"Okay?" Joan pressed for a commitment. "Hope's already said she c'n help."

*This thing is gunna happen. Joan had already made up her mind ta that, an', by God, ever'body was gunna help...or else.*

"I'll be here," not disguising my reluctance, "but not 'til after I'm off work at noon."

*There! Put my foot down on 'at 'un .*

"I'll be here," Danny.

Homer nodded. I said goodnight then left the room. I turned and stuck my head back in the door.

"Homer," raising my brows, "when ya have a chance, I need ta talk ta ya."

"Sure. Tomorrow soon enough?"

"Yeah."


I was beat. I pulled my boots off and lay on the pallet without taking my clothes off. Danny said his goodnights. I listened to each creaking step as he walked to his room. Homer, Joan, and Hope returned to talking about Homer's grandfather, Joan desperately trying to draw parallels between the Baha'i Faith and Homer's shamanism. JD was snoring loudly in the living room.


A car occasionally clattered its way down Tenth. The breeze through the open window was cool. Summer was on its way. In a few more weeks it would be staying in the seventies until midnight.

*Dust'll stop blowin' soon. Worst'a that shit's over f'r a while. Hate surveyin' in the dirt an' wind like 'at. Fuckin' sand blastin' the skin off y'ur face an' hands. Fillin' up y'ur ears an' nose. Makes ever'thing smell like...dirt.*

*Cold.*

*Shit.*

*Goddamn wind makes ever'body in town half crazy.*

*It's been worse. It's been worse.*

*The rivers.*

*Trompin' cotton.*

*Damn shame I've already racked up enough reference points 'at'd make surveyin' in a freezin'-ass sand storm look like easy money.*

*Sure would'a never even considered trompin' cotton four years ago.*

*Reference points.*

*Chief Osborne. Scott Osborne.*

*From Minnesota.*

*Told me all about reference points.*

*Back in the Navy.*

*Reference points're what's b'hind all of a person's decisions.*

Yawn.

*Ya start out with no reference points, then ya b'gin experiencin' things. Some good. Some bad. Soon, y're sayin' "worse" an' "better" an' comparin' things ta y'ur reference points.*

"Your best piece of ass is only going to be as good as your sorriest piece was sorry. And don't let anybody tell you there's no such thing as a sorry piece of ass."

*The chief swore 'at applied ta ever'thing in life.*

"The best thing you can do for some whiny son uv a bitch is to explain reference points to him then shove a mussel covered piling up his ass."

*That's what the chief called "referential therapy".*

A long, deep yawn.

*Eatin' crap.*

"Nobody gets through life without having to eat some crap from time to time, but call it what it is when it happens and, goddammit, have the balls to be discriminating about what kind and how much you're willing to choke down and be prepared for the complications whenever you decide not to swallow."

*I'm beginnin' ta see what he meant by that...the more crap ya manage to choke down, the less complicated y'ur life b'comes. The more crap ya eat, the less people're gunna fuck with ya.*

*He called it coprophagy...decidin' how much crap you're willin' ta eat in any given situation.*

*I'm beginnin' ta see that.*

*I should switch my major ta business. Sell the bike an' get a Mustang. A convertible. Get a job in a bank. Make more money. Wear a suit an' tie. Move inta a nice place by myself. Not have ta work outside in the cold an' wind an' dust. I could change a few things here an' there an'pro'bly have it a lot easier.*

I flashed on a grade school cafeteria wall poster in Beeville, Texas.

You Are What You Eat.

Another huge yawn accompanied by a shivering stretch.

*Reference points an' dietary decisions. That's the whole ball'a wax accordin' ta the chief.*

*Hugo an' the chief would'a gotten along fine. An' JD.*

*Wish the chief could...*

*Damn. Just plain damn...*

Something startled me awake.

Confused. Disoriented.

*Oh, shit! Was I snorin'?*

I held my breath, listening intently between exploding heartbeats.

*The Dylan poster...my guitar...Lubbock...*

I relaxed. I crawled to the window and eased my head out into the night.

Hushed voices. Someone was on the roof. I looked over at the clock on the chest of drawers.

*1:30? What the...*

I went to the toilet then worked my way to the kitchen as quietly as possible. The front door was wide open. The soft voices fell silent as I walked out onto the stoop. Joan's car was still parked in the drive. Jerry's van was parked along the curb on W. I climbed onto the bottom rung of the railing and peered over the top of the eave.

*Homer, Jerry, an' Joan.*

"Git me a beer," Jerry whispered.

I pointed at Homer. He nodded yes. Joan, covered with a blanket, appeared to be asleep on her side, head resting on her hands.

I took three bottles from the frig and stepped back out to the porch. Jerry's arm was dangling over the eave. I slipped the neck of a bottle between each of his fingers. Jerry carefully raised them up and out of sight. I climbed to the top rail and eased myself onto the roof. I sat down next to Homer. Jerry reached over and handed me my beer.

"We wake ya up?" Jerry asked.

"Nah. I'm always up dickin' around at 1:30 in the morn..."

"Pissy, pissy, bitchy, bitchy," Jerry cut me off. "I don't really give a shit. I wuz jus' tryin' ta be a fuckin' buddy, man. Fig'red ya could use a friend after gettin' shit canned at the bar after one night. I was countin' on yew keepin' at..."

"Joan need ta be anywhere t'morrow?" I asked Homer.

"Fuckin' loser," Jerry muttered.

"She didn't say anything about it," Homer answered.

"I wish she'd go ta wearin' dresses, man," Jerry cackled. "This'd be a good time ta find out whud only her hairdresser knows."

Homer shook his head. Joan stirred under the blanket.

"That's rude, ya pervert," she yawned.

" 'at's whu' ya git f'r listen' in on conversations you ain't invited to."

"Good evenin', Joan," I said.

"Good evenin', Gil."

Jerry, Homer, and I lit cigarettes then sat quietly staring into a star packed sky.

After finishing my cigarette, I leaned back on my elbows.

"So what's got ever'body up so late on a weeknight?"

No one answered right away. Jerry finally spoke.

"Couldn't sleep. Sometimes I jus' lay there with this feelin' I'm s'posed ta be doin' somethin' real import'nt 'r feelin' like I f'rgot ta do somethin' an' I'm gunna git busted f'r not doin' it. Like missin' a watch in the Marines 'r somethin'. Know whud I mean?"

I thought it over, cleared my throat, and sat up.

"I usually can't sleep b'cause I lay there feelin' like I should have some kind'a plan goin'. It's like…I know I gotta have one. Just can't figure out why 'r f'r what. It's a real pain in the ass," pausing. "How about you, Homer. You got a plan?"

"I guess I have a plan. Sort of."

"Damn. Jus' spill y'ur fuckin' guts," Jerry snorted.

"Sorry," Homer yawned. "California. I guess," lighting a cigarette.

" 'at's it? Jerry winced. "Californya? I *guess*? Tha's the *whole* fuckin' plan?"

"It's not the *whole* plan," sitting up. " It's kind of a start."

"That's not the kind'a plan I was talkin' about," scratching my forehead. "I was talkin' about a long range plan with all the moves figured out f'r the next fifty years 'r so. That's all I hear out on campus. Some'a those guys're already talkin' about when they're gunna buy a house, how much money they're gunna be worth when they're thirty, when they're gunna start havin' kids an' how many they're gunna have. When they're gunna retire, an' on, an' on. Ever' blessed step laid down pat. Fuck me. I can't figure it out like 'at. I just figure ever'thing's gunna be okay 'r I'll take care'a shit as it pops up. I mean, what's wrong with 'at? What gets me is how it makes ya feel like'a dip shit b'cause ya *don't* have it fig'red out like they do. Like I'm a fucked up 'r somethin'," then looked over at Homer and Jerry.

"Be careful, man," Jerry, rocking slightly. "When ya go ta

thinkin' that ya ought'a be thinkin' like *they* do...'at's when ya start fuckin' y'ur life up. 'at's why I stay the fuck away from 'at place. Excep' when I'm trollin', if ya catch my drift," and snickered.

"JERRY!" Joan squealed.

"Anyhow," Jerry continued, "whud*ever* ya do, *don't* go ta thinkin' f'r a split secon' 'at that shit them fuckers're shovelin' is anything else *but* shit. Don't go b'lievin' *y'ur* way'a thinkin's wrong. 'at's how they win, man...when *yew* go ta thinkin' an' actin' like 'em an' wantin' the same shit they want jus' 'cause *they* wan' it. 'at's how they win. When ya b'come jus' like 'em...they fuckin' win an' *yew* fuckin' lose. Ya wan'a know *why* ya lose? 'cause *yew* didn' start out like 'em. Ya let 'em *change* ya. 'at's the truth. 'at's whu' sellin' out's all about, man. Ya see, Gil, college ain't *all* about makin' ya smart. It also teaches ya how ta fuck people over. Ya learn ta be a doctor 'r a lawyer 'r somethin' else like 'at, but the big thing ya come away from Tech with is the *moves*. Ya learn all'a the fuckin' moves. If ya don't git the moves down then nothin' else ya learn on 'at campus is gunna do shit f'r ya. Gil, ya know how y're always knockin' on frats? Well, guess whut? They're the only motherfuckers learnin' the moves, man. Ever'body else out there's jus' wastin' their time."

"You through?" I asked real shitty.

"Hear 'at, Homer?" and slapped Homer's leg. "I went an' pissed him off. Hurt his feelin's."

"I'm not pissed off, but I don't agree with some'a what ya said."

"I still ain't through completely," starting to cackle, "but I could use a break. Educatin' yew about whu's *really* goin' on's wearin' my ass out," slapping Homer's leg again.

"In the first place," as I leaned forward to see around Homer, "there's a lot'a people out there just tryin' ta fig're things out. An' there's some 'at just like goin' ta school an' learnin' ever'thing they can. An' then there's some of us who appreciate bein' around people who've done more'n jus' looked at the pictures in some Bible somewhere an' then put it down thinkin' they've got all the answers."

"Yew slammin' me?" Jerry.

"*Now* who's pissed?" Joan, from under the blanket.

"I ain't pissed," Jerry snapped. "An' mind y'ur own damn b'ness, woman."

"Jerry," wiping my hand over my face, "an' I'm serious as a heart beat…I'm not goin' ta Tech ta learn any moves 'r ta try an' get rich…"

"With a degree in hist'ry," Jerry interrupted, "I don't think ya got anything ta worry abou' there," and broke up cackling.

*Fuck it.*

"Shit," Jerry snorted, "if yew got all 'at time ta waste an' all 'at goddamn money ta burn, hell, go ahead. Do it. Blow ever'thing ya got. Ain't my life, man."

" 'at's right. It *ain't* y'ur damn life."


Jerry took a long tug on his bottle then pulled a joint from his riding jacket. He lit up and offered me a drag. I took a hit then gave it to Homer. Jerry filled his lungs one more time before continuing.

"Ya know whud else I think about when I cain't sleep? Churches, man. Churches'll fuck ya up too. 'at's why I don't go ta church. Church people don't go ta church ta learn how ta be like Jesus anymore. They go ta church ta git the go-ahead. Ya see, college says, 'This is how ya fuck people' an' the church says 'Don't go feelin' bad about fuckin' people 'specially if they ain't the same religion as yew'. It ain't *God* sayin' 'at…it's the church. They're all a bunch'a motherfuckers. God an' Jesus ain't 'at-a-way. Know whud I'm sayin'? God's cool, man. I know 'at f'r a fact 'cause I'm makin' Him mad all'a the time, but…He un'erstands the way it is. He cuts a lot'a guys like me a lot'a slack 'cause He knows we're tryin', man. 'at's pr'tty fuckin' cool."

A long moment of silence.

"What'a about that, Homer?" scratching my beard.

"An' don't go spillin' y'ur guts like ya did with 'at plan'a y'urs," Jerry. "I cain't han'le any more'a y'ur 'motional outbursts."

"I don't know," Homer. "I've never spent much time thinking about church. I was always thinking about other things, I guess."

"Yeah," Jerry. "Like when the nex' train load'a canned gover'ment beef wuz gunna show up at the reservation."

Joan kicked Jerry in the ribs.

"Dammit, woman!" grabbing Joan's leg before she could kick him again. " 'at fuckin' hurt!"

"Didn't hurt as much as that last comment hurt Homer!" Joan.

"Shhhhh!" I hissed.

Jerry let go of her leg.

"What time is it?" Joan.

Nobody had a watch.

"It was 1:30 when I came top-side," I said. "That's been about an hour ago. Ya have ta work t'morrow?"

"No. I should be goin' though."

"Stay here," I suggested. "Hell, ya live here now."

"No thanks. I don't want anybody peekin' up my jeans," and kicked Jerry again.

"Don't be kickin' at me all'a the time, woman," he snarled while slapping her foot away.

Homer scooted over to the edge of the roof then eased himself down. His forehead was visible as he stood on the porch. Joan sat on the edge and let her legs dangle over the side. Homer reached up, put his hands around her waist, and then gently lowered her to the porch. Jerry and I climbed down and watched Joan go to her car. Waving goodbye, she drove away.

"Time ta go ta bed...again," I yawned.

"I'm gunna grab a beer an' walk aroun' a li'l bit. Min' if I sleep in y'ur drive t'night?" Jerry.

Homer shook his head.

"You c'n sleep inside if ya want," I offered.

"Nah. 'at's cool. The van'll work."

Jerry made his way into the kitchen then down the stairs with a beer in one hand and a cigarette in the other. We watched him head toward Broadway, slowly fading into the darkness beyond the street light.

"I'm gunna sit out here a while longer," Homer, lowering himself into a sitting position, and letting his legs dangle over the edge of the porch.

"Okay. By the way, 'at thing I wanted ta talk ta ya about? It's about..."

"Sonny?"

I wasn't sure if Homer really knew it was about Sonny or if he was only hoping it would be something about her. I sat down on the top step and lit a cigarette.

"She wan..."

"She wants you to apologize for her for what happened," cutting me off.

"Christ, Homer. If y're gunna carry this whole fuckin' conversation then I'll just go inside an' flip through a titty magazine. Come get me when I'm finished talkin' so I c'n get some sleep. Okay?" and began to stand up.

"No, no," placing his hand on my shoulder. "I'm being a prick. Go ahead. What's she want?"

"She wants ta see ya again...an' again, an' again, an' again 'cause she can't get enough of that groin arrow'a y'urs."

"She said *that*?" and smiled.

"Yeah, Homer," burying my face in my hands. "Those were her exact words. No...wait a minute, Homer. Her *exact* words were 'I cain't git enough'a his throbbin', blood gorged, warrioresque groin arrow.'"

We didn't say anything for over a minute.

Finally, Homer spoke.

"You sure she said *warrioresque*? That doesn't sound like a word she'd be using."

I stood up.

"She's workin' ever' night at a lounge in the Roadway over on Fourth. Know the place?"

"I can find it."

I moved toward the doorway then stopped and turned.

"Homer?"

"Yeah."

"She honest-ta-God wants ta see ya. I honest-ta-God think she likes ya."

Homer nodded.

*\*\*\**

I was about to shove three bales of alfalfa over the edge of the loft to the barn floor when I heard a hoarsely shouted, "Gil!" from below, followed by a throat clearing hack then a loud spitting sound.

"Goddamn," Roy, raspy as hell.

"Up here in'a loft!"

"Put it back in y'ur pants an' git down here! Hugo's havin' a nut over them tornadas 'at hit outside'a Amarilla last night!" More hacking and spitting.

I kicked the bales over the side. The barn filled with dust as they thudded to the ground.

"Goddammit, ya sorry ass son uv a..." Roy's voice trailed off as he moved outside to escape the cloud.

I walked over to the loft hatch and poked my head out.

"Allergic ta alfalfa?" looking down at him.

"Allergic ta stupidass sons'a bitches. Git down here quick."

I lowered myself through the hatch and dropped to the ground.

We walked back toward the office, Roy taking long, quick steps.

"Hugo wants us ta board up all'a the windows on the place an' git all'a his sorry-ass animals inta the barn. Then we gotta git those two queer-ass fightin' minnows out'a the tank an' move all'a the loose shit layin' aroun' the place inta the garages 'r the barn."

"Amarilla's a hun'r'd miles from here an' 'at was last night," trying to keep up.

"Too damn close f'r Hugo. It's late in'a season, but he says he wants ta be safe. It was a late 'un 'at flattened Guadeloupe last year. Fucked up a bunch'a places in the ghetto too. Killed some people."

"That's still the other side'a town," not convinced there was any real danger. "When's the last time one's come out this way?"

"It's been a while, so he fig'res it's our turn, I guess. Who the hell knows. He thanks it, so 'at's the way it is. Hurry up. Know anybody c'n come out an' he'p?"

"Maybe. How much ya gunna pay 'em?"

"Twice whut yew git 'cause they're pro'bly gunna be worth it."

"Ya really b'lieve one's gunna hit here?"

"I've been here since '54. Hugo's been right about half the time. None uv 'em hit exactly here, but he's been about fifty-fifty f'r Lubbock County. 'at's better'n the weatherman."

"Hey! Almost f'rgot. Did a new waitress start workin' at the Westerner last night?"

"Name'a Sonny?"

"That's the one. Homer's seein' her."

"Yeah, well, thanks ta yew, I had ta give her six orgasms b'fore she'd b'lieve I wudn' ever married to yew. She was pro'bly convinced after her fourth 'un, but she lied about it j'st ta squeeze a coupl'a extras out. Ya sure Homer knows how ta han'le somethin' 'at needy?"

When we reached the office, I called the piano shop. Homer answered the phone.

"Hey, Homer. It's me."

"Hey."

"Ya sound a little beat."

"Hung over. Should'a gone to bed when you did," mumbling.

"Hugo says a tornado's comin' an' needs some help out here."

"Yeah, I know. He was at the house looking for you right after you left this morning. He picked up Joan and now he's on the way to

Vann's to see if he can get Doug and Vann. Danny and Jerry are on the way. Once we're done here at the shop, we'll be coming out."

"That ought'a do."

"Ought'a."

"How long b'fore ya show up?"

"Couple hours. We're covering everything here with plastic sheets and nailing those pieces of plywood up front into place. Then we have to go to the strip. JD's run out of everything."

"Why don't ya stop an' have somethin' ta eat an' maybe catch a double feature at the movies while y're at it?"

"It's only a tornado. Have to keep the priorities straight. Have to go. JD's yelling for me. See you in a little while."

"See ya." I hung up and ran into the garage.

Roy'd removed two unsecured pieces of plywood from the garage ceiling. He was in the rafters pulling window sized pieces of plywood from the interior of the attic over to the opening.

"Grab these as I pass 'em down," Roy ordered. "Stack 'em in the same order they come down."

"I got hold'a Homer at JD's place. He said Hugo's on his way with some more help. Homer an' JD are comin' too," and took three pieces from Roy. "Where's Hope?"

"I put her ta chasin' the animals inta the barn."

Several Harleys roared up the drive. Seconds latter, Jerry drove right into the garage, loudly gunning his bike as it rolled to a stop. Two other choppers made a few circles in the parking area before easing up to the fence and stopping. The riders gunned their bikes a few times, then killed the engines.

"Whut the hell is 'at?" Roy.

*Christ. Roy's gunna have a ball with this. Three hippie bikers ta rag on.*

Jerry's engine died. He set the kickstand, leaned the bike over, and then stood up. Jerry, still straddling the bike, slowly removed his goggles and fingerless gloves. Roy stuck his head through the opening.

"Roy, this is Jerry," anxiously anticipating Roy's opening shots.

"Glad ta meet ya," Roy nodded politely.

Jerry looked up and nodded.

*What the shit?*

The two other bikers entered the garage.

" 'at's Eduardo," Jerry, pointing at the larger man.

Eduardo was stout. Husky. He was wearing the standard pirate tied bandanna on his head, a blue jean jacket, dirty, faded jeans, fingerless, oil and grease stained leather gloves, and a pair of scuffed, black riding boots. Sunglasses on a strip of leather dangled around his neck. Eduardo came across as being a friendly kind of guy, nodding at me and smiling broadly when introduced.

Jerry pointed at the second rider.

" 'at's Tomas."

Tomas was much shorter at around five foot eight or so. Round, but solid. Built low to the ground and compact. He was wearing a bandanna and a pair of goggles. The rest of his outfit wasn't exactly biker chic—tennis shoes, khaki pants, a clean, white tee shirt— sleeves stretched to the limit by telephone pole biceps. No gloves. Tomas nodded when introduced then looked away shyly.

"Glad ta meet all'a y'all," Roy. "Glad ya could make it," then waved before crawling back into the rafters.

*No hippie-biker remarks! No insults! That's…'at's bullshit!*

I walked over to Eduardo and Tomas.

*Roy's jackin' with me. That's what's goin' on.*

"Que paso?" Eduardo, smiling broadly while shaking my hand.

"Nada," I answered, returning his smile.

"Espanol?" Eduardo.

"Muy pokito."

"Si, bien, bien."

"Don't let him put ya on Ed," Jerry sneered. "Only Mexican Gil knows is how ta order a beer, tell a whore he loves her, an' ask her how many pesos its gunna cost him."

Danny and Tomas laughed.

"Quantos pesos por una hora?" I asked Tomas as I shook his hand.

More laughter.

"We been buddies since grade school," Jerry explained. "I wuz married ta their cousin. Ran inta 'em while I wuz walkin' aroun' las' night. Ended up at the piana shop gittin' wrecked with JD. Hugo come by this mornin' an' said there'd be beer an' some cash if we helped out."

"And women," Ed grinned. "Foxy white women."

Jerry looked around the garage.

"There is gunna be some beer ain't there?"

"As soon as JD an' Homer get here," I assured him. "They're on their way ta the strip right now."

Hope burst into the garage.

"Jerry! Why'd yew do that?" as she stamped her foot. "I almos' had all'a 'em ducks in the barn 'til y'all come drivin' up. Git out here an' he'p me gather 'em up again! All'a y'all!" waving her arms at Ed and Tomas. "C'mon!" then spun around and was gone.

"Bitch," Jerry, mumbling while following after her, Ed and Tomas close behind.

Roy stuck his head back through the opening, gazed at Jerry's bike, and then whistled softly. I stomped over to the hole in the overhead.

"How come ya let 'em off without a word?"

"Who?"

"You know who. Jerry an' 'em. Ya didn't say a damn thing to 'em about their clothes. Their bikes. Bein' hung over as shit. Why they're not workin' on a weekday. Nothin'! Not even a hippie joke."

"It's 'cause they ain't hippies. They're bikers. I respect bikers."

"I gotta fuckin' bike an' all ya ever give me is grief."

"But ya see, Gil, y're a *hippie* with a bike. They're j'st plain ol' bikers. There's a big-ass diff'r'nce, but I ain't got time right now ta enlighten ya, so, git y'ur hippie-ass movin'."

Hugo pulled into the lot. Joan, Doug and Vann were with him. Danny roared up the drive right behind them. The instant the bike shut down we could hear Hope hollering in the distance.

"Hey, Danny! Joan!" I yelled from the garage. "It's pro'bly best ya go help Hope an' 'em with the ducks an' stuff."

"On my way," Danny, heading for the gate.

Hugo, Vann and Doug entered the garage.

"Looks like a damn motorcycle convention," Hugo chuckled.

"Jerry brought some friends with him," I told him.

"Good. The more hands, the quicker we c'n get things tied down."

Hugo introduced Doug and Vann to Roy then headed to the house.

"Long time no see," as I shook Vann's hand.

"Finals," frowning.

"Hey, Doug. Haven't seen ya since Saturd'y night. Looked like ya was havin' a real good time."

"Uh...it...it was...," slowly moving his hands in front of his face as if shaping the sentence in clay. "Actually it...it was not a *real* good time, however,...it was...pleasant."

He seemed to be annoyed, nervous about something.

Roy came down from the rafters and explained the labeling system on the precut pieces. We began taking the pieces to the house and matching them up with the windows. The duck herders returned. They joined in carrying the window covers to the house. Homer and JD arrived and began putting the covers in place. The rest of us set about moving loose equipment into the garage. By 11:30 the whole place was secured.

Hugo gathered everybody in the parking area. Way to the north, barely above the horizon, a line of dark gray clouds was beginning to build.

"I really appreciate y'ur helpin' me out. I'm gunna give each'a ya a ten dollar bill," and began passing the bills out. "There's beer in the garage if anybody wants ta hang around here an' wait it out. Go ahead an' make y'urselves at home."

We looked off to the north.

"I'm gunna stick aroun' an' work on my carb'retor," Jerry. "C'n I use a few'a y'ur tools, Hugo?"

Hugo pointed at the toolboxes. Ed and Tomas needed to get back to town. They stuffed a few beers in their saddlebags. After thanking Hugo and saying goodbye to everybody, they mounted up and rumbled down the drive.

"Nice guys," I told Jerry. "I'm surprised they let a jerkoff like you marry inta the clan."

"Yeah. We been through some shit t'gether, man. They chop Harleys. They go ta Mexico City ever' year an' pick up a few police bikes dirt cheap at the auction. They bring' 'em back here, chop 'em an' then sell 'em. Tomas, the young guy...he's a hell uv a artist. Does custom air brush jobs on bike frames an' cars, an' vans, an' shit like 'at."

"How about a game'a poker?" JD, walking to his truck.

"I'm in," Homer.

Roy, Danny, and Hope all wanted to play. Hugo returned from the ranch house.

"How about yew, Hugo?" Roy. "Been a while since we played a hand t'gether. I'll reteach ya."

"Might as well sign the damn ranch over to ya right now, Roy," Hugo declined. "I'll be upstairs listenin' ta the weather reports."

Joan hurried to the door and slipped past Hugo just before it shut.

Roy turned to me.

"Ya gunna sit in?"

"Nope. Never learned how."

"Ya lyin' bastard. Four years in'a Navy an' ya never played poker? Git y'ur card-sharkin' ass over here."

"It's the truth."

"Y're a goddamn disgrace," shaking his head. "Yew sure yew was born in Texas?"

"Dallas."

"Shit to!" Roy, relieved. " 'at explains ever'thang," and walked into the garage as if that really did explain it.

Within minutes a make shift table was thrown together. JD supplied everyone with a beer. Hope went to the house and returned with an arm full of Dr. Peppers.

"Gil's gunna knit Hope a shawl while the rest of us play poker," Roy. "Ain' 'at sweet uv him, Hope?"

"Ya know, Gil," Jerry snickered, "I could use a wienie warmer if ya c'n git Hope ta size it for me."

Hope threw a can of Dr. Pepper at Jerry.

"Watch the fuckin' bike, man!" deflecting the can off his arm.

"I cain't b'lieve ya thank so little'a Hope 'at ya'd say 'wienie' in front uv her," Roy.

"Yeah, ya...ya," Hope stammered, struggling for a fitting insult without resorting to profanity.

"Cretin." I suggested.

"Yeah! Y're j'st a Cretin!"

I left the barn and walked over to the fence where Vann and Doug, bathed in sunlight, were sitting on the top rung watching the growing darkness to the north. The wind had picked up and the temperature had dropped.

"Been in one'a these b'fore?" I asked Vann.

"Yes. Yes, I have. I was here when the big one hit last May. Extremely scary. Extremely powerful. An excellent experience," without taking his eyes off the building storm.

"How about you, Doug? Were you out'a the Army f'r the big one last year?" and offered Doug a cigarette and a match book.

Doug raised his hands and began to fashion his response.

"Before I...uh...*first,* first...I *will* take the cigarette since you still owe *me* two cigarettes. Remember?"

"Yeah, I remember. It was in front'a the IHO..."

"So, you see...I can accept a cigarette as *repayment. If* you see it as a *loan*...then, I'll *have* to refuse...the...cigarette, since, uh...since you would expect me to...to repay you at sometime in the...future and," breaking into a nervous, quiet, snorting laugh, "and I, at *this* moment...I can't *guarantee* I will *ever* be able to...pay you back. I mean, I don't want to, uh...*obligate* myself. I don't want to, *owe* anyone anything. I don't want...*that* kind of an obligation at...*this* time," taking a deep breath then exhaling loudly. "SO, if you agree to your...your offer being a *re*payment, and, really, Gil, in all honesty, all bullshit aside, that is *exactly* what it is...a *re*payment...*then* I can accept the cigarette."

"Okay," handing over the cigarette.

Doug lit it with his own matches, then, with what looked a bit like a sneer, reminded me I still owed him one cigarette.

"Here," shaking another cigarette from the pack.

"No," waving his hand and smiling broadly. "You see, right now...*you* owe *me.* I like that...*you* owing *me.* I'm going to...to leave it that way for now," and broke into an extended, quiet, wheezing laugh, his deep blue eyes glistening.

"Whatever," and put the cigarettes back into my pocket.

"So, Doug," hoping to initiate something a little more like a conversation than what we'd just been through, "where were ya last year for the big tornado?"

Doug, without acknowledging the question, slid from the fence then asked me where the restroom was.

"It's in the main office. Go through the garage."

Dragging leaden feet, he slowly trudged away.

"How do ya live with 'at?" as I crawled onto the fence and settled down beside Vann.

"He's not that way all the time. He provides challenges for me. Mental challenges. He demands every statement be proven in its minutest detail before accepting it as valid. That is a painfully difficult thing to do. It is an excellent exercise."

"Dudn't it get on y'ur nerves sometimes?"

"Not as long as Jerry keeps the grass prices where they are," smiling. "However, I am *very* much looking forward to the day he finishes building his motorcycle. Gas fumes. Polish fumes. Grease. And I won't miss these two thugs who come by now and then. They hang around and talk with Doug about forming a motorcycle gang."

"Really? What's their names?"

"One is Spanish. Neil."

"I know about Neil. Jerry says he's a real shithead."

"The other one is a big, clumsy, white guy. Calls himself Monster. Very theatrical. He doesn't have a motorcycle. He rides on Neil's. I don't feel comfortable around either one of them. They stay long enough to smoke a joint or two. I think Doug lets them hang around to get a few free tokes."

"Ya know that Jerry won't sell grass ta Neil," I told Vann. "Dudn't trust him."

"I can understand why," nodding his head.


We sat quietly a few minutes, sipping our beers. I liked Vann. He was easy to be around. Quiet. Usually serious, like he was carefully studying everything he observed before categorizing the experience and filing it away. Vann had a calming affect on people, something like the way Hugo did.


Vann looked over his shoulder at the garage then turned back to the storm.

"Doug *was* here last year for the big storm," he said. "Quite a few smaller tornados hit all around the panhandle, but I'm jumping ahead of myself. Doug had begun reading some of my physics books. He ended up reading a lot about energy, some intriguing things about quantum mechanics, and a few biographies about Einstein, Schrödinger and some others. He was really getting into it. You know how he becomes? Terribly excited? One night he told me about his theory of energy and about the existence of an essence most people refer to as God. He decided that, since energy can not be destroyed and since thoughts are energy created as a result of electrical activity in the brain, then thoughts do not vanish. Even the energy produced by the molecular activity of a rock doesn't simply disappear. Instead, these different kinds of energy become part of an infinite, universal energy mass influencing everything that happens."

Vann paused and glanced over at me.

"Are you following this?"

"Think so."

"Doug decided that this essence people perceive as God is really this mass of energy. He decided he could get closer to this energy kind of God if he became more *energy-like*. To become more energy-like would mean he would have to give more and more of his essence over to generating greater energy producing thoughts. To have increasingly powerful thoughts he would have to become more and more intelligent. This would make him more like this God. The closer to God the more powerful Doug would become. The more powerful Doug would become the more control Doug would have over his life. Then...he had a revelation. He concluded storms are a *natural* source of *pure* energy. A person exposed to the energy of a storm and surviving the encounter, like being hit by lightening or smashed in a tidal wave, would absorb a certain amount of this pure energy and be more God-like than other people. Doug kept building on his theory all through the tornado season last year. The tornados kept touching down closer and closer to Lubbock. When the tornado warnings were broadcast for the big one last May, Doug jumped on my bicycle and took off. The tornado hit a little to the north of town about 4:00 in the afternoon. It did a lot of damage in that part of town. Nothing but some downed tree limbs and hail damage to roofs and cars in the ghetto. Doug didn't come home that night. In the morning Doug came walking up the alley. Every square inch of exposed skin was caked in dried blood or covered in mud. His clothes were in shreds. He was barefoot. Even his belt was missing. His hair was all matted with mud and blood. He was a mess. He didn't have my bicycle. He walked right past me and into the house without even looking at me. He laid down on his mat and went to sleep. That was it."

"He ever tell ya about what happened?"

"Weeks, later. We'd gotten fairly wrecked on some hash. He told me he had gone out to the old Lubbock airport the afternoon of the storm and climbed up a water tower that was there. He had tied himself to the railing on the gangway running around the water tank and ridden the tornado out to test his theory about absorbing energy and getting closer to God. After it was over and he'd had time to think about it...he'd decided he'd been *all* wrong. He decided humans are not supposed to get *that* close to God."

"Hell, I guess not if all it's gunna do is get the shit kicked out'a ya," scratching an ear. "Did ya ever get y'ur bicycle back?"

"No," sighing.

"Just proves what a dickhead God can be sometimes. First, he beats the crap out'a Doug then he rips y'ur bike off."

"Exactly. I guess that's why I gave up on the divine. How about you, Gil? Have you had any interesting thoughts about God lately?"

"Some readin' f'r my classes. Nothin' as original as Doug's energy thing."

"Still going to the Baha'i meetings?"

"Yeah. Off an' on."

"I haven't been to one since October or November."

"Didn't like it, huh?"

"It wasn't that at all. I finally accepted the fact that Joan was never going to sleep with me so there was no longer any point in going," nodding to the north. "That is really beginning to look bad. I'm going to go see what Hugo is hearing on the radio. By the way, don't tell anybody about Doug's run in with God," and slid from the fence. "It would embarrass him too much."

"I won't" and jumped down. "Vann?"

"Yes?"

"Can I ask ya somethin'?"

"About the arm?"

I nodded.

"I was shot. By an American."

That threw me.

"He didn't mean to," he said. "He failed to recognize the subtle physical differences between someone from the north and someone from the south."

"I'm...I'm sorr..."

"You don't need to apologize. How could it possibly be your fault? Besides," smiling, "I'll be the first one in my family to ever receive an American education. Isn't that what it's all about?" then walked toward the garage.

*I...it's...shit. What the fuck am I supposed ta say ta that? Just plain shit.*

I followed Vann into the garage.

"Hope's kickin' our butts!" Roy, as we entered the garage.

Homer was dealing.

"Where's Danny?" I asked.

"Shitter," JD.

"Head," Homer.

"Restroom," Hope huffed.

Doug was sitting on the floor next to Jerry. Jerry was explaining the carburetor.

JD was tugging at a bottle of Old Charter, while everyone else appeared to be working on their second beer.

"Gimme Danny's cards," JD mumbled as he reached across the table to pick them up.

" 'at's cheatin'!" Hope protested.

"It's j'st a game, missy," JD grumbled. "Why should yew care? Y're winnin' ain'ch ya?"

"I'm gunna tell," Hope declared loudly.

"Here," as JD tossed her the ace of diamonds from Danny's pile. "Gimme somethin' from y'ur hand ta replace it."

Hope paused, eyed the ace, glanced at her hand, and then looked back at the ace. She yanked the three of clubs from her hand, tossed it to JD, and then picked up the ace.

"I'm only doin' it 'cause ya made me," defending her decision to bend the rules.

JD traded the nine of diamonds from his hand for the ten of hearts from Danny's.

"Anybody else?" JD.

No response as they studied their hands.

JD slid three of Danny's cards to the dealer.

"Danny wants three," JD decided.

Homer flipped the ten of spades, the six of hearts, and the ace of spades onto the table.

Hope grabbed the ace, tossing the two of diamonds back.

"That's cheatin', missy," JD reminded her.

"Shut up," Hope snapped.

Vann headed for the office door.

"I'm going to find out if we are going to die this afternoon."

I followed him.

Danny was coming down the stairs from Hugo's office.

"Should we tell him about the game?" Vann.

"You don't have to. Hugo already took care of me," holding up five cards. "Same style, same color."

"Hope's holdin' a bunch'a aces," I warned.

"She better have six of them."

We could hear the radio upstairs.

"What's the word?" I shouted up the staircase.

"There's a report'a one touchin' down outside'a Throckmorton.

Whatever else is comin' is on its way pretty fast. They're already gettin' some hail out at the air base an' flights're on hold at the airport."

I turned to Vann.

"Should we tie Doug ta somethin'?"

\*\*\*

"You gunna call Hugo 'r ya want me to?" I asked JD.

"Yew," fumbling with the lock.

Trying to remain standing and unlock the padlock at the same time was proving too much for JD to handle.

"Lemme try," reaching around him and taking the keys.

I inserted the key and twisted it once. The lock fell open. I fed the chain back through the small hole in the door then yanked the door open.

"Where's 'omer? Where's 'omer, gahdammit?" JD demanded to know as I dragged him into the shop.

I sat him on his cot then pushed him onto his back.

"Where's 'at gahdamn 'omer?" slobbering. "Gahda go an' gid him, ya shicken shid muth'fug...,"

JD passed out.

I turned the lights on and rummaged through piles of papers, pizza boxes, and hamburger wrappers covering the top of his desk. A beer bottle fell to the concrete floor and broke. I found the phone and called Hugo.

"We're at the shop. Dudn't seem ta be any damage around here. Water's runnin' in the gutters about a third'a the way inta the streets. Some branches down here an' there. The radio must'a been talkin' about north'a Fourth Street. I could see some flashin' lights way up around Fourth an' University. Looked like a road block maybe."

"How's JD?"

"In his cot passed out. How's things out there?"

"They're either passed out 'r asleep. Hard ta say about some of 'em."

"What time is it?" I asked.

"Goin' on midnight."

"Well, I guess I'll head ta the house an' clean up. JD puked all over me."

"Dammit, Gil. I'm really sorry. Thanks f'r takin' him home. I'll make it up ta ya somehow."

"Don't worry about it. It's no biggy. After pukin' all over me, he wanted me ta puke on him so we'd be West Texas blood brothers."

"Haven't heard that 'un in a while," Hugo quietly laughed, "but that is how ya do it. Don't show up t'morrow 'til ya feel like it."

"I'm gunna have ta wait around 'til Homer shows up with my bike, no matter what."

"It might be a while b'fore he's sober enough ta drive it."

"That's the beauty'a that bike...when he's sober enough ta start it, he'll be sober enough ta drive it."

"If ya say so."

"Time ta hit the rack," I yawned.

"Good idea. Thanks again."

"G'night," and hung up.


I walked over to the piano stool next to Homer's pallet, sat down, and lit a cigarette. I was wrung out. JD nearly rolled off the cot while turning onto his stomach.

*What an ol' fart.*

I finished the cigarette, locked up, and walked home.


Upstairs I flipped on the light in my room and found Chad asleep on the pallet.

"Hey!" and kicked the wall. "Wake up!"

Chad rolled onto his back and squinted.

"What the fuck're you doin' here?" I yelled.

Chad eased into a sitting position and rubbed his eyes. He

reached for his shoes and began to pull them on without saying a word.

"Will already throw ya out'a his place?" walking over to the window to raise it. "That's gotta be some kind'a record for ya. What's it been? Three days?"

"You won't have to throw me out of the window like you did my clothes," Chad, wearily. "I'll walk down, thank you."

"My ways quicker."

Chad stood up and walked over to the door.

"The storm flooded Will's place," without turning around. "The roof leaks. Everything of mine *you* didn't ruin is soaked in filthy roof water," pausing in the doorway for my reaction to his plight.

"G'night, Chad."

"I'm going, I'm going," and stepped into the hall. "Let me get the others."

"Others?" following him into the hall.

Two girls, wrapped in sheets, stepped from the living room.

"What's wrong?" the girl with long, snow white hair asked sleepily.

"Whut's 'at smell?" the second one through a yawn.

I glanced down at my puke stained clothes.

"This is Bobbie and Shauna," Chad, pointing at each of them in turn.

"Is the tornado over?" Bobbie shivered. "Do we have ta go back there t'night? Ever'things all wet."

Chad looked over at me.

*Shit. Great positionin', Chad...set me up ta be the asshole.*

"Go back ta sleep," I mumbled and walked back to my room.

Muffled voices, then creaking footsteps approaching my room.
*Christ.*

Someone rapped lightly on the door.

"Can we talk?" Chad whined.

"I'm really tired, Chad. It's been a bitch of a day an..."

"It won't take long."

I thought a moment, trying to anticipate the direction this thing was going to take. I opened the door.

"They can move in. You can't. Ya can't even come visit 'em."

"Can we *please* talk?" he begged. "In the kitchen?"

"Make it fast," I grumbled.

I sat down across from him at the kitchen table and lit a cigarette.

"Will's decided to spend a year in Europe and India," Chad began. "He's leaving as soon as he gets his passport. He's already had his shots. He'll probably be gone in a week or two."

"So?" blowing smoke in his face.

Chad stifled a cough and turned his face away, fanning the air with one hand.

"You know anyone who might want to move in? It's a great place. Big. Five bedrooms, two baths, and a full basement for storage or parties."

"Hook my friends up with you? Are ya shittin' me? Chad, y're fuckin' unreal!"

"I was mainly concerned about the girls. It's cheap. If they lose the place, they'll have to give up their plans to go to Tech next semester."

*Jesus Christ, Chad. This is so weak.*

"I thought they were hairdressers?" I muttered.

"They are now, but they want to be...nurses."

My forehead hit the table with a thud.

*How fuckin' stupid does he think...*

"Please?" whinning again. "Please listen to the arrangement."

*Don't let him get started. Just throw his ass out. Let the girls stay, but...*

"It's two hundred dollars a month. With five people that's only forty per person. The rent can't go up for another year. Will's on a two year lease," pulling a folded piece of paper from his back pocket and handing it to me. "That's a better deal than what you've got here."

"Except y'ur roof leaks like a son of a bitch an' mine dudn't," as I unfolded the paper and read the terms.

"That will be taken care of."

"Two years at two hun'r'd a month *includin'* utilities startin' June 1, 1970," summarizing the lease out loud.

"Think about it, if for no other reason, for the sake of the girl's. They really are sweet. I honestly want to try and help them."

*Barf.*


I lit a cigarette and stood up.

"I'll think about it, but not b'cause I'm buyin' any'a y'ur crap about those girls. Ya screwed me out'a…"

"Eight Hundred dollars. I know, I know. I'm working on it," running his fingers through his hair.

"What're gunna do? Up y'ur grass prices?"

"It hurts me to know you believe every negative rumor you hear about me."

"Do somethin' that'll give me a reason not ta b'lieve 'em," and stepped to the hall curtain. "I want you an' Will's harem out'a here no later than…noon t'morrow."

"We'll be gone. Are you going to ask around for me?"

"Yeah," looking away. "I'll ask around."

"I need to know before June first."

"Okay, okay," as I left the room.


I shut my door, sat on the pallet, removed my boots, and then peeled the damp jeans from my legs. I sniffed the pants.

*Oh, damn! That's disgustin'. No wonder JD threw it back up.*

# CHAPTER THREE
## October, 1971

**M**-my round," as Jonas got up.

"O-o-o-o-kay," Jerry snickered.

Jonas ignored him. He worked his way through the crowd to the bar.

"Half way inta the semester an' I'm already bored shitless," then emptied my mug.

"Two hours into the weekend and I'm already snokered," Danny.

"Coul' be worse," Jerry slurred. "This time las' year yew wuz still in."

"I got out in August. An' ya know what? That's the last time I was eatin' regular," I grumbled.

"You can reenlist," Homer.

"I'll tromp cotton again b'fore reenlistin'. Things're pissin' me off, though. I'm still cleanin' shitters, moppin' floors, emptyin' fuckin' trash cans an' doin' any other goddamn shit job that comes along out at Hugo's 'r over at the lounge. I'm workin' two jobs, I'm on the GI bill an' I'm still broke all the time. I already spent ever' penny of the bill I'm gunna make this semester just on shittin' books an' fees. Just like last semester."

"Should have spent the summer in Albuquerque with me," Danny, lighting a cigarette.

"Well, ya know Daniel...I guess I *should'a* done a lot a things. I *should'a* changed my major so I wouldn't be spendin' ever' goddamn penny I make on a hun'r'd books I gotta read an' not one of 'em's in the fuckin' library. I *should'a* moved inta Will's when I had the goddamn chance. Then *I'd* be plankin' two different chicks all the time instead'a him," hitching my thumb in Jerry's direction. "I *should'a* told Sonny that first night at Dancer's that Homer was dyin' a syphilis so *I'd* be gettin' some'a that shit ever' night. Yeah, Danny, if ya wan'a talk about my fuckin' *should'a's*, I could keep ya up all night."

Danny looked a little surprised.

"I guess *I* should'a just told you how much I like the way you're wearing your hair tonight."

"Y're pissed 'cause my roomies do it an' y'ur roomies don't," Jerry cackled. "Ain't tha' right?" lifting his eyebrows and squinting.

Jerry was partly right. I'd given up on ever becoming the love of Joan's life. Wasn't her type I guess. After living under the same roof with her for almost five months now, I was sort'a glad I *wasn't* her type. Joan, at times, could be a real bitch-kitty on square wheels. And Hope...

*Shit.*

Hugo'd told me a long time ago she'd sworn off cigarettes and men. I was still praying for the day when she'd walk up and, out of nowhere, ask me for a smoke.

I shot Jerry the bird for being so fucking right.

"Whoa!" as Jerry jumped back. "He's *really* pissed now, man. Hit a fuckin' nerve 'r somethin'?"

"Blue balls make some people edgy," Danny.

"I'm ready ta take a fuckin' trip ta Juarez," I mumbled.

"Ya poor sufferin' bastard," Jerry. "Havin' ta drive all'a way ta Juarez an' pay f'r it," he sneered then continued to rub it in. "I got days I gotta pinch myself on'a ass ta make sure I ain't dreamin'. I'm gittin' it whenever I wan' it. Got a basement f'r the bike. Git free hair cuts an' scalp massages, an' home cooked meals an' I git it all f'r jus' fifty-five bucks a month. But, listen, man, I ain't tryin' ta make ya feel bad," glancing around the table and snickering. "I'm jus' sharin' my stuff with yew losers. Know whud I mean? Like how they used ta do back in church when ya stand up an' tell ever'body how good things're goin' for ya? Ya see...this here's whu's happenin'. Y'all're payin' f'r the way ya talk about Jesus all'a time. Tha's jus' a fact, man," squinting one eye while fully opening the other.

I wasn't listening. Something Jerry had said wasn't adding up.

"Yeah," continuing, "gittin' me moved inta Will's place wuz the bes' thing Jesus an' God ever done f'r me. 'at's why I'm all'a time stickin' up f'r 'em aroun' turds like y'all."

"How much rent're ya payin' at Will's?" furrowing my brow.

"Fifty-five f'r the rent an' then about twen'y more f'r the util'ties. 'at includes the phone too. An' it's nice havin' a phone f'r a change, lemme tell ya."

Jonas plopped three pitchers on the table.

"G-got three more..."

"S-s-spit it out," Jerry snickered.

"F-f-f..."

"Fuck you, Jerry," Danny, helping Jonas out.

"Yeah," as Jonas gave Jerry the finger then nodded at Danny. "T-thanks."

"Three more comin', right?" Danny.

"Yeah. Happy hours alm-most over," and headed back to the bar.

Danny filled all the mugs.

I leaned toward Jerry.

"How much rent're the girls payin'?" I asked him.

"Same as me...fifty-five plus util'ties."

"Ya sure?" getting all the ducks lined up.

"Yep. Seen Chad collectin' it from 'em b'fore. Don't worry, man...he ain't stiffin' me 'cause I ain't a chick," taking a big gulp from his mug. "It wuz cheaper when Will lived there, but the lease run out jus' when he left town. Chad had ta git a new 'un. Says he almos' had ta give the owner a blowjob ta keep it at fifty-five a piece."

"You see the new lease?" taking hold of my mug.

"Didn't have ta. I tol' the motherfucker I wudn' signin' shit. I know whud a maggot he is. My name ain't even on the phone thing. I ain't 'at stupid," cackling.

"Nah. You ain't *that* stupid," and took a swig of beer, "but ya *are* stupid enough ta be payin' Chad's share'a the rent an' then some."

Homer and Danny exchanged glances. Jerry set his mug down.

"See 'at?" Jerry, pointing at me while looking at the others. "See whud he's doin', man? Whud a fucker! Tryin' ta piss me off with a bullshit story like 'at," looking back at me. "Y're gunna have ta do better'n 'at, butthole," shaking his head and sneering.

*Oh, Jerry...hang on ta y'ur ass.*

"Last May," I began, "Chad showed me a two year lease Will had on the place. It was good 'til the first'a June, 1972."

Jerry's head fell back, eyes big.

"Will ain't aroun' no more so the ol' lease ain't no good."

"Ya *real* sure about that?"

Jerry's right eye narrowed to a slit as he threw himself forward and turned his head slightly to the right. His left eye, as open as it could be, glared across the table at me.

"Uh, oh," Danny.

Homer slowly ran his hand over his bandanna and played with the knot in the back.

"So...whu' y're sayin' is 'at," Jerry, slowly, "the ol' lease is still good?"

It didn't happen very often that Jerry would put a full sentence together without at least one cuss word in it.

"It's not the *old* lease," answering as slowly. "It's the *only* lease. Never was a *new* lease."

Jerry calmly chugged half the beer in his mug. Long, slow gulps. He leaned back, and held the mug in his lap with both hands. He belched loudly.

"So...how much *is* the lease?" he asked quietly.

I looked over at Danny and Homer. Danny pressed his lips together. Homer put his head down.

"Two hun'r'd a month," I told him.

Jerry squirmed a little in his chair as he started to simmer.

"Two hun'r'd?" repeating the figure as he began to slowly rock in the chair. "Util'ties included?" eyebrows raised.

"Utilities included."

Jerry began rocking faster.

"That'd be about...fifty bucks apiece f'r *ever'thing*," I informed him.

"I c'n do my own damn fig'rin'," boiling over.

Jonas returned, put the pitchers down, and then took his seat. He glanced at Jerry then turned to me.

"W-what's wrong?" he asked.

"Nothing...yet," Danny.

Jerry stopped rocking.

"I'll be damned. Tha's jus' a real nice fuckin' thing ta find out," slurring to himself.

"Make him pay you back," Homer.

"With interest," I added. "That'd be a fair thing ta expect."

"And a fine or something," Danny suggested. "Ten percent of what he owes you, maybe."

Jerry stewed a good two or three minutes, staring at his mug as the rest of us discussed several other possible ways to rectify the wrong that had been done. Finally, Jerry leaned forward.

"Gil, I consider ya a damn good frien'. Ya know tha' don'ch ya?"

"I know that."

"So...'at's why I'm askin' ya this firs'. Un'erstand?"

"I think so."

"Would it ruin things b'tween yew an' me if I wuz ta kill y'ur brother?"

"Hell no, Jerry," not requiring a split second's thought. "Not a bit! Damn," relieved. "Ya had me scared f'r a minute. Since he's my brother, I thought ya were gunna hate *me* b'cause'a what that little butthole did," reaching over and putting my hand on his shoulder. "You go right ahead, Jerry...kill his squirrelly little ass!"

"Ya mean 'at?" to be certain. " 'cause a frien'ship's worth a lot more ta me than gittin' even with some low-life maggot."

"Not a bit'a doubt in my mind, Jerry. An' I really appreciate y'ur askin' me about it first. It's gunna take somethin' a hell of a lot more serious than killin' Chad ta fuck things up b'tween us."

Jonas raised his mug over the center of the table.

"I'll d-drink to that," then stood up.

Danny, Homer, and I rose to our feet and placed our mugs alongside Jonas'. Jerry slowly got to his feet and toasted each mug separately.

"Ta buds," Jerry, and sat back down.

After refilling our mugs, Jerry leaned into the center of the table.

"T'morrow night, not t'night 'cause I been drinkin' an' I don't wan' nobody sayin' I did it 'cause I wuz drunk, so...t'morrow night," and looked at me, "I'm gunna have ta kill 'at motherfucker. Okay?"

"This is America, Jerry," nodding my head. "Ya do what ya want, by God."

"Damn straight this's Amer'ca," Jerry nodded. "An' lemme tell ya somethin' else about Amer'ca. Lemme say jus' four fuckin' words, man...jus' four words 'at'll say it all—Ee Wo Gee Ma. 'at's it. 'at's the whole Amer'c'n thing right in a nutshell," he declared while looking around the table with one eye squinting and the other wide open.

"Right!" the rest of us in loud unison. "Ee Wo Gee Ma!" and raised our mugs into the air again, sloshing beer onto the table.

The tables around us were becoming nervous. A group got up and left. Bo was beginning to watch us closely.

The conversation turned to a group of ladies at the table next to us.

"High class leg," Jerry observed. "Look'a them 'spensive, long-ass, tie dyed dresses."

"Wan'a buy 'em a drink?" I asked the others. "There's four'a us an' four'a them."

"Yew shittin' me?" Jerry. "Them sons a bitches're drinkin' pitchers'a margaritas 'r somethin' an' happy hour's over."

"Well," I burped, "one of us ought'a go over an, sugges' we pull the tables t'gether an' get aquaninted."

"Don't sen' Jonas," Jerry burped. "We'll be here 'til f-fuckin' s-s-sun up."

"F-f-f-f..." Jonas.

"Fuck you, Jerry," Danny helping Jonas out again.

"One more roun' an' I ought'a be ready ta talk some trash," I volunteered. "But, first...I've been playin' with this idea all day 'at could make us all rich."

I topped the mugs off then motioned for everyone to lean forward.

"Homer, how much church glass repairin' do you an' JD do?"

"Not much. Two more churches since the bunch you came and looked at back in May."

"Yeah, but didn't JD used ta do a lot of it? I mean, hell, one whole corner in the shop is nothin' but scrap glass an' he's got all 'em crates'a church glass against the wall."

"Yeah, I guess at one time or other he was into it a lot more."

I lit a cigarette before continuing.

"At least twice a week f'r the past two months Hugo's had a crew of us in Guadeloupe surveyin' lots ta rebuild houses...the one's 'at got knocked down in the '70 tornada. Yesterd'y we surveyed another church there. 'at's three so far. Two Catholic an' one Methodist. All of 'em have busted up church glass windows. I was talkin' ta this priest yesterd'y an' he tol' me they can't afford ta have theirs repaired 'cause they can't afford ta pay anybody ta come out from Dallas. 'at's the closest place he knew of 'at did those kind'a repairs."

"None of them had insurance?" Danny.

"You shittin' me?" squinting and shaking my head. "God's not gunna fuck with people 'at have insurance. What's the point?" turning again to Homer. "How much does JD charge ta fix church windows like 'at?"

He shrugged his shoulders.

"Don't know what JD makes, but he pays me two fifty an hour."

"Think we could learn ta do repairs?" I asked.

"Don't see why not," Homer.

"You better be damn sure you know what you're doing before you mess with it," Danny cautioned. "They might not be able to afford insurance, but I would imagine they could find some attorney money real quick if you screwed their windows up."

"We won't screw anything up," I insisted. "Listen, Homer, what if we lined up the jobs...do ya think JD'd take care'a the business end an' show us how ta fix 'em if we gave him a percen'age?"

"Don't know," Homer shrugged.

"Well, f'r now, let's say he would do it. Now, listen ta this. Guadeloupe's jus' one area'a Lubbock. Those tornadas were all over the place...Dalhart, Plainview, New Deal, Amarilla, Levelland...an' all of 'em have churches."

"Hell," Danny's interest growing, "for all we know, half the churches right here in Lubbock may still need repairing."

"Tha's a lot'a fuckin' money," Jerry, momentarily pulled from his brooding over the rent situation.

Danny went practical on me.

"Do you know why it costs a lot of money to have a stained glass window repaired? It might be because not everybody knows how to do it. Stained glass craftsmen, *real* craftsmen, spend years studying under a master craftsman to learn how to do it. How'd JD learn?"

"He taught himself," Homer.

"But he knows what he's doin'," I countered. "Dudn't he, Homer?"

Homer fiddled with his mug.

"I suppose. He can make a beat up old window look brand new. You can't even find the fixed pieces most of the time."

"Think he'd work with us?" I asked.

"Don't know. He's not too driven. He works enough to pay the rent and buy the basics...cigarettes, booze, grass. He might see this as too much of a pain in the ass."

"All he'd have ta do is kind'a keep an eye on us. Make sure we're doin' it right. Hell, repairin' windows can't be 'at hard if he c'n do it drunk on his ass. From what ya've seen, Homer, does it look all 'at hard ta do?"

"Not really. He does all the hard replacement piece cuts, but I'm getting better at cutting. I've got the soldering part down good."

"Whud about it Danny?" as I leaned toward him.

"Here's the deal. Let's see what JD says first. Then, if he agrees, we need to consider a number of other issues."

"Anything beats workin' f'r somebody else, man," Jerry.

"T'morrow afternoon," I said. "After I'm off work at Hugo's, let's all meet at JD's an' talk to him about it. I don't have ta be at the lounge 'til 6:00. I bet ya we c'n talk him into it b'fore it's time f'r me ta go ta the lounge. Whud'a ya say, Homer?"

Homer was hesitant.

"What's to lose?" I persisted.

"Yeah," Homer nodded. "You're right. It can't hurt to talk to him."

We all agreed to meet at JD's at 2:00 the next afternoon.

"Them ladies're still lustin' after us," Jerry hissed. " 'at skinny 'un cain't keep her eyes off'a me, man."

We glanced over at them.

"Go get 'em, Gil," Danny shoved me. "You're drunk enough now."

"Yeah. Jus' ask 'em ta come on over f'r a while," Jerry.

I looked at Danny.

"Y're right...they *wan'* us. Anybody wan'a go with me?"

"Too drunk," Danny.

"I'm picking Sonny up at the Westerner at 2:30," Homer.

"Jerry?"

"I still ain' cleaned up from work."

"Y're no dirtier'n me," slapping my jeans to raise a cloud of dust.

I continued to nurse my beer while putting the polish on the line of trash I was going to use. The others kept looking at me impatiently.

"You wait too much longer and you're gunna to be too screwed up to talk," Danny.

"All right, goddammit," and drained the mug. "I'll hit the head then talk to 'em on'a way back," and stood up.

I wobbled a little, caught my balance, and then, after plastering on a *huge*-ass smile, turned to the ladies. They all looked away. Shakily, I stepped away from the table. I felt the toe of my boot catch on Jonas' chair leg. I fell forward and crashed to the ground. The lights dimmed.

*Perfume?*

I looked up and caught a glimpse of panties and a bare thigh. My head exploded.

\*\*\*

My left eye wasn't working. Wouldn't open. The right eye would open, but was a little blurred. When I tried to raise up a sharp, crippling pain shot through the left side of my skull and down the left side of my neck into the shoulder. A constant, agonizing throb literally shook my entire head.

*Goddamn. Where...?*

*Jail?*

A soft, golden light filled the room.

*Sun up?*

242

*A chest'a drawers. Drawin' of a cow with a shitbird feedin' on a cow patty. Bob Dylan poster. Ferlinghetti poster. A guitar.*

*Not jail.*

I shut my eye.

*What day is it?*

I tensed my body and tried to sit up. The pain held me flat on my back.

*What time is it? Supposed ta be somewhere! Fuck...late for muster!*

I jerked violently.

"How you feelin'?" someone asked in a sleepy voice.

Joan's weary eyes were studying my face. She lifted something from the inoperative eye and winced.

"What happened?" I breathed.

"You got hurt," yawning. "Somehow you ended up with y'ur head under some girl's skirt and she hit you with a pitcher."

*A dress. Perfume. A bare thigh. Oh, my God.*

I rolled onto my side, looking away from Joan, moaning more from the pain of the memory flashes than from the injury.

"Don't move," grabbing my shoulder and returning me to my back.

"Where's my bike?"

"Homer pushed it home. He was too drunk ta start it. He got a ticket for not signalin'. Pro'bly gunna cost ya at least twenty-five dollars."

"How the hell c'n ya get a ticket when y're *pushin'* a bike?"

"Ask the judge."

"How bad's the eye?"

"Swollen. Real swollen. An' blackish-purple. About this big," and made a circle the size of a hardball with her fingers.

"Cut?"

"A little. As much as it bled you'd'a thought she'd shot ya 'r somethin'."

Joan wrung the face cloth out in a pan then placed the cloth over my eye.

"What time is it?" I groaned.

"7:00."

"Saturd'y?"

"Yep," standing up stiffly.

"How long ya been here?"

"Since 3:00. Hope watched ya first," her robed bosom inflating to bursting as she leaned back, stretched, and then yawned.

"Thanks f'r helpin' me out. Didn't mean ta be a problem."

"It wasn't a problem. More of a royal pain in the butt."

"Joan?"

"What?"

"Remember those old movies where a guy's hurt an' a lady takes care of him f'r like a week 'r so?"

Joan smiled tiredly.

"Remember," I continued, "how the hurt guy always wakes up naked under a blanket b'cause the lady's been givin' him sponge baths while he was knocked out?"

Joan lost the smile.

"Joan," softly, "would ya mind..."

"You haven't been out a week," interrupting. "And this isn't Hollywood," bristling. "I c'n*not* b'lieve you. Y're still half drunk."

"Can't hurt ta try," reaching up to adjust the face cloth. "Where's ever'body else? Anybody get in trouble? Cops come?"

"They're all still in bed, you've all been banned from Mother's for life, an' the police were called."

"What'd the cops do?"

"Nothin'. One of 'em knew ya."

"Knew me?"

"That's all I know. You'll have ta get the details from one'a the others. Danny an' Jonas're passed out here an' Jerry's at his place. I guess Homer's with Sonny. I'll be right back," and left the room.

I clenched my teeth and sat up. The face cloth fell into my lap. It was spotted with blood.

*Damn.*

I gently felt the swollen area.

*Jesus goddamn Christ!*

It took several seconds to focus on the clock.

*Shit! Gotta be at work at 8:00!*

I struggled to my feet, steadying myself against the chest-of-drawers. The eye throbbed painfully. I had a hot railroad spike in my left temple.

Joan returned to the room.

"What're you doin'?"

"Work," part groan.

"I don't *think* so!" rushing to my side. "You might have a concussion. You need ta rest."

"Can't afford to," wobbling to the door. "I'll feel better once I'm cleaned up."

"You need ta see a doctor."

"I don't need a doctor bill," and stepped into the hall, Joan right on my heels.

"You won't make it through the day."

"I'm only workin' 'til noon."

"What about the lounge t'night?"

"I'll worry about that t'night," entering the bathroom and shutting the door.

Joan knocked on the door.

"I'm goin' down ta Jerry's an' call Hugo an' tell him what happened. He won't want ya ta work."

"You don't know Hugo," I answered, placing a towel over the mirror to avoid looking at the damage.

It took forever to shower, every move setting the eye and head off. I pulled my pants on then stepped into the hall. Joan was waiting.

"Hugo'd already left," she huffed, "an' Roy's on his way ta pick ya up."

"I'm doin' a lot better. I'll be fine after a cup'a coffee, some aspirin an' half'a pack'a cigarettes."

"I'll fix the coffee," turning toward the kitchen, apparently giving up on trying to talk me out of going to work.

"Hot out'a the tap an' two full spoons'a instant, please."

I finished dressing and entered the kitchen. Joan told me she couldn't stand to look at me.

"Joan," reaching out and touching her shoulder. "I appreciate the concern. It means a lot, but it's been worse."

"That's supposed ta make us feel better?"

"Us?"

"Us...me, Hugo, Hope, Danny. Everybody else who knows y'all. Y'all are...I don't know...half there. We worry about you guys. You an' Homer's drinkin'. Jerry's, Vann's an' Jonas' dopin'. Doug's... Doug's everything."

"We're big boys. We can handle it."

"That really helps," sniffling.

"You cryin?"

"No," wiping tears away.

"I'm sorry," and dropped my head. My skull detonated.

Joan struck my chest with a closed fist.

"You *should* be!" wiping her nose on her bathrobe sleeve. "Y'ur eye was *bleedin'* last night. Ya wouldn't let us take ya ta the hospital. You could'a lost y'ur eye or somethin'. You bastards...all'a y'all," running her arm under her nose again while turning away.

"I'm really sorry, Joan. Honest-ta-God. I tell ya what...we're gunna change. We're gunna change, just f'r you. Okay? We'll stop drinkin', an' cussin', an' dopin', an' we'll sell the bikes an' buy regular cars an' all of us'll b'come business majors at Tech an..."

"Shut up!" spinning around and hitting me again. "Just wearin' underwear'd be an improvement f'r you guys," sniffing.

"How'd ya know..."

"Anytime I do the wash for any of ya I never find any underwear in y'ur bags," walking toward the hall.

"Maybe we throw 'em away after one wearin'? Maybe we think 'at's more sanitary than..."

"Don't forget y'ur coffee," before throwing the curtain in the doorway back and leaving the kitchen.

"Thanks f'r fixin' it," I whispered after her.

A horn honked in the street below. I grabbed my cigarettes and matches as I passed the table then hurried down the steps. Roy didn't stop honking the horn until I was all the way inside the cab. I sat and looked straight ahead, trying my best to deal with the pain, waiting for Roy to notice the eye and then eat me alive.

*He's gunna have so much damn fun with me t'day.*

Roy leaned all the way over to the passenger side and whistled softly.

"Ya know, Gil," starting in on me, "in polite society it's customary ta *ask* a young lady f'r her permission b'fore ya go stickin' y'ur head up under her dress. Leas', 'at's the way I was brought up."

"How'd ya find out?" surprised that he already had all the details.

"It's on the front page'a the Avalanche Journal bigger'n shit... 'Dope Crazed Hippie Injured In Muff Dive'."

"C'mon, Roy. How'd ya find out?"

"Homer," throwing himself back behind the wheel and clanging the transmission into first gear. "He told me last night when he come after Sonny."

Roy drove to the corner.

"This is where y'ur brother lives now, ain't it?"

"Yeah. Him, Jerry, an' two hairdressers."

Roy sat on the horn, leaned out the window, and then began to yell.

"Wake up ya dope smokin', fornicatin' bunch'a Godless hippies! Reveille! Reveille!" staying on the horn until he'd crossed the intersection. "Goddamn, I love it down here in'a ghetto," racing toward Broadway. "An' I cain't even *b'gin* ta tell ya how glad I am 'at yew could make it this mornin', Gil," grinning, gum line brown with chew. "Too damn bad we only work half'a day on Saturd'ys. Ya see, the more I look at yew, the better my hangover feels. Damn. Yew *do* look bad!"

We worked until noon. Roy dropped me off in the alley behind JD's shop.

JD took one look at me and scrambled off to his desk. He opened the bottom drawer and rummaged around until he found a small white bottle and a larger amber one. I came up behind him as he was shaking two pills from each bottle. JD turned around and handed me the pills, offering me his beer to take them with.

"Take these an' don't gimme no shit about it."

"What are they?" before popping them into my mouth and washing them down with a mouthful of beer.

"Pain pills. Veteran's hospital gives 'em ta me. By the truckload. It's the one reason I put up with the butchers," he growled, moving closer to study the mangled socket. "How the hell'd 'at happen? Ya fall off y'ur wheel?"

"Nah," as I went over to Homer's sleeping mat and sat down. "I fell an' hit my head last night at Mother's," avoiding the details.

"Medics come?"

"Don't know. I was passed out 'til this mornin'."

"Homer there?" and brought me a warm beer. "Got no ice," apologizing.

"Yeah. Him, Jerry, Jonas, an' Danny."

"Son uv a bitch," as he shook his head and stared at the eye again. "Lemme give ya a han'ful'a 'em pills…'nough ta last ya a week 'r so. When y're drinkin' alcohol, take about two extra'a each. Alcohol keeps a reg'lar dose from workin' right."

"How often?"

"Whenever it hurts."

"It hurts all the time."

"Lemme thank a minute," running his fingers through the silver-gray hair surrounding his bald dome. "Take two'a each pill ever' hour 'til ya notice blood in y'ur shit. Then ya cut back ta two uv each ever' three 'r four hours 'til the blood goes away. Then ya c'n go back ta takin' 'em ever' hour if thangs is still hurtin' bad."

"Okay. Thanks, JD. Feels like they're already beginnin' ta work. I'm gunna lay here f'r a while. Homer an' some'a the others're comin' over around 2:00. We got somethin' we wan'a talk ta ya about," yawning.

"What about?" while heading back over to the desk.

"Too tired ta talk right now," feeling my body go limp.

JD began pulling all kinds of pill bottles from the drawers and pitching them onto his cot.

"Thought I'd run out'a them kind," mumbling to himself.

I heard a bottle lid pop off, pills rattling, and then loud gulping.

I was beginning to drift, not drift off to sleep, just plain drift. It was a light feeling. Not floating. More like flying in slow motion. I was relaxed. My face still throbbed, but I didn't seem to care. My eye felt swollen, swollen and tight, but not much actual pain. My mind was churning. Ideas flooded my brain. The church glass. School. Coin operated player pianos in all the restaurants in town. How to meet women on campus. How ta pick up on Missy at the lounge. How ta fix the bike up.

*Poetry. Start writin' poetry. An' songs. I'm gunna start practicin' more on the guitar an' start playin' in places around town. Maybe take it ta Dallas 'r Houston.*

*California with Homer!*

*That's the plan I been tryin' ta find!*

*An' it was there all along.*

*Been so wrapped around the axle with the little things 'at I wudn't seein' how ever'thing was really fallin' t'gether the whole time. Damn! Ever'thing really was under control. Damn, what a feelin'! So…so…fine. Calm. What a…motherfuckin' feelin'. What was I gettin' all nervous about? Ever'things fine. Ever'things…*

\*\*\*

The slow, piercing screech of a large nail being removed from old, dry wood woke me. I remained still with my eyes shut.

"All this is opaque glass," JD was saying. "Ya cain't see through it. It's whut's called opalescent glass. Ya use it in lampshades an' almost all y'ur old church repairs. If y're gunna call anythang church glass, it'd be this op'lescent glass. All this colored glass is called stained glass though. No such thing as church glass."

ZZ Top was playing on a radio in the alley, the words barely audible over a noisy crowd. A bottle broke followed by an outburst of laughter.

"So how long will it take you to teach us to do a fairly simple repair?" Danny's voice.

"Teach ya as ya go," JD. "Homer here c'n cut glass a little. It ain' 'at hard. Most'a repair work is knowin' the tricks an' the shortcuts. Experience, 'at's most uv it. An' I got all'a 'at y're gunna need."

"When do you want to go look at the churches?" Danny.

"If Homer'll keep an eye on the place, we could go now. See if it's worth the time ta even mess with."

"I'll stick around," Homer. "*If* Gil wakes up, I'll fill him in."

"All the churches're in Guadeloupe?" JD, as the voices moved from the center of the shop toward me.

"Yeah," Danny. "I think Gil said three or four in all. He doesn't need to come along. We can drive around and find them."

"We'll pro'bly be gone an hour 'r so," JD told Homer. "Don't let 'em git too rowdy an' don't let 'em start ridin' 'em wheels up an' down the alley."

"Don't worry," Homer.

I didn't move as they walked past the mat. The alley door creaked open. The noise from the alley increased in volume then muted as the door slid shut behind them.

My head was throbbing again. Not as bad as before, but bordering on intolerable. My mind felt fuzzy, unfocused. I reached for the beer next to the pad, slowly sat up, and then took one each of the pills JD had given me earlier. I remembered his instructions about the alcohol and took two more of each.

The alley door opened. The noise level increased. Homer went over to the cooler at the end of JD's desk and retrieved a can of beer.

"It's 4:30," he told me.

"4:30? Can't be."

"Well, it is," walking over and sitting down on the piano stool.

"I've been out four an' a half hours?"

"Looks like it. Here," offering me his beer. "Take this and hold it against your eye. It's ice cold."

"I heard you guys talkin' when ya were openin' the glass crates," placing the can against my left temple. "Sounds like JD's gunna work with us."

"I guess. It took a while, but Danny sold him on it. He especially liked the part about him not having to do any of the heavy work, but…tomorrow he might not even remember talking to us."

Homer got himself a beer, popped it opened, and then chugged half of it down before returning to the piano stool.

"JD give ya these?" pointing at the pile of pills by my side.

"Pain pills," I told him.

"Yeah. I know," running a finger through the pile.

"You going to work tonight?" picking two light blue aspirin sized pills from the rest then washing them down with some beer.

"Yeah. I'm feelin' better."

*Much better.*

"If you say so," staring at my eye.

"I'm gunna have ta leave b'fore they get back. Will ya come up ta the lounge sometime t'night an' tell me what's goin' on with the glass an' shit?" as I slowly got to my feet.

*Whoa! Shiiiit, man! What a rush!*

My brain had to catch up with my skull. My body tingled.

"You all right?" a voice in the distance.

"Yeah. I'm fine. Just had a nice tingly kind'a rush. That's all."

"It's the beer. Never take pills with beer. Or wine."

"Did Jerry 'r Jonas show up ta the meetin' with JD?"

"Yeah. They're in the alley. Doug finally got his bike up and drove it over here. It still has some problems. They're working on it. Doug's acting like a new father. He keeps yelling 'Far out! Far fuckin' out!' over and over and wheezing. He's really happy."

"That'll make Vann happy."

"Yeah," standing and stretching. "Grab a cold can of beer for your head and give me that one if you're not going to drink it."

"Don't feel much like drinkin' right now," handing the beer to Homer. "Stomachs kind'a sour."

"You eat today?" heading for the back door.

"Some doughnuts this mornin'," following Homer into the alley.

It was hot outside. The noise subsided slightly as everybody stopped to stare at me. Jonas, busy blowing into a pulled gas line on his bike, looked up.

"Want a s-sack for that f-face?" he yelled.

Ed and Tomas were right outside the door.

"*Chingado!*" Ed hissed.

Tomas winced.

"You been to see a doctor, man?" Ed. "That looks *baaad*. You might be blind," shaking my hand.

"Thanks, Ed. That puts my mind at ease."

"Only telling you the truth, man. You got to be *reeeal* careful with your head. I would rather be hit in the nuts than the head, man. Too many things can go wrong when you get hit in the head."

Doug came over.

"See what I'm saying?" as Eduardo tapped his head with his index finger and nodded at Doug.

Doug, pointing at his bike, was one giant grin. His eyes were dancing.

"Can you fucking believe it?" in a wheezing laugh. "Far out!" bending his knees and throwing his head back. "Far *fucking* out!"

"Congratulations," and shook his hand.

"Wait until you hear it. Wait until you fucking hear it!" then pulled me to him and hugged me. He let go and returned to his bike.

Jerry was standing next to Doug's bike, sweat soaked tee shirt clinging to his back. Homer and I stepped over to Jerry.

Jerry shook his head when he saw me.

"Damn, Gil," squinting dramatically and whistling. "If ya ever git inta a fight with a *guy*...ya might as well jus' kill y'urself," snickering as his eyes flew open. "But then, yew ain't gotta worry much about tha' ever happenin' since ya cain't git y'ur head up a *guy's* blue jeans," breaking into a cackle as he returned to working on the throttle handle.

"Thanks."

"Listen, man," Jerry snickered, "I wuz right there for ya," glancing at Homer. "Ain' 'at right, Homer? The only motherfuckin' one 'at stayed cool. The *only* one."

"That's what happened," Homer agreed. "While the rest of us were trying to pull the lady off you and keep her friends back and stop the bouncer from jumping in, Jerry here's the one who stayed calm enough to remind her over and over again what a whore bitch she was."

"Guess I owe ya."

"How ya like whu' Dougy did with the gas tank?" Jerry.

The frame and tank were flat primer gray. Doug had used a black marker to shade and vein the tank. He really was a damn good artist. The tank looked exactly like a big-ass, circumcised penis.

"Looks damn good, Doug. Wish I'd thought of it."

*Ya won't make it past the first cop with 'at tank b'tween y'ur legs.*

Jerry handed a pair of needle nosed pliers to Doug. A small, stiff cable was gripped in its jaws.

"Hold this tight," Jerry.

Doug took the pliers.

"Keep the tension on it while I wrap it," Jerry.

Jerry struggled with the cable a few minutes.

"There," he puffed after working the ball tab into a groove in the throttle arm. " 'at'll be better'n doin' it with y'ur hand, anyway. It'll pro'bly still need a'justin'," stepping away from the bike.

Doug hopped on the bike and rotated the throttle a few times.

Homer and I followed Jerry to the back door of the shop. We stepped inside to escape the sun.

" 'at stupid mother," Jerry growled. "He hand throttled 'at fuckin' bike all'a way over here from Vann's. He jus' wraps the cable aroun' his hand an' takes off like he's ridin' a fuckin' horse. He'd be doin' five mile an hour then, BAM...up ta sixty, then down ta ten, then ninety, him screamin' 'Far out!' at the top'a his lungs all'a way over here. An' both uv us higher'n shit an' holdin'. The son uv a bitch ain't right. Out uv his fuckin' mind."

Jerry got a beer from the cooler.

"I'm so glad 'at damn bikes finally up. I could jus' shit. Ya know, ten more minutes with 'at whacky motherfucker an' I'd be as screwed up as he is. Talkin' ta ever' nut an' bolt. Blowin' weed smoke over ever'thing. Sleepin' on the damn parts. Kissin' 'em. Babblin' on all'a the time about 'functional essence' an' shit," lighting a cigarette. "If I had it ta do over, I'd'a found him a bike at's already put t'gether...like y'urs," pointing the beer can at me.

Doug's bike roared to life. The crowd cheered. Doug 's voice rose above the din.

"Listen to thaaat!" and gunned it. "Listeeen!" gunning it again and again.

We followed Jerry outside to watch Doug.

"But, ya know," Jerry yelled over the bike's roar, "I c'n dig it, man! Know whud I'm sayin'? I c'n dig it!"

The bike died. Doug removed his tee shirt and began to rub away at the grease spots and oil stains dotting the frame. The chrome springers sparkled in the late afternoon sun. The springers hadn't come with the basket case Jerry had found for Doug. The original forks were shitty looking shock tubes. Doug had ordered the springers brand new. He'd paid an arm and a leg for them and had ritually polished them everyday since they'd arrived. The bike's whole personality centered on those shinny chrome springers.

A Harley roared up the alley and slid to a stop. It was Neil. He killed the engine and launched into his dismount routine, ending the performance by slipping a pair of sunglasses on and stepping from the bike.

"How's Mr. Badass?" Jerry, sneered.

Neil dropped his head and looked at me over the top of the sunglasses.

"Better than some around here from the looks of his face. Gotta beer?" winking at the ladies in the crowd.

"Whu's left's been spoken for," Jerry told him.

Neil ignored him. He looked over at Doug.

"Hey, Doug…nice job. Looks good, man. Looks real good. Ready to do some jammin' tomorrow?"

"Maybe," Doug answered without turning around.

The group around Doug had thinned—one hippie looking guy and two nasty looking girls drooling over Doug's flexing muscles as he rubbed his bike down.

"How about you guys?" nodding at us, while attempting a snarl. "Can any of you make it up to Palo Duro Canyon and back without your bikes falling apart?"

Jerry walked over to Neil.

"I been thinkin'. Whu' kind'a Mes'c'n mama goes an' names her baby boy Neil? Wuz 'at the mailman's name 'r somethin'?"

Ed and Tomas glanced at each other. Neil slowly straddled his bike and began his departure routine. Jerry stepped closer to the bike and shouted over the roar of the engine.

"How come ya ain't changed 'at faggot-ass name to a *real* Mexican name?"

Neil peeled out, fishtailing the first ten feet. He flipped Jerry off as the bike turned out of the alley onto University without slowing for the stop sign. A siren cycled once before a police car tore past the alley, heading in Neil's direction.

Jerry pointed toward University.

" 'at's all 'at son uv a bitch is good for, man. Drawin' the cops. Always gotta be flashin' it," Jerry scowled. "He's fuckin' trash!"

"He doesn't even speak the language," Tomas.

"See there?" Jerry, pointing at Ed then Tomas. "Ed an' Tomas're *Mexicans*. Neil's a *Mes'c'n*. Even Mexicans hate Mes'c'ns. Fuckin' Germans got Hitler. Japs got…got what's his name, 'at Jap guy, an' Mexicans got Neil. Whud'a ya think?"

"I think he's gunna get real fucked up some night, find a gun, and then blow y'ur ass away," Homer.

"By the time he's that drunk," Eduardo, "he won't remember why he was getting drunk."

Homer nodded at me and tapped his wrist.

"It's late," he said.

"Yeah, I gotta go. Gotta be at work at 6:00. Hey, thanks f'r pushin' the bike home from Mother's last night."

"No problem. If I'd a been sober enough to start it I'd be half way to California right now."

"I doubt ya would'a gotten that far. Hell, ya couldn't even push it two blocks without gettin' a fuckin' ticket."

"Oh, yeah. Nearly forgot," pulling a waded up yellow receipt from his pant's pocket. "This is yours," and handed it to me.

"At least ya weren't speedin'."

"Here's the other one," retrieving a second waded ticket from his pocket. "I didn't have the headlight on."

"What the hell is goin' on?" furrowing my brow and staring at the tickets. "These're bullshit tickets!"

"Maybe you should trade the bike in for a VW or a station wagon, shave, get a haircut, change your whole attitude, and start going back to church again."

I walked over to Ed.

"Ed. Tomas. Come on up an' see me t'night an' I'll throw a coupl'a free ones on ya."

"I'll be there," Ed.

I turned to Homer.

"Make sure JD an' you guys come up ta the lounge t'night. We need ta get this glass thing goin'. I need the money bad now," waving the tickets.

"We'll be there."


As soon as I got to the house I put down two more pills with some tap water. I stood at the sink and looked down at the utility across the alley from us. It'd been empty all winter. A U-Haul trailer was parked behind it now.

"Gil?"

I turned. Hope and Joan were standing at the table. They both gasped and covered their mouths.

"It looks worse!" Hope exclaimed.

Joan approached me.

"I told ya not ta go ta work," she said angrily.

"It's all right. Dudn't hurt that much," touching it gently with my finger.

"It's still swollen shut," Joan.

"Pro'bly will be for a while. If I can't see after the swellin' goes down, then I'll go ta the doctor."

"Why bother?" Joan. "All he'll be able ta do for ya by then is pop it out. Or were ya gunna have Jerry do that for ya?"

Hope came over.

"We decided we could all chip in an' he'p ya cover a doctor bill."

"Thanks, but I'm gunna wait 'til the eye opens up some."

"I'm not gunna waste anymore time worryin' about it then," Joan, turning and walking away.

"Whut if ya go blind?" Hope.

"If I go blind it'll be b'cause neither one'a ya'd give me a sponge bath."

"Sponge bath?" Hope.

"Never mind," Joan. "He's just bein' his dirty self again," and opened the refrigerator.


Joan pulled a head of lettuce and some tomatoes out and then slammed the door shut with her hip.

"A salad won't hold me all night," I told her, stepping aside as Joan brushed past me on her way to the sink.

"It's not for you," stiffly. "Did ya blow y'ur nose in the sink when ya got home?"

"I told ya I wouldn't do that anymore. Nobody does 'at anymore. We go ta the porch an' huff it over the side 'r we..."

"I don't need ta hear the details, please," plopping the lettuce and tomatoes into the sink.

"Move over," Hope ordered and pushed me aside. She stepped to the sink alongside Joan.

"Who's all this for?" I asked.

"The Baha'i are havin' a potluck here t'night," Hope, turning the water on.

"If you'd come ta the meetin's once an' a while, you'd know that," Joan.

"Two nights a month over here idn't enough?" mumbling as I stepped over to the frig.

"What'd ya say?" Joan turned around.

"I'm hungry as hell."

"Walk up ta the Lotta Burger," Joan.

"No money," mumbling again.

"Ya should'a thought about that las' night while yew was spendin' ever'thang on beer," Hope.

I scrounged around inside the refrigerator.

*Cheese logs. Fresh mushrooms. Bag'a sun flower seeds. Raw bean sprouts.*

*Smells like vinegar.*

*No beer.*

"How could we be out'a beer..."

"It's downstairs in Jerry's van," Joan. "Remember the agreement...no beer in the refrigerator when the Baha'i come over? No visible alcohol, no grass smokin', an' no boinkin' 'r cussin' when the Baha'i are here," glancing over her shoulder at me. "Although the boinkin' hadn't turned out ta be much of an issue," giggling along with Hope.

"Those rules just apply ta regularly scheduled meetin's" I protested, ignoring Joan's last remark. "This thing t'night's an unscheduled thing. An' how c'n ya have a proper potluck without some beer 'r at least some Ripple? What the fu...what the hell kind'a potluck is 'at?" and stomped to the back door.

"Y're confusin' an orgy with a potluck," Joan.

"If it *was* a fuckin' orgy," under my breath, "you'd pro'bly have more people showin' up."

"Would you stop mumblin'!" Joan snapped. "That's all ya do anymore."

"I AM GOING TO GET A BEER!" slowly enunciating each word. "Unless," leaning against the doorframe, "Hope? Hope, would ya mind...?"

Hope turned away from the sink and wiped her hands on her tee shirt. Joan stopped slicing tomatoes and grabbed her arm.

"Don't you dare!" Joan cried. "Remember what we were talkin' about this mornin'?"

Hope paused then looked at me.

"Git it y'ur self. I ain't married ta yew."

She stuck her tongue out and returned to pulling the head of lettuce apart. She was giggling.

"Dammit, Joan," exaggerating a whine. "She won't be fit f'r marryin' if ya keep fillin' her head with all 'at woman's liber crap."

"Y're beginnin' ta sound more an' more like Jerry," Joan.

I ignored her.

*Christ! What else could I do but ignore her? Belt her one?*

I got a warm beer from the van then went back upstairs. The girls were still at the sink dicing mushrooms and cutting up bean sprouts.

"Can we use y'ur room f'r counselin' t'night if we need to?" Joan asked.

"As long as y're done b'fore I get home from work."

*Hell might freeze over an' I might get lucky at the lounge t'night.*

Joan came over and gave me a quick hug.

"Thanks. I've already picked it up an' vacuumed it," moving back to the sink. "Try not ta make a mess while y're gettin' ready f'r work."

I walked into the hall.

"And," she yelled, "clean up after y'urself in the bathroom an' don't pee all over the toilet seat! Raise it up!"

"I'll pee all over the goddamn wall if I wan'a," I mumbled.

"Y're mumbling again!" Joan.

*Damnation. She better be puttin' a coupl'a more inches on 'at bust line'a hers if she's plannin' on gettin' any bossier.*

I washed a pill down with a mouthful of foamy, warm beer.

I got to the lounge at the Roadway a little before 6:00. It was a small bar located at the back of the motel on the bottom level near the pool. The motel had sacrificed three rooms to provide Lubbock with one more watering hole.

# THE RAVING EUNUCH MONKS

It was a cozy, quiet, little place. Tables for two were placed along the front side of the room. Four tables seating up to six were arranged between the bar and two huge, plush booths at the far end of the lounge. The booths could seat four. They faced away from the tables and the bar. They were high-backed and arranged so anyone sitting in the booths had complete privacy.

The whole place was lavishly decorated in folds of black and red velvet, the floor covered in deep red carpeting. A small dance floor was located to the left of the bar. A jukebox on the dance floor left enough room for three or four couples at a time. Most of the songs on the jukebox were slow dry-humpers.

The lounge was kept dark. A chandelier hung in the center of the lounge. I could control its intensity with a dimmer switch located behind the bar, but the motel manager had instructed me to always keep it on low no matter how much the waitresses might bitch about the darkness. Small candles in burgundy globes burned at each table and in each of the private "make out" booths. All the waitresses claimed they felt like they were working in the bedroom of a French whore with bad taste. That wasn't too far off the mark.

The clientele consisted mainly of married men and women involved in affairs or traveling businessmen, truckers, and a few locals looking for company. Hanging out at the lounge wasn't cheap. I didn't know anybody who could afford it. You needed some bucks to sit around and get shitfaced. Either that or you had to know the bartender.

It was usually a pretty slow bar. The week nights were the busiest, but even then it never got that crowded. The tips could be outrageous. All you had to do was look at some guy having an affair then act like you were trying to remember his name and the son of a bitch'd leave you a five dollar bill. The waitresses could snag even more if they stumbled onto any action in the booths.

Hugo'd hit it off with the help and the hookers over the past few months. He'd drop in about two nights a week to shoot the shit with the waitress on duty or any of the working ladies that might be hanging around. It was a Hugo kind of place—small, quiet, out of the way, and had some Marty Robbins songs on the jukebox. He told me it was an atmosphere that encouraged stimulating conversation. Hugo's the only person I knew who'd go to a French whore's bedroom to discuss reincarnation, predestination, meditation, and whatever else that might come up along those lines. The working ladies and the waitresses thought the world of Hugo.

I relieved the day bartender. The day waitress had already taken off since it was so slow. I checked the schedule to see who'd be waiting tables for me.
*Missy. Good.*

I liked working with Missy. Hugo liked her too. She was one of a handful Hugo'd take to breakfast when the bar closed in the morning. Missy was twenty-four and a single mother of two. Divorced. Her husband had run off and left her or something like that. She had thick, wavy, shoulder length, red hair. Missy was about average height and build. Not fat. Not slim. Not stacked, not flat. She wasn't a raving beauty, but she was far from unattractive. Missy was one of those uniquely cute ladies so often overlooked because they don't come close to being a Raquel Welch or a Julie Christie. She was a little flaky, but intuitive enough to engage Hugo in some pretty heavy shit. Missy was a hoot to work with. I was positive she wasn't one of the waitresses whoring on the side.

I buttoned the top button on my white shirt and clipped on the bow tie the night bartender was required to wear. The waitresses had to wear tight, short, black skirts that barely covered their buttcheeks when they'd bend over to place drinks on a table. Their tops were skimpy little bras made of red velvet. It was a part of the managers plan to make the place more romantic. It seemed to work.

After watching a waitress all night, I was usually feeling pretty romantic.

Behind the bar a narrow aisle separated the sinks, cash register, coolers, kegs, and the drink well from the shelves where the glasses and call liquors were kept. Call liquors were expensive, usually running about twice what the house liquors cost. By taste, I couldn't tell the difference between them, although, when I kipped a shot, I'd always kipe a call liquor.

The wall behind the shelves was mirrored to make it look like there was more booze on them. The mirror was a pain in the ass to keep clean. It had to be polished at the beginning of each shift unless things were busy. The top of a set of butt-high cabinets served as the bottom shelf.

I'd begun removing all the bottles from the bottom shelf to clean the mirror when Missy came running into the lounge. She hurried to the bar, threw her purse down, dug through it, and then pulled out a cellophane package of panty hose.

"Hi, Gil. Hand me the bar knife," and looked up at me. "Oh my God," gasping. "Did yew fin'lly fall off 'at goddamn motorcycle? 'at's terrible. How c'n ya work like 'at? Yew cain't work like 'at! Yew'll scare the hell out'a the customers," rattling on as she stood up on the bottom rung of the stool and leaned across the bar. "Yew cain't even see out'a that eye, yew poor baby."

"It's not all that bad," I blurted quickly before losing my chance to get a word in.

"Ya sure?" sitting back down on the barstool. "It looks like hell!"

I handed the knife to her. She grabbed it and sawed the package open. Missy pinched the panty hose she was wearing and looked up.

"Run. Huge run. Ruined," hopping from the stool and coming around the end of the bar.

Missy stopped at the register, tossed the new pair of panty hose on the cabinet top I'd cleared, glanced at the door then told me to cover my eyes.

"I'm sorry," correcting herself. "Cover y'ur *good* eye."

She turned away from me and immediately unzipped her skirt, tugged at the hem until the skirt cleared her hips, and then let it fall to her ankles.

"Eye shut?" as she stepped from the skirt.

I raised my hand and covered the defective eye.

"Eye covered," I answered.

Missy stripped the ruined hose from her butt, pulled them down her thighs, and then bent over to push them off her calves.

*Oh, Jesus...red panties. Tiny, little, red panties.*

She straightened up, kicked the hose free of her feet, and then sat down on the bartender's stool. She placed her feet on the cabinet top, spread her legs, leaned forward between her knees and then grabbed the pair of new hose. I glanced in the mirror on the wall behind the shelves, then looked back at her bare thighs, hips, and all but naked ass. My stomach knotted.

*Oh, my God! I love her. I swear I do.*

I watched her extend a foot and ease the hose over brightly painted scarlet toe nails. Her calf and thigh muscles rippled as she moved her foot up and down, wriggling her toes to insure a snug fit. She repeated the procedure for the other foot. Using a series of slow, gentle tugs, she carefully slipped the hose up and over, first one calf, then the other. My eye darted from the mirror to her thighs, back to the mirror, then to her hips, then to the tiny red panties, back to the mirror, her butt.

*Missy McNeil. Oh, yes! It works. It's...beautiful!*

She straightened, placed her feet on the floor and stood up. She turned away from me slightly. She bent over and continued to slip the hose over...

*Those wonderful, silken thighs!*

She bent all the way over, reaching for her ankles.

*MY GOD! What a…! How could anybody in their right mind've walked out on that? Two kids 'r no two kids. She's absolutely gorgeous.*

She began straightening the hose, caressing each leg in turn with long, loving strokes. I watched her butt tense, then relax, tense, relax, over and over again, as she worked her way up her legs with soft delicate strokes. Smoothing up the outside then smoothing up the inside of those flawless legs.

Erect, she slid the panty hose over that perfectly sculpted butt. The sheer material slightly tinted the tiny red panties. She leaned forward a little at the waist and ran her hands between her legs, tenderly smoothing the panty hose snuggly into place.

*GOD, I swear, I'll raise all my kids in the church'a y'ur choice if ya'd just lemme touch that butt! That's all I want. Just lemme touch it once.*

*With my lips.*

*My tongue.*

She stepped into her skirt, bent over quickly and began pulling the tight little piece of material up her legs, wriggling her whole body, tugging at the skirt, undulating until it finally slipped back into place.

*G'bye sweet butt. G'bye tiny red panties…*

"Yew c'n look now," she announced.

Her voice sounded far away.

"I need he'p with the zipper," backing up to me.

I reached over and carefully eased the zipper to the top and clamped it. I was shaking. I was coming apart.

"Thank yeeeew," then pranced away smoothing the last of the wrinkles from the skirt.

"An', thank yew f'r bein' such a gentleman. I wouldn't feel safe doin' 'at with jus' anybody hangin' aroun'."

*The kiss'a death. She thinks I'm a safe kind'a guy. Safe guys spend their whole damn lives with a flashlight in a closet strokin' to a Playboy.*

*Fuck me dead.*

My face was throbbing again, my stomach hurt, and now my balls ached. I got a glass of water and took another set of pills. I crossed my arms on the bar and rested my head on them. I began to whip myself.

*I'm livin' with two eligible females. I'm livin' down the street from two horny hairdressers. I'm surrounded by hookers an' hot-ass waitresses at work. I attend a college with at least 15,000 women an' I know, almost f'r a fact, that at least a quarter of 'em put out like nymphos. Pro'bly.*

*I work my ass off, have a nice place ta live, study hard, own a goddamn chopper, an' have a pleasant enough personality. I'm not flat out ugly an' I have a decent lookin' body.*

*F'r Christ sake! What's it take ta get laid in this town?*

The lounge door jerked open. Chad strolled in with his arm wrapped around a stunningly beautiful young woman. He was decked out for Saturday game day—Red Raider red blazer, white shirt, no tie, black slacks. His whore was decked out in a Red Raider red, lady's cut blazer, a tight, white boobie-sweater, and a sprayed on, just-below-the-belly button length black skirt.

*Go Tech.*

"Hi, Chad!" Missy yelled in surprise.

"Not yet," smoothly, then pointing a finger at Missy and winking, "but...I'm working on it," followed by a low, subdued laugh.

"Y're nuts," Missy, as she walked over to give him a quick hug.

His date, still giggling at his dumbass remark, didn't seem to mind the show of affection. Chad introduced the two. They quickly sized each other up. Chad walked to the bar with Missy on one arm and his slut on the other.

"How's it been going, bubba Gil? I heard about the eye. Bummer, man...really."

"Bubba?" Missy, confused.

"Gil hasn't mentioned our being brothers?" Chad, pretending to be hurt by the oversight.

"No," she answered, studying my face then concentrating on his. "I'd'a never guessed it."

Chad's slut, trying not to stare at the eye, extended her hand.

"I finally git ta meet bubba Gil," and smiled warmly. "I'm Robyn Mills."

*I'm Robyn "Clap Queen" Mills.*

I shook her hand politely.

"Gil, where's the restroom?" Robyn.

*Where's the mattress, Gil?*

"The door next to the jukebox," and pointed.

She nodded then slithered off.

*Damn, she's so nice! So...nasty lookin'!*

Missy put a hand over her mouth.

"I jus' cain't b'lieve it! Yew two...brothers!"

I pulled a five from the register and handed it to her.

"Play somethin' f'r the customers, please."

"I'll be right back, Chad. We gotta talk an' catch up a little."

"Where the hell ya know her from?" I asked Chad.

"I had a friend in a duplex on Fifth Street. Missy was her neighbor. I'd watch her kids from time-to-time. The compensation arrangement we'd worked out must remain...confidential," and winked.

*Smack his ass! Knock 'at sleazy little grin right off his face.*

"Could I have a scotch on the rocks and a Mai Tai for the lady?" Chad.

"Missy's not supposed ta drink on the job," attempting a slam.

Chad executed this unnerving, silent laugh he'd developed— head back, eyes closed.

"Gil, Gil, Gil. That *is* rich," pointing his finger at me. "Seriously, a Mai Tai for Robbie and a scotch for moi," reaching inside the blazer for his wallet. "By the way," opening the wallet and producing five twenty dollar bills, "this will be the first of several payments I intend to make over the next few months toward satisfying my financial obligation to you," then placed the bills on the bar.

*Snotty little turd. Couldn't just say here's some'a the fuckin' money I stole from ya.*

Robbie exited the restroom and began to help Missy select songs. Judy Collins began to sing. Chad, back towards the ladies, was missing the butt bouncing show I was getting as they both leaned over the jukebox, tapping their toes to the music while making their selections.

*Time ta jack ol' Chad up.*

"Been by y'ur place lately?" I started.

"Picked up a change of clothes," turning and glancing at the jukebox. "I've had my hands full elsewhere these past few days. Why?"

"So ya hadn't seen Jerry t'day?"

"My God!" groaning dramatically. "What burr does he have up his ass now?"

I spread the twenties out on the bar.

"This one's mine," sliding a bill to the side. "This is Jerry's," sliding a second bill alongside my twenty. I separated the remaining three bills and tapped each in turn.

"This one's f'r Shauna, this one's f'r Bobbie, an' this last one gets divided among the three of 'em as a 'You Lyin', Cheatin' Motherfucker' penalty," then swept the bills up and stuffed them into my pocket.

Chad looked at me blankly.

"Ya see, Chad," and began making his drinks, "I've taken it upon myself ta help ya get honest with Jerry b'fore he kills ya."

"What?" surprised, but not *real* surprised.

"You been collectin' fifty-five dollars a piece f'r rent an' around twenty each f'r utilities. All the landlord wants is fifty a piece. Includin' utilities. Right?"

"NO!" grabbing the edge of the bar with both hands and throwing himself forward—classic Chad dramatics.

"Ya fucked up on this one, bubba," I growled. "Ya showed me the lease back in May. Remember? Ya gave me all the details. I know *exactly* what that lease says. Last night I found out what ya've been collectin' from ever'body at Will's."

"What did you tell Jerry?" nervously.

"Ever' motherfuckin' thing."

"But it's not true! It's not true. I had to sign a new lease. The landlor..."

"Save it, Chad. I'm not the one y're gunna have ta convinc..."

"Wait a minute! Just you wait a minute! The landlord found out Will had left and I had to renegotiate the lease!" face etched in sincerity.

"Well, if I was you, I'd show a copy'a the new lease ta Jerry as fast as I could 'r, I swear, Chad, he's gunna...well...there's no tellin' what he's gunna do."

I was dead serious.

"Of *course* I can show him a lease. That's no problem. No problem at all," slightly panicked. "It's at the house."

"I'll do ya a favor. You go find it an' bring it back up here. When he comes in t'night, I'll show it to him an' 'at'll take care'a that. Maybe. Ya see, Chad...I'm afraid that, as mad as he is about this, he's not gunna give ya a chance ta explain shit. He's gunna just start in poundin' an' cuttin'."

"What time will he be here?" frantically.

"Anytime," and placed his drinks on the bar.

Chad glanced at the Rolex on his arm.

"Damn," he hissed while turning to the jukebox. "Robbie! We've got to leave," then turned back to me. "I had no idea it was this late. Could you put those in plastic glasses or something so we can take them with us?"

"Against the law."

"I'm not paying for them if I can't drink them," anxiously glancing at the door.

"Whoops!" sweeping them from the top of the bar into the well. "My mistake. No charge."

"Thank you," huffing.

"Ya want me ta ask Jerry ta help ya look f'r the lease? I know just where he'd start...right up y'ur ass an' he'd go in boots first. I mean it, Chad...ya better have 'at lease up here t'night. Ya went an' fucked the wrong man this time. Chad, he's not college boy pissed," as a final warning. "He's *jungle* pissed."

Chad reached for his pocket, hesitated, and then pulled his wallet out. He handed me three more twenties.

"Tell Jerry," grumbling, "to let me know how much more I owe everyone. This is all I can spare right now."

I took the money.

Missy and Robyn came up alongside Chad. He hugged Missy, then told Robyn they were going to have to leave or be late for the game.

"Nice to meet you," Robyn called out over her shoulder as Chad ushered her to the door.

*Until t'night, sweet Robyn.*

Missy sat down at the bar.

"Yew an' him brothers. God, 'at's so hard ta b'lieve. Ya know, I remember him tellin' me he had a brother named Gil, but I never knew Chad's last name so when ya started workin' here I never put it t'gether. I swear. Yew two're as diff'r'nt as night an' day," shaking her head.

"How would ya know that?" bending over to clean up the mess I'd made in the drink well. "Ya never seen *me* naked," under my breath.

No response.

*She didn't hear me. Just as well. Shouldn't't'a said it. Just jealous b'cause I'll never get any off'a Missy. I'm too goddamn 'safe' ta...*

The light touch of fingers on my temple startled me. I looked up. Missy had leaned all the way across the bar. She was smiling sweetly.

"I don't know whut he told yew, but Chad ain't my type," easing back across the bar and settling on the stool. "He was kind enough ta he'p watch the kids f'r me a few years back when I was workin' some real strange hours at the Cotton Club. It was nice uv him ta do that. I'd have him over f'r dinner ever' now an' then 'cause I couldn't afford ta pay him nothin' else. He quit comin' aroun' when he broke up with my neighbor."

*Goddammit.*

"I'm sorry. I didn't mean ta assume. I was just bein' a shithead. Truth is, I think a lot'a ya. Y're one nice lady."

"Why, thank yew, Mr. McNeil," hopping from the barstool and curtsying. "Ya make me feel like one nice lady."

"Want me ta kick his ass f'r tryin' ta make it look like you two were...you know, that he was..."

"Hell no, Gil," laughing. "He'll git his someday. It's like Hugo says, what goes aroun', comes aroun'."

"I suppose."


The Stones. "Lady Jane".

Missy hurried over to the jukebox.

"This is one'a my fav'rite songs," she told me.

When it was over she turned and looked at me.

"If it stays slow t'night, would yew mind dancin'a few songs with me?"

"I'd love to, but things're gunna pick up I'm afraid. Danny, Homer, JD, Jerry an' some others're supposed ta show up anytime now."

"How about Hope an' Joan?" moving back to the bar.

"They won't be in. They got some kind'a Baha'i thing goin' on at the house t'night. A potluck. With no booze."

"So 'at's why ever'body's comin' up here. They ain't got nowhere else ta go."

"Any port in a storm."

"No matter," she chirped. "Cain't he'p but have fun with 'at crowd."

"That's the truth."

I downed a set of pills with a shot of Old Charter.

*How many's 'at been since...since...?*

*Relaxing. Make me feel..happy?*

*Yeah. Damn happy.*

*T'night's gunna be a hoot.*

"Ya know if Hugo might show up?" Missy.

"No. Haven't seen him since Frid'y mornin'. He might be goin' ta the potluck."

Missy looked disappointed.

"But," I added, "he'll pro'bly drop by if he's in the neighborhood. He likes it here."

She smiled and went to her normal post, the stool at the end of the bar next to the wall. Reaching over the bar, Missy found her purse, pulled a romance paperback out and began to read with the help of a small key chain flashlight.

Ten minutes later the door popped open and Jerry stumbled in. He was dressed in a filthy, sleeveless, olive drab tee shirt, gloves, a bandanna, his goggles, and ridding chaps over the same pair of jeans he'd been wearing for the past two weeks. The parking lot must have been empty or Jerry would have stripped the gear off outside as a part of the dismount. That was one of the unwritten dismount rules—if there's no audience in the parking lot of a bar then you take the show inside.

Jerry, eyes still adjusting to the dark interior of the lounge, plowed right into the table closest to the door. He knocked the candle over and nearly fell to the floor.

"Fuck, man...whu' the..." in his hissing slur.

"Jerry!" Missy squealed.

She put her book down, skipped over to him, and then gave him a big hug. She let go and righted the candle on the table before it went out. Missy took Jerry's hand and led him to a barstool. She reached up, removed his goggles, and placed them on the stool next to him. Jerry tossed his head back, squinted one eye, and fixed the other, wide open, on Missy.

"So, t'night, after ya git off work, we'll go ta y'ur place, pick up the kids, drive ta Mexico an' tie the fuckin' knot. Whud'a ya say?"

Missy threw her arms around his neck.

"Whut else c'n I say?" excitedly. "YES, YES, YES! Oh, my *God*! I'm so damn *thrilled*! Lemme see the rang! I wan'a see the *rang*!" jumping up and down.

"Aw come on, man," hitting his head on the bar a few times. "Don't go layin' 'at ring shit on me again, Missy. I love ya. Ain' 'at enough? I'll git ya a fuckin' ring in Mexico. I promise."

"No rang?" taking her hands from around his neck and planting her fists on her hips.

"Did I say here wudn' a ring? Huh? Is 'at whud I said? Damn, woman. Course there's a ring. I jus' ain't got it yet 'cause...'cause I want *yew* ta pick it out. 'at's the *only* reason I ain't got one on me right now. Ya gotta b'lieve me, sweetheart. This is the f'r real thing, man," then turned to me. "Bottle'a Bud."

"Hear 'at, Gil?" Missy angrily. "He wants me ta run off ta Mexico an' hand him my virginity on a silver platter b'fore I even see a rang!"

"He's a cad," as I opened the Bud and handed it to Jerry. "No doubt about it."

She slapped him on the butt.

"Glad ta see ya," pecking him on the cheek before returning to her reading corner.

"How's the ol' eyeball?" Jerry, leaning closer for a better look.

"Pr'tty much the same. Hurts like hell."

"Shiiit, man," peeling the bandanna from his head and stuffing it into his back pocket. "I been ridin' Doug's bike," and took a gulp of beer.

"How'd that go?"

"Fuckin' death trap. Brakes're all fucked up. Leaks gas under the tank. Wirin' shocks the shit out'a ya. Springers ain't a'justed right. Han'le bars're loose. Fuck me, man. I'm lucky ta be alive," brows raised, eyes squinted.

"Y're the one helped him build it."

"Yeah, I did, but damn…I also tol' him 'at it wudn' safe ta ride yet. 'at it needed a lot'a tweakin'," followed by another big gulp of beer. "Is he gunna listen ta me? Fuck no. Whu' the hell do I know? Right?"

"I'm kind'a su'prised he let ya ride it."

"No choice. Hell, he got so fucked up at JD's, he couldn't drive it back ta Vann's. I wuz gunna drive it for him, but two blocks wuz enough. Fuck it. I drove it ta my place an' put the bike an' him in the basement. Then…an' then," bouncing up and down on the stool, "shit, man, y're gunna love this! Guess who's movin' in ta 'at li'l house b'tween me an' yew guys?" emptying the bottle then burping. "Am I payin' f'r this?" momentarily distracted from his story.

"The bar'll catch the first one."

"Ya should'a tol' me tha' b'fore I wasted my freebie on a cheap-ass Bud! I'll pay f'r the Bud an' yew c'n let the bar buy me the secon' drink. Gimme one'a 'em expensive imports, man. Mos' expensive one ya got."

I reached into the cooler and retrieved a Coors.

" 'at shit ain't imported," he frowned.

"Bullshit. Comes all the way from Colorada. Most expensive beer in the place."

Jerry snorted and took it from me.

"Anyways," bouncing again. "Guess who's movin' inta tha' white shack?"

"No idea, but I saw the U-Haul this evenin'."

"Yew ever seen 'at big, long haired, jerkoff 'at rides aroun' on Neil's bike ever' once in a while? Yew know who I'm talkin' about. Neil's *bitch*?"

"Oh no! Don't tell me that."

" 'at's right, motherfucker," and leaned forward. "I don't know if it's Neil 'r the bitch, 'r the both uv 'em, but the bitch wuz unloadin' the U-Haul t'night."

Jerry took a cigarette from my pack.

"Want one?" he asked and shook one out for me.

I took it and sat down heavily on the barstool.

"Goddammit," I muttered.

"No shit, Godda…no shit," muttering back.

Jerry put my pack of cigarettes in his pocket, lit the cigarette, inhaled deeply, and then exhaled the whole smoky breath through his nose.

"We could run him off," as I lit mine. "It pro'bly wouldn't take long ta do if we put a real effort into it."

"Nah. I'm jus' gunna kill him. I'll kill him the same night I kill y'ur fuckin' brother. I got it all fig'red out, man. I'll tell Neil 'at Chad wants ta give him a blowjob. When Neil comes over ta the house lookin' f'r Chad, I'll shot 'em both an' make it look like a lover's fight. 'at .45 I got ain't registered. Cops'll jus' think it wuz Chad's 'r Neil's. Whud'a ya think?"

"We gotta do somethin', Jerry," not answering the question. "Seriously. I'm not takin' any shit off a him an' if they start harassin' the girls…"

"Hey! He starts pullin' 'at shit, an' he's all mine," Jerry snarled.

"Speakin'a shit," as I reached into my pocket to retrieve all the twenties Chad had given me, "Chad saw the wisdom in payin' ever'body back the rent money he's been stealin'," and placed the wad of bills on the bar in front of Jerry. "He wants ya ta figure out how much more he owes ever'body."

Jerry's eyes popped open then, suddenly, squinted fiercely.

"I'm still gunna kill his ass f'r fuckin' with me, man," Jerry growled.

"Get the money from him first, then kill him."

Two couples entered the lounge and went directly to the privacy booths. The guys, wearing red Texas Tech blazers, were in their mid forties and balding.

The girls had been in before. They were working girls.

*Pro'bly told their wives they were goin' ta the game. Scummy bastards.*

"Don't go starin' at the ladies when they come in," I told Jerry.

"Wudn' starin'. I wuz jus' lookin' close. Wonderin' about it."

"I thought ya said ya had all ya could handle at the house."

"Nobody's ever OD'd on pussy," turning back to the bar.

"Ya know how long it's been since I got laid?" I mumbled.

"Overseas?" snickering.

"Did I already tell ya?"

"Nah, but it shows, man. Y're all tense all'a time. Actin' kind'a squirrelly. Ya start droolin' an' y'ur head starts ta jerkin' when y're aroun' chicks. Joan tol' me ya make her fuckin' nervous sometimes."

"I'm serious as hell. I can't think'a anything else *but* pussy anymore. It's drivin' me batty. I walk around 'at goddamn campus with a boner all day long. I wake up with a boner. I hear one'a the girls walkin' down the hall at the house an' I raise a chubby. I'm fuckin' dyin'."

"Whu's stoppin' ya from beat..."

"Not the same, Jerry an' ya know it."

"I don't know *shit* about touchin' on myself," snickering. "I never had ta do tha' shit, man."


Missy came up to the bar and ordered two White Russians, a bourbon and water, and a martini, extra dry.

*One'a the adulteratin' suits must be a fuckin' alcoholic.*

Jerry and Missy talked while I got the drinks. She took the order out, returned to her stool, and began reading again.

"I'm not shittin' ya, Jerry," continuing the conversation where I'd left off. "I'm gunna take a pay advance at Hugo's an' spend next weekend in Juarez. I don't have a choice anymore," whispering so Missy wouldn't hear me.

Jerry grimaced, rubbed both hands over his face then leaned forward.

"Yew gotta relax some. In'a firs' place, 'em whores in the booth back there'd be cheaper 'an whud its gunna cost ya ta go all'a way ta Mexico, git a room, stay drunk, eat, an' ever'thing else. So if y'ur gunna buy it, buy it local. But...yew ain't gotta pay f'r it, asshole. Yew'd know 'at if ya wudn' sperm blind."

"Sperm blind?" sensing a Jerry special.

"Yeah. 'at's when ya go so long without it 'at all 'em li'l spermies backs up inta y'ur head an' keeps ya from seein' a piece a willin' tail even if she's buck naked, spread eagle right in front'a ya. 'at's whu' yew got, man...sperm blindness." Jerry leaned closer. "Ya know who Bobbie is, don'ch ya?"

"The Bobbie at y'ur place? The skinny one with the white hair. Always paintin' on y'ur front porch?"

"Yeah. She's so fuckin' hot f'r ya, she steams her silk when she jus' hears y'ur name."

"She tell ya this shit b'fore ya thump her 'r after ya thump her. Or do ya hear her callin' out my name while Chad's layin' her?"

Jerry snapped away from the bar, leaned way back and raised his brows high. Missy looked over and smiled. Jerry slowly moved back toward the bar, gradually coming to rest on his elbows.

"Ya dumb turd," he whispered. "Ya sit aroun' feelin' sorry f'r y'urself an' fabr'catin' all kinds'a shit up about who's doin' who," shaking his head. "Y're one stupidass turd, man."

"I know damn well y're fuckin' her. Ya said so last night. An' I know f'r almost a fact Chad's pro'bly nailin' her too."

"Oh, right, right. Yew know jus' about ever'thing there's ta know about ever'thing, don'ch ya, Mr. College Man? Shiiit. Yew don't know *squat*. Yew really think I'd go puttin' my thing where Chad's had his? Whu' kind'a guy ya take me for? 'at hurts deep, man. Ya might as well'a…I don't know…said somethin' about my mother as ta go an' say I'd sloppy secon' Chad," placing his head on the bar.

"So Chad *is* humpin' her."

Jerry raised his head.

"Did I say 'at? Did I fuckin' say 'at? Look. I'm jus' gunna tell ya this one time 'cause, like, it ain't my balls turnin' purple. Un'erstand? One time only, so listen good. I wuz only kiddin' aroun' about Bobbie las' night. I ain't kiddin' about me an' Shauna, bu' tha's a whole diff'r'nt thing. So…*I* ain't doin' Bobbie an' *Chad* ain't doin' Bobbie. *Nobody* ya know's doin' Bobbie. There's this asshole zoomie from the air base 'at keeps comin' aroun', but Bobbie's had it with him. She tol' him ta fuck off, but he keeps comin' aroun'. I even tol' him ta watch his ass. I think he used ta beat her up now an' then b'fore I moved in with 'em. She's been tryin' hard ta git him ta stay away. 'specially since she foun' out yew ain't gittin' any off Joan 'r Hope. I ain't shittin', Gil…she's got the hots f'r ya, man."

"What'd Bobbie do, walk up an' say 'Hey, Jerry, I got the hots f'r Gil'?"

"Better'n 'at. I c'n hear 'em talkin' when I'm in'a basement workin' on'a bike. Git this…they think Chad's a fuckin' clown. But, anyhow, 'at's how I know Bobbie thinks y're a stud muffin."

"She dudn't act like it."

"Are yew shittin' me? How many times a week ya see her up at y'ur place? Six? Seven? Ten?"

"She's learnin' yoga from Hope an' she talks ta Joan about Baha'i stuff."

"Will ya listen ta whud I'm sayin'?" raising his voice.

Missy looked up.

"Don't start y'ur arguin'!" she warned.

"I swear ta God!" lowering his voice. "She's usin' 'at shit f'r an excuse. She ain't inta 'at shit, man. She's a damn hairdresser from Tahoka, f'r Chris' sake."

"Is 'at what ya hear through the floor? That she's hangin' around ta get my attention?" still finding it hard to believe him.

"Damn, Gil. How easy ya want me ta make this for ya?" banging his head on the bar. "It ain't like she's sittin' there tellin' Shauna an' 'em she wants y'ur peter in her heater. She says shit like, 'I jus' love his fuckin' sense'a humor'. An' tells 'em how much she likes seein' ya ridin' y'ur bike with y'ur shirt off, an' how much she likes y'ur beard, an' how damn smart ya are 'cause y're in college. An' 'at wuz even *after* I tol' her about how ya damn near flunked out."

"I wudn't even close ta flunkin' out," I protested.

"Don't go missin' the point an' the point is she wants ya like a rabbit in heat an' yew been too stupid ta see it."

"How come ya never told me this b'fore?" still suspicious.

"I jus' fig'red ya didn' like her. Didn' know yew wuz jus' bein' plain-ass retarded about it."

"How come *you* never made it with her? She's not bad lookin'… kind'a plain, but she's got a nice little figure."

Jerry finished his beer then leaned forward.

"I'm gunna tell ya somethin' 'at'd embarrass the hell out uv her if she wuz ta ever know I told ya. Ya gotta promise ta never tell anybody. I swear…if she knew anybody else knew it'd kill her."

"You about ta jerk me around with some more'a y'ur bullshit?"

He reached out and gripped my arm tight enough to make it hurt.

"No. It'd kill her."

"Okay. I understand," preparing myself for a possible kick in the ass.

He paused to light a cigarette before beginning.

"Fact is, Gil," coughing lightly "I could'a made her. We wuz in her bed an' I wuz havin' a smoke while I wuz lettin' her git used ta bein' there naked with me. I like a lady ta feel relaxed, ya know. I want her ta enjoy the whole thing as much as I do. 'at'a way they keep comin' back f'r more. Know whud I mean? So, anyways, we wuz jus', ya know, makin' small talk an' she starts tellin' me how her daddy wuz originally from Tahoka. Her daddy died when she wuz a baby so her an' her mom moved back ta Nevada where her mama's from. Her folks'd met in Mississippi durin' World War II. Bobbie'd come out ta Lubbock after finishin' high school las' August ta see Tahoka an' some'a her relatives f'r the firs' time since she's a baby. She was gunna go ta Fr'isco after leavin' here an' get inta art school 'r somethin' like 'at. Anyway, she ended up stickin' aroun' here 'cause she ran out'a money. So, we wuz talkin' about Tahoka an' she starts tellin' me about all her relatives in Tahoka. Guess the fuck whut, Gil? Bobbie's dad's my mama's brother. My fuckin' uncle. I wuz layin' here naked as sin with my own damn cousin, an' jus' three cigarette puffs away from jumpin' her. I knew I had a cousin floatin' around somewhere, but until 'at moment, I never suspected it was Bobbie. Ain't that the shits, man?" raising his brows high.

*Liein' bastard.*

"I mean," continuing, "the idea'a doin' a cousin dudn't bother me none, 'specially if *she* dudn't know we wuz cousins, but I decided ta tell her first jus' ta keep things up front an' make sure it wuz cool with her."

"What'd she say?"

Jerry took a deep breath then exhaled slowly.

"Fuck, man...she didn't take ta the idea at all."

"What'd she do?"

" 'member 'at two weeks in June when I went ta California?"

"Yeah."

"Well...I wudn' in California. I wuz stayin' with a friend down in Sinton. Ya see, after I'd run all 'at by Bobbie...she kneed me four 'r five times in the nuts so hard it took two fuckin' weeks b'fore I could walk again."

"No shit?" relieved.

"No shit. Gil...I honest-ta-God thoughd I wuz gunna lose 'em both. They got big as soft balls an' turned dark purple. I couldn't keep food down f'r a week. Couldn't piss. She hurt me, man. JD gave me a bunch'a painkillers. If it hadn't been f'r them, I swear, I'd'a died. It hurt worse than when I got shot. Fuck, man, I'd'a rather been shot. Even after the swellin' went down I had ta keep eatin' 'em painkillers f'r a coupl'a weeks. Damn near got addicted to 'em."

"Those pills'a his're addictive?"

"Hell yeah. They're fuckin' narcotics. Straight up narcotics, man. Shit, did JD give ya some'a his pills f'r y'ur eye?"

"Yeah. I've been eatin' 'em like candy all day. Gotta. Takes that many ta keep the pain under control."

"Don't go gittin' caught with 'em. It's five ta ten if ya do. Jus' be real careful with 'em."

"They make me feel mellow. *Real* mellow. Relaxed...real calm."

"I know. That's whut gets ya hooked on 'em. Anyways, about Bobbie...jus' don't *ever* tell her whud I jus' tol' ya. An' 'member this, Gil, the way she worked me over, I swear, she might be a li'l bit psycho."

"Pro'bly runs in the family," I joked.

"Hope not, man. It's scary ta think I could git 'at'a way."

"Just one more thing, Jerry. Did she figure out I was available *b'fore* she was gunna make it with ya 'r *after* she kicked ya in the nuts?"

"Whu' the fuck diff'r'nce 'at make? Chicks git horny too."

"It makes a difference ta me."

"Lemme see," rubbing his chin and looking up at the ceiling. "I don't think she knew yew wudn't gettin' any 'til after I got back from Sinton...after she'd kicked me in the balls. Ya see, whud I heard in'a basement wuz 'at Hope an' Joan'd pr'tty much told Bobbie an' Shauna ever'thing there wuz ta know about y'ur sorry-ass sex life. 'at's when Bobbie got real inter'sted in 'at Baha'i an' Yoga shit," sneering.

Jerry pulled my cigarettes from his pocket and lit up without offering me one.

"So whud'a ya think?" he snickered. "Still wan'a run off ta Mexico? She's a kind'a homely, but after livin' aroun' her f'r a while, I'm seein' she's a damn nice person. 'cept f'r 'at mean streak. An' ya know whud else? Them clothes she wears make her look boney, but I'm tellin' ya, man...don't let tha' throw ya. When she's naked, she's a real turn on kind'a skinny an' her nipples..."

"Jesus, Jerry! That's y'ur own damn cousin y're talkin' about."

"Hey!" defensively. "It ain't like I fucked her, man. I'm jus' talkin' about the shit I saw *b'fore* I knew she's my cousin. It ain't wrong ta talk about the stuff I saw *b'fore* I knew she's my cousin. Right? I wuz jus' tryin' ta help ya make up y'ur mind. 'at's all. I wudn' tryin' ta be nasty," grumbling.

I got Jerry another beer and thought it over.

"Ya swear y're not just settin' me up. That this idn't a joke? She *really*, honest-ta-God wants ta go out with me?"

"Fuck," Jerry snorted then took a drink. "I don't know if she wants ta be seen in public with ya, but I'm damn sure she wants ya ta dick her blind...'mong other things."

I put my elbows on the bar and rested my chin in my hands.

"She does have nice hair."

"She's a hair dresser. Whud'a ya expect?"

"No, I mean the length...down past her waist. Soft lookin'. White as snow. She pro'bly bleaches it."

"She does," Jerry, casually. "She's either bleachin' her head her dyein' her crotch blac..."

"Shut up, dammit! I don't wan'a hear it!"

"SHHHHHH!" Missy again.

"Yew gunna talk to her?" he asked in a whisper. He was wearing one of those "I already know the answer" sneers.

"Lemme think about it. F'r some reason it's gettin' harder an' harder ta b'lieve anything ya tell me anymore."

"Take y'ur time, man. An' while y're thinkin' it over, jus' incase I *am* lyin' to ya about her nat'ral hair color, yew c'n be askin' aroun' town ta see if black pube dye c'n make ya sick if ya swallow it."

"Goddammit, Jerry! If she starts seein' me, y're gunna have ta quit talkin' about her fuckin' pubes aroun' me...'r anybody else. Got that?"

The door opened and JD hobbled in. Danny and Jonas were right behind him.

As dirty as they all were, Missy went over and hugged each one, saving JD for the last and longest.

"Yew started drankin' again!" Missy scolded JD.

"Shud up, winch. I never stopped. B'sides, yew ain't my ol' lady," and reached around her to plant a single, gentle pat on her butt.

"Watch 'at!" she warned. "Jerry pr'posed ta me t'night. He'll kick y'ur ass."

"He couldn't kick my ass even if I..."

"Don't go pissin' me off ol' man," Jerry snarled.

"Put a beer f'r me on jerkoff's tab, Gil," as JD pointed at Jerry.

JD settled into a chair at the large table alongside the dance floor. Jonas shook my hand then joined him.

Danny flopped onto the stool next to Jerry.

"Thanks, man," Jerry frowned.

"No problem," Danny. "Thanks for what?"

"Sittin' on my fuckin' goggles."

Danny jumped up. Both of the lenses had popped out of the soft rubber frames. One lens was cracked. Danny picked them up and handed them to Jerry. Jerry examined the damage.

"Hell, Jerry...a little glue. Some tape. A few staples," Danny.

"They cost me nine hun'r'd dollars," tossing them onto the bar. "They wuz made custom ta my face."

"If I bought you a really expensive beer, would that make things even?" Danny, pursing his lips.

"Nah. 'at Coors shit tastes like piss. This 'un's gunna cost ya. I wan'a shot'a Jack."

"Bar keep!" Danny. "My friend here, who evidently is a connoisseur of urine, would like a shot of Jack," placing his hand on Jerry's shoulder.

"We ain't been friends since the secon' ya butt-cheeked my fav'rite pair'a ridin' glasses ta bits."

I placed the shot glass in front of Jerry.

"Two pitchers of Bud," Danny, holding a five dollar bill up.

"Make 'at three!" A waded bill flew from the table, hitting me in the chest.

"Four!" as another bill wad hit the shelves.

Jerry and Danny carried the mugs and pitchers to the table as I filled them.


After all the pitchers had been delivered Danny joined me at the bar.

"Draw a pitcher for me and I'll sit here and describe to you how rich we are about to become," Danny.

"Looks that good?"

"It looks that good," smacking his lips.

It was encouraging that Danny was impressed. I placed the pitcher in front of him then filled his glass from the tap. Danny took a long slow drink then leaned heavily on his elbows. He began rolling the glass between his palms.

"All right," smacking his lips. "Here's the deal. We found the three Catholic churches and a Methodist church with broken windows. JD estimated all four church repairs would bring in fifteen thousand dollars."

"Fifteen thousan' dollars?" nearly choking.

"Yep. And that's a lot cheaper than what the out-of-town studios would charge."

"How much an hour would we be payin' ourselves?"

Danny fell forward, touching his chest on the bar.

"Gil...stop thinking in hourly terms. This is going to be much bigger than hourly."

"Just wonderin'."

"Now listen," going back to his elbows while taking a deep breath. "I'll give you the next year in a nutshell. Hold your questions until I'm finished."

Missy went to the back of the room to check the make out booths.

"This is what we've got," Danny began. "We've got fifteen thousand dollars worth of repairs in churches that can't afford fifteen thousand dollars. JD says no studio in the country allows a client payment plan. So, that's what *we're* going to do so we can get the business. We'll also build new windows on a payment plan for poorer churches that've been turned down on loans for windows. We found a fifth church in Guadeloupe that didn't have *any* stained glass. JD estimated he could design a pretty nice set of windows, build them, and install them for around six thousand. We'll ask for twenty percent down and X number of payments. *But*, that's just the beginning. Think of how many churches there are within a hundred miles, hell, two hundred miles of Lubbock? What if only a quarter of them needed repairs or wanted new windows? Guess what else? Storm glass. Install storm glass outside the stained glass windows to protect against vandalism and the weather. And what if something still happens to the windows, like a plane flying through them? Insurance. We'll provide a low cost insurance policy. And there's more. Remember all those art students from Tech who hang around JD's asking him about how to work with stained glass? Get this, we're going to teach them how at Lubbock Art Glass Studio. And where are they going to buy their supplies? Lubbock Art Glass Studio."

Danny took a drink then looked at me, brows raised.

"What do you think?" he asked.

"Well..."

Missy stepped up along side Danny.

"Another round f'r the love booth," slipping her arm around Danny's waist. "How's it goin' big guy?"

"Could *not* be better, Missy," Danny smiled. "You certainly are looking sweet tonight."

"Why, thank yew, sir. F'r that, yew don't have ta tip me," with a wink.

"He wudn't gunna tip ya anyway," I said as I placed the White Russians on the tray.

"Don't be mean," Missy ordered. "If he had it, he'd be tippin' royal," coming to his defense.

I got the wine, marked a round down on the ticket, and then placed the Martini on the tray. Missy blew Danny a kiss and was off. Danny watched her in the mirror as she swished back to the booth.

"I love her, Gil," Danny sighed heavily. "I'd marry her in a heart beat," and watched her walk back to the party table after delivering the drinks.

"Let's get back ta this glass thing," tapping Danny on the shoulder. "It all sounds good an' I'm willin' ta see how it plays out, but I've got immediate concerns…immediate financial pressures ta deal with. How much would I be able ta make in a weekend? Say in…ten, maybe twelve hours?"

"A weekend?" Danny, as if in pain.

"Ya told me not ta think hourly."

"Gil, if it eases your mind, then I'll put it this way. A *restoration specialist* doing a repair would be paid six to eight dollars an hour."

"Six ta eight an hour?" eyes wide.

"That's the specialist, Gil. The business is charging ten to twenty dollars an hour per repaired piece, depending on whether it's painted or whatever. JD says a good worker can replace three pieces an hour using the tricks he'd teach us."

"Christ, Danny, even at six an hour, that's more'n *three* times what I'm bein' paid at Hugo's or here."

Danny smacked his forehead into the palms of his hands.

"You're not grasping the big, big picture, Gil. Let's look at the repairs alone. One worker makes the business twenty- four to thirty dollars an hour. After labor, materials, and overhead, the business takes home, and this is conservative, somewhere around fifteen bucks an hour. That's our money also."

"So I'd be gettin'…twenty one bucks an hour?" I exclaimed.

"No…well, yes, however, the fifteen the studio makes would be divided between expanding the business and an investment portfolio."

"So when would I get my share'a the fifteen?"

Danny stared at me, then dropped his head to the bar.

"Never mind," frustrated. "I'll take care of everything," raising his head and looking at me. "I'll handle the business end and help repair glass, JD will be the supervisor, and you and whoever else wants to, will fix the glass. We'll all be paid six to eight dollars an hour depending on how difficult the repair job is as a whole. JD will make that decision."

"F'r now, that's all I need ta know," a little irritated at his treating me like an idiot. "When do we start?"

"I'm working with JD tomorrow to pick up some more of the stained glass lingo and develop a better feel for the technical requirements. Monday I'll begin hitting the churches in Guadeloupe and swing some deals. We should be ready to start by the end of the week."

"Hot shit! Six 'r eight bucks an hour!"

Danny shook his head.

"What about y'ur classes?" I asked.

"Setting this up won't take that much time. I'll miss a few classes next week, but that'll be all."

The door crept open. A blast of Aqua Velva filled the room. Eduardo and Tomas cautiously entered the lounge. They both had on clean, starched jeans, short sleeve sports shirts, and polished cowboy boots. Their black shiny hair was pulled neatly back. Everyone yelled out.

"Hey, Tomas, Eduardo! Come on in! Grab a mug!"

"Shiiiiit, man!" Eduardo, grinning broadly as he walked up to the bar. "You motherfuckers are *druuuunk*, man!"

Tomas tentatively followed, looking as if he was expecting someone to tell him to leave. Ed walked behind the bar and grabbed my hand.

"Shiiiiit," looking around the lounge. "This place is *niiiice*. Thanks for asking us to come," crushing the life out of my hand.

"Mi cabaret es su cabaret, amigo. Buenos nochas, senior Tomas. Como usta usted?"

"Better than your Spanish," he replied softly while glancing around uncomfortably.

I handed Ed and Tomas a mug.

"Grab a seat," pointing at the table.

Danny stood up from the barstool, shook hands with Ed and Tomas, then followed them to the table. I began filling six more pitchers of beer.

"How many more ya bringin'?" Jerry yelled.

"Six comin'," I yelled back.

I was pelted with waded paper bills. I set the pitchers on the bar along with two more mugs. Danny and Ed moved everything to the table. Missy started to remove two empties from the table.

JD stopped her.

"Leave 'em here, Missy. I gotta keep track'a whud I'm a drankin' so I don't git drunk an' make a Jerry out'a myself."

"Whu's 'at, ol' man?" Jerry, doubling up a fist and cocking his arm.

"Yew heard me, ya little pecker hea…"

"Am I gunna have ta intr'duce myself ta these two fell'a's?" Missy interrupted.

Jerry pointed at Ed.

"This here's Ed Ocampo. The smart lookin' one's his brother, Tomas Ocampo."

Ed and Tomas reached across the table to shake Missy's hand.

"O'Campo," Jerry cackling. "They're Mexican-Irish. Git it?" glancing around the table.

No response.

"O'Malley, O'Rielly…O'Campo," he explained. "Them's Irish names, man. Git it now?"

Still nothing.

"It's a fuckin' joke!" slamming a fist on the table.

"I guess you would have to be Irish," Tomas.

Everyone cracked up laughing.

"Whud *I* said wuz funnier 'an 'at! Y'all're jus' tryin' ta piss me off."

And so the evening went.

Hugo never showed. Missy didn't seem to mind. She was the lone female at the table. She ended up kicking her high heels off and dancing every dance. JD got good and drunk and ended up drinking some beer from one of Missy's shoes. Tomas finally relaxed and ended up at the bar talking bikes, painting, and music with me. The couples in the booth had a final round then split, tipping Missy ten bucks and me five. No other customers came in the rest of the night. We all got shitfaced. At 1:00, they all cleared out and went to the IHOP. I closed and cleaned up so Missy could go with them. I was tired as hell, but still feeling pretty good. I took a few more pain pills then locked up. It'd been a damn good night.

I got back to the house around 2:00. Down W street, between Main and Broadway, I could see a lone figure struggling with a bike. The figure slowly crept through the dim, golden glow of light from one of the ghetto's ancient street lamps. I lit a cigarette and watched the bike and the figure fade into the night, heading in the direction of Vann's place.

I crawled up the stairs as quietly as I could. I went straight to the bathroom and showered. I was tired. Feeling heavy. I took two more pills, wrapped a towel around me, and then headed to bed. I stepped into the room and let the towel drop to the floor as I shut the door behind me.

*Perfume?*

I felt for the light switch.

"Don't," someone whispered.

"Christ!" I gasped, cupping my hands over my crotch.

"Shhh," as a figure rose to its knees on my pallet, clutching a sheet to its chest.

"It's all right. It's me...Bobbie."

*Bobbie?*

"Jerry talked ta me a little while ago," continuing to whisper.

"He was on his way ta get somethin' ta eat. Do ya think this is... slutty?" Bobbie, lowering her head.

I dropped to my knees in front of her.

"No," I answered, barely louder than a breath. "Don't think that. Don't go thinkin' that at all."

\*\*\*

A glove with the fingers cut out placed two beers in the rain gutter. A dirty red bandanna popped into view. Jerry flopped his chest onto the roof then pulled the rest of his body up over the edge. He took the beers from the gutter and duck-walked his way over, coming to rest in a cross-legged sitting position alongside me. I brought my knees up, locked my arms around my legs, and then lowered my forehead to hide my face. Jerry opened the beers and poked me. I took a bottle without making eye contact. Jerry lit a cigarette and handed it to me.

Several minutes passed. The belltower at the Baptist church tolled the beginning of the 8:00 o'clock service.

"Yew been up here all night?" Jerry, coughing.

"Yeah."

"Fuckin' church song woke me up," he mumbled. "Bast'rds."

Several more minutes passed.

"Ya gunna stay up here all day?" Jerry, staring straight ahead.

"No," after thinking it over. "At some point...I'm gunna jump."

"Tha'd break ol' Bobbie's heart," taking a drink then lighting a cigarette for himself.

More silence.

"Ya talk to her this mornin'?" I asked quietly.

"Yeah. A li'l bit. After I got back from the IHOP. About 4:30 this mornin' I guess. She said yew'd jus' gone back ta y'ur place. She was sittin' on the porch smokin' a joint."

"She say anything?"

"About whut?"

"Anything. You know...about me?"

"Damn! Ain't *yew* the stuck-up snot. Like two people cain't sit out on a porch an' have a conversation without y'ur fuckin' name comin' up. Y're worse than 'at brother'a y'urs sometimes."

*Wonder if Bobbie told him about what happened last night? Wonder if that's why he's here now?*

We sat quietly for two or three minutes.

"My fuckin' brains killin' me, man," Jerry, rubbing his head furiously. "This is the worse damn headache I've had in a long time. Still got some'a JD's pain killers?"

I leaned back and removed four or five pills from my pocket. I handed them to Jerry. He kept two and returned the rest.

"Only need two," before washing them down with some beer. "One thing I found out when my balls wuz achin' wuz 'at if ya take too many a JD's pills at one time, ya cain't git a fuckin' hard-on."

*Shit fire!*

"How many's too many?" trying to sound conversational and not concerned.

"Ohhh, I don't know...six 'r eight in a day. 'at might do it f'r a wimp-ass pussy, but ya see, I wuz takin' about four hun'r'd a day. 'at's how many'a them puppies it took ta keep this bad boy down," patting his crotch. "Tha's no bullshit either."

"How long b'fore ya was back ta normal?" and faked a yawn.

"Ohhh, lemme see...one, two, three, four, five..."

"Five fuckin' days?" anxiously.

"Weeks."

"Five weeks?" and fell back onto the roof with a thud.

"*Nine* weeks. Ya didn't lemme finish countin'. I'm pr'tty sure it wuz aroun' nine weeks."

I rolled onto my side, facing away from Jerry.

"But, then, my nuts wuz *all* fucked up," cackling. "I'd imagine it'd jus' take a coupl'a days if all 'at wuz wrong with ya wuz a...a broken finger, 'r a...a fucked up eyeball, 'r somethin' like 'at," sliding to the edge of the roof to leave. "Three days at the mos'," before dropping onto the porch and clomping down the steps.

I stood up and moved along the peak of the roof to the alley end of the house. I saw Jerry looking in the window of the little house we guessed Neil was moving into.

Jerry backed up, looked around, and saw me.

"Nobody home," he said then threw his beer bottle through one of the front windows.

The sound of breaking glass filled the street.

"Fuckin' whoops," cackling as he continued on home.

I squatted and gazed at Bobbie's bedroom window. The curtain pulled back. It was Bobbie. She gave me a little wave. I waved back.

*She knows. Jerry pro'bly told her what went wrong.*

I dropped my head and stared into my lap.

*Three days.*

*Fuck me dead.*

\*\*\*

The girls screamed. I turned and looked through the opened door to the stoop in time to see Jerry collapse on the porch and a bottle of sun tan lotion fly through the air. Jerry reached up and snagged a bikini top as it sailed over the edge of the roof.

"You bastard!" Joan.

Jerry entered the kitchen, exaggerating a limp and dusting his pants off.

"Didn't hear ya comin' up the steps," as I shook his hand.

"Ain't that the whole idea'a sneakin', man. How's the eye?"

"Better," and looked away.

Jerry tossed two tin foiled cubes the size of sugar lumps on the table.

"Tell Homer 'at's the best I c'n do f'r him. I'm gunna have ta git a little cash from him to. Fuckin' hash's gittin' expensive as hell. Motherfuckers're pro'bly rippin' me off, man," he grumbled.

"I'll tell him," and took the cubes to Homer's room where I put them in a book he'd hollowed out.

Joan was yelling through the pads of the water cooler on the roof. I went to the cooler switch and turned it off so I could hear her.

"What?" I yelled back at her through the vent in the hall ceiling.

Footsteps back to the cooler. The refrigerator door slammed in the kitchen.

"Didn't you tell him we were up here?" Joan shouted over the noise of the dripping water pads.

Jerry stepped into the hall swigging a beer. The bikini was around his neck like a scarf.

"Man, I'm real sorry," Jerry shouted back. "I mus' be...like... delir'ous from this unseasonal heat wave 'r somethin'," snickering the whole time.

"Pervert! Throw my top back up here!" Joan. "An' wipe that nasty smirk off y'ur face."

"I didn' see nothin'," as Jerry moved closer to the cooler vent. "The sun wuz in my eyes. Honest. I wudn' tryin' ta pull nothin'. I wuz jus' comin' up ta work on the ol' tan. I didn' know y'all's up there."

"L'ar!" Hope in the distance. "Yew know the roof schedule. Tuesd'y's f'r the women."

"I thoughd I wuz somewheres else," Jerry cackled. "It wuz a mistake."

"Gil! If he's cacklin' would ya kick the shit out uv him f'r me?"

" 'at Missy?" Jerry, forehead furrowed as he moved to stand beside me under the vent.

"Yeah," I confirmed.

His eyes popped open.

"Honey bunch! I come over ta git ya. I got roun' trip Greyhoun' tickets ta Vegas. I got us a chapel rented an' ever'thin…"

"I ain't marryin' no peepin' Tom," she shouted back. "Now I'll never be able ta trust ya again!"

"Leave her alone, ya heart breaker," Sonny yelled.

"But I love ya, baby!" Jerry.

"Throw my top up here!" Joan demanded.

"Soon as me an' Gil's done with it."

"What'd he say?" Joan.

"Nothin'!" I answered.


The music volume increased. I switched the cooler back on. A little boy stepped out of the living room.

"Where's mommy?" rubbing his eyes.

"On the roof," and walked toward him.

He shot back into the room. I could hear his muffled footsteps running across the carpeted living room, his little body barely creaking the floor boards. I walked over to the door and looked in. Jerry came up behind me. Tyler'd hopped back onto the couch, lain down, and then pulled his blanket over his head. His little sister was still sleeping soundly on the other couch.

"You ought'a be watchin' 'em," I told Jerry as we walked back to the kitchen. "Y're the one's always proposin' to her."

"When she starts playin' wife with me, I'll start playin' daddy with 'em," snorting. "Who all's up there?"

"Sonny, Missy, Joan, Hope, an' some lesbian friend'a Joan's visitin' from Amarilla."

"Lesos," snarling as we entered the kitchen.


We sat down at the table. Jerry pulled the bikini top from his shoulder and sniffed at it.

"What's it smell like?" I joked.

"Lactate," and placed it on the table.

"Lactate?" surprised. "Where'd ya pick up a word like lactate?"

"There ya go doin' it ta me again, man," lighting a cigarette.

"Doin' what?"

" 'at shit. Treatin' me like I'm some kind'a dumbass. Like I wouldn't know a word like lactate."

Jerry leaned toward me.

"I know all about lactate an' a lot'a other shit too," snickering as he fell back in the chair, downed a mouthful of beer, and then burped loudly. "I def'nitely posses an innate propens'ty f'r the in'ellectual," he slurred.

"You been readin' the graffiti on the shithouse walls out at Tech?"

"Nah. 'at lactate stuff's from a fuck magazine, but I been pickin' some other shit up here an' there. Been talkin' with Hugo, an' listenin' ta Vann an' Doug argue shit while I'm over at their place, an' I been listenin' ta yew an' Danny when ya start showin' off."

"Showin' off?"

"Yeah, man. Showin' off. Talkin' y'ur shit. Usin' 'em big words. I know y're jus' showin' off an' I know y'all think I'm kind'a stupid, but ya know whut? Yew two ain' the only one's been readin' shit. Them books a y'urs I borrow' ta pick up chicks with on'a campus? Hell...I look through 'em. An' ya know whut?" raising his brows and closing one eye.

"What?"

"It ain' that damn hard. I mean, learnin' a bunch a big words an' knowin' a lot'a shit about whud a lot'a other people think about things is a piece'a cake, man. Ya jus' read it an' remember it. But rememberin' a lot'a big-ass words is a waste'a time in my min'. I ain't the only one feels 'at'a way, either," leaning closer and lowering his voice. "Most people ain't got the fuckin' time 'r the need f'r a nine letter word if a four letter word'll do jus' as good. Know whud I'm sayin'? An' ya know whud else, man? Who gives a fuck about whud a bunch'a other sons a bitches have ta say about whut *they* think life's all about? 'at's their life they're writin' about. It ain't mine. I gotta whole differ'nt thing goin' on an' they don't know squat abou' that. Wan'a know somethin' else I fig'red out?" becoming more serious. "Smart asses c'n change the way a thing looks by changin' the words they use ta describe the thing they're talkin' about. Jus' like magic."

"Like?"

"Like sayin' 'police action' instead'a 'war'. Or sayin' 'attrition' instead'a sayin' 'dead'. An' there's a whole lot'a other words they fuck with," turning to stare out the door a few seconds. "I should'a been payin' more attention, man," mumbling to himself.

Jerry swung back around then slowly edged his way across the table top toward me. He stopped about halfway and raised his brows.

"An' then...I put tha' slant-eyed bitch onta her knees an' did her doggie style. I had her soundin' like a baby sheep gittin' nailed by a crazy elephant 'r a badass donkey 'r somethin'," withdrawing to his chair and cackling. "I thought that 'un up all by myself, man. An' I wuz straight when I did. An' I'm the only motherfucker aroun' 'at knows whud it means," smugly.

I didn't know what to say. This was strange, even for Jerry.

"An elephant doin' a sheep," I nodded. "That'd damn sure hurt."

"Yeah. Like a son of a bitch," and rubbed his face with both hands. "Like a full time son of a bitch."

We sat in silence for over a minute. It was uncomfortable for me.

"Listen ta this 'un," he finally said. "Moral imperative."

"Damn. That's slick."

"Roy taught me that 'un. Like...it's a moral imperative f'r a guy ta let his ol' lady have a orgasm. Somethin' like 'at, anyways."

"Damn, Jerry! That's great!"

" 'at's pro'bly how yew an' Danny'd say it too 'cause ya cain't live without them big words. Here's how *I* say it…'Ya owe the bitch a nut'. See how much quicker 'at is?"

"WATER!" Joan ordered.

"COMIN'!" as I stepped out onto the porch.

I hauled in a trickling hose dangling over the rail.

"Ready?" I shouted.

The radio was muffled by a towel.

"Ready!" all the girls in unison.

I partially covered the end of the hose with my thumb while directing the spray onto the roof. The girls shrieked.

I slowly fanned the hose back and forth.

"That hittin' ever'body?"

"Yes!" they squealed.

They called for a halt. I dropped the hose back over the side and worked the nozzle to the ground.

"Thank Yew!" almost in unison.

I stepped into the kitchen, took a beer from the frig, then sat down.

"So, how come ya ain't workin' t'day?" Jerry.

"Went ta that funeral f'r Hugo's friend."

"Oh, yeah? How wuz it?"

"Not bad. Real traditional."

"Oh?" Jerry huffed, "like there's somethin' *wrong* with 'at?"

"I didn't say that."

"Didn' have ta. It wuz jus' there."

"The guy was eighty-eight," ignoring him.

"Eighty-eight," scratching his chin. " 'at ain't bad. I ain't gunna make it that long. Ain't no way."

"I doubt I will."

"Yew bes' be prayin' y'ur ass off 'at ya live f'*rever*, man."

I didn't respond. It didn't matter. Jerry was off and running.

"See…the way yew b'lieve about things, an' the way y're always sayin' the 'G' word, an' the things ya say about Jesus…all 'at stuff's got y'ur sweet butt in Hell. I'm gunna be laughin' my ass off in Heaven when ya find out jus' how bad ya fucked up. An' I won't be the only one," rocking in his chair and snickering. "Jesus'll come off liberty when he hears *y're* showin' up," rocking faster. "The angels're gunna have a big-ass raffle ta see which one uv 'em gits ta boot y'ur li'l fanny inta Hell."

"You gunna come an' watch?"

"Damn straight. I'll be standin' at the Pearly Gates with my arm aroun' one'a 'em big-titty strip joint angels."

"Y'ur Heaven's got titty bars?"

"Ain't *my* Heaven, man. It's God's Heaven. God's an' Jesus'."

"So where exactly in the Bible does it say there's strip joints in Heaven?"

"It says in the Bible 'at Heaven's gunna be a happy place ta be an' titty bars damn sure make *me* feel good."

"Jerry, there's no way the Baptists're gunna allow a bunch'a strip joints in Heaven."

He leaned forward and gave me the Jerry one-eyed squint.

"Gil...there ain't gunna *be* no Baptists in Heaven."

We both broke up, me laughing and Jerry cackling like mad. He was proud of that one.


"What makes ya so positive *y're* goin' ta Heaven?" I asked.

" 'cause I b'lieve in Jesus," confidently.

"It's that easy, huh?"

"Ain' all *'at* easy," seriously. "Ya gotta *really* b'lieve in Him 'cause God c'n tell if y're bullsh...lyin' to Him jus' ta git inta Heaven. 'at's whut's gunna blow all 'em church people away, man. They'll be standin' there at the Gates gettin' their bus tickets ta Hell an' watchin' me ride right on in ta Heaven on my bike. They're all gunna be sayin' 'Whu' the fuck, man?' an' I'll be laughin' my ass off an' shootin' 'em the bird."

"If Hitler b'lieved in Jesus, would he be in Heaven right now?"

"Git serious, man! Ain't no way 'at son uv a bitch b'lieved in Jesus. Ain't no fuckin' way."

"How da ya know?"

" 'cause he wuz...damn...there ain't words f'r whud he wuz. Ya jus' don't go doin' the kind'a things he did if ya *really* b'lieve in Jesus. 'at's one'a the ways God fig'res out if y're lyin' about b'lievin' in Jesus. He jus' looks at the shit ya done an' 'at's how he c'n tell."

"Ya know who Billy Graham is, don'ch ya?"

"Hell, yeah," looking insulted by my even having to ask.

"Would Billy Graham go ta Hell if he *didn't* b'lieve in Jesus? I mean, if he was still a nice guy an' all but he was a Buddhist 'r...a Hindu 'r somethin' other than a Christian?"

Jerry hesitated, momentarily stumped.

"No," he decided. "He wouldn't go ta Hell," shaking his head. "Why?"

" 'cause people 'at don't go aroun' makin' ever'body eat shit an' people who ain' jus' plain evil, git one last chance."

"For what?"

"Ta b'lieve in Jesus."

"After they die?"

"Yeah. Right after they die. 'at's whu' the last judgment's all about. If ya lived *like* ya b'lieved in Jesus, but never said ya did 'r ya never heard uv him while yew wuz on earth, then y're tol' all about him right after ya die. Ya pro'bly even git ta meet him, like in a li'l room jus' outside the Pearly Gates. If ya *still* don't b'lieve in him then it's all over for ya no matter *how* good ya wuz, but if ya start b'lievin' in him...then y're saved. 'at's pro'bly how it works 'r somethin' like 'at. The trick is ta live like Jesus did, man. An' 'at's a bitch 'cause there's so many shitheads fuckin' with ya all'a the time. 'at's why a lot'a church goers're gunna burn their asses off. They *say* they b'lieve in Jesus, but God knows they're full'a sh...knows they're lyin' 'cause they don't *live* like they b'lieve in Him."

"An' all this is in the Bible?" amazed by the Gospels according to Jerry.

"Not *exactly* like the way I jus' said it. Some things're jus' un'erstood by some'a us," with a hint of superiority, brows raised, eyes squinting. "See whud I'm sayin'?"

"Well," locking my fingers behind my head and looking up at the ceiling, "I see what y're sayin, but I don't see how ya c'n b'lieve…"

"Fuck it, man," cutting me off. "Yew don't b'lieve none'a whud I'm tellin' ya an' I ain't gettin' inta it with ya again."

Jerry finished his beer and got another. He flopped back into his chair then leaned toward me, squinting with one eye and zapping me with the other wide opened eye.

"Jus' one las' thing then I'm gunna shudup about the whole damn thing, man. The bottom line is 'at ya either b'lieve the truth 'r ya don't b'lieve the truth an' yew c'n go fuck y'urself if ya don't b'lieve the *real* truth," eyebrows raised.

"And my opinion dudn't…"

"Let's talk about somethin' else," putting down a few hard gulps. "Y're jus' gunna try ta piss me off. Let's talk about Chad. When's the last time ya seen 'at butt-wipe brother'a y'urs?"

*He was right. We'd just end up hollerin' at each other.*

"Saturd'y, I guess. Up at the lounge. Hadn't he been by the house?"

"Nah. I gave the girls their share'a the money he gave ya. If ya see him…tell him I ain't gunna kill him anymore."

"Will do."

Jerry pulled a joint from his jacket pocket, lit up and then took a long drag before offering it to me. I took a tug and returned it. Jerry cleared his throat and coughed.

"So," Jerry began, "how's…how's ever'thing else goin'?" and took a drink while staring out the door.

"Nothin'. Still can't, ya know, see shit. An' this is the third day. I'm gettin' a little nervous."

"Third day?" Jerry repeated in a hush. "Hell," speaking up, "it won't be too much longer. Try lookin' at some fuck mags. 'at might help…"

"JERRY!" Joan again. "I need my top up here! Give it ta me right now!"

"Yew got some dish soap?" Jerry, getting up and walking to the sink.

"In the cabinet underneath the..."

"Got it," and squeezed a tablespoon full of the slimy soap into each cup.

"JERRRYYY!" Joan again. "Hurry up! I got things ta do."

Jerry walked out onto the stoop.

"Here ya go!" tossing the top up and over the edge.

Two, maybe three seconds later,

"OH, MY GOD!" Joan shrieked. "WHAT DID YOU DO?"

"Whud *IS* it?" Hope squealed.

"Git it away from me!" Missy.

"Yew two're sick!" Sonny.

I moved to the door.

"It's just dish soap!" I hollered.

"It's still *sick*!" Sonny.

"The whole *idea* is sick!" Joan.


Jerry waved goodbye.

"Gotta go help Doug work on his bike an' see if he wants ta work t'morrow. T'morrow's We'n'sd'y ain' it? T'day is Tuesd'y idn't it?"

"Yeah. Tommorrow's day four for me."

"Don't sweat it, man. Ya won't be blin' f'rever," as he plodded down the steps.

Joan must have heard Jerry leaving.

"YOU STAY AWAY 'TIL YA GET PROFESSIONAL HELP!"

\*\*\*

"Gettin' ready for the Baha'i meetin'?"

I spun around. It was Bobbie. We hadn't been this close since early Sunday morning when things had gone to shit.

"Yeah. Ever' Tu'sd'y night we have ta hide the booze 'til it's over. It can't even be in the house b'cause it gives off bad vibes accordin' ta Joan," closing the van door.

"How's the...swelling?" glancing at my crotch.

"Uh...it's...it's better. Should be able ta, ya know, ta see... anytime now."

Bobbie stepped closer and took my hand

"Don't be embarrassed. I know that's why ya hadn't been over ta see me. It's all right. I understand."

My stomach knotted.

*Good God, I want her.*

My brain was one throbbing erection.

"It's beyond embarrassin', Bobbie. I can't describe what it makes me feel like," and looked away.

She stepped closer to me, reached up, put her hand behind my head, and then eased my face onto her chest.

"I'm in no russsh," whispering in my ear. "Okay?"

*Oh, Jesus!*

I shivered from head to toe. I straightened up.

"What was 'at?" I managed to squeak out.

"I'm in..."

"No, no. Not like 'at. Tell me like ya did just then," and lowered a cheek back onto her chest. "Now...whisper it again. Real slow."

Bobbie giggled then whispered once more into my ear.

"I am in no russssssh," quickly nibbling my ear lobe before pushing my head away. "Maybe that'll speed things up."

I was dizzy. I was reeling.

"Damn," I breathed.

"Comin' ta the meetin' t'night?"

"I don't have ta work," struggling to pull myself back together, "so I guess I'll be around. Gotta read a little. Tryin' ta get ahead so when...when the eye's well I won't have ta think about anything else."

Bobbie vamped it all the way up the stairs, her long snow white hair brushing rhythmically from side to side over her ass.

"Y're not makin' this any easier," I frowned after she'd reached the stoop.

Bobbie paused and turned around.

"I don't wan'a make it easier," leaning over and rocking her shoulders. "I wan'a make it as hard as I can," then slipped through the doorway.

*Damn! Damn! Damn!*

A station wagon of regular meeting goers pulled up. Everyone took turns shaking my hand and giving me a hardy Allah'u'Abha, Persian for "Praise the Lord and how the hell are ya, buddy" rolled into one. I'd always answer each one with an "Ali Baba". They'd smile and nod. Under their breaths they were probably thinking, "Y'ur gunna burn, you infidel motherfucker". I grabbed a few cans of beer from the van and wandered over to Jerry's. I looked in the basement for his bike.

*Gone. Not home yet. Wonder how his day went with Captain Duh. Shit.*

*That was raw. Doug can't help it.*

I sat down in the dirt and leaned against the house. The kitchen door was wide open. I could hear Shauna talking on the phone as she clattered around making Jerry's dinner.

*Smells Mexican...onionie an' hot pepperish. Lintel burritos pro'bly. Cheap eatin'. Smells good.*

"Puff the Magic Dragon" was on the record player. Jerry's favorite song. I opened a beer and listened in on the phone conversation.

Girl stuff. Somebody at work looked like shit in whatever it was she'd worn today. One of the other girls didn't know squat about hairdressing and ought'a be canned. The owner's a whore. Everybody knows she's doing all the lesbian hairdressers in town. Shauna's looking for a different shop to work in. Shauna thought Jerry might be right about her trying to open a barbershop, but *forget* that shit about a *topless* barbershop and calling it the "Boober

Shop". She thought she'd probably get rich with a topless shop, but it wouldn't be fair ta poor Bobbie if Bobbie came ta work there because Bobbie's so flat.

*Bobbie's not that flat.*

Shauna laughed then agreed it was a mean thing to say.

Her voice dropped to an excited whisper.

"It ain't a rumor," she said. "Bobbie an' Gil *did* do it an', accordin' ta Joan an' Hope, it was embarrassin'. She was so *noisy*. She's *never* been like 'at f'r anybody else an' I been her roommate ever since she moved ta Lubbock."

*What the fuck is 'at all about?*

The conversation turned to Bobbie's old boyfriend, some butthole named Luther. Shauna couldn't believe Luther'd come over last night, that he actually had the balls to come back after what Jerry'd told him the time before. If Jerry hadn't been here last night, Shauna thought that dickhead would have knocked the door down and beat Bobbie up again. Shauna *really* thought Jerry would shoot him if Luther ever came back. Luther better have believed Jerry *this* time. Shauna agreed with the phone—dumping that prick was the best thing that could'a happened ta Bobbie. Especially since Gil's come along.

*She dumped a guy f'r me? She must be serious about us. I don't know if...no...'at's okay.*

*No problem.*

*I could use somethin' kind'a steady. A mild kind'a commitment. She might be hopin' f'r somethin' a little more serious, but that's okay too. I can handle 'at.*

*She is cute.*

*'at goddamn long, white hair fries my loins. It'll look fine trailin' b'hind us when we're out ridin' around on the bike. An' Jerry was right about her figure...it's a sexy kind'a skinny. I've always had a thing f'r Twiggy an' Mia Farrow types. Last Sund'y mornin' was like havin' both of 'em in bed with me at the same time. She even looked a little like a shorter version'a Cher. Cher, Mia, an' Twiggy all in one package. I could have her*

*dress up like 'em! Oh, damn. I bet she would if I asked her to. One night'd be Cher night, then a Twiggy night, an' then a Mia night.*

*And a Bobbie night...just so her self-esteem dudn't go down the crapper.*

*Then start the cycle all over again. She'd do it. I know she would. Hell, I'd be willin' ta dress up like Clint Eastwood 'r whoever she want...*

"How long yew been here?" Shauna, standing on the little porch, a trash bag in her hand.

I jumped to my feet.

"Y're gunna have ta speak up," cupping my hand to my ear. "I worked out in 'at sand storm all afternoon an' I can't hear a thing!"

It didn't look like she'd believed me.

Shauna stepped down from the porch.

"I thought yew'd be at the meetin' with Bobbie."

"Yeah, well," taking the trash bag from her, "I got some studyin' ta do."

"Ya study better when y're sittin' in my backyard drankin'?" sarcastically.

"Takin' a break."

We strolled across the yard to the trashcan in the alley.

"Gil, c'n I ask ya a question?"

"Y're gunna ask me about Bobbie. Right?"

"I know it ain't none'a my business, not *really*, but..."

"I like her. I like her a lot. I think about it...*her*, ever' wakin' minute. That's all I c'n tell ya right now."

She beamed.

"Ya know, Shauna...it wouldn't bother me one bit if Bobbie was ta find out I felt that way about her. If ya know what I mean?" raising my brows.

"I'll try my best not ta let it slip out," brimming over with happy. "As soon as Bobbie gits home."

We exchanged grins.

She leaned to look around me in the direction of an approaching Harley. It was at least a block away.

"Jerry don't usually come up Tenth," brushing some hair from her face.

The roar of the bike grew louder. I looked toward Tenth.

"Dudn't sound like his bike," I said.

Neil drifted around the corner, crept past the house then, at the last second, swung off the street into our driveway, barely missing some late Baha'i arrivals. He swerved to miss the van then crossed the thin strip of dead grass between the drive and his patch of front yard. The bike rolled to a stop, wheels straddling a disintegrating cement walk.

"I'm goin' back ta the house. Jerry don't like this shithead an' I don't either," turning to leave.

Neil shut the bike down. I walked over.

"I'd appreciate y'ur avoidin' my driveway in the future," forcing friendly.

Neil, still seated on the bike, casually looked over his shoulder at the drive. Some more people were arriving. Joan was on the stoop glaring down at us. Neil had an audience and wasn't going to let the moment pass without some Hollywooding.

"You don't own the driveway," loud enough for those in the back row of the theater to hear him.

"But, I am rentin' it," much quieter, hoping to take some of the pressure off him. "Use the alley...not the driveway."

"I'll think about it," slowly dismounting. "And you think about not throwing bottles through my window," attempting surly.

"Fair enough."

Neil must have misread my effort at diplomacy as some kind of weakness or fear thing. The fat bastard went cocky on me. He looked in the direction of Jerry's place and waved. I turned around. Shauna was watching from the porch. I turned back to Neil. He was blowing her a kiss.

*This movie needs a new motherfuckin' director.*

"Ya know, Neil," voice slightly shaking and substantially louder than before, "do that again, an' you can f'rget about the bottle through y'ur window deal."

"You renting her too?" sneering.

"Worse...f'r you anyway. Jerry owns her."

*Goddammit! Where the fuck did that come from?*

"That so?" still sneering while continuing to stare at Shauna. "I'd like ta hear her version of that."

"Neil, you'll never get that close to her," close to a growl.

*Shit! I can't stop! Why the fuck am I lettin' this happen?*

"Time, Gil...it's only a matter of time," and waved at Joan, still watching from the stoop.

*CUT! THAT'S A TAKE!*

*Fuck me.*

I headed back to Jerry's.


"Whu'd he say?" Shauna.

"Nothin'," I lied. "He'll use the alley from now on. He didn't mean ta cause any trouble," as I picked up my other beer and opened it.

"I'll *bet* he said that, the filthy pig. He...he jus' looks so...so slimy. When he looks at me, I feel like he's spittin' on me."

"Yeah, well, don't go mentionin' any'a this ta Jerry 'r we'll have a murder on our hands. Okay? Neil's all blow. He's scared shitless'a Jerry. He's not gunna be seriously botherin' anybody."

Shauna invited me inside.

"No thanks. I'm gunna sit out here a while. Watch the sunset."

"C'n I call this person I know from work an' tell her about whut I'm not gunna tell Bobbie as soon as she gits home t'night?" hands clasped at her chin, eyes wide.

I smiled and plopped to the ground.

"Go ahead."

Shauna clapped her hands and bounced into the house.

*She'll have me an' Bobbie engaged by the time she hangs up.*

A dust cloud was moving up the alley and coming fast. I could tell it was Homer by the clinking beer bottles and the clatter of cans in his truck's bed. He shot from behind a utility, braked, and then slid to a stop next to Neil's place. A thick, swirling cloud of dust washed over the truck like a huge, silent, tan colored wave. He eased the truck around the corner, parked it in the drive behind the van, and then crawled out.

"HOMER!"

He turned around. I lifted my beer into the air and pointed at the van with my other hand. Homer waved, pulled a six pack from the bed of his truck and began to walk toward me, cutting across Neil's front yard as he came.

"These've been on ice!" stepping right past Neil's bike without so much as a glance at it.

*That'll kill Neil if he's watchin'.*

Homer collapsed beside me and opened a beer. It spewed everywhere.

"Hi Homer!" Shauna from inside.

"Good evening, ma'am!" pulling a joint from behind his ear and lighting up.

Homer took a hit then handed it to me.

"Been busy?" he asked.

"Not really," and took a deep hit. "Same ol' shit I guess. Went ta that funeral earlier t'day. Jerry came by for a while. He was in'a weirdass mood. Saw Sonny this afternoon."

"Yeah. She said she was coming over to sunbathe. How's your eye?"

"The swellin's goin' down. Still sore as hell," pushing on it to confirm the report.

"Not going to church tonight?" nodding at the house.

"Nah. Hadn't been up to it lately."

"Where's Bobbie?"

"The house."

"Lover's spat?"

*What the...*

"Where's ever'body comin' up with this shit? First Joan an' Hope're doggin' me ta come ta the meetin' t'night b'cause it'd be *sooo* fuckin' cute if Bobbie an' me were ta be there t'gether, then Shauna wants ta know why I'm not with her, an' now y're actin' like we're married 'r somethin'."

"No shit? Joan said *fuckin'* cute? She *never* says the 'F' word around me," lighting a second joint then motioning for me ta keep the first one. "Danny home yet?" settling against the side of the house.

"Nah."

"Saw him this morning," he grinned. "He was all dressed up in a suit. Shaved his goatee. Had a hair cut."

"Short?"

"Not real short. Short enough to sell used cars, but not short enough to sell insurance door to door."

"He was gunna finalize those glass repairs in Guadeloupe t'day."

"Yeah. That's where he said he was headed. Looked sharp. Like he knew what he was doing."

I dropped my chin onto my chest.

"Ya know what worries me about that?" I asked.

"What?"

"Danny's a talker an' he's gunna end up signin' a contract with ever' motherfuckin' church in West Texas an' committin' us ta deadlines we can't meet without workin' ourselves ta death."

"And pissing JD off. He doesn't like pressure. He falls apart when we're down to a single six pack in the ice chest."

We sat quietly. Five, ten minutes passed. The grass was working all the knots out. It was beginning to feel like I owned the moment. I got lost in all the evening shades of fiery red and orange splashed with hues of blue and turquoise above the ghetto rooftops.

*Sunsets're such cool places ta get lost in.*

*Hawaii had cool sunsets. Just a kid.*

*Growin' up on Guam. Nothin' b'tween you an' the sunset. Beautiful sunsets.*

*Same thing way out at sea. Huge sunsets at sea.*

*Philippines had nice sunsets.*

*Vietn...*

"How's things goin' with you an' Sonny?" I asked. "Still hot an' heavy?"

Homer waited a bit before answering, finally leaning forward and sighing.

"I don't know. I guess things are all right. Definitely still hot and heavy."

Several minutes passed as we nursed the joints, listening to Shauna speaking in low, excited bursts on the phone. A hushed Hank Williams was singing "I'm So Lonesome I Could Cry" on the radio.

I looked over at Homer. He'd pulled his bandanna off. His hair tumbled over his shoulders and down his back. A few thick strands came to rest on his chest. His white tee shirt made his hair as dark as a raven. The dying twilight tinged it with shiny streaks of the deepest purple.

*Damn.*

On occasion, in the right light and from the right angle, Homer's profile would rattle me to the core. Like being slapped by a clap of thunder that's close by. His strong chin, the high cheek bones. His solid, sweeping brow furrowed in thought. He sat there, legs crossed, dark, moist eyes fixed on something I'd never be able to see no matter how long I might end up knowing him.

His head fell forward. His eyes closed. His shoulders drooped.

The long strands of his hair slipped forward, exposing a bit of tortured scar.

I was suddenly frightened for him.

My chest felt like a weight'd been placed on it.

An icy breath of air swept over me.

I needed to hear his voice. I struggled for something to say. A reason to call him back.

"Homer?"

Homer rolled his head and looked at me.

"I...uh...how'd ya keep y'ur shirt so clean t'day?"

"Didn't work much. It was a worry day."

The weight lifted.

"Sounds serious," relieved. "Wan'a talk about it?"


Homer waited a while, then stretched out, situating himself on his side. He was facing me, resting on his elbow.

"I've been writing a lot of things down," he said slowly.

"Like what?"

"Stuff about...spiritual things. Or something like that."

"Stuff y'ur grandpa told ya?"

"He never talked that much," taking a hit. "I've been thinking about all the stuff he *showed* me in the things he *did*. All the important stuff he told me, I think he told me with his heart. I'm remembering the things he told me with his heart. I'm remembering things he did and I'm writing down what I think he was trying to tell me when he did them."

"You could stub y'ur toe pretty hard when y're tryin' ta guess why people do some'a the things they do. You'd have ta know the person pr'tty damn good."

"I'm beginning to feel like I knew him a lot better than I thought I did."

"So what're ya comin' up with?"

After a long pause.

"I'm writing my own spiritual...viewpoint, I guess you could call it. It's not a religion. It's more like my own explanation to myself about what I think are spiritual...things. Attitudes, maybe."

I thought it over before responding.

"Nothin' wrong with 'at. You have a God'a some kind in it?"

"Not really a God," taking a long hit and chasing it with a hard swallow of beer. "Maybe some people would say it's a God. Christians might, but…it's really closer to being a spirit. An essence. A presence maybe."

"Like the Great Spirit?"

"No," frowning at me. "That sounds like something Tonto would say to the Lone Ranger," looking away again. "That makes it sound like there are a lot of different spirits…some more powerful than others and at the top of the heap is a King Spirit running everything. That's too much like a religion. I don't feel comfortable with that."

"That's a good sign."

"I was having a lot of trouble trying to describe it to myself. Then, I had a thought. It can't be described in words, because it's *all* the things words describe individually. It's *everything* all at once. To describe it would take a word that was all words at once."

Homer took a long hit, sat up, popped opened a fresh beer, and then chugged half of it.

"You got a name for it?" I asked.

"*It* doesn't have a name. If it did, you would never be able to speak it to its end. It would go on forever, but…I really don't think it has a name," downing some more beer before taking a deep hit. "You can *hear* its prescence all around you, though. It's the sound a cloud makes when it moves across the sky…the sound between the stars. It's…it's the *invisible*. The invisible *between* all things and it holds all things together to make all things one big thing. It's the universe breathing."

*Damn. Chill bumps.*

"And you can *feel* it, but it touches you *inside* first then works its way outward."

More chill bumps.

"That's all, Gil. That's my…my whatever it is. No rituals. No chants. No name. No way to describe it in a holy book. Grandpa spent his whole life trying to understand its bigness, its everywhereness, its everythingness. The clearer your understanding becomes of its nature, its...you know...its *invisibility*, the more you become *like* it. It draws you into itself so you...you begin to fade. Fade into it."

I took a hit and a gulp.

"An' ya got all this from watchin' y'ur grandpa?"

"Yes. He lived in those spaces between things," beginning to rock a little.

"Everyone always thought he was going crazy, but he wasn't. He was becoming invisible. He was becoming *it*. Whatever *it* is," turning to me. "I want to find the strength to become invisibile. I want to become Spirit."

Homer was smoked up, probably a little drunk and, on top of all that, may have taken some of JD's pills. I was smoked up and beginning to feel the effects of the beer, but...,

*If this sounds as good straight as it does right this exact moment... damn.*

"I honest-ta-God don't know what ta say, Homer. It sounds so...so...," I was truly stuck for words.

"Exactly," he nodded. "It sounds so...something."

"There's this thing I read about last semester," scratching my head. "This thing in the Hindu religion called Neti, Neti. It means 'not this, not this'. Your thing is a little like 'at, maybe."

"A little. Maybe."

"You run this by anybody else?" I asked.

"JD and Hugo."

"What'd he have ta..."

"And I've mentioned it to Danny and Roy. I've tried talking to Sonny about it, but she's not into talking about this kind of thing. All she wants to do is party, have sex, get smoked up, have sex, get coked, have sex."

"Life's a bitch, man."

I guess he didn't hear me.

"Lately, Sonny and I seem to be arguing a lot."

"Just a minute. Just a fuckin' minute," running my fingers through my beard. "It sounds ta me like I'm the last motherfucker on earth ta hear about y'ur...y'ur Neti, Neti. I thought we were shipmates. I should'a been the first one you'd a wanted ta tell about it. Bein' last ta find out about it kind'a hurts, Homer."

"Don't take it personal," reaching over and slapping my leg. "You never come up to the Westerner. That's where it comes to me...my whiskey visions."

"So the birth place'a the world's newest spiritual revelation is a cowboy dance hall?"

"That and JD's place. Late nights and early mornings. Hashing it out with JD."

I took a long hit and mulled over what Homer had said.

"So," I finally said, "God goes ta Oklahoma, appears to a hashed up, ex-Marine, Cherokee prophet named Homer an' tells him ta go to a shitkickin' bar in Lubbock, Texas where he'll receive a vision revealing that all the answers ta life an' God an' shit're in a place ya can't see an' 'at the one hope ya've got, the absolute *only* thing ya have ta look forward to in this miserable, fucked up world...is ta disappear."

Homer was grinning.

"Is *that* what I said?" hitting the joint then the beer.

" 'at's what I *heard*."

"I guess...I guess I need to work on saying it the way I mean to have it heard."

"Why? It's y'ur own personal spiritual thing. If *you* hear it the way ya say it...that's all that should matter."

"Yeah," lowering his voice. "That's all that *should* matter."

Homer burned the joint to a nub then washed it down with the last of his beer.

The deep growl of Jerry's bike grew louder as it crawled up Main. Shauna ran to the back door. He turned onto the once bricked, dirt driveway behind the house, rolled up to a concrete ramp descending into the basement, and then dropped out of sight. The house shook. Shauna ran into the basement after him. When they came back into view Shauna was carrying his backpack and tool belt. They had their arms around each other. Jerry looked beat.

"Whu' the fuck is 'at shit y're smokin'," Jerry slurred. "I could smell it all'a way from Nineteenth. Some New York hippie rip ya off on a lid'a shredded tire?" cackling. Jerry took my joint and finished it off. He nodded in Neil's direction.

"Whu's El Dickless up to?"

Neil had pushed his bike around to his back porch and was chaining it to one of the support posts.

"Looks like he's lockin' his porch to his bike," he snickered. "Like somebody'd wan'a steal 'at ugly lookin' porch."

Shauna giggled.

"Hey!" turning his attention to Homer and I. "Whud're yew two doin' sniffin' aroun' my back porch?"

"There's a song in there somewhere," Homer.

"No shit, Sundown," I agreed. "Did...uh...what's his name," head buzzing, "Doug. Did you an' Doug work on his bike this afternoon?"

"Yeah. 'at's where I been since I left y'ur place. Helpin' him take his bike back down so we c'n work the bugs out. I'm goin' nuts. 'at fuckin' guy's as remote as yew c'n git, man," stepping onto the porch, Shauna hanging on his arm.

"Comin' out ta join us later?" I asked.

"Nah. I'm tired as shit. Gotta be up early. Gotta pick Doug up, an' then find this house goin' up south'a town. Take 'em cans with ya when yew damn vagrants're done. I don't need ta have the neighbors thinkin' any white trash lives here," then pushed Shauna through the doorway.

"Well, I guess we just about wore our welcome out," slapping Homer's arm.

"Yeah," Homer grunted.

"Let's wander," and struggled to my feet.

"Did you like that shit?" Homer, standing up. "The grass," sniffing the lid. "It doesn't really smell bad, does it?"

"Nah. Jerry's fuckin' with ya. It's some *real* good shit. Who'd ya buy it from?"

"Chad."

"Really?"

"Yeah. But, I'm not supposed to tell you that."

"Wha'd he stick ya?"

"Twenty."

"Twenty bucks f'r a lid?" choking. "Why didn't ya just beat the shit out of him an' take it? Damn, Homer! Twenty fuckin' dollars?"

"Yeah. Gave him a five dollar bill and told him to deduct the rest from what he still owes you."

"Then half the lid's mine," and reached for it.

"This is my half," jerking it away. "We just smoked your half."


As we reached the alley a big Lincoln Continental with tinted windows turned onto Avenue W from Tenth. It swung over to the curb and parked in front of Neil's house.

"You order a whore?" as I came to a stop in the middle of the alley.

The door swung open and Danny hopped out.

"Got a minute?" walking around the front of the car.

His sleeves were rolled to the elbow. He opened his collar and loosened his tie while approaching us. With the slacks, the haircut, and the shave, Danny looked like a real wheeler-dealer.

"Lookin' good Fast Daniel," I complimented him. "Lookin' real tight."

"Hey, Dan," Homer.

Dan came up to us, squeezed his lips together, and then looked down. He struck what I guess he thought was an appropriately authoritative pose for the information about to be imparted—arms crossed tightly over his chest, feet parted and firmly planted.

"Here's the deal," looking up at us. "When can you guys start working?"

"Ya bagged some glass work already?" I asked.

"I've been busting ass the last two days. As of an hour ago, I've met with *all* of the churches in Guadeloupe. Two of the Catholic churches I met with yesterday called back today and want us to come up with a formal contract. I'll meet with JD tomorrow and take care of that," explaining in a starched, business-like tone.

"I'll be damned," reaching out and shaking his hand. "Congratulations!"

"Good job," Homer, shaking Danny's hand.

"We'll get the paperwork end wrapped up on Friday. So, when will everybody be available?"

Homer and I exchanged glances.

"I don't know," shrugging my shoulders. "How about Sund'y. An' I'll work somethin' out with Hugo ta take Saturd'y mornin's off. If I drop Sociology, I won't have any classes on Tuesd'y an' Thursd'y. I only need ta carry twelve hours ta keep the full GI Bill comin' in. I c'n work at Hugo's one day an' do the repairs the other day."

"I don't have a schedule," Homer. "I could start whenever JD says I can."

"How about Jerry and Jonas?" Danny.

"I'll find out b'fore Sund'y. Let's make Sund'y the first work day," I suggested.

"That'll work," Danny.

Homer nodded in agreement.

Danny turned back to the Lincoln.

"Gotta take the car home."

"When'd y'ur dad take up pimpin'?" as I pointed at the car.

"Shhh!" finger to his lips. "He told Mom he needed it for a part time job delivering pizzas at night," opening the door.

"Ya gunna be back t'night?" I asked.

"I'm beat. I think I'll go ahead and spend the night out there," making his point with a loud yawn.

"Okay. Say hi ta y'ur folks."

Danny hopped into the car, honked, and then drove away.

We walked across Neil's lawn. Neil was watching us from behind a large piece of cardboard he'd put in the window Jerry'd broken out.

"Goodnight, Neil," Homer waved.

Neil popped out of sight.

"Didn't I tell ya Danny'd pull it off?" and slapped Homer on the back.

"I never said he wouldn't," as we squeezed between the van and his truck.

"Still, we're gunna have ta keep his ass on a leash. I don't wan'a kill myself over this."

We went over to my bike. Homer sat on the bike and lit a cigarette.

I sat down on the dead grass and leaned against the rear wheel.

"When the Baha'i come down," I reminded him, "we gotta ditch the beer. Okay?"

"Okay."

"When ya pickin' Sonny up?"

"I'll head up there about midnight."

"Ya sounded a little down when ya mentioned her earlier."

"Yeah, I guess I did. Don't get me wrong. I'm still crazy as hell about her. It's hard to sit and talk with her, though. Sometimes I want to talk to her about things like we talked about tonight. It never seems to happen. When she has a night off, we're out dancing or partying with her friends. She's got some strange friends. Don't have much in common with them."

"Ya talk to her about it?"

"Yeah. Last night. Ended up in a big blow out. Locked me out of the bedroom."

"That bad?"

"That bad. After an hour she got horny so, we made up. She promised to stop trying to run things so much. I guess that's why she was over here this afternoon. Probably talking it over with the other girls."

"Hell, ya should'a heard 'em all. There was four 'r five of 'em up there squirtin' lotion at each other, squealin', laughin', an' talkin'."

People were on the steps shouting goodbyes, Allah'u'Abhaing each other, and laughing. Homer and I emptied our beers, crushed the cans, then saucered them into the front yard. The whole gaggle made a point of coming over to Homer and me to say hello, ask us how we were doing, ask me about the eye, and tell us how much they missed us at the meeting. Ahmed tried desperately, but unsuccessfully, to obtain a promise from us to be at the next meeting. It took about twenty minutes for the place to clear out. Bobbie wasn't with them.

Homer coughed then cleared his throat.

"So…how's it feel being the talk of the ghetto?"

"Didn't know I was."

"I'll *bet* you don't," looking over at me. "You probably started the story."

"What story?"

"Sonny told me all about it on the phone before I left JD's this evening. She got it from Hope and Joan while she was over here this afternoon. Your love making is the hot topic."

*First Shauna now Homer. What the hell's goin' on?*

"Yeah," looking over at me. "to hear her tell it, you're quite the stud. According to Hope and Joan, you and Bobbie were thumping so hard the lamp on Hope's dresser was shaking. Noisy too. Joan told Sonny you guys woke her up three times. Three times in an hour and a half."

*Bobbie must'a told Hope an' Joan what really happened an' now Hope an' Joan are makin' all this shit up ta cover for me.*

"Nothing to say for yourself?" Homer.

"What could I possibly add?"

"You like Bobbie?"

I didn't answer immediately.

"Well?" Homer pushed.

GLYNN E. THOMPSON

"Yeah. Yeah. I like her a lot."

"*GOOD* answer!" Joan.

I looked up. Hope, Bobbie, Joan and her friend from Amarillo, had crept about halfway down the steps.

"How long ya been out here?" as I got to my feet.

"How long wuz yew an' Jerry listenin' ta us on the roof this afternoon b'fore we knew *y'all* wuz there?" Hope.

Homer stood up and bowed.

"Good evening, ladies."

"Good evening, Sirs," in unison.

"Can ya come in an' help finish off the food?" Joan.

"Yeah," Homer. "I can handle that."

"I'm gunna hang around down here a while," and looked at Bobbie.

All of them except Bobbie clomped back up the stairs and disappeared into the house. Bobbie waited until they were in the kitchen before descending. She came over to me, holding her hands behind her.

"What ya said ta Homer was sweet," smiling.

"Oh Yeah? How sweet would it'a been if you'd'a snuck down here an' caught us lightin' each other's farts?"

"I was tryin' ta be romantic," frowning and slapping my arm.

I took her hand and walked toward Tenth.

"Let's wander around the block."

"Did ya mean what ya said ta Homer or did ya know we were on the steps?" quietly.

"I wouldn't jack with ya like 'at. I meant it. An' we didn't know ya were on the steps."

Bobbie squeezed my hand. She didn't say anything for a while.

"What classes do ya have on We'n'sd'ys?" she finally asked.

"How'd ya know I have classes on We'n'sd'ys?"

"I can see ya leave in the mornin'. I know y'ur whole semester schedule. On Mond'y, We'n'sd'y, an' Frid'y ya leave at 8:00 ta go ta school. Then ya survey in the afternoons at Hugo's. I've met Hugo at the meetin's. He's a nice man. He thinks a lot'a ya. On Tu'sd'ys and Thursd'ys ya go ta Hugo's in the mornin' then school in the afternoon only ya didn't go t'day b'cause'a the funeral. When ya work on Saturd'y mornin's Mr. Butthole in the orange truck picks ya up an' he wakes up ever'body in the neighborhood when he yells an' honks his horn."

"Roy. He's a nice guy...just has a weird sense'a humor. An' I'm cuttin' class t'morrow ta work out'a town with him so, I guess ya won't be able ta sleep in late t'morrow. Anyway, ya figured all 'at out about me just by lookin' out y'ur window?"

"Yeah. Plus Jerry told me ya work Mond'y, Thursd'y, an' Saturd'y night at a lounge."

I stopped and looked down at her. She was sparkling. Her long white hair absolutely glowed silver in the moonlight.

*Angel's hair.*

"I didn't have any idea," as I lit a cigarette. "Why didn't ya say somethin'?"

We continued to stroll.

"I thought ya had a ton'a girlfriends," shyly. "You work in a lounge with all those women. Ya live with two good-lookin' ladies. At first I thought one of 'em was y'ur girlfriend...or somethin'. An' what about all those women at Tech ya see ever'day. Lemme see, what else kept me from sayin' anything? I think you're...that you're handsome enough ta have anybody you'd want. I don't think I'm the *only* one watchin' when ya take y'ur shirt off ta wash y'ur bike 'r work on it. All in all, I didn't figure I had much of a chance an'..."

"If I'd'a known ya were lookin' I'd'a left my shirt on," I lied.

"Maybe 'at's why I didn't say anything," giggling. "Plus, I was afraid ta say anything to ya b'cause ya might think I was too young for ya."

"Wait a minute. Y're makin' it sound like I'm an ol' geezer. I'm just twenty-two. Turn twenty-three this month."

"Really?"

"What'a ya mean *really*?" How old did ya think I was?"

"At least as old as Jerry b'cause he said you were in Vietnam about the same time he was."

"How old's Jerry?" I asked.

"Twenty-six."

"I'd'a guessed *fifty*-six."

"He does act like an old man sometimes," she laughed.

"How old're you?"

"Nineteen. Had a birthday in July."

"When did ya graduate from high school?"

"1970."

"So...is twenty-three too old for ya?"

"Is nineteen too young?"

"I like 'em young," as I imitated a dirty old man—bent over, tongue hanging from my mouth, and mumbling in a deep, gravelly voice.

She giggled.

"I like older, more experienced men," presenting her imitation of a dirty old man. "Anyway...I had this big, long list'a reasons why I thought ya might not wan'a like me, ya know...in a certain way."

"So What happened ta change y'ur mind."

"Jerry."

"Jerry?"

"Yeah. Sometime in late June. I asked him about ya when he got back from California. That's when he said ya weren't...stop. Wait a minute."

Bobbie dropped my hand, removed the bandanna from my back pocket, and then hopped in front of me. She reached up and pulled the cigarette from my mouth. The filter stuck to my lips.

"Damn! Careful. My lips're dry."

"Sorry."

Bobbie placed the bandanna on her head and let the cigarette dangle from her mouth at an exaggerated angle. She opened one eye wide, squinted with the other, then forced her brow as far up as she could get it to go.

"Gil?" she snarled. "Yew fuckin' askin' me about Gil?" slurring like Jerry. "Shiiit to, woman. All's I know about Gil's 'at he ain't gittin' any from nowheres an' it's makin' him crazy...cackle, cackle, snort, cackle, heh, heh, heh."

"Damn! Throwing my head back and laughing. "That's perfect. He seen ya do that?"

"Oh, no. It'd hurt his feelin's but, Shauna an' me imitate him all the time b'hind his back. Like the way he lifts his eyebrows *all* the way up and squints one eye real tight then opens the other eye real wide? We call that the 'Jerry Eye'. Shauna can do a perfect Chad, too. No offense, but y'ur brother's such a dipshit."

"None taken."

Bobbie returned the cigarette, put the bandanna around her neck, and then stepped back to my side. She took my hand as we began walking again.

"So, when I found out ya weren't seein' anybody...I caught myself thinkin' about ya more an' more. I still didn't feel like ya, ya know...like ya really noticed me. I guess that's why I didn't pester ya."

"Ya should'a pestered me. I've been scopin' ya from a distance f'r sometime now."

*Wondered about what it'd be like ta do ya.*

"Ya pro'bly only thought about me when ya were drunk, horny, or lonely."

"That's not true. In the first place, I don't think at all when I'm drunk. In the second place, I've got too many roommates ta ever be lonely."

It took a few seconds to register.

Bobbie stopped and elbowed me in the ribs.

"So ya only thought about me when you were horny?"

"Just kiddin'," and pulled her along.

After turning onto Avenue X she stopped again, stepped in front of me, and then looked up.

"I guess now ya know how...how attracted I am to ya?" she asked quietly.

"Yeah. I got a p'rtty good idea about that."

Bobbie looked down at the ground.

"Would ya like ta hear me say it?" softly.

"That'd make me feel real good, Bobbie," and meant it.

She looked up.

"I like you very much," slightly cocking her head.

I bent over and gave her a quick kiss on the lips, then hugged her tightly.

"I like *you* very much also," whispering in her ear.

It made her shiver.

*Jesus. This all feels so...I don't know. So...nice. So right.*


We continued on, arm-in-arm, turning left onto Main and slowly walking back toward her place. Three houses from the corner Bobbie froze. She covered her mouth with both hands.

"Oh, no!" terrified.

"What?" frantically looking up the street then back to her.

"It's Luther's car," pointing at a white Impala parked at the corner on our side of the street.

She was sobbing, bending slightly at the waist, shaking, and slowly backing up.

"It's okay, Bobbie," pulling her to me and putting my arms around her. "It's okay."


Luther must have seen us. All four doors of the Impala opened. Four men exited the car, each loudly slamming a door behind them.

Bobbie's knees buckled. I held her tightly to keep her from dropping to the ground.

The driver hurried ahead of the others as they walked towards us.

Two shadowy figures, one a large hulk, the other short and stocky, darted from Jerry's front porch. The hulk stopped at the sidewalk while the shorter figure slipped around the pack and quickly stepped up along side the one in the lead. The shorter figure placed his hand to the man's temple. I could here the metallic click of a handgun being cocked.

The leader froze. His army scattered.

*Holy shit!*

"Git her inta the house!" Jerry ordered.

Bobbie couldn't walk. I had to pick her up and carry her. I stepped off the sidewalk to get around Jerry and the prisoner. I carried her inside, gently placed her on the couch, then left her with the girls.

I went back outside and stood alongside Homer. He was keeping an eye on the three deserters who'd regrouped back at the car.

"Tell y'ur chickenshit frien's ta git back in'a fuckin' car," Jerry growled.

"GET IN..."

"Not so fuckin' loud, man," Jerry, putting the .45 to Luther's lips. "There's a bunch'a college kids aroun' here tryin' ta study."

Luther quaked and cleared his throat.

"Get in the car," in a loud, harsh hiss.

His buddies, stumbling all over each other, scurried into the car. Three doors slammed in rapid succession.

Homer was laughing.

Jerry took a deep breath then exhaled slowly. He shook his head and squinted at Luther.

"Ya know, Luther...gittin' yew ta un'erstand 'at yew ain't welcome aroun' here's like tryin' ta teach a fence post ta spit."

Luther was quivering, eyes crossed while staring at the gun to his lips.

"Ya know who the short guy is over there?" Jerry, hitching his head in my direction.

Luther couldn't respond. I walked over to Jerry and Luther. I reached down, took Luther's hand, and then shook it vigorously.

"Glad ta meet ya Luther," I smiled. "Ya spineless cunt."

Jerry was cackling. I dropped Luther's hand.

"Me an' Bobbie're engaged," I told him. "What'a think about that shit, Luther?"

Jerry uncocked the .45 and slowly lowered it. Gripping Luther's wrist, Jerry forced him to take hold of the gun. Jerry then raised Luther's hand and put the muzzle to his own forehead. The silhouettes behind the screen door of the house, gasped.

*Oh, Fuck.*

Homer stepped towards us.

"Jerry," he said quietly.

"Go ahead," Jerry told Luther. "Pull the trigger. It'd be self-defense. Hell, it's *my* damn gun. Kind'a."

Luther, shaking, shut his eyes.

"Stay away from Bobbie an' ya do whut ya can ta avoid me from now on. Them's the rules. If ya don't like 'em…best ya shoot me right now 'cause if ya break the rules…I'm gunna kill ya."

Long moments.

Jerry finally let go of Luther's hand. Luther's arm fell to his side. Jerry took the gun back. In a flash, Jerry slammed his knee into Luther's crotch. Luther groaned loudly and collapsed, his forehead crashing against the sidewalk. He rolled over on one side and doubled up. Jerry looked over at Luther's cohorts cowering in the car.

"Git this dog turd off'a my lawn an' then git the fuck out'a here," Jerry ordered.

They scrambled to obey. In less than a minute they were on their way, speeding down Main toward University.

"Sons a bitches're so scared, they f'rgot ta turn their lights on," Jerry sneered. "Where's a fuckin' cop when ya need one, huh?"

Joan and Shauna ran out of the house.

"Goddammit, Jerry!" Shauna cried. "Don't yew *ever* do *anythang* like 'at again! He could'a killed yew!"

"Where's Bobbie?" I asked.

"Kitchen," Joan.

I ran inside and found Bobbie at the kitchen table, Hope sitting on one side, Joan's friend, Connie, on the other. Both had their arms around her. Hope and Connie got up, kissed Bobbie lightly on the head, and then left the room. I sat down beside her and took her hand. She grabbed it with the other and squeezed hard.

"I'm sorry," dropping her head onto my chest and sobbing.

I gently stroked her hair and told her there wasn't anything to be sorry about.

"Shauna...Shauna," she stammered, "said Luther'd been waitin' for me for over thirty minutes. Shauna an' them couldn't find us ta warn us. Homer an' Jerry decided ta wait until we showed up an' see what Luther was gunna do."

I told her not to say anything. I slipped my bandanna from around her neck and began dabbing the tears from her cheeks. Bobbie pulled my hand to her nose and quickly ran the bandanna under it.

"I look so nasty," tearfully. "I'm so sorry."

"Stop worryin' about it, Bobbie. Y're pr'tty as hell. Red eyes, snot, an' blubberin' b'comes ya."

Bobbie poked me hard with her elbow.

"Shut up," she managed.

Things gradually settled down. Homer went to pick up Sonny. Joan, Connie, and Hope went home. Shauna settled in with Jerry. He was the hero of the night and Shauna couldn't wait to be with him. It was just me and Bobbie, alone in the living room, her head in my lap. She was curled up into a tight little ball, fast asleep. She looked so small. I gently ran my fingers through her hair.

*God I love her hair.*

Eventually, I carried her into her room and placed her on the bed. I kissed her on the forehead. Bobbie didn't move a muscle.

*Damn. Why am I fightin' this thing?*
*Why not just let it happen.*
*Son of a bitch.*

It was going on 2:00 in the morning when I got back to the house. I slowly, quietly made my way up the steps, eased the door open, and then entered the kitchen. On my way to the bedroom I heard someone in Homer's room. His door was cracked open a bit. I peeked inside.

There, in the moon lit room, two bodies were pounding away at each other with such ferocity the window was rattling. The lady had her knees pulled up along side her head. The man on top of her, pumping furiously, was grunting and whispering obscenities. Suddenly the lady straightened her legs, dug her heels into the carpet, thrust her hips upward and screamed.

"Shhh. Shhh. Not so loud," Chad.

*That's who the girls heard the other night! Chad's been sneakin' sluts over here ta avoid Jerry.*

I slipped into my room and laid down. The smacking kisses, skin slapping, low moans, and hurried whispers continued for a while longer. It gave me butterflies. My groin ached. As I drifted off to sleep, I thought I felt something stir.

\*\*\*

The next morning the roar of Jerry's bike kicking over startled me awake. I opened my eyes and looked around the room. I covered my right eye and focused on the shitbird drawing. It was fuzzy, but it was better than yesterday. I sat up. The room was chilly. I crawled on my knees to the window and lowered it. Jerry's bike was sputtering and coughing as it warmed up. Yawning, I got to my feet, stretched, scratched...

*OH, SWEET JESUS!*

I grabbed my jeans and began pulling them on, first one foot, then the other, as I hopped out of the bedroom and into the kitchen. Buttoning the top button, I flew down the stairs. I skipped painfully across the graveled driveway then broke into a full run toward Jerry. He was sitting on his bike toking a joint. I came up alongside him.

"My eye!" pointing at the bruise. "Is Bobbie awa...,"

Bobbie appeared in her bedroom window right next to us. She was wrapped in a large pink bath towel. I held my fist up, gradually extending my index finger. Her mouth opened wider as the finger slowly straightened.

"I c'n see again!"

She hopped up and down excitedly while motioning for me to come inside. I turned back to Jerry.

"Gotta go!"

Jerry nodded. He was sneering again.

Behind me a horn honked several times. Roy's orange pickup was in our driveway.

"Goddammit," I groaned loudly.

*It can't be that late.*

Jerry, cackling, looked at me. He cupped his hands over his mouth and yelled.

"Looks like y're gunna have ta bring 'at tree down with the ol' five finger hatchet." He gunned the bike a few times before roaring off, cackling all the way.

Roy spotted me as he was getting out of his truck.

"Yew ain't trippin' again are ya?" he bellowed. "It's We'n'sd'y. October, 1971. 'member? Y're s'posed ta have 'at half naked ass'a y'urs in this fuckin' truck so we c'n git ta work!"

"Gimme a minute!" as I ran to the back porch. I threw the door open, charged through the kitchen and living room, then burst into Bobbie's room.

Bobbie, sitting on her feet in bed, hands folded delicately in her lap, had slipped into a sheer, light blue colored negligee, her face an expression of painful distress as the horn sounded again.

"It's Roy," as I hurried over to her.

"I know. I know," close to whimpering.

Bobbie rose up on her knees and moved to the edge of the bed, put her arms around my bare waist, and then pulled me to her.

"An' ya have ta leave," sighing in frustration.

She dropped her forehead to my chest and looked down.

A tiny moan.

Her arms slid from my waist. I could feel her fingers gently easing the unfastened fly open. I gasped as she slipped her fingers inside the fly and found me. I shivered.

"Oh God!" she breathed.

I placed my hands on her butt and slowly crushed her body against mine. Bobbie yielded, raising her head without letting go of me. She feverishly peppered my neck with quick kisses and little nips, as she continued to hold me.

HOONK! HOOOOONK!

I dropped my head to her shoulder, hers fell to mine. Bobbie whispered in my ear.

"If we hurried, we cou..."

HOOOOOONK!

"Come on ya fuckin' lazy-ass hippie!" Roy. "Le's go!"

"Shut the fuck up!" Neil's voice.

I kissed her as I eased her hands from me.

"Nooo!" she whinned.

"Damn," my entire body electrified.

HOOOOOOOONK!

"I'm gunna call the cops!" Neil.

"Fuck yew!" Roy. "It's seven-goddamn-thirty in'a mornin'! Ain't yew got a fuckin' job ta go to ya freak?"

I stepped to the door.

"When do ya get off t'night?" I asked hurriedly.

"5:30," sitting on her legs again, pouting.

"I'll be back at around 4:30. I'll pick ya up at the parlor. Okay?"

She brightened and popped back to her knees.

"Bring Jerry's van!" excitedly. "An' some blankets 'r pillows 'r somethin' like 'at!"

HOOOONK!

"T'night!" charging out of the door.

"GIL!" she cried.

I grabbed the edge of the doorframe and yanked myself back into the room.

"What?"

"I...I like you very much," softly.

Her arms were outstretched, her negligee wide open.

It'd been dark in my room last Sunday morning, only the moonlight. This was the first real shot I'd had of her.

The negligee closed. She fell onto her side giggling.

"I like you very much," I told her.


I charged across Jerry's backyard. Neil, his shirtless gut hanging over the top of his jeans, was faced off with Roy in front of Roy's truck. They were loudly exchanging profanities.

"Gimme a second!" I called out to Roy then dashed up the stairs. I grabbed a shirt, a pair of socks, my work boots, and then darted back down the steps.


Roy was leaning against the truck, legs slightly spread, arms folded across his chest. He was stuffing a wad of chew in his mouth. I didn't see Neil.

" 'at fuckin' freak says he's gittin' a goddamn gun," Roy fumed.

"You gunna drive 'r do ya want me to."

"Yew drive, goddammit," continuing his mumbling.

Roy got his chew going while watching Neil's front door.

"I'm too goddamned upset ta drive," spitting into Neil's yard before hollering wildly, "How about it ASSHOLE? Let's see 'at fuckin' gun'a y'urs, ya goddamn piece'a FREAK SHIT!"

Nothing from Neil's place.

Roy snorted, spit again, opened the passenger door, and then climbed in.

"J'st git me the fuck out'a this shithole," grumbling as the door slammed shut.

I jumped in behind the wheel and threw it into gear. Roy hung out the window and yelled one last time.

"Gil's gunna kick y'ur cowr'dly ASS when he gits home t'night! Ya done pissed him off good ya yell'a piece'a MONKEY FUCK!"

Roy pulled himself back into the cab as I crept down the street. My eyes were fixed on Jerry's place.

"Yew will take care'a 'at for me t'night?" Roy, calmly. "Won'ch ya, Gil? If it ain't out'a y'ur way?" leaning over and tapping the speedometer. "Let's go! Let's go! This son of a bitch's got a second gear ya know," then looked in the direction I was staring. "My *Lord!*" he gasped.

Bobbie was standing in her window waving, holding her towel in front of her.

"Would ya look at that hair?" Roy sizzled. "So, *'at's* whut's been goin' on," whispering to himself. "Ol' Gil done went an' fell in love while I wudn' lookin'," then started snarling. "*Shit.* It was hard enough gittin' a days work out'a ya when ya was sufferin' from azure testicularitis. Now yew've gone an' caught poontheria."


I waved at Bobbie as we approached the house. I could feel another erection coming on.

*Hot damn! It feels so good.*

Roy whistled softly and waved as we got closer.

"Is 'at her nat'ral hair color?" spitting out the window. "Bet ya git asked 'at a lot, don'ch ya?"

Roy waved at her and tipped his hat. Bobbie curtsied in return then blew a kiss.

"See 'at?" he snickered. "Blew my ass a kiss. Right smack in front'a ya. Whud're ya gunna do about it, pussy?" reaching over and slapping my arm.

I smiled and peeled out.

"C'mon now. Is it 'r ain't it? 'r am I gunna have ta find out f'r myself?"

"I guess y'u'll have ta find out f'r y'urself."

"Fuck it. I'll ask Chad 'r Jerry."

"C'mon, Roy. Don't be talkin' about her like 'at, okay?"

"My wife's brunette," ignoring me. "Top ta bottom. Now it's y'ur turn ta tell me about *y'ur* lady," with a sleazy grin.

"That's not a fair deal, Roy. Ever'body in Lubbock knows what color y'ur wife is from top ta bottom."

"Prick," grumbling before spitting out the window.

"Where we goin'?" as we turned onto Broadway and headed toward University.

The sidewalks were already busy with students hurrying to class.

"J'st this side'a Turkey. Got an ol' Spanish land grant ta find the corners on. We'll have ta use the vera chain."

"When're we gettin' back?" sensing a possible problem.

"Listen ta that. C'n ya make it ta supper time without blowin' a gonad gasket?"

"I got plans. That's all."

"I bet ya do, ya horny little Pooh bear."

"So how long's this gunna take?" becoming irritated.

"Damn! Hair's already kinkin' an' we ain't even out'a town yet."

"Serious, Roy, goddammit. I need ta know," fully irritated.

"7:00 'r 8:00. We won't be back in time f'r me ta fiddle t'night."

I hit the brakes and cut the steering wheel sharply to the right, barely having enough time to make the turn onto Main.

"Whut the...!" Roy.

I floored it, as we screamed down Main back to Jerry's.

"This won't take a second," I told him.

"Poontheria!" hanging on to the dash with both hands as we accelerated past 50 miles an hour. "Once ya start gittin' it reg'lar off somebody," shouting over the screaming transmission, "ya go aroun' all day long crackin' fatties 'cause ya know whut's waitin' f'r ya back at the house. Poontheria makes ya do dumbass thangs like goin' sixty mile' an hour in a goddamn thirty mile an hour zone! I ain't payin' the ticket, goddammit!"

I screeched to a halt in front of Jerry's, hopped out and rushed into the house. Bobbie was in the kitchen fixing a cup of instant coffee. She was wearing a faded flannel Barbie robe tied shut.

"Bobbie?"

"Oh, no," covering her mouth with both hands.

"We won't be back 'til 7:00 'r 8:00."

"That's all?" moving her hands to her chest.

"Well...yeah. Idn't 'at bad enough?"

Bobbie rushed over and hugged me tightly.

"I thought ya'd...gone blind again."

I hugged her hard.

"I'll make dinner for ya," she promised then stepped back and winked. "Now, go ta work."

I turned and charged out of the house. Roy was in the driver's seat. Bobbie came to the front door and waved. Roy and I waved back as we drove away.

"Ya Know what the female version of poontheria is?" Roy, serious as hell.

"I don't really care, Roy."

"Dicktheria. Git it? Dyptheria...dicktheria?" chuckling to himself. "I j'st made 'at 'un up," proudly. "Hot shit. Hung over as hell. No sleep. Damn near shot by a crazy-ass Mes'c'n, then damn near killed by a dope addict, sex fiend in a car crash, an' I *still* got it."

I shook my head.

Roy spit out the window.

"Ya know how ya cure poontheria?"

*Christ. He was on one'a his rolls.*

"I don't really care, Roy."

"Ya don't cure it. It j'st goes away. Ya start gittin' bored with the same ol' stuff so ya b'gin shoppin' aroun' again. She finds out an' throws y'ur ass out. Then guess whut happens?"

"I don't really care, Roy."

"Blue balls again," spitting out the window. "It's a goddamn vicious cycle, but I'm gittin' the feelin' 'at ya don't really care about any'a this," leaning over to turn the radio up. "Ya lack a healthy sense a curiosity, Gil," shouting over a hog feed commercial.

"Mark my words, boy...'at's gunna prove ta be a major hindrance ta y'ur developin' inta a full-blown, honest-ta-God intellectual."

\*\*\*

Roy pulled up to the drive and dropped me off. It was going on sunset. It'd blown sand all afternoon. I'd cut line all day through thick mesquite scrub using an old, rickety handled machete. I'd worked blisters around the calluses on both my hands and I'd burned over my sun tan. I was filthy. I was beat.

Jerry, sitting next to a case of beer on his kitchen porch and smoking a joint, motioned for me to come over. I trudged toward him. He looked freshly showered, his hair still damp and slicked back. He tossed me a beer and held the joint up. I caught the beer and took the joint.

"Bobbie here?" I asked.

"Oh yeah," he growled. "She's here,"

"What's wrong?"

"Wrong? Whu' the hell makes ya think anything's wrong?" brows raised to the max. "Jus' 'cause I been tol' ta git the fuck out'a my own house an' ta stay away yew go an' think somethin's wrong?"

"What happened?"

"Whut happened?" glancing over his shoulder into the kitchen. "This whut's happened, man," and took the joint back. "Bobbie's cookin' a romantic dinner for ya, an' she told the rest'a us ta hit the bricks f'r the evenin' so y'all c'n be alone," finishing with a snort. "Whud'a ya think abou' tha' shit. Throwed out'a my own damn house."

"Really?" as I looked into the kitchen. "She mentioned somethin' about fixin' dinner for me, but I wudn't expectin' anything fancy. Where's she at now?"

"I'll tell ya where she's at. Shauna's helpin' her git dolled up so she'll look real hot when she serves ya dinner t'night. 'at's where Bobbie's at. Joan an' Hope wuz over here earlier helpin' her. Damn. How many people's it take f'r Bobbie ta git ready f'r a date? She retarded 'r somethin'?" getting up an' slapping my arm. "Yew lucky shithead," he cackled.

"I'll be damned. Fixin' a romantic dinner an' sprucin' up just f'r me."

"Yeah. Shauna an' me're gunna go see a skin flick at the drive-in so we won't be in y'ur way. An' don't go thinkin' 'at wuz my idea, man. Joan said she'd kill me if I didn't take off. Like I said…throwed out'a my own damn house jus' so yew c'n bang my roomy. Ain' 'at the shits 'r whut?"

"Hey," grinning, "I appreciate the sacrifice. I'm hungry as hell…if ya know what I mean?"

"Hungry ain't the word f'r a man in y'ur condition," cackling. "If I wuz in y'ur shoes, I'd be damn near starved," and turned on the Jerry Eye. "Y're gunna be goin' from finger san'iches ta rump roast t'night."

"Better let her know I'm back," as I stepped onto the porch.

Shauna ran through the kitchen, threw herself against the screen door, and then latched it.

"Ya cain't come in yet! Go git cleaned up an' stay away 'til the porch light's turned back on. It'll be about forty-five minutes," slapping the wall. The porch light went out.

"Don't come back 'til the lights turned on!"

336

"Okay. Tell Bobbie it sure smells good an' that I'm so hungry I could eat a horse."

"Among other things," Jerry snickered.

I jumped off the porch.

"Damn."

"Damn right, damn," Jerry. "We pro'bly won't be back 'til aroun' 1:00. 'at gunna give ya enough time?"

"It's been so long, I can't remember how long it takes."

"Takes me three 'r four hours, but then, not ever' ladies as lucky as Shauna," snickering again.

"How'd Doug do t'day at work? He gunna make it as a bricklayer?"

Jerry buried his face in his lap and groaned.

"The son uv a bitch laid brick f'r an hour then wouldn't work anymore 'cause he felt like brick layin' wudn' nat'ral."

"Layin' brick's unnatural?"

"Accordin' ta him it is," slowly smoothing his hair back. "He ended up shinglin'. F'r some reason roof shinglin' *wuz* nat'ral."

"But he worked all day?"

"Yeah. I dropped him off at Vann's about thirty minutes ago."

We were both startled by a figure charging past the corner of the house. It was Doug. He had a crow bar in his hand. Vann, seconds behind him, spotted us and stopped. He stooped over and gripped his side with his hand. He was panting heavily, his stub twitching uncontrollably.

"Somebody broke in," Vann gasped, "and stole Doug's bike parts," continuing to fight for air.

Doug had reached Neil's place and was slamming the crow bar against the side of the house, demanding that Neil come out.

"Doug convinced himself Neil did it," Vann panted. "I couldn't stop him."

The three of us took off running through the backyard.

"I called Homer at the shop," Vann shouted while trying to keep up with us. "Eduardo and Tomas were there. They're all on the way."

Doug was working his way around to the back of the little shack, leaving a trail of deep gashes as he went. We got to the alley and stopped.

"He's gunna kill him," I told Jerry.

"That's what he said he was going to do," Vann. "Beat him to death."

Doug's blows were increasing in ferocity.

"Let's jump him," I suggested. "Take the crow bar away."

"No," Jerry, studying the situation. "Tha' won't...leave him be."

Neil's bike was chained to the porch. Jerry ran over to the bike and kicked it to the ground.

"SON UV A BITCH!" and began to stomp on the rear spokes. "FUCKIN' SON UV A BITCH!"

Doug stopped hammering on the house and turned to watch Jerry.

"Motherfuckin' son of a bitch!" Jerry, continuing to stomp on the spokes.

Doug attacked the bike. Jerry backed away and rejoined the rest of us.

Homer's truck was burning up the alley, dust bellowing into the air behind him. Tomas then Ed rounded the corner at Tenth and slid to a stop in front of Neil's. Homer drove into Jerry's back yard. We turned our heads while the dust cloud rolled over us. Homer jumped from his truck and ran to Jerry's side, not stopping to shut the door. Tomas and Ed hurried over. They didn't bother taking their riding gear off. Doug was furiously thrashing away at the bike. He ripped at the wiring and the hoses. He pried the battery loose then tossed it against the house.

"Is that motherfucker inside?" Eduardo, seething.

"Don't know," I answered.

Ed and Tomas ran around to the front of the house. We heard a loud crash then a lot of yelling and shouting in Spanish from inside. Doug, beginning to tire, continued to bash away at the bike. He knocked the head lamp free of the front forks then began smashing the head pans.

The yelling inside intensified. Neil suddenly appeared in the street. He scurried across W Street then waddled up the alley away from us, looking back every other step to see if anyone was going to give chase. Doug, busy with the bike, never saw the escape.

"Should we go after him?" I asked.

"Hell no," Jerry. "Let him go f'r now."

Doug, wet with sweat and close to spent, was on his knees, weakly striking the gas tank. Ed opened the back door of the house and stepped onto the little porch. Tomas appeared behind him. Ed held a set of springers up.

"DOUG!"

Doug looked up as Ed stepped down from the porch. Doug stopped hitting the bike, struggled to his feet, and then let the crow bar fall from his hands. The crow bar clanged against the frame one last time. The dust cloud Doug had raised while assaulting the bike settled.

I looked up at our stoop. Danny, Connie, Joan, Hope, and Hugo were gathered in a knot. Joan was clutching Hugo's arm. Danny had his arm around Hope. Hope, hands to her face, appeared to be crying. The occupants of the apartments below ours were standing around in the yard—staring, whispering among themselves. The hippies across the street where gawking at the spectacle.

Doug staggered over to Ed. He paused and examined the springers before reaching out and slowly running his finger over a number of long, deep scratches in the shiny chrome. He touched a few spots where the plating had chipped when Neil had removed them from the frame. Without looking up, Doug gently took them from Ed, stood motionless a few seconds, and then backed away. Turning around, Doug took several slow, heavy steps toward the alley. He stopped, raised the springers over his head, and then heaved them through the air. They crashed to the ground and slid a few feet before coming to rest against a gas meter in the alley. He walked over to Jerry, Vann, Homer, and me.

"I don't...*think*...you know...*those* scratches...can be...polished out," speaking loud enough for Tomas and Ed, still near the porch, to hear. "Those are deep, deep...*deep* scratches, man," looking at the springers and pointing. "And chipped. The fucking chrome is...*all* chipped," looking back at us, eyes frenzied. "What do *you* think, Jerry? Gil?"

We didn't say anything.

"How about you, Homer?"

Doug turned to the porch.

"Tomas? Eduardo? Do you...know of a way to...to make *those* kinds of scratches go away?"

Doug walked over to Ed and shook his hand.

"Thank you. Thank you for finding them. Thank you for helping." turning to face the rest of us. "Thank you...*all* of you. Sincerely," stepping toward W Street and waving to the spectators. "THANK YOU!" grinning wildly. "Thank all of you for allowing me to share this moment with you," and broke into a light, wheezing laugh. "Thank you for coming!"

He waved at everyone on the stoop then slowly walked back to Homer.

"Would you...mind taking me somewhere, Homer. I would... appreciate it."

"Get in the truck. I'll be right there."

Doug, feet dragging, in a kind of stupor, headed for the truck.

"I'll keep him at JD's tonight," Homer.

Tomas and Ed walked over to their bikes without saying a word. The stoop at the house slowly cleared. Homer drove through Jerry's backyard, empty beer bottles clinking loudly in the bed of the truck as it eased over the curb onto W. The bikes roared away. Within a minute, the only sounds remaining were those of a rapidly squeaking water cooler fan in the distance and a Jefferson Airplane song drifting up the alley from a utility. The dust settled. No one moved for a while.

Jerry finally spoke.

"Whud're ya doin' t'night, Vann?"

"I feel like I should go to JD's and help keep an eye on Dou..."

"Nah. 'at's a fucked idea. Y're comin' ta the skin flicks with me an' Shauna. I'll pay. We'll ask 'at Connie chick ta go. Sort'a like she'd be y'ur date," cackling.

"I heard she is a lesbian," Vann said quietly, studying Neil's mangled bike.

"She ain't *all* leso," Jerry snickered. "Joan tol' Shauna 'at Connie swings about six 'r seven diff"r'nt ways. No such thing as a *real* leso anyway, Vann. There's only challenges," then danced his eyebrows up and down a few times. "An' from whud I hear when I'm in'a basement, I kind'a think ol' Connie could be talked inta tryin' a little bit'a Vann *lap xuong*. Don'ch ya think so, Gil?"

"Strong possibility," I answered flatly, still sorting out what just happened.

"Anyways, there ain't no better way ta steam a' oyster open than at a skin flick. Ya know whud I'm sayin', Vann? It's kind uv a sneaky way ta slip the conversation aroun' ta sex an' shit."

Vann hesitated.

"Does she know I am Vietnamese?"

"Pro'bly wouldn't make a shit to her, but if y're worried about it, tell her y're a Chinaman 'r somethin'. Hell, y'all look alike."

"A *skin* flick," Vann, considering the offer. "Connie does seem to be a nice lady."

"Damn straight she's nice. Jus' a li'l fucked up an' li'l heavier 'an I like 'em. Don't really matter," Jerry snickered. "By the time y're ten minutes inta a *good* fuck movie ever'body starts ta lookin' like Raquel Welch. Skin flicks ain't against y'ur religion are they?"

"No. Not at all," smiling. "Hedonists are encouraged to take part in depravities of all kinds."

Jerry furrowed his brow.

"Yew ain't shittin' me are ya?" laying on the Jerry eye. "There really is a religion 'at allows 'at kind'a thing?"

"Hedonism," Vann repeated.

Jerry thought about it.

"They b'lieve in Jesus?" brows raised, biting his upper lip.

"You are free to believe anything you like."

"I'll be damned!" Jerry, turning to me. "Yew pro'bly got about twenty 'r thirty minutes left b'fore 'at porch light goes on. Yew best be movin' it," nudging Vann toward Doug's springers. "So, Vann... how many times a week y'all git t'gether an', yew know, pray an' shit?"

Jerry bent over to pick the springers from the dust. Their voices trailed off as they walked to Jerry's.

Hugo and Danny came over from the house to look at the bike.

"Where'd Homer take Doug?" Hugo.

"Over ta JD's f'r now."

"The police'll pro'bly be lookin' for him if Neil files charges," Hugo, shaking his head.

"How c'n Neil file charges?" I asked. "He's the one who stole Doug's bike parts."

"Two separate matters," Hugo. "Listen...I'm takin' the girls out ta the house with me in case this thing hasn't completely blown over. I think they'd feel more comf'tr'ble out there t'night."

"I'm going with them," Danny.

I said goodbye, jogged past Neil's and then took the stairs two steps at a time. I paused on the stoop to look back at Jerry's house. The light was still off.

I found Joan in her room, throwing some things into a small overnight case.

"Vann, Jerry, an' Shauna're goin' ta the drive-in," I told her. "Vann was hopin' Connie might wan'a go along."

"I c'n ask her. She's awfully shy. When're they leavin'?"

"About thirty minutes…little less than 'at, maybe."

"I'll tell her," and stepped toward me. "Gil?"

"Yeah?"

"Wear somethin' nice t'night when you go ta Bobbie's. She's gunna be wearin' an evenin' dress Sonny gave her."

"Christ. I don't have a suit 'r anything."

"I meant somethin' clean and not all wrinkled. And put on some underwear…just for decorum's sake."

"Gotch ya."

"And…have a *real* good time," she winked.

The house was empty by the time I'd finished showering. I tossed some clean clothes on the pallet then sat down by the window to smoke a cigarette. Clean felt good. The cool air felt nice after the hot shower.

*Fuckin' Neil. What a bastard.*

I relaxed and looked over at the shitbird drawing. I closed my good eye to test the lame one.

*Still blurred.*

*C'n read the big black letterin' on the reel-to-reel tape boxes. 'at's a good sign.*

*Dammit.*

*Wish I'd hung onta the tape deck. T'night'd be perfect f'r some'a the hump music.*

*That was the whole purpose'a buyin'all 'at shit overseas.*

*The sound system. The tapes. All part'a the pussy trap I was gunna have after gettin' out.*

*Oh, well.*

I yawned, flipped the cigarette butt out the window, and then stretched out naked on the mat.

*Five minutes. Then splash some Old Spice on.*
*Everywhere.*
*Get dressed an' then...chow time.*

\*\*\*

Something was on my chest. I eased my eyes opened.
*Bobbie.*

Her hands and head were resting on my chest, her knees drawn up, touching the side of my head. Bobbie was looking at me and smiling. Her long hair, silver in the moonlight, streamed delicately over her shoulders. She was wearing her Barbie rob. I yawned deeply and glanced around.

*Shit!*

*I'm in my bedroom!*

I tried to sit up.

"It's okay," Bobbie, pushing me back.

She raised up beside me, leaned on her elbow, and then rested her head in the palm of her hand.

"I'm such a maggot," I mumbled.

"Don't say that," gently touching my face.

"Well, I sure fucked this up."

"You didn't fuck anything up," resting her head back on my chest, tucking her arm under her side.

We lay quietly as I combed my fingers through her hair, raising my hand into the air then watching the silken strands slip away and float back to her shoulders.

"I love y'ur hair. It's so soft...so beautiful."

When I'd said "love" she'd picked her head up slightly and looked at me sweetly.

"I love y'ur chest," and gently kissed her way back and forth across it.

My spine tingled. My temples were pounding.

"I waited thirty minutes after turnin' the light on," laying her head back down and closing her eyes. "I thought somethin' might be wrong 'r that you were really upset about Doug an' the bike. I was afraid ya weren't gunna come."

I placed my hand in the small of her back.

"I came over ta see if ya were all right," she continued. "You were snorin'."

"I don't snore."

"Yes ya do. An' you were naked. I was watchin' ya. You look good naked. Especially in the moonlight," shuddering. "How'd ya get these?" delicately running a finger over scars on my left shoulder and right side.

"Car wreck," I lied. "Big one."

"Were ya alone?"

"No."

"Were ya drivin'?"

"No. I was just along for the ride. Joan's gunna kill me," turning the conversation away from the scars. "Jerry's gunna kill me."

"No they won't. I went back ta the house an' fixed ever'thing so it looks like we had dinner an'...went ta bed. I messed the covers up so it'd look like we made lo...like we had a good time."

"You thought ta do all'a that? Just so I wouldn't look like a jerkoff?"

"Yeah. An' I left a pair'a panties on the livin' room floor."

"Jesus."

"An' draped my hose over the back'a the couch an' put a sexy lavender garter belt in Jerry's bed an' messed his bed up," giggling.

"Y're kiddin'!"

"He'll love it. I put the evenin' dress Sonny loaned me in Chad's room. The high heels're in Shauna's room. I left a note tellin' 'em we'd decided ta spend the rest'a the night over here."

"Y're somethin' else."

She placed her hand over mine in the small of her back.

"Tighter. Hold me closer."

I pulled her to me, as close as I could get her.

I tensed and gasped.

Her head shot up. She looked at me, twinkling eyes wide.
"That's y'ur...your..."
"Yeah. I b'lieve so."
Bobbie leaned forward and put her lips to mine.

# CHAPTER FOUR
## February, 1972

*C*old! *Goddamn! Bitter cold!*
    I ran up the steps, frozen breath puffing like a train. The living room light was on, the stoop window curtain drawn. *Already dark an' it's hardly 5:30.*

I hurried into the kitchen and shut the door. I was blasted by the heat. It felt good. All the burners on the gas stove were on high. I removed my gloves, went over to the stove and began rubbing my hands above the flames.

Voices in the hall.

"Bobbie! That you?"

"We have company," she answered as she pushed the door curtain aside and stepped into the kitchen. Bobbie came over to me, went up on her toes, and then kissed my ear.

"Good God, Gil! Y're freezin'!" dropping from her toes and reaching up to place a hand on each ear. "Are you all right?"

"Just cold. Roy sits in the truck between shots. Me an' Stan're the one's out in it all afternoon. Roy dudn't remember how goddamn miserable it is."

Bobbie put her arms around me and hugged me.

"But do ya still like me very much?" purring while nibbling at my ear.

"Yeah," and picked her up. "I still like ya *very* much."

The eyes on the stove sputtered as I spun her around. I set her down with a pat on the butt.

"Ya got a letter from the Police Department t'day," and reached for a brown envelope on the table.

*Shit.*

"Lemme see it," and took it from her.

I ripped the letter open and began to read while Bobbie put her hand in my pocket and started rubbing me.

"I got hot for ya t'day," she murmured.

"Ya always get hot for me on y'ur days off," as I read the letter again to be certain I wasn't missing something.

"Want me ta take more..."

"Remember the tickets Homer got a coupl'a months ago when he was pushin' the bike home? Not signalin' an' no headlight on?"

"Didn't ya take care'a of 'em?"

"Don't have to now. They've been dropped."

"Maybe they figured out how stupid it made 'em look ta give a ticket ta somebody who was *pushin'* a motorcycle."


Danny walked into the kitchen.

"Did Bobbie tell you about what happened?" upset. Very upset.

"About the tickets?" I asked.

"You can tell him the sucky news," Bobbie told Danny.

I looked at Danny.

"What's wrong?"

Danny handed me a letter addressed to J.D. Grubb. I read through it quickly.

"Failin' ta meet the specifications of the contract? What the fuck's 'at mean?"

"Let's go into the living room," Danny, as he stormed from the kitchen.

I looked back at Bobbie.

"Jerry says it's no big deal," shrugging her shoulders and lifting her eyebrows. "He says Danny's bein' an asshole."

I stripped my coat off and set it on the chair. Bobbie grabbed it and put it on.

"Gimme y'ur boots. I'm gunna run over an' see Shauna an' Connie. Gimme y'ur gloves too."

I kicked off my heavy wool boots. Bobbie stepped into them. They came to just below her knees.

"There's some fried chicken in the refrigerator," as she clomped to the door.

I walked down the hall and entered the living room. It was thick with cigarette smoke and the sweet, heavy smell of hash. Jerry, Jonas, and Tomas were stretched out, one on each of the three couches, Homer stretched out on the floor. Danny was in the rocking chair, studying the letter again. I fell into one of the three bean bags. Two pieces of crumpled tin foil were floating in a sea of cigarette butts in the ashtray. A dozen empty beer bottles were scattered around the room.

"Christ. How long's ever'body been here?" I asked.

"I got here righ' after lunch," Jerry slurred. "Cain't pour decent concrete in this cold-ass shit."

"About an hour," Tomas. "Danny called me."

"J-just got here," Jonas.

I kicked Homer's foot. Homer snorted, covered his eyes with one arm and began to snore.

"He's, uh...wasted, man," Jerry snickered. "He'd already done a cube before I got here."

"Here's the deal," Danny huffed. "This letter's from a church we did a while back. Remember the one with the big picture window behind the baptismal? The one with Jesus holding the lamb?"

"The jerkoffs who didn't come up with the last two thousan' they owed on the job," I added.

"Yeah. Their attorney says he's gunna sue us because you guys deliberately fucked up two of the repaired pieces in the window. They've had to put duct tape over the pieces."

"It says *that*?" leaning forward and reaching for the letter. "A church's lawyer said 'fucked up'?"

Jerry and Tomas began laughing.

"IT'S NOT FUNNY!" Danny.

*Fuck 'at shit!*

I flew into him.

"JUST HOW THE HELL C'N THEY SUE US WHEN IT WAS 'EM 'AT RIPPED US OFF F'R TWO FUCKIN' THOUSAN' DOLLARS TA B'GIN WITH?"

Homer jerked and rolled onto his side. Jerry struggled to his feet.

"Be cool, man. Be cool," quietly walking over and slapping Danny's shoulder then tapping me on the head with the bottom of his beer bottle. "This vol'tility shit sucks, man. Be cool," returning to the couch and flopping back down.

Danny and I exchanged glances.

"Go ahead," as I turned away. "Didn't mean ta lose it,"

"Same," Danny mumbled.


Danny paused a bit before starting over.

"As far as their right to sue us, I'll come back to that later. First...what the hell is he talking about? I checked those windows myself. They were perfect."

Silence.

Tomas sat up. Jerry rolled his head to look at Danny.

Jonas slid from the couch to the floor, somehow managing to end up in a sitting position.

"Nobody has any idea what they're talking about?" Danny pressed.

"Well," I mumbled, "maybe a wild-ass guess."

Jerry, Jonas, and Tomas sputtered as they fought to contain their laughter. Danny was ready to blow again. I coughed and cleared my throat.

"Remember when I called ya an' told ya the preacher was hintin' that he didn't like the repairs so he was gunna hold the last payment 'til he talked it over with some fuckin' committee 'r other?"

Danny nodded.

"Danny...I was raised around those bastards. That son of a bitch'd already made up his mind there wudn't any way in hell they were gunna pay us the rest'a the money. I know for a fact that, from the very start, he was pro'bly never plannin' on makin' the last payment. Anyway, we still had the final polish left ta do. While we were doin' 'at, Tomas made some changes to a few'a the pieces in the window. That's all…just a coupl'a minor touch ups ta some painted pieces. We didn't even fire 'em in the kiln. Just used some lacquer an' spray. They c'n scrape it off if they want."

"We don't need ta be tellin' 'em maggots 'at," Jerry. "Make 'em think they gotta learn ta fuckin' live with it f'rever."

"Live with what?" Danny. "Learn ta live with what?"

"The roach clip," quickly brushing my hand over my face.

"The roach clip?" Danny, shutting his eyes.

"Yeah. Ya see, we decided since the preacher was blowin' smoke up our ass about the last check…"

"He thought we wuz jus' a bunch'a dumb-fucks," Jerry interupted. "Showed his ass," raising his head enough to share a sneer with Tomas and Jonas.

"Anyway," I continued, "while we were polishin' up the windows an' pickin' up ta leave, Tomas painted a roach clip in the hand Jesus was holdin' the lamb with. Beautiful job, Danny. You'd'a almost had ta known it was there ta notice it."

"I c-couldn't see it at all p-past the third row," Jonas agreed.

"Same way with the fuckin' beer can, man," Jerry. "Tomas did a hell uv a job with the beer can."

Tomas covered his face, embarrassed by the reviews his work was receiving.

"Beer can!" Danny, jerking forward.

"T-Texas Pride," Jonas.

"Yeah. You can just barely make out about a third'a this Texas Pride beer can in the bushes on the right side'a the rock as y're lookin' at the window," I explained.

"Beau'ful job," Jerry. "Really beau'ful job."

Danny let the letter slip from his hand to the floor, leaned back in the rocker, and then shut his eyes. He began to rock slowly in the chair, gazing down at the letter and massaging his temples with his thumb and index finger.

"Listen," he sighed deeply. "I talked with dad and he's gunna talk with an attorney for us. He's gunna *shit* when he hears this. Outright shit. That church is probably gunna try to stiff us for every bit of what little we have."

"HAH!" as I lurched forward. "Did I see this one comin' 'r what? If we'd'a plowed ever'thing back inta the business like *you* wanted to, then this fuckin' preacher'd be gettin' a lot more'n what he's gunna get now!"

"Fuckin' deejay vu, man," Jerry. "Good job on 'at 'un, Gil."

"Premonition," Danny corrected wearily.

"Whu's 'at?" Jerry.

"Never mind," Danny, to himself. "I need to call Dad tomorrow and give him the details."

In an instant, Jerry lost interest in the whole conversation.

"Yew workin' at the lounge t'night?" he asked me.

"Yeah. Comin' up f'r a while?"

"Too fuckin' cold. I'm leavin' here, takin' a hot bath, an' then draggin' Shauna inta the sack with me," looking over at Jonas. "Don't 'at make y'ur drawers a li'l lumpy, Jonas?" Jerry cackled.

"I g-got my own l-leg.".

"I'll bet she loves it to. Y'ur orgasms mus' las' twen'y minutes with 'at stutter'a y'urs," Jerry snickered.

"Shiiiiit, man," Tomas.

"Ya liked 'at, didn' ya?" as Jerry turned to take aim at Tomas. "Y're gunna go home an' be up all night in front'a the mirror practicin' ta stutter...t-t-t-t-g-g-g-g-d-d-d-d. Ain' 'at right Tomas? Practicin' f'r 'at twen'y minute nut," cackling.

"Maaaan," Tomas covering his face. "Twenty minutes is a long time. I don't know."

Jerry chambered another round.

"Yeah," he cackled wildly. "An' then y'ur ol' lady'll wake up an' hear ya an' she'll be yellin' 'Tomas! Yew in there stutterin' again?

Y're gunna go fuckin' blind, man. Knock 'at shit off, Tomas! Ya hear me?'"

Tomas, shaking his head, reached for the six-pack on the table.

"Oh shit, Tomas! I'm sorry, man," Jerry, serious as could be. "I f'rgot...Mexican guys don't like talkin' about loppin' the ol' mule. F'rgit I even mentioned it," snickering.

Danny snatched the letter from the floor and stood up.

"I give up on you people. I fucking give up. I'm gunna cancel the three big contracts we haven't started on. We'll do the First Baptist repairs and the two Methodist church repairs. No more big ones. If all you guys want out of this is to work the petty-ass nickel and dime jobs, then fine. I'm gunna stop busting my ass to make this thing happen."

He left the room in a huff.

"Jesus fuckin' Christ," I grumbled, fighting my way out of the bean bag. "Danny!" and chased after him.

"You okay?" as I entered his room.

Danny was looking out his window.

"Yeah," grunting and turning to face me. "This could have worked. This had the potential to really go big."

"It still does an' it still might. Just not as fast as you'd like ta see it happen."

Danny sat down on his mattress on the floor and scooted backwards until he was against the wall. I sat down by the window, lit a cigarette, and then cracked the window.

"Cigarette?" offering him the pack.

"Nah."

Minutes passed.

"While you guys were gone," Danny finally said, "I spent the whole four years jumping from one thing to the other. Every, I mean *every* fucking one fell through. From apprenticing as a blacksmith to trying to break into the commodities market. Nothing's worked out. It's getting old. I want *something* to work. I'm not gunna spend my life eating everybody else's shit."

"An' ya won't. You'll figure it out. All of us will. We got lots'a time. Hell, we're only, what, twenty-three, twenty-four years old? Y're puttin' way too much pressure on y'urself."

A few more minutes passed. The snow was getting heavier.

"Let's keep the church job in Juarez," I suggested. "It's good money. JD says it'll be easy money. Then there's the cheap beer an' hot women."

"The Juarez Chamber of Commerce advertises it as cheap women and hot beer," Danny.

"We could do it over spring break. Think that'd work?"

"You want the truth?" Danny snorted.

"The truth?" wincing in pain. "Fuck 'at shit, Danny. Who's got time f'r *that*?" and flicked some ashes out the window. "Lie ta me. Tell me what I wan'a hear. Tell me how rich this Juarez thing's gunna make us an' how it'll be fast, easy money, an' shit."

"Okay. If all you can handle is bullshit. I can do that. Juarez will be the fastest, the easiest money you've ever made and you're gunna come back to Lubbock in a stretch limo…"

"Yeah! That's what I wan'a hear! Tell me more! More lies! Tell me how *big* it is, bitch!" pretending to bounce someone up and down on my lap and panting heavily.

"And the limo's gunna be packed bumper to bumper with nasty, naked women."

"YES! YES! Lie ta me, slut," lifting my imaginary partner high into the air then crashing her back into my lap over and over again. "Tell me I'm the best…"

"And they'll all be lighting cigarettes with hundred dollar bills."

I suddenly stopped and looked at Danny.

"I b'lieve 'at's *exactly* how it'll be, Fast Daniel," becoming serious, "b'cause I just will *not* b'lieve it c'n be any other way. I just won't fuckin' b'lieve it."

Danny looked down and swept his hand across his shirt a few times, brushing away invisible cigarette ashes.

"I believe it'll happen *something* like that," he said quietly.

I smoked another cigarette and watched the snow come down.

After a few minutes, Danny coughed into his fist.

"What if Jerry gets the post office job he applied for and can't go with us?"

I glanced at the door before answering.

"He's not gunna get that job," I whispered. "He won't make it past the first interview. Get real. Would you hire him ta deliver y'ur mail after talkin' to him f'r two minutes?"

Danny agreed.

"Homer still wan'a go?" he asked.

"Yeah."

"Eduardo and Tomas?"

"Don't know. Depends on when the Harley auctions are in Mexico City."

"How about Jonas?"

"He wants ta go ta Mexico City with Ed and Tomas."

Danny asked for a cigarette.

"Does JD want to go?" Danny.

"He wants to," handing him one. "I wouldn't count on him, though. Homer says he's either too drunk 'r too hung over ta do much'a anything lately," tossing him a book of lounge matches.

"More than usual?" lighting his cigarette.

"Must be. Has ta be pr'tty bad f'r Homer ta notice it."

"How's Hope working out?"

"She's doin' great. Caught on fast. We keep usin' her more an' more. She's a hoot ta work with. Why? You considerin' takin' her ta Juarez with us? I mean...Hope in Juarez?"

"JD says we'll need at least five people to do it in less than two weeks."

"At least that many."

"How long is spring break?"

"Eight...ten days."

Danny laid on his back blowing smoke rings for a while. He finished his cigarette, spit in his hand, and then carefully extinguished the cigarette in his palm. "Here's the plan," making his decision. "Let's keep Juarez, but let's wait until the end of the semester. We'll concentrate on wrapping up what we've got around here and go to Juarez without anything pressing us to a deadline. I want it to go as smooth as we can make it down there. I mean it, the first time you guys begin jacking around...I'm walking away from it."

"We'll be in an' out'a Mexico so fast we won't have time ta fuck it up," I promised. "Time ta clean up an' head ta work," as I stood up. "What're ya doin' t'night?"

"I'll be helping Connie rearrange some things to free a room up for Doug when he comes back. He's not expecting to have his own room. Should be a nice surprise for him."

"I'm surprised Connie hadn't moved in with Vann just ta get away from Jerry's raggin' on her all the time about bein' bi."

"Vann likes the sex, but he told me he wants his privacy more than an accessible piece of ass after doing his time with Doug. Plus, Connie likes ragging on Jerry about his being a simpleminded, rednecked, male, chauvinist pig as much as Jerry likes ragging on her."

"Poor Doug. He'll be leavin' one nut house an' movin' right into another."

"He'll have an advantage, though. He'll be medicated."

I crossed the hall and glanced into the living room. Tomas was back on the couch. Jonas had stretched out on the floor. Homer and Jerry hadn't moved a muscle.

Danny came out of his room.

"I'll clean up around here before Joan gets back."

"Her an' Hope at yoga?" as I peeked into Hope's room.

"Nah. Hugo took them to a lecture on campus. Some travel

program about Spain. I think he's nearly got Joan talked into going to Europe with him this summer."

I ate, cleaned up, and got ready to take off. Bobbie still had my coat and boots.

*Dammit. I can't wait any longer.*

I put on my jungle boots, bucked for the cold, and then stepped onto the stoop.

*Christ! Cold, windy, an' snowin' again.*

My nostrils froze shut.

Bobbie was running across the alley, kicking snow into the air with every other step. She looked like a little kid. She waved as she headed up the stairs. I stepped back into the house. Bobbie bounced through the doorway, cheeks red, sniffling, and laughing.

"Stay home t'night, pleeease. We can make snow ice cream an'…"

"Gimme the coat…c'mon, c'mon. I'm gunna be late."

She deflated.

I took the coat from her and pulled it on, brushed her forehead with a kiss and started for the door.

She reached out and touched my arm.

"I like you very much," softly.

I stopped and dropped my head.

*Dammit. Don't be such an asshole.*

I turned, stepped back to her, and gave her a long hug.

"I like *you* very much. I'm just tired an' I hate this fuckin' cold weather."

"It won't last forever. When will you be home?"

"10:00 'r 11:00," releasing her from my grip and stepping once more to the door. "This snow's gunna keep ever'body away t'night. I can't see it bein' any later than 'at."

"I'll be waitin'," and held up a small paper bag. "Shauna got me somethin' nasty I wan'a show ya."

"If it fits in there, it's gotta be pr'tty nasty."

I waved and left.

The lounge didn't run a Monday afternoon shift. I opened the bar and began to get things ready. Missy called while I was preparing to clean the mirrors. She didn't want to come in tonight due to the weather. I told her I'd call if it got real busy, but not to expect it. I finished all the chores behind the bar, grabbed my book, and settled in.

A working girl came in about 8:00. Actually, more like a working lady since she was probably in her late thirties. Marcy was a regular at the lounge. She was a beautiful woman—sensual, elegant. Always dressed like she was on her way to a formal dinner party or something fancy like that. She never approached looking cheap like some of the younger working girls. Marcy looked confident. Expensive.

*Pro'bly gets at least two 'r three hun'r'd a throw.*

She waved and went to one of the back booths. I made her a double Chevas on the rocks, began a tab with her name on it, and then took the drink out to her.

"Evenin' Marcy. How's it goin'," as I set the drink down.

"Hi, Gil."

"Ya look pr'tty as hell t'night, but, then, ya always do."

"Why thank yew," tipping her head and toasting me before downing half the drink.

"Need another?"

"Please. Might as well. It's b'ginnin' ta look like this 'un's not gunna show. Been waitin' in the room since 5:00. Don't matter. Ever'thing's already been paid for. Well, almost ever'thing," swirling the Chevas around in the shot glass.

"I'll help ya out on 'at. Sometimes I f'rget ta write ever' order down. Especially when it's as busy as it is t'night."

She gave me a quick grin.

I brought her a double. She was lighting a cigarette, a sure sign she'd given up on the guy since the girls never smoked until they found out if their customers objected to it or not.

"What kind'a music ya want?" I asked.

I could hear her kicking her high heels off under the table. She reached up and pulled a few clips from her hair and shook her head. Her dark locks tumbled down. She brushed the hair back from her face.

"Play ever' slow song ya got on 'at thing," quietly and reached for her drink.

I made my selections at the jukebox, returned to the bar, and continued to read.


About 9:00, right after delivering another drink to Marcy, Hugo came in.

He looked around.

"You are open aren't ya?" drawling, as he removed his hat.

Marcy's head popped over the top of the booth then dropped back out of sight.

"Opened just f'r you Hugo. Want y'ur regular?"

"Only if y're gunna let me pay f'r it."

"Never the first one."


I mixed a whiskey and water in a short glass—no ice, no straw, no coaster.

"It's been a while since it was just you an' me shootin' the bull," Hugo, after taking a sip and nodding his approval. "Seems all I do is say howdy an' g'bye to ya anymore," each gentle word, each leisurely gesture, each slow, measured bob of the head massaging the space around him.

"I know," I agreed. "Seems like ever'body's been gettin' busier an' busier."

"I should throw a get t'gether out at the place as soon as it warms up ta put ever'body in one spot at one time f'r a change," sipping his branch. "So, Gil, what's new?"

"I won't thaw out 'til May. Schools borin' as hell. Not the

subjects. It's the routine. Danny's keepin' us hoppin' on the church repairs. I guess ya know about ever'thing else."

"How's Bobbie. Haven't seen her in over a week."

"She's fine. She's only workin' four days a week now. She likes 'at."

"I know it's none'a my business, but...what're the chances'a that takin' a serious turn?" while rolling his drink between his palms.

"Livin' t'gether's pr'tty serious."

"You know what I mean," looking at me from over the top of his glasses.

"Well, f'r the time bein' nothin's gunna change much."

Hugo reached across the bar and squeezed my arm.

"I gotta tell ya...you two make a smart lookin' couple."

"Damn, Hugo. Is 'at what's goin' on b'hind my back? Ever'body havin' me married ta Bobbie?"

"When a fell'a leaves ever'body guessin' about such questions then ever'body'll go ta makin' up their own answers," chuckling.

"Maybe she dudn't feel 'at way about me."

"Oh, don't go kiddin' y'urself, young man. You know how much 'at little lady thinks'a you."

"Yeah, I guess," dropping my head to the bar and moaning. "I just can't think in terms'a *us* 'til I get some kind'a idea about what I'm gunna do with myself. I don't even know where ta start with 'at one."

"C'n I make a suggestion as ta where ya c'n start?" seriously.

I raised my head.

"Yew c'n start with gettin' me another branch," and smiled.

I got his drink and passed it over the bar.

"I understand ol' Doug's due ta be released Frid'y an' he'll be movin' in with Jerry an' 'em."

"Afraid so," glad he'd changed the subject.

"What's wrong?"

"I don't know, Hugo. Maybe the judge screwed up when he

sent him to a nut house f'r just ninety days. It might be he's not gunna be any better off than he was b'fore he was sent away an' he's gunna come straight back here an' step right back inta the same shit again. If nothin' else, he should think'a goin' somewhere other than Lubbock."

"Where should he go?"

"I don't know. Sometimes I think he dudn't fit in anywhere. Ya ever talk ta JD about planets an' orbits?"

"I've known JD since 1947. Met him out at Tech. There's not much we *haven't* talked about at one time 'r other."

"Well, I think that JD's orbit theory applies ta Doug's problem in a way, but Doug's not ever gunna find his orbit. He's this planet screamin' through the solar system an' he's gunna keep goin' 'til he either burns out 'r crashes inta somethin'."

"You really b'lieve 'at?"

"I don't wan'a b'lieve it, but damn, Hugo, when I listen ta Doug...when I watch how hard he tries ta piece things t'gether an' see how hard it is for him ta do simple things like meet people 'r make any kind'a normal conversation...I can't help but b'lieve 'at way. Sometimes I wan'a slap him 'r somethin' an' yell at him 'Hey, Doug! Goddammit! It's not that fuckin' difficult!' Does 'at make sense?"

"Yes...it does," Hugo nodded sadly.

"It's like he goes aroun' hurtin' all the time. Like he's in this foreign country an' he can't speak the language, dudn't know the customs, dudn't know the laws, dudn't have any identification, no drivers license, no skills, no idea where he's from, where he's supposed ta be 'r where he's supposed ta be goin'," leaning forward and lowering my voice. "I know this sounds raw, but most of us agree that, in Doug's case...suicide'd be damn near a valid alternative. That's how Danny puts it."

Hugo frowned and dropped his head.

"You gotten around ta readin' any Camus yet," he asked.

" 'Myth'a Sisyphus', " I nodded. "If Camus'd known Doug he might'a had a different take on the subject."

"Have ya seen the letters he's been writin' Vann?" he asked.

"No, but Vann says they're pr'tty scary."

"I wouldn't characterize 'em as scary. They are explicitly... strange."

"You read 'em?"

"Yes. Vann wanted someone ta look at 'em. He wanted an opinion as ta whether he should show 'em to the Veteran's Administration. He thought they might wan'a reconsider releasin' him if they saw the letters."

"Damn. What's in 'em? Does he talk about killin' Neil?"

"No, nothin' like 'at. It's much more abstracted than 'at. Very obscure observations regardin' authority, power, an' symbols uv power. I told Vann the VA pro'bly screens his mail so they'd already know what he's written. If they aren't worried about it then maybe we shouldn't be worried about it."

"Do the letters ramble like the way he talks?"

"Somewhat. I've sat through a few of his impromptu lectures... long streams'a unrelated thoughts. No constructed arguments. No direction."

"Yeah. I heard somethin' about what happened over at Jonas' place when Doug ended up jumpin' through a window."

"Yes. I remember," tugging on his ear and shaking his head. "Homer, Vann, Jonas, Chad, Doug, an' I. We'd smoked some grass an' were sittin' around in the dark discussin' Revelations. Vann told me latter 'at Doug had dropped some acid with Chad an' Homer earlier in the day. At any rate, Doug took off on an hour long tangent. All of a sudden the fire light over the intersection outside Jonas' house started ta flashin' yellow. The engines came screamin' down the street from the firehouse. The whole room was filled with red, orange, an' blue lights, an' noise from the fire engines...sirens, an' horns. Poor ol' Doug...he looked terrified. He jumped up an' dove through the window. Crashed right through! We ran outside, but by the time we got around ta the side'a the house he was gone. Vann said Doug didn't show up at his place f'r a week."

Hugo finished his branch and asked for another.

"Yeah," he continued as I fixed the drink, "that evenin' I saw how tenuous a grip 'at poor boy has on each singular moment he lives in…an' it don't seem ta take 'at much of a breeze ta shake him loose."

"Exactly my words," I laughed.

"Didn't mean ta sound like a shrink, although I've spent enough money on those bastards ta have most'a their bullshit down pat."

Hugo looked up and furrowed his brow.

"Ya know…I don't b'lieve I've seen 'at rascal Chad since Doug jumped through that window. Way back in August if I remember correctly."

"He's still around."

"He an' Jerry work things out over 'at rent scam?"

"Wudn't much ta work out. Jerry wanted a refund on all the extra money they'd been payin' him. If he didn't pay up, Jerry swore he'd kill him. Chad went ta Abilene 'at next weekend an' told mom he needed money f'r a cancer operation 'r some shit like 'at. Whatever it was, she bought into it an' coughed the money up. He was in an' out'a town b'fore Dad found out about it."

Hugo was laughing.

"Cancer, huh? Y'ur poor mama."

"Once all that was evened up, ever'thing pr'tty much got back ta normal. Little faggot still owes me six 'r seven hun'r'd, though."

"Is he still livin' on the corner?"

"No. He moved in with a coupl'a sluts somewhere in the ghetto. He hardly ever comes around. 'scuse me Hugo. Gotta go see if Marcy's doin' okay."

"Marcy's here with somebody?"

"Nah. Guy didn't show."

"I b'lieve she likes…Chevas?"

"Ye'sir."

"Go ahead an' take her one. Put it on my tab an' say hello for me."

Marcy, stretched out on the booth, smoking a cigarette, was ready for another drink.

"You doin' all right?" I asked.

"Yeah. Keep the music goin' if ya don't mind."

I placed the drink on the table.

"It's from Hugo. He says hello."

"Well, I wudn't gunna have any more, but I don't wan'a hurt his feelin's. I'll finish Hugo's, then you cut me off. Thank him for me. He's a doll."

"Mind if I play a few Marty Robbins songs f'r Hugo?"

"Go right ahead," reaching for the drink.

I went over to the juke box, punched in over a dozen songs, turned the volume to low, and then returned to the bar.

I settled back in behind the bar as Marty began to croon "El Paso".

"Marcy says thanks."

Hugo nodded.

"Thanks f'r playin' ol' Marty."

"So, what's Joan think about Spain?" I asked.

"Don't ya mean ta ask me if she's gunna go ta Spain with me f'r a while this summer?"

"Well, ye'sir. I've heard a few people mention it."

"Damn. Ya can't change toilet paper brands in this town without ever'body else findin' out about it."

"Well? Is she gunna? Or is it a secret?"

"I hadn't come right out an' asked her ta accompany me yet," rubbing his face with both hands.

"I wudn't talkin' about Spain. Is she's gunna change toilet paper brands?"

"None'a y'ur goddamn business," he smiled.

Hugo finished his drink then glanced at his watch.

"Almost 10:00. Think I'll go grab a bite at the IHOP, then come back an' spend the night in town. Don't feel like puttin' up with 'at storm t'night," standing to put his coat on. "How much?"

"One branch."

"Bullshit," and tossed a twenty on the bar. "Buy the lady another 'un if she wants it. The rest is f'r you."

"Ya don't hav…"

"If I had ta, I pro'bly wouldn't," turning and walking to the booths in the back.

I could hear his soft, deep, drawling whisper then Marcy's light, gentle laugh. Hugo walked to the door and waved.

"Buenos noches, amigo," before stepping into the blizzard.

At 10:00, I began cleaning things up so I could close as soon as Marcy left.

When I finished, I settled into my book and began reading again.

Several pages later Marcy slid up beside me.

"One more, please," placing the empty rocks glass on the bar. "I don't wan'a keep ya up all night."

She looked as poised as she did when she'd first come in this evening. The alcohol didn't show a bit. I guess it takes practice. I asked her how she was getting home, concerned about the weather and the amount she'd already had to drink.

"I am home. F'r t'night anyway," sliding onto the barstool and turning sideways.

I could hear the delicate scratching of her nylons as she crossed her legs.

"I'll be spendin' the night here," patting her hair while looking in the mirror behind the bar. "Might as well. Room's paid for. Breakfas' is paid for. I'm paid for."

"Don't get upset 'r anything, Marcy, but unless ya c'n show me a room key, I'll have ta switch ya ta coffee."

"Are yew suggestin' 'at I may be too intoxicated ta drive?" pretending to be offended.

"That's some bad weather outside. Hugo's even stayin' in town t'night," avoiding the intoxication issue.

GLYNN E. THOMPSON

Marcy emptied the contents of a black velvet purse onto the bar—lipstick, a silver cigarette case, lighter, perfume, a toothbrush, a compact, small tube of K-Y jelly, breath mints, car keys, a few Trojans, and some tampons. She used the long glossy finger nail on her index finger to separate the room key from the other items.

"Room 124...five doors down," leaning toward me. "I thank I c'n walk 'at far," placing her hand on my knee. "Satisfied, daddy?"

My stomach fluttered. She put everything except the key back into her purse.

"Wouldn't ask if I didn't give a damn," I told her.

I set my book down, slipped from the stool, and then went behind the bar. I got a clean glass and fixed her a single shot with a shot of soda. Marcy reached for my book and pulled it to her.

"Spirituality and Man," reading the title out loud.

"Required readin' in my religions class," and placed the drink in front of her.

"Studyin' ta be a priest?" as she took a sip. "Yew poisoned it!" she frowned.

"That's better for ya."

"Yew could'a at least warned me," bracing herself before taking the next sip. She made a face.

"Sorry."

"Ya have ta take religion courses ta be a doctor? I thought one'a the other girls said yew told her yew were gunna be a doctor."

"I Pro'bly did. I use 'at line when I'm tryin' ta hustle some... meet the ladies."

"Does it work?"

"Hadn't yet. Can't seem ta get 'em ta b'lieve me. I'm workin' on my delivery."

"I'll b'lieve anything as long as it's written on a note in an envelope with a few hun'r'd dollar bills."

*I was right...she's fuckin' expensive.*

Marcy leaned on the bar and cocked her head a little to one side.

"I imagine yew don't have ta try all *'at* hard ta...meet the ladies," grinning.

*Is 'at a seductive kind'a grin 'r just a normal grin?*

"The truth of it would make ya weep," looking away.

"Hugo mentioned once 'at yew were livin' in some kind'a commune with four 'r five *sexy* young things."

"Yeah, well...," getting nervous, "I share a place with some guys an' a coupl'a gir...females. I don't know if you could call it a commu..."

"Y're not close to *any* of 'em?" she pressed. "The females, I mean," sipping her drink.

"Not really," without hesitating.

*Damn! Why'd I say that?*

"That sounds a little evasive," reaching for my cigarettes on the bar, removing one, and then placing it between her fingers.

"Wudn't meant ta be evasive," lighting the cigarette for her.

"So," blowing a thin line of smoke from between her lips, "y're completely unobligated?"

"I guess ya could put it that way."

*GODDAMMIT! STOP!*

"It's late," holding the drink up. "I'll finish this in the room. Would ya mind walkin' me ta my door. I'm a tiny bit tipsy," she purred.

I hesitated before answering. Marcy removed the perfume from her purse, put a little on her finger, then touched behind each ear. The scent was overpowering.

*Oh, shit.*

"Let me close up."

Marcy picked up the key, her purse, and the book then glided slowly to the door. She left the glass behind.

*Tipsy my ass.*

When we reached her room she unlocked the door then stepped inside, pulling me along with her. She tossed the book onto the bed before turning to face me.

"Would ya mind undoin' this for me b'fore ya leave?" placing a finger on the dress clasp at the back of her neck. "It's hard enough ta undo when I *hadn't* been drinkin'."

When she'd reached up the movement nearly forced her breast from the dress. She maneuvered around me, turned her back to me, and then eased the door shut. She remained with her back to me. I couldn't move.

"Well?" softly.

I stepped up to her and unfastened the dress.

"Could ya bring the zipper down a little? It's still too high for me ta reach."

I lowered it about six inches and stopped. The back of her bra was exposed.

"A little further, please," purring again.

"Tell me when it's low enough," continuing to lower it slowly.

The zipper crept down her spine, gradually revealing the dimpled small of her back. Marcy didn't say anything. The zipper traveled as far as it could go. The top of her buttocks was visible.

I was dangling by a thread.

The door lock clicked.

"Could ya stay a while?" she whispered, without turning around. "I mean...yew don't need ta be anywhere else right now, do ya?" as her dress slipped to the floor.

*Sweet Jesus.*

It was probably the garter belt. Or the panties and the hose. Maybe the perfume or the delicate curves of her body. Or possibly that near naked butt. Whatever it was, the thread snapped.

\*\*\*

I stepped from the room, shut the door behind me and collided with Hugo.

"Whoa, partner," as he grabbed me. "Still workin'?"

"Uh...ye'sir. One last room delivery. Now I c'n go."

The door to Marcy's room opened. Marcy leaned out, exposing a firm round breast as she extended her arm.

"Yew forgot y'ur book."

I took it from her.

"G'night," she winked then said goodnight to Hugo.

Hugo touched the brim of his hat and nodded.

"G'night," he said.

Marcy closed the door. The lock clicked. The safety chain rattled against the door as she put it in place.

I looked down at the ground, too damned ashamed to say anything.

"Don't worry, son," drawling sadly. "I won't say anything ta anybody. I'm sure 'at's y'ur main concern right now."

It was a painfully placed shot—especially since it was so true. I felt his hand on my shoulder.

"Gil, a year from now," tightening his grip, "I want ya ta remember somethin' for me...ever'body creates their own Hell. Will ya remember 'at for me?"

I nodded, unable to make eye contact.

"Look at me," easing his grip.

I looked up.

"A year from now," Hugo continued, "if ya can't be man enough ta accept responsibility f'r the decisions y're makin' t'day an' ya can't accep' the consequences'a those decisions...don't bother comin' around. I c'n damn near overlook anything in a man except his not acceptin' responsibility f'r his own damn life. Un'erstand?"

"Ye'sir," and looked away.

Hugo took his hand from my shoulder.

"Now, get on home. I'd imagine somebody's b'ginnin' ta get worried about ya."

I listened to the crunching ice as he headed to his room.

*Oh, God. What have I done? What have I gone an' done?*

I tucked the book under my coat and headed home. I was oblivious to the bitter, freezing wind as I walked to the house. My insides were torn to shreds. I couldn't come up with a board big

369

enough to beat myself with and if I had, I wouldn't have been able to hit myself hard enough with it.

There was a loud crack as the kitchen door broke free of the iced up threshold. Bobbie jumped from the chair at the kitchen table, clutching her Barbie robe closed. Recognizing me, she fell back into the chair and covered her face with her hands.

"You *scared* me," sleepily. "What time is it?" running her fingers through her hair.

"Midnight," as I removed my coat and approached the table. "It was crazy up at the lounge t'night. Lot'a people stranded with nothin' ta do but sit in the bar an' get drunk." I bent over and kissed her hair.

"What's 'at smell?" wrinkling her nose.

"Perfume. A few'a the girls got pr'tty drunk an' ended up in a perfume sprayin' fight," and turned away from her.

"It smells like...mosquito spray 'r somethin'," she yawned.

She got up, hugged me, and then walked toward the hall curtain.

"I was startin' ta worry. I'll try ta stay awake for ya while ya shower," before entering the hall.

For the longest time, I sat at the table, numb with regret. I slowly, mindlessly scratched, first my head, then my beard, my head. Beard.

Finally, a thought.

*You fuckin' asshole.*

Followed immediately by a second.

*You sorry, motherfuckin' asshole.*

I smoked a cigarette then showered.

I crept into the bedroom. Bobbie was curled up under the covers on my side of the bed. I carefully slipped under the blankets and settled in beside her. She still had her rob on. Her feet were freezing. She stirred and, more asleep than awake, murmured,

"I like you very much."
I could barely hear her. I didn't answer.
I was sick to my stomach.

\*\*\*

The ice and gravel crunched loudly as Jonas' truck pulled into the drive. Everyone crowded around the living room window that looked out onto the stoop. The headlights on the truck died. Two bundled figures hurried up the stairs. Everyone backed away from the window. I picked up the champagne bottle and positioned my thumbs under the lip of the plastic cork. The kitchen door opened and closed. The floor creaked noisily as the two men made their way down the hall. Jonas entered the living room. Doug was next. I popped the cork. The bottle went off like a geyser. The room filled with cheers and shouts. The ladies swarmed over Doug, hugging and smothering him with kisses.

Doug, genuinely surprised, began stammering "thank you"s and wheeze-laughing. As one of the ladies would let go and back away, one of the guys would step up and shake his hand. Jerry placed a lei of joints around his neck.

"Speech! Speech!"

Everyone fell silent. Doug was nervous. After stumbling a few times, he managed a good run.

"I...I don't know what to, uh...to say. I, honestly, did...*not*...expect...*this*," and waved his hand around the room. "I'm very...very...very...*very* glad to be back," then bowed smartly and broke into a huge smile.

Everyone shouted and clapped. The ladies swarmed again. I handed Doug the bottle of champagne. Danny cranked up the record player—Hendrix.

The party was on.

Hugo came over to me.

"I c'n see now why ya asked f'r t'morrow off," drawling.

I'd been around Hugo four or five times since Monday night and he'd hardly acknowledged me. He'd spoken to everybody in the room tonight except me while we were waiting for Doug.

"Ya think a Saturd'y an' a Sund'y're gunna give ya enough time ta sober up?" he asked.

*Damn, it's good ta have him talkin' ta me again.*

"I'm not takin' t'morrow off ta sleep in. Danny an' me are meetin' with the janitor of the First Baptist Church. We gotta line things out f'r the window repairs we're doin' there. Might even start it t'morrow."

Hugo patted me on the back and went over to Doug.

I wanted to call Hugo back over and tell him how bad I felt about what'd happened at the lounge. I wanted to tell him I'd decided that if I ever wanted to rack it with anyone else again, I'd break it off with Bobbie first. I wanted to tell him that if I didn't want it bad enough to end things with Bobbie, then I didn't want it bad enough. I wanted to tell him, but decided not to. I already knew what Hugo would'a said—"Don't tell *me*, show *her*".

Or something along that line.

I slipped up behind Bobbie. I brushed her hair aside and put my hand on her butt then squeezed. Bobbie jumped and spun around.

*God, she's lookin' hot.*

I told her so. She motioned for me to bend down. I leaned over. Bobbie brought her mouth to my ear, tugged on my ear lobe with her lips, and then stepped back. Her hair, flowing to midthigh, shimmered. She'd said she was growing it longer because she knew I liked it that way. I made a fist and slowly extended the index finger. Bobbie winked and went over to talk with Hope.

I stepped over to the crowd surrounding Doug right as Doug asked Homer where Sonny was.

Silence.

"Oh, man. I didn't mean...to...," Doug struggled. "Nice...nice fucking weather today. Nice fucking day to get out of a...a hospital," nervously.

"Sonny went back to Dallas," Homer, smiling to help Doug over the bump. "We still write and talk on the phone now and then."

Doug looked relieved.

Late in the evening, Homer, Jerry, Ed, Doug, and I were on the stoop smoking a joint while catching some fresh air. Chad came charging across Jerry's backyard. Three fairly big guys were closing in. Chad scampered half way up the stairs before coming to a halt. Panting heavily, Chad turned to face his pursuers who had stopped at the foot of the stairs after seeing all of us on the stoop.

"Come on you cowards!" Chad yelled down at them before glancing over his shoulder at us. "What's wrong, pussies?" continuing to taunt them. "What're you waitin' for, pussies?"

Jerry moved from the center of the stoop then took a few steps down the stairs.

"Whu's goin' on, man?" slurring.

"These pussies wan..."

"Shut the fuck up!" Jerry. "I wudn' talkin' ta yew, maggot. I wuz talkin' ta them," and waved his beer at the three panting, smartly dressed men.

Wherever they'd left from to chase Chad, they'd left in a hurry, leaving their coats behind. The biggest of the three moved onto the bottom step.

"We wuz sittin' up at Dancers when this li'l bast'rd starts flirtin' with our dates," drawling.

A second one spoke up.

"He bought 'em a round'a dranks even after they tol' 'em they's with us."

"Then," the first one again, "he slips 'em a note askin' 'em ta ditch us an' go to a party with him!"

"Bullsh..."

"Shut up, turd!" Jerry.

Jerry descended the steps and stopped on the one above Chad.

"So, Chad," leaning over and snickering, "ya drug 'em over here ta let us whoop up on 'em?"

"They were going…"

"Shhh," putting a finger to his lips. "Yew don't move."

Jerry straightened up and addressed the three men.

"Gimme a minute," and then ascended the stairs.

"Chickenshits!" Chad yelled at the men.

Jerry shook his head.

Once he reached the stoop, he asked me what I thought.

"I think I'm freezin' my ass off," I shivered. "Let's go back inside."

Eduardo, closest to the door, opened it and hurried in, blowing warm air into his cupped hands as he went. We all followed Ed.

"Hey!" Chad screamed and ran up the steps. "Where are you going?" reaching the top as the door slammed shut.

I stepped to the door and looked out the window. Chad was knuckling the pane, frantically demanding to be let in. Turning to the living room window, he slammed away at the frame, pleading for somebody to raise the window.

"No hablo ingles!" Tomas.

I heard the three men bolt up the steps. Chad looked at me in terror before stepping to the edge of the stoop. He lowered himself over the side then dropped to the ground. The thunder on the stairs reversed. I opened the door, walked to the railing, and spotted Chad running, balls to the wall, down W Street toward Ninth.

"I'm gunna tell mom!" Chad. "I'm gunna tell mom!"

"Slow down, dammit!" I answered. "Y'ur gunna slip on some ice an' hurt y'urself!"

One of the men waved to me as they raced after him.

Back inside, Jonas was ripping out some blues riffs on his harmonica. After a while I grabbed my guitar. We sat around for a good hour playing as the ladies sang along—Dylan, Hank Williams, Peter, Paul, and Mary, Marty Robbins, Buddy Holly, George Jones. Some Stones. Everybody knew all the words to at least one song. We decided we sounded so good Hugo should finance a record. We'd go over to Clovis, New Mexico, and use the same studio Buddy Holly used when he started out.

By 2:00 in the morning the party had tapered to a dull roar. Bobbie dragged me into the bedroom, pushed me onto the bed, and then lit some candles and incense. She turned the light out, telling me to shut my eyes. I listened to the soft swishing sounds of her clothing as she removed her blouse then her jeans. I heard the rustle of a paper bag.

"You can look now."

She was posing sexily in a nasty little see-through teddy.

"Like it? You've stayed up late studyin' ever' night this week. I hadn't been able ta show ya what Shauna gave me the other night. Remember? The little paper sack?"

*I remember. Just been feelin' too damned guilty ta feel like doin' anything else but study.*

Bobbie moved to the side of the bed and placed a knee on the mattress along side my leg. Her hair, a cascading veil of silver, flowed over her breasts to between her legs, concealing more than the sheer material of the teddy.

*Damn. I want her more now than I've ever wanted her. Why'd I beat myself up all week? Ever'body fucks up now an' then.*

At the moment, as the candle light danced on her skin, as I gently traced every curve of her body with my fingers, it felt like Monday night never happened. And if it did, it didn't really matter anymore.

I guess, in the long run, lust weighs heavier than guilt.

\*\*\*

Danny and I walked to the church in the morning. It was brisk, but not near as cold as it had been earlier in the week. We were both hung over, but functioning.

"How long did Doug stay last night?" I asked.

"Too long," sounding disgusted.

"Oh, no. What happened?"

"He started explaining his letters to Vann. Before it was over he'd tried to get everybody involved."

"Anybody's feelin's get hurt?"

"Only Doug's. He didn't feel like we'd gotten excited enough about his theory of power in society."

"Any damage?"

"We'll know if we don't see him for a few weeks."

"What was he sayin'?"

Danny waved his hand as if to brush the whole thing off.

"Ask Vann," grumbling. "I'm tired of trying to analyze every fucking thing that comes out of his mouth."

Danny coughed, spit into the street, and moved the topic to business.

"We want to use all the gear they've got...ladders, buckets, brooms. I don't want to waste a lot of time loading and unloading the truck every day. We want to try and keep the glass up there also. That'll save some time."

We crossed Broadway then cut through the four million acre parking lot of the First Baptist Church. I felt like I was approaching Oz. Danny had been here a month or so ago to put together the estimate the church eventually accepted. We entered through a metal door at the rear of the castle-fortress and proceeded down two flights of stairs to the dungeon. I followed Danny into a huge supply room.

"Art!" Danny called out.

A slight, balding, elderly man looked up from a table piled with light sockets, toilet tank floats, and corroded faucets.

"Danny!" and jumped up.

Danny introduced us.

Art's grip was powerful.

"Glad ta mee'ch ya," he smiled.

"Ready ta show us around?" Danny.

"Yep. Let's have a look see at the 'quipment room an' see if thare's anythang in thar y'all gunna be needin'."

Art led us down the hall and through an open double doorway. The room was packed with ladders, extension cords, overhead projectors, ropes, big carpet cleaning machines, buffers, and a vast collection of hardware.

*There's more shit in here than Monkey Wards.*

As we walked the aisles between the shelves, Art tied strips of red plastic flagging around the items Danny said we'd need.

"Is there a store room close to the auditorium?" Danny. "We could use a small storage closet to keep a few things we'll need during the day."

"Got one 'at might do ya. The broom locker in the men's room j'st outside'a the main auditorium. Lemme show ya an' then y'all c'n tell me wutch ya thank."

We hurried along behind him, up stairs, down corridors, and through hallways lined with classrooms, meeting rooms, and a few minichapels. The closer we got to the main auditorium, the more polished and ornate things became. Art eventually stopped at a shiny mahogany door with large, gleaming brass door grips. Danny and I followed him into the men's toilet. The floors were sparkling white marble. The bottom half of the walls were paneled in a deep, rich mahogany. Sumptuous, cream colored, felt wallpaper with raised, light blue angels, opened bibles, crosses, water lilies, and fish covered the wall between the ceiling and the top of the paneling. All the stalls were made of polished mahogany. All the fixtures were shiny brass. Danny and I exchanged glances.

"So this is how..."

"Not now," Danny stopped me.

377

Art took us to the back of the toilet and stopped at a much smaller mahogany door. After fumbling with a ring full of keys he selected one, inserted it into the keyhole, and then unlocked the door. Art opened it, flicked on the light, and then stepped aside. Danny and I walked in. The room was about ten or twelve feet square containing all the necessary supplies required to maintain a royal shitter. Danny and I decided it would be perfect for our needs while executing the repairs.

Before leaving the locker, I wandered to a set of shelves against the back wall. The shelves contained two state-of-the-art TEAC reel-to-reel tape decks, three or four amplifiers, a set of headphones, a microphone, and several small yellow boxes wired to the amplifiers.

Art came up behind me.

"Danged fancy, ain't it?" beaming. " 'at's why I keep it locked up all'a the time."

"One hell of a stereo rig," I mumbled while studying a tangle of wires feeding into a number of holes in the wall above the equipment shelves.

"It's the heart'a the music system f'r the bell tower."

"How's it work?" and stepped aside so Art could approach the shelves.

"These here's the tape machines. This 'uns got the hourly an' half-hourly bell chimes recorded on it. This here's the timer f'r the chimin' tape player," pointing to one of the small, yellow boxes. "This other player's got the recorded music. The tape reel on thar right now's got three hours'a the same song, "Onward Christian Soldiers". Dang good song. Ya ever hear it?"

"Yeah. Once 'r twice."

"This here's the timer f'r the music tape machine," pointing at the second yellow box. "I ain't gotta rewind this tape but once ever' two months since the tape jus' plays the same song over an' over... timer starts it, timer stops it, timer starts it, timer stops it. Same with the chime player, but the chime machine's tied inta a electric clock somehow an' I gotta rewind the tape thang once a week."

I followed Art from the closet. He shut the door behind me and locked it.

"This gunna do ya?" Art.

"This is fine." Danny.

"I'll open it when ya git here uv a mornin' an' y'all c'n lock it behin' ya when ya leave in the ev'nin'," leading us back into the main lobby of the church. "When y'all plan on gittin' started?"

"Maybe this afternoon," Danny.

"How long ya reckon it's gunna take?" he asked Danny.

"Four, maybe five..."

"No sooner than next Saturd'y," I interrupted. "Late Saturd'y at the earliest."

Danny looked at me curiously.

"Well, I'll be a leavin' it to ya. Come git me if ya need me," and scurried out of the lobby.

"What was that all about?" Danny, once we were alone.

"This is one fucked week I got comin' up. Two mid term tests an' a mid term research paper review. I wanted ta give myself some breathin' room."

Danny nodded.

"When do you want to begin?" he asked.

"Homer an' Jonas can start Mond'y. I'll help when I can."

"That'll work. Be certain to stress that this could be some fast cash if..."

"If we don't fuck it up?"

"Something like that."

"Danny, we're gunna make ya so goddamn proud'a us. Y're gunna weep with joy."

"One way or the other, I'm sure I'll be in tears," mumbling.

We went to Broadway Drug and had some breakfast then strolled back to the house. It had warmed up enough for us to take our coats off. Doug and Connie were sitting on the front porch at Jerry's drinking coffee. Connie was in her bathrobe. Peter, Paul, and Mary were singing "Puff the Magic Dragon" in the living room.

I waved as we approached.

"Heeey, Doug. How's it goin' this first mornin' on the outside?"

"It's...I'm hung over. Just...hung over," Doug answered before taking a hit from the joint he was smoking.

Danny nodded at Doug.

"Hey, Doug," politely.

"Want some coffee?" Connie smiled.

"Yes, ma'am, " and raised my hand. "I'll take a cup."

"Danny?" Connie looked at Danny.

"No, thanks. I've got to get a move on," waved and disappeared around the corner of the house.

Connie went to get the coffee.

I sat down next to Doug, waving away a turn on the joint.

"Your brother...he...fuck, man," in his wheezing laugh, his head bouncing up and down. "He didn't make it too far last night."

"Ya seen him this mornin'?"

"Yeah."

"Real bad?"

"Yeah," dropping his head between his knees and continuing to wheeze. "I'd, uh...I'd say...yes."

"Is he inside?"

"Yeah. He's on the couch. WOW! Three correct answers. First, have I seen him...meaning Chad. Second, is it bad...meaning his... face. And third...is he...inside, meaning the house," snorting and wheezing. "Very good. *Very* good."

"Is he alive?"

Doug furrowed his forehead and thought a moment.

"I would guess so," then paused before continuing. "I mean... what *exactly* do you mean by...*alive*?" eating the butt.

*Jesus Christ, Doug. Y'ur whacky bag's just as full as it was on the day ya left f'r that nut house.*

"Is he breathin'?" trying to be more specific.

"Yes! Oh, yes!" Doug shot back. "Yes. Chad *is* breathing. *Actually*, he's, uh, snoring. I think...because his nose seems to be very...very swollen."

Connie returned with the coffee, sat down on the other side of Doug, and then lit cigarettes for the three of us.

"So," Doug began, "how's Neil?" wheeze-grinning.

I wasn't expecting that.

"I heard he was in Californya," I told him.

"Oh! Really! I was...looking forward to seeing him again," followed by the wheeze laugh.

*It's not a real lie. Nobodys seen Neil since the incident so, he could be in Californya.*

Jerry, wearing a pair of fatigue boxer shorts and red socks, came out to the porch with a cup of coffee in one hand and a joint in the other. He looked bad.

"Damn it's *cold* out here," in his usual slurring grumble before breaking into a raspy, coughing fit, clearing his throat, and then spitting over our heads into the front yard. Jerry sat down next to me then farted loudly.

" 'scuse me," and leaned forward to address Connie. "I mos' sincer'ly hope 'at I have not offended y'ur delicate sens'bilities," still sounding shitfaced.

"What about me?" wrinkling my forehead.

" 'at's chow call f'r yew, squid," snickering and giving me the Jerry Eyeball. "Ya know, Gil...y'ur bubba's one *ugly* son uv a bitch when he's had the shit stomped out uv him. He don't swell up pr'tty at all," cackling.

"That's what I heard. What time'd ya go ta bed last night?"

"Damn near didn't," coughing. "Lef' y'ur place an' come back here an' had a room warmin' party f'r Dougy. He's gunna be sleepin' in'a same bed Bobbie used ta roll aroun' in all naked an' shit. 'at bother ya any Gil?" Jerry snickered before breaking into a hacking fit.

"I hope ya feel free ta engage in any sexual fantasy about Bobbie that ya want to," I told Doug.

"Uh...I already have," Doug wheezed through a wicked grin. "But thank you for...for your permission."

"Yeah, it's good ta have ya as a roomy, Doug," Jerry hacked, "but if ya go ta havin' sex'al fantasies about Shauna...I'm gunna have ta charge ya for 'em. Yew'll be on a kind'a honor system."

"That sounds...fair. I'm going to...I'm going to...well, I guess I forgot what I was going to say. Anyway...I'm glad I'm here."

"Gil!" Jerry, raising both eyebrows. "Ya don't b'lieve it's gunna upset the neighbors when they find out ol' Dougy here's been in a insane asylum do ya?"

Doug grinned.

Jerry patted Doug on the back.

"Only kiddin' ya Dougy. Yew ain't crazy. Y're jus' fucked up a li'l bit, but who ain't? Right? Yew jus' got caught at it. The trick is 'at ya don't go freakin' out in public, man. Jus' do it aroun' y'ur friends an' shit."

"With you around Doug's gunna look perfectly normal," Connie snipped at Jerry. "An' I'm sure he's gittin' tired'a yew makin' fun uv him," getting up and going inside.

"Don't pay her any attention," Jerry. "Yew know I'm jus' kiddin' ya. Deep down inside...I'm hurtin' for ya, Dougy. No shit."

I don't think Doug had been aware of a single word that'd been spoken during the past few minutes. He simply grinned and nodded.

Jerry turned to me.

"I need ta borrow one'a y'ur hist'ry books f'r a day 'r two," he told me.

"Weren't ya tellin' ever'body on campus you were an international marketing major?"

"Tha's only f'r 'at one bitch. She figur'd out somehow 'at I wudn' a frat so 'at 'un's over," and took a hit from a joint Doug had fired up.

"So ya think a hist'ry major won't care if y're in a frat 'r not?"

"Listen. Whu's really goin' on is," quickly glancing over his shoulder at the door and lowering his voice, "I been watchin' this one bitch an' she's always carryin' a bunch'a hist'ry books. She comes by here on Mond'y, We'n'sd'y an' Frid'y mornin's jus' b'fore I git up. I c'n see her out'a the window while I'm still in bed. The bitch knows I'm watchin' her too, man," cackling. "She wears this short coat, no matter how cold it is, jus' ta make sure I c'n see a l'il a whu' she's got. She looks over at the window real quick an' then starts ta swingin' 'at ass'a hers. I swear ta God...if it wudn' f'r Shauna bein' there ta jump, I'd be in worse shape than yew wuz b'fore Bobbie lowered her standards."

Jerry offered me the joint. I took it and handed it to Doug without taking a hit.

"Whu's the matter?" Jerry snickered. "Mama don't wan' her li'l boy ta have no weed? She afraid he might go crazy 'r git addicted an' shit?"

"Nope. Lately, my teeth start hurtin' ever' time I smoke a joint. They feel real sensitive...like they're real dry an' somebody's sprayin' 'em with cold air."

"Whu'!" leaning forward to reach around me and take the joint from Doug. "C'n ya b'lieve 'at shit, Doug? It makes his fuckin' teeth hurt, man!"

Doug grinned and began wheezing, apparently aware once again of what planet he was on. Jerry, turning serious, came back at me.

"Hey, man, I didn't mean ta make fun'a ya abou' tha' shit. I pers'nally know whu' y'ur goin' through. I had a frien' once 'at smoked a whole lid an' then ten minutes after he wuz done, no shit, all'a his fuckin' teeth *fell out*...I mean it, ever' fuckin' one uv 'em fell right out," eyes wide. "Course...steppin' in front'a 'at Mack truck while he wuz all fucked up might'a had somethin' ta do with it too, but *I* think it wuz the grass, man. It's evil shit. It's uv the devil. First y'ur teeth're fallin out then it's y'ur fuckin' peck..."

"I'm not shittin' ya, Jerry," getting pissed.

Doug, eyes sparkling, was wheezing uncontrollably.

"For some reason the last coupl'a times I've smoked grass my teeth've hurt like a bitch."

"Gil," shaking his head slowly, "if y're scared y're gunna git busted f'r smokin'…'at's one thing, but don't go bullshittin' me about y'ur fuckin' teeth hurtin'," sneering and glancing at Doug. "'at's bullshit. How fuckin' stupid ya think I am?"

"It's not bullshit!," I insisted. "It hurts like hell."

"I'm sure it does," winking at Doug.

"Fuck you, then," finally pissed.

"Fuck yew, then," Jerry doing a whining imitation of me.

"Want that book 'r not?"

"Hey!" Jerry stiffened. "Don't go jackin' with my sex life jus' b'cause y'ur sense'a humor went ta kah kah."

We sat quietly a minute or two as the joint back and forthed its way to death between Doug and Jerry.

"So," Jerry broke the silence, "ya over y'ur li'l piss fit? Ya gunna help a fell'a war vet git some strange 'r not?"

I lit a cigarette.

"You can use one'a my books from last semester."

Jerry snickered.

"First ya gotta tell me ever'thing I need ta know about hist'ry, but shorten it up. Jus' tell me the import'nt stuff."

Connie returned to the porch and sat back down by Doug.

I thought about it a few moments then began the short course for Jerry.

"First there was nothin' on earth an' then the cavemen came along…"

"An' dinosaurs," Jerry added. "Don't go leavin' out them big-ass motherfuckers."

"An' dinosaurs," correcting the oversight. "After the cavemen there were the Egyptians an' the Jews. The Egyptians made slaves out'a the Jews…"

"Jews wuz niggers back then?"

"What?"

"Jews. They wuz slaves? Yew know...nig..."

"JERRY!" Connie, genuinely angered. "BLACKS, FOR GOD'S SAKE! BLACKS!"

"Fuck it," Jerry muttered. "I wuz only kiddin' aroun', man."

"Then," I continued, "the Greeks came along, then the Romans, an' then Jesus was born..."

"Yew jus' now gittin' ta when Jesus wuz born?" Jerry, impatiently. "C'n ya speed it up some?"

"No sweat."

*The goddamn abbreviated short course.*

"After Jesus and the Romans, the crusades came along with the knights'a the round table. Then there was this big-ass plague, then Columbus discovered America, an' then America told the British ta fuck off. Next came the Civil War an' the slaves were freed. Then Japan surrendered. Then TV was invented, an', in the '50s Buddy Holly invented rock an' roll, an' then grass was invented in the '60's, an' now it's the '70's."

"Tell me a few parts where nig...," catching himself, "*black* people're in it. Like slavery an' the Civil War."

"Is this lady black?" I asked.

Connie leaned over and eyed Jerry suspiciously.

"Whu' wuz 'at look s'posed ta mean?" Jerry growled at Connie. "We're talkin' about my damn dentist, Connie. Don't go thinkin' up a bunch'a shit, man."

I rephrased the question.

"Is y'ur *dentist* black?"

"Light black," correcting me.

"Gray?" Connie snipped.

"Maybe she's just a *sick,* uh...white woman," Doug, frowning and nodding. "You...I mean, a person can turn gray when...when they're *really* sick. Sometimes."

"No way," Jerry insisted. "Not with 'em lips."

"Does she have a bone in her nose?" Connie again.

"Fuck yew, bitch," Jerry flared. "Quit tryin' ta make me look like a nigger hater. I ain't got shit against nig...blacks, man!"

"As long as one of 'em dudn't move in next door 'r marry y'ur sister?" Connie.

"I'd rather have one'a *them* marry my sister than one'a *y'ur* kind."

*Oh, shit! Left hook.*

Connie stormed back into the house. Doug fidgeted uncomfortably.

"That was a cheap shot," I said.

"She'll git over it," he snorted. "If she don't like the way I talk, she c'n jus' move her leso ass in with Vann."

"I don't like the word either," I mumbled.

"Whu' wuz 'at?" Jerry, squinting.

"You heard me," speaking up.

Jerry threw his hands into the air.

"I fuckin' give up. I fuckin' give up. I never thoughd I'd ever live ta see the day when I couldn't speak my min' in my own fuckin' house in front'a frien's. Damnation, man," as the Jerry Eye crept across his face. "Okay. Okay. No more sayin' nigger, *but*...but...listen ta this shit, man...*yew* gotta quit climbin' up God's as...yew gotta quit slammin' God an' Jesus, an' the Bible when I'm aroun'."

"That, uh...sounds fair," Doug. "And...no more saying...leso. I would, you know, think...that's also fair. For Connie."

Jerry and I looked at each other.

"I can live with 'at," I nodded.

Jerry hung his head and snickered softly.

"Shiiit."

"Well? You agree?" I pressed. "No more nigger, no more leso, an' no more crackin' on Jesus?"

"Hell," after hesitating, "I guess." Then added sarcastically, "We don't wan'a go hurtin' anybody's feelin's, now, do we?"

We sat for some time, sipping our coffee and smoking our cigarettes. The period of silence was broken by Jerry.

"Well," coughing, "ain't this the shits? Now we done los' our damn freedom'a speech, all we got left ta talk about is the fuckin' weather."

"It was, uh...snowing when I left...Fort Collins. Yesterday," Doug, nodding his head, pursing his lips.

Jerry slapped Doug on the leg and started cackling.

"It wuz fuckin' nine hun'r'd an' twenty-seven degrees when ya left Fort Collins yesterd'y, Dougy! A damn heat wave. 'at wudn' snow yew wuz seein'. It wuz static. It wuz all in y'ur head," and broke up.

Doug began rocking wildly.

"Yes! That's...*that's* what it was! Static!" wheezing himself into a coughing fit.

\*\*\*

"Ready?"

Homer's voice echoed in the cavernous church toilet.

"Yeah...almost," I answered from the storage closet. "Lemme check ta see if we got ever'thing," as I picked my seabag up and moved to the back of the little room. "Gimme a second."

Several minutes later I stepped from the closet, pulled the door closed, then checked to make sure it was locked.

"*God,* I'm glad this bitch is over," I hissed. "It's been too much like work, but I *will* miss this shitter," as I looked around one last time at the posh surroundings. "Reminds me'a the heads in Vegas."

We exited the men's room then walked up the hall to a barricade of huge mahogany doors at the enterance to the main auditorium. We pulled one open and stepped inside.

"I wonder how much money they piss away just ta heat this place?" mumbling to myself.

Homer grunted as he adjusted the bandanna on his head.

"And look at that swimming pool," as I pointed at a large tank of water built into the wall immediately above and behind the choir loft. "You could float a goddamn boat in it. They use it when they baptize converts."

"Were you baptized when you were going to church?"

"Yeah."

"What did you wear?"

"A white robe. People were usually baptized on Sund'y 'r We'n'sd'y nights. The curtains ya see up there on both sides'a the tank're usually closed. They turn all the lights out except the ones around the tank, then they open the curtains. Ya walk down some steps inta the tank. The preacher walks down steps on the other side. He puts one'a his hands over y'ur nose and mouth an' then dunks ya. From then on, y'ur ass is covered."

"Hugo told me a person can be thrown out of the Catholic church if they screw up. Can you be *un*baptized if you screw up?"

"That's the beauty of the Baptist thing...once y're in, y're in f'r good. Baptists get off ta jackin' the Catholics up f'r b'lievin' a person c'n go out an' kill 'r rape somebody an' then all they gotta do is go ta confession an' they're f'rgiven. That way they can still go ta Heaven. Baptists have 'at beat *all* ta hell. Once a Baptist is saved, he's saved f'rever." I poked Homer in the arm, "Wan'a go take a few laps in the tank just in case they're right?"

"Nah. I'll risk it."

"In Abilene, where I was baptized, the church was a lot smaller so the tank wudn't even a quarter the size'a this one. The preacher in Abilene had a big fish tank in his office with about ten 'r twelve fancy lookin' little fish."

"Like Hugo's?"

"Colored like 'at, only not as big. Anyway, this guy I knew, real crazy fucker, took the fish from the preacher's office durin' church services one Sund'y night an' turned 'em loose in the baptismal...the water tank."

"No shit?"

"No shit. He thought it'd be a hoot ta have all these shiny, different colored fish swimmin' around when the curtains were pulled back f'r the baptism ceremony at the end'a the evenin' service. Well, nobody looked in the tank before openin' the curtains at the end'a the sermon. The water had a ton'a chemicals in it ta kill germs. When they opened the curtains there was all these fish floatin' around. Ever'one of 'em tits up. Deader'n hell. Nobody got baptized 'at night."

We began pulling on our coats and gloves.

"Ya know, Homer, I squeezed my first boobie in 'at church. It was when I was a sophomore. Carla."

"Right in church?" doubtfully.

"Well, in this construction area where an addition ta the older part'a the church was bein' built. Carla was a year younger than me but already had a big set of jugs. She was a little chubby. Not all 'at pr'tty. She was a little bit of a loner. I started talkin' with her. Bein' friendly an' shit. Not friendly enough ta sit with her durin' church services, though. Sittin' next ta somebody durin' church services was like announcin' ya had the hots f'r whoever it was ya sat with. I didn't wan'a be linked to her in 'at way. One Sund'y afternoon b'tween Trainin' Union an' choir practice, we were hangin' out with each other in the new construction part, just walkin' around shootin' the shit. Somehow it came up 'at she wanted ta kiss me. So I let her. Somethin' like a sympathy fuck, I guess. One thing led ta another an', b'fore ya know it, she'd let me put both my hands up under her bra. I was squeezin' away like mad. My first titty feel. I was goin' out my mind."

"Was it good for her?"

"Idn't funny, Homer. I'm serious as hell. It's one'a the things I did in high school I still look back on an' feel bad about. That an' a girl named Jana. Pro'bly damaged Jana pr'tty good too. Anyhow, I could'a at least sat with Carla in church a few times after tittin' her, but...I didn't. She quit comin' ta church a few weeks later."

"Why'd you quit going to church?"

"Parts of it didn't make sense."

"What parts?"

"The virgin birth. Dead people comin' back ta life. Angels. The whole idea that it's the Baptist way 'r no way at all. Or the

Catholic way, 'r the Church'a Christ way, 'r whatever way ya wan'a plug in. There was a lot'a stuff 'at was botherin' me about the whole thing. Stuff 'at dudn't matter anymore. And then there was this thing 'at happened."

"This *thing?*"

"Yeah. We'n'sd'y night service was called prayer meetin'. Less formal than Sund'y services. You could wear school clothes 'r whatever. At the beginnin' of the service the choir director'd always ask people ta call out their favorite hymn number. He'd pick a few f'r the congregation ta sing. So ya had all these people hollerin' out numbers…'183!, 322!, 234!', an' shit. One night I hollered out 'BINGO'!"

"You're kidding me?"

"Nope. You'd'a thought I'd yelled out 'WHO WANTS TA SEE MY DICK?' 'r somethin' like 'at. Anyway, Dad an' the preacher an' ever' motherfucker in the church got pissed an' wanted me ta make a public apology. I wouldn't do it. Hell, Mick Jagger wouldn't have. Right? There was this big stink an' Dad finally said I didn't have a go anymore."

"Bingoed your way inta Hell."

"Nope. I'd been baptized. My ass was covered," and lit a cigarette. "Let's get out 'a here. It's depressin' me."

We walked through the lobby and exited the building through the towering front doors. I checked the door. It'd locked behind us.

"Well," shouldering my seabag, "I told Danny we'd be done b'fore Sund'y mornin' services an', by God, we are."

"With half the night to spare," as Homer reached down, grabbed a handful of snow, and then put it in his mouth.

"Looks like it's dumped a few more inches," I mumbled. "Wonder what time it is?"

Homer looked up at the sky.

"Can't tell. Moon's behind the clouds."

"Don't gimme 'at shit, Homer. Even a full blood Cherokee can't tell time by the moon an' stars. Least not down ta the half hour."

"I know, but without the moonlight, I can't see my watch."

"You don't own a watch."

"Then why'd you ask me what time it was?"

"I was talkin' more ta myself."

"Are you working at the lounge tonight?"

"Nah. One'a the girls is coverin' me. It's too cold f'r there ta be any kind of a crowd. Plus it's Saturd'y night. It's never busy in 'at place on a weekend night. All the hubbies're home with their families. It's a killer f'r tips. Hardly worth workin' at all."

We hurried up Broadway toward University.

"Bobbie said ya got a letter from Dallas yesterd'y," I mentioned casually, avoiding Sonny's name.

Homer didn't say anything.

"She say if she likes Dallas?" trying again.

"She doesn't like it now as much as she did before that guy she ran off with dumped her."

"She plannin' on comin' back ta Lubbock any time soon?"

"Look," Homer, ignoring the question.

He was pointing at the front yard of the first mansion on fraternity row. Two dozen frats and sorority girls were putting the final touches on a thirty foot snow penis with balls the size of VW bugs. What it lacked in aesthetics it made up for in mass.

*It's gunna take a whole division'a Bible bangers ta stomp 'at one inta oblivion.*

We crossed the street mid-block and picked up the pace, frozen jeans burning our skin with every step. We were in a run as we turned onto University. In less than a minute we were standing inside Little Italy's, a pizza joint masquerading as an Italian restaurant around the corner from Mother's. We'd begun hanging out at Little Italy's back in October right after we were all hit with a lifetime ban from Mothers' because of the head-up-the-dress incident. We still weren't allowed into Dancer's because of Danny's decking the head bartender. The only other bar in the ghetto, the Tenth Street Saloon, was partly owned by the owner of Mother's so we weren't welcomed there either.

Italy's had a bar off the main dining room. The area could seat thirty or forty people. It had a small, antique, six-stool bar at the back of the room. The place was more like a tavern. It was *the* place for Texas Tech liberal arts undergrads and grad students. At first, we weren't wild about it, but what choice did we have? Until some establishments changed hands or something else opened, we were stuck with it.

The owner, Rupert, was as big a lush as JD, about the same age, and damn near the same height and build. With that much in common, a tight relationship had developed between the two over the years, not to mention Italy's being directly across the alley from the piano shop.

By the end of November, we'd staked out a few tables alongside the bar which were generally accepted by all the other patrons as ours, "ours" meaning "the bikers". The other regulars would go out of their way to get to know us so when they came in with their dates they could impress them by buying us a pitcher and calling us by our biker names.

We were just expected to have biker names. To avoid bursting any bubbles -and to insure the free pitchers would keep coming -we'd all reluctantly assumed nicknames. Mine was Doorstop. Homer's was Toilet Seat. Jerry's was Jarhead. Eduardo was Big Mex. Tomas was supposed to have been Little Mex, but he insisted on Zapata. We couldn't get him to understand that Zapata was just another name and not really a nickname. Danny officially became Fast Daniel and Stutterin' Jonas became Skip. Doug, although bikeless, was still part of the group. Doug took the name Little Mex, arguing, in typical Dougian terms, that there couldn't be a

Big Mex if there were no Little Mex. Someone had pointed out that Doug, as an Anglo, couldn't legally carry the name Mex. Doug won out by arguing that a kind of precedence for bending the biker rules had been set when we'd allowed him to be in our motorcycle gang although he no longer owned a chopper. This had opened the way for Vann to be a member. He'd once owned a Vespa in high school. Vann became Lefty since his left arm was missing, a moniker the academics considered appropriately dark, biker humor.

Going to the "bar" had become synonymous with going to Little Italy's. It was at Italy's that we, as a group, were allowed to make our particular contribution to the cultural ambiance of the student ghetto by virtue of our newly recognized station within ghetto society—biker trash.

Homer and I, shivering uncontrollably, walked into the restaurant. Homer patted his bandanna and looked at me. I nodded. We entered the bar area. It was standing room only. The space was filled with smoke. Dylan was singing "Don't Think Twice". We worked our way to the back, stopping twice to talk with people who told us to put a pitcher on their tabs. Three tables had been pulled together in front of the bar. Four chairs had been tipped, indicating they were being saved. People standing along the walls weren't challenging the reserved status of the seats.

Almost the whole gang was present, Doug and Connie being absent. We waved to everybody as we reached our table. I slid the seabag under the table then peeled the winter layer of clothing off before sitting down next to Bobbie.

Bobbie leaned over and kissed me.

"Done?"

"Yep," scratching my head furiously.

Bobbie, partially anesthetized, reached up and straightened my hair.

"Ya need a perm," giggling then leaning against me.

"His beard's long enough ta perm," Shauna, a little wrecked. "We ought'a give his beard a perm!"

"How long's ever'body been up here?" as I glanced around the table.

"Since 6:30," Bobbie.

Danny, at the far end of the table, threw a soggy napkin at me. I looked over.

"Finished?" Danny yelled.

"Yeah," I yelled back, "We're out'a there!"

Hugo, Joan, and JD were arguing some point of the Baha'i faith. Hope and Danny were discussing the repair job in Juarez. Hope had hinted to me earlier in the week that she wanted to go with us real bad. Jonas and Eduardo were trying to talk Rupert into buying a Harley. Vann, smiling to himself, eyes closed, was sitting back in his chair, evidently pretty wasted. Jerry's head rested on crossed arms on the table while Shauna rubbed his neck. Tomas was at the bar talking with Charlie, the bartender.

"One more hour an' they'd all been passed out," I told Homer.

Homer, agreeing, filled our mugs. Bobbie blew in my ear and asked me if I'd heard the news.

"About what?" shivering and rubbing the goose bumps she'd given me.

"Connie an' Doug."

"What about 'em?"

"They moved inta the same room this afternoon."

"Holy shit. What about Vann?"

"That's the weird part. Doug asked Vann for his permission for Connie ta move in with him."

"I wudn't aware 'at Vann owned her."

"He didn't mean it that way. You know how Doug is? He didn't wan'a hurt Vann's feelin's."

"So I guess Vann didn't mind?"

"He helped 'em make the move! He really dudn't seem ta care.

He said he was gettin' shitfaced t'night ta celebrate their happiness. A Vietnamese thing 'r somethin'."

I looked over at Vann. He was definitely shitfaced.

"Hey! Vann!" I yelled across the table.

Vann struggled into a sitting position and leaned forward.

"Been meanin' ta talk with ya about Doug's new theory," I told him.

"Oh! Yes!" trading places with Homer to avoid having to scream. "It's extremely interesting."

"Does it involve space ships an' alien abductions?"

"No."

"Parallel universes?"

"No."

"Reincarnation, psychic evolution, talkin' with dolphins..."

"Baptism?" Homer.

"I...I don't think so," looking puzzled. "What is baptis..."

"Never mind," I said. "Whole diff'r'nt story. How about astrology, teletransportation..."

"No! No!" Vann laughed. "None of those things."

"Well, hell, this one just might have half a chance."

"Although it seems to be well thought out, it is still *exclusively* Dougian, if you understand what I'm saying."

"Yeah," lighting a cigarette. "C'n ya gimme the short version? Danny said he went on about it f'r an hour 'r so at the party then got pissed b'cause nobody got all excited about it."

"Yes. I can make it very short. Very short."

Bobbie pushed me back from the table and crawled onto my lap.

"I wan'a hear too. I was busy with *you*. Remember?" and kissed me on the forehead.

I pecked her on the cheek in return and scooted the chair back to give her more room.

Vann took a drink from his beer then began.

"Doug believes it is all about power and control and power and control are the true gods everyone worships and fears. Only a few people ever have power or control. Those who are *perceived* as powerful and in control within a society, are considered so, *not* because they are physically strong, intellectually superior, or wealthy. They are perceived as powerful and in control because they posses certain *symbols* of authority. Strength, intellect, and money are a means to secure the symbols, but without the symbols, a person never has *real* power and is always controlled by those who *do* possess the symbols. When members of a society see someone who possesses a symbol of authority, then the general population will submit to the will of that person or group of people. He cited the Jews in Germany before World War II...they were smart and rich, however, they were powerless in the face of a bunch of thugs with swastikas on their uniforms."

Vann paused for questions. None, so he moved on.

"Doug has decided all you have to do to become powerful and take control is to somehow come into possession of the *symbols* of authority."

"What kind'a symbols?" Bobbie.

"He mentioned things like a priest's collar, anything having to do with law enforcement, like a badge or a uniform, a judge's robe. Things such as that. Each new generation learns to recognize a culture's authority symbols through a strictly enforced *socialization* process everyone is exposed to in the schools, the churches, the media, and the family."

"Rich kids learn ta wield a battle-ax, poor kids learn first aid. That's the whole socialization process anymore," I mumbled.

"Isn't that a little like the point Doug is trying to make?" Vann.

"Maybe," I shrugged. "Anyway, I'm guessin' he wants some power an' control now."

"Of course! Of course!" Vann.

"How's he gunna get hold'a the symbols ta get the power?" Bobbie.

"Run f'r Lubbock County Sheriff?" I joked.

Vann laughed.

"He's still working on how to acquire the symbols," rubbing his chin. "I'm certain he'll let us know when he has an answer."

I squeezed Bobbie and asked her what she thought about all of it.

"It kind'a makes sense," she said, "but it's pro'bly more complicated than 'at."

"It is! It is," Vann. "I've only told you about one of the conclusions he reached. There are over a hundred pages of argument contained in his letters from the hospital. What I've given you are the basics of his revelation, and the short version at that."

Jerry raised his head.

"Good," he snorted. " 'cause it's all a bunch 'a shit. Fact is, powerful people're powerful 'cause they got money an' money's power unless y're a Jew 'cause the Jews killed Jesus. Period," then plopped his head back onto his arms.

Vann and I exchanged glances.

"I'm too tired ta get inta that one with him t'night," rubbing my neck while looking at Jerry.

"And I'm too drunk," Vann, stretching and yawning. "If I don't leave now, you'll have to carry me out of here. It's been fun," and stood up.

Vann made his way around the table kissing the ladies goodbye and shaking hands with everyone else.

"It is gettin' pr'tty late," as I looked around the room. "I best start tryin' ta snag some company 'r I'll be sleepin' cold t'night."

Bobbie, still sitting on my lap, reached between her legs to grab my crotch then buried her tongue in my mouth. She withdrew as suddenly as she had attacked.

"That's y'ur point'a reference for the night while y're lookin' around," she giggled. "Happy huntin'," and slid from my lap. "Restroom. I like you very much," she winked.

By 10:30 the bar crowd was beginning to thin—people moving

onto parties, Dancers, or, for those with a currently fashionable interest in goat roper dancing, the Cotton Club outside of town. Our table was invited to several of the parties. Ruth, the owners wife, and Charlie were scurrying around clearing tables. I overheard Danny ask Hope to his parent's house for Sunday dinner. Hope accepted. Hugo and Joan excused themselves, said goodbye, and left. Rupert, JD, and Jonas, all three approaching incoherent, were ironing out the final details of a drunken plan to serve pizzas to the Saturday and Sunday afternoon crowds in the alley once it warmed up again in the Spring. Shauna wanted a band to play one Sunday a month.

Jerry asked if anybody was hungry. We all were.

"Let's head ta the house an' cook somethin' up," Jerry.

"You got ten 'r twenty pounds 'a somethin' ta eat at the house?" I asked.

"Yew sell us some meat an' some bread?" Jerry yelled at Ruth as she went behind the bar with a tray of empty mugs.

Ruth set the tray down.

"I gotta a better idea. If y'all'd he'p clean up, I'll put some spaghetti on an' we c'n finish up 'at left over sauce. It won't keep 'til Mond'y."

" 'at's a deal," Jerry, turning to Shauna. "Why don'ch ya help Ruth clean this place up so we c'n eat."

"Why don'ch ya kiss my fanny!" Shauna answered, imitating his slur.

"Don't go ta talkin' ta me like 'at in front'a my frien's, woman!" giving her the Jerry Eye. "I'll pop 'at sweet ass'a y'urs right here an' now if 'at's whud it takes."

Shauna jumped up and pulled her jeans to midthigh then threw herself across Jerry's lap. Jerry quickly removed the bandanna from his head and covered her butt.

"Damn, Shauna," wincing and rolling his head around. "Why'd ya have ta go an' do that, man. Daaaamnation. An' yew wan'a be the mother'a my childr'n?"

"Is 'at a proposal?" squealing excitedly as she jumped up and wriggled her jeans back over her hips.

"Whu' the fuck yew talkin' about?" brows furrowed, squinting tightly.

Eduardo agreed loudly that it sure sounded like a marriage proposal. Tomas suggested we go find the Priest down the street at St. Elizabeth's.

"No way, man!" Jerry protested. " 'at ain't whud I said. No fuckin' way," putting his arm around Shauna's neck and gently pulling her to him. "Whud I said wuz 'at if ya c'n keep y'ur damn pants on in public places, *then* yew'll be fit 'nough a lady ta be a proper mother ta my chil'ren, but there ain't *ever* gunna be no fuckin' weddin'.'"

"If there ain't *ever* gunna be no fuckin' weddin', man," Shauna, in Jerry's drawled slur again, "yew c'n have y'ur own fuckin' kids," sticking her tongue out and joining the clean up.

The ladies went into the kitchen to help Ruth throw the meal together. The rest of us sat back down at the tables. The bartender closed the register out, drew a pitcher of beer and then joined us.

"So, Charlie," Jerry, snickering, "yew give Rupert a pr'tty good price on all'a the body parts ya drag over here from the hospital?"

"Better deal than what I give Furr's Cafeteria," filling his mug.

"How long ya been a surgical...guy, 'r whudever y're called?" Jerry.

"Tech. I've been a surgical tech f'r two years."

" 'at shit ya got on now...ain' 'at part'a y'ur uniform?" as Jerry focused on the red stained smock.

"Yeah. I was in a rush this afternoon when I got off work. I had enough time to change 'r get high, so...I got high."

"You been in the kitchen at all t'night?" raising my brows.

"Nope," sipping his beer.

"So...whud ya spill all over y'urself?" Jerry.

"Nothin'," Charlie answered casually.

*Fuck.*

*Nah...it couldn't be.*

Charlie leaned toward Jerry.

"Can I buy a joint from ya?"

Jerry pulled one from his blue jean jacket pocket and gave it to him.

"No charge if ya share it," Jerry.

"No problem. Can't get too fucked up. Gotta go back on duty in the emergency room at midnight."

They got up, pulled on their coats, and then shuffled their way down the narrow passageway past the kitchen toward the alley door.

"I almos' forgot," as I sat down next to Danny. "Ya find out when Ed an' 'em're goin' ta Mexico City?"

"The bike auctions four days after we begin working in Juarez, so Tomas, Jonas, and Ed won't be going with us."

"Ya know, Danny...I heard Hope askin' ya if she could go."

"She'd like to, but I don't know."

"I had my doubts at first too, but how much safer could she be than with Homer, you, me, an' Jerry. She does good work an' she's fast. Never hung over. Won't take smoke breaks. Won't be hittin' on the nuns. Damn model employee."

"Let me talk it over with her some more. Make sure she knows exactly what she's stepping in."

I spotted Hope at the end of the bar watching Danny and I talking. I raised my hand and, without Danny seeing me, touched the tip of my index finger to the tip of my thumb for the okay signal. Hope put her hands together, smiled broadly, and began to hop up and down. She silently mouthed an exaggerated "Thank you." then vanished back into the kitchen.

"Yeah. You can ask her at y'ur folks house t'morrow," I said.

Danny reddened.

"I think it's neat," slapping his back. "Why haven't ya asked her out b'fore?"

Danny thought a few seconds.

"She makes me feel guilty for wanting...for wanting her in a, you know, a physical way. I mean, she's so damn sweet and she's been through so much shit. Every time I imagine the two of us in a sexual context, I feel like I've peed all over her or something. But, at the same time, goddammit, my libido can't handle any more fucking Plutonic relationships. First, Joan. Then this philosophy bitch in Albuquerque last summer. Then Missy. My balls can't take it anymore."

"Missy?"

"Yeah. Missy," rubbing his face with both hands. "Looked good until Hugo began taking her to breakfast after she got off work. Guess she thought she had a chance at him and decided what he had to offer her was better than what I had to offer her. Once Hugo began pulling that shit, all she wanted me to be was one of her closest friends," then emptied his mug.

"Ya should'a just kicked Hugo's ass. Hell, he's old. You could'a taken him."

"I'm trying to be serious, Gil," frowning

"Sorry. The thing with Missy...that why ya quit comin' around the lounge so much?"

"Yeah, I guess," picking my pack of cigarettes from the table, shaking one out, and then lighting up. "Even goddamn Neil has a bitch."

"But she's one *ugly* dog."

"I'm about ready to do a dog. You know what? If I did try to get something going with a dog, you know what would happen? I'd end up spending every goddamn night listening to her rave on about whether there's a doggie heaven or not or debating whether God is a Saint Bernard or a German Shepard."

"He's a Bassett," as I lit a cigarette off his. "Listen," putting my hand on his shoulder. "Ya need a distraction. T'morrow mornin' I'm gunna be gettin' ya up at 7:15 ta witness somethin' I just know y're gunna enjoy. Okay?"

"Fine," not paying any real attention to me.

It was close to 1:00 in the morning when Bobbie and I got back to the house. We'd had a good time. She was a hoot to get drunk with and nasty as hell. It was never right out in the open. Nothing cheap or embarrassing—just private and sexy. I'd felt really close to her tonight. I was glad we were together. Glad she was my friend. I was glad she was my lover.

***

At 7:29, Danny, Bobbie, Joan, Hope, and I - blanketed, shivering, hung over, and bitching - were huddled on the stoop. I'd had to physically drag everyone from their rooms. Icicles broke free of the steps and porch and fell to the ground as we stomped our feet to keep warm. Some tits and peters had already sprung up in the freshly fallen snow. It was dead calm. The early morning sky was cloudless.

At 7:30, the brisk morning air of the ghetto filled with the all too familiar sputtering crackle of the First Baptist Church speakers as they prepared to commence the Sunday morning bombardment. Bobbie covered her ears. The speakers roared to life. A male's voice echoed throughout the student ghetto twice as loud as "Onward Christian Soldiers" had ever been played before.

"GIMME AN 'F'!"
" 'F'!" a crowd screamed in response.
"GIMME A 'U'!' the male voice again.
" 'U'!" the crowd.
"GIMME A 'C'!"
" 'C'!"
"GIMME A 'K'!"
" 'K'!"
"WHAT'S THAT SPELL?"
"FUCK!"
"WHAT'S THAT SPELL?"
"FUCK!"

# THE RAVING EUNUCH MONKS

## "WHAT'S THAT SPELL?"
## "FUCK!"

Bobbie'd dropped her hands from her ears. Everybody's mouths and eyes were wide open. The speakers crackled for a quick moment. The crackling was followed by the hard driving guitar licks of Led Zeppelin's "Whole Lot'a Love". The window in the kitchen door was rattling.

Residents of the cramped utilities, the crowded subdivided houses, the trashy makeshift apartments, began stumbling into yards, alleys, and out onto porches. At first they were quiet. Then, yard by yard, alley by alley, street by street, students began clapping, laughing, throwing snow into the air, raising clenched fists, shooting the bird skyward, and waving frozen fingered victory signs. On the stoop we could hear the closest shouts and cheers—everything from "Fuck yeah!" to "Praise the Lord".

At 7:38, before the song ended, the speakers went silent. The whooping and hollering population of the ghetto was left to itself. The din slacked off, then grew again in intensity, this time with profane, outraged demands for more.

By 7:45, it was over.

The yards, porches, and alleys emptied. The ghetto fell quiet again.

We returned to the warmth of the kitchen. I was hit with an avalanche of questions. How did I know about it? Did I do it? And, if I did, *how* did I do it?

Danny looked over at me.

"I wish you'd have waited until I'd picked up the last check tomorrow."

The next day, in the Monday morning addition of the Lubbock Avalanche Journal, way in the back, a two paragraph article mentioned something about a case of vandalism at the First Baptist Church. On Tuesday the headline of the University Daily at Tech read "Ghetto's Touchdown Irks Baptists". On Wednesday, the entire editorial page of the Journal was filled with ravings concerning the reprehensible deed.

> ...This despicable incident defiled the House of the
> Lord and mortified every Christian in the city who
> was unfortunate enough to have experienced so
> unforgivable an act of sacrilege. It exposed innocent
> women and children to a word so vile, surely,
> the devil himself was left sickened on Sunday past.

On Friday morning God struck back with a vengeance. The son of a bitch just couldn't take a joke.

Homer woke me up.

"You have to come with me," handing me my pants. "Right now."

His face was drawn, his voice strained.

"What's wrong?" Bobbie, frightened.

Homer looked at her, shook his head and stood up.

"Hurry," he urged as he left the room.

I slid from bed and pulled my pants on.

Bobbie jumped up.

"I'm goin' too," grabbed a few things and then ran into the bathroom.

We got ready and piled into the truck. Homer turned down the alley, nearly lost it on some ice, and then floored it. Within minutes we were at JD's backdoor. Bobbie and I followed Homer to the front of the shop. Homer slowly rounded the end of an older upright player piano and stopped. The lid of the player appeared to be propped open a bit.

"Wait here," I told Bobbie, then stepped around the end of the piano.

"Jesus motherfuckin' Christ," I moaned.

JD's butt and legs were hanging limply from the top of the piano, his torso and arms hidden inside the upright.

"He's dead," Homer.

Bobbie gasped and covered her face.

"Call an ambulance yet?" I asked.

"No."

I asked Bobbie to call an ambulance and then to call Hugo. Sobbing, she ran to the phone. I stepped over to JD. He'd vomited inside the piano and crapped his pants.

Homer moved to a folding chair and sat down.

"I found him like this when I got here this morning."

"Heart attack?"

"Don't know. Might have choked on his own…," throwing his head back. "GODDAMMIT! I shouldn't have slept at the house last night! I could have helped if I'd been here."

"Fuck 'at shit, Homer. Stop thinkin' 'at way."

I heard Bobbie sobbing, her broken voice trying to tell the operator she needed the number to the hospital. I ran to her and gently took the phone from her quivering hand.

"Operator, there's been an accident an' a man's dead."

I gave the lady the address then called Hugo.

"Dead?" in disbelief.

"Ye'sir. Homer found him a little while ago."

"I'm on my way," and hung up.

Bobbie clung to me as she continued to cry softly.

"Do ya wan'a go back ta the house?" holding her tightly.

She shook her head.

I cleared JD's chair off and eased her into it.

"Are ya warm enough?"

Bobbie pulled her coat tight around her and nodded.

"I'm gunna go see how Homer's doin'. Will ya be all right f'r a minute?"

Bobbie squeezed my hand then let go.

"I'll be right back."

Homer was still sitting in the folding chair, staring at JD's legs.

"There's nothin' ya could'a done, Homer. Don't go beatin' y'urself up over this."

Homer rested his elbows on his knees then buried his face in his hands.

Sirens approached in the distance.

\*\*\*

If a person could have designed a Lubbock day in February for a funeral it would have come out looking like the day we buried JD. It was one of those rare winter days in West Texas when the wind's not blowing and the temperature's approaching civil. About thirty people showed up at the funeral home. I recognized several of them as alley regulars. Rupert was drunk. Ruth had stayed home. Me, Vann, Eduardo, Tomas, Jonas, and Doug were smoked up. Homer and Jerry were trashed on some of JD's pills. Roy was hung over. The girls, including Joan and Hope, had shared a ceremonial joint before leaving the house. Danny and Hugo were sober as judges.

I noticed one couple I'd never seen before. The man looked to be in his mid to late forties. Clean shaven, tall and skinny with thick, close cropped, graying hair. He was wearing a tailored western cut suit and gray, lizard skin boots. The lady, slightly shorter than the man, was probably in her late thirties, her blond hair short and wavy. Slender. Very attractive.

Hugo'd found two notes in an envelope marked "upon my death" while going through JD's papers at the shop. One note was dated December 10, 1971. It was a kind of will leaving the contents of the shop to Homer. The second note was dated August 16, 1968. According to Hugo, it must have been written several months after JD'd had his first heart attack. The note requested he be buried in his Army uniform, that the ceremony not be of a religious nature, and designated the songs he wanted played. He wanted a "festive wake" to be held immediately after his interment.

Honoring his request, Hope read something from Kahil Gabran, Joan read a Rod McKuen poem, and then Hugo spoke for several minutes about JD's life. Roy played Swing Low Sweet Chariot on his fiddle as everyone passed by the casket. JD's uniform looked sharp—a Purple Heart and a Silver Star among the medals covering his left chest.

Six of us on bikes followed the procession to the Lubbock cemetery. The unknown couple was present at the gravesite. Hugo played a recording of two player piano selections JD'd wanted— "Beer Barrel Polka" followed by "Blue Skies". The casket was lowered while Roy fiddled taps. Everyone pitched a shovel full of dirt into the grave.

The ladies wept, the men were sullen.

And then it was done with.

Start to finish, Homer never spoke a word.

The funeral party went out to Hugo's place. Hugo'd catered a big barbecue—JD's favorite. Rupert had supplied a keg. Homer got pretty drunk and ate a few more pills. He finally said something about how we were "exhuming" JD's Spirit so JD could become part of the between places of the universe. The idea freaked Doug out for some reason, but he was respectful.

Homer came up beside me.

"Gil...I'm going to try and keep the shop going. I think that's why he left it to me."

"Can ya afford it?"

"Think so. It's three twenty-five a month plus utilities and then the phone. I don't know how to repair a player all the way so I thought I'd keep one that works and sell the others. Maybe have an auction."

"Let's talk ta Danny about usin' some'a the glass money ta cover rent an' expenses. That'd be fair. JD wouldn't take anything, but it's different now."

Homer nodded. I called Danny over and ran the idea past him.

"I don't have any problem with that," Danny, "but you're forgetting something. First, we don't have any glass money."

"JD left me close to six hundred dollars in cash," Homer told him. "Hugo says three hundred more was in his account that I'll eventually get. I can use the cash to cover March and April. We can finish the Methodist repairs by then. After that there's the Juarez job. Like I was telling Gil, I'm going to auction off all but one of the pianos. That should bring in a good amount."

Danny scratched his chin and began to dissect the idea.

"The contracts are in his name," shaking his head slowly. "I'm not sure what kind of problem that presents."

"Who has to know he's...," I paused and looked at the ground.

"No longer the owner?" Danny put it nicely.

"Yeah," and looked back up.

"We can find a way around that," Homer. "We can figure something out."

Danny went back to scratching his chin.

"How complicated are the Juarez repairs?' he asked. "Did JD tell either one of you about what was wrong with them?"

"He just kept sayin' it'd be easy money," I told him.

"We can figure that one out too," Homer.

Danny crossed his arms over his chest and pursed his lips.

"Okay," he mumbled. "I'll stick with it, but here's the deal. If I'm gunna put anymore effort into this, you guys are gunna have to help me. You're gunna have to take it a lot more seriously than you have been. From now on, it'll be my name on any new contracts."

"I can agree ta that," and turned to Homer.

"Sounds good," Homer nodded.

Homer left soon after that, telling me he was going to spend the night at the piano shop and not to worry about him.

I got a joint from Jerry then wandered out toward the barn. I ended up at the water tank sitting on the top rung of the buffalo fence, lost somewhere in the late afternoon horizon.

I heard someone walking up behind me. I looked over my shoulder, expecting to see Bobbie.

It was the mystery lady.

The jeans she'd changed into molded to every curve of her slender figure. Her golden hair bobbed as she approached. I climbed down from the fence and watched each shift of her hips as she drew near.

*What a sweet little smile.*

"Hi," stopping a few feet from me and extending a delicate, almost fragile looking hand. I took it in mine and gently shook it.

*She's pro'bly a little older than I'd guessed. Maybe in her forties.*

The tanned, graceful contours of her face made her look something like a model.

*Pro'bly was a model at one time.*

She was a hair taller than me, but that might have been the boots she was wearing.

She introduced herself in a quiet, sultry voice.

"I'm April Ratliff."

"Gil. Gil McNeil."

"Yes," letting go. "I know."

Mrs. Ratliff removed a pack of cigarettes from her coat pocket and offered me one. I took it then lit hers before lighting mine.

"I wudn't expectin' that," smiling. "I'm not used ta bein' around a gentleman."

*Was 'at a wink? Could'a been the sun in her eyes.*

"I was brought up ta treat a lady like a lady," smiling back at her.

*Good! Real good. She liked that.*

"It's very much appreciated," slightly tilting her head to one side.

*Oh, yeah. No mistake. She's winkin'.*


Mrs. Ratliff walked to the fence, turned and leaned back against it.

"I need ta speak ta somebody about some stained glass windows f'r my house. I understan' JD taught some of ya how ta do the glass work?"

"Taught all of us. Where'd ya know JD from?"

"I'm his ex-wife. We were married f'r about six years, but that was a long time ago."

*JD, you lucky stiff. How did ya...WHY did ya fuck this up?*

"He was a nice man," I said. "We all liked him a lot."

"There was a lot ta like about him," sadly.

"Was JD gunna make some windows for ya?"

"Yeah," drawing on her cigarette, the tip of the filter barely touching the light pink lipstick. "He was gunna make me some windows ta repay a loan I'd given him. I still want the windows, but I'll pay f'r 'em now. That was JD's debt, not Homer's."

"Why don't ya come by the shop an' talk ta us about it sometime this week?"

"When will *yew* be at the shop?" cocking her head.

*She flirtin'?*

"Any Mond'y, We'n'sd'y, 'r Frid'y evenin'," feeling a bit uneasy. "I bartend at a lounge on Fourth the other nights."

"The lounge in the Roadway Inn at the corner'a University an' Fourth?"

"Yeah."

"Why don't I brang my drawings up ta the lounge on...Tu'sd'y night? Would that be convenient?"

"Uh, well...yeah," nervously.

For some reason I looked toward the house to see if I could find Bobbie. I didn't spot her.

"That'd be fine," nodding my head. "Anytime after 7:30 'r 8:00. It'll be slow an' we c'n talk it over."

"Fine," she chirped.

Mrs. Ratliff put her cigarette out in a patch of last week's snow still surviving in the shadow of the fence post.

"See ya then," and swayed away.

*Damn, her ass is nice. Two firm, well defined cheeks. Not skinny like Bobbie's. Not that Bobbie has a lousy ass. I love her ass. It's cute as hell. But, April's ass has a different, I don't know...quality about it. A different...personality.*

I let Mrs. Ratliff reach the parking area before I headed back. Roy, feeling no pain, met me at the gate.

"See ya met JD's ol' lady," he sloshed.

"Yeah. She wants a stained glass window made."

"Bullshit, compadre. I was watchin' her talkin' with ya out at the tank an' I was watchin' her watchin' ya all through the funeral. I know all abou' tha' lady," burping loudly. "Whut she wants is *yew*, an' she's gotta a way'a gittin' damn near anythang she wants when it comes ta saddle time."

Bobbie came up and pinched Roy on the butt.

"Don't stop now, li'l lady," he grinned. "Ya done went an' got this cowboy's attention."

"At ninety years old, you'll forget all about it in a few seconds," she laughed.

"Ninety years ol', my ass! Who told ya 'at? "

Bobbie looked at me.

"Yew sorry son uv a bitch!" growling. "I'm gunna git my gun out'a the truck an' kill myself a lyin' hippie," then walked away in the direction of the keg.

With the sun going down, it was turning cold again. Bobbie said she was ready to go.

We said our goodbyes and walked to the bike. Danny came running over to us waving a coat.

"Homer forgot this. He'll need it tomorrow if it's gunna be any colder than this in the morning."

"I'll drop it off on the way home."

I started the bike. Bobbie put Homer's coat on over her coat then pulled it up over her head. As I rolled slowly out of the parking area, Mrs. Ratliff gave me one of those cutesy, fingers only waves and, I swear, I think she winked at me again.

The fifteen minute ride across town all but froze us to death. I dropped Bobbie off at the house before driving up to JD's to return Homer's coat. I got to the shop and left the bike running while I ran inside.

A soft orange light flickered on the walls, the ceiling, and the window pane up front. A large shadow moved eerily from wall to wall, slowly making its way around the room. The shop was a cloud of burning incense. I heard a measured shuffling and an occasional, low moan. I laid the coat down and rushed to find Homer.

All the pianos had been arranged in a large circle. I looked between two of them. Homer, naked, hunched over, hair dangling, scar fully exposed, was slowly turning around and around while circling a few large candles. Several of his grandfather's paint pots were next to the candles. His grandfather's pelts were scattered on the floor.

Homer was holding the eagle's wing in his hand, raising it into the air then lowering it as he moved about. His body glistened with sweat. Half his face was painted black, the other half red. Drops of red sweat were spattered across his right shoulder. Drops of black sweat speckled his left shoulder. Gray dots the size of quarters covered his chest and arms. The dots were beginning to lose their shape as the red and black sweat mixed with the gray spots then trickled down his arms and chest in tiny rivulets. Homer was whispering to himself while making his way around the candles. He groaned deeply from time to time. I slid between the pianos and watched.

After several turns he noticed me standing there. He stopped, gazed at me for a moment, and then came over. The gray dots weren't painted on. They were dabs of ash, probably from the burned incense. He was completely wasted.

*Acid? Got some coke from Jerry?*

Whatever it was, it'd kicked Homer's ass all the way to wherever.

Homer addressed me in a calm, quiet voice.

"His Tohkahm was big. His Sahdahk small. In his own way, he was a spiritual man. In some ways...he was crazy like Grandpa. Now, he has become Tahnkahnyehwah. I am dancing to Tahnkahnyehwah."

"Does all this have somethin' ta do with the stuff you were tellin' me about b'fore? Remember? That night Jerry pulled the gun on 'at Air Force turd?"

"I...I think so."

"You said it couldn't have a name an' there wudn't gunna be any," looking around, "any rituals. No ceremonies."

"I guess...I was wrong, then," sluggishly. "I changed my mind. It has to have a name, even if it's the wrong name. If it doesn't have a name...it can't be spoken. If it can't be spoken...how can I chant? If I can't chant, my heart has to stay silent. Sometimes...my heart needs to speak to it...has to speak to it."

Homer looked consumed by sadness.

"What'a the dots mean?" softly.

"The spots are Sahdahk thoughts and feelings I have. I have to dance until they are washed away."

"An' y'ur face? What's the red an' black mean?"

The question seemed to throw him. After ten or fifteen seconds, his face expressionless, Homer answered.

"Black and red are Texas Tech's colors."

*Holy shit.*

"Ya feel all right?" worried.

"Yes. I have to keep dancing. If the spots aren't gone by first light, my Sahdahk will grow."

Homer shuffled back to the candles, hunched over a little, and then slowly raised the eagle feather into the air. Moaning, he began his dance again, rhythmically raising up onto the toes of one foot before easing the heel back down just as he rose up on the toes of the other foot to slide it forward in a graceful arc. Homer alternated the sliding step while slowly turning, making a large circle around the candles, the paint pots, and the other relics he'd rescued from his grandfather's place. The only sounds were his breathing, an occasional moan, and the unbroken swishing of his bare feet on the sandy floor.

I stepped out of the circle of pianos and watched. It was hypnotizing—each step flowing into the next. Every move, before its completion, melting into the next. It was all so intensely natural. I felt like I was watching something…

*God, I hate the word…*

…something sacred.

I stopped worrying. Wherever Homer was, I was convinced that whoever he was there with wouldn't let anything happen to him. I caught myself wanting to dance that way. I wanted to be a part of his ritual, with all its paint and incense and strange sounding words. I wanted Homer's invention to be a part of an answer, a universal expression of some kind because, at this moment, it simply felt like it should be.

*Fuck me.*

I turned away and hurried outside.

# CHAPTER FIVE
## June, 1972

I stepped out of the bathroom, pulled my jeans on, buttoned up, and then slipped my tee shirt over my head. I walked to the side of the bed and sat down.

"Gotta go," I mumbled.

"So soon?" April whined softly.

She eased from her side onto her back, slid her right foot over to where I was sitting, and gently pushed at my butt with her toes. As I turned to look at her she raised her left knee from the mattress and let her legs part slightly. I turned away and pulled my socks on. It'd only been thirty minutes, but I could already feel the tension in my groin returning. April reached for the champagne glass on the nightstand and took a sip.

"Hot date b'fore goin' ta Juarez?"

"Takin' Bobbie to a dinner an' a dance Hugo got tickets to," pulling my boots on.

"How sweet. C'n I come?" bringing the glass to her lips again. "Afterwards we could make it a threesome."

I stood up and looked at her angrily.

"Calm down, silly," she smiled.

April brought her knees together and reached up to grab my arm. I sat down beside her.

"I'm sorry," running a hand over my face. "I've got a lot on my mind with this Juarez thing. I just wan'a get it over with. I need the money bad."

"Anythang else botherin' ya?" as she slipped her hand under my shirt and gently scratched my back.

"Nah. Nothin' else. Just tired."

"Gil?"

I turned and looked at her.

*Goddammit. She's so beautiful.*

"If y're b'ginnin' ta feel uncomf't'rble about this…then it should stop. Or we could cut it back ta once a week."

I looked down at the floor and folded my hands in my lap.

"If y're not enjoyin' it," she said, "I cain't either. Honest, Gil, the guilt'll ruin it f'r us an' f'r yew an' Bobbie.

April rose up and put her arms around me, resting her head on my shoulder.

"Whut we're doin' ain't wrong. We're just enjoyin' each other. I love ya, Gil, but in a way 'at's special ta us. If I loved ya the same way I love Jake an' then slep' with ya…then *I'd* feel guilty. That's what would make me feel like I was cheatin' on him. Yew don't feel about me the way ya do about Bobbie, so, ya see…there's nothin' wrong with what we're doin'."

"I can't help it. Sometimes it just dudn't seem right."

She began running her fingers through my hair.

"We c'n stop seein' each other f'r a while if ya want some time ta thank about it," slipping her hand back under my shirt. She began to draw slow circles around my navel. It gave me goose bumps. April picked up on my response.

"Yew think about it while y're in Mexico," whispering into my ear.

*Oh, Christ!*

I wanted her again and it pissed me off. I stood up and hurried to the door.

"Gil."

I turned around. April was lying down again, her legs straight out on the bed and slightly parted, her toes pointing at me. She'd covered her lap with both hands and brought her elbows together to push her breasts up.

"I'll see ya in a few weeks," smiling wickedly, gently rocking her shoulders.

I twisted sideways and looked away. If I hadn't, I would have been all over her.

*She is so...*

"I...I really don't know right now," I told her. "I need ta sort some things out. Away from you *and* Bobbie."

"Yew'll be back," she teased.

I spun around and glared at her.

"Ya sound awful damn sure about that."

"I *am* sure. Wan'a know why?" removing her hands from her lap.

I turned and reached for the doorknob.

"Because," giggling, "I'm more...*experienced* than Bobbie."

I jerked the door open.

"An' y're havin' too much fun," before the door closed behind me.

I rushed downstairs, got the bike kicked over, and then looked back up at the second level walkway of the motel. April was leaning over the rail with a sheet wrapped around her.

"An' y're gittin' away with it!" she laughed.

Her short, wavy blond hair was mussed, a lock falling across one eye to her cheek.

*Marilyn Monroe. Marilyn Monroe at...forty-six 'r so.*

She threw me a kiss and waved. I waved back before roaring off.

Pissed. Pissed as hell.

*Goddammit. She's right. On all counts.*

***

"Gil first!" Joan shouted down the hall.

I left the bedroom and entered the living room. Joan, Shauna, and Hope were gathered around Bobbie. Hugo, in a tuxedo, stood behind the girls.

*Oh my God.*

Bobbie was wearing the dress she'd worn the night I was supposed to have had dinner with her at Jerry's. Her dazzling white hair, reaching to well below her tiny waist, was pulled over one shoulder and draped across her breast. The long black evening dress, slit to midthigh, fit her wisp of a body like a glove. Her high heels intensified the sleek lines of her delicate figure. Her smile was electric, eyes filled with anticipation. She was about to bubble over. She looked hot and she knew it.

I approached her on a cloud. I was spellbound.

"Ya look...beautiful, Bobbie."

She blushed.

"You don't look too bad y'urself. The tux'd look nice on the bike."

"Listen ta them!" Hugo grinned. "You'd think they'd never seen each other b'fore."

Joan stepped over to me and gave me a big hug.

"Yew clean up real good," she said.

"Wait 'til ya see Jerry," I told her.

Joan, in a dark green, ankle length gown straining desperately to contain her bosom, stepped back to the doorway.

"Y'ur turn Jerry!"

Shauna nervously ran her hands over her midnight blue dinner dress, smoothing an imagined line here, removing an invisible speck of lint there. She reached up, patted her hair, and then turned to Hugo. He winked at her. She reddened. The girls formed a screen in front of her.

Jerry, also in a tuxedo, entered the room. His hair was cut short, his beard close cropped and neatly trimmed. He looked completely uncomfortable, tugging at the collar of his shirt with one hand, clutching a beer in the other. He was about to say something when Shauna stepped from behind the girls. Jerry went dumb. He stared at her, set the beer down on an old crate next to one of the bean bags, and then walked over to her. He looked like he'd been hit with a board. A big one. Shauna was beaming. She hadn't known what to expect. Jerry's reaction thrilled her.

"Damn, Shauna. Ya look like a...a...fuc...a...," he couldn't finish.

Shauna ran over and wrapped her arms around him. Tears were coming down her cheeks.

"Don't ruin the makeup!" Joan, jumping to Shauna's side. "Don't get anything on the tux!"

"Okay, Danny!" an excited Bobbie, hands clasped together under her chin, elbows tucked in.

Hope, in a black evening dress stepped to the front of the crowd. Her long red hair had been done in a pile. A lone curl drifted down the side of her face. Hugo stepped up to her and whispered something in her ear. It made her smile, look down, and giggle. Danny strolled into the room.

"My God!" Hugo exclaimed. "Ya look like a 1920's robber baron at a presidential inauguration."

I doubt Danny heard him. The same board that'd floored Jerry had put Danny down. Hope and Danny slowly approached each other. Danny began to put his arms around her then hesitated as Hope momentarily pulled back. With tears in her eyes, she glanced at Hugo. Hugo smiled at her and nodded to Danny. Hope slowly reached out, took Danny's hands, and placed them behind her back. She suddenly sobbed, dropped her head onto Danny's chest, and threw her arms around his waist.

"I'm sorry," she cried, "I cain't he'p...help it."

*Jesus Christ! They're all cryin'.*

The girls gathered around Hope and kept hugging on her. Hugo looked as proud as a father seeing his only daughter off to the prom. Joan, dabbing tears from her cheeks with a handkerchief Hugo'd given her, ordered us to the kitchen so the ladies could regain their composure and redo their makeup.

I stepped over to Hugo.

"Ya didn't have ta rejoin the country club ta snag all those tickets ta this 'Do' did ya?"

"Oh, hell no," chuckling. "They're always tryin' ta reel me back in. Not that they like me all 'at much, but they damn sure like those membership fees."

"Well...thanks. I didn't know how much it was gunna mean ta the girls. Hell, Eduardo said his wife's been a wreck all week."

"I swear, son, it doesn't take much ta keep 'em happy when there's some strong feelin's involved. This shindig t'night's just icin' on the cake in their minds. Remember that for me," unnervingly serious.

It felt as if Hugo suspected something.

"I will."

*Dammit. It was like he'd been in the room watchin' me an' April this afternoon.*

"I'm so happy the other ladies decided ta come," Hugo, head bobbing slightly. "I'm lookin' forward ta meetin' the better halves'a that crowd."

"Jonas and Holly still coming?" Danny.

"Far as I know," Hugo. "Maybe I shouldn'a put 'em on the spot like 'at by askin' 'em ta come. That Holly's one brave lady."

Jerry stepped over.

"Holly's brave?" growling and raising his brows. "Hell. Anything happens it's gunna be all'a us guys gittin' into it. Ain't gunna be her, man."

"Nothin's gunna happen, Jerry," Hugo.

"Nothin' we cain't handle," Jerry snorted.

Hugo slapped my arm.

"Best be gettin' the corsages out'a the refrigerator," he told me. "I hear 'em comin'. I'll do the pinnin' since we're fallin' b'hind schedule."

One by one the girls passed through the kitchen as Hugo fixed the corsages to their gowns. Each in turn locked arms with an escort then headed downstairs. It took ten minutes to neatly pack all of us into Hugo's station wagon. Finally, with every seat taken and all the men's laps occupied, we were off to the Lubbock Country Club. Hugo'd paid for it all, even the tux and gown rentals.

"Too bad Doug an' Connie couldn't make it," Hugo.

"Connie wanted to," Shauna huffed, "but Doug didn't. All b'cause he wanted to show her 'at he's the boss. The bastard."

"Homer said he couldn't find a date?" Danny.

"He didn't even try," I said.

"Vann sure wuz excited about goin' ta Hong Kong," Hope. "He ought'a have a real fun summer."

"He deserves it," Danny.

"Yew ever been ta Hong Kong?" Hope asked Danny.

"Nope."

"Yew ever been ta Hong Kong?" Hope, turning to me.

"Yeah. Two 'r three times."

"He cain't remember if it wuz two 'r if it wuz three times 'cause he wuz so fuc...," Jerry, catching himself, "screwed up. Dammit, Hugo!" frustrated. "I cain't think about whud I'm talkin' about if I gotta be concentratin' all night on not cussin', man."

Shauna planted a quick kiss on Jerry's lips.

"Yew c'n do it f'r one night," she said.

"Did ya like Hong Kong?" Hope asked me.

"It was okay."

"It wuz okay," Jerry mimicked me. "Shiiit, man! Gil tol' me he went through two thousan' dollars in seventy-two hours an' didn' have nothin' ta show for it 'cept the crabs."

"Dammit, Jerry!" I snapped angrily.

"You had crabs?" Bobbie shrieked and pushed away from me.

The look of horror on her face turned to one of pure revulsion.

"It's not like I still got 'em."

"But...the *crabs*!" Joan grimaced. "How *nasty*."

"That was three years ago, f'r Christ sake!" I cried. "If any of 'em survived the powder, they'd all be dead'a old age by now!"

"Eeeewww!" Hope, covering her face. "Dead ol' crabs all over y'ur body."

"I've showered a few times since then," glaring at Jerry. "Thanks a goddamn lot, Jerry," and jabbed him. "At least I caught mine from a lady an' not a bunch jarheads."

Shauna pulled away from Jerry.

"Yew had crabs too?" astonished.

"Ever'body got the crabs, man," Jerry, squeezing his eyes shut and wrinkling his nose.

"But," Hope, stunned, "yew wuz a preacher Marine...how...,"

I caught Hugo looking into the rear view mirror at Jerry. "Preacher Marine?" he mouthed silently.

"The li'l bastards wuz ever'where," Jerry, looking over at me to see if I was going to blow the whistle on him about his not having been a chaplain's assistant.

"Jungle crabs can jump thirty feet," deciding to corroborate his story. "They're real light an' in a good blow they can be carried up to a coupl'a miles. Medics, nurses...preacher Marines. Ever'body got 'em."

*Son of a bitch owes me big time now, the buddy fuckin' jarhead.*

"Yeah," Jerry, glancing at me in relief. "Jonas said his whole platoon got 'em when they passed six clicks downwind uv a whore house once."

I whistled.

"Six clicks?"

"Couldn't we change the subject ta somethin' a little more pleasant?" Hugo interrupted.

"How *stupid* do you think we are?" Bobbie, stabbing Jerry in the shoulder before turning her attention to me. "Was she good lookin'?" crossing her arms and glaring at me.

"Jesus Christ, Bobbie. I was nineteen years old an' single. Not even a girlfriend back home. What'd ya expect me ta be doin' when I had a little time on my hands?"

"Would ya've done it if we'd known each other back then?" sternly.

I looked over at Jerry and grinned.

"Well, I'd'a damn sure been a lot more careful about pickin' a cleaner one."

"You *bastard*!" and tried to slap me.

I grabbed her wrists. She butted me with her forehead.

"C'n any'a y'all waltz?" as Hugo tried again to change the subject.

"I c'n two-step," Jerry. "Sort'a."

"It's a little differ'nt than 'at," Hugo chuckled.

"I *never* have," Hope. "Not the real way like in the movies."

"I'll teach you," Danny. "When Dad was stationed in Spain, all the officer's kids had to take ballroom dancing lessons."

"It's been a long time, but I think I can remember," I said.

"Good for you," Bobbie snipped. "Maybe there's gunna be a good lookin' Chinese hooker there you can pay ta dance with ya," leaning forward and resting her elbows on the back of the front seat.

"She wudn't Chinese," I mumbled.

Bobbie stuck her tongue out at me.

"Is 'at the kind'a shit they'll be playin' t'night?" Jerry moaned. "Tha' waltz shit?".

"Some'a the time," Hugo.

"Looks like me an' Shauna're gunna be puttin' in a lot'a table time then," Jerry.

"Bullshit to!" Shauna declared, tapping Hugo on the shoulder. "Yew'll dance with me, won'ch ya Hugo?"

"I intend ta dance several dances with ever' one uv you ladies this evenin'," Hugo promised. "It'll be an honor."

"And, Danny," Shauna turned to Danny. "Yew'll dance with me? Right?"

"With my escort's permission, I would be happy to."

Hope giggled.

"I'll have ta thank about it. I might wan'a keep him all ta mahself."

423

"Whut the fuc...the shit *is* this, man?" Jerry, exasperated. "Yew guys're soundin' like a bunch'a pansy-asses."

"I like it," Shauna.

All the girls expressed their agreement.

"Hey!" Jerry snorted. "Yew knew I wuz a sow's ear when ya met me an' I ain't changin' f'r nobody."

Shauna put her lips to Jerry's and kissed him passionately while wriggling wildly on his lap. She broke the kiss off then leaned back.

"One night," he snickered, "but tha's it, man. Ya want it steady like this shit," tugging at his tux coat, "then ya best be doin' some shoppin' aroun' at the dance t'night."

"I wouldn't *want* ya ta be like 'at *ever*'day," and kissed his forehead, "but it's fun ta dress up an' pr'tend ever' once in a while."

Bobbie looked over her shoulder at me.

I pulled her to me then gave her a hug.

"You are so beautiful," whispering in her ear.

She broke out in goose bumps.

"I like you very much," she whispered back.

Hugo pulled up to the front of the country club. His trashy station wagon looked a little out of place alongside the Continentals, Cadillac's, and European luxury cars arriving and departing the covered drive. A spit shined college kid in an all white tux opened the doors for everyone. We stood alongside the curb while the ladies made last minute adjustments. At last we were ready.

Bobbie took hold of my arm. In her heels, she was nearly as tall as I was.

"I'm so nervous. I didn't get ta go ta my prom. This is like a prom...only fancier."

I looked at her and smiled.

"Once we're inside," I assured her, "you'll see. You're gunna be the pr'ttiest one here."

She hugged me.

Hugo led us into the lobby, Joan on his arm. We all clumsily imitated his every move. Danny and Hope were behind Hugo. Hope appeared to glide over the bright red carpet on the walkway, her shoes barely touching the ground, one foot floating gracefully in front of the other. Jerry and Shauna followed. They made a good looking couple. Jerry's stout frame and dark skin gave him the appearance of a rich cattleman. Shauna glowed, taking everything in and grinning madly. Ready to party. Bobbie and I were last.

"Does this dress make my boobs look too small?" she whispered. "We had ta take so much of it in b'cause Sonny had such big ones."

I released her arm and hugged her tightly.

"Y'ur boobs're perfect," taking her arm again. "An' if I catch anybody lookin' at 'em t'night, I'm gunna kick their ass."

As we waited in the lobby to be taken to our table a snotty looking elderly gentleman approached Hugo and handed him a note. Hugo read it, furrowed his brow then excused himself. Several minutes passed before Hugo returned with Eduardo and Tomas, escorting their wives, and Jonas escorting Holly. The wives appeared shaken. Holly, her jaw set defiantly, was ready to put some lights out, her fiery eyes darting around the room, challenging every stare.

Hugo waited until everyone was gathered together then spoke to us.

"There was a little misunderstandin' at the door," and bowed. "Ladies, I sincerely apologize. Please, don't let this rough start ruin the evenin' for ya," clearing his throat then addressing the guys. "Gentlemen, this is *their* night," gesturing to the ladies. "Let's don't let anything *we* do ruin the evenin' for 'em. If anything's said to ya that's out'a line t'night, please...let me handle it. Agreed?"

Jerry, Danny and I exchanged glances. Jerry turned to Jonas and Holly.

"Somebody call y'all niggers?" Jerry asked Jonas angrily. "I swear ta God I'll kill the motherfu..."

Eduardo put his hand on Jerry's shoulder.

"Nothin' like that happened, maaan. Some shithead said, uh... he was telling me I'd parked in the wrong place and we got into this argument. It's all cool now."

Jerry didn't look like he was buying Eduardo's explanation.

"T-that's all it was," Jonas, his voice strained.

"I b'lieve some introductions're in order," Hugo drawled softly while turning to Ed and Tomas.

By the time everybody'd finished with the handshakes, hugs, and quick pecks on cheeks, whatever it was that had happened out front seemed to have been pretty much put in its place. Once seated at our table, everyone settled in quite comfortably. I glanced around the room at the panhandle's social elite. The community's moral watchdogs. The smug, moneyed self-righteous. They glared back, and to a person, looked pissed as pissed could get.

*Eat me, you sorry bast'rds...*

...and laughed.

Bobbie smiled.

"What's so funny?"

I kissed her forehead.

"Nothin'. I just feel real good at the moment."

I guess everybody has the right to a perfect block of time showing up now and then. A block of time where all the expectations are met and once it's all over, y're left with one grand memory that helps keep some of the crap at bay for a while. I believe that's what all the ladies were hoping for and I believe that's what they got. Chairs were held, hands were kissed after returning to the table from the dance floor, and the conversations deliberately avoided any profoundly crude subjects.

Even Jerry's getting a little too drunk and saying the "F" word a few times didn't ruin it for Shauna. With Hugo's coaching, she had her gentleman for an evening. Emma and Leticia were being courted by Eduardo and Tomas again. Our table damn near had the dance floor to ourselves whenever Jonas danced with one of the ladies in our group. Danny and Hope danced all the slow numbers with each other. All the ladies were living the fairy tale and loving every minute of it.

There were low moans and objections when Jonas announced he'd been accepted into the vet medicine program at the University of Nevada in Reno. He and Holly would be moving in August. There were loud cheers and a round of applause when Joan announced her decision to accompany Hugo to Spain during the summer. Everyone toasted the newly negotiated lease Jerry had signed, since Will had decided to stay in Katmandu indefinitely.

Bobbie and I spent a lot of time talking. Talking and touching—touches that felt more like caresses at times. I kept telling her how much I was going to miss her while I was in Juarez. Bobbie kept changing the subject. I knew she wanted to tell me she loved me. And that hurt. Maybe it was the moment, but *I* wanted to tell *her* I loved her.

But I didn't.

And I couldn't figure out why.

I wished to God I hadn't spent the afternoon with April. I was certain of one thing—after spending the evening watching Bobbie, feeling her touch, joking with her...something felt different. Whatever it was, I decided I was never going to cheat on her again.

*An' this time...I mean it.*

\*\*\*

By noon Saturday, despite the hangovers, Jerry's van and Homer's truck were loaded and we were ready to whip over to the house, pick up some clothes, say goodbye to Shauna, Joan and Bobbie, and then pack it off to Juarez.

At the house Bobbie led me into the bedroom and shut the door.

GLYNN E. THOMPSON

"Thanks for last night," and wrapped her arms around me. "There won't ever be another night like that ever again. I felt like Cinderella."

"You looked pr'ttier than Cinderella. You were beautiful. Ya still are," as I hugged her tightly.

"This'll be the longest we've been apart," tearfully.

"Ten 'r twelve days'll go fast as hell," I promised her with a big hug.

"I want more than a hug," kissing my chest.

I held her head in my hands, gently tilted it back, and kissed her. Bobbie unsnapped my jeans and slipped them from my hips. She pushed me onto the bed then shed her dress. There was nothing under it. She lay on top of me, brought her knees up to straddle my hips then, leaning over, continued to kiss me. Bobbie dropped her head forward and moaned deeply as she eased herself onto me. Her snow white hair danced across my face like silken brush strokes as she began a slow, gentle rocking motion, eyes closed, lightly panting in uneven breaths. She made love to me.

***

Three hours later the caravan was half way to Juarez.

"C'n we trust Fast Daniel ta be alone with Hope in the truck?" Jerry sneered as he looked over his shoulder out the back of the van. Jerry offered the last of the joint to Homer.

"Shit," I said. "Hope'll have his balls on the rear view mirror like a pair'a fuzzy dice if he tries somethin' she dudn't want him to."

"It's beginning to look like she might want him to try something," Homer.

Jerry snickered.

"Then be lookin' f'r Danny ta be hangin' Hope's panties from the rear view mirror."

"Y're such a romantic fuck," I mumbled.

"Shauna seems ta think so," Jerry.

"She's fakin' it. She's puttin' up with y'ur shit just b'cause y're

428

gettin' 'at high payin' Post Office job. I still can't figure out how ya manag…"

"Whudever it takes ta keep 'at ladies tail b'tween my sheets, man. Whudever it takes. If y'all had any idea how hot an' nasty 'at lady c'n git, yew'd be hidin' in'a bushes waitin' ta smack my ass with a shovel 'r somethin' so yew could git at it. I'm tellin' ya," slowly sucking air between his teeth, "of all the pussy I got overseas 'r in TJ, 'r east Lubbock, 'r off 'at campus she's…she's…. fuuuck, man. Look whud I went an' did ta myself."

I glanced over at Jerry. He was pointing at his crotch.

"See 'at Homer?" Jerry howled, eyes wide. "See 'at joint gazer look over here at me?" cackling wildly. "Y're a fuckin' joint gazer, man. Stop this van an' lemme out," pulling a baggie from his boot.

He pulled some papers from the bag and began to roll a joint.

"I'm gunna have one more smoke then crap out f'r a while. Yew wake me up when y're tired an' I'll drive."

"Yeah, I'll be able ta rest real easy with y'ur smoked up ass b'hind the wheel."

"Fuck y'urself. I'm a hell uv a lot better a driver when I'm smoked…when I'm relaxed an' all."

"Gil!" Homer from the back of the van. "When you get tired, I'll take over. He'll end up killing us."

"Okay. Thanks."

"Oh, goodness!" Jerry in a high pitched voice. "I'm *so* afraid ta die. Shiiit, man," slurring as he finished rolling the joint. "Ya know, Gil, sometimes I jus' c'n*not* b'lieve 'at son uv a bitchin' sissy-ass injun wuz ever in'a Corps. He's a shittin' embarras…," stopping to look back at Homer. "Y're a shittin' embarrassment ta the Corps, Homer," raising his voice. "I wish ya'd start tellin' people yew wuz in the Air Force 'r the," looking over at me and slapping my arm, " 'r the Navy."

"Is it gunna be like this for the next week an' a half?" I grumbled.

"Like whu'?" pretending to be at a total loss. "Whu's wrong

now? I say somethin' wrong?" cackling while lighting the joint. "No fuckin' sense'a humor," before taking the first drag and holding it. " 'at's whu's wrong with this whole-ass world, man. No fuckin' sense'a humor," exhaling slowly. "Damn! This shit'll give ya a sense'a humor. This's some *bad*ass shit."

We stopped in Alpine, grabbed a bite to eat, checked to make certain everything was still secure, and swapped out drivers. I ended up with Jerry and Danny in the van. We couldn't talk Jerry out of driving. Homer and Hope were in the truck.

It was late afternoon by the time we got rolling again.

"The spackling powder's no good," I mentioned to Danny. "It's all lumped up."

"I thought you checked everything yesterday," Danny snapped.

"It's no big deal!" surprised at his reaction. "It's cheap as shit."

"It's the idea of it," Danny, irritated. "We could 'no big deal' ourselves broke down here."

"We ought'a switch ta spray cleaner, man," Jerry. "It don't do 'at bad a job. I hate tha' fuckin' powder. Makes me sneeze my ass off. Gives me headaches."

"Powder's a hundred times cheaper than spray," Danny. "I'll pick up twenty pounds before crossing the border tomorrow. I wouldn't know where to find it in Juarez. We need anything else? I don't want to cross back and forth over the border any more than I have to."

No one could think of anything.

Danny laid down in the small space between the seats and the glass crates.

"We've got to be careful," he cautioned.

Jerry held an unlit joint out to Danny.

"Here. Ya need ta mellow out a li'l, man. Quit sweatin' the small shit."

"Some ones got to," refusing the joint. "Right now I'm sweating out all the grass in this van."

"They don't check ya comin'," Jerry. "Only goin'. Tomas an' Ed told me they ain't never been searched goin' south an' they go at least twice a year," handing me the joint.

I lit up.

"So how come they decided they weren't going to take any dope with them when they go to the bike auction next week?" Danny.

"Jonas," Jerry sneered. "He kep' whinin' about drug dogs an' Mes'c'n jails an' shit. Fuck, man. If it'a been me, I'd'a left the li'l maggot behind."

"Well, if you guys want to take any dope across in the van, Hope and I are taking the pickup across. If you're nailed...you're on your own," Danny.

"Shit, man," Jerry hissed. "Ain't nothin' gunna happen. Y're jus' bein' par'noid an' 'at's gunna make me par'noid an' then I'll fuck up an' somethin' *will* go wrong. 'at's the way 'at shit comes down," reaching for the joint in my hand.

"Hell no!" jerking it away. "Not while y're drivin'."

"Yew Bogartin' motherfucker," Jerry mumbled.

"I mean it," Danny warned us again, "and you can tell Homer this too, if any of you screw up while we're in Juarez, you're on your own. For the money involved here, I don't understand why you can't lay off of it for a few days."

"Fuck yew, man," Jerry, getting pissed. "Yew sayin' I'm a fuckin' pot head 'r somethin'? If ya felt 'at'a way about it, why didn't ya leave me b'hind with Doug? Ain' 'at why he got uninvited? 'cause'a his shit?"

"Jesus Christ!" I jumped in. "*Nothin*'s gunna happen!"

They both shut up.

"The only thing's gunna happen," I continued, "is that we're all gunna make some damn decent money. Right?"

" 'at's a damn fact," Jerry slapping my arm. "An' I'm gunna need ever' fuckin' dime so I c'n check inta a junkie hospital somewhere when we git back an' do somethin' about this pot addiction I got."

Danny didn't say anything. He didn't have to. I knew Danny was worried about the drug thing. That *was* the reason we'd talked Doug out of going. Doug was planning on bringing along all the pills, hash, and acid he could carry so he could "experience" Juarez. Even Jerry realized taking Doug would have been asking for trouble.

"Whud'a ya think?" Jerry asked me, as if my opinion really meant a damn thing to him. "Yew think I'm a fuckin' pot head jus' 'cause I stay lit a li'l bit? Yew think I'm a weed weirdo?" giving me the Jerry Eye and drooling. "Yew think I'd kill my own mama ta git the last toke off'a dooby she's burnin'? Huh? Yew think grass's fucked me up?" sneering as he slumped over the steering wheel.

In all honesty, in the pale light of the dashboard, Jerry did look a little questionable.

"Nah," I answered. "It wudn't grass 'at fucked ya up. I think you were pro'bly born...

*kind'a twisted...*

a little different. That's why society's always fuckin' with ya."

"Think 'at's why they're always up my ass?" seriously. " 'cause I'm diff''r'nt? Ya think God picked me ta be like...like, uh...Jesus 'r somethin'? 'cause God knows I c'n handle it?" slowly rubbing his chin, staring over the dash into the night. "Hell yeah," talking to himself. "I could'a handled it back then, man. I could'a handled bein' Jesus," then quickly added, "Excep' 'at nail shit in'a hands an' feet. I don't know abou' tha' shit. 'at's gotta hurt like a bitch," and whistled softly. "If I'd'a been Jesus, I'd'a talked God out'a tha' part uv it. Like, I'd'a said, 'Hey, God...whu's wrong with a fuc...a firin' squad 'r somethin', man'. Know whud I'm sayin'?" still staring into the dark.

I dozed off listening to Jerry's mumbled ravings, Danny's snoring, and the hum of the tires on the highway.

We got into El Paso around 8:00 and checked into a cheap-shit motel a few blocks from the Cordova crossing into Juarez. Danny,

Jerry, Homer, and I shared one room. Hope got a room to herself. After grabbing a bite to eat, Danny and Hope took the truck and went to find some spackling powder.

Homer, Jerry, and I walked to the bridge.

"Smell 'at?" Jerry, sniffing the air. "When's'a last time ya smelled 'at, man?" snickering.

"Bangkok," Homer.

"Kowloon," I whispered.

"Fuckin' Olongapo," Jerry cackled. "O'po. R an' R."

All three of us were grinning.

" 'course, ol' Gil here, he cain't touch shit. He c'n only look 'cause Hope's gunna be watchin' him the whole damn time. Ain' 'at right, Gil?" Jerry, slapping my arm.

"Dudn't matter. All I'd planned on doin' was ta watch you catch ever' fuckin' disease they've got down here."

Homer put his arm around Jerry's shoulder.

"What's gunna keep Hope from telling Shauna about everything *you* do?"

" 'cause it don't matter ta me if Hope does tell Shauna," pushing Homer's arm away. "Shauna knows I'm gunna be deep fryin' the ol' fat. I don't hide nothin' from Shauna. Got to much respect f'r the lady. 'at's why our shit's so tight, man. I tell her ever'thing," lighting a cigarette.

"So ya told her right out you'd be fuckin' around down here?" I asked doubtfully.

"Hell no, but she knows. It's one'a them unsaid things."

"How unsaid is it that she might go up to Dancers and sniff out some strange of her own," Homer.

" 'at won't happen. Wan'a know why? She ain't gunna risk pissin' me off an' losin' me. Nah...she'll sit aroun' f'r two weeks buildin' up steam in the ol' love engine f'r when daddy comes home," cackling.

"So it's okay f'r you ta screw around on her, but she can't screw around on you?" I asked.

"In'a firs' place, it ain't screwin' aroun'. It's diversifyin'. Got that 'un from Roy."

"That's a perspective that puts a lot of issues to rest," Homer nodded.

"Hell yeah it does," missing the sarcasm.

"Whatever," shaking my head. "Shauna's not allowed to *diversify*, but you are?"

" 'at's right. Whu's wrong with 'at? Listen, man. Yew don't like the arrangement, then don't go fallin' in love with me," cackling and glancing at Homer. "Right, Homer? Damn straight I'm right," answering for him.

We stared at the far side of the dry river bed for a while.

"Let's go across and have a few beers," Homer. "It's not even 9:30."

The three of us exchanged glances.

Jerry, digging in his pocket, turned to Homer.

"How much gas money ya got left?" Jerry asked him.

Homer reached into his pocket, pulled out a few bills and some change then began counting. Jerry counted his money.

"About twelve-fifty," Homer.

I had close to three dollars.

"I got twenty-two an' some change," Jerry.

"That's b'cause we didn't gas up when we got in t'night," I pointed out. "That's money from t'day's budget that's gotta go ta gas. If we spend it t'night then…"

Jerry put his hand over my mouth.

"One Danny's enough," he frowned. "It ain' like we're gunna drink *all* uv it up. Ten bucks at the mos'," turning his palms up, holding a shrug, and raising his brows. "Right?"

"Just ten bucks?" raising my brows, seriously doubting that, once we got started, any of us would notice hitting a ten dollar wall.

"Ten bucks, then we come back," Homer, pulling his bandanna tight then making sure his long hair covered everything on his neck.

The three of us mingled into the Saturday night statesiders crossing the bridge for a night of cheap thrills in Juarez.

"Look f'r a titty bar!" Jerry, as we stepped onto Mexican soil and headed south on Av. Lincoln.

I was overseas again on R and R. Rest and recreation. Going on liberty in some shithole sailor town. I glanced at a set of storefront windows as we hurried by. I'd almost expected to see myself dressed in a sparkling white liberty uniform, starched jumper flap bouncing slightly with each step, tailored bellbottoms swishing against each other, white hat cocked, resting on the right eyebrow. For a split second I thought I saw two or three other sailors on either side of me, all of us laughing and joking with each other. Anxiously discussing the evening's possibilities. Speculating about how bad tomorrow's hangovers were going be. Pitying those poor bastards back there working the rivers *as we spoke.*

I felt an unsettling twinge in the pit of my stomach.

I stopped. Jerry and Homer stopped. I returned to stand in front of the window. They joined me, one on either side. We stared at the images facing us; Homer's bandanna pulled tightly over a growth of hair now reaching halfway down his back; my beard, thick and bushy, at least six inches long and a full head of wavy, wind blown hair down to my shoulders; Jerry looking worn out, going on old.

All three of us were so ragged.

A reflected kaleidoscope of dazzling neon signs shrouded the gaunt shadows in the window in a shimmering halo of colors.

It was a little unnerving.

*It's the lighting here. That's all it is.*

We stood in front of the window a good minute, each lost in our own thoughts.

Jerry brought an end to the moment.

"How'd yew squids party all night an' keep them fuckin' white's clean?"

"We didn't. All the recruitin' poster pictures were taken when we were on the way *inta* town. Not comin' back. America's mother's couldn'a handled the comin' back pictures."

"Wuz it hard ta git the blood out'a them whites?" Jerry.

"What blood?"

"From when a Marine'd whip y'ur ass."

"Wouldn't fuckin' know, Jerry. Never came across a jarhead who could whip my ass."

"Shiiiit," he hissed and continued up the street.

Homer and I exchanged quick grins before hurrying after him.


As we were coming out of the third dive a raspy voice called out.

"Boys! Hey, boys!"

We turned and found an older, emaciated looking black man in dirty slacks, a wrinkled, burgundy sport coat over a tee shirt, and a pair of scuffed, dusty, white loafers.

"Y'all boys lookin' fo' somethin' special," slurring through a sly little smile.

I poked Jerry.

"It's y'ur daddy! I thought ya had a speech defect, but I guess it's just inherited."

"Fuck yew, man," he snapped.

"Yeah, he's too tall to be Jerry's daddy," Homer.

"Damn good action at a *damn* good price, gentlemens," the old man continued. "Cos' ya five each an' no mo'. Bes' money y'all could be ta spendin' t'night," and cackled softly.

"I c'n git laid twice by myself f'r five bucks, ol' man," Jerry growled.

"Two bucks!" bargaining. "Beautiful youuuung womens at fair prices in a place ya ain't neber gwan'a fin' by yo'se'f. Beeeauuu'ful young 'uns. An' clean. Rooms upstairs be free if'n ya spends more'n ten dolla's on drinks fo' the lady. O' ya c'n gib da man five up front an' git righ' to it."

"Let's go," Jerry, still not impressed.

"Dey be strip dancin'," eyes wide. "All da way down. Sometime it be right on yo' table. Fo' nuffin' extree."

"C'mon, Jerry," I said. "Y'ur own daddy wouldn't lie to ya would he?"

Jerry pointed at the old man.

"He ain't no diff'r'nt than any'a these other motherfuckers standin' aroun' tryin' ta git ya ta come in an' watch a bunch'a hags slap their saggy tits all over the place," leaning forward and squinting at the old man. "There ain't a bitch in this shittin' town under sixty, is there?"

The old man broke into a deep laugh, stooped over, put his hands on his knees, and shook his head. He looked up at Jerry.

"Whut if'n y'all boys keeps y'alls money 'til we gits dere. If'n ya ain' happy...ya leaves," straightening up. "If'n ya stay mo'n ten minutes...ya pays me two dolla's each. Sho beat walkin' yo ass off'a night an' gittin' nowheres."

We looked at each other.

"How far's it from here," I asked.

"Fi'e minute walk. No mo'."

"Why not?" Homer.

Jerry, cussing under his breath, reluctantly agreed.

About five minutes later, after navigating several smaller streets, we entered a short unpaved alley ending in a large, dirt square the size of two football fields laid side to side. Cabarets, saloons, bars, taverns, strip clubs, sleazy flop hotels, and tattoo parlors surrounded the vehicle packed square.

"So, ol' man," Jerry snarled. "ya don't b'lieve we could'a found a place this damn big by ourselves?"

The old man shook his head and laughed.

"Sho y'all could'a, but by da time ya did, y'all'd be dead broke an' too damn drunk ta git it up," cackling like Jerry.

We walked around the square. It was impressive—half naked,

nice looking, young ladies dancing in windows all over the place and inviting us in. Others, standing in front of their places of business, were flashing tit shots and grabbing at our crotches as we walked past. Jerry was sneering, cackling, and grabbing back at the girls as we worked our way down the south side. The old man stopped in front of a place with no windows and no girls out front.

## JUAREZ GENTLEMEN'S CLUB

was painted in large gold letters on a scarlet background above the door. It looked a little rundown.

"Dis be it," the old man announced.

"This is a fuckin' graveyard compared ta the other places aroun' here," Jerry.

"Ten minutes. Ten minutes an' all'a y'all leaves din ya owes me nuffin'. If'n y'all stays din one'a y'all comes out an' pays me six dolla's."

"C'mon," as I grabbed Jerry's arm. "What'a we got ta lose?"

Homer wasn't waiting for Jerry to make up his mind. He'd already stepped to the door of the place and was holding it open for us. Creedence Clearwater was playing inside.

Jerry, mumbling to himself again, followed me through the door.

"Ten minutes, " Jerry warned me, "then we're gunna go lookin' f'r some *real* action."

Homer shut the door.

We were facing a heavy, red curtain inside a small carpeted foyer. Glowing felt paintings of life-size, big breasted, redheaded caucasian women hung on the walls either side of us. Jerry eased the curtain back and peeked in. He looked back over his shoulder at us then stepped through the curtains.

Homer and I were right behind him.

We entered a smoky, dimly lit room about forty or fifty feet square. A quarter of the room was occupied by a raised, centrally located stage. A sturdy brass pole rose from its center to the ceiling where it was swallowed up by a dome of plush velvet folds. Surrounding the canopy were a series of red, blue, yellow, and green stage lights that slowly dimmed then gradually intensified again. Wispy layers of cigarette smoke, catching the soft glow of the changing hues, leisurely undulated over the polished wood floor. A foot wide counter ran around the perimeter of the stage with the exception of a narrow break used to access the dance area. Shining brass handrails flanked the steps. Chairs were packed around the platform. A handful of men sat, elbows resting on the ledge, drinking and staring at the empty stage.

On the left side of the room, a narrow aisle separated the chairs from a second raised platform a little higher than the stage. A brass rail ran the length of the raised section with a break at the far end for entering the area. A string of tables filled the platform. Several men, speaking in hushed tones occupied a few of the tables. They kept glancing at the stage impatiently. The remainder of the floor space in the room was packed with tables. A thirty foot service bar was built into the right wall of the room. Three bartenders were furiously making drinks, pouring wine, or popping caps off beer bottles.

A curtain on the wall across the room suddenly ripped open as a lady rushed through carrying a tray covered with empty glasses and mugs. The splash of light from the room on the other side of the curtains was like a flashbulb going off in our faces. The girl, wearing only panties and a bra, dashed towards the bar, dodging tables and chairs as she went. She set the tray down and rattled off an order in Mexican. Every inch of elastic in her panties was pressing a paper bill, folded length wise, to her flesh. She harvested about half of them, handing the fist full of bills to one of the bartenders who then stuffed the money into one of ten or more cigar boxes on a shelf behind the bar. The Stones were coming from the other side of the curtain.

"Buenas nochas," a voice on our left.

We turned and faced the voice.

"I am Hector Gonzalez," extending his hand. "Welcome to the Juarez Gentlemen's Club," smiling generously.

Jerry tore his eyes off the waitress to shake Mr. Gomez's hand.

"How ya doin'? This is Homer an' 'at's Gil," pointing to Homer and then me.

Mr. Gonzalez bowed slightly then shook our hands enthusiastically. He was a short, stout man smartly dressed in a light toned leisure suit. It was impossible to tell exactly what color the suit was in the slowly changing stage lights. His dark hair was slicked back, his thin moustache neatly trimmed.

"You the manager?" I asked.

"I am the *owner*," proudly. "I make a special effort to greet all the customers and explain the house rules," pausing to light my cigarette for me.

His accent had a snappy classiness to it. Sophisticated.

"Enjoy yourselves," Hector. "The ladies, however, do expect to be treated as the ladies you will, no doubt, find them to be. Should efforts you make to become more...*familiar* with a lady be considered less than appropriate and the lady asks you to behave yourself, I suggest you do so. This *is* a gentleman's establishment. If you feel you can not conduct yourselves as such then you should consider going elsewhere," continuing to smile graciously. As Hector finished, he pulled his suit coat back far enough to expose the handle of what appeared to be a large magnum handgun in a waist belt holster.

"All the bartenders and security personnel are in *complete* agreement with me regarding the treatment of the ladies and are as prepared as I to enforce the house rules," letting the coat fall back into place.

"Damn good rules," Jerry. "Keeps the fuckin' riffraff out. I like a place like 'at. Makes it easier ta relax."

"Exactly," Mr. Gonzalez smiling and nodding.

The curtain tore open again. A tall, nasty looking redhead in a garter belt, mesh hose, fancy corset, and high heels backed through the opening. Her flesh was snow white. She spun around and ran the table obstacle course on her way to the bar. Her long red hair flowed to her knees. She chattered an order in some kind of European accent and began gathering the bills from her outfit.

"Somebody git the ol' man his six bucks," Jerry ordered, eyes glued on the waitress.

"Did an elderly black gentleman escort you here?" Hector.

"Yeah," I answered. "He's out side waitin' ta be paid. Two bucks a piece."

"Don't worry about Marcus. He's already been compensated. He sometimes becomes…greedy. I'll take care of it for you," stepping to one side while graciously extending his arm in the direction of the curtain. "Don't forget our floor show at midnight…about twenty minutes from now. We have a live band every Tuesday, Wednesday, and Thursday night. Vaya con Dios," and winked.

We strolled past the stage. The longed haired white lady, balancing a tray of drinks on one hand, pulled the curtain back for us with her free hand, and then curtsied with a smile.

*Damn. She smells good.*

We entered the room.

*Christ! This place is as big as a gym.*

One mirrored corner served as a dance floor. A topless woman in a G-string was riding the lap of a drunken soldier at a table to our right. A pile of one dollar bills was building in the center of the table. She looked over her shoulder at the pile and slowed to a stop. One of the soldiers threw a dollar on the pile and the rider was off again, sliding furiously up and down over the man's lap.

"My kind'a gen'lemen," Jerry.

"My kind'a ladies," I added.

A waitress in a see-through teddy led us to a table close to a wide, red carpeted staircase. We ordered beers and sat back to take it all in.

Somewhere around eight or ten ladies, wearing different styles of lingerie and under things were scurrying around the room. They darted from table to table swapping fresh drinks for empty glasses. They would hesitate at each table and allow the patron's to stuff money into their outfits. It looked as if anywhere was a fair place to make a deposit. The ladies would slip between the curtains to return several minutes later with a tray of fresh drinks, bills missing from the more popular deposit sites.

A another set of ladies sat at the tables drinking and laughing it up with the customer's. The girls were dressed in everything from hot pants and hose to evening gowns. Four girls, wearing panties or nothing at all, were performing various routines at tables throughout the room—dancing, riding laps, squatting over beer bottles to pick them up.

*Not as nasty as the places overseas...but it's close.*

"See 'at?" Jerry, pointing at a bottle lady. "I knew a bitch overseas 'at could sign her name with a pen 'at'a way," his brows raised. "When I turned nineteen, all my buddies chipped in an' got her for me f'r a whole night."

"Ya have her autograph y'ur forehead?" I asked.

Jerry, seriously distracted, hadn't heard me.

"C'n ya b'lieve this shit, man?" Jerry drooled.

"This *is* pretty damn colorful," I answered. "And it sounds like they've got some good songs on the jukebox. I like it here."

Jerry emptied his pocket onto the table. Homer and I did the same.

Our waitress returned. She stood beside Jerry, bending a little at the waist to reach across the table and give Homer his beer. The waitress repeated the move as she gave me mine. With each delivery her butt came to within inches of Jerry's face.

"Damn!" Jerry cried out. "How the fuck ya say 'I wan'a kiss 'at sweet ass' in Mexican?"

The waitress reached for the money on the table, snatched a dollar bill from the community pile, and then bent over, offering her butt to Jerry. Homer and I got a free tit shot while Jerry kissed each cheek.

"You are a gud keesser."

"How much f'r a Frenchie?" Jerry snickered.

"Don't talk dirty!" she laughed.

Jerry took his time planting another dollar bill in the crotch of her teddy bottoms.

She curtsied and was gone.

"I'm fuckin' in love," Jerry, eyes wide. "No shit," looking around the room. "I'm in love with ever' fuckin' one uv 'em."


A soldier and a girl descended the stairs to our right and headed back to a crowded table. All the men, howling like wolves, toasted him as the lady took the hand of one of the other young men at the table and led him back to the stairs. His buddies whooped and hollered.

" 'at's buddies, man," Jerry cackled. "*Sharin'* shit. 'at's whud it's all about."


We had two dollars and some change left when we finally got back to the motel. It was going on 2:00. We passed by the pickup as we made our way through the parking lot. It was sitting in the last row of spaces facing south toward the twinkling lights of Juarez.

"The dumbass used up two spaces," Jerry grumbled. "We bes' move it," and headed for the truck.

Homer grabbed Jerry's arm. Jerry jerked free. He was about to say something when Homer pointed at the rear window of the cab. Somebody was inside, sitting in the driver's seat, leaning against the door. We quietly slipped up the passenger side of the truck and looked in. Danny was asleep. Hope, cuddled up against his mass, was holding the arm he'd draped over her shoulder.

"Ain't tha..."

Homer slapped his hand over Jerry's mouth and dragged him away from the truck.

"Shhh," Homer.

Jerry nodded. Homer let go.

We went to our room and flipped a coin to determine who would sleep on the floor. I lost. Several minutes after lights out, Jerry started mumbling.

"C'n ya b'lieve 'at dancer? I should'a paid Gomez ta tie me ta tha' pole, man. Damn. Ol' Hector's got some nice stuff in 'at place. An' a variety'a makes. I done foun' myself a home down here, boys. Whud'a ya think?" raising his voice. "Wan'a go back ta Hector's t'morrow after work?"

Homer was already snoring. I was too tired to respond.

"Fuckin' bunch'a pansy-asses," Jerry grumbled.

\*\*\*

Danny laid his body, face down, across the hood of the truck and began tapping his fingers.

"Two dollars?" in disbelief without raising his head.

"An' some change," I reminded him.

"Thirty-four cents," Homer, shaking the change in his hand.

Danny slowly peeled himself from the hood then leaned back against the fender. He crossed his arms over his chest, pursed his lips, and looked down at the ground. He didn't move for over a minute. Danny finally pulled a small notebook from his hip pocket and a pencil from his shirt pocket. Using the hood as a desk, Danny scribbled away for several minutes then spun around.

"Listen," sounding disgusted. "Here's the deal, the *revised* deal. Forget the original plan. It was," shaking his head, "seriously, seriously flawed. It failed to address a significant reality. That was my fault. The new plan will correct my oversight."

Silence.

"Here's what we're gunna do," looking down at the notebook. "We'll pay ourselves seventy-five dollars a day, in cash, every day. We can do that with what's left of the down payment," looking up from the notebook. "If you guys want to spend every goddamn dollar you make, every goddamn day...fine. Go ahead. We'll divvy it up as we go along so I don't end up paying for your blowjobs."

"An'," Jerry squinted, "we still git our twenty percent uv the second five thousan' when we're done?"

"Yeah," Danny. "And you can run through your share of that too if you can find a whore who's willing to let you run a tab."

We exchanged glances then nodded in agreement.

"Ya sure this is all right with ya?" I asked.

"What other choice do I have?" throwing his hands into the air. "I'm not about to leave here broke and you three aren't planning to leave here sober."

We looked down at the ground.

"I'm planning on making as much as I can on this damn thing. Setting it up like this, you get what you want, I get what I want, and no one gets pissed. Sound fair?"

"Ain't ya gunna ask Hope?" Jerry.

"If she's not happy with the arrangement...I'll kill myself. Satisfied?"

"Don't go killin' y'urself, man," Jerry, serious as a heart beat.

"He's kiddin', Jerry," shaking my head.

Jerry glanced at Danny then looked at Homer. Homer nodded.

"Damn, Danny," Jerry frowned. "Ya shouldn't be kiddin' about shit like 'at."

GLYNN E. THOMPSON

Danny looked off into the distance then cleared his throat.

"This is how it'll all work. I'll cross the border, every fucking day, and draw it from the bank. I'll find a bank branch downtown somewhere," frustrated, pissed.

"T'day's Sund'y," Jerry, quietly.

"If we pay the hotel in Juarez for only one night. We have enough cash on hand to manage until tomorrow. I'm gunna go get Hope," and stormed away from the truck.

As soon as Danny was out of sight, Jerry slapped Homer on the arm, then slapped me. Jerry gave us both the Eyeball and began cackling.

"C'n ya b'lieve 'at shit?" Jerry, breaking into a little jig.

I threw my head back and joined in.

"I mean," pausing in his celebration, "ain't no way none uv us c'n go through seventy-five dollars a day down here, man, but" raising his brows to the max, "it's nice ta know it's there...if ya know whud I mean," and began jigging again.

We crossed over into Juarez without incident at 8:30 and then drove south through town. Jerry, Homer, and I were in the van, following Danny and Hope. On the southern outskirts of town, Danny pulled into the dusty, potholed parking lot of a run down, single story, adobe motel. The son of a bitch didn't even have a name. It was one long, crumbling, twelve unit structure sitting perpendicular to the blacktopped road. The sunbleached lime doors had probably been green at one time.

Fifty yards away, across a gravel lot, a deteriorating adobe baked in the morning heat. It was the only remaining building between the motel and the nothing that stretched to the southern horizon. "Oriental Pagoda Cabaret" was painted in red-gone-pink block letters on the wall of the building. Among all the other messages written on the wall, there were two in English.

HAPPY HOUR

followed by a splashed patch of black paint.

The second one advertised nude dancing everynight.

A large, sloppy arrow painted on a piece of ragged plywood was propped against a mangled, rusty, fifty gallon drum. The arrow pointed to door 12. "Officia" had been scribbled in black marker above the number on the door.

We got out and met Danny in front of the van.

"Ya lost?" Jerry.

"Hell no I'm not lost," Danny snapped. "This is JD's idea of a motel."

"So," as I looked the place over, "this is where ol' JD'd planned on stayin' f'r two months doin' the windows by himself?"

"It's got everything he would have wanted," Homer. "A bed, a bar full of naked females within walking distance, and all for just four bucks a night."

Danny walked to the truck and stuck his head in the window. Returning, he told us he and Hope were going get a place in El Paso since he was going to have to cross over every day anyway.

Jerry snickered.

"How about lettin' me throw in on 'at 'un an' we c'n make it a three-way?"

"Come on, Jerry," Danny. "This is Hope we're talking about."

Jerry tugged at his nose then scratched his ear.

"Yeah. Y're right," swatting at a swarm of sweat gnats buzzing around his face. "I wuz jus' jokin' aroun', man. This ain't a very nice place f'r a lady," pointing at the motel. "Pro'bly be best she don't stay here. Pro'bly got rats an' no tellin' whud else."

"Maybe you guys should do the same thing," Danny suggested.

Homer, Jerry, and I looked over to the cabaret and quickly talked it over. We decided to give JD's shithole a try for a few nights.

"After all," Jerry pointed out, "We knew this wudn't gunna be no picnic. We're down here ta make some money, not throw it away on fancy digs," sarcastically referring to Danny's earlier lecture.

"Then let's check you in," Danny, ignoring Jerry.

We walked to room 12 and knocked on the door. Hope got out of the truck and stood in the shade of the adobe. An elderly Mexican man with thick, graying hair pulled the door open and stepped outside. The man was wearing sweat pants, leather sandals and no shirt. He was sturdy looking, just beginning to develop a beer gut.

"Buenos dias," as I extended my hand. "Hablo Ingles?"

The old man looked at me awkwardly and squinted.

"What makes you think I *don't*, you presumptuous son of a bitch," with only a trace of a Mexican accent. "I'm a goddamn U.S. citizen," he growled. "You with JD from Lubbock?"

"Yes, sir," I nodded.

"I *like* that," sneering. "Sir. Anglos with respect for…their elders. I like that. You wanted five rooms?"

"Three. For tonight," Danny.

"What? JD told me five rooms for ten or twelve days! That's why I gave him the discount," looking toward the vehicles. "Where's JD? He'll straighten this shit out."

"JD's not coming," Danny, hurriedly.

"Wha'd he do? Go and drink himself to death?"

Danny glanced at us, then broke the news.

"JD died a few weeks ago. Heart attack."

The old man's head jerked a few times. He'd been caught off guard, but recovered quickly.

"That bastard! He still owes me over a hundred dollars for girls he had when he was down here at Christmas. Swindling son of a bitch," grumbling as he moved into the shade of the building. "Last time I ever give credit to a goddamn Anglo," turning away from us to stare out at the road.

"So, how much is it without the discount?" Danny.

"How much is what?" he mumbled.

"The rooms. How much without the discount?"

He swirled around and glared at Danny.

"I can't talk about that now, goddammit! Can't you see I have something on my mind?" the accent more pronounced.

He stepped from the shade and tossed a hand into the air.

"Me and JD go back a long way, goddammit! Why the hell didn't you tell me this when you called last week? Why did you lie to me about it?" waving a fist in Danny's face.

Danny stepped back. Jerry took a step closer to Danny.

"I should kick your goddamn ass!" the man's eyes blazing.

Homer stepped to Danny's side.

"I...I didn't realize you two were friends," Danny managed while closely watching the crazed old man.

"FRIENDS? I said we went back a long way! I never said he was a friend! Friends don't go running tabs on your girls then go and die to beat the goddamn bill," returning to the shade.

He thought a few seconds, head down, sweat forming on his leathery, brown back.

"Four dollars," slowly rubbing his forehead. "A deals a deal. Four dollars a night."

Danny looked at us. We nodded.

"We'll take it," Danny.

"And no tabs on anything!" raising his voice and shaking his finger at us. "Not the liquor, not the girls, not the food. All cash," and stomped into his room.

He stomped back out and handed Danny three keys.

"Twelve dollars," grumbling. "Check out time is 11:00...11:30. Sometime around there. My name is Albert Munoz. I'm the owner of the motel *and* the cabaret over there," pointing at the other adobe building. "So don't fuck with me."

Danny paid up. We returned to the vehicles.

Hope left the shade to join us.

"Well?"

"They're staying, we're going," Danny.

"Did ya explain ever'thang to 'em?" Hope, embarrassed. "Tha' we ain't gunna be..."

"There ain't nothin' ta explain," Jerry. "It kind'a cuts all uv us ta the core ta have ya thinkin' we'd question y'ur...y'ur..."

"Sense'a morality," I offered.

"Yeah," Jerry pointing at me. "Y'ur morality."

Hope looked up shyly.

"Thanks, Jerry," smiling sweetly and brushing a loose strand of hair from her face. "I guess 'at wuz whut I was wantin' ta know."

" 'at's cool," Jerry. "B'sides, Hope, ever'body an' his brother knows Danny's queer as a three sided cue ball."

Hope lunged at Jerry, pounding his back as he doubled over.

"I thought yew wuz bein' serious yew...yew...Grecian!" Hope shrieked while pummeling and kicking him mercilessly.

"Cretin," I corrected her.

"Cretin!" she screamed.

Jerry broke away and hobbled to the other side of the truck. Hope was in hot pursuit. Danny latched onto her as she passed by him.

"Bitch," Jerry.

"Cretin," Hope.

We looked at the rooms and dumped our personal gear. We had the first three rooms off the road. They weren't bad. A few roaches. Some mouse turds in places accessible only with a serious floor sweeping effort, but, for the most part, pretty clean. Cleaner than me and Homer's old place. Hope was laughing in the room next door. Bed springs were squeaking loudly. She came running into my room, jumped onto the bed, then began bouncing up and down on her knees. My bed was relatively quiet. Jerry entered the room.

"Homer's is the noisy one", Hope. "His room's b'tween yew an' Jerry's so, when Homer finds a girlfriend," giggling, "he's gunna keep the two'a y'all up all night. Did yew brang a pi'ture'a Bobbie?" turning to me.

"Damn straight he did," Jerry. "I paid him five dollars ta lemme keep it f'r the night," cackling.

"I ain't never talkin' ta yew again!" Hope, throwing a pillow at him. "Not *ever* again!"

The truck honked.

"Let's go!" Danny.


We arrived at the church at about 11:30. Two cars were parked in the graveled lot. We got out and looked around.

"It's Sunday," Homer. "Where's everybody at?"

"I don't know. I'm not Catholic," Danny.

We looked around for someone to check in with.

"The guy in charge'll be wearin' like a crown kind'a hat," Jerry informed us. "One'a them tall lookin' things."

"I don't think so," Danny.

" 'at's whut they're wearin' all the time in the pictures ya see."

"Those're Popes 'r Bishops 'r somethin'," I told him. "Ya won't see anything like 'at hangin' around in Juarez."

"His name's Father Addison," Danny, as we entered a garden area on the east side of the church.


The garden separated a second, single story, adobe structure from the chapel building. The chapel was an old, two-story, adobe. From the garden we could see eight tall stained glass windows. They were around three feet wide by twelve feet high, gradually arching to a peak at the top. The windows had three strips of thin borders, light violet on the outside, pale green in the middle, and light blue on the inside. The borders surrounded a field of amber diamonds. Each diamond looked to be about six inches high and four inches across. A round medallion, about a foot in diameter, was centered in the fourth panel of each window, seven or so feet above the sill. The medallions were kiln fired, painted scenes from the bible. None of the painted pieces were broken. The panels were buckling where the wire ties had either rusted away from the support rods or torn free of the lead line they had been soldered to. Several diamonds were broken in each window.

"Piece of cake," Danny. "Right?" turning to us. "You guys can handle this, can't you?"

"No sweat," Homer.

A heavy wooden door opened. A tall, blond, athletic looking man wearing black slacks, a black short sleeve shirt, and a priest's collar entered the garden.

"May I help you?"

"We're from J.D. Grubb in Lubbock, Texas," Danny, approaching the priest. "We're here to fix the windows."

"Father Jay Addison," and shook Danny's hand.

"Danny Wright," then turned towards us. "This is Hope, Homer, Jerry, and Gil," pointing at each of us in turn. "Mr. Grubb is ill and won't be joining us until later."

"I'm sorry to hear that."

The priest shook hands with each of us then stepped back.

"Mr. Wright," motioning to the door, "this way, please."

"I'll be right back," Danny.

The priest said we could look inside the church and pointed at a heavy door at the rear of the chapel. He smiled warmly at Hope, and then followed Danny into the building.

We moved in single file toward the door the priest had pointed out.

"Ya see the way he looked at Hope?" Jerry snickered.

"Jerry!" Hope whispered harshly. "He's a *priest!*"

"So? A priest don't git horny?"

"It don't make a diff'r'nce. It ain't right ta talk 'at'a way about preachers 'r priests an' people like 'em."

We entered the church and looked around. All the pews had been removed. A set of scaffolding in the center of the room rose to a freshly stuccoed ceiling. Canvas throws covered the floor. The statuary behind the pulpit was covered in large sheets of stucco splattered and paint speckled clear plastic. The tallest statue was a white robed, bigger than life Jesus standing with arms open, bleeding palms facing out. I walked over to Jesus and looked under the plastic.

"Sorry about Jerry makin' fun'a that priest," I apologized to the statue. "He didn't mean anything by it."

"Dammit," Jerry. "It's one thing ta knock on a priest, but, man, don't go slammin' on Jesus. 'at's dang'rous, man. 'member the deal we got? I don't say nigger an' yew don't go jackin' with Jesus?"

I dropped the plastic and turned to Jerry.

"Sorry," seriously. "It slipped my mind f'r a moment."

"Damn," he mumbled and walked away.

"They must be renovating the whole place," Homer.

"Makes it easier on us with all the tarps down," as I turned to Hope. "You mind gettin' somethin' ta write on from the truck? Me an' Jerry'll inventory the west side. You an' Homer c'n do the east side."

Danny was gone about an hour, long enough for us to complete the repair inventory. Father Addison had told Danny the Catholic Church was refurbishing three chapels in the Juarez area. Services weren't being conducted at any of the sites we'd be working at. We wouldn't have to worry about working around Mass schedules. The chapel was open around the clock, with a security guard at night. We could work whenever we wanted for as long as we wanted. The priest was going to let us keep all our supplies in the chapel.

Danny took our inventory and checked it against the one JD'd done when he'd bid the job in December. Both inventories were close enough to not alter the bid. We all agreed to work through lunch the first day to get things moving along.

By early afternoon we were unloaded, had the saw horse tables up, and the jigs set to rip out four inch amber strips for the diamonds. The afternoon and early evening was spent cutting the diamonds out and carefully "leafing"—raising—the lead faces away from the broken pieces in the windows. At 7:00 Danny called it a day.

"Hope and I still have to find a place to stay," stretching.

Hope glared angrily at Jerry.

"An' don'ch yew go sayin' nothin' mean!"

I slugged his arm.

"Yeah. Ya pervert."

"Go ta hell," Jerry.


Danny spoke to the security guard then paid each of us sixty eight-dollars dollars a piece for the day.

"What's this?" Jerry, upset. "We're s'posed ta be gittin' *seventy* a day."

Danny hitched his thumb at the guard.

"He said he needed coffee money to make sure he stayed awake."

"The motherfucker," Jerry scowled.

The guard smiled and waved.

"Is everything out of the van and the truck?" Danny.

"I'll go check," Hope.

"Which one you want," I asked Danny. "The van 'r the truck?"

"We git the van," Jerry.

"Hoping to save on a bump room?" Danny.

"Ever' penny counts," Jerry sneered.

"What time in the morning?" Homer.

"Here's the deal," Danny crossing his arms and scratching his chin. "The banks won't open until 9:00. I can't be here before 9:30, so let's do this. Hope and I'll start the clock at 9:00 in the morning and go until 9:00 tomorrow night. You guys put in twelve hours for the day whenever you want, but everybody's *got* to get twelve a day or we won't stay on schedule."

Jerry's eyes popped open.

"Hell, yeah. 'at's a damn good schedule."

Homer and I agreed.

Hope reentered the chapel.

"Ever'thangs out'a the truck an' the van."

"Okay," Danny waved. "See everybody tomorrow."

Hope gave Homer and me a hug.

"I ain't gunna hug yew," she told Jerry, "I'm still mad at yew."

"I don't want one'a y'ur damn hugs."

Hope turned and walked away, one foot delicately floating in front of the other—the Hope glide.

"Liberty call! Liberty call!" using my cupped hands as a megaphone. "Liberty to expire on board t'morrow mornin' at zero any fuckin' time we want it to."

Hope came prancing back into the chapel, arms at her sides, hands bent at the wrists so her fingers pointed straight out. Her shoulders swayed with each bounce. She hurried over to Jerry, gave him a big hug, and then pranced back out the door.

*Damn. 'at felt good.*

Jerry, having been taken completely off guard, scratched his chest, collected himself, and then turned towards Homer and me.

"Nice hug," Jerry noted, nodding his head. "Needs a li'l work. Good thing I gotta few days ta...*tutor* the sweet young thing," cackling. "If ya know whud I mean," then darted his tongue in and out of his mouth like a lizard.

And with that, he had repaired whatever it was he thought Hope had damaged with her show of forgiving affection.

We got into the van and headed back to the rooms.

"We'll wash up, eat, an' then what?" I asked.

"That'll make it somewhere around 8:30 or 9:00," Homer.

"I'm goin' back ta Hector's," Jerry. "Whut yew do's up ta yew."

"Hector's sounds good," Homer.

"I'll tag along," I said.

"Tag along?" Jerry, snickering and shooting me the Eye. "Is 'at whud he said? Tag along? Shiiit, man. Yew might be taggin' f'r a while, but yew ain't shittin' nobody," digging in his ear with a finger. "Yew'll be beefin' somethin' b'fore midnight. If ya make it *that* long."

We cleaned up then regrouped in the parking lot where we decided to eat at the cabaret. We entered a huge room. More like a banquet hall. A forty-foot bar was centered along the left wall. Paintings of nudes decorated all the walls. Paper Chinese lanterns dangled from the ceiling among a confusion of flickering Christmas tree lights. Fake palm trees, also strung with twinkling lights, were scattered throughout the room. Worn, gray paths in the green painted floor spidered among tables surrounded by rickety bamboo chairs. Dim runway lights outlined a carpeted area at the far end of the room. A door was centered directly behind the carpeting. "Abbey Road" blared from a jukebox located near the dance floor. Two girls were sitting at a table next to the carpeted area. Their heads rested on folded arms. They appeared to be sleeping. Other than Alberto and the two girls, the place was empty.

"SHOW TIME!" Al, from behind the bar. "Come in! Come in!" exhibiting a one hundred eighty degree turn in attitude from this morning.

A short, oriental girl with bleached blond hair done in ponytails reaching to her waist strolled to the jukebox. She was wearing a small, tight tank top, a tiny pair of shorts, and white, knee high go-go boots. The girl reached behind the jukebox and fiddled with something. "Yummy, Yummy, Yummy I Got Love In My Tummy" preempted "Abbey Road". She flicked a switch on the wall. A set of recessed, blue strobes spotlighted the carpeted area. She tossed her ponytails over her shoulders and broke into a listless dance number.

We strolled to the bar, sat down on the creaking bamboo stools and ordered beers.

"Twenty-five cents a beer," Al, reaching into a cooler under the bar.

I caught all three.

The other girl, a little taller and not as athletically built as the dancer, slowly got to her feet, stretched, and then began drifting back our way. She was wearing a red, tight fitting Chinese working girl's evening dress slit up both sides to her hips. Her straight, dark hair didn't quite touch the top of the dress's high, stiff collar.

"Whu's on the supper menu?" Jerry, scrutinizing the approaching figure.

"You want to eat?" Al, somewhat surprised.

"We hadn't eaten all day," I answered.

"Not now!" Al yelled at the girls. "Let them eat first."

The dancing girl stopped, hit the light switch, fiddled with the back of the jukebox and returned to her seat as "Dock of the Bay" filled the room. The lady approaching us made a slow turn around a table then headed back to the dance area, her hips slipping from side to side as she slithered away.

Al tapped a plastic stirring rod on the bar to regain our attention then pointed to a set of shelves behind him. An assortment of cans were neatly stacked on the bottom shelf—Spam, canned beef, Vienna sausages, chicken, some stews and soups, tamales, chili. Everything a hungry man could want if he wanted it out of a can.

"What's it going to be?" he asked, sounding a little put out.

"Got any C-rats?" Jerry, sarcastically.

"What was that?" Al, leaning toward Jerry.

"Nothin'. C'n ya warm 'at shit up?"

"Of course. You don't think I would charge a dollar American for a goddamn cold meal, do you?"

Al was putting some rudder on for another attitude course change.

"Anything else come with it?" Homer.

"A slice of bread."

I asked for a salad.

"Goddammit!" Al barked. "People normally come here to get laid, not to eat a goddamn gourmet meal. It's a deal I made with all the fancy restaurants in town…their waitresses don't give blowjobs and I don't serve anything you have to set fire to at the table."

Jerry looked around the place.

"It's a damn good thing I don't want either one. This place is a fuckin' graveyard, man."

"Sunday is *always* a slow night," growing more agitated.

Homer pointed at the cans.

"I'll take a tin of Spam with a can of chili on top of it."

"Fry the Spam or broil it?" shutting his eyes.

"I though' ya said this wudn' a *fancy* rest'rant," Jerry.

"Fry it, please," Homer.

"I'll take a can'a tamales," placing my order.

Jerry wanted a can of beef.

"Ya got ketchup don'ch ya?" he asked.

"What kind of restaurant would this be without ketchup?" Al.

"Where's the head?" Jerry, looking around.

"Over there," Al, without indicating where "there" was.

Jerry turned to Homer and me and danced his brows. He was having a ball with Al.

"Al?" Jerry, dripping civility, "If ya don't min' I'll take another beer, please. 'at last 'un wuz simply marv'lous. I think it wuz the way ya opened it 'r somethin'. I cain't wait ta see whut comes'a that can'a beef in the hands uv a master cook like y'urself," then headed to the men's room. It was a good thing he did. One more comment and I think Al would have lost complete control.

I got comfortable and gave the place a closer going over.

"Nothin' but oriental ladies workin' here?" I asked.

"The finest imported delicacies you can find in Mexico," mumbling. "And the cheapest," as he slid our canned dinners to the end of the bar where a hot plate, a toaster oven, and a large sink were located.

Jerry returned and we ate. We bought a round of beer, moved to a table, and stretched out. The ponytail went to the carpet and began wiggling to "This Diamond Ring". The second girl stayed put.

"Damn," Jerry yawned loudly. "If Al had some hotter lookin' stuff floatin' aroun'...I b'lieve I could jus' settle in here f'r the night."

We listened to the music, watched the uninspired gyrations of the dancer, sipped our beers and, after obtaining Al's permission, smoked a joint.

"Shit, man," Jerry, leaning forward and rubbing his eyes. "If I don't git movin', I'm gunna go ta sleep," then emptied his bottle. "Let's git out'a here," and stood up.

Homer slowly got to his feet. I remained seated.

Jerry looked at me.

"Ya wan' us ta carry ya, Gil?"

"Nah. I'm gunna sack out early an' start fresh t'morrow."

"Ohhh, now ain' tha' sweet?" Jerry, starting in on me. "Ol' Gil's gunna hang aroun' the house thinkin' about Bobbie an' poppin' shame-on-me's all night."

"Nothin' wrong with 'at," I shot back.

"An' yew still think whud *I'm* doin' is?" brows lifted.

"I didn't say that."

" 'at's whut ya meant."

"You can fuckin' read my mind, now? I just wan'a hang around here a while an' then hit the sack. That's all. You wan'a put any more into it than 'at...go right ahead."

"That's no problem," Homer. "If we had any brains that's what we'd be doing."

"Whut?" Jerry. "Yew think I ought'a sit aroun' here all night gettin' Shauna-ons?"

GLYNN E. THOMPSON

I shot him the bird. Homer pulled Jerry to the door.

"When ya wan'a go ta work t'morrow?" I asked.

"Wake us up at 6:00," Homer.

"7:00," Jerry.

Jerry broke free of Homer's grip, returned to the table, and then pulled a ten from his pocket.

"Hey! Al! Make sure dopey gits drunk an' laid t'night!" waving the bill in the air before placing it next to the ash tray. "Enjoy y'urself," then saluted me.

"Same to ya," saluting back.

Jerry cackled all the way out the door.


Al came over and sat down.

"Want to see a dance or maybe buy one of the girls a drink?"

He'd calmed down considerably.

"What's the name'a the one in the dress?"

"Mitsko. She's a little stuck up, but she's hot. She was one of JD's favorites this past Christmas," and lit a Swisher Sweet. "She's one wild ride," staring at Jerry's ten dollar bill. "Stays very busy. If she didn't have a habit, she could have bought this place by now. Especially if it was still as busy as it used to be."

"Hard times, huh?" not really interested.

"Yes. It's been better," sighing. "About six months ago Fort Bliss began cutting back. This place used to be a mad house every goddamn night. For three years I even ran a bus from the main bridge. Everything is slowing down now. It's been so bad some nights, I've had to grease a few of the girls myself to make sure they don't start squeaking."

"Seems like ya could find somebody ta take 'at job from ya pr'tty cheap."

"Did you know JD very well or did you just work for him?"

"Knew him pr'tty well. Not as well as Homer. They were tight. JD left ever'thing he had ta Homer."

Al looked over at me.

"What did that amount to, if you don't mind me asking?"

"Little bit'a money. Some pianos. The glass. A truck."

Al shook his head slowly.

"He would spend a fistful down here every Christmas and then again during his summer visit. Do you need another beer?" getting up.

"Yeah," and slid the ten over to him. "Take the ladies somethin' too."

Al started to motion for the girls.

"Send the drinks ta their table," I told him. "They don't have ta come over here if they don't feel like it. Ever'body deserves a night off."

"It's your dime," shrugging his shoulders.

He fixed the drinks and took them to the girls. They waved at me and smiled.

Al returned to my table.

"So, how often did JD come down here?" I asked.

"Twice a year. June or July in the summer and always at Christmas."

"How'd ya meet him?"

"Working in the oil fields around Midland. Right after the war. Around '46 or so. He'd been in the Army. Pacific."

"He was buried in his uniform."

"Good," nodding solemnly. "That's good," pausing for a moment. "Anyway, we became friends and started hanging out together. I had a chance to buy this place when an uncle of mine died so I jumped on it. It beat the shit out of rough necking. JD'd been hurt in the war. He wasn't holding up to the oil field work so he moved to Lubbock. He surveyed a little. Worked for a piano tuner. Learned how to repair old players and nickelodeons. Some of the fancy ones had broken colored glass in them so he taught himself how to fix the glass. Wasn't long before he was repairing churches and doing colored glass work for homes and restaurants."

"Y're still a U.S. citizen aren't ya?"

"Hell, yes," he barked. "One of these days the States will legalize prostitution, and when they do," snapping his fingers, "I'm going to have the first goddamn whore house in Carmel, California. You ever been to Carmel?"

"Once 'r twice when I was goin' to a military language school f'r six weeks in Monterey."

"Beautiful little place!" his accent flaring as he looked to heaven. "I'll be able to ask a goddamn decent, fair price on the girls and live like God intended a man to live. No more of these dollar blowjobs and two dollar quickies. You can't make a living that way," sounding disgusted.

"Did ya ever meet JD's wife, April?" I asked.

"Yes," Al nodded vigorously. "Was she at the funeral?"

"Yeah. What happened b'tween 'em?"

Al locked his fingers behind his head, leaned back, and looked up at the ceiling.

"She was still a kid. Sixteen or so. She married JD to get out of the house, not because she was ready to settle down. She ended up fucking every goddamn thing with pants on. Male or female. It took JD a while to admit it. Five years. Goddamn. She was," shaking his head slowly, "she was a beauty. He should have known better," pausing before continuing. "I lost touch with him while he was married to April," falling forward to lean on the table. "After the divorce he began to come down here again," spreading his arms and glancing around the room. "JD liked it here. He liked the girls and they liked him. He would fall in love with one of them. Take her to dinner. The movies. Shopping. Then he'd fall in love all over again with a different one the next time he'd come down. One thing for sure...Christmas won't be the same without JD. He was like Santa Claus to the girls. Santa Claus with a hard-on. I'd have a good time while he was down here too. We'd both stay drunk. I even gave him discounts on everything to make sure he'd keep coming back."

"Will the discounts be part of Homer's inheritance?" I joked.

"Inheritance?" sadly staring across the room. "I can't believe he's...that he's..." then shot to his feet. "Hell, no! No more discounts, no freebies from the girls. I'll fire them if I find out that shit's going on," and chugged his beer. "Nothing is free around here. Including those goddamn drinks you bought the girls," turning to the ladies up front. "Susie! Get to work! You think that damn drink was on the house? Mitsko! Don't you want to thank this gentleman for that goddamn drink?" then headed for the bar. "You want to buy them two more?" without turning around.

"Yeah," I yelled back before "Helter Skelter" completely drowned me out.

Susie cut loose on the carpet. Mitsko, all smile, dripping sex, approached the table.

"May I?" as she placed her hand on the back of the bamboo chair where Al had been sitting.

*Hot-ass perfume.*

I stood up and motioned to the chair.

"Thank you," nodding and tossing her head as she reached for my cigarettes. "Do you min'?"

"No, go right ahead," striking a match to light the cigarette for her.

Mitsko looked toward the dance floor where Susie was gyrating wildly.

"She do her nose. She be crazy now," then turned to me. "She dance jus' a fo' you. You tip big time o' maybe you no' go Heaven. Be safe...tip big, okay?"

If Mitsko had been tied in a gunny sack her accent alone would have given me a boner.

"I sure as shit don't wan'a go ta Hell," I said.

"I know. Dey no pussy in dere," laughing. "Wha' you name?"

"Gil."

"Mitsko," nodding her head as she took my hand and shook it gently.

Her hands were small and soft.

"You stay Al's?" she asked.

"Yeah. Be workin' in Juarez for two weeks."

"Two week?" her eyes brightening while scooting her chair closer to me. "Two week rong time."

"I suppose."

"You cou' fa' in ruve in two week," she teased.

"I c'n fall in love in two *minutes* if the moods right," I teased back.

"You maybe fa' in ruve wi'h me?" moving quickly from tease to flirt. "Big 'a discoun' you fa' in ruve two week straight," moving as quickly from flirt to business woman.

I honest-to-God wasn't interested in a hooker for two weeks. But, I was curious.

"How *much* 'a discoun'?" mimicking her.

"Onry be fifty dahra fo' ah night," eyes wide, like she was cutting me the deal of the century.

"Christ!" slamming my head to the table then looking up at her. "If I got ta lovin' ya that much, I'd just go ahead an' marry ya."

"Then it be *doub'o* discoun'!" followed by a short burst of laughter.

"Can't swing fifty a night for two weeks," shaking my head. "Don't get paid that much."

"Okay. Jus' a fo' you...two week specia'. Jus'a fo'ty dahra each a night," placing my hand in hers then slowly massaging between my fingers.

"Twenty," I countered. "Plus I'll take ya dinner ever' night."
*Just havin' a little fun here. Nothin' more'n 'at.*


Mitsko lifted my hand to her face, eased my middle finger all the way into her mouth, pulled it half way out as she sucked on it, then chewed it gently. She repeated the maneuver several times. She finally removed the finger, stroked it lightly, then leaned toward me to nibble my ear lobe.

"Twenty fi'e."

I was coming apart. I was aroused and hated myself for it.

*I don't want this. I really do not want this. If I did, I'd'a gone inta town with Jerry an' Homer.*

Her tongue slipped in and out of my ear. I wanted to push her away. Mitsko placed her hand on my crotch.

"Twenty fi'e an'a dinn'a. Tha' ve'y che'p," whispering in my ear while beginning to gently rub me.

On the carpet up front, Susie was easing her short-shorts from her hips. There was nothing underneath.

*This's gone far enough.*

Before I could speak she'd buried her tongue in my mouth and tightened her grip on me.

"Okay. Twenty-five," I shuddered.

*Goddammit!*

"I come back," Mitsko, turning me loose and hopping up.

She made a mad dash to the bar.


Al looked over at me while Mitsko spoke to him. They began to argue in hushed voices. Al pulled the towel from his shoulder, threw it to the floor, and then stormed around the end of the bar. He practically ran over to the table, threw himself into the chair, and then glared at me.

"Do you know how much I make on her in one night when it's busy?"

"When's the last time it was busy?"

"You want her for only twenty-five goddamn dollars?" painfully. "For *all* night? I'll only see fifteen of that and nothing on the goddamn room since you already have one. And what's it going to cost me while she's not here hustling drinks and pulling quickies?"

"That's all I got f'r this kind'a thing," not budging, hoping like hell he'd tell me ta fuck off and the whole moral dilemma'd be resolved.

Al planted his elbows on the tabletop and slammed his forehead into the heels of his hands. He held the position, breathing heavily for a good thirty seconds before raising his head and glaring at me again.

"She can't leave the bar before 11:00," Al insisted.

"9:00," doing my damnedest to keep it an offer Al couldn't possibly accept.

Al pounded his fists on the table.

"Goddammit! You pig-ass Anglo bastard! If she was your *daughter*, would you want her to work that cheap? That's not a *compassionate* price! You have *NO* compassion for these poor girls!" then immediately lowered his voice to continue. "It doesn't even start hopping around here until 8:00. Be goddamn reasonable," he hissed.

"Yeah," stretching and faking a yawn. "I kind'a noticed how much it starts hoppin' around here after 8:00."

"It's Sunday night!" wailing. "It's *never* busy on Sunday night!"

"Twenty-five, dinner, an' I pick her up at 9:00," repeating the offer.


I could tell by the look on his face that there was no way Al was going to let that fly.

*I hope Bobbie's happy as shit.*

"Deal," Al huffed.

"What?"

"It's a goddamn deal," angrily.

*Fuck me dead.*

"Twenty-five a night. Pick her up at 9:00," Al, repeating the terms. "Starting tonight."

*It wudn't like I had ta screw her. I could take her ta dinner, enjoy her company then send her home.*

"What time is it now?" I asked.

Al pulled a pocket watch out and looked at it.

"10:15."

*NO! I can't do this. I'll end up screwin' her.*

*I'm callin' it off.*

"Al," and looked toward the dance floor.

*Oh, Jesus!*

Susie, down to just go-go boots, was humping a chair back, head slowly rolling, eyes closed, face twisted in artificial ecstasy as a third or fourth or fifth phantom orgasm swept over her.

"What now?" Al, hostile as hell.

"Never mind."

*I am one spineless, sorry, weak-ass bastard.*

I pulled my money out and paid Al twenty-five dollars. Al stomped off grumbling to himself in Spanish. He called Mitsko over to the bar and spoke with her. When they were done, Mitsko nodded, turned, and then blew me a kiss.

*Dinner.*

*Conversation.*

*Send her home.*

Al made a round of drinks. Mitsko returned to our table with her Singapore Sling and my beer.

"You ca' me Mitsi now," sipping her drink.

*I feel like trash...from the waist up.*

***

The wind-up clock went off at ten minutes before 7:00. I found it on the floor next to the bed and killed it. Mitsi, on her back, stirred and kicked the sheet from her body. She'd slept in the nude.

It wasn't a bad body. It was, in its own way, pretty nice, but it wasn't exactly what the dress had led me to expect. She had stout, shapely legs and a little tummy—what you'd call a pecker belly. Her waist was pinched. Her breasts were full, but not big, although they were bigger than Bobbie's.

*Bobbie. Dammit. Goddammit.*

I got up pulled my pants on, went outside, and banged on Homer's door until he responded with a deep groan followed by a prolonged coughing spasm. I hit Jerry's door once.

"Yeah, Yeah. I heard ya," bellowing then breaking into a loud hacking fit.

I returned to my room. Mitsi was in the bathroom. I lit a cigarette and sat outside the door on a railroad tie parking curb with the number '3' hand painted on it in yellow.

I'd made it through the night without cheating.

We'd come back to the room around 11:00. She'd showered. When Mitsi'd stepped out of the bathroom I'd pretended to be asleep in the big, overstuffed chair next to the window. Mitsi'd turned out the dim table light on the dresser and crawled into bed. She'd pulled the sheet back on my side of the bed before turning on her side and going to sleep. I'd stayed up for an hour, congratulating myself between erections for not succumbing to temptation, struggling desperately not to think about Mitsi's nakedness. I'd finally slipped into bed alongside her, avoiding contact. I don't know how long I laid there before I went to sleep.

Mitsi came outside as I finished the cigarette. She'd pulled on a pair of panties and had draped a towel around her shoulders. She was holding it closed over her chest. Mitsi squatted down behind me then asked for a cigarette. I lit one and gave it to her. She went back inside then returned with a towel. She placed it on the tie and sat down next to me.

"You no' make ruve with me," pouting.

"Too tired," faking a yawn.

"You no' kinky me when I as'eep?" angrily.

"I no 'kinky' you."

*Wonder how perverted somethin' would have ta be f'r her ta consider it kinky?*

"You change'a you min' about two week?" apprehensively.

"No, hell no," and looked over at her. "You were tired. I was tired. It just wouldn't'a been very good. That's all," I lied.

*T'night I'll take her ta dinner then cut her free.*

"You sti' no' get'a you money back. No' make ruve you fau't, nah me."

"Don't worry about it," I assured her. "It's no big deal."

"Today, I s'eep ah day. Go wo'k at'a six o'c'rock an' be fresh at 9:00 when you come fo' me. I no' be s'eepy. You no' wo'k a hawd today an' nah' be s'eepy too."

"Look, I'm gunna give ya some cab fare an' some money ta get ya inta town. You go get some breakfast f'r y'urself."

"You no' eat a brea'fas'?"

"I never eat a brea'fas'."

"Mos' impo'tan' a mea' fo' day," she advised me.

"Well, eat an extra one f'r me."

"No way! Ge' fat."

I stood up and stretched.

"I won't be back 'til after ya've gone ta work t'night. Al dudn't want me ta come over ta get ya 'til 9:00."

"Nooo! You see Mitsi dance! You come see...I ver' goo'. Make you *hot*."

"I'll ask Al. Anyway, we'll go somewhere fancy f'r dinner after ya get off work."

"I know goo' prace," getting up and following me into the room.

The door noisily scrapped shut.

"Wha' time you go now?"

"In about ten, fifteen minutes," as I turned around.

Mitsi dropped the towel.

*My God! She's gotta be one healthy fu...*

I was up again.

*Damn her! Damn me! Damn Bobbie.*

"Look, Mitsi," and turned away, "let's just save it f'r t'night, okay? Let's make it special."

Mitsi came up behind me and put her arms around my waist. She pressed her breasts into my bare back.

"I make it *ver'* specia'," and bit my back.

It stung, but I didn't pull away.

*Goddammit! Maybe she'll be killed in a car crash on her way ta breakfast this mornin'. That'd solve the whole fuckin' problem.*

\*\*\*

Danny and Hope were busy leafing lead when we got to the church at 9:00.

"Going to have to work until 9:00 tonight if we want to stay on schedule," Danny.

"No problem," I answered.

"Git the money?" Jerry, hoarsely.

"Every penny of it."

Jerry and Homer were feeling a little better after smoking a joint and downing a few of JD's pain killers.

"Fall in love last night?" Hope yelled down from the ladder to Homer.

Jerry walked over and looked up at her.

"Hope," his voice rasping, "Homer here wuz a perfec' gen'leman. Yew'd'a been proud as shit uv him."

"Whut're yew lookin' at?" and brought her legs together.

"Ya know, Hope," Jerry, sounding seriously concerned, "when a ladies workin' on a ladder, a real loose dress is safer ta work in than 'em tight-ass jeans. Tight dresses 'r jeans'll cut off the circ'lation in y'ur legs an' then they'll go numb an' then yew'll fall an' hurt y'urself."

Hope looked down and stuck her tongue out.

"Gil says 'at in some cultures when a female shows her tongue ta a man it means she's wantin' him!" Jerry snickered.

Jerry got his ladder then dropped it as he was carrying it over to the windows he'd been working on the night before.

"If you're still drunk," Danny snapped, "sleep it off before you screw something up."

"Fuck y'urself Daniel," Jerry snarled. "I only had two beers las' night, man. Don'ch ya go worrin' about me one bit."

Jerry dropped the ladder again as he swung the rear end of it into the scaffolding. "Fuuuck," he whispered, waiting for Danny's reaction.

Nothing.

I helped Jerry with the ladder then helped Homer place his.

An hour later Jerry was a changed man, becoming more hung over than drunk. By noon he was recovering and by the time late afternoon rolled around, he was ready for Hector's again.

"Yew really gunna work 'til 9:00?" Jerry asked me.

"Twelve a day," I nodded. "That's the deal."

"Shiiit, man," slurring. " 'at's four more fuckin' hours."

Jerry lumbered to the work table to load more diamonds into his apron.

Homer came down from his ladder and approached me.

"Joint?" he offered.

"Sure."

We stepped into the garden and lit up.

"So, how was it last night?" while I held the first hit.

"Damn nice," Homer, taking his hit. "Had a good time. Met a real nice lady."

"An' 'at's all he did wuz meet her," Jerry, coming up behind us. "He's in love, man," intercepting the joint on its way back to me.

"No kiddin'?" putting my hand on Homer's shoulder. "*True* love?"

"Didn't feel like screwing around last night."

"Whu's gunna be y'ur excuse t'night? Gas?" handing the joint to me.

"I suppose you fucked away ever' dime ya had?" before I took a deep hit.

"Don't know. Hadn't looked in the ol' money belt yet. How late yew stay at Al's place?"

"Around 11:00 'r so."

"Ya make any frien's?" Jerry snickered.

"Yeah. Yeah, I did as a matter'a fact."

"How many times?" poking Homer and winking.

"We just shot the shit," a little on the defensive side.

"Yew gunna shoot the shit again t'night?"

"Pro'bly. I kind'a like the place."

"Pro'bly. I kind'a *like* the place," mimicking me in a high, squeaky voice. "I bet y're plookin' the blond."

"I'm not plookin' anything."

"Somethin's got ya hangin' out there. I know ya *that* well," Jerry.

"B'lieve me...I just don't feel like raisin' a lot'a hell. Period. That's it," standing my ground.

Jerry didn't accept that.

"I'll jus' ask ol' Al. He'll tell me," sneering before returning to the church.

Homer and I lit cigarettes and walked through the garden to the parking lot. Late afternoon was giving way to early evening.

"You goin' back ta Hector's t'night?" I asked.

"Yeah," without hesitating.

"Gunna see the same lady?"

"I'd like to. I really enjoyed talking with her. Can't speak much English, though."

"Gee whiz, Homer. I wonder why the fuck not?"

Homer grinned.

We walked around the lot and stopped at the gate.

"I don't really want to do what Jerry's doing," clearing his throat. "Not that what he's doing is wrong. It's...I don't know what it is. Last night it was fun to just get drunk and joke around with that girl."

Homer turned away and looked back toward town.

"I paid ten dollars to keep her at the table," and paused a moment. "Stupid, huh?"

"Nah," tempted to tell him about my night, but deciding against it.

"I'll probably do it again tonight," he said.

"If 'at's what ya feel like doin', then 'at's what ya ought'a do. Don't listen ta numb nuts. He took the hobble off his dick the second we crossed the bridge from El Paso."

Homer laughed.

We went back inside the chapel and finished up the evening with a minimum of conversation. Hope quietly hummed cowboy songs to herself while puttying the replaced diamonds.

At a little before 9:00, Danny called it quits. Hope sat on the floor, removed her boots, and then began to rub her feet.

"This is the longest I've stood in a stretch f'r I don't know how long," she groaned.

"If ya cain't hack it, don't...," Jerry ducked as Hope threw a spackling bag at him.

He wasn't fast enough. With a powdery puff, it glanced off the top of his head leaving behind a white mark the size of a baseball.

"Dammit, Hope!" reaching up and slapping the dust from his hair.

After policing things up Danny assessed the day's work. He was satisfied with the progress. We agreed to start at 7:00 the next morning.

"Anybody want to eat with me and Hope on the other side?" Danny.

"Maybe t'morrow night," Jerry answered quickly.

"How about yew, Homer? Hungry?" Hope.

"No thanks. I'll wait until tomorrow."

"Gil?" Danny slapped my shoulder. "You wan'a come? I heard about the gourmet meal you had last night."

"I think I'll wait too," glancing at Hope. "I just wan'a go back, clean up, have a few beers with Al then..."

"Pork six 'r seven uv his hookers," Jerry.

"Shudup!" Hope.

"Dammit," Jerry grumbled. "I thought we done left Joan in Lubbock."

Hope, once again forgiving Jerry, handed out her goodnight hugs before following Danny into the garden.

"Hope!" I called out.

She waited for me to catch up to her.

"Listen. I tried callin' Bobbie last night an' the phones were all messed up. Could ya call her from y'ur hotel an' tell her…tell her I, uh…miss her an' I'm thinkin' about her."

" 'at's *all?*" she coaxed.

I paused a moment.

"Yeah. F'r now."

"Okay," sounding disappointed. "Should I tell her y're b'havin' y'urself?"

"Yeah. An' make it sound f'r real."

"I'll cross my fangers b'hind my back j'st in case," giggling.

At 9:45 I was walking across the parking lot to Al's.

*Forty-five minutes late. She'll be waitin'.*

About six or so dusty cars and pickup trucks were parked haphazardly along the wall of the cabaret.

My stomach was growling.

The plan was to take Mitsko for a steak somewhere, have a few drinks, and then return to the room. We'd talk for a while then I'd send her on her way.

*Nothin' else, dammit.*

The cabaret was pulsating to "She's A Rainbow". Several scantily clad girls were sitting on laps, quietly staring at the stage area. I stood near the door and looked around for Mitsi. I couldn't seem to find her. I looked at the girl performing on the carpeted stage and gasped.

# THE RAVING EUNUCH MONKS

*Mitsko.*

She was down to a G-string with some cheap-ass feathers stuck to it, slinking her way through a gymnastic routine in time to the song. She was on her shoulders, hands on her hips as her arms held her butt aloft. Her legs extended straight into the air. They slowly parted, opening until they were parallel to the floor. Mitsi rolled to an upright position, keeping her legs fully spread. She faced the mesmerized crowd of ten or twelve soldiers and civilians. In a single flashing move she was sitting sideways to the audience, legs together. Slowly arching her spine, Mitsi pulled her shoulders back, gradually reducing her breasts to little mounds. She leaned back until the top of her head touched the floor, her back remaining arched, her stomach and chest taut. She lowered her spine to the floor, lifted her legs, and then brought her knees to her lips. She slowly rolled back onto her shoulders, slipped her hands under her hips, and then eased her legs past her head. She bent at the waist as her toes came to rest on the floor above her head. Mitsi was folded in half, her navel touching her chin. She parted her legs slightly, lifted her head from the floor, and then kissed herself. The customers exploded as she shot to her feet then breezed through a series of full splits and backward somersaults. Finally Mitsi turned her back to the audience spread her legs, locked her knees, and then bent over until her head touched the floor.

*Oh, my God.*

A bar girl ran onto the stage and stuffed a bill under the G-string. Mitsi held the pose while several men jumped onto the stage to cop quick feels as they roughly stuffed money under every available inch of elastic the G-string had. On the last beat of the song Mitsi straightened up, jumped to the door directly behind the carpeted area and vanished. The dozen or so customers sounded like a hundred as they clapped, whistled, and howled for more.

My gut ached. I was painfully aroused.

*Walk out the door right now. Don't think...just start movin'.*

Al had slipped up beside me.

"Goddammit!" grumbling. "The second I sell off the hottest bitch in the place for two weeks a goddamn army of stiffs shows up."

"That's hardly an army, Al," nodding at the occupied tables immediately around the show carpet.

*Good God. I'm shakin'.*

"Y're late," he snapped. "Mitsi was getting worried. It affected her performance. I'll tell her y're here. Meet her around back," then walked away.

I hurried out the front door and started across the lot.

*Get in the room, lock the door, an' write Bobbie a long letter.*

I stopped.

*Mitsi might take it wrong...like there's somethin' I didn't like about her.*

*Wouldn't be right ta hurt her feelin's.*

I trotted to the rear of the building.

*I'll tell her the deals off an' that it's got nothin' ta do with anything about her personally.*

For twenty minutes I worked on how I was going to tell her how pretty I thought she was and how much I'd enjoyed her company last night, but I was having to back out of the whole thing.

Mitsi emerged from the back door of the cabaret in high heels and a short, untied, silk bathrobe. I could see it all—from her glittered toenails to her short dark hair, still damp from a shower. She smelled sweet, fresh. She was holding a large bag at her side.

"You see dance?" cocking her head.

Her body, drenched in moonlight, radiated white.

*She absolutely...fucking...glows.*

"Yeah. Yeah, I saw it."

*Stop lookin' at it! Turn the fuck away!*

"What you think?" knowing what the answer would be.

"It was…was…," shaking again.

"Hot!" laughing. "I know. I know," stepping up to me then placing her hand on my crotch. "It make you ho'ny!" pretending to be surprised as she covered her mouth with a tiny hand.

"Hell no. The dancin' dudn't have anything ta do with 'at. It's…it's the way y're wearin' y'ur hair. That's what's doin' it."

"You fu' bu'shit!" and bounced to my side.

*NOW! Tell her now! Then run like hell!*

"Uh…listen," faltering.

Mitsi stepped in front of me, went to her toes, and kissed me passionately, rubbing her knee up and down between my legs several times. The instant she stopped the thigh rub she placed my hand between her legs and held it there, slowly broke the kiss off, and then whispered in my ear.

"We go make ruve *now*," dropping the sack to take hold of me with the freed hand. "I nah hungry now. I s'eep ah day in you room," while nibbling away at my neck. "I ah rest up jus'a fo' you."

***

On Thursday afternoon, at around 1:00, we dusted the last of the spackling powder from the final window.

They were nothing short of brilliant.

Father Addison came out, quickly walked through the chapel, and then hurried off. Moments later he returned with four nuns. They excitedly walked around the inside of the chapel, mouths open, gasping in surprise.

"They look like new!" the priest finally exclaimed.

The nuns, in broken English, agreed enthusiastically as they scurryed from window to window, touching the previously bowed areas, trying to remember which pieces had been cracked. One of them began crying. They all shook our hands, chattering away in Spanish. The priest told us they were saying they wanted to kiss the hands God had blessed.

" 'at's whu' the ladies at the Club been tellin' me ever' night," Jerry whispered in a low cackle.

The windows did look nice. I'd never considered repairing church glass as anything more than another job. Like surveying, or mowing lawns. The windows bathed the chapel in a warm, golden light. If you took a moment to let them, they made you feel different. The place suddenly became special for some reason—apart from other places. It wasn't spooky or religious. Just special. Watching the nuns made it that much more special.

Hope came over and took Homer by the hand.

"I wish JD wuz here," she told him.

Homer nodded.

The priest motioned for us to follow him into the garden. We left the nuns inside to continue their thrilled critique.

"What you have done is a marvelous, marvelous thing," as the priest shook our hands again. "At one time, the Bishop was considering taking the glass out and replacing it with solid sheets of colored plastic. Your bid was so much lower than the others, we were afraid you...you might not be," struggling to find a nice way to say he thought we were going to fuck it up.

"You thought maybe we were gunna rip ya off?" I joked.

Father Addison waved his hand without answering.

"We wouldn't fu...," Jerry stumbled, "we wouldn't mess with the Pope, man," glancing at the rest of us, proud of how he'd caught himself.

The priest smiled.

"Are you Catholic?" he asked Jerry.

"Nah. I think I'm a hedon..."

"He's a little bit'a ever'thing," I jumped in.

"An eclectic," the priest nodded.

"In his own peculiar way," Danny added.

Jerry, frowned. He wasn't sure if he was an eclectic or not. He suddenly broke into a grin, evidently deciding that if a priest called him an eclectic without giving him an "eat shit" look then it probably wasn't a bad thing to be.

"Will you begin the rectory this afternoon?" the priest asked Danny.

"We'll probably move everything over to the other church now, but wait until tomorrow to start. We've been putting in twelve hour days and got a little ahead. We're knocking off early today."

"I'll call Father Torres and tell him what you intend to do. He will have a key for you to access the rectory while you are working there. The windows are all that remain to complete the restoration there."

Father Addison bowed and walked away. We packed up then drove to the rectory. It was about ten minutes away.

Father Torres was waiting, standing in the middle of a freshly blacktopped parking lot. The lot still smelled like tar.

"Welcome! Welcome!" greeting us excitedly with firm handshakes all around. "I've heard all about you...your work. Father Addison said it is magnificent!" smiling broadly.

The old priest was short and thin. His hard, wrinkled features gave the impression he'd been through a lot of shit in his time. He reminded me of one of the ancient, gnarled, sun baked mesquite trees scattered throughout the area. Father Torres took us immediately to the rectory library. It was empty.

The windows were small, a foot wide by six feet tall. Peaked at the top. All the windows were constructed of three inch by two inch amber opalescent diamonds in half inch, flat faced lead. They were strong, heavy looking windows. Both the east and west walls had twenty windows each. The windows were about two feet apart. Thirty feet of wall extended beyond the last window at each end of the room. The room was approximately eighty feet wide. The refinished oak floor looked like a giant mirror. Tarps, held in place by adobe bricks, formed a six-foot wide walk along the walls all the way around the room. The adobe had been freshly stuccoed then painted a shiny white. The wood ceiling, about twelve feet high, was a lighter shade than the floor. Two dozen hand made, tin lanterns hung from the ceiling.

Father Torres turned the lights on and led us around the room, continually looking over his shoulder and reminding us to stay on the tarps. He pointed out all the broken amber diamonds they had found and had marked with small pieces of masking tape— one hundred thirty-eight cracked or shattered pieces. We couldn't see any bowed windows and noticed a few wire ties rusted free of support rods. Grunge build-up on the windows appeared to be the biggest problem the windows had. Overall, it was going to be a pretty slick job.

We stowed our materials in a small out building behind the rectory, set the tables up, and moved some sheets of glass into the library. By 4:00 we were ready to leave.

Danny and Hope went into Father Torre's office to get a set of keys. Homer, Jerry, and I wandered out to the van where Jerry removed a joint from his pack of cigarettes and fired up.

"Yew gunna sleep the afternoon away when we're done here 'r come on downtown with us?" Jerry snickered.

"What's wrong with' catchin' a little extra sleep?"

"Nothin' at all…if 'at's whut y're really doin'," turning on the Eye.

"What's 'at s'posed ta mean?"

"Don't mean shit, man," while lighting the joint. "It's jus' 'at I been talkin' with ol' man Munoz an' he seems ta think ya might be goin' sweet on one'a the whores in 'at shithole'a his."

Jerry exhaled and handed the joint to me. I took a deep drag and held it as I passed the joint to Homer.

"Al's just a dirty ol' man," holding my breath. "I go over there an' buy this one girl a few drinks, watch the others dance, an' I get drunk," then exhaled loudly. "She gets off work an' I take her ta dinner. We eat. She goes home. It's no worse than Hugo takin' Missy ta breakfast after she gets off work at the lounge," trying to sound as casual as I could.

"Yeah, well, I'm sure it happens somethin' like 'at," Jerry, taking the joint from Homer.

"It happens *exactly* like 'at," aggravated.

"I'm sure it does," glancing at Homer and nodding.

"Fuck you," I mumbled.

Jerry extended another invitation.

"Come on down ta the club with us t'night. Yew c'n hang with Homer, here. Hell...he's as safe as c'n be," handing me the joint. "The dumb fuck goes an' falls in love the firs' night with the ugliest one in'a place, buys her f'r the night *ever'* night, an' then he says he ain't even pokin' her."

Homer grinned.

"Whud'a ya say ta tha', Gil?" Jerry snickered. "Is 'at some sick-ass shit 'r whut? Both'a y'all're sick shits, man. Comin' down here ta fuckin' hooker heaven 'an one'a ya holes up in a flea-bag motel room an'a other son uv a bitch goes an' falls in love. Damnation," he hissed.

I gave the joint to Homer.

"I might be by later on," I told Homer.

"Yeah, right," Jerry.

I ignored him.

"You still seein' the same one you were talkin' about before?" I asked Homer.

"Yeah," nodding and exhaling. "Elida. I like her," as he passed the last of the joint to Jerry. "She's easy to talk to," he added before breaking into a dry cough.

"Talk?" Jerry yelped. "Is 'at whu' ya call all 'at gruntin' an' sign language?" turning to me. "Ya ought'a see it, Gil. Looks like two deaf people carryin' on. Hands wavin', fingers pointin' 'at shit. All night nothin' but 'Huh? Whu's 'at ya say? I don't un'erstand! Draw me a fuckin' pi'ture'," Jerry grumbled. "Yeah, she's *real* easy ta talk to," finishing the joint, dabbing it on his tongue, and then swallowing what was left.

Danny and Hope stepped out of the rectory and came over to us.

"We're going to grab a bite and then hit the history museum," Danny. "Anybody want to come along?"

"Damn," Jerry, shaking his head. "I wished I'd known yew wuz goin' b'fore I bought them op'ra tickets."

Jerry jumped back as Hope kicked at him.

"I'm headin' back an' hangin' out at the motel," scratching my head with both hands. "I'm beat."

"I'm going to take Elida to dinner before she has to go to work," Homer.

"I guess I'm the only one honest enough ta admit he's gunna go git a b..."

"I don't wan'a hear it!" Hope, as she covered her ears and stamped her feet. "If I know about it an' Shauna asks me then I gotta tell her."

"*Bath*, woman!" Jerry. "I'm gunna go git a *bath*. Whud'd ya think I wuz gunna say?" acting hurt. "Damn, Danny. How ya put up with a potty mind like 'at?" jerking his head in Hope's direction.

"Come on and get your money," Danny grinned and turned to the truck.

After paying us, Danny and Hope said their goodbyes then took off, Hope hanging out the window and waving wildly.

Homer, Jerry, and I went back to the motel where they hurried into their rooms to clean up and grab a change of clothes. I sat down on the railroad tie in front of my room and started fumbling for a cigarette. I tossed two broken ones into the parking lot before finding a third that, although painfully crippled, was at least in one piece. I lit up and began unlacing my work boots.

The door to my room scraped loudly over the rough concrete floor. As I turned, a man darted from the room, charged past Homer's then Jerry's door, and then whipped around the corner of the building. I jumped up and ran after him, stopping after turning the corner.

*What if he's got a knife 'r a gun?*

The man disappeared behind the adobe, his dust hanging in the still air. A door slammed shut. I stepped back and saw Mitsko, half naked, running toward the opposite end of the building, big bag in one hand, overnight case in the other. I started to shout, but remembered Homer and Jerry were still here. I ran after her. Mitsko jumped into Al's room. Al stepped outside. I slowed to a fast walk then halted. He glared at me for a moment then stepped back into the room, slamming the door behind him.

*Just plain fuck it.*

I stood there, fuming. Pissed. Hurt. Pissed at and hurt by the apparent betrayal. I turned, and walked back to my room, closed the door, lay down on the bed, and stared at the ceiling.

*What a fuckin' slut!*

*Pro'bly been screwin' guys in here ever' goddamn afternoon since we started our...thing. Our "deal".*

*Pro'bly been chargin' 'em ten bucks f'r the room. What a goddamn bitch! We had a fuckin' understandin'!*

*That lyin', cheatin'...whore!*

Around 5:00 I heard Homer and Jerry take off to the Club. I thought about going with them.

*That'd teach the cheatin' bitch a lesson.*

Instead, I laid there.

A few minutes later someone knocked at the door. I rose up, but didn't say anything.

*It's pro'bly her. Pro'bly realized how bad she fucked up an' she's gunna try ta patch things...*

"It's me. Alberto."

The door creaked and scrapped open a few inches.

"Are you decent?" Al, sticking his fists into the room, each holding a dripping quart of beer.

I hesitated a second or two, debating whether I wanted to talk to him. I was damn near as mad at him as I was at Mitsi. Al clomped in uninvited, leaving the door open. He tossed me a quart and sat in the chair near the window. I pulled a church key from my pocket and opened the bottle. Al braced the cap of his bottle against the window sill and slammed the heel of his hand down on it. The cap popped off.

"Don't let me catch you doing it like that," leaning back in the chair.

I took a tug off the bottle before asking if he knew anything about what had been going on.

"Knew about it? Hell. I encourage such…uh…*initiative.* That kind of *enthusiasm* for their job. Why? You're not mad at her are you?"

"I'm pissed as hell, goddammit!" getting up from the bed and stepping to the door.

"Why? She's a goddamn working girl. If she isn't turning, she's not earning. That is the economics of pussy vending, compadre. If you don't want her fucking around, then marry the bitch. Take her back to Lubbock and knock her up six or seven times. Until then, amigo, you're just another customer."

"We were gettin' along, though. It wudn't like it was just a…a quickie 'r somethin'. I was startin' ta think she was beginnin' ta feel the same way. That we had a special arrangement 'r somethin'."

"*That* is what you *paid* her for. *That is* what you *wanted* and *that* is what you got…the "Mitsi Bullshit Romance Special". Everything that is good about the real thing without all the hassle of the real thing and with only *one* obligation…pay her when it's over. It's a hell of a good deal," pausing to gulp down some beer. "If you started taking it serious then that goes to show you how good she is at what she does. I would say you were getting your goddamn money's worth. You should tip her like a mother…"

"Bullshit!" and spun around. "I wudn't lookin' at it like 'at! All I wanted was a fuck! I'm pissed b'cause I thought we had an understandin'…she wudn't supposed ta be fuckin' anybody else while she was with me."

"She wasn't with you," he laughed. "She waited until you were gone for the day."

"It's not funny!"

"Look, Gil. If all you'd wanted was a hot shot of leg you would have jumped Susie the first night then somebody else the next night, and so on, and so on. You stayed with Mitsi after the first time because she picked up on the kind of production you wanted and she gave it to you...the old 'let's be sweethearts' shit. Taking her to dinner, the movies, shopping. It's the *same* movie JD would make every time he came down here but, he never forgot it was just a movie."

"I stayed with her b'cause the price was right."

"Of course you did," waving his hand in the air and looking away. "I'm sure that's all there was to it."

I put my hand on the doorknob.

"I'm tired. I wan'a clean up an' rest a while. Tell Mitsi...Mitsko the arrangement's canceled."

"Taking your letter jacket back? Just a week before the prom? It will break her heart."

"Eat me," I mumbled.

Al rose stiffly from the chair.

"Speaking of broken hearts, what are you going to do tonight to fix yours?"

I looked out the door at the club.

"I'm pissed, okay? Just plain ol' pissed. Nothin' else."

Al slapped me on the back on his way out.

"I'm going to set you up with Susie. Fifty dollars for the rest of the night after her last dance at 11:00."

"No."

"If 11:00 is too late we can set it up for...say...forty bucks from 9:00 to 11:00. Special deal for you only," scratching his chin. "I'll send a pint of cherry brandy with her. Susie loves that goddamn cherry brandy."

"Damn, Al! I may be a fuckin' hist'ry major, but how's forty dollars f'r two hours a deal when ya just offered her to me f'r all night f'r fifty?"

*Why the hell am I even arguin' about it. It's out'a the question. I'm tired'a the guilt, an'...*

"Make me an offer."

"I don't *wan'a* make an offer, Al. I wan'a eat an' I wan'a get some sleep. Nothin' else."

"For one night I will make you a *super* special deal so you can see she's worth *every* penny. For tonight...twenty dollars from 9:00 until 11:00 and half price on the cherry brandy."

"Thanks f'r the beer Al," easing him out the doorway.

"Susie's different. If you live through it, you will never forget it," promising me as I shut the door. "Nine o'clock sharp!"

I fell back into bed.

*What the hell's wrong with me?*

*Been here five days an' hadn't written Bobbie so much as a post card.*

*Nothin' but guilt after ever' nut with Mitsi an' now 'at that's over, I'm wonderin' what it'd be like ta plank Susie.*

*Fuck.*

*Al's pro'bly exaggeratin' about her, anyway.*

I got up, showered, lit a cigarette and then sat naked on the side of the bed without drying off.

*It's hard ta b'lieve 'at Susie's got anything on 'em girls overseas.*

*Christ. I can't imagine what she...DAMMIT!*

*Stop thinkin' about it! This shit's over.*

*No more.*

*When...if Susie shows up, I won't answer the goddamn door.*

*Eat one'a the Spams an' work on 'at quart'a Jack Daniels.*

*A little b'fore nine I'll take a walk.*

*Won't even be here if she does show up.*

*Come back ta the room an' write Bobbie a long-ass letter. Tell her how much I miss her.*

I fixed a stiff Jack and water, then lay down on the bed.

*So sick'a bein' such a bastard.*

*Bobbie's pro'bly thinkin'a me right this minute.*
*Wish she was here so I could tell her...tell her 'at...that...*
*Shit.*
*Tell her I like her very much?*
I leaned over and snatched the clock from the floor.
*4:15.*
I set the alarm for 8:45.
*Get up at 8:45. Take a cab ta Hector's b'fore Susie shows up. If she*
*shows up. Get drunk as shit with Jerry an' Homer.*
*That's the plan.*

At 8:30, the sound of wood scraping over concrete startled me
awake.

\*\*\*

The alarm was buzzing. I rolled over onto my stomach and
turned it off. My back felt like it was on fire. Susie slid from the bed.
She sat down at the table, pushed an empty bottle of cherry brandy
aside, and then removed a piece of foil from her purse.
I looked down at my chest.
*Bite marks?*
The insides of my thighs were a series of hickeys.

Susie did a line of coke. Her ponytails were still in place. Her
body melted into the chair. I watched her a minute or two. She was
a cute, innocent looking thing, built like a healthy pubescent still
in the process of shedding the last of her baby fat. If it weren't for
her habit, she'd probably be a chubby little butterball. Everything
about her gave you the impression she wasn't quite ripe. Her taut
little breasts. Her round, angel face. The light patch of fluff between
her legs.
Al swore Susie was twenty-two, but was probably way off. The
thought was upsetting.
She opened her eyes. They had a dreamy, unreal quality to
them now.

She staggered into the bathroom.

I shut my eyes and watched quickly flashing reruns of the night before.

*Al may'a lied about her age, but he was dead-on about the ride.*

She returned to the room, sat down beside me and squeezed a large amount of body cream into her palm.

"Ro' ob'r," she ordered.

Painfully I made it to my stomach. I tensed and moaned while Susie began spreading the lotion over my back. A warm sensation gradually replaced the initial stinging. The pain eased. She worked her way along my spine, over my butt, and then down the back of my thighs.

"Tu'n ob'r," she ordered again.

I rolled onto my back and felt the wounds on my chest catch fire. She had me put my arms over my head and spread my legs. She applied the lotion to the under sides of my arms where several bite marks glowed red. She rubbed my chest and stomach in slow circular motions. Gradually the stinging subsided. She moved to my ankles and began to work her way up my legs. I felt a tightening sensation in the pit of my stomach as Susie kissed her way up the inside of my thighs and began massaging me.

"Oh, Jesus," I murmured. "There's nothin' left, Susie."

I was wrong.

I threw on some pants and a tee shirt before stepping outside. I fired up a cigarette.

*Damnation. It hadn't even taken her five minutes.*

I walked over to Homer's door and pounded on it.

Nothing.

I tried several more times with no response. I moved to Jerry's door.

"Jerry!" as I banged on his door. "Is Homer in his room? He won't answer up!"

Jerry's door flew open. He stumble-staggered through the doorway.

"No," he spit out, coughing and gagging into his hand before falling back against the wall and scratching himself. "Shit, man... I...," then lurched to the edge of the building, doubled over and puked his guts out.

I came up behind him.

"You gunna be okay?"

Jerry straightened up, spit toward the road, and then wiped his mouth on the back of his arm.

"Shit, man," a bit fogged.

"I've got some Pepto in the room," I offered.

"Nah," waving the idea off with one hand while holding his stomach with the other. " 'at shit'll jus' make me sick."

I followed him back inside.

"Gimme ten minutes," panting through a dry heave as he hurried across the room and entered the bathroom.

The shower sputtered. I looked around the front room. Clothes were scattered everywhere. The room smelled like stale smoke and do-it—sweat, semen. Crotch. Lime rinds covered the floor. I glanced at the table where a couple of empty Tequila bottles, a salt shaker, a wet package of Zig Zags, some grass, more rinds, an open pin knife, and an overflowing ash tray were all stuck in a mucky goo. Two naked ladies, out cold, lay stomach down on the bed. Both were a little on the plump side, like the old paintings of nudes in art history books. One appeared to be much older than the other one. From what I could see of their faces, they didn't appear to be that bad looking. Maybe even a little on the attractive side if they hadn't been rode hard and put away wet.

Jerry had probably gotten his money's worth.

I stepped into the bathroom. The shower curtain was wide open. Steam was pouring from the stall. Jerry was squatting on the floor of the shower, head locked between his knees.

"You gunna live?" as I reached into the stall.

No response.

I turned the hot water off.

"Fuuuck, maaan!" Jerry moaned as cold water poured down. "Ooooh Jeeeezuuuus."

I walked back into the front room. The older of the two had rolled onto her back.

She looked to be a tough, seasoned meat grinder.

I heard the shower shut down. A moment later I heard pills being shaken from a bottle. I returned to the bathroom.

"That some of JD's shit?"

Jerry, eyes closed, shook his head slowly.

"Got 'em from Hector," and handed me the bottle. "I'll be cool," gagging, "if I c'n jus' keep a han'ful'a these bas'ards down long enough for 'em ta work."

"Will these keep ya from gettin' a..."

"Yew think Hector'd gimme somethin' 'at'd put me out'a commission?" Jerry managed in a deep, dry, raspy voice. "My peter's...," hacking something up then spitting. "My peter's makin' him rich."

I put two of the pills in my pocket, popped two more into my mouth, and then swallowed them with a mouthful of water from the sink spigot. I leaned against the wall outside the bathroom door and lit a cigarette.

"Ten minutes," I told him. "Okay?"

"Ten. Gimme a cigarette."

"Where's Homer?" lighting his cigarette.

"With 'at whore'a his," coughing and gagging.

I bent over and placed the cigarette between his lips before leaving the bathroom. I heard the pill bottle rattling again. Running water in the sink. Jerry slurping.

"This lady he's with, is she the same one you were kiddin' him about yesterd'y?"

"Yeah."

"What's she like?"

"She's a Mexican Indian 'r Columbian 'r somethin'. She ain't all 'at great."

"Ugly?"

"Nah. Jus' real plain. Come by t'night. See f'r y'urself. I swear ta God," gagging loudly, "he's done gone blin' since Sonny run off."

"She better lookin' than these two hogs out here in y'ur bed?"

Jerry staggered through the bathroom door, brows furrowed. He stepped to the side of the bed, leaned over, and then closely studied the two women.

"They ain't ugly," he snorted in relief. "B'sides, they had a long night. Whud'a ya expect 'em ta look like?" returning to the bathroom.

"How's Homer gettin' ta work?" I asked.

"Don't know."

"What about these two?"

"Taxi. I'm leavin' 'em five bucks f'r breakfas' an' a cab."

I walked across the room to the door.

"Ten minutes," I reminded him.

"Won' take me 'at long," through a coughing fit. "There any'a 'at Tequila left?"

"Nope. Dudn't look like it."

"Got anything at y'ur place?" .

"Some Jack…"

"Bring me some. I'm out'a mouthwash."


I stepped outside. Susie was standing in the parking lot, butt-naked, smoking a joint. I rushed over to her and ushered her back into the room.

"Stay inside until we leave," I ordered sternly.

She fell back onto the bed and giggled.

"You ready one'a mo' time?"

"I gotta go ta work."

"*I* make'a you wo'k," still giggling.

"Just stay inside until we're gone," pointing my finger at her.

"You frien' wan…"

"My friend's gotta go ta work too."

"I make'a *both* you wo'k," raising onto her elbows. "Two fo' one cos'."

"Some other time."

"When uhda time?"

"I don't know when uhda time," grabbing the Jack Daniels bottle. "I'll ask him. Okay?"

"Okay."

"Snort some more shit 'r smoke another joint 'r somethin'," before stepping outside.

I glanced at the clock

*8:00. Fuck. Danny's gunna be pissed as shit.*

I pulled the door shut then took the bottle to Jerry.


He was half dressed, on his knees, head in the toilet.

"Throwin' up?" as I put the bottle down beside him.

"Nah," barely audible. "Jus' gittin' somethin' ta drink."

It sounded like a bucket was over his head.

"I'll be waitin' outside."

Dry heaves from the toilet bowl.


Jerry and I entered the library a little after 9:00. Homer was stripping out diamonds. Hope was on a ladder leafing lead away from cracked pieces. Danny came over.

"I didn't expect you before noon," he grumbled. "Homer really surprised me," pointing across the room. "He got here at 8:00."

"Car trouble," I coughed. "I was too fuckin' drunk ta crawl out'a bed an' start it."

"My folks wuz killed in a car wreck," Jerry slurred. "I had ta arrange some things. I'm gunna need t'morrow off f'r the…yew know…the thing," wrestling with a dry heave.

"Send flowers," Danny, and walked away.

"Bast'rd," Jerry mumbled.

I walked over to Homer and pulled a cigarette out. Homer laid his cutter down. He looked up from the cutting table.

"Nice set of hickies," he whispered.

I slapped a hand to my throat.

"Yeah. It got a bit crazy on the dance floor last night," watching Homer to see if he'd bought the bullshit.

"Whatever. Hope is the one you're going to have to convince," and returned to stripping out diamonds.

I glanced over at Hope.

"Tell her I was at Hector's last night an' ya saw what happened."

"What about Jerry?" looking at Jerry who was beginning to break cracked pieces from the panels.

"As fucked up as he must'a been last night, he wouldn't know if I'd been there 'r not."

"Good point," Homer nodded. "I'll remind him you *were* there."

I lit the cigarette.

"I hear y'ur lady took ya home last night," hacking my way through the first drag.

"Yeah," without looking up from the table.

"Sounds serious," nodding my head.

Homer said something under his breath.

"What?" leaning toward him, brows raised.

"As serious as it can be down here," speaking up a little.

I could tell he didn't really want to discuss it at the moment.

"Guess I best get busy b'fore Danny starts bitchin'."

I tied my apron on and moved a ladder to one of the windows Hope had leafed. I climbed up and began breaking diamonds out.

Everybody stayed to themselves for the rest of the morning. Homer stripped glass. Danny and Hope leafed cracked pieces. Jerry broke them out. At noon, we went to a restaurant down the street from a statue of Benito Juarez. It was a tourist joint, but Jerry, Homer, and I wanted a decent meal. Something uncanned.

493

"A fuckin' steak costs more'n a piece'a as...," Jerry stopped. He looked up from the menu at Hope.

Hope was glaring at him.

Jerry began over.

"This place is kind'a expensive."

"Rather," I agreed.

"Quite," Danny.

All of us ordered hamburgers and fries, the cheapest thing they had, then settled into our chairs.


Hope finally noticed the dark spots on my neck, leaned forward and squinted.

"Whut's 'at on y'ur neck?"

I covered the spots as best as I could with my hand.

"Hickies!" in horror, her eyes wide.

"It's not what it looks like," Homer. "It got a little crazy on the dance floor at Hector's last night."

Jerry looked confused, brow furrowed.

"He wudn' at..."

"He showed up after you took those two ladies to dinner at 7:00," Homer cutting him off. "You never came back."

"Wuz it 'at early?" Jerry, unsure.

"Must'a been," I answered hurriedly. "When I got ta Hector's at about 7:30, you were gone."

Hope examined Homer and Jerry.

"How come y'all ain't got any?"

"Shiiit," Jerry. "Homer's sweetheart'd carve anybody up tryin' ta love on him. Ain' 'at right?" slapping Homer on the back. "Ya see, Homer's in love," cackling across the table to Danny and Hope.

Homer dropped his chin to his chest.

"Look 'a tha' shit, man, " Jerry continued. "He's embarr'ssed."

"Shut up!" Hope, throwing her napkin at Jerry. "Jus' 'cause he idn't sleepin' with ever' hooker in town dudn't mean yew c'n make fun uv him like 'at. I thank it's sweet."

Jerry went wild, leaning almost all the way out of his chair, pointing at Homer and giving him an exaggerated Eye.

"Hear 'at? She thinks 'at shit's sweet!"

Homer, in a flash, reached over and pushed Jerry out of his chair. Jerry hit the floor cackling. He crawled back into his seat and turned serious.

"Shit, man," rubbing his arm as if he'd sustained a major injury. "I wuz jus' kiddin'. No fuckin' sense'a humor," grumbling.

"Y're jus' jealous," Hope.

"Uv whut? I'm in love with six 'r eight uv 'em," smiling wickedly. "An' they all love me," cackling again.

"I could say somethin'," Hope frowned, "but I won't."

"Somethin' about Shauna?" Jerry snarled, brows high.

"Well," glancing around the table. "How'd ya feel if she wuz sleepin' aroun' on yew the whole time yew's down here?"

"If I don't know about it then it never happened," Jerry, as if it were some kind of universal truth.

"But, what if ya wuz ta find out she wuz?"

"I'd have ta kick somebody's ass then, wouldn't I?"

Hope exploded.

"Yew ever hit Shauna an' I'll..."

"Not Shauna, stupid," Jerry wincing in pain. "The bast'rd 'at talked her inta doin' it. Damn, Hope," and threw himself back into his chair. "Whu' the fuck kind'a guy ya think I am? Whud've I *ever* done ta make ya think I'd *ever* hurt tha' lady?"

"Yew don't thank it'd hurt her if she wuz ta find out about yew runnin' aroun' on her?" she snapped.

Jerry, with a sincerely hurt expression on his face, looked at Hope.

"It ain' 'at'a way at all," squinting. "If Shauna wuz ta ask...I'd tell her. She ain't never gunna ask, though. It jus' ain't 'at important to her. Un'erstand?"

"I thank 'at's how *yew* wan' it ta be, but I don't thank it's how she feels about it. Not deep down inside anyways," becoming upset. "Ain't no woman c'n feel 'at'a way about somethin' like 'at," eyes moistening.

"Damn," dropping his head to the table.

"The weather's really been a bitch lately, huh Homer?" Danny, loudly then resting his hand on the back of Hope's chair.

"A real bitch," Homer agreed.

"No shit," I added. "Can't remember the last time it was this much of a bitch."

The table fell silent. Hope slumped into her chair, crossed her arms, and then glanced at Danny. A good half minute crept by.

"I apologize f'r buttin' in," Hope, rapid fire. "I s'pose it ain't none'a mah b'ness. At least 'at's whut I been told," frowning at Danny.

"Got tha' shit straight, man," accepting her apology with an air of victory. "Whoever told ya tha' it ain't none'a y'ur b'ness is one smart son uv a bitch," snickering and pointing at Danny.

"But yew know whut, Jerry?" Hope hissed, suddenly straightening up.

"Whut, Hopeless?"

"I done fig'red out that yew pro'bly wudn' a preacher Marine. I thank yew wuz j'st as nasty as Gil wuz when yew wuz over there."

"How'd I get sucked inta this?" I protested. "An' whud'a ya mean by callin' me nasty?"

"Ya got the crabs didn' ya?" she huffed.

The hamburgers arrived. Everyone busied themselves with condiments.

Hope reached across the table and tapped Jerry's plate with her knife.

"C'n I ask Homer some questions about his girlfriend without yew makin' fun uv it?"

Homer squirmed.

Jerry put his burger down, turned his palms up, and glanced at the rest of us.

"I been makin' fun'a him?" looking pained.

"Jus' tell me yew won't interrupt with anythang dirty."

"I don't know whut y're talkin' about, woman."

Hope moved her knife to Homer's plate and taped.

"Whut's her name?"

"Elida."

" 'at's Mexican f'r 'woof'," Jerry.

"I'm warnin' yew!" Hope, pointing the knife at Jerry.

"Where's she from?" turning back to Homer.

Homer wiped his mouth on the cloth napkin.

"Columbia."

"The ugly part'a Columbia," Jerry again.

Hope kicked at Jerry under the table.

"Watch it!" reaching down to rub my leg.

"Sorry. Tha's s'posed ta be f'r big-mouth."

I slugged Jerry hard in the shoulder.

"That's from Hope."

"How'd Elida end up in Juarez?" Danny.

"She met a girl in New York City from Juarez. They were sewing dresses or something. Her friend's husband was busted for not having papers so he was deported back to Mexico. Her friend got real sick so when she wanted to go back to Juarez and hook up with her husband, Elida went with her to see that she made it."

"How long has she been here?" Danny.

"About a year," Homer.

"She tryin' ta get back state side?" I asked.

"Nah. She wants to go home. Back to Columbia."

Jerry pushed his chair away from the table and looked at Hope.

"As much money as Homer's been throwin' at her," he said, "she's gunna be able ta rent a private jet back ta Columbia by the end'a the week."

"I'll git yew later," Hope glared.

With no attack imminent, Jerry pulled his chair back to the table.

"She's a hostess," Homer. "Not a working girl. She's paid for dances and the drinks she pulls in."

Jerry was in shock.

"Y're payin' all'a tha' money jus' ta keep her off'a the floor?"

"Who cares?" Hope shouted.

People at tables around ours looked over.

"She's already met Jerry. And Gil," Homer added quickly.

"Yew like her?" Hope asked me.

"Nice lady," winging it. "She's not ugly either," tossing a fry at Jerry. "She's cute as a hell."

"Mus' be the damn water down here," Jerry. "Mus' dick y'ur sense'a beauty up somehow."

Hope threw a bigger fry at him.

"She speak English?" Danny.

"Little bit."

"I *luf* you, gringo boy," Jerry. "You buy me *biiiig* drink?"while dodging another Hope fry.

Homer ignored him.

"She shares a two room place with five of the girls from Hector's," Homer continued. "It's crowded so," hesitating, "so I...the last few nights anyway...we've been staying at a hotel near the bar. Twin beds."

Jerry went into double shock.

"Y're payin' ta keep her off'a the floor *an'* gittin' her a room an' ya ain't even..."

"Don'ch yew say it, Jerry!" Hope jumping up.

Jerry pushed his chair back, ready to bolt in case Hope started around the table to clobber him.

"I wudn't gunna say shit," Jerry snarled. "I wuz jus' bein' curious. 'at's all."

Hope sat back down and looked at Homer.

"I'll wait 'til *he* ain't aroun' b'fore I ask ya anythang else," she huffed.

Jerry wrinkled his nose at her.

Danny steered the conversation to business so we could finish the meal in relative peace. After lunch we headed back to the rectory.

The rest of the day went fairly fast. About a quarter of 9:00 I wrapped it up and went out front to smoke. I dropped the tailgate on Homer's truck and lit a cigarette. It was muggy. Very still. A thick haze of dust and smoke dulled the lights on the hills in El Paso. I thought about calling Bobbie.

*Dammit. I hate my ass.*

*Wish I could start the whole damn thing all over.*

*Not fuck around on her this time.*

"Am I interrupting anything?"

I looked up. It was Father Torres.

"No, sir. Not at all."

I stood, put the cigarette out, and then sat back down, moving over to make room on the tailgate. Father Torres seated himself beside me.

"You must enjoy what you do with the glass," he started.

"Ye'sir. It's okay. It can be pr'tty borin'. Like diggin' ditches after a while."

"You've dug a few ditches in your time?" smiling.

"A few."

"What were you doing before you got involved in stained glass?"

"Military. Land surveyin'. Bartendin'. Tromped cotton for a while."

*Shit. Shouldn'a told him about the trompin'.*

"What branch of the military?"

"Navy. Four years."

"Did you go overseas?"

"Ye'sir."

"Did you visit the Philippines?"

"Ye'sir."

"I'm from the Philippines."

"No kiddin'?" surprised. "What happened ta y'ur accent?"

"You mean my 'Peeropino' accent? I spent twenty two years in South Africa before coming here eight years ago."

"You get home much?"

"Every two or three years. How did you like the Philippines?"

"Loved it. It's a pr'tty place."

"And Subic?" grinning at me.

*Uh-oh. Olongapo.*

I was embarrassed.

"Well, I'd go out ta Grande Island mostly. O'po made me nervous."

"You're not Catholic are you?"

"No, sir."

"Then I guess it's all right for you to fib to a priest," he laughed.

"Well...I guess I did go inta town a few times, but I didn't..."

"We better change the subject. I'm not certain how many fibs you are permitted as a non-Catholic," laughing again. "What denomination are you?"

"I was brought up in the military so we were p'rtty much Christmas-Easterites. Protestant brand. My folks became Baptists when I was in junior high. Somewhere around then."

"And you?"

"Oh...I guess I was Baptist for a while. I'm not really anything at the moment."

"Sounds as if that might change someday."

"Ye'sir. It might. I'm lookin' inta a lot'a different things."

Father Torres thought a moment then asked me if I believed in God.

"I'm not a hun'r'd percent sure. I *am* convinced I don't b'lieve in the God most religions seem ta b'lieve in. No offense, sir."

"Would you mind my asking another question?"

"No, sir. Go ahead."

"Imagine, for my question, that there is a God and he pays you a visit. What *one* question would you ask Him? Only one question. And take your time."

"Mind if I smoke around ya?"

He shook his head. I lit up. About half way through it, I cleared my throat, coughed lightly, and then turned to face him.

"I'd wan'a know, I mean…I think I'd ask him just exactly what it is He expects from ever'body. No BS, no fables, no magic, no dead people comin' back ta life 'r whales swallowin' people. Nothin' that could be twisted 'r misinterpreted. Just straight out tell me 'This is the way it is'. This is what it's all about."

Father Torres tugged at his ear.

"And none of the writings in existence today can provide you an answer to your question? To *your* satisfaction, that is?"

"Can't say. Haven't read ever'thing 'at's out there."

"That would take some time," he nodded.

"That's why I'd ask him that one question."

"What would you do with the answer?"

I thought while I finished the cigarette.

"Well," I began as I stepped on the butt, "I don't know f'r sure. I know one thing f'r sure…I wouldn't hop on a space ship ta Mars an' try ta shove it down all the Martian's throats an' kill the one's who wouldn't swallow."

"Yes…many mistakes have been made."

Jerry and Homer came out of the chapel.

Father Torres yawned.

"Thank you for your candidness," standing up and shaking my hand.

"Well, I wudn't gunna go lyin' to a priest. Again."

Father Torres grinned then slowly walked away.

*That was kind'a fun.*

*A redneck preacher would'a beat me ta death with his bible for what I'd said.*


The next five days passed uneventfully. I let Al know I didn't want anything more to do with Mitsko or Susie. As it was, there wouldn't be enough time for all the scratches to heal and hickies to completely go away before returning to Lubbock. I settled into Hector's and made good friends with Elida. Jerry was so full of shit—Elida wasn't bad at all. She'd never end up on a nudie calendar, but she was a far cry from being ugly. She was uniquely cute.

I made a few friends among the girls, joking and dancing with them, but resisting the temptation to go any further than that. It was difficult at times. I had to stop watching the strip shows in the front room. That was only making it harder. Actually, I was beginning to feel pretty proud of myself for towing the line. I still hadn't written Bobbie, but I *had* gotten her a gold necklace. At least it was supposed to be solid gold. I'd also picked up some nasty bedroom things. Kind of a present for the both of us.

We finished at the rectory and moved on to the final church. It turned out to be a piece of cake, mainly taking some bows out, resoldering some ties, replacing a few broken pieces, and a good powdering to polish them up real good. Three of the nuns worked right along side us to learn how to do it themselves. It damn near drove Jerry nuts. He was having enough trouble as it was trying not to say "fuck" around Hope.

Evenings and the wee hours of the morning remained reserved for Hector's. The hangovers and the lack of sleep were wearing all three of us to a nub, but it was fun.

And we could see it coming to an end soon.

Watching Homer and Elida at Hector's was a trip. It was like they were dating. Even Jerry quit making fun of them. Every evening Homer would buy her out of the bar, take her to dinner, then they'd go to a movie or something. Around midnight they'd show up, have a drink or two, dance a few slow dances, and then head back to their hotel. Homer had to drag a guy outside one night—the son of a bitch wouldn't leave Elida alone. Hector didn't say anything when it'd happened. I think Hector didn't mind having Homer around as a free bouncer.

# THE RAVING EUNUCH MONKS

Hector liked all of us. We were courteous to the ladies and we didn't *start* any trouble. He finally conceded that even the "Marine Hymn" incident wasn't really our fault. One of the week-night house bands was a German um-pah band—a tuba, accordion, snare drum, and a clarinet. They wore German um-pah clothes, like lederhosen and knee socks, but big-ass sombreros for that south-of-the-border touch. They could play anything from Hank Williams to Jimmie Hendrix. Once you were drunk enough, you could even dance to it. Much to Jerry's satisfaction, they knew "Puff the Magic Dragon". The band would play requests for a nickel. Jerry paid for a dollars worth of the "Marine Hymn" one night to fuck with a bunch of noisy Army turds. After the sixth or seventh time it'd been played, a fight broke out. Hector forgave Jerry when it was all over, not losing sight of the fact that Jerry was, after all, laying out sixty dollars a night at the Gentlemen's Club.

Jerry was fucking himself silly. He was in hog heaven, sometimes literally since Hector did have a few less than perfect female specimens working at the Club. That didn't seem to bother Jerry. He'd set himself a goal to screw every hooker in the place before returning to Lubbock and by the time the last night rolled around, Jerry was going back to his favorites for a second dose.

Our last night was a hoot. Danny and Hope even showed up. Hector got plowed with us. When Hope entered the dance hall, he'd stood up on a table, waved his .357 around, and announced to the crowd that if anybody touched Hope or Elida or said anything foul to them, he'd shoot the guys testicles off. Hector said he'd deliberately used "testicles" instead of balls or nuts out of respect for Hope.

Homer got legendarily hammered. He was on the dance floor with Elida for every slow dance that came up. Hope and Elida, even with the language barrier, chatted all night like two girls at a high school dance.

About midnight, Danny and Hope announced their departure.

"Be at the church at noon," Danny. "Hope will meet you at the church to load everything up. I'm staying on the other side to pick up the last check and put it in the bank. You'll pick me up at the bank at around 2:00. Hope'll remember all this. All you have to do is make sure y're at the church at 12:00."

"Be at the church at noon," I repeated.

I think.

Hope hugged everyone goodnight, including Hector. She asked me to say goodnight to Jerry when he came back from upstairs, hugged Elida one last time, and then exited, hand in hand with Danny. The last time I remember asking Hector for the time it was going on 2:30.

Or maybe it was 3:30.

Somewhere around there.

***

It must have been the vicious throbbing in my temples that woke me up. That was the first sensation that registered anyway. The bed shook with each exploding heartbeat. My mouth felt like it was glued shut. I struggled to part my lids. They felt pasty and swollen.

*Oh shit. Triple vision.*

The wall was jittering, the table was a blur. I was sick to my stomach. I rolled my head, very slowly, very painfully, to one side. The door was wide open. The day's heat was already filling the room. I eased onto my back and drew my knees into the air. I felt like I was spinning. Tumbling. Falling. Shutting my eyes made it worse. I tossed my arms out to my sides. My right arm came to rest on something next to me. A vice slammed shut on my brain as I jerked my head in the direction of the object. It took a few seconds to focus.

*Mitsko.*

*Oh, Christ Jesus!*

I squeezed my eyes shut.

*Fuck me dead.*

I tried desperately not to think. I wanted to not-think myself into some Mitskoless place. I looked to my right again. It wasn't working.

Mitsko was still there.

*This is real.*

I slid my legs over the edge of the bed and slowly sat up. Within seconds I began to gag. I stumbled into the bathroom, fell to my knees and began vomiting, one gut wrenching, stomach-emptying spasm after another for a good thirty seconds. I fell onto my butt and leaned against the wall, letting strings of drool dribble from my mouth to my chest. It hurt to breathe.

*Good God. This is so foul.*

Minutes passed. I made several leaps to the toilet as a succession of false alarms wracked my stomach. Miserably dry heaves. After an eternity I reached for a towel and wiped my face and chest. I stood up shakily and returned to the front room. I needed a cigarette. I consciously avoided looking at the bed while tieing the towel around my waist. Quaking, I lit up then broke into a coughing fit that doubled me over the instant the smoke hit my singed lungs. Slapping my hand over my mouth to avoid waking Mitsko, I ran to the door. Once outside I pulled the door shut, leaned against the wall and dropped my chin to my chest. I was gasping for air.

An engine roared as tires growled on loose gravel. I was pelted by a shower of pebbles. I turned my back and covered my face. As soon as the barrage let up, I looked over my shoulder. A cloud of dust was churning behind Jerry's van as it tore across the lot. Homer's door flew open. He ran stark naked from his room into the parking lot. The dust ball swerved just in time to miss the cabaret then turned onto the blacktop. The dust cleared from around the van as it sped away. Homer, halfway across the lot, slowed to a walk.

He came to a stop. He stood there, arms at his sides, watching the van shrink into the distance until it evaporated in the shimmering heat waves rising from the road.

Homer remained motionless for some time.

Long, quiet minutes.

I stepped into his room and got his pants and his bandanna. I walked out to him, stopping a few feet behind him and clearing my throat. Homer didn't move a muscle. His eyes remained fixed on the horizon.

"You, uh," I faltered, "Ya want y'ur pants?"

Homer, smelling strongly of whiskey, turned at the waist and took them from me. He looked back at the road, holding his pants in front of himself, letting the bandanna fall to the ground. I stayed put, not feeling comfortable about leaving him alone at the moment.

"We got married this morning," he finally said in a low voice. "About three hours ago. I guess...I guess she decided to go home and tell her parents about it."

"Want me ta call the poli..."

"No."

I waited a while then walked back to the room.

\*\*\*

The cab we'd taken to the church peeled out, the cabbie flipping us off and cussing in broken English. I'd thrown up all over the back seat. I found Hope and told her about what had happened.

"Stol't Jerry's van?" shaking her head as if she'd misunderstood me.

"Yeah."

"Does Jerry know?"

"Well," looking away and shuffling my feet. "I'm not sure where Jerry is," quietly, "but I think I know where he might be. More'n likely."

Hope spun around and slapped her hand to her forehead.

"Dammit! The van's been stol't, Jerry's missin', an' Homer went an' got married," turning back to me. "Anythang happen ta yew last night?" she yelled.

I stepped back.

"Uh...nothin'. Just got drunk. Terrible drunk."

Hope stomped over to the truck where Homer was sitting on the tailgate fidgeting with his bandanna. Homer stood up and looked down at Hope. His face was expressionless.

Hope squared off in front of him, her head tilted back as she looked up into his weary eyes. I couldn't see her face. Several seconds passed. Her shoulders drooped. Hope reached over, squeezed his hand, and then told him to lean down. She adjusted his bandanna. Homer began to straighten up. Hope pulled him back down to her, quickly kissed him on the head then let go.

She turned and walked back to me. Tears were working their way down her face.

"Where ya thank we c'n find Jerry?" running the back of her arm across her face.

"He's pro'bly still at Hector's."

I felt like she was wanted a more positive report.

"I'm certain 'at's where he is," I nodded.

"Let's load up an' git on out'a here," heading toward a tarp beside the church.

I motioned for Homer to follow.

It took longer than expected to load the truck since we had to find places for what would have gone in the van. At 2:30 we were on our way to Hector's, hoping to find Jerry. I ran inside and shot back to the dance hall. The place was busy. I spotted Hector and rushed toward him. Hector pointed at the stairs. He raised his other hand and held up three fingers. I veered off in the direction he'd pointed and ran up the stairs. I found room 3 and knocked on the door. I heard footsteps behind me and turned around. Two of the bouncers walked up to me. Both were grinning and shaking their heads. One of them opened the door. I stepped inside. The room was hot. It stank. Jerry, alone, was passed out. The two bouncers picked him up and carried him past me, his head bobbing with each step. I followed them down stairs where Hector, looking like death, was waiting.

"Here's his wallet," Hector, his voice low and hoarse. "The wallet is empty. He spent everything he had and then some."

I pulled my wallet out and removed some bills to pay the balance of Jerry's bill.

"No, no. That's all right," and pushed my hand away. "Bring him back sometime and let him pay me in person. All of you come back again."

"Sure thing, Hector," as I shook his hand. "Thanks f'r ever'thing. It's been a real hoot."

"Have you been to the hotel to get Homer yet?"

"Uh...no."

*He pro'bly dudn't know about the weddin' much less her cuttin' out.*

"Why?" playing dumb.

"Tell Elida she doesn't have to come in tonight. I have a feeling it is going to take her a while to get over Homer leaving."

"Yeah. I'll tell her."

I shook his hand one last time, waved goodbye to the girls, and then left.

Outside, Homer and Hope were trying to decide where to stuff Jerry. After rearranging a few things, we managed to make some room at the back of the truck bed between a glass crate and the tailgate. We went through his pockets to make sure he wasn't carrying any dope. We found some pills and threw them into the parking field.

"He smells so...awful," Hope commented as she settled into the cab between Homer and me.

"He's gunna feel worse than he smells when he finds out about his van," I mumbled as I put the truck into gear and drove away.

"I'm going to give Jerry a thousand dollars when I tell him about the van," Homer.

"That thing idn't worth a thousand dollars," I said.

"Probably not, but it's what I'm giving him."

Hope took Homer's hand and held it all the way to the border. Homer stared straight ahead. I kept trying to remember what had happened the night before, debating if it was really like cheating on Bobbie if I didn't remember a goddamn thing about it.

*That's how Jerry'd handle it.*

I pulled into the shortest line at the crossing. Even so, it looked like we were in for at least a thirty minute wait. We wouldn't be at the bank to get Danny before 4:00.

*He's gunna be one pissed off motherfucker.*

Hope leaned against Homer and fell asleep. Homer rested his head against the door and stared out the window. I watched a Mexican border guard slowly walk down our line of cars. The guard would bend over, quickly glance into the front seat of a car, then the back seat before strolling importantly to the next vehicle.

We gradually inched forward, finally meeting the advancing guard. He peered into the cab, stepped to the truck bed, pulled a flashlight out, and then checked under the tarp immediately behind the cab. The guard asked me something in Spanish. I stuck my head out the window, smiled stupidly, and shrugged. Dropping the tarp, he walked to the rear of the truck and spotted Jerry. He laughed. The guard stepped onto the bumper and looked into the glass case then reached inside and fumbled with something. Using both hands, he removed a five-pound box of spackling powder from the crate, lost his grip, and dropped it to the pavement.

*Shit.*

I opened the door to get out. I stepped from the cab and turned toward the rear of the truck. The guard, wide eyed and crouching behind the bumper, was pointing a handgun at me.

"ALTO!" he roared.

His shoes were coated in white powder.

I tripped over myself as I fell back against the open truck door. The guard put a whistle to his lips and began blowing. The shrill screech startled Hope and Homer. I looked into the cab. A guard appeared at the passenger window, thrust a shotgun into the cab, and then started yelling in Spanish. Hope screamed and threw her head into Homer's lap. Homer leaned forward and covered her. The guard slammed the muzzle of the shotgun into the side of Homer's head and held it there, repeating his command in Spanish. I felt a quick, dull thud at the base of my skull then a sharp, painful blow to the top of my head.

*** 

My wrists were burning. It felt like salt in a cut. I had a blinding, skull-splitting headache. My ears were ringing.

*Asleep? I've been asleep? Hung over?*

It was pitch dark. It smelled like a sewer.

*Where the fuck...?*

I tried to move.

More sharp pains in the wrists and a clanking noise.

*What the...,*

I was being restrained.

I tried moving again. More pain accompanied by the sound of...

*Chains!*

*Holy shit! I'm in motherfuckin' chains!*

"Stop movin' aroun', dammit," a whispered voice hissed. "Ya got chains on. Sit up an' lean for'ard! Lean for'ard an' put y'ur hands on y'ur knees."

"Jerry?" searching the dark.

"Yeah. Now do whud I told ya ta do."

I followed the directions. The pain eased to bearable.

"What the fuck is goin' on?" thrashing my head about. "I can't fuckin' see!"

"Shud up, dumbass! Ya got a blindfold on."

Someone between Jerry and me was moaning lowly with every breath.

"Is 'at Homer?" I asked.

"Yeah."

I felt a chill sweep over me.

"What'd they do to him?"

"Beat the shit out uv him. Whu's it soun' like they did to him."

"F'r what? What happened?"

"How the fuck would I know? I come to an' here my ass wuz. We must'a got inta some trouble at the bar last night."

"Where's Hope?"

"With Danny. They both better be doin' somethin' ta git our sweet asses out'a here," he slurred. "I cain't b'lieve 'at son uv a bitchin' Hector let this happen, man," growling. "One'a us must'a killed somebody f'r us ta be chained up like this, man. Yew 'member killin' anybody?"

"Didn't have anything ta do...," an unbelievably sharp pain in my head prevented me from finishing.

"Whu' wuz 'at?" Jerry.

"Jus' a minute," gritting my teeth. "Feels like my brains bein' electrocuted. Hurts ta talk. Gimme a second."

It took several minutes for the pain to let up.

"Jerry?"

"Yeah."

"You were passed out when it all happened, but...I think we got arrested at the border."

"Arrested? F'r whut? Shit! Was Homer carry..."

"Lemme finish, goddammit," panting in pain.

I paused to allow the pounding to subside then began again.

"The border guard dropped a box'a spacklin' powder. I got out ta help clean it up. He pulled a gun on me. Next thing I know, Homer's got a shot gun in his face an' then I got hit in the head. From b'hind I think."

" 'at's it? Ya don't remember nothin' else?"

"Not at the moment."

*Jesus! I think I'm gunna pass out.*

"Somethin' pissed 'em off," Jerry. "Ya sure ya didn't call him a stupid spick 'r somethin' when he dropped the pow...,"

Jerry groaned. An extended groan.

"Fuuuck, man," he whispered.

His chains began to rattle violently. As suddenly as the clanking had begun, it halted. I could hear Jerry growling lowly.

"Jerry? What's wrong?"

"Spacklin' powder," Jerry blurted. "It wuz the fuckin' powder, man. They mus' be sayin' it's heroin 'r coke 'r somethin' like 'at. Don't make no diff'r'nce. Our ass is fucked."

"But it's *not* heroin! Once they test it they'll see that an' we're out'a here. Right?" hoping like a son of a bitch I was right.

"They knew 'at shit wudn' coke 'r heroin five minutes after they thumped ya on 'at rabbit-ass brain'a y'urs. They're holdin' us ta see if they c'n git some money out'a this thing. They're gunna claim it's coke 'r somethin', schedule us f'r a fuckin' hearin' 'at's ten thousan' fuckin' years from now then give us a chance ta call somebody stateside an' arrange bail," clearing his throat and spitting. "As soon's they git the money...they let us go. Then we skip back over the border an' 'at'll be the end uv it. I'm kind'a su'prised they ain't let us call by now. All they want's the fuckin' money."

"How come ya know so much about this shit? I mean, how do ya know they're not just gunna keep us here f'rever?"

" 'cause 'at's how it happened ta some other people I know only it was baby powder. Bet ya they're runnin' a scam somethin' pr'tty damn close ta that. Yew'll see."

"What about Hope? They got her chained up like this somewhere?"

Jerry didn't answer.

Homer stirred, his chains clanking and clattering. He moaned loudly before falling quiet.

"Homer?" I whispered.

"He's still out uv it," Jerry. "They must'a whacked him pr'tty fuckin' hard."

We sat quietly. My back and legs were cramping from holding the forward leaning position. My ass felt like I was sitting on a pile of sharp rocks. I tried to find a more tolerable position. The burning, searing pain in my wrists worsened. I returned to the old position, remaining as still as possible.

"How long ya think we been here?" I asked.

"Can't say f'r sure. I been awake about six...maybe seven 'r eight hours."

"Damn."

"No shit, damn."

"Ya think Danny knows what's happened?"

"I been wonderin' abou' that. I'm pr'tty sure he knows about us by now. 'at's po'bly why they ain't had us make a call ta somebody ta raise some money. He's pro'bly swingin' a deal with 'em righ' now."

"How much ya think it's gunna cost?"

"Shit, I don't know. Once they fig're out we ain't workin' f'r some big-ass, rich company, it pro'bly won't come ta all 'at much."

A few minutes passed.

"Jerry, I'm...I'm really worried about Hope."

Jerry went off.

"Don't be thinkin' abou' that shit, man! Don't go mentionin' it again! Un'erstand?" and then began mumbling. "Don't *even* go fuckin' thinkin' about it, man. There ain't a fuckin' thing we c'n do about it righ' now."

I guess about thirty minutes passed. Homer stirred and moaned. He took a deep breath then broke into a gurgling cough.

"What if Homer needs a doctor?" I asked.

"Whud if he does? I ain't got a dime f'r the fuckin' phone call," Jerry answered.

"Homer?" I whispered.

"Yeah," weakly.

"You gunna live?"

"Yeah. What's wrong with my...my wrists're..."

"They put us in chains," Jerry. "The only way ta take the pressure off y'ur wrists is ta bring y'ur legs up, rest y'ur arms on y'ur knees, an' lean for'ard a li'l bit. Y're also blindfolded."

Chains clanked as Homer maneuvered into the position Jerry had described.

"Where are we?" Homer.

"Some kind'a Mexican jail 'r somethin'," I answered.

"My balls are asleep," Homer groaned.

"Y'ur whut?" Jerry.

"My balls," raising his voice. "My nuts. They're numb."

"Gil," Jerry snorted. "Reach over an' rub some feelin' back inta Homer's nuts."

"Whud'a ya think my balls feel like?" I grumbled.

"Anything else wrong?" Homer.

"Thirsty," I told him. "Head hurts. Sore. Hung over."

"How about you, Jerry?" Homer again.

"Hung over. Pissed off."

"How long have we been here?" Homer.

"Six 'r eight hours 'r so," Jerry. "I cain't see the clock radio next ta my bed here with this fuckin' blindfold on."

"I'm gunna try to stand up," Homer.

"Don't!" Jerry snapped. "There's a chain aroun' y'ur waist. Ya cain't stand up. It's attached ta the floor b'hind us somehow."

"Shit," Homer.

"No shit, shit," Jerry. "Since we can't leave ta get somethin' ta eat we're gunna have ta send out f'r pizza an' ya know how expensive 'at..."

"Dammit, Jerry," I interupted. "One goddamn asshole wise-crack after the other. Is there somethin' about dungeons 'at brings the comedian out in ya?"

"Ya know...if this wuz the *worst* I'd ever seen then, yeah, I guess I'd pro'bly be cryin' about it too."

"I'm *not* cryin' about it, motherfucker," pissed.

"Did I say ya wuz?"

"That's what you were hintin' at."

"I wudn' hintin' at shit, turd. I don't go hintin' at things. I tell it like it is cocksucker."

"Jerry, y're so full'a..."

"No, man. Listen ta this. I'm gunna tell ya somethin' *exactly* like it is an' yew ain't gunna like it one bit. I ain't worryin' about none'a this 'cause Jesus..."

"Fuck Jesus!" raising my voice.

"Nigger, nigger, nigger, nigger!" Jerry, back at me.

"HEY!" Homer's voice echoed in the chamber.

Quiet. For a long time.

"Where's Hope?" Homer breaking the silence.

No response.

"They beat the shit out of me when I tried to keep them from putting handcuffs on her. That's all I remember."

"Then 'at's all we know," Jerry.

*She's okay. She's gotta be.*

Footsteps echoed in the vault as someone approached our cell. The footsteps halted. Keys clinked. The sound of metal against metal then a loud creaking noise. The footsteps crossed the room.

*Sixteen steps. Eight paces. Forty, forty five feet or so.*

My blindfold was pulled down around my neck. The guard stepped over to Homer and then Jerry. We were each given a drink of water from a canteen. The guard left without saying a word.

The room was dimly lit. I could make a few things out. We were shackled to a concrete pillar about six feet high in the center of a circular, brick room probably a hundred feet across. The ceiling, made of corrugated metal, was around twenty feet above us. Four evenly spaced slits were located at the top of the room. The concrete floor slanted downward and away from the pillar.

Sets of shackles like ours were set in the brick wall surrounding us. A single chain with a lock in the last link was attached to an eyebolt sunk in the floor. The eyebolt was about four feet from the wall and directly opposite every set of shackles. This was the waist chain preventing us from standing. The wrist shackles were two feet long and attached to an eyebolt a yard or so from the floor. This arrangement didn't allow a prisoner to rest his hands in his lap. The prisoner was forced into a sitting position when trying to ease the pressure of the shackles on the wrist.

"Is 'at sunlight?" Jerry, looking up at the slits.

"Sunrise," Homer, nodding his head

"We were picked up at 5:00 'r 6:00," I said. "We've been here ten 'r twelve hours."

"Fuck me," Jerry, mumbling. "I thoughd It wuz the room 'at stunk."

I looked over.

"I fuckin' puked all over myself," Jerry.

"If it makes ya feel any better," I coughed, "I've been pissin' in my pants all night."

We spent the morning squirming from one painful position to another, occasionally speculating about what time it was, the efforts that might be underway to get us out, bitching about our luck, cussing our fate, and demanding, from no one in particular, an answer to "Why us"? The room gradually heated up like an oven. It was stifling. I was sweating constantly. During what we figured to be late afternoon a guard brought us some more water.

By evening, as the space darkened, things began to cool down again. We were given a bowl of bean soup. I slopped it down. It was cold and didn't taste like anything at all.

"Looks like we're here f'r the night," Jerry, " 'r they wouldn'a fed us."

"I can't feel my hands any more," I said. "An' I'm not whinin' about it, either. Just sharin' an observation," without looking over at Jerry.

Jerry cackled lightly. The guard returned, collected our bowls, gave us a drink of water, and then departed.

Silence for quite a while.

I wasn't really thinking about anything. I lapsed into what was more of a daze than anything else. A thick, dark haze.

*Survival, escape, resistance, and evasion.*

*SERE school.*

*'67. Oak Harbor, Washington.*

*'at's what this reminds me of. Fuckin' SERE school.*

*Simon an' Garfunkel. "Feelin' Groovy".*

"You know what?" Homer's voice.

It thundered in my head. Jerry stirred, but didn't say anything.

"What?" my answer sounding more distant than Homer's voice had.

"I believe I'd rather be tromping cotton," Homer, in a dry, raspy voice.

I paused before answering.

"Yeah. Me too."

Jerry broke the next period of silence.

"Maybe God got tired'a listen' ta yew two bitchin' all'a the time about trompin' an' decided ta give ya somethin' diff'r'nt ta bitch about."

"Well," I grumbled, "if he got tired'a hearin' me bitch about trompin', he's never gunna hear the end'a this one."

Several minutes passed.

"It's not as bad as what it was over there," I said.

Jerry and Homer agreed in a heartbeat.

"Then, it idn't all 'at bad," I mumbled. "I mean...it's been worse."

Jerry whistled softly.

" 'at's fuckin' scary, man."

"It's not as much scary as it is pathetic," Homer.

"Damn!" Jerry.

"What's wrong now?" right as my nose caught it. "Goddammit, Jerry! Is 'at you?"

"And you're not sitting right next to him," Homer gagging.

"I got the runs," Jerry.

The cell gradually darkened. Two guards, one with a flashlight, returned and removed the shackles from our hands. We busied ourselves rubbing every sore muscle we could reach.

"I c'n lie down," Jerry, sounding almost content.

Homer and I shifted around, eventually managing a position on our sides.

"This ain't half bad," Jerry, yawned. "If I had a cigarette, I'd damn near be comf'tr'ble."

My butt felt like it was on fire as the blood rushed back into it.

We settled in and listened to a conversation in Spanish drifting down to us from one of the four tiny slits at the top of the room— loud, rough, boisterous voices occasionally interrupted by outbursts of deep sinister sounding laughter.

"Think 'at's other prisoners?" I asked.

"Pro'bly," Jerry.

"What'a ya think they're sayin'?"

"Pro'bly tryin' ta decide which one'a us they want the guards ta drag up there so they c'n butt-fuck him all night," Jerry. "They're gunna want the bes' lookin' one. Guess I best be uglyin' up real quick," he mumbled.

"Listen ta that," as I slapped Homer's leg. "He really thinks they're gunna wan'a have anything ta do with some filthy, puked on, hung over scum bag with the runs."

"They don't give a shit about the puke 'r the runs," Jerry. "All's they wan' is good lookin', young, an' tight," Jerry.

"I'm younger than you."

"Yeah, but y're a hell uv'a lot uglier," Jerry.

"Homer? Seriously...which one'a us would you wan..."

"Gill...don't even think of asking me a sick-ass question like that," Homer.

The iron door creaking open woke me at dawn. I was chilled. Shivering.

Three guards, two with shotguns, entered the room. A third guard was dragging a hose. Jerry and Homer began to stir. The two shotguns positioned themselves along the wall of the chamber and pointed the guns at us. The hose man shouted something in Mexican. The hose belched, snaked a little, spit a few times, and then erupted. We covered our faces as Capitan Asshole drenched us in freezing water. Asshole wandered around, squirting us from every angle. The shower lasted three or four minutes, the guards laughing the whole time. After hosing us down, Asshole expertly began directing bits of feces, streams of foaming urine, and scurrying cockroaches toward a drain located at the base of the wall. Before leaving the room they approached Homer and took a closer look at his scar.

More Mexican followed by laughter.

Capitan Asshole, along with his asshole buddies, left the room, squirting us one last time as the door clanked shut.

"F-fuck!" Jerry, wheezing and hugging himself tightly. "It's f-fuckin' c-cold, man," teeth chattering.

"No s-shit," I chattered back.

"They g-give you a s-shower and you're s-still not happy," Homer.

By mid morning the room was heating up again.

"Try to remember what the shower felt like," Homer. "This afternoon we'll be sweating our asses off again."

"We won't be here this afternoon," Jerry, swatting at one of several hundred flies sharing the cell with us. "They're lettin' us out this mornin' 'r they wouldn'a hosed us off an' they'd'a fed us somethin' by now. We'll be out'a here in a coupl'a hours," confidently.

We stretched out and listened intently for the sounds of approaching guards.

At last, somewhere around late morning, heavy steps in the passageway outside the cell door. A guard opened the screeching gate then entered. A second guard, armed with a shotgun, followed him. The unarmed guard released us from the waist chains then pointed at the gate. We wobbled, legs numb, muscles weak and cramping, to the exit. We were led through a series of halls to a heavy, wooden door. The unarmed guard kicked it open. The sunlight blinded me as I was pushed into a dirt lot filled with dusty police cars, box trucks, and vans.

It was later than I had guessed. More like mid afternoon rather than late morning. One of the windowless box trucks, back doors open, had been placed outside the exit. The guards hurried us into the truck's box, motioned for us to sit on the floor, and then slammed the doors closed. The box was like an oven. They'd probably deliberately left it closed up and in the sun all day just for us. It was difficult to breathe.

*DON'T faint, goddammit. Jerry'd never let ya live it down.*

We remained quiet as the vehicle began to jerk and rock its way over a bumpy road. Traffic sounds—horns, reving engines. Some occasional music. Stop-and-go driving. After what seemed to be a good fifteen minutes the van came to a halt. Commands in Mexican. Shuffling feet. The crisp, metallic click of rounds being chambered. The doors swung open. The sun blasted my eyes again. I rose into a crouching position, moved to the door, and then hopped out. I fell to the ground. A guard roughly pulled me to my feet. I squinted in the direction of a line of uniformed, AK-47 wielding Mexicans. I turned to watch Jerry, then Homer struggle from the box, both straining to adjust their eyes in the glaring afternoon sun. We stumbled several times as we were shoved down an aisle of policemen toward a walk-bridge. The area was unfamiliar. At the end of the armed escort one final guard indicated we were to continue on over the bridge. I looked up and saw a lone figure standing at the top.

"Hugo," I whispered and smiled.

The closer we got to Hugo, the easier it was to see the hard, taut lines of his face. Hugo didn't appear to be as happy to see us as we were to see him.

I slowed as we drew nearer, stopping a good ten feet from him. Even that felt too close.

"How's Hope?" Homer asked.

"Fine," expressionless.

We all broke into smiles, nodding our heads like idiots.

Hugo slowly removed his sunglasses. He glared at us, head bobbing, lips pursed tightly, sweat running down his face, bulging eyes unblinking.

Long, miserable seconds crept by.

Homer shuffled his feet. Jerry kept clearing his throat. I rubbed my wrists, hoping Hugo might notice we were already injured.

Finally.

"You boys all right?" his voice deep, strained.

We all nodded, avoiding eye contact.

"The Border Patrol has y'ur things. It's about three blocks east'a here."

I began to step toward Hugo. He raised his hand. I halted.

"Ya each owe me five hun'r'd dollars," Hugo.

"Hell, 'at's no problem," Jerry. "We c'n pay ya as soon as Danny cashes the..."

" 'at's five hun'r'd each Danny was short after givin' the Mexicans ever' blessed dime you sons a bitches didn't spend on whores an' liquor," his voice shaking.

The news hit us hard.

"Ever'thing?" Jerry managed.

"Ever' goddamn penny uv it," eyes flaring. "You boys went an' fucked this 'un right inta the dirt, didn't ya?" way beyond disgusted.

He pulled his wallet out, removed three twenties, stepped up to us, and then handed one to each of us.

"Cigarettes, gas, food, booze, whores, ointment f'r them wrists," fighting to maintain his composure. "I don't care what ya do with it. J'st yew make damn sure all three'a ya show up t'morrow at the office ta start workin' 'at five hun'r'd, excuse me, five hun'r'd an' twenty dollars off. I expect it ta be paid off by the time I get back from Europe in September. Do we have an understandin'?" his voice cracking in rage.

We nodded. Hugo pulled a bandanna from his pocket and handed it to Homer.

Jerry cleared his throat.

"Hugo, it wudn' like we done anything wrong here. It wuz jus' some spacklin' powder f'r...,"

Hugo turned and walked away.

"...f'r...cleanin'," Jerry's voice trailing off as he looked up the dry river bed. "Fuck it," to himself.

We watched Hugo cross the bridge, enter a parking lot, get into his station wagon, and then drive away.

"Shit, man," Jerry grumbled as we made our way for American soil. "All 'at fuckin' work f'r nothin' an' I'll bet ever' fuckin' one'a my tapes an' the radio's been stole from the van. I'm su'prised they didn't jus' take the whole damn van."

Homer glanced back over his shoulder at me.

"Jerry," Homer, proceeding cautiously, "I guess I have something I should tell you about the van. It kind of slipped my mind before now. Didn't seem as important as being thrown in jail."

It took three hours to get the truck released from the Border Patrol lot. Jerry railed on Homer the whole time. At one point Homer signed the title of his truck over to Jerry, promising to give Jerry an additional five hundred dollars as soon as possible. When we were about to leave, Jerry pulled the truck title from his shirt pocket, waved it in Homer's face, and then took the keys from Homer. Jerry hopped behind the wheel. He started it up then stared straight ahead while Homer and I got into the cab. Jerry peeled out.

It was going on 5:00.

We stopped to buy cigarettes and a case of beer then grabbed something to eat. The waitress kept staring at our raw wrists and filthy clothes like we might be escaped convicts or something. Nobody said anything as we cleared the El Paso city limits. Homer had Jerry pull off the road long enough for Homer to remove a canvas sack from under the frame. It contained a few joints and some pills.

*My fuckin' God. I can't b'lieve this shit.*

"I don't feel like sharin' no weed with any'a yew right now," Jerry grumbled as he edged back onto the highway and popped open a beer.

I snatched a beer up. Homer downed a few pills after returning the joints to the sack.

It was after sunset when I finally drifted off to sleep.

Homer's snoring must have woke me up. He was leaning against the passenger door, an oily towel serving as a pillow. I'd slid over and ended up resting against him. I was holding an empty beer can. A milepost, momentarily lit up in the headlights, slipped by.

## LUBBOCK 4

I could see a glowing dome on the horizon. I continued to brood over the whole disaster.

*What a fuckin' nightmare.*

*What a fuckin' waste.*

*Supposed ta be comin' back rich an', instead, all we've got is a bunch a broken glass an' a Mexican police record.*

*Fuck.*

I watched the yellow dashes in the road click by and rekicked myself in the ass over everything. Blowing the job. Losing all the money. Running around on Bobbie.

The truck seemed to wander slowly to the left until the center line stripes were lined up with the middle of the hood. I looked over at Jerry. His head was down, chin resting on his chest, eyes closed. It didn't immediately register that Jerry was asleep.

It was too late anyway.

The truck swerved sharply to the left, front wheels digging into the sandy shoulder. The rear end jacked around and then the truck began to roll—one time, two times. It came to rest on the passenger side. The cab smelled like gasoline. Jerry was scrambling all over me while Homer was trying to shove me away. Both were yelling "What the fuck?"s, "holy shit"s, and "Jesus Christ"s.

"STOP!" as loud as I could. "Ever'body fuckin' stop!"

They froze.

"Jerry! Y'ur window's broke out! You gotta climb out first! We'll push!" still shouting for some reason.

The smell of gasoline was growing stronger. Jerry pulled himself to the driver's door. Once his head was in the window Homer launched him from the cab and out onto the door. I rose up and reached for the steering wheel. Jerry grabbed my hand and pulled while Homer pushed. I shot from the cab. Homer, sack in hand, was right behind me. We tumbled to the ground then scrambled to the roadside. Flames immediately followed a whooshing pop. Within seconds the truck and the gas soaked weeds around it were ablaze.

We stood by the road and watched in silence, not bothering to check for injuries or realizing the gas tank might explode. We watched the flames dance higher and higher. My eyes watered as thick, acrid smoke from burning plastic and rubber drifted over me.

Gradually the flames died down. No one said a word, even after the flames in the weeds had died to weakly flickering embers and all that was left of the fire in the cab was a set of glowing seat springs and puddles of smoldering, shiny black, gooey plastic. We stood and stared at what was left of the truck, our tools, the glass crates, our clothes, until only the occasional clinking of a cooling piece of glass disturbed the quiet night.

Eventually Jerry reached into his pocket and removed a folded piece of paper—the title Homer had signed over a few hours before. Jerry stuffed it into Homer's back pocket, jerked the canvas sack from Homer's hand, and then removed a joint. He handed the sack back to Homer then lit up before starting down the road to Lubbock, rubbing his right shoulder as he went. Homer, limping, followed at a distance. I fell in behind Homer, wiping some blood from a small cut on my arm.

Without a doubt, we would all have better days in Hell.

A man in a stake bed truck picked us up at the city limits. He dropped us off at Tenth and University. Jerry went straight to his place without so much as a goodnight. Homer and I crept up the stairs to the stoop. I glanced at the clock on the kitchen wall.

*Five.*

Homer got two beers from the frig and offered me one.

"Lemme check on Bobbie first."

I ran smack into Danny as I pulled the hall curtain aside.

"Shit. Ya scared the crap out'a me," I whispered.

"No need to whisper," and looked down. "She's not here. She's moved out."

"What're you talkin' abou…"

"Joan said she left two days ago."

I rushed into the bedroom and turned the overhead light on. The bed was missing. All her pictures and posters were missing. Three empty ceiling hooks where her hanging plants used to be. I walked over to the closet and looked inside. Her clothes were gone. Shoes. Jacket. Hair dryer. Everything. I stepped over to the chest of drawers and picked up a stack of postcards. Three were from Hope, one was from Jerry, one from Homer, one from Danny. The floor creaked behind me.

"Bobbie left a letter with Joan," Danny. "Joan gave it to me."

I turned and took the letter.

"Before you read it," his voice failed. "Before you read it," starting over, "could you come into the kitchen?"

Danny looked ill. Drawn and gray. Eyes swollen and red. I nodded and followed him from the room.

Homer was leaning back in the chair. I sat down, clutching the letter in my hand. Danny placed his back against the refrigerator then slid into a squatting position on the floor, ending up staring into his lap.

*Somebody's died!*

Danny coughed, raised his head, and then began.

"Hugo thought it was best you weren't told about this until you got back to Lubbock. You'd already gotten into enough trouble down there."

"Tell us what?" Homer, eyes narrowing.

A chill swept over me as I watched Danny wipe some tears away. He took a deep breath then, quietly, his voice quivering, told us Hope had been raped by the Mexican police while in custody.

I went cold.

I could feel the blood rushing from my head. I was dizzy, reeling. My temples caved in. I felt a stabbing pain in my chest.

Homer stumbled out onto the stoop. I could hear him retching over the side.

Bobbie's letter fell from my hand. I attempted to get up, but couldn't stand.

Homer thundered down the steps.

My ears were roaring. I was coming apart. Completely apart.

"Where's she now?" I asked weakly.

"Hugo's not saying."

Numb.

I retrieved Bobbie's letter from the floor and carefully opened it, trying not to rip the envelope. I hesitated before removing a single sheet of paper. As I unfolded it, a lock of white hair tied with a piece of pink ribbon fell onto the table. I picked it up and read the short note.

> Dear Gil,
> I will always like you very much.
> Bobbie

Down the street I heard a long, anguished wail. It was Jerry.

"YEW GODDAMN BASTAAAARDS! YEW SON UV A BITCHIN' BASTAAARDS! I'M GUNNA KILL EVER' GODDAMN ONE'A YAAAAAA!"

The hair on the back of my neck stood up. I was covered in chill bumps.

Shauna was crying, begging Jerry to come back into the house.

Danny broke down crying.

My stomach knotted, a series of dry, choking sobs wracked my chest. I lowered my head to the table and shut my eyes.

Twenty minutes? Thirty maybe? I had no idea. It didn't really matter.

One thought kept repeating itself over, and over, and over—Father Torres' asking me what one question I would ask God if I was allowed to ask him something.

## GLYNN E. THOMPSON

*I wan'a know...the one question I'd ask him would be...why is it that... that you seem ta get such a kick out'a...out'a crawlin' up ever'body's ass an'...an' takin' a switchblade ta all the tender places?*

*Why is 'at?*

*Jesus goddamn motherfuckin' Christ.*

# CHAPTER SIX
## August, 1972

Bobbie and me are gettin' married," I announced. Homer and Jerry exchanged surprised, no, shocked glances. It took a few seconds for the news to sink in.

Jerry reached across the table and slapped me on the arm.

"Knocked her up, huh?" snickering.

"She's pregnant," put off by his portrayal of the situation. "She's *not* knocked up. There's a big-ass difference."

"Yeah," raising his brows. "I'm sure there is," with a smirk.

Homer downed a swig of beer.

"This is exactly why I wanted ta tell you an' Homer b'fore anybody else," glaring at Jerry. "Homer b'cause he'd understand. I wanted ta tell *you*," sticking a finger in Jerry's face, "so you could get all y'ur nasty-ass, filthy little comments out'a the way b'fore sayin' somethin' stupid in front'a Bobbie."

"Hey!" firing back. "Don't go gittin' pissed at me, man. I ain't the one 'at..."

"I'm not pissed! Why should I be pissed?" then lowered my voice. "I...I love her."

Homer and Jerry looked at each other. As a declaration of love, I guess it had lacked a convincing degree of passion.

"I honestly love her," trying again. "I'm glad this happened. It'll force me ta make a commitment I know's right an' wouldn't have the guts ta make otherwise."

I put my cigarette out and watched the last flimsy string of smoke disappear above the dying butt.

Jerry cleared his throat and shifted around in his chair.

"I gotta ask ya somethin', man. And don't go freakin' out on me when I ask ya. Okay?"

I looked up from the ash tray, ran my hands over my face, and then nodded.

"And don't be lyin' about it," Jerry squinted. "It's a serious damn question."

I nodded.

Jerry cleared his throat again.

"Okay," glancing at Homer. "Did ya decide ta love her *b'fore* ya knoc...b'fore she, uh...b'came with child 'r was it *after* ya found out she wuz with child?" raising his brows.

Both Jerry and Homer sat motionless, quietly anticipating the answer.

"I think I've pro'bly always loved her," I answered slowly. "In a certain way. Just never admitted it ta myself."

Jerry's brows relaxed.

"Tha' sounds good. Real good," nodding his head "Sounds like ya, you know...like ya mean it," slapping Homer on the arm. "Sort'a," under his breath.

"I mean it a lot, goddammit!" I flared.

"There ya go again! Gittin' all pissed off."

"If ya don't want me gettin' all pissed off then quit makin' it sound like I don't love her an' that I'm not happy as hell about all this."

"I ain't tryin' ta make ya sound anyway, man," Jerry, turning to Homer. "Am I sayin' he don't love her?"

Homer shrugged.

"See? Homer don't think I'm fuckin' with ya. I'm jus' tryin' ta get ya ta see how ya gotta be real careful about some'a the things y're thinkin' right now," leaning back in his chair and locking his fingers behind his head. "I'm jus' tryin' ta git ya ta fuckin' think straight, man. I mean, if y're marryin' her jus' 'cause she's havin' a baby..."

"I'm marryin' her b'cause I *want* to," as calmly as I could. "Not b'cause I feel like I *have* to."

"Let me finish, man!" angrily. "Don't go cuttin' me off like 'at. This is fuckin' serious shit, man. Yew gunna lemme finish?"

"Yeah. Go ahead," looking out the open kitchen door.

"Okay," lighting a cigarette. "Why can't ya jus' start livin' with her again an' see how things go with a kid aroun'? People git preg... c'n I call it bein' pregnant without you gittin'..."

"Yeah," waving my approval. "Pregnant's fine. Go ahead."

"People git pregnant all the time an' don't go runnin' off an' gittin' married. Yew git married an' then decide it ain't gunna work," shaking his head slowly, "tha's a whole differ'nt thing. 'at's some badass shit ta be stuck in. B'lieve me, man. I know," gazing down at the floor.

He looked saddened.

Homer cleared his throat.

"Jerry's right. You're not doing anybody any favors by getting married if you're not sure you, you know...you really love her. And," shuffling his feet nervously, "there's other ways of handling it," voice becoming a whisper.

"Abortion?" I grunted.

"No fuckin' way, man!" Jerry exclaimed. "Ya don't go killin' y'ur own baby, man."

"I know," sighing. "I know. I couldn't ask her ta even consider that. She dudn't think 'at way."

"Damn straight," Jerry, relieved. "I still can't b'lieve 'at's whut Carol went an' did. Even if it wuz Doug's kid. Damn good thing she went home ta Denver, man. I'd'a kicked her leso ass if she'd'a come back here after her killin' her own baby like 'at."

"Well," Homer lighting a cigarette, "like Jerry suggested, why don't you move in again with Bobbie for a while? You don't have to get married right away. Take it a little at a time."

"Yew don't even b'lieve in marriage," Jerry pointed out.

"Dudn't matter," rubbing my face. "*She* does. We talked about the whole thing when I found out she was pregnant. She said she b'lieved in marriage, but only for love. Not b'cause a person gets pregnant. Said she didn't wan'a marry me at first b'cause she'd always feel like I'd married her just b'cause she was pregnant. Took me all night ta convince her I really wanted ta marry her b'cause I...you know...loved her too."

"When did she find out she was pregnant?" Homer.

"While we were in Mexico. I think that's why she moved out b'fore we got back inta town. That an' some other things, I guess."

I let my hands fall to the table.

"Listen, I gotta ask you two somethin' that's eatin' me up."

They both nodded.

"I...I need ta know if...if either of ya thought I was runnin' around on Bobbie in Mexico."

Jerry stirred uncomfortably, glancing at Homer.

"Well," Jerry, glancing once more at Homer before continuing, "yeah. We knew. Ol' Al couldn't shut up about the deal he'd cut ya," raising his shoulders and turning his palms up. "So whut? It's no big deal, man."

Homer got a beer from the refrigerator then sat back down.

"Did Hope know?" I asked.

They looked at each other.

"I didn't tell her," Homer.

"I didn't say nothin'," Jerry, looking back at me. "Nah. There's no way she could'a knowed. Danny didn't know either. He'd'a said somethin' if he'd'a knowed. Somethin' shitty."

"Then how'd Hugo know?" I asked. "How'd he find out?"

"I didn't know he did," Jerry, surprised.

Homer shook his head, brows furrowed.

"On the bridge. When he said something about all of us blowin' ever'thing on booze an' whores. Remember?"

They thought it over.

"Hell," Jerry. "He wuz jus' guessin', man. He wuz pissed as shit. He didn't know f'r sure who was doin' what, man. 'specially yew. I don't give a shit if he knowed about me," he growled. "Fuck him anyways."

"Did ya say anything ta Shauna?"

"I didn't say *anything* ta *anybody*," angrily. "In'a first place, it wudn't none'a her b'ness and second, I don't go spreadin' 'at kind'a shit aroun' about people. Un'erstand? I ain't that'a way."

"I didn't mean ta make it sound like I was accusin' ya of anything."

Jerry relaxed.

"It's," rubbing my forehead, "it's just *real* important for me ta find out if..."

"If *Bobbie* knew," Homer.

"She's retarded if she didn't at least suspect it," Jerry.

"Are you thinking about telling her?" Homer, looking like he might have been holding his breath.

"Damn," Jerry hissed. "Like a confession?" eyes wide. "Don't..."

"Fuck, no," waving my hands in front of me.

" 'cause there ain't no reason ta tell her *shit* about whud ya wuz doin' down there," Jerry, emphatically. "No reason at all. I mean, I wuz tellin' y'all I didn't give a shit if Shauna knew, but I damn sure wudn't gunna come back ta Lubbock an' tell her up front about it. Goddamn, man. I didn't say *nothin'* ta Shauna about it. Not even after she come down with the clap."

I thought Homer's eyes were going to pop out of his head. I know mine felt like they had.

Jerry, realizing his slip, let his head crash to the table.

"Shiiit," he moaned.

"You gave Shauna the clap?" Homer, I swear, turning pale.

"Jesus Christ," I whispered.

"It's okay. It's okay," Homer assured him. "We're not going to say anything."

"No way," I agreed, "but...I gotta know, Jerry. Jus' gotta...how the hell'd ya give her the clap an' not have her walk out on ya? Damn! That's...that's..."

*Unfuckin' b'lievable!*

Jerry slowly raised his head from the table, slumped back into his chair, and then let his chin come to rest on his chest.

"It wuz," he mumbled, "an honest-ta-God bitch, man. It took three fuckin' days ta convince her it wuz this old infection thing from when I was overseas an' 'at all the drinkin' I done in Mexico made it come back," closing his eyes. "Three motherfuckin' days'a her cryin' an' yellin' an' callin' me ever'thing she could think uv."

"Didn't she have ta see a doctor?" I asked. "I mean, how'd ya get a doctor ta go along with a line'a shit like 'at? Christ, Shauna's not stupid."

"Didn't go to a doctor. This friend'a mine knows a guy whose ol' man wuz a doctor. His dad died a few months ago, but this guy c'n still get inta the clinic. His ol' man had all kind's uv shit layin' aroun'. This guy told Shauna whut I wuz sayin' wuz the truth then he fixed us up with some pills."

"Damn. That's slicker'n snot," I said.

He gave me the Eye and leaned toward me.

"How the hell'd *yew* keep from catchin' somethin'?"

*Should I tell him?*

*Shit. Why not?*

"What makes ya think I didn't?"

"You gave "Bobbie the clap?" Homer, eyes wide.

"How could I? She wouldn't even talk ta me when we first got back."

Jerry tapped his finger on the table in front of Homer.

"How about yew?" brows up. "Yew got any secrets?"

"Nah," Homer. "Elida wasn't like that. She was...she was different."

Things got uncomfortably quiet. It was apparent Homer still hadn't completely gotten over Elida.

"We knew that, man," Jerry, breaking the silence.

"When's the baby due?" Homer, moving things away from Elida.

*God, that sounds scary...when will my baby be born?*

*When will I be a...a father?*

"Sometime in January," I told him.

"When's the weddin'?" Jerry.

"I want it b'fore school starts next month. Just ta get it over with," immediately wishing I'd phrased it differently.

Homer and Jerry exchanged glances. They hadn't liked the sound of it either.

"That's not what I meant. What you guys're thinkin'. What I meant was the weddin' needs ta be as soon as possible for all kinds'a reasons."

"Sure, Gil," Jerry, reaching for Homer's beer. "We know whut ya meant."

"Where you going to live?" Homer.

"Well," pausing before continuing, "we were hopin' we could..."

"Stay here?" Homer nodding his head.

"That's what we were hopin'," nodding my head. "For a while, anyway."

"Hell, yeah!" Jerry. "It'd be like havin' a li'l pup runnin' aroun'. Call him Harley. Teach him ta do tricks an' shit."

Everybody was laughing. The tension in the kitchen dissipated noticeably.

"Got a name yet?" Homer

"Not yet."

"Where ya gunna have the weddin'?" Jerry.

"Not sure."

"What kind'a wedding's it gunna be?" Homer.

"Biker wedding!" Jerry. "With ever'body naked an' drunk as shit!"

"I don't know about that either. I'm leavin' all'a that up ta her."

"Listen at that," Jerry, grimacing. "Ain't even married an' she's makin' all the decisions. Tha's some sick shit, man."

"Pussy-whipped already," Homer, swatting me on the arm.

"We s'posed ta be keepin' this a secret f'r now?" Jerry, standing up.

"I've told Hugo. That's all so far."

Someone outside was shouting. We walked onto the landing. It was Vann.

"Congratulations, Gil! Shauna informed me of the impending nuptials!"

I waved and smiled down at Vann.

"Yeah, Jerry," I said, "let's keep this bitch a secret for a little while longer."

"Guess I best be getting' this fuckin' mail delivered," Jerry.

He picked his mail pouch up then lit a joint. He was wearing rubber shower shoes, cut-off jeans, a sleeveless ZZ Top tee shirt, and a red bandanna tied in a wide band around his head.

Homer and I watched him descend the stairs.

"I can't b'lieve they hadn't fired his ass yet," I told Homer.

"They're probably afraid to make him mad," Homer.

Jerry offered Vann a hit as they passed each other on the steps. Vann declined.

"I am extremely excited about the news," Vann, reaching the stoop. He grabbed my hand and shook it wildly.

"Oh, hell. Well," trying to approach his level of enthusiasm, "I'm pr'tty happy about it myself."

"Shouldn't we be leaving for Hugo's?" Vann, glancing at his watch.

"Don't want to be late for your first day," Homer.

I ran inside to grab my riding gear.

Vann followed me down the stairs then over to the bike.

"You sure you don't mind my riding on the back of your bike?" Vann.

"Hell, no," over my shoulder. "That crap about a guy ridin' bitch on a bike is a bunch of macho crap. Anybody says anything, we'll just kick their asses."

"Badass biker dudes," Vann laughed. "Kicking everyone in the ass."

Homer waved goodbye before stepping back into the house. Vann and I mounted up.

"What're you doin'?" looking down at Vann's hands gripping my belt buckle.

"I'm hanging on."

"Not like 'at y're not. Grab the fender an' hang on."

"What if you hit a bump? Won't the wheel smash my fingers?"

"It's a hard-tail. That wheel's not goin' anywhere."

Vann took his arms from around my waist.

"Okay," nervously. "I'm ready. I think."

The ride was nowhere near as embarrassing as I'd anticipated. No cat-calls. No whistles. It was like nobody cared I had a male riding bitch.

*Maybe that's just a chopper-guy thing.*

At least it was beginning to look that way until we got to Hugo's and found Roy standing in the parking lot with a shit-eating grin on his face. I pulled along side Roy's truck to let Vann off before shutting the bike down.

I remained seated while Roy slowly made his way over to us.

"How ya doin', Vann," shaking his hand. "Would ya mind seein' if Stan needs some he'p there in the garage?"

Vann nodded then headed for the garage.

Roy stood quietly beside the bike for a few moments, staring at the ground. Finally, slowly shaking his head, he looked up at me.

"Cute," wrinkling his nose and smiling. "Yew two looked real cute."

"I knew you'd appreciate it," staring over his shoulder into the distance.

"Yew've had a busy week. First, ya go an' git engaged. An' now this," winking at me. "I mean, comin' out'a the closet about y'ur true nature an' all."

"Yeah, Roy," closing my eyes, "it's been one taxing son of a bitch," opening my eyes. "Thank God f'r friends like you ta help me through times like these."

"Acquaintances," Roy frowned. "We're j'st acquaintances. I don't friend up with...homo biker trash."

"Right," dismounting. "Acquaintances."

"I'm leavin' Vann in charge uv this fence paintin' detail," Roy snickered. "That way I'll know it'll git done ta Hugo's exactin' specifications."

"Good thinkin', Roy," and started for the garage.

"The fence is out here," Roy.

"I need ta speak with Hugo before gettin' started."

"Damn slacker."

Vann and Stan were pulling things together for the painting project.

"I'll be right back," I waved and entered the office.

I stopped at the foot of the stairs.

"Hugo! Can I come up an' see ya f'r a minute?"

"Certainly, Gil. Come on up," his voice soft and calm.

I climbed the stairs then settled into one of the chairs in front of his desk.

"Marty Robbins?" hitching my thumb in the direction of the record player.

"It's Frid'y. I c'n listen ta whatever I want," chuckling lightly. "What c'n I do for ya, Gil?"

"It's about the weddin'."

Hugo tensed.

"It's still on," I blurted.

He relaxed.

"I'd like ya ta be my best man," and smiled.

"I'm surprised it's gunna be so traditional," as he stood up.

*Dudn't seem to excited about the idea.*

Hugo walked over to the phonograph, turned it off, and then sat down in the chair to my left. He ran his hands over his face before locking eyes with me.

*Oh, no. He's goin' inside my head.*

"Gil...I want ya ta listen very closely," in his slow drawl. "I don't want ya ta misunderstand what I'm about ta say."

I nodded, an uneasy feeling creeping over me.

"Y'ur askin' me ta be best man an' then me acceptin' won't change a thing b'tween you an' me as far as what happened ta Hope down in Mexico."

My stomach tumbled. I looked into my lap.

"Look at me, Gil. This is important."

I looked up.

"Gil, I can't help but feel like y're hopin' 'at, if I was ta be y'ur best man, then things'd be like they were b'tween us b'fore ya went ta Mexico."

Hugo was laying it down hard.

Things *had* changed. Dramatically. I just didn't want to admit it. He'd distanced himself from me and wasn't budging. He was right about my hoping that having him be the best man might begin to close the gap, but it wasn't going to happen. I'd crossed some kind of line. Hugo'd had enough.

*Damn. Just plain...damn.*

I looked away.

"Y're pro'bly right," sadly. "That's pro'bly what I was thinkin' deep down inside."

Hugo leaned over and touched my arm.

"I j'st...I can't put it out'a my mind like 'at. It's not a matter'a givin' it some time 'r a question of f'rgiven anybody. It's all about how much I still hurt f'r that little girl. It's a pain like no other I've ever had. I can't seem ta find the strength ta shake it."

"We all hurt for her," somberly.

"You'd have ta be one sorry son uv a bitch if ya didn't."

We sat silently for a moment.

"Hugo...do you hate me f'r all'a that?"

"No! Not at all!" hurriedly assuring me. "Don't go thinkin' that at all, Gil," squeezing my arm. "There's some out there who, no matter how hard I've tried not to, I hate enough ta shoot if I could get away with it an' I'm tired'a lyin' ta myself about feelin' that way. But…I don't hate you 'r Jerry 'r Danny 'r Homer," easing his grip on my arm.

A long silence.

"Could ya kill the one's who raped Hope?" I asked in a hush.

Hugo looked out the small window behind his desk for a moment. Then his eyes seemed to wander all around the room, fixing on this or that for a second before moving onto something else. He finally folded his hands in his lap and stared down at them.

"A coyote got inta the chickens one night. Long, long time ago. I shot him. I didn't shoot him b'cause I hated him. I shot him b'cause he proved ta be a threat. Dangerous. I shot him then went back ta bed an' didn't lose a bit'a sleep over blowin' his scurvy little ass away. He was j'st one more animal encroachin' on my world," pausing for a moment. "What they did ta Hope was…," shaking his head slowly, unable to finish. "If they'd been a pack'a starvin' dogs, they'd'a had her f'r dinner. Torn her ta shreds an' devoured her. No thought of her pain 'r concern about the life they were destroyin'. Those animals in Juarez b'haved the same damn way only they were hungry f'r somethin' else. There wudn't a damn thing human about 'em," trembling slightly. "Yes," sighing deeply. "I could kill ever' goddamn one uv 'em that laid a hand on her. I could kill 'em b'cause, in my mind, they've lost their status as human beings," looking out the small window.

*He's talkin' to himself. I might as well be on the moon.*

Hugo slowly got to his feet.

"Ten years ago," reaching for his hat on the desk, "I had this notion that I should do somethin' about changin' the way I felt about such things," waving his hat at the book cluttered shelves. "I thought that thinkin' some people deserve ta die was...well, that it wasn't right ta feel 'at way about people. I thought somethin' in those books might help me b'come a better person. A more compassionate, f'rgivin' soul. I was gunna b'come a shinin' example f'r others. But I was wrong. I wasn't wrong about all those books bein' able ta change me. They could'a changed me if I'd'a let 'em. There's just too damn much in 'em that contradicts most'a what I've seen'a this world. It's been like tryin' ta do the two-step ta Ravi Shankar," he grinned. "No, sir,...where I was wrong was ta think I needed ta change the way I felt about such things. It's an imperfect world...an' there's not a shittin' bit a difference one more Holy man's gunna make. I don't know what the hell I was thinkin'," putting his hat on.

I felt drawn to say something. Anything that might make him feel better.

"Maybe a person's not supposed ta work on changin' the whole world. Maybe a person should just concentrate on the part of the world he's in."

"My portée?"

I shrugged my shoulders, having no idea what that meant.

"Influencin' those in my immediate circle," he explained. "Within my reach."

"Ye'sir. That's what I meant. You've influenced *all* of us, Hugo. We all look up to ya. You've shown us a lot about things."

"Yeah. Ever' time I turn around I c'n see the positive effect my influence has had on all'a y'alls lives."

That hurt.

"I'm tired," he sighed. "Think I'll go ta the house f'r a while," and headed for the stairs.

I followed him into the parking lot. Roy and Stan had left. I went over to Vann.

"What's wrong with Hugo?" Vann.

"Tired. He gets that way," picking a brush up.

"He looked sick."

"Uh...no, he...," trying to shake the effects of the conversation. "Hugo's got this...some kind'a thyroid thing. That's why his eyes bulge a little. It also makes him tired all of a sudden."

I dipped my brush in the paint and began stroking.

"That's not how you do it," Vann informed me.

I stopped and looked at him.

"Roy said to put it on, like this," as he dabbed a freshly dipped brush along a two foot length of board. "Then," going back over the paint, "you smooth it out. Smooth it with each stroke going in the same direction."

"What?" squinting.

"This is how Roy wants it painted," without looking up.

"Damn, Vann. Right out'a boot camp I helped paint the whole goddamn USS Ticonderoga. A fuckin' aircraft carrier, f'r Christ sake. I think I know a little bit about how ta paint somethin'."

"Roy said you would be like this."

"Like what?"

"Difficult to work with."

"Shiiit," hissing loudly.

"He also said you would call him a stupid fuck."

"I was gettin' ta that. The stupid fuck."

*** 

"That's disgusting," Missy cried out.

"What?" digging dried paint from under my fingernail with the fruit cutting knife.

"That!" pointing at the knife.

"It's just paint," continuing to dig.

"Paint an' ever' other thang 'at lives under them nails."

The door to the bar opened slightly. Bobbie, smiling brightly, slipped inside.

I swear to God, something in my chest fluttered. Then, and notably it was after the fluttering, I noticed how hot Bobbie looked—tight, tiny shorts, thin tube top. No bra.

*Bite-size. Goddamn. I want her. Right now.*

Missy ran over to Bobbie and hugged her tightly. She let go and stepped back.

"Y're not even showin' yet," Missy whined. "It's not fair."

Bobbie blushed.

"It won't be long," gently patting her stomach.

I tossed the knife into the liquor well and stepped out from behind the bar. I took Bobbie's hands and kissed her on the cheek.

Missy giggled.

"Yew two go ta one'a the booths ta talk. I'll watch thangs out here."

Thanks," and escorted Bobbie to the rear of the room.


We slid into the booth and immediately embraced. We told each other how much we loved each other, *really* loved each other. And I honestly believed I meant it.

I slipped my hand under the tube top. She pulled my hand away.

"Just hold me," she whispered.

*Of course. She just wants ta be held. A tender moment. I can understan' 'at. No problem. Let her relax for a bit.*

Long, agonizing, tender moments dragged by.

We slowly released each other. She leaned back against the booth and shut her eyes.

*Damn. She's beautiful. Even with her hair cut shorter.*

"How'd it go in Tahoka?" I asked.

Bobbie smiled and opened her eyes.

"Well, after the initial shock, everybody went crazy. They seem ta be really happy for us. I don't think a Justice'a the Peace wedding is gunna work."

"What'a ya mean?" uneasily.

"I mean...my aunts. My uncles. Actually, it was everybody. They want a...*wedding* wedding."

"A *wedding* wedding?" tensing.

"You know?" looking into her lap. "A kind'a...church wedding."

"A *church* wedding."

*This was not at all a part'a the goddamn deal.*

"Well, it wouldn't have ta be *inside* a church," hurriedly presenting an obviously well thought out alternative to a full-blown church wedding. "It could be at my aunt an' uncle's house," snuggling up to me.

"With a minister?" trying to stay calm.

"Preacher," whispering in my ear.

Goose bumps. Chills.

*Think fast. Yes 'r no. This is crucial.*

Bobbie nibbled my ear lobe.

*It's just a weddin'. Wouldn't it be hypocritical of me ta make a big deal out'a somethin' I'm not supposed ta think is 'at big a deal? Fightin' this thing…is it worth the consequences. Short an' long term.*

"We could still write our own vows," moving to my neck.

Everywhere—electrifying, tingling chill bumps on top of goose bumps.

"It doesn't matter," I softly moaned.

*And it dudn't. Not when a person really gets right down to it.*

"What's important," I whispered, "is…is that we're t'gether."

Bobbie's eyes moistened. She drew me to her. We kissed passionately.

"God. I love you, Gil."

I rested my hand on her chest. She pulled the tube top up.

*There. That's settled.*

\*\*\*

Bobbie's uncle, Ted, was a brutish little redneck who'd never been any further from Tahoka than to Sweetwater, right down the road, for the annual rattlesnake roundup. Ted did some mechanic work and house painting to keep his "landscaping" business in the black. He was the closest thing to a father Bobbie had for the moment and had decided to play the part to the hilt. As such, Uncle Ted had expressed a desire to spend some time with me before blessing the foregone. Uncle Ted refused to set foot in Lubbock, a sin-filled college town which, without a doubt, provided the kind of Godless environment where such evils as out-of-wedlock pregnancies thrive. Consequently, I would have to go to Tahoka for the meeting.

On a cloudless Sunday, Bobbie and I drove Hugo's beat up station wagon to Tahoka. I would have preferred the bike, but even Jerry thought the chopper would send the wrong message to Uncle Ted. We arrived in time for Sunday dinner. Ten or so people had shown up. Bobbie and I were the only ones at the table who hadn't been in church since sunup.

Conversation centered on the sermon Bobbie's cousin had delivered during the *early* morning service. David, at least ten years older than Bobbie, was the first one in the history of the clan to have been to college: the Oral Robert's Full Armor of God Evangelical Locked and Loaded Crusaders for Christ Bible College located somewhere around Quitman in east Texas. It was close enough to a real college for Bobbie's bunch.

Everyone at the table had been seriously impressed with how David had so authoritatively crushed every argument against the Bible being *the* word of God and, as such, was the singular undisputable source of truth in the universe. They all expressed an eager anticipation for next week's sermon when David promised to prove, beyond all doubt, what God had in store for those who choose to live outside the "Revealed Truth".
*Halle-fuckin'-lujah.*

After dinner Uncle Ted invited me to join him in the backyard. We seated ourselves opposite each other in rusting metal lawn chairs. Ted eyed me suspiciously as I lit a cigarette.

"How long ya been a smoker?" obviously disapproving of the practice.

"Couple years, I guess," considering putting the cigarette out.

Ted cleared his throat then spit an after dinner lunger into the grass by his chair.

"Ya ought'a quit. It's a filthy habit. Bobbie don't smoke."

*Unless she's drunk, pissed off, 'r post orgasmic.*

"Ya love mah niece?" he growled.

*No, but she gives great head.*

"Ye'sir. I love her more than anything."

"Would ya be marryin' her if she wudn't pregnant?"

*Not if I'd known more about her gene pool.*

"Sir, we'd discussed marriage several times b'fore she was pregnant," straight faced as hell. "It was just a matter'a time."

Ted grunted.

"Y're in college?"

"Ye'sir. Texas Tech. Just finished my sophomore year."

*Would he even know what year that'd be?*

"Whut're ya gunna be when ya finish up?"

"I haven't declared a major yet."

His face blanked. I tried again.

"I'm still not sure what I wan'a do."

The blank look changed to disbelief.

"Bobbie done tol' me ya spent four years in'a Navy."

"Ye'sir."

"So, ya spent four years in'a Navy an' ya been in college f'r a while an' ya *still* don't know whut ya wan'a be?" smirking.

"Well it's…"

"I knowed whut I wanted ta be b'fore I even dropped out'a high school! 'at's why I dropped out…ta start mah own business. Be mah own boss. One'a the easiest durn decisions I ever had ta make."

*Where would the difficulty be in decidin' ta b'come an ignorant fuck-wad?*

"That's impressive," nodding my head. "Ever' now an' then I've thought about droppin' out an' startin' my own business, but I keep thinkin' 'at bein' a teacher might be a p'rtty good deal too," hoping to justify my staying in school.

"A *teacher*?" contemptuously. "Seems like a lot'a *women* go inta teachin'. 'at an' nursin'."

"A *shop* teacher," going for a save. "Or maybe a vocational agriculture instructor."

He nodded approvingly.

"So ya like workin' with wood?"

*I shouldn't do this, but...,*

"My father was a carpenter," I nodded, lips pursed.

"Really? I built a few houses in mah time. It's hard, honest work."

"Dad loved it," smiling like I was up to my neck in a fond memory.

"Bobbie said y'ur folks wuz in Abilene."

"Ye'sir. Actually..."

*Oh, shit. I can't stop myself!*

"...my step dad lives in Abilene. My real dad was beat ta death by some niggers in Dallas about ten years ago," gazing into the distance. "They were helpin' him build a house, but he fired 'em when he figured out they were stealin' some'a his tools. They...they beat him ta death with one'a the very hammers they'd stolt from him."

"MY GOD!" Ted, eyes wide, nostrils flaring. "That's *exactly* why I refuse ta work with niggers! They'll rob ya blind!"

*I'm in.*


"Ya know whut, Gil?" leaning forward and scratching his chin. "I thank I got somethin' ya might be inter'sted in considerin'."

*A cross burning? Having sex with a chicken?*

"How much money ya got goin' inta this marriage? Includin' the cost'a the baby?"

"Well...not a lot. I'm sellin' my bike...my motorcycle. Pro'bly get around seven fifty for it. I'm workin' two jobs an' got the GI bill money comin' in."

"By the time the baby comes, Bobbie said that'd be in January, will ya have four thousand in the bank?" brows raised, certain of the answer.

"Hell...uh, no. Not even close."

"Listen here. I gotta friend in Lou'siana 'at runs shrimp boats in the gulf. It's hard work an' ya'd have ta stay out all season, but ya could put away at least a thousand a month b'tween September an' January. Whud'a a ya thank abou' that?"

*I think y're full'a shit. Why aren't you cashin' in on it?*

"I thought about goin' down there mahself a coupl'a times, but from whut I been tol', there's too many damncath'lics down there. It's all'a 'em Cajuns. Ever' one uv 'em's a damncath'lic. They don't even call a county a county down there! Call it a *parish*! Un'erstand why that'd keep a man from takin' his family down there?"

"Yeah," frowning in disgust. " I un'erstand completely. An' there's nothin' a fell'a c'n do about it. It's math'matical...one Cajun, one Cath...*damn*cath'lic. Ten Cajuns, ten damncath'lics."

"Exactly! But in y'ur situation...j'st show up, rake in'a money then head on back home. Should I call mah friend an' tell him y're inter'sted?" like there really wasn't a lot to think over about such a good deal.

"Four thousand in the bank?" stroking my beard.

"At least," ready to swear on the Bible. "Bobbie could stay with us. Yew'd be livin' on the boat. Yew wouldn't hardly have no expenses."

I hesitated, seriously treating it as a possibility.

"Don't ya thank ya kind'a owe it ta tha' baby? Thank'a Bobbie. Wouldn't it be best f'r her ta not have ta worry about all 'em bills? The cost'a baby food. Diapers. Doctor visits."

*Sit out for one semester. Pull in enough jing ta cover ever'thing plus some. It makes sense. That's a little frightenin'...Uncle Ted makin' sense.*

"I need ta talk it over with Bobbie."

"Is 'at how y're gunna han'le things in y'ur fam'ly?" he sneered.

I eased forward and rested my elbows on my knees.

"Tell ya whut, Uncle Ted," and glanced at the back door, "call y'ur friend an' ask him when he'd want me ta be down there. I'll tell Bobbie when we get home it's just gunna have ta be this way."

Ted slapped me on the shoulder.

"F'r the baby," he nodded.

*Good God was this gunna take some talkin'.*

*Four thou' in three 'r four months though?*

*I'd be stupid not ta try it. I can talk her into it. She'll go along f'r the baby's sake if f'r nothin' else.*

Uncle Ted and I discussed a few more details before going back inside the house.

Bobbie was ready to leave. We said our goodbye's. Ted and I exchanged knowing glances as Bobbie and I pulled off their front lawn and drove away. Bobbie slid over next to me and squeezed my leg.

"What'd you say to Uncle Ted? He thinks y're wonderful."

"He said I was *wonderful?*"

"No," and poked me in the side. "You know what I mean."

"I told Uncle Ted," pecking her on the cheek, "how much I loved ya and how excited we were about the wedding and the baby."

*Wonder how close I'll be ta New Orleans?*

Bobbie sobbed softly. I looked over at her. She was gently crying. I put my arm around her and hugged her tight.

*Emphasize the part about it bein' f'r the baby's sake.*

\*\*\*

I found Doug at the foot of the dock, standing under a leaning, weathered lamp post.

"The Captain thinks it'll be at least six hours b'fore we get underway," I told Doug.

"What time is it?" Doug.

"Eight...eight-thirty. If there was a hotel around here, I'd check in, get a shower an' grab some sleep."

"That...that would be nice," Doug, nodding.

"Let's find a bar," I suggested.

Doug snapped his head in my direction and looked at me as if I'd lost my mind.

"I don't...I mean, that...that isn't...," looking away while shaking his head nervously. "Haven't you noticed what kind...*who* we've been working with the past two weeks? Rebel flag tattoos. Shaved heads. What they, uh...say about long hair. Long beards," glancing at me. "I don't think...going to a bar here would be...very, uh, you know...smart."

"The key words in all that are 'two' an' 'weeks,'" Doug. We been humpin' it for *two* solid weeks," stepping to the other side of the old, rickety dock and pointing down a gravel road at what there was of Cameron, Louisiana. "See that? Just one block away. A cozy, friendly lookin' little tavern. Now...what could possibly happen that we couldn't out run in a block. Especially if they're all drunk-up. Seriously, Doug. We've earned a beer 'r two. Don'ch ya think?"

Doug stepped over to where I was and looked down the road at a sign that read TAVE N in orange, jittering neon. He lit a cigarette, inhaled deeply, and then let the smoke slowly slip out.

"I'm not going," he said quietly.

"Dammit, Doug. There won't be any trouble. If it looks bad when we walk in, we'll just turn around an' leave."

"We might...get drunk and...miss the boat."

"Ya can't get that drunk in six hours."

"However...you *can* spend a great deal of...money in six hours," holding a finger up and grinning broadly, like he'd delivered the inarguable, knockout consideration. "We are supposed to be *saving*...everything we make. Four thousand dollars. Remember? Isn't that what you told, uh...Bobbie? Four thousand dollars...for the baby? And...four thousand for me. For school so I won't have to, uh...work for a year. With the GI Bill."

"Y're assumin' we'll be down there drinkin' f'r six hours. I only want a beer 'r two," lighting a cigarette. "Goddamn pack'a cigarettes cost more'n 'at," waving the lit cigarette in front of Doug.

"I'm...not going," Doug, glaring at me. "And I'm beginning to feel like...like you think I'm not going because...I might be *afraid* of the...the shrimpers and *that*...*that*...is *not* the reason, although... if...

*Shit! He's tangenting.*

...*if* I *feel* like *you,* uh...are thinking *that*...then I will *have* to go to the tavern and...and *prove* to you I'm *not* afraid to...get into a fight, and...*and* I will *have* to *start* a fight to..."

"Doug, Doug," interrupting him. "Listen," speaking slowly, softly, but emphatically, "I would *never* think you were ever afraid of *anybody*. Okay? Y're just bein'...concerned. Y're considerin' all the possibilities an' 'at's good. I understand. B'lieve me. Okay?"

Doug looked at me, unsure about whether I was bullshitting him or not.

"Doug, I'm gunna go have *one* beer an' come right back. That dudn't mean I'm braver 'r...meaner 'r...'r anythinger than you. Okay? All it means is 'at I'm beer thirstier than you at the moment an' I, honest-ta-God, don't think anything's gunna happen. Understand?"

He nodded hesitantly, struggling with what I really might be thinking of him. I waited for several minutes, watching for a sign indicating he'd accepted the idea that I didn't consider him a complete, one hundred percent coward for not wanting to join me. His expression didn't budge. I took that as the sign I was looking for.

"Doug, I'll be right back," and started toward the tavern, glancing over my shoulder for any sudden signal shifts.

None.

*Good. Real good.*

I picked up the pace.

*Hot damn! A two beer reprieve from an eternity with Doug.*

Doug, once hearing about the shrimping deal I'd fallen into, had, more or less, guilt-tripped me into cutting him in on it. He was convinced it was the last shot he was ever going to have at turning his life around. Just the prospect of putting himself on any kind of track had completely altered his behavior—more up beat and excited about things in general. In the end, I was left with little choice but to get him hired on.

*I'll survive it.*

About one hundred feet from the tavern a beat up, old, white DeSoto crept from an alley I'd passed. I could hear the tires crunching over the gravel as it eased up along side me. Suddenly, it lurched ahead, throwing two tracks of small rocks into the air. The car came to a stop in front of the tavern. Five sleazy looking, lanky, shaved heads emerged from the rusting tank. They gathered around the tavern entrance.

"Whe' yuh be ta go'n'?" one of the dirt bags snarled as I attempted to step around the knot.

Several men, sporting mean looking sneers, were staring out of the plate glass front of the bar. They rested their cue sticks against the window then moved to the double screen door to my right. Two of the car's occupants had stepped behind me. I was surrounded.

"Whu'ch yah gots har?" a fat, sweating pig standing behind the screen doors snorted.

"Nah f'r raht sho," one of the riders behind me. "It gots a b'ard so it t nah be a gahl ah nah thankin'."

"Ah thank a dahmn queeah," another one of the riders.

"Ah'm thankin' same tang," the pig.

Everyone, except me, was laughing hard. They went from Cajun-English to Cajun-Cajun in excited twinkles of the eyes.

I looked back up the road. No one was under the weak night light at the foot of the dock.

\*\*\*

Pungent odor of creosote.
Water slapping on creaking piles.
Hot. Humid.
Smell of rotting river moss and old mud.

Sun breaking the tree tops on the eastern horizon.

West side of a steaming Mekong River glowing deep gold.

I rolled onto my back, stretched, yawned loudly, and then stared up into a deep purple.

*Diesel fumes.*

The muffled, deep throated growl of an idling river patrol boat.

Voices. Familiar voices.

Familiar faces.

Tiredly ordered commands. Familiar commands. Unnecessary commands.

*It's all so routine. Ever'things nothin' more'n a routine anymore.*

Benelli, elbows resting on a fifty gallon drum to steady the high-powered binoculars pressed into his face, anxiously scanning the far bank.

*Always with the glasses. Son uv a bitchin' paranoid. Never relaxes. Fuckin' drivin' me nuts.*

A hushed burst of profanity from the area of the forward .50 cal gun tub.

*Ron.*

*Goofy bastard. Funny goofy, not stupid goofy. Gutsy. Damn good drinkin' buddy an'...*

"You awake?"

*Doug?*

He was in cut off fatigue shorts and an open flack jacket with no tee shirt under it. His helmet had a bullseye painted on it.

"Hey," gentle nudging.

I opened my eyes. It was dark. The lone dock light was suspended in a dirty yellow mist.

"Uh...Gil? You have to, uh...wake up. We have to get out of...you know...leave. Leave here. Get out of Cameron."

I glanced around and panicked.

*What the fuck is goin' on? Where'd ever'body....*

I doubled up.

*Dreamin'.*

"You okay?" Doug asked. "You in pain? Bad?"

"Yeah," below a whisper. "I'm hurtin' all over," and flashed on the beating I'd received.

*Goddamn them son of a bitchin' bastards.*

"Think you can, uh...walk? Now? The Captain and the... sheriff...they said we had to...leave. Get out of...Cameron as soon as, you know...you woke up."

"Got some water?" swollen lips cracking.

"Yes. Water. Right here," and placed a canteen in my hand.

Doug helped me into a sitting position. It hurt. Terribly.

"I got some...some pills down you. About...an hour. No. An hour and about...ten or...maybe eleven or twelve minutes ago. They're probably helping you. A little. Maybe."

Doug must have noticed my reaction to a trace of blood I'd left on the lip of the canteen.

"You...y're cut. Here and there. Bruised. Very bruised up."

"I been fired?"

"Yes. We...are fired. And asked, actually...*ordered* to, uh... leave. Cameron. Now."

"A bunch of Cajun trash kicks the shit out'a me for no goddamn reason an' *I* get canned?" drooling a puddle of bloody saliva onto my pants leg.

"*We.* We...get canned."

"Goddammit, Doug," I whispered, "I'm sorry. I'm so damn sorry I..."

"No!" shaking his head. "No. It is the way it is because... because it was *not*...this whole trip...was *not* supposed to happen. *Or*...it would not be the way it...the way it is. I *really* don't think that, *you* got us fired. I really don't. We were fired because...because *none* of...*this*...was supposed to happen the way we planned it. *Or*...it *would* have happened the way we planned it."

"Yeah, but, Doug..."

"Yah ready ta gots the hell oud'a har," a fat figure yelled as he stomped down a gangway between the boat and the dock. It was the captain we'd been out with the week before. I felt the dock shiver with every thundering step.

The sweating lard ball stopped beside Doug.

"Gots 'it up an' gots da hell goned," scowling down at us.

Doug's eyes flared. His face tightened. Hoping to distract him, I slapped his back and asked him to pull me up. Doug slid a hand under my armpit then brought me to my feet. He continued to glare at the smelly sweat gland. I bent over, grasped the strap on my seabag, and then took a deep breath before slowly straightening up.

*My GOD, that hurts.*

Doug, on the verge of losing it, spun around and quickly walked away, hands behind his head, fingers interlocked.

"Doug!" I called out.

Lard ball was sneering.

"Y'ur duffle bag!" I yelled.

Doug kept walking. I bent over painfully and grabbed the strap of Doug's bag.

"Yuh gahl frien' she mad," sneering.

I shouldered my seabag and hurried after Doug, dragging his bag behind me.

"Kiss my ass, ya fat motherfucker!" over my shoulder.

"Queeahs!" he roared.

"Eat me, ya sorry-ass, inbred bastard!" trying to catch up with Doug, wincing with every agonizing step.

As I approached the end of the dock a car's headlights flashed on.

*Shit! A fuckin' cop car.*

Gritting my teeth, I double timed it to reach Doug. He suddenly wheeled around then stopped. The cop car's lights flashed a few times, as if to signal Doug to keep moving. Doug started back toward me, jaws locked, eyes blazing. I let go of the bags and stepped in front of him. He tried to storm around me. I threw my arms around him and hung on.

"Doug! Listen ta me!"

He stumbled, struggled to break free then came to a halt. I let go and positioned myself directly in front of him, placing the palm of my hand on his chest. Doug was beyond himself, completely consumed by rage.

"Doug! Don't think!," I ordered. "Stop thinkin'! Go blank, Doug!"

He was shaking from head to toe, glaring wildly over my shoulder at the cop car.

I took my hand from his chest.

"Stop thinkin' about anything, Doug," lowering my voice. "Just...stop...thinking."

His eyes shut.

The cop car honked. Its lights went to brights.

Doug's eyes popped open.

"Don't think, Doug. Stop thinkin'," as I took hold of his shoulders and tried to turn him away from the cop car.

The car was creeping toward us, gravel growling deeply as it closed in.

"Ya wan'a go ta jail in Louisiana?" wiping a stream of blood from my chin. "That's what'll happen, Doug. You'll be in jail in Louisiana. *Think* about *that*, Doug."

Several seconds passed before a look of sad resignation swept over his face. Doug slumped, seeming to shrink. He allowed me to turn his back on the car. I eased him into a leaden footed first step. A second. A third.

*Good. He's movin'.*

Doug paused long enough to retrieve his duffle bag then continued to drag himself up the road. I followed, the cop car right on my ass.

We walked for a little over an hour, me maintaining my distance behind Doug, the cop gradually slipping further and further behind. The graveled road became a patchwork of potholes before ending at a black-topped, two way county road. Doug stopped at the intersection. The cop car closed to about thirty yards before coming to a halt, its head lights illuminating a mile post on the other side of the road.

### NEW ORLEANS
followed by an arrow pointing east.

### BEAUMONT / HOUSTON
followed by an arrow pointing west.

The cop flashed his lights on and off and honked several times. Doug, without turning around, dragged himself onto the blacktop and turned westward. I followed. The car made a slow, crunching u-turn and crept back toward Cameron.

We walked for a long time, only stopping to take a few pills. I was hurting, but the pain pills took the edge off, allowing me to keep up with Doug's dragging pace.

I couldn't even guess how far it was to Houston. Actually, any town would have worked.

*Need a bus station.*

*B'tween us, we pro'bly have enough money ta get tickets back ta Lubbock.*

*At least Abilene. Mom an' Dad could...*

*Oh, Jesus. Dad'd love 'at.*

*This'd make him look like a fuckin' prophet. "I told ya so! Didn' I? Didn' I warn ya? Ya wouldn't get a haircut. Ya wouldn't shave 'at damn beard. Ya wouldn't..."*

*Christ. Dad's out.*

*We'll get as far as we can on the bus then hitchhike ta Lubbock 'r...*
nearly running Doug over.

He'd stopped and was pointing up the moonlit road at what appeared to be a large log or something stretched across the blacktop. It was around eight or nine feet long, maybe thirty yards or so away.

It moved. More like a huge twitch.

"Alligator," Doug.

"Think so?"

It twitched again.

We stealthed to the side of the road where Doug picked up a handful of small rocks.

"What the hell're ya doin'?"

He didn't answer. Doug cocked his arm back.

"Don't go pissin' him off," grabbing his arm. "They can charge ya!"

Doug broke free and launched the missiles down the road. A few stones bounced off the gator's back.

More twitching.

"We can go around him," I suggested.

Doug edged forward. I stayed put.

Within twenty yards of the beast, Doug cupped his hands to his mouth and shouted.

No twitch.

Doug backed up to where I was.

"C'mon," I whispered. "We can get inta the water an' sneak around him at the tail end."

"I...," Doug, pausing to look at the reed filled, moon-silvered swamp surrounding us. "What about *other* alligators? And water moccasins? And cottonmouths?"

*Damn good point.*

We fired a few more volleys of rocks and shouts.

Nothing but the occasional twitch. The butt-wipe liked it there and, by God, that's where he was set on staying.

"We can't wait here f'rever," I grumbled.

"He will...have to move...if...if a car comes. We'll have to, uh...wait for a car. Or...something," and sat down on his duffle bag in the middle of the road, face to the gator.

I sat down on my seabag, facing the opposite direction in case another gator might try to creep up on us. I immediately became aware of how exhausted I was. And the pain. I got some more pills from Doug then settled in as comfortably as I could on my seabag.

It was hot and muggy, the dead air swarming with every kind of noisy, biting, stinging swamp thing a menstruating Mother Nature could possibly think of creating. I ruled out rubbing mud all over any exposed skin, thinking a driver was going to have enough trouble, as it was, deciding to let the two of us in his car. I shut my eyes, tilting a bit this way, a little that way, back this way, trying to locate a point of balance on my spine that would permit me to remain upright with a minimal amount of effort. It was impossible. The dive bombing night creatures weren't going to allow it.

I'd killed about a million or so of them when the sound of Doug's voice interrupted my war.

"What was 'at?" I asked.

"Understanding and tolerance," Doug repeated. "Those... people. Those Louisiana people back there...and everyone like them...everywhere. *Those* kind of people will never...*understand*... people like...*us*," ending the statement in a quiet, wheezing laugh.

I turned and looked at him. He was grinning broadly, eyes wide and sparkling.

*Fuck me dead.*

*A two ton alligator in the road in front'a me. Cameron b'hind me. A snake infested swamp on both sides'a me.*

*An' now Doug's havin' a goddamn revelation.*

*How'd Dante miss this level'a Hell?*

"Everyone, you know...preachers...and teachers...and other people like that, they...they keep insisting on...*understanding.*

Everyone must try...must bust their asses to *understand*...everybody else," nodding in agreement with himself.

*Virgil didn't miss this level of Hell. He didn't have the balls ta go there.*

I repositioned my seabag and faced Doug to give him the impression I was mortally interested in what he was attempting to divulge. If he suspected otherwise, it would only make matters worse.

I stifled a yawn. I was safe. He hadn't noticed.

"Imagine a...this...object," slowly shaking a finger as he started to make his point. "This object is...suspended in space," glancing at me to see if I was listening. Doug looked back toward the swamp. "Now, imagine a person...standing in a...a fixed position...some, uh...some distance away...observing this...this object. Now...starting at where the...the person is...draw a circle around the object and...and place another, uh...person...at every degree on the...the circle you've drawn around the...object. That would be...three hundred and sixty people. Now imagine...*draw* a globe...around the object. And...and on the globe there's...there is this grid. Lines going north and south and east and west...one degree apart and...a person...standing at every, uh...intersecting point on the grid. Then imagine three planes...each with its own grid...and a...a person at every intersecting point on...*that* plane. Now see the whole thing...slowly...revolving around the...the, uh...object. There are 86,400 seconds in a day. There are 365 days in a year," pausing to break into a wheezing laugh. "Man, can you, uh...see where this is...what this...this *means*?" turning to see if I did.

I raised my brows and tried to appear as if I did.

"I've got to...to do some figuring," excitedly turning away. "I have to, uh...have that...that number," pulling a small notebook from his back pocket and a stubby pencil from his front pocket.

Doug positioned himself to take full advantage of the moonlight and began scribbling away.

*Good. That'll keep him busy for a while.*

The gator was snoring. I relocated my balance point and drifted off.

"Gil," Doug, excited.

"Yeah?" yawning and stretching. My seabag chair had become my seabag pillow. I pulled myself from the road.

"This is it," and handed me his notebook. "The, uh... number."

I gradually brought the number into focus.

*1,470,000,000,000,000.*

"Damn good, Doug," doing my best to sound impressed.

"That number is a...*minimum.* That is the *minimum* number of, uh...perspectives *one* object will have. One object...will, *minimally,* have *that* many...observers, each having his *own* interpretation...his own perspective of the object," beginning to wheeze laugh.

"What's the max number?" trying to sound as though I really gave a shit about any of it.

"Large," in a hushed voice. "If the degrees were, you know, broken down into...minutes...and then seconds...the number would be, uh...*very* large. BUT...the minimum number works to...well... it works to prove my...my point," fading back to a hush.

*Point?*

"You see...no *one* person can...understand, not *fully* understand...that many other different...different ways of, you know, of...seeing the same thing. The same object," suddenly standing and waving a hand about. "It's...it's fucking *impossible!*" Looking to me for agreement.

I nodded.

"SO...*understanding,* as an answer to...to, uh...getting along... to live with all the different...opinions...the different perspectives concerning the object...is *impossible.*"

I nodded again.

"What *will* work is...*tolerance,*" grinning broadly and wheezing. "*Everyone* can be taught to...*tolerate* other perspectives. They don't have to *understand,* uh, shit. They only have to *tolerate* the differences.

Instead of learning to...understand, at a *minimum,*" pausing to retrieve his notebook, "one four seven zero zero zero zero zero zero zero zero zero zero zero zero zero, uh...different perspectives...all a person has to do is learn *one* concept...*tolerance.* By learning that *one* thing...*everybody,* I mean *EVERYBODY,*" growing more excited, wheezing louder, "everybody in the whole world...can get along," eyes sparkling. "Can you dig it? Can you fucking *dig* it?" ecstatically.

"I can dig it, Doug. I can fuckin' dig it."

"It's *not* about *understanding* at all! It's all about...*tolerance!*" locking his fingers on top of his head. "Fucking...*tolerance.*"

Doug held that position for several long seconds before throwing a finger in my face and grinning at me.

"Those...those...back there," glancing over my shoulder toward Cameron, "those people...they could *never* understand what *you,* uh...are *about.* How could they?" laugh wheezing again. "BUT! If... *if* they had been taught...taught to *tolerate* your *different* perspective on things...then...then nothing would have happened. They would have...*tolerated* your long hair. Your long beard. *Everything* that, uh...was *different*...about you. They didn't know *how* to...tolerate you. They only knew how to...*not*...understand you. SO...you got the shit beat out of you! See?"

"Yeah," nodding.

*Now idn't the time ta get inta a debate about how the precepts'a asshole redneckism an' all concepts'a tolerance are mutually exclusive.*

"That...that number is, uh...a...a *tolerance* sum. That's what I'll call it. The Tolerance Sum, and," barely pausing to take a breath," those...those people in Cameron...they...they didn't *understand* us and were...they felt...threatened, and so *that* is why they...they did what they did. The captain. The sheriff. Those punks. They felt like...they'd lost *control* because...they didn't understand us and... they thought they had to at least make sure *we* knew that...*they* were in control. In *their* minds, anyway...that was the situation. BUT," raising a finger and locking eyes with me, "even when *they* thought they'd reasserted control...*I* was, in reality...*still* in control."

*So that's the hair he's got up his ass. It's all about the control thing he's always so eaten up with.*

"I was still in control because...because I was in a position of *tolerating*...their difference. I remained in control. I wasn't threatened by that difference. I was, the whole time...in reality...in control. Not them."

"Damn straight ya were," I assured him. "You were in complete control."

"And," gazing in the direction of Cameron, "they, uh...they need to be...be made aware of *that*, uh...fact. They need to know that *I* was, in fact, in control and that...*I*...was *not* threatened by *them*. I wasn't *afraid* of them. *They* need to know that."

*Shit. He's startin' ta misfire. Think fast.*

"Y're in control b'cause ya know about tolerance an' they don't. You go explainin' it to 'em an' then they'll know as much as you an' then they'd be...they'd be...

*Think! Think, goddammit. They'd be what?*

"Equal! They'd be *equal* ta you. Right? You'd lose the edge 'at knowin' about tolerance gives *you* over *them*."

Doug became sullen, eyes fixed on Cameron.

"How do I know...that...that, if I don't go back, it's because... I *let* you talk me into believing I wasn't afraid to go back there and not because, *subconsciously,* I *am* afraid to, uh...go back."

*Jesus Christ, this is wearin' thin.*

"Doug," and nudged him.

He faced me.

"Doug, ya just came up with this...this *inspired* explanation f'r why nobody can get along an' then ya came up with the solution. Right? Idn't 'at what the Tolerance Sum's all about?"

He didn't flinch.

"Wouldn't y'ur goin' back there an' kickin' all their asses just invalidate y'ur...y'ur goal of ever'body gettin' along? It's *y'ur* fuckin' idea, for Christ's sake. If *you* can't apply it ta *y'ur* life, damn, Doug... nobody's gunna even *try* ta apply it ta theirs. Nobody's gunna give it a second thought."

Doug appeared to be distracted by something. I turned and saw a set of headlights approaching in the distance. We moved to the side of the road and waited in silence.

Several minutes later a rambling wreck of a pickup truck rolled to a stop beside us. The alligator looked twice as large in the truck lights.

"Ha yah?" the driver smiled.

I think he was asking how we were doing.

I stepped forward.

"Tired. Been walkin' all night," hinting for a ride.

The passenger door squeaked open. A young boy slid out, pulled a length of two by four board from under a pile of sleeping bags, and then started toward the gator. The kid was wearing blue jeans and a Boy Scout shirt. The other boy in the cab and the driver were both in Boy Scout shirts.

"Boy Scouts?" I asked stupidly, watching the first scout nearing the gator.

The driver nodded.

"I was an Eagle scout," I said. "Also got the God an' Country Award."

The boy in the cab snickered.

"Hush up, 'ere," the driver barked, elbowing the boy. "He coo' be dat he be a young'n," staring at my bloodied beard and tangled locks.

WHOP! from the direction of the roadblock. I jumped and watched the alligator slither into the swamp, tail swishing angrily. The kid, hands in the air, was doing a victory dance. He ran back to the truck, tossed the board into the bed, and then hopped back into the cab.

Doug came up behind me.

"Whe' yah to?" the driver.

Doug and I glanced at each other.

"Whe' y'all goin'," the driver cackled.

The boys were giggling.

"Houston 'r Beaumont" and began nodding my head stupidly, attempting to out dumb them and increase our chances for a ride. "Anywheres we c'n git ta a busy highway so's we c'n hitch it on home."

"Whu' happen yuh face?"

The two boys leaned over for a better look.

"Gahdamn," one hissed.

"Shiiiut," the other.

"Min' yah damn mout's," the driver snapped then turned back to me. "Yew gone been whoop on, yeah?"

"Yeah. *Big* time gone been whoop on," touching a swollen eye.

"T'row yuh se'f an' tangs in'a bake," hitching his thumb toward the back of the truck.

Doug and I picked our bags up and tossed them into the truck bed. The engine roared. The tires growled loudly. The truck leapt away from us.

Doug grabbed the tailgate, lost his grip, and then tumbled to the ground.

One of the kids was hanging out of the passenger window yelling something about faggots and haircuts. Doug was on his back, slightly stunned. I ran over, cussing like mad under my breath.

"Ya all right?" as I inventoried the scraps and cuts.

No answer.

He lay motionless for a short while then struggled to his feet, jerking his arm away when I tried to help him up. Doug stood there quivering. Slowly, he raised two clenched fists into the air and trembled violently. His eyes shut, his head fell back. He didn't make a sound. I waited nervously for an explosion.

Nothing, just a heavy, rapid wheezing.

Several minutes passed.

Doug's arms finally dropped heavily to his sides.

"They, uh," mumbling, "they took the...our...medicine. The pills."

Doug began dragging one foot after the other down the road toward Houston.


Behind us, on the horizon, a sliver of bright red was painting the underside of a long line of clouds dark orange. The swamp was becoming more detailed in the predawn light. I started after Doug.

*Motherfuckin' shit.*

*Had that seabag since boot camp, goddammit. I've lived out of it since '66. It can't be replaced.*

*Those sorry-ass motherfuckers.*


Just after the sun broke the horizon behind us, we came across our things in the road.

*My seabag!*

I broke into a fast, heavy limp around Doug.


I picked it up. My heart sank. It had been slashed from top to bottom. Doug left his pile and came over to me.

"There's...there's this, uh...," speaking for the first time since the hold up, "this canvas company in...in Lubbock. They can, you know, fix it."

"Yeah. At least they didn't keep it," and began stuffing my scattered clothes through the gash.

"You know what?" Doug, returning to his things.

"What?" continuing to stuff.

"For the past, uh...mile or so...or however far it...it was. For a while anyway. Since the...the clothes were taken...stolen...I've been feeling...feeling...different. Calm. Very, uh...peaceful."

I looked up at him.

Doug was nodding, rubbing his chin, and grinning.

"For a while...a *very* short while...there was nothing left for...*them* to take," continuing to wheeze and grin. "They...they *motherfucking* had it, uh...*all*," starting to wheeze laugh. "I was... motherfucking *FREE*! Like in that, uh...that Janis Joplin song."

Doug scooped his things up, walked to the edge of the road, and then tossed it all into the swamp.

"FREE!" raising his hands over his head.

"What're ya doin'?" as I ran over to him.

"MOTHER...FUCKING...FREE!"

I stepped into the murky water and immediately sunk to my knee in mire. I lost my balance. Doug grabbed my arm and pulled me back onto the road.

"Let them go," wheeze-laughing like mad. "I...I don't *need* them anymore. I don't *want* them anymore."

*Shit. On top'a ever'thing else, he's gone completely mental on me.*

"Get a fuckin' grip, Doug! They got y'ur money, too. Without the money we can't get bus tickets. Without bus tickets we gotta hitchhike. Ya hadn't changed clothes in two weeks. Ya stink like dead skin an' rotten shrimp, for Christ's sake. Nobody's gunna give us a ride with you reekin' like 'at. "

Doug gazed at his muck-trapped clothing. He stopped wheezing.

"Then," solemnly, "then...I'll walk all the way, uh, back. I'd rather walk...*all* the way back than worry...worry about...that," pointing at his clothes, "that kind of thing. You know? Worry about somebody, uh, stealing them again. I like it like...this," quickly adding, "Except the pills," and nodded sadly. "I *will*, uh...miss the, uh...medications. And the money. I guess." then trudged on.

Around mid-afternoon we reached a toll ferry and were turned away. The tollman threatened to call the police. We walked up the channel to an area thick with tall reeds. We cleaned up then changed into the freshest things I could find in my seabag. It was a squeeze for Doug, but it was a definite improvement. After returning to the ferry crossing we waited for the tollman who had run us off to be relieved. The new guy let us on with no problems. It was 4:15.

The ferry ride, a dollar a person, left me with eighteen dollars. Neither one of us had eaten since the day before. We bought a loaf of bread, some bologna, a six pack of beer, and two packs of cigarettes at a seedy little bait shop. As we exited, a Louisiana State Patrol car cruised by. The patrolman gazed at us suspiciously. Doug and I exchanged glances.

"Let's keep walkin' 'til we're out'a Louisiana," I suggested.

Doug nodded and picked up the pace.

At sundown we stopped at a rest stop inches inside Texas. For some reason, it was comforting to be back. Doug sat down at a concrete picnic table and began making a sandwich while I went to a phone booth to call Tahoka.

*Tell her what happened. Get her ta borrow some money. Wire us enough f'r bus money. Get this fuckin' nightmare over with.*

A female grudgingly accepted the collect call.

*Bobbie's aunt. Sounds pissed.*

*Bitch.*

"Is Bobbie there?"

"We ain't got nothin' ta say ta yew, Gil an' don't go callin' back. I won't be acceptin' no more calls from ya."

Silence. Click. Prolonged buzzing.

*Fuckin' whore! Goddamn fuckin'...*

"SHIT!" and hammered the receiver against the phone.

Doug jumped to his feet. I rested my head against the booth.

*They already know. Wonder what version'a the story they'd gotten about what'd happened. Bobbie's pro'bly pissed as hell. Beyond pissed.*

My appetite was gone. All I felt like having was a beer.

*What now?*

*Hugo's in Europe.*

*Bad idea anyway. He'd croak.*

*No more botherin' Hugo with my shit.*

"I was plannin' on askin' Bobbie to wire some bus money to us," I told Doug.

"That, uh...that would have been...nice," chewing on a bite. "What...what happened to, you know, your...plan?" as he sat back down.

"Didn't get a chance ta ask. Her bitch aunt hung up on me. Wudn't plannin' on her answerin' the goddamn phone."

"Well, not to be...not to make you look...dumb, but...her aunt, you know...*does* live there and..."

"Yeah, Yeah. I know, Doug. It was a fucking dumbass idea from the start," I snapped.

All conversation came to an end while Doug ate another sandwich and I drank another beer.


Doug burped, cleared his throat then stated flatly,

"Plans are...a waste of, you know...a waste of time. In our, uh, situation anyway," lighting a cigarette.

I opened a beer, thinking that was the end of it.

"Because," raising a finger in front of his face,

*Oh, God, no. I can't take anymore'a his...*

"...because...too many, *way* too many things...like other people, bigger events, uh...bigger things, and...the plans that...that *powerful* people make, uh...*those* plans get in the way of...*our* plans. See what I mean?" grinning.

"No," risking hurting his feelings, but not really giving much of a shit at the moment.

"It's like this," slowly moving his finger back and forth in front of his face. "*Our* plans work *IF...IF*...they don't interfere with *their* plans or with...with events *greater* than our...our, uh, our *pathetic*, little lives," nodding, wheezing, grinning, slowly shaking his finger at me, obviously feeling he was successfully making his point. "*We*...are at...*their*...mercy," adding a slight rocking to all the other gestures of certainty.

"So we shouldn't even try?" rubbing my face with both hands. "We shouldn't make *any* plans?"

"*We* should find...*our place*...in *their* plan. *We* don't have a choice."

"So, *we* should just plan ta eat whatever crap *they* allow us to eat in *their* plan? Our plans should be restricted to whether we plan ta eat their crap with a spoon or suck it through a fuckin' straw?"

"What other choice *is* there?" repeating himself.

"Bullshit, Doug. I'd rather have ever' motherfuckin' plan I ever make fall flat on its ass than ta...ta..."

*Surrender?*

"...surrender ta a goddamn idea like y'urs. I got a *right* ta my own plans."

"You may have, uh...the *right*, however,...you do *not* posses the *power* to exercise that...that right," sneering now.

"Fuck you, Doug," truly angry.

"*Their* plan," hissing at me, "is the...the *only* plan that matters."

"Well, Doug," disgusted, "whether ya like it 'r not, we gotta figure out how ta get our sorry asses back ta Lubbock on ten dollars an' 'at calls f'r a plan."

"Our plan should be...to start walking. Then...sleep when we're tired. Drink when we're thirsty. Shit and pee wherever...whenever we, uh...want to," wheeze laughing. "Eat whatever we find. Use a spoon. Use a straw."

"Don't ya think some power mogul will fuck with it?"

"Uh," back to wheezing, " I, uh...don't see that we...*this* plan could be much of...of a *threat* to...to anyone. Or thing...event," grinning broadly. "I think...I think whatever plan we make to get back to Lubbock...it will be, uh...safe. Probably. No! Wait! *Possibly.*"

A dark brown car with a light bar on top, tinted windows, and a spotlight mounted on the passenger side eased into the rest area.

*Another fuckin' cop!*

It came to a stop at a point as close to our table as the access road would permit.

"Don't move!" thundered from a speaker hidden somewhere under the hood. "Keep your hands on the table!"

Doug, pale as a corpse, froze. I could feel the blood draining from my head.

A uniformed figure got out of the car and cautiously made his way toward us, a hand resting on an unclipped holster.

He stopped about ten feet short of the table.

"Pardon me, I need ta see some identification," politely enough.

I pulled my wallet out and started to get up from the table to hand it to him.

"Hold it," backing up a few steps. "Toss it over here. Underhanded. Nice an' easy."

I did as he directed.

"Put y'ur hands back on the table, please."

I followed the soft spoken request. Doug, face stiff, was trying hard to maintain.


The officer opened the wallet and removed an expired Washington state driver's license. He looked at me then back at the license picture of a male in a closely cropped beard and short hair.

"Washington?" holding the license up.

"That's from when I was in Whidbey Island, Washington. That was my last duty station in the Navy."

"When'd ya git out?"

"September, 1970. My discharge papers're in the wallet. B'hind the Texas Tech ID."

"Texas Tech?"

"Ye'sir. I go ta school in Lubbock."

"Yew been livin' in Texas since September '70 an' ya still ain't got a Texas driver's license?" fidgeting with the wallets contents.

"Well, I…I, uh," glancing around nervously, mind blank.

"This the discharge?" holding up a folded square of glossy, yellowing paper.

"Ye'sir."

The cop unfolded it and started reading. He appeared to be a little confused.

"Don'ch ya have ta git shot ta git a Purple Heart?" looking up at me.

I nodded.

"How'd a guy in the Navy git shot? I thought y'all's on ships. Where it's safe."

"I was on PBRs. River patrol boats. Real small boats on real small rivers. You been in?"

"Nah," folding the discharge paper and slipping it back behind the Tech ID. "How about yew?" nodding at Doug. "Yew got some identification?"

"I, uh...I," Doug stammered loudly, beginning to panick.

"We were workin' in Cameron, Louisiana on shrimp boats," I blurted.

*If Doug lapses inta Dougian we're as good as dead.*

"I got beat up on the dock. We, me an' Doug, we got fired. We've been walkin' since midnight last night. Officer. Sir," trying my best to convey the highest degree of respect for his authority that I could. "Halfway out'a Louisiana, early this mornin', I swear ta God, a pick up truck full'a Boy Scouts stole our things. They took off with 'em after we'd put 'em in the truck. They took off b'fore we could get in. Honest-ta-God, Officer, it was a bunch'a Boy Scouts in their uniforms an' ever'thing. We found the bags on down the road. Mine'd been cut open," starting to reach for the bag at my feet.

"Hold it," the officer. "Hands on the table."

"Ye'sir. Sorry, sir," damn near kowtowing. "They kept his bag," nodding at Doug, "an' his wallet an' money an' ever'thng 'at was in his bag."

The officer moved a few steps to the right and examined the slashed seabag. His expression softened. I felt like he'd decided to believe me.

"Stay where ya are," and walked back to the car.

I hissed at Doug to get his attention. His head jerked.

"Listen, Doug," whispering slowly. "Doug, this is important as hell."

He stared at me.

"Doug, let *me* do *all* the talkin'. Okay. Don't say a word," enunciating each word dramatically.

His stare changed to a smoldering glare.

*Good, God, I hope he understands.*


Ten or fifteen minutes passed before the policeman returned and handed me my wallet. His holster was secured.

I relaxed.

"Is it okay ta...?" and turned my palms up.

"Yeah. No problem. Yew checked out. Just a few more questions," putting his pointed, gray, lizardskin cowboy boots on the edge of the concrete seat. He hitched his thumbs in his front pockets.

Doug remained stiff as a board, staring across the rest area.

"Y're tryin' ta git back up ta Lubbock right now?"

"Havin' ta walk it," avoiding hitch. "Only got about ten dollars."

*Shit! Stepped on my dick! How much money do ya have ta have ta not be a vagrant?*

"We had a lot more," hurriedly, "b'fore them Boy Scouts ripped us off. Most'a the money was in Doug's duffle..."

"Git y'ur things an' come with me," turning to the car and walking away. "We're takin' ya ta town an' buyin' ya some bus tickets out'a petty cash," over his shoulder.

Doug's face lit up.

"Can I, uh, you know...talk now?"

"Wait just a little longer. Okay. Once we're on the bus."

"All right," quietly standing up. "I guess that...that I should try to, uh...try to think of something to...to talk about then," looking challenged.

*He's fuckin' amazing.*

Silence for twelve miles. Two blocks into a ratty little town made up of one rusting, antiquated mobile home after the other, we pulled into a space in front of a fairly new brick building. "SHERIFF" was spelled out in large, aluminum, seagull shit streaked, block letters above a set of glass doors. Doug and I were led into the lobby of the building then hurriedly ushered through a single glass door marked "County Sheriff" in gold lettering. We faced a long, chest high counter. At the far end, to our left, a heavy metal door had been stenciled with six inch black letters.

## JAIL

Doug, standing in front of me, glanced over his shoulder at me. He looked nervous.

An ugly looking, grossly overweight tumor with no neck, instructed us to stand beside each other at the counter. An unseen stool creaked loudly with every heaving breath the malignancy took. Two more officers entered the room and positioned themselves behind us. The cop who'd brought us in turned a rumpled envelope up side down above the counter.

A lone, withered Camel cigarette butt fell out.

I looked at the cop. A number of serious questions were thrashing about in my skull.

"Found this on 'em," our cop told the sweaty growth behind the counter.

One question suddenly stood out among all the others clamoring for attention.

"What the fuck is goin' on?" I bellowed.

In the next instant my face was being held to the counter top by the two cops standing behind me. Doug was restrained, his hands cuffed behind his back in a split second. I felt cuffs tighten around my wrists. It was slick and fast. They'd obviously had a lot of practice. Doug, probably in shock, glared out the window behind the counter, nostrils flaring, body quivering.

"Don't think, Dou..." I managed before having my head bounced on the counter a few times.

"Y're both under arrest f'r suspicion uv possession uv marijuana," tumor-man smirked. "We're gunna have ta hold ya'll 'til we git it tested."

"It's a Camel," Doug. "It says Camel right on...,"

Doug winced as the deputy jerked the cuffs up, painfully pulling on Doug's shoulders.

"DON'T THINK!" I yelled.

Headbang, headbang, headbang.

"Yew mus' really like kissin' 'at counter top, boy," tumor-man.

The others laughed.

"I fuckin' love it," I shot back then smashed my head into the counter without any assistance.

In the movies, that would have been one cool-ass move—a really classy statement of defiance. Instead, having miscalculated the trajectory of my forehead, my nose burst. Blood gushed everywhere.

"Gahdammit!" the growth yelped, nearly falling off his stool. "Git 'em out's here!" slapping at a few spots of blood on his uniform.

We were hustled down the counter and practically tossed through the open metal "JAIL" doorway. I was choking on what bloody snot I wasn't slinging everywhere. The guards taking custody of us were cussing us up one wall and down the other.

I kept expecting Doug to explode. I constantly reminded him not to think throughout the whole humiliating booking process—strip search, delousing, face and head shave.

We were issued oversized, orange jump suits, "PRISONER" stenciled on the back. No underwear. No tee shirt. Only the jump suit.

Our final stop was a thirty foot by thirty foot cell brightly illuminated by three large industrial ceiling lights. The room was already occupied by five inmates who were stretched out on five of eight available bunk beds. A seatless commode squatted in one of the corners of the cell, a roll of toilet paper on the floor next to it. The floor gently inclined toward a drain in the center of the room. A big floor fan, located outside the cage, stirred the disinfectant laden air. At a glance, it appeared to be one hell of an improvement over Juarez.

The cage door slammed shut behind us. None of the inmates moved a muscle. I looked at Doug for a melt down reading. He was pale, but apparently maintaining. Gazing into nothing, Doug leaned back against the bars of the gate then slowly slipped into a squatting position, knees pulled up under his chin.

I eased down beside him.

"Ya did good, Doug. Real good."

After a while, Doug began wheezing. I looked over.

*Oh, shit. He's grinnin'.*

"*This*...this," starting slowly, under his breath, more to himself than to me, "this is as *free* as...as I will *ever* be," wheezing louder, grin growing, eyes shining. "I...I have done it. I am *completely*...free. There is nothing else to fear. *True* freedom is living in a fearless state of being. There is *nothing* else *anyone* can, uh...do to me. Nothing left to fear," turning to me. "I...*we*...are," wheeze laughing, "...*free*," then slapped his version of an amen on it. "Can you dig it?"

*Let it pass.*

I sat, seething.

*No. I can't take anymore'a his...his...bullshit!*

"Doug," voice deep with weariness. "This may piss ya off, but if I don't tell ya this then I'm gunna go out'a my rabbit-ass mind."

Doug's brow furrowed as he turned to face me.

"I know y're lookin' at this from some esoteric, some deep philosophical angle an', yes, I agree...a person *can* remain *free*, in an extremely restricted sense, *even*...even if 'at person's in chains,'" pausing to brake the rising emotions. "*BUT*," placing a finger in the space between us the way Doug does when making a particularly important point, "but, Doug, goddammit...we are in a fuckin' *jail*. I *fully* understand where y're comin' from, but no matter *how* goddamn free ya *think* we are at the moment, *this*," clutching a cell bar, "*this* fucking *SUCKS*," hissing loudly. "And if *this*," trying to rattle the iron bar, "if *this* is y'ur weirdass idea of a *pure-ass* form'a freedom, then...then your fuckin' idea of freedom fuckin' sucks."

His face sagged. Doug rested his head against the bars. His eyes glazed over.

*Shit. That didn't feel anywhere near as good as I thought it was gunna feel.*

\*\*\*

The bus rolled to a slow stop. Doug and I had walked out of Cameron forty-three days ago. Arriving back in Lubbock I finally felt like the whole damn thing was really over.

I spotted Bobbie and Hugo standing outside the passenger loading door. Bobbie was waving wildly. Hugo just stood there. I ran to Bobbie and grabbed her up in big hug.

Hugo placed his hand on my shoulder.

"Careful, Gil," he said. "Y're huggin' on two now."

I backed up and looked at Bobbie's tummy. She was showing. I placed my hand on the tiny bulge and smiled. Bobbie started crying as she put her hand over mine. I gently pulled her to me and gave her a long hug. She was trying hard to stop crying.

Hugo cleared his throat. I eased away from Bobbie and, clutching her hands, addressed Hugo.

"Hugo, thanks for helpin' me an' Doug...,"

*Doug!*

"Damn, Hugo! Have ya heard anything about Doug?"

"Homer's got the story. Ask him about it," slipping me a folded piece of paper.

I opened it and nearly choked. It was a bill. A big bill.

"See ya at the office in the mornin'?" Hugo, brows raised. "Same arrangement as b'fore?"

I nodded and reached out to shake his hand. Hugo pretended not to see it, kissed Bobbie on the cheek, and then walked back into the terminal.

"Goddamn him."

"Don't get upset at Hugo," Bobbie, squeezing my hand. "You're lucky he decided ta step in at all this time."

"He's not even givin' me a chance ta explain what happened."

"Doug convinced him y'all weren't drunk the night ya got beat up. An' told him about the Camel cigarette. Hugo b'lieved Doug."

"But he wouldn't b'lieve me?"

Bobbie shrugged her shoulders.

"What matters is 'at he decided ta take care'a things an' now y're home," pulling me into the terminal.

"Damn sure took him long enough ta make up his mind," mumbling.

"Maybe he was tryin' ta teach ya a lesson."

I ground to a halt.

"What possible lesson was there ta learn?" angrily. "Never take a better payin' job? Never leave the house again? Kill the next cop who pulls me over? There's no fuckin' lessons here," and headed for the exit, Bobbie in tow. "I appreciate his help, but Hugo's actin' like a goddamn baby. This wasn't my fault. Not *this* time."

Bobbie stopped. I spun around.

"Goddamn, I missed ya, Gil," her eyes tearing.

I choked.

*It'd been just as hard on her.*

*You fuckin' asshole.*

I grabbed her and held her to me.

"I'm sorry, Bobbie. I'm...so sorry. I'll never leave ya again," closing my eyes.

She began crying.

I was hurting. Hurting for Bobbie. Hurting for the baby.

*Good, God. They both deserve better than all this.*

"Y're crushin' me," through the sobs.

"I'm sorry," releasing my grip. "This'll take some gettin' used to," smiling down at her stomach.

"Don't get too used to it," through a sniffle. "It's not lastin' f'rever."

We walked arm in arm to JD's old truck. I asked about Doug as we got in.

"He's in the veteran's hospital in Houston, but he's okay. He's not hurt. He's in the mental part."

"What the hell happened?"

"That's all I know. That's all I wanted ta know. Homer's been talkin' with Doug's folks. He can tell ya at the house."

Bobbie pulled away from the curb and made a left on Broadway, heading toward the campus.

"Where ya goin'?" I asked. "We're not goin' ta Tahoka?"

"Don't need to. I moved back inta Tenth. We're bunkies again," still lightly sniffling.

I moved to her side and kissed her neck. Bobbie scrunched her shoulder up and shivered.

"Pull over," I told her.

"What?"

"Pull over," jerking the wheel to the right. "Now."

She eased over and parked in front of a grubby duplex.

"What..."

I put a finger to her lips then took her hand from the wheel.

"B'fore we get there...home. I wan'a make sure ya know how much...how much I love ya. And the baby. Our family. Bobbie, Im really happy an' things are gunna change. I'm gunna change. I don't wan'a lose this. I don't wan'a lose what I've...we've got. You've gotta b'lieve me."

Bobbie, crying again, threw her arms around my neck. We sat by the curb until she had pulled herself together. I got out and slid in behind the wheel. She couldn't have gotten closer to me. I headed on down Broadway.

Bobbie started talking. And talking. She told me about how she'd decided to move out of her aunt and uncle's house because they wouldn't stop bad mouthing me after I'd been fired. She was afraid the baby might be listening. Homer and Jerry had helped her move back to the old place four days ago, once she was sure I'd be getting out of jail. She was working six days a week at the beauty shop and all her steady customers were tipping like crazy due to the baby. Homer had sold two old pianos and given her the money as an early baby present to help us get back on our feet. Jerry had gotten a thousand dollars for the bike and had given his commission to us as a present to help out.

"But you already know about that. I wrote ya about it. What ya don't know, b'cause Jerry thought it would make ya mad, is he sold it to a guy out at the air base. Anyway, everybody at the house agreed ta give us the livin' room since everybody always ends up in the kitchen ta talk an' we needed extra room for the crib an' the dressin' table. OH!" clapping her hands, "I forgot ta tell ya! Hugo bought us a brand new crib and a changing table with a little baby sized tub in it! It's so cute! Wait 'til ya see it," excitedly. "It's got a..."

"Bobbie," I interrupted.

Bobbie looked over at me.

"You gunna take a breath?" I asked.

"Oh, my God," slapping her hands to her mouth then dropping them into her lap. "I've been ramblin'. I can't help it. I'm so excited! Everybody's tryin' so hard ta help an' ever'thing is..."

"Bobbie," again.

"And guess what else?" either not hearing me or ignoring me. "I *have* ta tell ya this an' then I promise ta shut up."

She'd heard me.

"Danny's cousin decided not ta go back ta Tech. He was an art major! He gave me five huge stretched canvases, a big box of acrylics, a ton of other supplies, an' some books!" absolutely thrilled. "For the past three weeks I've been paintin' in Jerry's basement after work b'fore goin' out ta Tahoka. Jerry's been callin' it my studio. The basement," patting my leg. "I'm done. Nothin' more," and smiled. "For now, anyway."

I pulled into the driveway, turned the truck off, and then looked at Bobbie.

*She's so damn pretty. Red eyes an' all.*

I was suddenly aware of how much I wanted her, physically needed her.

*I wan'a be naked b'side her. Right now. Make love to her.*

She hopped out of the truck and hurried over to the steps, her sweet little butt tightly bound by a pair of fading blue jeans.

*God. I've missed her in so many ways.*

"C'mon! C'mon," she urged

I chased her up the stairs, through the kitchen, down the creaking hall, and into the living room. Our bedroom.

It was nice. She'd done a good job redecorating. All the couches and pieces of crate furniture were gone. The bed was centered on the bank of windows across the room from the door. Tan curtains replaced the old, yellowing, rain stained curtains. The grungy white wall paper had been painted a pale brown, just a shade darker than the curtains. A worn, over stuffed easy chair occupied one corner. Her clock radio, sitting on a dark wicker night stand by the bed, was softly playing James Taylor. Her plants hung from the ceiling.

And then, against the wall to my right, a crib and a changing table.

I shivered. I didn't say a thing.

"Don't ya like it?" Bobbie, quietly.

"Uh, yeah," staring at the baby things. "It's perfect," pulling her to me.

Bobbie put her arms around my waist and rested her head on

my chest. I shut my eyes for a few seconds. When I opened them again,

*Oh, God.*

...the crib and baby table were still there.

*This is f'r real. This is actually happenin'.*

A heavy, dark feeling overwhelmed me. It was frightening.


"What do you think?" Homer's voice behind me.

It startled me. I let go of Bobbie and turned around.

"Nice haircut," he smiled and took my hand. "Grow the beard back as fast as you can," grimacing.

Homer gave me a bear hug then stepped back and examined me from head to toe.

"Not too bad for the wear," he nodded.

"Ya sure this arrangement is okay with ever'body?" I asked.

"It's the best way for me to insure my God child is properly cared for," slapping me on the back. "Had anything to drink since getting out?"

*Since gettin' out.*

A chill ran through me.

*That sounds so...wrong. It sounds...unreal.*


The past six weeks rushed by. The beating in Cameron. The haircut and dry shave. The cell. Three days of pill DTs. The parade of drunks peeing and shitting all over themselves. Cleaning up after them. The criers. The screamers. Lights on all the time. The pig-ass guard who made wise cracks all through the weekly shower. Doug sitting on his bunk all day, gently rocking, occasionally engaging me in abstracted conversations which gradually became more and more incomprehensible.

"What'a ya know about Doug?" switching off the nightmare.

"Let's get a beer first," Homer, stepping into the hall.


Bobbie and I followed him into the kitchen where Homer held the chair for her then tucked her into the table.

"Thank, you," and dipped her head slightly.

"Tryin' ta make me look bad, Homer," I mumbled and took the chair next to her.

Bobbie jabbed me with an elbow.

Homer got two beers and a glass of orange juice before taking a seat.

"Bobbie's not allowed to drink alcohol," pointing at the juice.

"Or smoke," Bobbie.

"Hugo's orders," Homer added.

"Well," glancing at Bobbie, "that makes sense," a little agitated about Hugo taking charge of everything.

I sipped the beer. It was so good.


"This is what I know about Doug," Homer began. "He left the bus station in Houston and started back east. Toward Cameron."

"That's why I had ta catch a later bus. I looked all over for him. I thought he'd gone outside an' got lost 'r somethin'. That's when I called ya."

Bobbie began massaging my shoulders. Homer continued.

"Doug walked up to a Highway Patrol car parked alongside the road outside of Houston and tried to get the guy to let Doug have the car, or least give him his badge or uniform."

"Y're shittin' me?" eyes wide.

"I shit you not. He wasn't being hostile or anything. You know how Doug gets so polite and formal when he's really off the wall about something?'

I nodded.

"That's what the cop noticed. Doug got lucky. This guy'd worked as an orderly in a mental hospital before becoming a cop. He suspected something right off. He called for backup then kept Doug occupied until they arrived. Instead of arresting him, they just took him into custody. To make a long story short, he ended up in the psych ward at the VA hospital in Houston. Guess what his mother said to me?"

I shook my head.

"I asked her if there was anything we could do to help. She said we'd already done enough. Said it real shitty. Then she hung up on me."

"Bitch," I grunted. "Doug kept bringin' up all his 'symbols of authority' crap the whole time we were locked up. Still, I damn sure didn't see this comin," swigging my beer.

"How long will they keep him?" Bobbie, a hint of apprehension in her voice.

I put my arm around her shoulder.

"A lot longer than Fort Collins did."

"Yeah," Homer. "Trying to talk a cop into giving him his squad car looks a little crazier than using a crow bar to reconfigure a motorcycle."

"I feel sorry for Doug," Bobbie taking my hand.

"Better feel sorry for Cameron if the VA lets him out too early."

A herd of elephants was noisily making their way up the steps.

*Shit. I need some Bobbie time, goddammit.*

Bobbie read the look of disappointment on my face and squeezed my hand.

"Everybody wants ta see ya," wrinkling her nose. "Later," she whispered in my ear.

"I FOUND HIM FIRST!" Danny, as he crashed into the kitchen. "I get the reward for recapturing him," laughing.

The second I was on my feet I was caught up in his arms and lifted from the floor. From over Danny's shoulder I watched Eduardo, Tomas, and Vann file into the kitchen. A few minutes later, Shauna arrived. I was being beat and hugged to death. It was a nice beating. We ended up sitting in the hall, popping beers and lighting joints. Bobbie brought her radio from our room and started running up and the dial trying to find, at my request, anything that wasn't country. I'd had my fill of anything remotely redneck down south.

Within an hour I was kind'a drunk, kind'a smoked up, and kind'a pilled. I was all the way relaxed and it felt absolutely *grand* to realize I was somewhere around three or four million miles from everything that had happened.

*I'm...HERE. Not...THERE. EVERYthere.*

*But here.*

*Oh, crap. I sound like Doug. Too much exposure ta Dou...,*

Joan stepped around the curtain from the kitchen. The hall fell silent.

*Those tits!*


I hadn't seen her since the night before leaving for Juarez. She cutely, fingers only, waved to everyone. She looked uncomfortable. Bobbie jumped to her feet and bolted over to her. Shauna was on her tail. They tied themselves into a hugging knot and broke down crying. Eduardo began a slow, steady clapping. Everyone joined in. Danny started to repeat Joan's name in time with the clapping. Immediately the hall filled with "Joan, Joan, Joan, Joan..."

*Goddamn. This feels so...so...fine.*

*This is as real as the cell was. This is as real as the beatin'.*

*Bobbie's real. The baby's real. Danny...all of 'em. They're all as real as all the assholes out there.*


I spotted Jerry. He must have slipped in during the Joan thing. He leisurely made his way over to me like nothing had happened, as if the past sixty or so days had been an exaggerated second. Jerry bent over in front of me, hands on his knees, chin on his chest. His filthy bandanna was right in my face. He held the position for a few moments then raised his head up enough to peer over the top of his sunglasses. His eyes were bloodshot.

"Ya know," flopping into a sitting position and removing his shades, "this is how *I* see things, man. If yew wuz ta take this multiple choice test," staring into my eyes, "an' all ya had ta choose from wuz 'A'...no 'B' 'r 'C' 'r 'D' answers. Just a 'A' answer ta choose from...yew'd still fuck it up," brows high, lips pursed.

I grinned and looked over his shoulder, head nodding.

"Thanks f'r sellin' the bike. I 'preciate it."

"I sold it ta some queer-ass air force turd. Don't tha' bother ya some," smirking.

"Nah. That thousan' dollar's gone a long way toward assuagin' any negative feelin's I have about that."

Jerry dropped his head and shook it.

"Yew ain't even been talkin' ta me f'r ten seconds an' y're already tryin' ta make me feel stupid with a big-ass word."

"Which one?"

He looked up.

"Eat me," and slapped me on the shoulder. "Yew okay?"

"Yeah. I'm settlin' in. Doug's the thing 'at's botherin' me real bad."

"There's nothin' none'a us c'n do f'r Doug, man. He's where he needs ta be f'r now. He's diseased, man. Sick. We ain't shrinks," looking around the hall.

"I'm tryin' ta see it that way."

"Joan's lookin' damn hot," he said. "Yew notice how we come in t'gether?" sneering.

"I noticed how you two got here at about the same time."

"Shit to, man. Maybe we got somethin' goin' since yew been gone," cackling low.

"I don't think so, Jerry. I don't think Shauna'd be too happy about that an' she seems ta be in a pr'tty good mood right now," nodding at the girls.

"Shauna's eat up with compassion, man. She un'erstands 'at Joan's got needs 'at maybe I'm the only one c'n satisfy," dancing his brows.

"An' maybe y'ur showin' up at the same time as Joan was just a cosmically coinciational event."

" 'at's a made up word," he huffed.

"If you can make up fantasies about Joan then it's legal f'r me ta make up words."

"Fantasies? Well, if thinkin' 'at makes ya feel better...then go right ahead," cackling.

"I missed fuckin' with ya, Jerry," serious as hell.

"Yew ain't got the gray matter ta fuck with me, turd," and slapped my leg.

"Jerry," putting my hand on his shoulder, "Y're so full'a shit."

"Yeah," nodding, "I know. I know," laboring to his feet. "Nice fuckin' haircut. Now git y'ur beard back, man. Y're killin' us. By the way, man...glad y're back," then lumbered over to Shauna.

That's as serious as Jerry was going to get about our reunion. It was serious enough. It felt good.

I watched Joan, now sitting cross-legged across the hall from me. She suddenly turned her head and looked at me. Smiling, she patted the empty space beside her. I went over to her on my knees then sat cross-legged, in front of her, our knees close to touching.

"How was Louisiana?" cocking her head.

"Not as much fun as Europe, I'd guess. I can't tell ya," softly, "how good it feels ta hear y'ur voice," momentarily overcome by an unnerving feeling of intimacy.

"You'd better get used to it," tossing her head to one side, "I'm movin' back in ta help with the baby," watching for my reaction.

I lit up like a search light.

"Bobbie's idea," she said.

"I thought, after ever'thing that's hap..."

"Don't worry," placing her hand on my knee. "I had to get over those feelin's. It was...it felt so," gazing into her lap, "It was eatin' me alive."

"What's Hugo think about it?"

"He's not overly happy about it, but he does think Bobbie could use some help."

*Damn. The whole world's fallin' back inta place.*

\*\*\*

Roy spit a wad of tobacco from his mouth.

"I had enough trouble gittin' a honest days work out's ya when ya wuz j'st a damn, unwashed, hippie freak," he growled. "Now y're a damn, unwashed, hippie freak jailbird. Not ta mention y'ur provin' ta be such a damn duplicitous son uv a bitch."

"Duplicitous?" I winced.

"Look at ya," pointing an accusing finger at me. "Short hair. Barely any beard. Sold y'ur Harley. Institutionalizin' y'ur relationship with Bobbie," shaking his head in disgust. "Y're a goddamn hypocrite, Gil. The minute thangs got the least bit rough ya went an' turned y'ur back on y'ur whole damn culture."

"What's duplicitous mean?" Stan.

"Don't worry, Stan," I said, "It dudn't have anything ta do with bein' a homo."

Roy came at me for one more stab.

"Y're a goddamn ethical an' moral chameleon. Look at poor ol' Stan," pointing at Stan. "He done thought the world'a ya f'r y'ur staunchness of commitment in the face'a ever'thang a decent, God-fearin' society had ta throw at ya. Yew wuz his hero. He's done tore ta shreds."

"Yeah. My ass is all tore up," he drawled.

"Speakin'a tore up asses," Roy, "how many times ya git poked in the yah-yah while yew wuz in?"

"F'r fun 'r f'r money?"

"Damn, Gil!" Stan groaned loudly. "Don't even kid abou' that shit."

"What makes ya think I'm kiddin'?" walking toward Stan with a slight swing in my step.

"Git the fuck away," backing up.

"Seriously," Roy, keeping it going, "How'd ya like it at'a way?"

"Shut up!" Stan, hands over his ears.

"Personally," Roy speaking up so Stan would hear, "it might

not be all 'at bad. 'specially if there wudn't anythang else aroun'. Whud'a ya thank, Stan?"

"SHUT UP!" stomping off toward the office.

"That there's one close-minded buckaroo," Roy, shaking his head. "He'p me load some flags an' stakes," then walked to the truck and slid in behind the wheel.

"How ya gunna help me load things up if y're sittin' in the truck?"

"It's a sad thang ta see how the slammer turned ya inta such an unpers'nable hardass," shutting the cab door. "Ya used ta be such a lack'daisical kind'a fell'a."

That was my answer.

I began transferring bundles of stakes and flags from the garage to the bed of the truck. Roy, whistling quietly, played around with some folded blueprints in the cab.

Stan stormed out of the garage.

"We gotta talk!" glancing angrily in my direction. He stopped short of crashing into the truck and squared off with Roy.

"This ain't right," he shouted. "I gotta do house plats with Hugo 'cause he don't wan'a be aroun' him," jabbing a finger at me as I approached. "Yew know I hate house plats! An' I won't git no overtime workin' with Hugo. I'm gittin' my ass kicked f'r *his* goddamn fuck ups," hitching a thumb in my direction.

I dropped a bundle of stakes in the bed then stepped over to Stan.

"Hugo dudn't wan'a work around me?" hoping I'd misunderstood.

Stan looked down, realizing he'd let something out of the bag. His reaction answered my question.

I exploded.

"Hugo's pissed b'cause some swamp scum beat the shit out'a me an' a fuckin' redneck cop wanted ta send me up f'r life on a bogus drug charge?"

"That's not it at all," Roy shaking his head while exiting the cab. "He ain't...pissed. Not out right, anyway," removing his chew from a back pocket. "He's j'st a little...upset. Tha's all," calmly cutting a plug off and sticking it in his mouth. "Hell, he'll git over it. Ain' no biggie."

"What exactly has he said about me?"

Stan, still looking at the ground, eased some bits of gravel together with the toe of his boot. Roy crossed his arms over his chest. He wouldn't make eye contact.

"Fuck it," I mumbled. "I'm not workin' here if he thinks I'm a total fuck up. I'm not workin' f'r any asshole 'at thinks I'm a...a piece'a shit."

"WHO!" Roy flared. "*Who* thinks I'm a piece'a shit," and put his face right into mine. "An' ya best be tryin' ta keep thangs in their honest perspective. Un'erstand?"

"So you think I'm a piece'a shit too? Ya want me ta quit?"

"Nobody's said nothin' 'bout wantin' ya ta quit," Roy, spitting on the front tire.

"But, ever'body's pr'tty convinced I'm a goddamn fuck up. Right?"

Roy paused before answering.

"I won't lie to ya, Gil. Ya need ta start un'erstandin' how things look from where ever'body else stands," spitting at the tire again. "F'r sometime now yew been gittin' inta some shit that's..."

"Ya think I *asked* to get beat up?" angrily. "Ta get thrown in jail down there?"

"Yeah!" Roy right up in my face again. "Ya sure as shit did an' ya need ta accep' 'at. Anybody goin' inta that part'a the world with a two foot beard an' hair down ta his goddamn ass is all but beggin' 'em sons a bitches ta shit all over him! Up here bein' diff'rent gits ya a few oddball looks. Down there...it c'n git ya killed."

"Easy Rider," Stan, nodding.

I turned away.

"So it's all my goddamn fault?"

"Yew've damn sure gone out'a y'ur way to set y'urself up f'r ever' goddamn thang 'at's happened, by God. Git a firm grip on 'at 'un 'r...," his voice trailed off.

It sounded vaguely like some kind of ultimatum. Or maybe a prediction. I got the feeling they'd all hit some kind of threshold.

I turned back around.

"I...I don't like this," I said. "The way this whole...this conversation's goin'."

Roy and Stan nodded. I felt myself sag.

*Fuck me.*

*Their pro'bly right.*

*I'm a piece'a shit.*

"I'm sorry," shaking my head. "I didn't realize...I mean, I never thought about..."

Roy slapped my shoulder.

"It's gotta lot ta do with...with respect, too," he said.

"Yeah," Stan, planting his feet apart and crossing his arms over his chest. "I respect all'a the shit ya went through in the service an' all 'at. An' I respect how ya keep tryin' ta make thangs better f'r y'urse'f an' all 'at. Ya work hard an' carry y'ur own weight, but damn, Gil, some'a the shit ya do...well, it's j'st...j'st plain wrong by my way'a thankin'," glancing at Roy. "The way ya seem ta...ta drag ever'body inta ever'thang ya git into an' the way ya act like ya...well, ya act like ya don't seem ta care how it's effectin' ever'body else aroun' ya. Sometimes it feels like ya don't seem ta care about that. Like ya ain't got much respect f'r us," stuffing his hands into his pockets and looking down. "I thank 'at's wrong. That...that's whut's been botherin' me more'n anythang else lately."

"I couldn'a put it better myself," Roy, resting his hand on Stan's shoulder. "I thank ya hit the nail on the head."

An uncomfortable silence set in.

I cleared my throat.

"Why ya keep puttin' up with it? Why don't ya just kick my ass 'r somethin'?"

"Ever'body hits rough spots," Roy. "I c'n handle a fell'a hittin' some rough spots as long as he's truthful about all the circumstances."

"Me, too," Stan, looking up.

"An' don't f'rgit" Roy winked, "If we c'n make a good, God-fearin' white man out'a ya then we're set solid f'r a spot in Heaven. Ain' 'at right, Stan?" poking Stan in the arm.

"Yeah," Stan grinned. "An' it's kind'a cool bein' in the ag department at Tech an' havin' ever'body know I'm friends with a dope smokin' hippie."

"Hear 'at?" Roy yelped. "Son uv a bitch went an' said '*cool*'! Ya done went an' corrupted him!" pointing an accusatory finger at me.

Stan spun around and tossed his hat to the ground.

"Damn!" he wailed.

"Now git y'ur sorry ass inta this truck," Roy, sliding back behind the steering wheel.

I got in the cab. Stan shook my hand firmly then slapped me lightly along side the head.

And that was the end of that. There probably wouldn't be anything more said on the topic. I got the impression, however, that I'd just about run out of rope.

Roy and I headed down the lane.

"When's Bobbie due ta calve?" Roy, turning Buck Owens up.

"Around mid January," turning Buck Owens down.

"If it's *real* ugly, ya gunna put it ta sleep?"

"Jesus Christ, Roy! That's...that's fuckin' evil. How can ya even *joke* about somethin' like 'at?"

"Ya gotta think about thangs like 'at when ya got a baby comin'," spitting out the window. "Hell, yew start showin' up ta family reunions with some hideous lookin' creature an' they'll stop tellin' ya where they're havin' 'em."

"Y're sick, Roy. Y're not at all right," and settled against the door.

"Thank ol' Doug c'n pull some strangs an' git me inta Whacko University down there in Houston?"

"They wouldn't have enough shrinks f'r the two of ya."

\*\*\*

"January tenth," Hugo. "Right on schedule. I like punctuality in a baby," chuckling.

Hugo and I stood side by side peering into the nursery through a wall of glass. All my attention was focused on a red faced, tight eyed new born squalling in plastic container number 16. Both his fists were clenched.

"Tripp McNeil," Hugo mused, head gently bobbing. "Thanks f'r not usin' my first name. I never liked Hugo. Sounds awkward."

"I thought Tripp worked better with McNeil," wondering if the screaming baby was in any real pain or only raising hell.

"Mr. Mc Neil?" from behind.

"Yes ma'am," continuing to watch the baby.

"Could yew *please* go ta the lobby an' speak with some folks claimin' ta be Mrs. Mc Neil's husband?" exasperated.

I dropped my head.

"It's already started," Hugo patting me on the back. "I'll go down an' take care'a things. You wait here ta see Bobbie. Ya don't wan'a miss y'ur chance ta hold 'at young 'un."

\*\*\*

I lit a cigarette then leaned over the tank to stare into the frozen water.

Top to bottom, solid ice.

*Must'a dropped ta way b'low zero last night for it ta do this.*

The prize fish still looked impressive—the shiny blues, greens, oranges and yellows as vibrant as they were when the fish were still swimming around. Their long feathery fins and flowing tails looked like they'd been delicately arranged by a Neiman-Marcus window dresser.

Then locked solid in ice.

Freezing, killing ice.

Crunching steps approached from behind. I couldn't take my eyes off the fish.

Roy stepped up beside me.

"Damnation," his breath clouding the air. "They never looked pr'ttier," bending over and thunking gloved knuckles on the icey tomb. "The ice kind'a heightens their natural brilliance."

"I was in a hurry ta get out'a here yesterday afternoon so we could take Tripp ta Tahoka. Bobbie was all excited about it. She was dyin' ta show him off."

"She wudn't the only thang dyin'," he mumbled.

"I forgot ta plug the tank heater in before leavin'. Just flat ass forgot."

"Ya know somethin'?"

I looked over. His moustache was caked with frost.

"Yew ain't never, ever, *ever* gunna git out'a debt ta that man," slowly shaking his head.

I looked back at the fish.

"Ya know whut, Gil? As p'rtty as they look, yew could make a poster uv 'em an' sell 'em ta pay Hugo back. Lots'a people'd be willin' ta buy a poster 'r a calendar with a pi'ture uv a coupl'a five hun'r'd dollar, pure bred, imported fightin' fish froze solid in a West Texas stock tank. Talk about surreal, I mean, the whole damn concept..."

"You finished?"

I was in no mood for a humorous take on things.

"J'st tryin' ta comfort ya a bit b'fore Hugo rips y'ur head off an' shoves it up y'ur ass," quietly.

"How the fuck am I gunna tell him," using the back of my jacket sleeve to wipe some snot from my nose.

"I'll take care uv it," putting his hand on my shoulder and gently squeezing. "Y're too upset right now."

"Would ya?" thankfully.

"Don't worry about it," then looked toward the office barn.

I followed his eyes. Hugo was crossing the parking lot.

Roy let go of my shoulder patted me on the back then cupped his hands to his mouth.

"GIL KILT Y'UR DAMN FISH!"

"Goddammit, Roy!" and shoved him as hard as I could.

He stumbled backwards a few steps.

"Don't ya feel better f'r gittin' it all out in the open an' over with? Damn y're one hard SOB ta please," he huffed.

I turned away, pissed as hell.

"He ain't stupid, Gil. He'd a known somethin's wrong. When's the last time he ever saw the two uv us standin' around the tank at 7:30 in the mornin' in b'low zero weather?"

Hugo, taking short, quick, heavy breaths, got about half way to us then stopped.

"That ain' normal breathin' f'r Hugo," Roy.

Hugo spun around and headed back for the office—long, fast strides, slipping and sliding a few times on the ice.

"Damn good thang ya went an' named 'at kid'a y'urs after Hugo. 'at may be the one thang 'at keeps him from poundin' ya ta death," starting toward the lot.

I crunched along behind, following him into the garage.

"I'll wait f'r ya here," he mumbled.

I entered the office, stomach churning.

*God-fuckin'-dammit.*

Hugo was coming down the stairs. We met in the middle of the room.

"Hugo, I..." stammering.

"Here," and handed me a folded piece of paper.

*Shit. I know what this is.*

"Gil, I know how distracted yew've been lately," drawling softly. "Especially this past week with the baby comin' an' all. Startin' a new semester out at Tech..."

"That's no excuse," hoping to impress him with my willingness to assume full responsibility.

"Goddamn right that's no excuse," he shot back. "I'm tryin' ta do my best ta ease the pain'a this f'r the both of us," back to a calm drawl. "Yew must feel terrible about inflictin' such...such a cruel death on so innocent an' magnificent an example'a God's handiwork. This must be eatin' y'ur ass alive," shaking his head sadly.

*He's pissed as hell. He's gunna make this hurt like a bitch.*

"Yew knew they had names, didn't ya?" as he glanced at the floor.

"Yin an' Yang," wiping my melting moustache.

Hugo started toward the stairs then stopped. He turned and asked me to tell Bobbie he'd be dropping by the house this evening to look in on his name sake.

"I wan'a make sure he's bein', well...that he's stayin' warm while this norther's blowin' through."

*Jesus. That was almost too low. That was a crotch shot.*

I unfolded the piece of paper and read it.

*One hun'r'd dollars?*

"One hun'r'd dollars?" looking up in relief. "I thought they were around five hun'r'd dollars a piece?"

"What?" surprised, brows furrowed. "Five hun'r'd dollars f'r a goddamn fish? Who in their right mind'd pay five hun'r'd dollars f'r a goddamn fish?"

"Uh...I don't know," stumbling.

His eyes popped open wide.

"Is 'at whut ever'body thinks I paid f'r them fish? Y'all think I'm some kind'a nut? A crazy ol' eccentric?" chuckling. "I'll be damned."

Hugo walked back up stairs, muttering a string of "I'll be damned"s as he went.

I stepped into the garage. My lungs seized up from the cold.

Roy spotted me and started honking. I coughed my way to the truck then hopped in.

"Still got any ass left?" peeling out on the frozen blacktop.

"He didn't even yell," through a cough.

"How much're them Nip fish gunna cost ya?"

"A hun..." catching myself. "Guess."

"I thank he paid five hun'r'd for 'em. My God!" Roy looking at me in shock. "He ain' gunna hit ya f'r five hun'r'd dollars is he?"

"Five hun'r'd each," assuming a crushed posture.

"That ain't *half* right," snorting. "That ain't half right at *all*. Tell ya whut I'm gunna do. I'm gunna make the monthly payments on 'at for ya 'til yew've paid all the other shit off ya owe him."

"Serious?" surprised he'd believed me.

"Serious as a heartbeat. Here's the deal. Ever' time I make a payment, ya j'st send Bobbie up ta the Westerner after I'm done f'r the night an' I'll have her back home in time f'r her ta cook ya breakfas'."

"Y're a classic turd, Roy," and slumped down in the seat.

We called it a day at 3:00, both to numb to keep going. On the way back to the office, Roy, out of nowhere, asked me if I was still seeing April. I was taken completely off guard. I ignored him.

"C'mon, Gil. I ain't stupid. I know ya started seein' her sometime after JD's funeral."

I paused, considering whether I should deny it.

*Fuck it. He wouldn't have brought it up if he didn't know f'r sure.*

"Who else knows I've been with her?"

"Pro'bly nobody. She wouldn't'a said nothin' ta anybody. I j'st fig'red it out on my own. She's not the kind ta kiss an' tell. That's whut's so great about her. An' that's why I'm havin' this conversation with ya," looking over at me.

Roy was serious.

"This idn't a lecture," he told me. "It's some advice 'at could save y'ur marriage...y'ur family someday."

I nodded.

"It's some advice on...wanderin'.'"

"Wanderin'?"

"Yeah. Ya know all those waitresses an' all those slutty little reg'lars 'at hang out at the Westerner? Well, I've never had a single one of 'em. Not one."

*Bullshit!*

"When I...wander, I don't go wanderin' in my own backyard. Un'erstand?"

"So where do ya meet..."

"Dudn't matter where I find 'em. The important thang is...be careful. Be discreet. Ya don't want that baby losin' his family over a piece'a ass. Be smart about thangs."

I thought it over for a minute.

"You ever feel bad about it? You know, guilty?"

"If I felt like I wuz doin' somethin' wrong I pro'bly would feel bad, but it ain't wrong. If God hadn't intended f'r our species ta enjoy the orgasm, an' I mean *ever'* chance we git ta enjoy it, he'd a put carpet tacks an' ground glass in semen an' lined vaginas with 36X grit sandpaper."

"Baptists think God made it feel so good so it'd be a test of their obedience ta God. Has ta do with findin' strength in the Lord ta resist temptation then feelin' guilty as hell when ya blow it. Goes all'a way back ta Eve bein' told not ta eat the apple. I think 'at's what makes me feel guilty sometimes. Some kind'a residual thing from the way I was brainwashed early on."

"Ya know, Gil...ya kill my ass. Ninety-nine point nine percent'a ever'thang yew got ta say about religion has ta do with how fucked up they are then ya go an' home in on one aspect of it an' treat it like there's some kind'a credence ta that one part. Damn, boy, y're talkin' about *religion*. If a religion ain't *all* the way true, then it's *all* the way flawed. Y're still as eat up with issues as ever'body else. Residual Baptist bullshit 'r not...make up y'ur damn mind. Anyway, jus' f'r the record, I don't thank God wastes his time playin' pissant temptation games like 'at."

"Roy?"

"Yeah."

"Why'd you start...wanderin'?"

"I'll be as truthful as I can with ya , Gil," rubbing his eyes. "I guess ever'body's got their own reasons. F'r me, it's...it's b'cause I c'ain't he'p wantin' ta love on ever' damn one of 'em an' there ain't *shit* I c'n do about it."

"Ya love bein' *with* 'em 'r do ya *love* love 'em? I mean, do ya have strong feelin's for 'em?"

"Have I ever loved one of 'em as much as I love my wife 'r kids?"

"Somethin' like 'at, I guess."

"Hell, no. An' I won't ever let it happen. Ain't worth it. An' 'at brings me back ta April. Gil, she's the perfect, yew know, *other*...if y're gunna have one. She's got the rules down pat."

"Dudn't matter anymore. We broke it off. I slept with her one time right after comin' back from Juarez, but that was it."

He eyed me skeptically.

"No shit, Roy. Bobbie'd left me. I got drunk at the lounge one night, April showed up an', BAM...just like 'at, it happened. But only once. Not that I wanted it that way, but...," and stopped.

"But whut?"

"Well," looking away and mumbling.

"Whut?" leaning closer.

"I gave her gonorrhea," then covered my face with both hands. Quiet.

Roy turned the radio off.

"April, one'a the hottest lookin', horniest, most experienced, most discreet pieces'a free in North America, an' yew went an'...gave her the clap?"

I looked over at him.

"I didn't mean to. I was drunk. Horny."

More quiet, only the whir of the heater on low, Roy's soft, even breathing, a faint humming from the engine, and the wind whistling in the passenger window that wouldn't roll all the way up.

Roy eased into the lane, slowing to a stop in the lot. Then, like a shattering explosion, he blew the windows out with laughter. I jumped right out of my skin. Roy was beating his palms against the steering wheel, throwing his head back and forth, laughing harder than I believe I have ever seen anybody laugh before. Tears streamed down his face. Roy couldn't catch his breath. He began to cough, struggling to bring the outburst under control. I began laughing. He gradually settled down.

"I can't even get April ta talk ta me anymore, much less fuck me," I said, knowing what that would do to him.

Roy went off again. I was laughing right along.

It took a good two minutes before he could even try to say anything.

"My, God," gasping for air, "I...I can't b'lieve it!" wiping tears away. "Ever' thang yew touch," choking, "turns ta *shit*!" busting up. "*Ever'thang!*" he managed to squeal in a rushing gasp. "I'm hurtin', Gil!" falling against the steering wheel. "Y're fuckin' killin' me," panting heavily. "I cain't take no more! Oh, sweet Jesus. I swear, I ain't *ever* gunna blame yew again f'r a goddamn thang 'at happens to ya," slapping me on the leg. "Y're *cursed*!" he howled. "Y're goddamned *cursed*!" laughing hard, eyes running again.

"Don't you dare tell anybody about any'a this," I told him.

"How the hell could I?" trying to settle down. "I wouldn't live through it," sniffling and patting his eyes with a bandanna.

Hugo, his face one big question mark, was tapping on the driver's window. Roy, still sputtering, rolled it down.

"Whut the hell's goin' on?" Hugo grinned.

Roy and I exchanged glances then cracked up.

Hugo shook his head and walked away scratching his head.

# CHAPTER SEVEN
## May, 1973

HUGO!" as I hurtled through the backyard of the house. "HUGO!" banging on the backdoor with both fists. The door popped open. Hugo looked scared shitless.

"Somebody's shot some'a the goats! Two that I could find right off."

"Shot the goats? Who'd shoot..."

"An' at least three'a the ducks. One of 'em's Copernicus," stepping aside.

Hugo bolted by me.

Roy's truck rolled into the parking lot. I frantically motioned for him to follow us.

Hugo slowed as he came up on the first downed goat. It was Faith.

The goat was in a crumpled pile, still breathing.

"See whut ya c'n do for her, Gil," then rushed over to Darwin.

I gently turned Faith's head and looked at her eyes. The pupils had rolled out of sight.

I went over to Hugo. He was kneeling by Darwin, examining the body.

"Shot," he whispered. "At least six times."

One of the rounds had hit Darwin in the muzzle about halfway between the eye and the nose.

Roy came to a stumbling stop beside Faith.

"How many ducks?" Hugo, looking around the yard.

"I found three."

"All dead?"

"I'm not sure. I went an' got you b'fore..."

"Well find out, Goddammit! They've suffered enough!"

"I'll git my rifle from the truck," Roy.

"They're ducks, Roy! Wring their goddamn necks!"

"It's f'r Faith!" obviously as upset as Hugo.

They stared at each other for a few seconds. Hugo looked away. Roy turned and ran back to his truck.

"Show me the ducks," Hugo, in a deep voice.

He followed me to the north side of the barn. Copernicus and Galileo had been so shot up they were more blood than feathers. Aristotle, barely alive, was nestled in some tall grass along side the barn, his head turned, resting on his blood stained back. Hugo knelt down and gently stroked him. Aristotle didn't move.

Hugo snapped the duck's neck.

He carried Aristotle into the barn, placed him on a bale of hay, and then began exploring the bullet holes with a pocket knife. Hugo retrieved a small, bloody piece of metal from one of the wounds then held it up for closer examination.

"Twenty-two," Hugo, trembling in anger. "Kids. Had ta have happened b'fore 11:00 last night. I didn't hear a thing after I got home at 11:00."

Roy hurried into the barn, rifle in hand.

Hugo glanced up.

"Go ahead," he said.

Roy walked away. Seconds later a shot rang out. All the animals in the barn yard scattered in a panic.

Hugo shut his eyes.

Roy returned.

"Where ya want 'em buried?" Roy asked quietly.

"Buried?" Hugo flared. "Put 'em in feed sacks an' take 'em to the dump."

"I told ya a year ago this wuz gunna happen!" Roy came back at him. "I knew damn well it'd only be a matter'a time b'fore 'em damn kids in 'at housin' project'd git tired a shootin' at tin cans an' rabbits! Didn't I tell ya ta move further south 'r git rid'a the animals?"

Hugo stomped out of the barn. Roy followed. I stepped over to the door.

"An' it's gunna happen again, an' again," Roy yelled after him, " 'til there ain't a single one uv 'em left! Not even the goddamn buffalo!"

Hugo started walking faster. We watched until he disappeared into the garage.

"Goddammit!" Roy as he kicked the barn door.

Fine grains of dust from the rafters, sparkling gold in the streams of morning light pouring through several cracks in the east wall, drifted to the floor of the barn. Some settled peacefully on Aristotle.

"Yew heard him," Roy. "Find some feed sacks an' bag 'em up," then walked toward the lot.

Stan was pulling in beside Roy's truck. Stan's greeting went unacknowledged as Roy entered the garage. Stan slowly got out and looked in my direction. I motioned for him to join me. He slowed to a crawl once he was close enough to realize what had happened. He waited until he was next to me before speaking.

"It's 'em kids, ain't it?" Stan frowned.

"Pro'bly."

"Hugo callin' the police?"

"Don't know. Roy an' him been yellin' back and forth at each other since findin' out."

"Who found 'em?"

"Me. Two goats and three ducks. Then I got Hugo. Ten... fifteen minutes ago."

Stan went over to Faith.

"Sons a bitches," nudging Faith with the toe of his boot. "He say whut he wants done with 'em?"

"The dump."

603

"Where's the dump?"

"Don't know. Never had a reason ta go there."

"The goats're too big ta throw out along the road anywheres. Somebody'd see us. Maybe we could douse 'em in gas an' burn 'em."

I cleared my throat and walked over to him.

"Stan, ya know...I don't think Hugo really meant it when he told us ta take 'em to the dump. I think someday he'll regret gettin' rid of 'em like 'at."

Stan thought it over.

"Y're pro'bly right," he decided. "He was attached to 'em. More like pets than animals. He's j'st upset f'r now."

"Exactly," as I bent over to grab Faith's front legs.

"Where should we bury 'em," Stan, taking hold of her back legs.

"North side'a the barn. That way he won't see us diggin'. We'll tell Roy an' then Roy can tell Hugo we took 'em to the dump. When Hugo starts feelin' bad about it, then Roy can tell him what we really did."

" 'ats a...a nice thang ta thank uv, Gil. Real nice."

"Yeah. I'm Captain Sensitive. One walkin', talkin', fully exposed nerve endin'."

We gathered up the other bodies, placed them in a row, and then began digging a mass grave.

Forty-five minutes or so into the burial, a Lubbock police officer turned the corner on the barn. He looked familiar.

"Eddy Dyer?" I asked.

"Yep," walking over and smiling.

After shaking hands I introduced him to Stan.

"Hadn't seen Eddy since high school," I told him.

"Hadn't seen yew since the night that bitch coldcocked ya at Mother's," Eddy.

"What?"

"About a year or so after I dug ya out uv a snow bank in 'at alley in the ghetto."

*I'll be damned. Eddy's the one.*

"Ever'body kept tellin' me about this cop showin' up ever' time I got in...ever'time I had a problem an' how he'd tell ever'body he knew me."

"J'st tryin' ta keep ya out'a jail," Eddy smiled.

"How about the bike tickets? Pushin' a bike with no lights on an'..."

"Them too."

"Damn, Eddy. Thanks. Those tickets would'a busted me flat," shaking his hand again.

"I'm gunna git somethin' ta drink," Stan, stabbing his shovel into the mound of dirt we'd excavated. "I'll bring some back f'r yew. Nice meetin' ya," nodding at Eddy.

Eddy touched the brim of his hat.

I sat on the mound, pulled a pack of cigarettes from my shirt pocket, and then held the pack out to Eddy.

*SHIT! Is this the pack with the joints?*

"No thanks. Quit."

*Holy Jesus, that was close. Holy fuckin' Jesus.*

"Yew all right?" Eddy asked.

"Uh, yeah...I'm still a little pissed about what happened," nervously returning the pack to my pocket. "This was a bad way to start the day," pointing at the row of bodies. "How long ya been with the LPD?"

*He's lookin' at me kind'a funny now. Does he suspect somethin'?*

"About four years. Did nearly two years in the Army. Got an early discharge," holding up his left hand.

His little finger and the one next to it were missing.

"Happen overseas?"

"Yeah," as he looked away.

"Vietnam?"

"Third month. Pro'bly saved my life," rubbing the scarred hand.

"Pro'bly."

"I got most'a the info I need f'r my report from Mr. Tripp," Eddy, turning to business. "Gotta ask yew a few questions ta wrap it up," pulling a notebook from his utility belt.

"Sure. Sure," glancing at the corpses. "Go ahead."

Stan returned with a canteen of cold water as Eddy finished questioning me. I took the canteen and gulped half of it down.

"Thank ya c'n make it up ta Fat Dawgs sometime?" Eddy, returning the notepad and pen to the utility belt.

"Pick a time. I kind'a feel like I owe ya pitcher 'r ten 'r twelve."

Eddy waved the debt off.

"I'll be in there ever' night 'til closin' f'r a while. Startin' at midnight t'night."

"Vacation?" I asked.

"I wush. Admin suspension while they investigate me."

"For what?" exchanging glances with Stan.

"Don't ya read the paper 'r watch the news? I'm famous."

"Too busy studyin'."

"Y're not the guy 'at shot a car up f'r runnin' a stop sign are ya?" Stan.

"It wuz a car load a *Mes'c'ns*," Eddy scowled. "An' they failed ta slow down properly f'r a yield sign."

*Whoa. I don't like the sound'a this.*

"C'mon up ta Fat Dawgs t'morrow night an' I'll tell ya the whole story. I'm bein' railroaded b'cause somebody don't like the way I'm doin' my job. Bunch'a goddamn, small town politics," he snorted.

"Well," a little uneasy, "I'll try ta make it..."

"It's a hell uv a story. Yew ain't gunna b'lieve it," looking as if he really needed to talk with me about it. Or anybody, for that matter.

*Ya owe him at least this much.*

"Around 6:30?" I suggested.

"Don't matter. I'm gittin' there at 2:00. Soon as they open."

"I'll be there at around 6:30."

Eddy shook my hand, waved at Stan, and then left. Stan and I finished the funeral detail then headed back to the office.

We ran into Roy and Hugo in the garage. Things appeared to be back to normal between them. Hugo walked over to me.

"I want to apologize for the way..."

"You don't owe me an apology for anything, Hugo."

Hugo nodded then walked toward the house.

Stan removed his hat as Hugo passed by.

"Got them animals bagged up?" Roy.

"Me an' Stan, we buried 'em behind the barn. North side," not sure how he would react. "It was my idea. Stan just helped because I asked him to."

"But, I liked the idea too," Stan, glancing at me, trying to let me know I wasn't going to hang alone if there was to be a hanging.

Roy looked at the ground, took his hat off, and then wearily ran his hand over his graying, thinning hair.

"J'st as well," looking up at us. "Don't tell a soul," sternly. "Not f'r now anyways."

\*\*\*

I'd never been in Fat Dawgs, a red neck dance hall catering to Tech and air base wan'a be John Waynes. It was located across from the northeast corner of the campus. Ads in the University Daily boasted of local cowboy bands on the weekends and a juke box offering, not only the newest country tunes, but the largest selection of country classics between Amarillo and Abilene. It was *the* place to be seen if you were of that persuasion.

I smoked a joint at the house to settle my nerves before heading over. I wasn't exactly excited about the whole thing.

Right at 6:30 I strolled into the bar and looked around. It

appeared to be large enough to hold around three hundred drunks. The place was packed. I immediately caught the attention of several "cowboys" with an obvious aversion to anyone into deviant self-expression. I caught myself stroking my beard. I wandered through the crowd for a few moments, carefully avoiding the more hostile looking tables. I spotted Eddy sitting alone at a small, two chair table against the wall by the stage. I hurried over and fell into the seat. He was one big smile.

"Glad ya could make it," Eddy, filling a mug apparently reserved for me.

"We may have ta move to a larger table if my friend shows up," more conversational than concerned.

"No pro'lem," he slurred.

*He's drunk. Drunk as shit.*

"So, how's it feel ta have all this free time on y'ur hands?" maintaining the conversational mode.

"Sucks! Hate it! Ain't right!" growling loudly.

*Should'a asked him how he liked havin' firecrackers lit off in his ass.*

"Them sons'a bitches are after me 'cause I'm the only one in the whole goddamn department tryin' ta enforce the laws," gulping down the remainder of his mug then refilling it. "Tha's the whole damn pro'lem, Gil."

His demeanor was one hundred and eighty out from the straight laced, professional figure he'd cut at Hugo's the day before. The alcohol had transformed him into a sloppy, sulking, overweight troll.

"Third fuckin' suspension," he barked. "Assholes gunna git their way this time. I'm gunna git fired this time."

"Well," scanning his clouded horizon for anything resembling a silver lining, "maybe y're better off leavin' the LPD if they hate ya 'at much."

Eddy glared at me.

"Ain't the LPD's after my ass! It's 'at goddamn bunch'a suit an' tie spic lovin' lawyers from Austin! They been all over me ever since

I had ta take a night stick to a coupl'a beaners when they pulled a knife on me," banging his fist on the table.

"What?" pretending to be as outraged about it as he was. "Wouldn't that'a been self-defense?"

"Another bunch'a fuckin' beaners watchin' the whole thang went an' lied about whut happened. Said I didn't start hittin' 'em 'till they wuz handcuffed an' 'at there wudn't a knife. Lyin' bas'ards."

A revised, mostly negative opinion of Eddy was taking shape in my mind.

"Coupl'a months later I got suspended f'r bumpin' inta a spick tryin' ta run away from me."

"Bumped into him?"

"Yeah. Barely tapped him with the squad car," matter-of-factly. "Should'a nailed his ass 'stead'a j'st tryin' ta slow him down. Anyways, I seen him throw his stash out the window when he passed me. I was parked near a four-way stop 'at the Mes'c'ns are always runnin' in Guadalupe. I hit my lights an' siren. He pulls over, jumps out an' starts runnin'. Whut else could I do? Son uv a bitch had a head start on me."

"So ya...bumped him?"

"Tapped him. Had ta stop him somehow didn' I? I mean, 'at's my goddamn job, idn' it? Anyways, when we couldn't find the stash, I knew 'em taco bendin' lawyers wuz gunna be all over me again. The second 'at baggie hit the road some other spic must'a picked it up. I know 'at's whut happened to it. Try ta git a bunch a spic lovin' lawyers ta b'lieve 'at, though."

"Was the guy hurt?"

"Not much. Broke leg," rubbing his chin. "Not hurt enough," sneering.

*Damn.*

"So the other night, I went after this car full'a wetbacks 'at'd j'st barely slowed down f'r a yield sign. I knew they's up ta somethin'. I hit the lights an' the siren an' one'a the li'l bas'ards sticks a handgun out'a the window. I put three rounds into the trunk an' they were gone. I shot at 'em twelve more times an' they still wouldn't stop.

In my mind, 'at j'st proved they's tryin' ta hide somethin'," gulping his beer. "Yew ain't gunna b'lieve this, but, them spicks...*they're* the one's shootin' at *me* with a handgun, *they're* the one's with a trunk load'a stolt TV's, *they're* the one's drivin' all aroun' town gittin' all fucked up on drugs an' booze, *but*...guess whut happens?" leaning forward, squinting, upper lip a mixture of sweat and beer foam.

"What?"

"The back-up unit shots the tires out on *MY* car," hissing like a stepped on snake.

"That's, uh...crazy," scratching my forehead. "Listen, just out'a curiosity, did ya find a gun in their car?"

"Hell no. They pitched it."

"Any dope? Beer? Anything?"

"Pitched 'at, too," looking at me suspiciously.

*Careful. He's drunk, he's bigger than me, an' he's crazy as a loon.*

"How many, uh, TV's were in the trunk?"

"Whud're yew hintin' at?" turning his head slightly and squinting at me.

*Leave. Tell him y're goin' to the head an' then cut the fuck out.*

"Nothin'. Just curious," pushing my chair away from the table. "That's all."


My shoulder was gripped from behind. I looked around. It was Homer. I looked back at Eddy. He was glaring at Homer. Homer extended his hand. Eddy remained motionless, strangling his mug with both hands.

"This the frien' yew's waitin' for," Eddy, keeping his eyes on Homer.

Homer withdrew his hand and lost the smile.

"Yeah. This is Homer. My best friend."

"He's a Mes'c'n," angrily.

"I'm Cherok..."

"That's right, Eddy," glancing at Homer. "He's a *Mexican*."

Eddy wobbled to his feet.

"I don't drink with Mes'c'ns," he slobbered. "An' yew better watch y'ur ass from now on, Gil," he snarled. "I done got yew fig'red out."

Homer's jaws clenched. Eddy stumbled away from the table and meandered for the front door, bouncing off several patrons on the way.

Homer sat down in Eddy's chair.

"You ever invite Jonas to a Ku Klux Klan meeting?"

"Homer, I swear ta God, I had *no* idea he was such a...such a fuckin' Nazi."

"That's no way to be talking about your guardian angel," filling Eddy's mug. "Isn't that how you described him to me last night?" taking a drink.

"Gimme a fuckin' break," topping my mug off. "Yesterd'y was the first time I'd seen him, well, the first time I *remembered* seein' him since high school. He wudn't like this back then."

"I'm jacking with you. *But*, if it weren't for Jerry sharing his hash with me...that bastard would be in the hospital about now."

"Let's kill this pitcher then get the hell out'a here. There's bound ta been a reason for why he felt comfortable hangin' out in this shithole."

"I'm taking my time," Homer, smiling and raising his glass to a pretty young thing two tables over.

Her partner, about two foot four inches tall, pretended he hadn't noticed.

"CALL AN AMB'LANCE!" from near the entrance. "GIT THE COPS!"

A crowd of people surged toward the front doors.

" 'nother damn fight," a male off to our left.

"Startin' kind'a early," another.

Gradually, rumors of a shooting in the parking lot drifted back to where we were.

Twenty or so minutes later the overhead lights came on. The

juke box stopped. A policeman climbed onto the bar and ordered everyone to vacate the premises in an orderly fashion. Several helmeted cops moved through the mass of pitcher gulping, mug chugging, pissed off customers.

Outside the front doors a line of flashing cop cars separated the evacuees from what was apparently a crime scene. As we passed down the line of cars, Homer froze and gripped my arm.

"Look!" pointing at a body doubled up on the ground.

I jostled about trying to see over the squad car and between the medics and police standing around the bloodied mess.

*Holy, shit!*

"Eddy," I whispered.

"That's probably who nailed him," Homer, pointing at a frightened looking Mexican kid sitting in the back seat of a cop car parked inside the police barrier. We were pushed along from behind. Homer and I proceeded on to his truck, dropped the tailgate, and then sat down. We lit up and watched the traffic jam develop as a hundred car loads of Fat Dawg's patrons tried to occupy Fourth Street at the same time.

Several minutes passed before Homer asked me what the final dead animal count was at Hugo's.

"No change," answering mindlessly, thinking about Eddy. "Two goats. Three ducks. One goose an' two chickens hit, but they'll live."

"Hugo still upset?"

"That kid, the one in the cop car," turning to face Homer. "He did the right thing. All things considered. Didn't he?"

Homer, after a short pause, barely nodded.

"I don't have any problems with it," he said.

"I mean, seriously, Eddy…he was…dangerous. A threat. He was like an animal prowlin' around. What that kid did dudn't seem all 'at wrong."

"Only illegal."

"That dudn't make it wrong," I snorted.

"Right an' wrong doesn't matter anymore. There's just legal and illegal. Ever heard of Wounded Knee?"

"Some army guys used Gatling guns on a bunch'a old Indian men, women, an' children."

"Yeah. They walked off this shitty little reservation. That was the only right thing to do given the circumstances. But...it was illegal. Shooting them all down was wrong, but...it was legal. That crap goes on all the time. In one way or another. Did you know some of the machine gunners at Wounded Knee got the Congressional Medal of Honor?"

"Y're shittin' me? F'r *what*?"

"I don't know," rubbing his forehead. "Marksmanship, I guess."

Fourth street was becoming reasonable.

"I'm going to the shop for a while," Homer, standing up. "Want to come?"

I could tell he wanted to be alone.

"Nah. Think I'll head ta the house. Spend some time with Bobbie an' Tripp for a change."

"Good plan," digging in his pocket.

"Homer?"

He looked up.

"One more question," slamming the tail gate shut. "Okay?"

"Okay."

"How old were ya when ya killed y'ur first animal?"

"Frogs an' lizards count? Snakes?"

"No. That dudn't compare ta what happened out at Hugo's."

Homer thought for a moment.

"I guess by the time I was seven or eight I'd shot quite a few coyotes, but that's not like what happened at Hugo's either. They were into the hen house all the time. We lived off those eggs. And they'd kill our cats every chance they got."

"Predators have it comin'," I mumbled. "Blind goats an' crippled ducks don't kill chickens 'r eat house pets."

"You ever kill anything?" he asked.

"Not any animals."

He'd asked without thinking and I'd answered too quickly. That pure, unguarded instant was overwhelming. When we turned to face each other we found ourselves staring at each other across a million miles of desolate landscape shrouded in hazy, formless questions. We'd have to skirt this place for now, make our separate ways around it.

"Be careful," I managed.

"Sure. I'll do that," sliding behind the steering wheel.

We waved at each other as he drove off, beer cans rattling in the bed.

I went across the street to the lounge and got drunk, running a tab against next week's paycheck. I think it was around 11:30 when I got home. The clock was too blurry for me to be sure.

*12:30, maybe. Have ta wait f'r mornin' f'r Bobbie ta be in my shit. Good God will she be in my shit.*

I crept into our room. Bobbie slipped from bed and, taking her pillow with her, walked by me and out the door. I stumbled noisily to the bed, tore the top sheet off, and then wobbled into the hall. I found Bobbie in Joan's room.

"Go back ta bed," I slurred.

I turned and managed to make it back down the steps without waking Tripp. Tossing the sheet under the staircase, I fell onto it and passed out.

\*\*\*

History 301 MWF
French Revolution
Today is: September 3, 1973

## THE RAVING EUNUCH MONKS

CHECK YOUR SKED NOW: Are you where your parents paid
for you to be?

was scribbled on the blackboard behind an ornately carved, wooden lectern. Two darkly tanned frats wearing tennis shorts and muscle shirts were sitting in front of me. They were arguing about who'd gotten more snatch over the summer—Bob, who'd spent all three months in Barbados, or Tom who'd hung out in Cancun.

*Fuckin' douche bags.*

They fell silent when the most beautiful woman I'd ever seen entered the classroom. I could hear hard-ons slapping against desk bottoms all around me.

She was five foot four, with brilliant, jet black hair down to the waist. Her skin was a golden almond.

*Chinese or Polynesian? Chinese. The eyes slant too much to be a Polynesian. Her legs...my God.*

*Petite.*

*Petite breasts. Petite ass. Petite waist.*

*Delicate.*

She sat in the front row. The frats moved to the row behind her.

*Turds.*

I watched her every move as the hour dragged by. The instructor eventually dismissed us. I remained seated as the classroom emptied. When she stood to leave, I was up and right on her ass. I followed her across campus, hypnotized by the rhythmic shifting of her hips.

*It'd be so easy ta love somethin' like 'at. It'd be so easy ta do whatever it took ta make her happy.*

I followed her into the student union where she hooked up with a fruitcake in slacks and a crisp, white, long sleeved shirt and tie.

*Spiffy. Very spiffy.*

*Pre-law?*

*Bastard.*

I exited the union. Pissed.

*Get a fuckin' grip! Anything like 'at's out'a reach now. Accept it.*

*Fuckin' depressed.*

*About ever'thing. The work routine. The school routine. Broke all the time. Tired all the time. Bobbie's off an' on bitchiness.*

*What's it been? Over a week with no sex? Christ. I was gettin' it more often when I wasn't gettin' it at all. Damn near, anyway.*

*Why am I in school?*

*Don't wan'a teach. Don't wan'a go ta grad school. Don't know what the fuck I want. No idea what I'm doin'.*

*Can't live like 'at when ya have a family. Can't just drift along anymore. It's not my life anymore.*

*Goddammit. How the hell'd I come ta this?*


No one was at the house. I found a note in Tripp's crib. Bobbie and the baby were in Jerry's basement. I grabbed a beer then wandered over to her "studio". Bobbie's back was to the doors. She was lost in a four by four canvass that appeared to be nearing completion. Hard to tell since everything Bobbie did was abstract.


I liked her paintings - all the subdued shades and subtle tones. The way the lines would sweep me from one side of the canvass to the other, plunging me into one pool of vibrant contrasts after the other. I would tumble softly through the whole gentle confusion. It was calming, especially when I was smoked up.

*Wonder where she gets the ideas ta paint like 'at? Where it comes from.*

I liked to think she was good. A good artist. It always embarrassed her when I told her I felt like she was good.


Tripp was asleep on a pillow in a blanket lined box. I went over and picked him up. He wriggled in my arms, clinging to my tee shirt with both hands, eyes remaining tightly shut. I sat down on a milk carton and placed him face up in my lap. After a little squirming, he yawned, vibrated through a stretch, and then went limp.

*Eight months old. He's really grown. Smaller than most babies at eight months. Doctors aren't worried. He's just a small baby. I was a small baby. He's so…so handsome.*

*Can babies be handsome?*

*Gettin' some good hair on top…long, fine, blond locks. Hugo figured it'd pro'bly turn more brown as he got older. Blue eyes. Crystal clear. Soft, pink skin. No blemishes.*

*Bobbie's a good mother. Tripp looks so clean an' fresh all the time.*

*Wonder if he's pickin' up on the feelin's I'm havin' about him right now? My vibes? I do love him. He just scares the shit out'a me at times.*

*All that crap this mornin' on campus…I just panicked.*

*Bobbie's not really a bitch. She just gets scared, too. This is pro'bly what I've always wanted.*

*It's just not exactly what I thought it was gunna be.*

I lightly ran my finger over his forehead. His lips twitched into a frown, his eye lids tightened. I looked over at Bobbie, tapping her foot to a tune in her head, dabbing a wadded piece of wet paper towel here and there around the canvas. She'd put a little weight on since Tripp was born. Not much. It wasn't likely to go away. She still made me hot. I wanted her right now. I wanted her bad.

Tripp jerked and squeaked, blew some bubbles then drifted away again.

Bobbie turned to check on him, screamed and jumped back,

"You scared the hell out'a me!"

Tripp stirred. I brought him to my chest and walked over to her.

"I like it," nodding at the painting.

"Really?" pleased.

"Really. Can we hang it in the hall over at the house when y're done?"

"It *is* done," frowning.

"Oh," flatly. "Then we should hang in it the hall as soon as it's dry."

Bobbie leaned over and kissed Tripp on the cheek.

"We'll see what the others think about it first," she said. "Got a good hold on the baby?"

"Well, yeah," squeezing him a bit tighter. "Why?"

Bobbie gently ran her hand between my legs. I shivered from head to foot.

"What's this all about?" she grinned nastily. "Couldn't help but notice it when ya stood up. You've been sittin' over there havin' dirty thoughts, haven't ya?"

"More filthy than dirty," I moaned softly as she continued to toy.

Bobbie took Tripp from me and carefully returned him to the box. She turned around and removed her tee shirt and bra then unbuttoned her cutoffs before simultaneously stripping her panties and shorts from her body. She held her hands behind her, shoulders rocking seductively.

"It's been a while," she mewed.

I glanced at the opened doors.

"Nobody'll see," walking over to me. "I don't care if they do."

By the time we got back to the house I was running late for work. Bobbie put Tripp on the carpet. He started scooting all over the place. Bobbie and I, holding hands, sat on the edge of the bed and watched. She laid her head on my shoulder.

"Bobbie, I'm sorry about the way I've been. All the drinkin'. Doin' that instead'a spendin' time with you an' Tripp."

She squeezed my hand, but didn't say anything.

"I love ya Bobbie."

"I love you, too, Gil," looking up at me. "I love you more'n anything. An' Tripp. I don't think I could live without him now he's here," putting her face to my chest. "I miss ya so much when y're not here an' it seems like y're never here."

"It'll get better. You'll see."

She hugged me tightly.

"I'm callin' Hugo an' tellin' him I can't come in this afternoon," I whispered.

"Can we afford that?" head still on my chest.

"We'll worry about it later. An' I'm not goin' inta the lounge t'night either."

Bobbie sat up.

"I *know* we can't afford that, but I appreciate what y're tryin' do," walking to the baby's chest of drawers for a tissue.

"I'm goin' ta Jerry's an' call in sick," pecking her on the back of the neck as I moved toward the door.

"I'll sign up for overtime hours at the parlor if I have ta," she told me.

I spent the afternoon studying, watching Tripp, and talking with Bobbie. Talking and touching. In the evening we strolled through the neighborhood, out to the campus, then came back to the house and made love in the shower. I studied on the floor between our bed and Tripp's crib, quite content, occasionally stepping onto the stoop for a cigarette.

*See how good this feels? How easy it is ta do the...the right thing? The responsible thing? This is how it should be. Ever' night.*

House traffic was steady all through the evening. Not noisy, but steady. I was rarely there during the evening and had lost touch with that part of the house's daily routine. Joan, Homer, Jerry, Shauna, Danny, all of them, at one time or another, rapped lightly on the door, peeked in, said hello, loved on Tripp, and then went about their business. Joan and some friends of hers we're up late in the kitchen theologizing.

Around one in the morning I slid into bed alongside Bobbie, trying not to wake her. As I laid there in the dark, Tripp softly snoring, the smell of baby powder and Bobbie's shampoo perfuming the air, it suddenly occurred to me that I hadn't had any alcohol for over twenty-four hours. No pills. No grass.

*How'd that happen? Stone sober a whole day.*

I looked over at Bobbie. She was looking back at me.

"Can I make love to ya again?" I whispered.

She smiled sleepily and edged to my side.

***

I was using a red, felt tipped pen to highlight the date, April 25, 1974, under The University Daily banner. Jerry, Dan, Eduardo, and Homer were fidgeting with beer mugs. Hugo motioned Charlie for a branch. Kriss Kristofferson was halfway through "Silver Tongued Devil". We remained stone silent while Hugo ruminated, head bobbing, face frozen. Charlie delivered the drink.

Hugo leaned forward, crossing his arms on the table. His sweat stained felt hat was shoved way back on his head. Hugo cleared his throat, snuffed his cigarette out, and then sipped the drink.

"Let's hear whut ya've got," in his thickest West Texas drawl.

We glanced around the table at each other.

"An' it better be good if y're askin' me ta consider givin' yew five yahoos ten thousan' dollars," he chuckled.

"Investing," Danny corrected, "You'd be an equal partner," somewhat uneasily. "Or more, if that's what you prefer."

We all nodded. Hugo kept chuckling and sipping.

"Mr. Tripp…"

*"Mr. Tripp?"* Hugo laughed, cutting Danny off. "Whut the hell happened ta Hugo?"

"Hugo," Danny began again, "It's a solid, established business with an excellent reputation for satisfying the entertainment preferences of a large, sophisticated clientele who bring a sizeable amount of disposable income to one of the busiest tourist areas in the world."

*Damn. He's good.*

We all smiled and nodded vigorously. Everybody but Hugo.

Hugo glanced around the table.

"Gentlemen, would any'a y'all be offended if I were ta request that all'a y'all, except Daniel, go across the alley ta Homer's place an' wait f'r us there?"

We were a little surprised, but I don't think anybody's feelings were hurt. We shook our heads.

"Good," Hugo pursing his lips. "Let's do that then."

We sat stupidly for a moment. Danny, frowning, hitched his head toward the back. In a burst of noise we scrapped our chairs away from the table and filed by the bar, waving to Charlie as we passed.


It was pouring rain out. Homer darted across the alley, unsnapped the padlock, rattled the chain through the hole in the door, and then pushed it open. He jumped inside the shop. He'd gotten drenched in the short amount of time it'd taken to execute the maneuver. The rest of us splashed through the alley river and into the shop. We wandered to the front of the building, passing between rows of opened glass crates and a set of shelves filled with square foot sized pieces of different colored opalescent and cathedral stained glass. We settled onto tall stools scattered around three large work tables.


Jerry immediately produced a joint.

"What're ya doin'?" I snapped.

"Whu's it look like, asshole," putting the joint between his lips.

"We're tryin' ta come off as businessmen," I pointed out. "He'll smell 'at shit the second he walks in."

"He knows we smoke up," Jerry, pulling a book of matches from his pocket. "Hell, he smokes up."

"A guy in the afternoon class is a cop," I lied. "*He'll* smell it."

"No bullshit?" convinced I was lying.

"No bullshit," not budging.

Jerry glared at me like he thought I was being a pussy about it. He pocketed the joint.

"You still getting lots of people in the glass classes?" Eduardo, combing water from his hair.

"Five and six in every class," Danny, keeper of the books. "Not as many as when we started them up."

"Selling a lot of supplies?" Ed.

"It's picking up," Danny. "We're actually about to run out of our first order of soldering irons, solder, and foil. Certain glass colors. What we need to do now is make a bigger order of everything so we can get a price break and increase the profits."

Ed flicked water from his comb onto the floor.

"Makes sense."

"It's still the repairs making the rent," Danny.

"An' 'at's thanks ta me," Jerry huffed. "I'm the only son uv a bitch doin' any *real* work aroun' here anymore."

He was ignored.

"Gil, did you tell Bobbie what we're talking to Hugo about?" Homer, shifting focus back to the matter at hand.

"I told her Hugo was interested in investin' in a business."

"I'm su'prised she's talkin' to ya at all," Jerry.

"Why wouldn't she be talkin' ta me?" agitated.

"F'rgit it," Jerry, stretching.

"What am I supposed ta forget, Jerry?" more agitated. "Tell me. I wan'a know."

"Well, Shauna seems ta think 'at Bobbie's all pissed as hell about yew never bein' at home an' shit. How ya always come home late smellin' like beer."

"That so? That's what Shauna's sayin?"

"Hell, yew asked, motherfucker."

I turned to Homer.

"Bobbie said anything ta you ta make ya think she dudn't understand how hard it is ta be in ten fuckin' places at the same goddamn time? Workin' at Hugo's. Workin' at the lounge. Classes.

The library. Teachin' stained glass up here. I've only got so much fuckin' time ta work with," beginning to lose it.

"Shit, man," Jerry, shaking his head and glancing at the others. "Ever'body knows ya spend all'a y'ur lib'ary time bar hoppin' all over the place. An' ya don't even go ta half y'ur classes."

I was on the verge of coming completely unglued. I glanced at Homer and Ed to see how they were reacting to the accusation. They wouldn't look at me. I didn't like it, but they seemed to be siding with Jerry. They weren't going to play the game the way Bobbie does.

"So, I guess ever'body in Lubbock thinks I'm one gigantic asshole?" I asked loudly.

"Hell, no!" Jerry. "Jus' the one's 'at know ya," cackling.

Eduardo and Homer broke up.

*Fuckers.*

Hugo entered the building, shaking rain from his hat. Danny was behind him. Hugo came straight to me. He was holding his breath, cheeks puffing out, fighting to keep from laughing.

*I sure hope this is a good sign.*

"So," sputtering a bit, "ya needed ten thousan' dollars'a my money ta buy a whorehouse in Juarez?" barely getting it out before bursting into laughter.

*Not good.*

Hugo removed his glasses then wiped his jacket sleeve over his eyes.

"My, Lord," trying to maintain, "You boys take the goddamn cake. I swear," back to his usual chuckle. "Were ya gunna let me rename it ta 'Hugo's Land Surveyin' And, Oh By The Way, Whorehouse'?" roaring with laughter, obviously liking that one. "'at's ten thousan' dollars worth a neon tubin' right there!" liking that one even better, gasping for air, beating the table with his palm.

I guess right about then we all realized how absolutely insane the whole idea had been. I'd suspected the proposal might have had a certain far fetched quality to it that would keep Hugo from wanting in on the deal, however, it wasn't until right now, at this very instant, watching Hugo laugh his ass off, that it dawned on me just how completely doomed the whole project had been from its inception.

That started me laughing. My laughing got everybody else going.

Hugo, weak after the workout, slowly shaking his head as it did its little bobbing thing, held a hand up for silence. We quieted down.

"I can't tell ya how damn much it means ta me 'at y'all came ta me first with this...this marvelous opportunity," hoarsely. "It's truly an honor I'll never f'rget as long as I live, but, boys, I'm...I'm gunna have ta pass on this 'un if ya don't mind."

Hugo shook our hands then walked to the backdoor, waving without turning around. He disappeared into the deluge.

We were quiet for a while. We lit cigarettes, shifted around on stools. Softly coughed.

I couldn't take it any longer.

"What turned him off ta the idea?"

"Everything," Danny. "He wanted to know what we knew about owning a business in Mexico. You know...taxes, licenses, insurance, permits. Payoffs to the police."

"Whu'd ya tell him?" Jerry.

"That we didn't know anything about any of it at the moment, but we..."

"Goddammit!" Jerry. "We could'a fig'red all 'at out!" jumping to his feet.

"There was a bigger issue," Danny, looking down.

"Hope?" I blurted.

*FUCK!*

I knew the instant I heard her name I'd screwed up.

"I'm sorry," I said. "I didn't mean ta…"
*There's no apology for that gross a fuck up.*
*Just leave it.*

We had to regroup before continuing, although there wasn't an awful lot to continue on about. I think everybody wanted to smooth things out instead of breaking up in a huff. After a piss break we took up our previous positions. The tension had eased.

"Yew sure we couldn't talk Alberto inta lettin' us make payments?" Jerry, having trouble accepting his dream business had slipped right through his fingers.

"Not with Hector waving ten thousand cash in his face," Danny.

"It's over, then," I sighed with an air of finality.

"It's over," Eduardo, sadly nodding his head.

"Hugo must think we're a bunch'a complete idiots now for comin' up with an idea like this," I said.

"This proposal didn't add or detract from his opinion of us," Danny. "Just confirmed a few things."

"I look at it like this, man," Eduardo. "Look at how close we came to owning our own *whorehouse*. Most people never even get a chance to own their own whorehouse. See what I'm saying?" grinning broadly. "Shiiit, man. It was a goood feeling, man."

We ate up the better part of a minute while silently considering Ed's perspective.

"He's right," I said. "I could hardly wait ta call Dad up an' tell him I'd cut my hair, shaved my beard, started goin' back ta church, changed my whole attitude, an' bought a whorehouse in Mexico."

Homer smiled.

"I wuz thinkin' uv a chain'a places, man," Jerry. "Like Pizza Hut only call it Piece'a Butt," seriously.

Laughter all around.

"Whu's so damn funny?" Jerry frowned. "We'd'a got rich, man."

"This whole week's been cool," Ed. "Walking around seeing everybody looking at me like everything was still the same for me. The whole time, me thinking 'Wait until next week, man...wait until next week when I own a gentleman's club in Juarez'. Damn... *that* was a *goood* feeling."

"You should've seen the look on Hugo's face when I told him what type of a business it was," Danny. "His head actually stopped bobbing. He was stunned."

"This may sound stupid," I said, "but, ya know what? I think I'd rather have things fall through on a whorehouse deal than get into a sure thing insurance business."

"Or a car salesman," Jerry.

"Or a guy working in a bank or something like that," Eduardo groaned.

"Anything like that," Homer frowned.

"I'm serious as a heart beat," I continued. "Think about fifty years from now when y're sittin' on the porch'a some old folks home in a wheelchair an' y'ur grandkids show up. Which story're they gunna wan'a hear? How ya ate shit y'ur whole life ta b'come the big wheel president 'r owner of some shit hook accountin' business *OR*...hear the story about how close ya came ta ownin' a whorehouse once?"

Laughter.

"If my grandkids want to hear the shit eating story," Ed, smashing a fist into the palm of his hand, "I'll disown them!"

Sustained laughter.

"Don't get me wrong," I continued. "It'd be a lot less stressful ta spend the next fifty years rakin' it in at some asshole job 'r other, but I feel an obligation ta my unborn grandkids ta give 'em somethin' more'n 'at. I'm willin' ta make the sacrifice."

A brief period of "damn straight"s, "fuckin' A's"s, and shoulder slapping was followed by a period of quiet.

Eduardo stood up.

"I want to thank you guys for inviting me to be a part of all this," he said sincerely. "Even if it didn't work out. It was really cool, man."

"Couldn'a *not* done it with out ya," Jerry.

The rest of us applauded. Ed, smiling, bowed deeply.

"What time's it gettin' ta be?" I asked.

"One thirty," Danny.

"Gotta set up for the afternoon class," as I slid from the stool.

"Need any help?" Danny, standing and stretching.

"Nah. I got it."

"Then I'm out'a here," Jerry.

They all shook my hand before plunging into the gulley washer outside.

*They're good people. Damn good people.*

I got busy setting up for the class. Danny had finally convinced the rest of the group there was a lot of potential in teaching "hobby" stained glass cutting and in the subsequent retailing of stained glass supplies. He'd been pushing the idea from the start. We'd create our own market that could, over time, prove to be quite lucrative providing, of course, we—we being everyone involved excluding Danny—didn't find some way to fuck it up. The first classes had started in January.

I liked teaching the glass classes. It was an ego boost. I was treated like some kind of stained glass master by the students, an image I couldn't keep myself from encouraging with a few bullshit stories I'd steal from The Stained Glass Quarterly. I shared the position of master craftsman with Homer and Joan who had also learned how to pass themselves off as experts. Danny didn't teach, deriving much more ego fuel from his management image than from that of a glass guru. Jerry didn't want any part of either roll, simply preferring to portray himself as self-employed rather than just being a mailman.

The Saturday afternoon class ran from 2:30 until 4:30. Currently the group consisted of two ex-decoupage housewives, two college girls, and one well-behaved homo. The evening class started at 5:00. Five women were in the current evening class. One of the ladies drove up from Midland, about two hours south of Lubbock. Tonight was to be their last night. Graduation. Hopefully I'd instilled in them the degree of confidence they'd need to drop a ton of money on supplies and glass for home projects larger than the one foot by one foot, five piece, copper foil training "panel" they would be taking home.

The evening class, running late, came to an end at a little after 8:00 with four of the five ladies carrying a combined total of around three hundred dollars worth of tools, solder, foil, glass, and patinas out the door. They couldn't wait for the upcoming craft show at the fairgrounds. They, like the sixty or so other graduates before them, were going to get rich.

Kristina, the lady from Midland, remained behind. She was still at her table doodling on a piece of paper. I walked over and pretended to be interested in the design.

"Let's skip drinks," Kristina, without looking up from her design. "Let's go straight to the room."

# CHAPTER EIGHT
## July, 1974

S omebody was knocking on the bedroom door.
"C'mon in," Bobbie.

Vann entered, went straight to Tripp, swept him up in his arm, and then spun around. Tripp, pulled away from his crayons, protested loudly. Vann, whispering in Vietnamese, returned him to his coloring book then sat down in the big chair.

"I saw Doug a few minutes ago," he announced.

"Where?" Bobbie and I in unison.

"Joan and I were stopped at the intersection at Nineteenth and Q. He was with his mother."

Bobbie was counting on her fingers.

"You sure it was Doug?" rubbing the back of my neck.

"Yes. We're positive."

"Did he see you?"

"He *may* have. I'm not sure."

"It's been around a year an' ten months 'r so," Bobbie, having completed her calculation.

"Wonder how long he's been in town?" I mumbled.

"Joan and I decided it couldn't have been too long or we would have seen him sooner," Vann.

"Ya think he's spent the whole twenty two months locked up?" as I got up and moved to the stoop window.

Vann shrugged his shoulders. Bobbie darted over to Tripp and removed a crayon from his mouth.

"Is it me or are you feeling a little, well, odd about all this?" Vann.

"I'll be honest with ya," and pulled the curtain back to look out the window. "I'm a little uncomfortable about anything ta do with Doug anymore," glancing at Bobbie.

She was watching me closely.

"But," trying to ease Bobbie's mind, "I'm not gunna lose any sleep over it. He's not dangerous. Never has been. He's just one perfectly fucked up human being."

"Of course," Vann, struggling from the overstuffed chair.

"When he's ready ta see us," I said, "he'll come around," walking down the hall with him.

"Yes. Yes," rubbing his chin. "He has been in an especially unique environment for some time. He will have to readjust at his own pace," stepping out onto the stoop.

When I returned to the bedroom I found Bobbie sitting on the bed watching Tripp doze off. I sat down beside her.

"Y're still worried. Aren't ya?" and kissed the back of her neck.

"Yeah. Doug's crazy an' crazy people can be dangerous."

"But he's not mean. An' he's been in the hospital for a long time. I think we're all gunna find out he's doin' a lot better than he was."

"I'd just as soon not find out one way 'r the other."

A horn honked loud and long in the street below.

Bobbie leaned against me.

"Ever'time he does 'at, I can't help but think'a the mornin' you came runnin' over ta Jerry's half naked an' yellin' about y'ur hard... y'ur eye gettin' better."

"I wudn't yellin'," moving my hand to her thigh.

"The first time we made love," extending her leg to encourage the gentle stroking, "What did ya like best about it?"

I nibbled her ear lobe. She broke out in chill bumps.

"The orgasm," I whispered.

"You bastard," slugging me in the stomach.

HOOOOOONK!

"Gotta go," and stood up.

"Good," she huffed.

I pulled her from the bed and hugged her.

"T'night I'll tell ya what part I *really* liked the best. It'll make a good bedtime story."

"I'll be too tired for a bedtime story," pouting. "I've got three hair appointments this afternoon."

HOOOOONK!

"We'll see. I love ya," swatting her on the butt.

I jumped into the cab of the truck.

"Three minutes after twelve," Roy growled. "Yew do that shit ta me j'st ta piss me off don'ch ya?" pulling away from the curb.

I poked my head out the window and looked back at the house. Bobbie hadn't come out onto the stoop to wave goodbye.

"Where we workin' this afternoon?" pulling my head back inside.

"Whut differ'nce does it make?"

"Just wonderin'," inspecting a tight little ass making its way up Broadway.

"Y'ur knowin' won't change nothin'," pointing at the lady I was watching. "An' I saw her first, dickless."

"I wanted ta have some kind'a idea about what we'd be doin' so I could prepare myself mentally."

"F'r God sake! Y're hammerin' metal rods inta the ground, boy. How much mental preparation does 'at take?"

"It's a Zen thing," drooling out the window at a nasty pair of shorts.

"Whut yew know about Zen pro'bly wouldn't fill a gnat's ass."

"Eat me," smiling at the little slut as we drove by.

"If Hugo ever gits wind'a a the way I let ya talk ta his only field supervisor he'll be firin' my ass. I'm layin' the welfare'a my entire family on the line j'st f'r puttin' with 'em obnoxious, turdful ways'a y'urs."

Roy went straight through the light at University and entered the Texas Tech campus. Working on the campus would be a first for me.

*This'll be entertaining.*

After wiggling his way through a narrow maze of streets, Roy eased over a curb and stopped on the grass down from the front of the main library.

"Here?" I asked.

"Would there be any other goddamn reason I'd be stoppin'?" as he grabbed his chew from the dash.

"You hung over worse than normal this mornin' 'r just pissed off about y'ur pathetic station in life?"

"Git the tripod down," ignoring the question. "An' the two hun'r'd foot chain while I mentally prepare myself f'r the task at hand," as he began whittling out a plug.

I reached for the transit box on the seat between us. Roy slapped my hand.

"Don't go touchin' my transit," he grumbled. "It's bad luck."

"Hugo lets me set his transit," I protested.

"Move it," stuffing the plug into his mouth.


I removed the tripod from the bed of the truck then set it up, forcing each brass pointed leg a good six inches into the turf. I tested the tripod for resistance.

*Stuck hard. Good. Grumpy-ass bastard.*

Roy got out of the cab, carried his transit over to the tripod, and then placed the transit over the tripod threads. After screwing it tightly into place he grabbed two of the tripod legs and lifted. His hands slid up the legs, smashed into the base of the transit, and then raked their way over the scope.

"Goddammit, yew sorry son uv a bitch!" shaking his left hand up and down. "Yew fuckin' happy now?" sucking on his thumb knuckle. "Damn near cut my thumb off!" in exaggerated pain.

"Y're not even bleedin'."

"Prick," dramatically grunting like a weight lifter while working each of the tripod legs free.

Roy moved the tripod to an X chiseled in the sidewalk a few feet away. He set the transite on point with the plumb bob, and then leveled it up. Returning to the truck, he retrieved a clipboard from the front seat and began scribbling on a blueprint clipped to it. I picked up the chain and waited, checking out all the scantily clad leg running around.

*Oh, my God.*

"Roy!" I gasped. "Roy! Quick!" jumping to his side in a panic. "It's her," nodding toward the library steps. "The bitch I've been talkin' about all year. Soong. From my history classes."

Roy studied the library steps,

" 'at short, warty lookin' one?"

"There's no time for 'at shit. Ya gotta help me out," watching Soong float down the steps.

"Whud'a ya want me ta do? Hold her down for ya?"

"Lemme get b'hind the transit an' act like I'm the party chief," as Soong hit the bottom step.

Roy moved to the transit. I was right behind him.

"C'mon, Roy. *Please.*"

Roy studied the approaching figure.

"Yew wudn't lyin' one inch about her, was ya," licking his lips.

"Roy!" beside myself.

"Well," stepping away from the transit. "All right, but ya owe me one, by God," handing me the clipboard.

I put it under my arm then flung myself behind the transit. I began to alternate between knob fidgeting, scope eyeing, and level bubble checking, pouring everything into the preoccupied, engineering genius role. Roy stepped back a few paces, presumably assuming the character of an underpaid, slothful, apathetic survey crew ape.

Soong closed to twelve yards before recognizing me. She cocked her head, sending long silky strands of raven dark hair wafting over the delicate features of her brightly smiling face. She reached up and brushed the hair back with her free hand.

My stomach was twirling.

"Hello, Gil," so softly I could barely hear her.

I smiled as warmly, as sweetly, as lovingly as I believe I have ever smiled in my whole life.

*Impressed. She's impressed by the transit. The blueprints on the clipboard.*

*Say something!*

She stepped onto the grass to walk around the transit.

Roy whacked me in the back of the head with his ball cap.

"Git the hell away from 'at transit, boy!"

I dropped the clipboard and sucked my head into my shoulders like a turtle withdrawing into its shell. Soong, startled, hurried around me, hopped to the sidewalk, and then practically broke into a trot.

"Go git y'ur sledge hammer an' play with 'at if y're bored," Roy continued as he pushed me toward the truck. "J'st try not ta break the son uv a bitch this time."

Soong glanced back at me, "retard" written all over her face. Within seconds she had whipped around the corner and disappeared from view behind a thick hedge.

"That was funny as hell, Roy! *Real* goddamn funny!"

"Yew mind pickin' the clipboard up f'r me?" groaning while rubbing his lower back. "I seemed ta have strained somethin' when I pulled 'at tripod from the ground. Thank there's a lesson somewhere in all this?"

"All I learned was just how big an asshole you can be," picking up the chain, undoing it, then dropping the looped sections as I angrily walked down the line we were going to shoot.

"If ya hurry," Roy yelled after me, "yew c'n catch up with her an' show her a chainin' pin. 'at's kind'a technical."

We worked until 5:30 then wrapped things up.

"Ain't ya gunna thank me?" Roy, while driving me home.

"For embarrassin' me all afternoon?" tiredly.

"F'r savin' y'ur goddamn marriage," acting surprised at my having misinterpreted the effort he had put into making me look like a moron every time a female had come near us.

"Y're a real pal, Roy. I guess I'm just a stupidass, selfish, ungrateful son of a bitch."

"Don't be so harsh on y'urself," snickering. "Yew ain't all 'at selfish."


I found a note on the bed. Bobbie would be late getting back from the salon. I should go ahead and fix something to eat without waiting for her. Joan was watching Tripp.

She loved me.

*Fix dinner. Yeah, right. Like I'm up ta that. Dammit.*

Joan entered the room. Tripp began squirming and reaching for me the moment he saw me. She handed him over. He was fussy, looking around the room for Bobbie.

"Doug is over at Vann's," as she fell back into the chair.

"So, I guess he did see ya this mornin'," nibbling on Tripp's neck.

"Jerry was there for a little bit. He came over about an hour ago an' told me Doug wants ta get t'gether with ever'body over here t'night."

*Shit.*

"Why here?"

"He didn't think you'd mind."

*There goes my library time.*

"Is this gunna be like a party 'r a discussion group 'r what?" bouncing Tripp on the bed to humor him.

"Jerry thinks he wants to say something real quick then take off. He doesn't seem ta think it's any big deal."

"What time?"

"Around 8:00."

Joan watched Tripp while I showered. Bobbie was home by the time I finished. Joan had already told her about Doug coming over. Bobbie wasn't exactly happy about it. I calmed her down as we walked up to the Lot A Burger for dinner out. We stopped several times on the way back to shoot the shit with some of our fellow ghettoites. I'd met some of these people as long as three years ago—in classes, the bars, at parties. A year or two from now and they'll all be gone.

*We'd be gone too. I guess. Ta somewhere. Doin'...somethin'. Still hadn't figured that one out.*

Tripp loved the attention he was getting from everyone. He seemed to enjoy all the music spilling into the street as we strolled along—country giving way to classical giving way to rock giving way to folk. He was thoroughly entertained, riding on my shoulders, tightly hanging on to my hair.

It was going on 8:00 when we got back to the house. Bobbie took Tripp to shower with her. I grabbed a beer from the frig then sat down on the top step of the stoop. A wall of darkening blue was gradually forcing a fiery sky below the roof tops of the ghetto.

*Be good t'night, Doug. I don't feel like puttin' up with any shit.*

*Been too nice an evenin' an' I'm tired.*

*Tired'a workin' all the time. Tired'a studyin' all the time.*

*Tired a you, Doug, gettin' ta be the only one who's allowed ta be crazy.*

*Ya do nothin', absolutely nothin', but ya get ta be crazy. Ya don't deserve 'at privilege. There's a whole lot more of us out here who've worked our asses off for the right ta be fuckin' nuts.*

*Dudn't seem fair at all.*

\*\*\*

Doug, guarding a standard size, spiral notebook, sat at the kitchen table, head nodding, eyes gleaming, grinning like a...

*Madman?*

Vann was next to Doug, Jerry and I seated across the table from them. Danny, obviously uneasy, had joined Homer on the sink. Shauna, Joan, and Bobbie had retired to our bedroom after welcoming Doug back. The girls had been nervous. Everyone in the kitchen had a beer except Doug who had explained that he couldn't mix alcohol with the medicines he was taking. We all enthusiastically agreed he shouldn't do anything to keep his medicine from working.

"First," Doug, still grinning, "I want to thank...*all* of you for staying in...in such close contact with me," dropping the grin.

*Damn. Didn't waste any time gettin' 'at off his chest.*

I glanced at Danny. Vann shut his eyes. Homer slid from the sink to his feet then rested back against it.

Jerry leaned forward and scowled.

"Y'ur mamma wouldn't tell us where yew wuz at. The VA hospital in Houston wouldn't tell us *shit* about where they'd sent ya 'cause we wudn't fam'ly. Yew never wrote any'a us ta tell us were yew wuz at an' then, when ya get back ta town, yew don't tell a fuckin' soul, so don't go startin' this little git t'gether off by tryin' ta put y'ur foot up ever'body's ass."

Doug had been stopped in his tracks.

"I was...I was...just kidding," bringing a weak smile back and glancing around the room. "It was only a...a joke."

The room was silent.

"May I continue?" asking no one in particular.

More silence.

Doug took that as a go.

"Please, bear, uh...with me," opening his notebook. "This is... this *will*...this is *intended* to be, after everything has been said...an apology."

We nodded in turn.

"All right, then," clapping his hands together.

*Here it goes. Time to find out if modern psychiatry is worth a shit.*

Doug began reading from the spiral.

"I know I have caused numerous problems for all of you," in a cadence approximating the measured beat of an inexperienced typist laboriously pecking out a memo one letter at a time. "I owe each of you and many others so much for helping me. I have found a way of thanking you and paying all of you back for all the trouble I have caused. I have come to realize we are all participating in a process of evolving from finite energy points to merging with and becoming absorbed into the infinite God-Energy, a completeness unto itself existing as its own cause and its own effect. God-Energy is the beginning, the middle, and the end, all existing in the same instant and spatially occupying the same place in that instant. It is pure God-Energyness," looking up and quietly wheezing through a big smile, eyes gleaming.

*He honest-ta-God b'lieves he's got somethin' here.*

Doug continued to read from his notes. He explained how this evolutionary process consisted of our growing awareness in a long series of phases we evolve through and, eventually, out of. While still in one phase we become aware of our potential to evolve into the next, more evolved phase. We then enter the next phase where we, existing as a developing energy point, continue to develop our potential. We will remain there until total phase awareness—our fullest potential in that phase—is reached. Through evolutionary energy phasing we eventually merge with the infinite totality of the God-Energy. Our sole purpose is to phase until mergence is achieved.

The phase we were all in at the moment is intended to demonstrate the reality of our existence as energy thus making us aware of the reality that material existence is an illusion. None of *this* is substantively occurring, *however,* it *is* substantially experienced as a *false* reality. Once we recognize our true nature as energy in our current phase we increase our potential and can then evolve to the next phase.

*Christ. How much longer is this gunna take?*

The others were starting to fidget.

Doug ignored all the signals.

"To initiate evolution to the next phase," he continued, "one must destroy the illusion of the body as a reality," pausing without looking up from the notes.

*Destroy the illusion of the body?*

"All the suffering we experience in this phase is essentially a purposeless distraction. None of it has any meaning until the illusion is brought to an end."

*Brougt to an end?*

"For all the things you have done for me and for all the problems I have caused you, I present to you this gift, the knowledge that your purpose here is to evolve out of this phase and that this evolving requires ceasing to be."

*Ceasing to be?*

By the look on everyone's face, I wasn't the only one having a serious problem with the terminology.

Doug closed the notebook then surveyed the room for reactions. He was evidently waiting for something much more animated than questioning stares. His growing disappointment was palpable as the period of silence lengthened. It finally occurred to him that there wasn't going to be an excited, enthusiastic, post revelation discussion culminating in his being accepted as a savior-genius of some kind.

"I have to, uh...go now," standing up. "Thank you, uh...for your...for your time," then quickly walked out the door.

The second Doug cleared the bottom step, Jerry was sharing his opinion about Doug's "gift".

"He's plannin' on blowin' our brains out. That's how he's gunna say thanks an' even things up."

"No fuckin' way," I said.

*He is. He's plannin' on blowin' our brains out.*

"Whut else could 'destroy' an' 'cease ta be' mean, man?" Jerry snarled.

"But...but," Vann stammered, squinting hard, "this is so *completely* illogical! Even for Doug!"

"He didn't come up with this idea by taking any Aristotle County roads," Danny. "He hopped on the Doug super freeway and got right into the express lane."

"If he really b'lieved what he was sayin', he'd'a just shot us without sayin' a thing," I argued. "He wouldn'a bothered with tryin' ta convince us. He'd'a shot us then we'd look him up in the next phase and thank him for gettin' us the hell out'a *this* phase. I think he's fuckin' with his own head. I think he must'a finally realized in the hospital how responsible he is for causin' ever'body a lot'a bullshit. He's told us about this truth he's invented an' somehow that relieves him of any guilt feelings he's got. If we wan'a take advantage of it, fine. If not, fine, but Doug won't be the one destroyin' us 'r causin' us ta cease ta be. He's leavin' 'at part up ta us."

*Maybe.*

"I think y're right," Vann, saging his chin again.

"That would definitely be a Dougian way of handling it," Danny.

"He's gunna blow our brains out as soon as he gets his hands on'a gun," Jerry, remaining unconvinced.

"Can he get his hands on a gun?" Homer, wavering between the two opinions.

"If he's staying with his folks," Danny, "he may have access to a hand gun his father used to own. His dad chased Doug out of their house with it back in high school once."

"I remember that," nodding my head, "but he's *not* thinkin' about shootin' anybody."


Bobbie poked her head around the hall curtain.

"Who left?" she asked.

"Doug," Danny told her.

"Was he mad?" her brows raised.

"Not at all. His medicine makes him tired," Danny, mater-of-factly. "Things went real well. He apologized for being such a pill."

Bobbie wasn't buying it.

"I have a right ta know if somethin's goin' on."

"We all do," Joan's voice from the hall.

We looked at Danny, silently appointed spokesman for the rest of us.

"Y're right," Danny nodded. "Doug...Doug isn't as well as he needs to be," his brain processing an acceptable version of the meeting.

"What's that supposed ta mean," Bobbie's concern growing.

"He may be thinking about killing himself," softly.

*Good one, Fast Daniel! That'll fly.*

We were all nodding sadly.

"Oh, no!" Joan bursting into the kitchen. "Is that exactly what he said?"

"Not exactly," Danny frowned. "We need to talk to Hugo about it. See what he thinks. Make sure we're not over reacting."

Bobbie glanced at me. She wasn't falling for any of it. She was mad. Bobbie dragged Joan from the kitchen.

Jerry stood up and walked toward the stoop.

"Y'all do whut ya want, but, by God, I'm sleepin' with a loaded .45 an' the doors locked 'til I c'n think'a some way ta convince somebody 'at motherfucker needs ta be locked up again. Yew'll see, man. Yew'll see," stepping onto the porch and rapping on the bedroom window. "Let's go Shauna," Jerry ordered then started down the stairs.

Shauna hurried through the kitchen, waving and smiling as she went. Homer followed Shauna, barely waving. He looked worried. Seriously worried. I think he may have come down on Jerry's side of the fence. Vann was next. Danny and I swapped whispered "goodnight"s before going to our rooms.

I undressed then slid into bed beside Bobbie—no hug, not

even a peck on the cheek. She wasn't going to talk to me. She wasn't going to be able to relax until she laid there for a while, staring up at the ceiling, torturing me with her silent bitch stick.

I couldn't sleep. I was up and down. On the porch with a beer. On the roof smoking a joint. Restless. Uneasy. I stole a white light bulb from a house a few doors down and replaced our yellow bug light. At 2:30 the last light went out at Jerry's. I went inside and crawled back into bed. I laid there, listening.

About an hour later I heard the steps creaking. I slipped from bed and crawled to the window. I eased a corner of the curtain back and peered out. Doug was on the stoop, gun in hand.

"DOUG!" from the bottom steps.

It was Jerry.

Doug turned and looked back down the stairs.

I ran across the room and grabbed Tripp while yelling for Bobbie to wake up. She shot into a sitting position, dazed. After pulling her from the bed, I thrust a screaming Tripp into her arms.

"Doug's here," pushing her to the window opposite the stoop. "Get out on the eave, shut the window an' wait."

Joan came into the room. I repeated the instructions then charged toward the kitchen. Danny stepped into the hall. Joan yelled for him to come with her.

I went to my knees at the kitchen door and listened.

"...the whole point," Doug speaking. "Whether *you* shoot me and free me or, uh...*I* free *myself*...what's the difference? Either way, I evolve," wheeze laughing.

*Jerry must have his gun.*

"THE POLICE'RE COMIN'!" Shauna, from the porch of their house.

I looked under the kitchen door curtain. Doug, seemingly calm as could be, was waving a finger down the steps. A pistol was in his right hand, down at his side.

"Be sensible, Jerry," Doug was saying. "If *you* shoot me...you go to jail. Probably. I don't want to have you...have that happen, you know, I mean...that's simply creating, uh...*more* problems for a...*another* friend. So...I don't, huh, *really* have any other choice," and began to raise the pistol to his head.

"NO!" Homer's voice.

*Holy fuckin' shit!*

I tore the door open right as a weapon was fired. I covered my head and fell back into the kitchen.

The girls and the baby were screaming.

Doug was writhing in agony, clutching his knee. Blood was everywhere. Jerry flew into sight, crashing down on top of Doug. Homer appeared in the doorway, jumped over me and ran to the sink where he ripped some dish towels from their racks then scooted back by me.

"We're going to need more towels!" Homer.

In an instant I was on my feet and running for the towels in the bathroom. I thought I heard sirens. I wasn't sure. My head was throbbing. When I returned, the kitchen was flooded in a blinding white light and quick flashes of red.

"Don't come out," Homer yelled to me.

I could see Jerry standing on the stoop with his legs apart, hands behind his head, facing the street. Doug, rolled into a tight ball around his bleeding knee, was moaning deeply.

"He's goddamn bleedin' ta death!" Jerry, yelling angrily into the light.

"HOLD Y'UR POSITION!" blared from a bull horn.

I heard Tripp screaming and ran back through the house to the eave window. My heart thudded to a stop as I looked out at the three of them tightly huddled together. The girls were sobbing, sobbing uncontrollably.

Danny was doing his best to calm them down.

*Oh, Jesus.*

I helped them back into the room then reached for Tripp.

"Get away from me!" Bobbie screamed and backed away, quaking violently.

Tripp began to wail, worn out from crying, lower lip quivering.

"Don't come near me! Get out'a here!" completely undone. "Get out'a here! NOW!" she shrieked.

"Just for a while, Gil," Joan sobbed, moving to Bobbie's side. "Please."

"Bullshit," Bobbie, sobbing along with Joan. "You get out'a here an' don't *ever* come back, goddamn you! You don't give a goddamn about us! I'm surprised you was even here t'night an' not out drinkin' an' whorin' around somewhere!" through a flood of tears.

"Please, Gil," Joan nodding toward the hall.

I slowly moved to the door. I paused before stepping into the hall where I was blinded by a slew of flashlight beams. I was commanded to freeze.

\*\*\*

The sun was coming up by the time I got around to calling Hugo from Jerry's.

*Goddammit. I'm so sick'a this shit.*

Hugo caught the fifth ring.

"Gil?" wearily.

"Ye'sir. Is ever'thing okay out there?"

"As well as c'n be expected. Shauna's havin' the most trouble. Poor thing. I gave her a few'a my sedatives."

"I get so sick an' tired of apologizin'..."

"We'll talk it over later. Yew need some sleep as much as they do."

"Is Bobbie still mad..."

"We'll talk it over later."

"You we're pro'bly on Doug's hit list too Hugo. That scares the hell out'a me."

"Put it out'a y'ur mind f'r now an' get ta bed."

"Hugo, I...it's about Jerry."

"He'll need an attorney an' some bail posted," Hugo, a sound of resignation in his voice.

"How much do ya think bail's gunna be for possessin' a .45 stolen from the Marines?"

"Is 'at all they're chargin' him with?"

"There callin' the shootin' self-defense. As far as me, Jerry, an' Homer are concerned, Doug was gunna shoot Jerry."

"Well...I guess 'at's good news. Shauna'll be glad ta hear that. I have no idea what the gun charge is gunna come to."

"Hugo, thanks for..."

"I gotta go, Gil. Yew get some sleep," and hung up.

*Damn.*

I went to the basement and sat on the floor in front of the painting destined to hang at the house. I suddenly wanted, needed, to hold Tripp close to me. I needed to kiss his hair. Kiss his chubby little hands. My chest ached. My eyes began to burn and my throat tightened.

*Cry, goddammit.*

Nothing.

I waited.

More nothing.

*Fuck me.*

I got up from the floor and returned to the house.

# CHAPTER NINE
## October, 1974

Vann, passed out, was sitting cross-legged, back against the brick wall in the alley behind Little Italy's. His mouth was hanging open. Jerry, sitting next to him, nudged Vann on the shoulder. Vann slipped along the wall until coming to rest against Homer.

"At least he ain't drunk no more," Jerry slurred.

I was sitting on the other side of Jerry, knees up, head against the wall. I dropped my head forward and barfed all over my boots.

"Damn," Jerry, edging closer to Vann.

I quaked and barfed again. Liquid. There wasn't anything else to bring up.

"Y're next, Jerry. Everybody else has puked except you," Homer.

"An' I ain't gunna. Feel like I'm drinkin' with a bunch'a ladies," he snarled.

"Whu' time's it," I slurred.

"Out'a booze time," Jerry burped. "Out'a grass time. Out'a money time. 'at's whut time it is. This's whut jail's gunna be like. Might as well be in jail righ' now."

"Y're not going to jail," Homer.

"Yeah," I agreed. "It's not like ya stole a tank 'r somethin'. It was jus' a .45 f'r Chris' sake."

"Borrowed," Jerry corrected me.

"They keep postponin' things y'ur gunna die'a ol' age b'fore they get ya ta trial," I said.

"When I git out'a jail, an' when Doug gits out'a the nut house I'm gunna shoot him again. In the head this time."

"Y're not going ta jail," Homer reasserted.

"If I'm so damned innocent," growling, "Why'd the post office fire me?"

"It was bound ta happen someday," I mumbled. "Ya weren't playin' by the rules."

"Bullshit. I played it by the rules."

"Deliverin' mail barefoot an' in'a speedo bathin' suit an' stayin' high all shift idn't exactly playin' it by the rules. You go out'a y'ur way ta break *any* kind'a rule. All the rules, not just the ones at work. How many times ya get written up f'r insubordination?"

"Them write ups don't mean shit. B'sides, the main problem ain't that I keep breakin' all the damn rules, man. The *real* problem's that *they* keep makin' 'em. I wuz still the bes' goddamn carrier they ever had. They fired me f'r takin' 'at gun. Shithead turds."

"They fired ya f'r bein' insubord'nate, *an'* b'cause ya demonstrated a willin'ness to resort ta violence when dealin' with a stressful situation rather'n seekin' a peaceful resolution," I explained.

"Ya shot somebody," Homer, clarifying my effort.

"That's what I said," I nodded. "It didn't have a thing ta do with y'ur ep'lepsy."

"Ep'lepsy?" Jerry squinted.

"He meant kleptomaniacy," Homer. "Stealing the .45."

Vann curled into a ball, his head ending up in Homer's lap. Vann moaned, then threw up again. Homer didn't move a muscle.

"Damn, Homer," Jerry winced. "Git him off'a ya."

"Don't want to wake him up."

"Ya know," I sighed, "I thought it was gunna be so damn easy."

"Whut was gunna be easy?" Jerry.

"Pullin' it t'gether. Fig'rin' it all out. I was gunna get out'a the Navy, go ta college...fig're it all out. Get the answers."

"Sue the shit out'a Tech, man," Jerry. "Tha's a lot'a money ta be out an' not git whut y're payin' for. I'd be suein' their asses off, man."

"Wudn't their fault. I thought I was gunna find some kind'a, uh...absolute somethin' 'r other that was gunna put me on some kind'a path ta...ta somewhere," my voice trailing off.

"You know what Roy says about absolutes?" Homer.

"Yeah," nodding my head. "Huntin' for absolutes is like settin' Unicorn traps."

"Why ya stayin' in'a loser thing like history?" Jerry. "The way y're always goin' off about weird shit...ya should'a thought about switchin' inta philosophy 'r somethin' like 'at."

"Tried," I grunted. "Kept failin' Logic 101."

"Ya know what I want?" Homer.

"A white squaw an' a bottle'a firewater?" Jerry.

"I want to find a place that's pretty much far away from anything," blowing Jerry off. "Some place near a desert and with some mountains close by. Deserts visitors are afraid to go into. Mountains with lakes nobody knows about except the people who live around there. A place with four seasons. In the winter it'd be covered in snow. In the summer it'd be sunny everyday. The spring and fall would look like one'a Bobbie's paintings...lots of mixed up colors everywhere you turned. I'd call it the High Place."

"Like 'dope' high?" Jerry.

"Dope high without the dope," Homer.

"That'd be cool," Jerry nodded. "Too bad there ain't no places like 'at left anymore. Not in the United States anyway," he snorted. "Somebody finds a place like 'at an' it ain't no time at all 'til ever'body hears about it an', BAM! It gets all fucked up."

Vann stirred slightly at the "Bam".

"Even if ya found a place like 'at," I added, "How ya gunna make a livin'? Gotta do somethin' ta eat."

"Live off the land," Homer. "Hunt. Fish."

"Paint y'ur face up an' sell Indian blankets an' flutes an' shit at a highway rest stop in the area," Jerry snickered.

I ignored him.

"Can't live like ya could a hun'r'd years ago," I said. "Looks good from a distance, but I just don't think a person c'n get away with 'at anymore. No game left. Can't drink the water. Can't eat the fish. You'd have ta look long an' hard f'r a place like 'at."

"I didn't say I was *going* to do it," Homer, sadly. "I said that's what I *wanted*."

"A man might stand with his mouth open f'r a thousan' years b'fore a duck flies into it," rolling my head to look at Homer. "Buddha said 'at. Know whut it means?"

"Means," Jerry burped, "Buddha don't know shit about huntin' fuckin' ducks, man."

"It means," Homer, "I'm going to have to get off my dead ass if I'm going to find it."

"Somethin' like 'at," and let my chin fall to my chest.

"If there's a place like 'at," Jerry, "I'll move there with ya. Me an' Shauna."

"Me an' Bobbie, too," I yawned. "That'd be a good place ta raise Tripp."

"Yew could cut a deal with Homer ta sell the blankets an' shit at the rest stop," Jerry.

"Wouldn't have to if my book sells big," I muttered.

"Whut book?" Jerry, squinting.

"The one I been workin' on f'r the last year 'r so. Thinkin' about callin' it 'Dolphin Recipies'."

"Ain' nobody gunna buy a book called 'Dolphin Recipies', man. Ya ought'a call it...lemme see...ya ought'a call it 'Her Steaming Cooze' 'r somethin' like 'at. Son uv a bitch'd sell like crazy, man."

"Whut's it about?" Homer.

"It'd be about this prison f'r nympho..."

"Not your book, asshole. Gil's."

"Some of it has ta do with Lubbock," I said.

"Am I in it?" Jerry's eyes popping open.

"Yep."

"Ya talk about how big my schlong is?" shooting me the Eye.

"Yep."

Jerry leaned forward to slap Homer on the shoulder.

"Hear 'at, Homer. Now the whole damn world's gunna know about the Crotch Cannon," brows at his hair line, eyes lost in a tight squint.

"But ya lose it in a knife fight in the first chapter," I told him.

"Whu'?" brows crashing to the bridge of his nose.

Homer was laughing.

"An' then Shauna runs away with the guy who cuts it off."

"Fuck y'urself," he growled. " 'at ain't funny."

"It's not s'posed ta be funny. It's a tear jerker. It'd have ta be with you in it, but I tell ya what. Gimme fifty dollars an' I'll have the doctors sew it back on in chapter two," laughing along with Homer.

"No. *I'll* tell *yew* whut. Use my damn name an' I'll sue y'ur goddamn ass, man. 'at's how I'm gunna support *my*self in Homer's high place, man. By suin' y'ur ass."

"It's getting cold," Homer.

"It's fuckin' October," Jerry. "Whud'a ya think it's gunna be like at 2:30 in the mornin'?"

"I'm goin' in," as Homer eased Vann's head from his lap and propped him against the wall. "I'm stayin' in the shop t'night."

I helped Homer transfer Vann into the building where we laid him on a make shift pallet of piano blankets.


Jerry and I staggered down the alley. It was cold and damp. A fine mist held the street lights in halos of tiny, sparkling dashes.

"I got some pills at the house," Jerry, as we approached his backyard. "Want a few. They'll mellow y'ur ass out big time. Sleep like a baby."

"Naaah," after thinking it over. "I'm way to drunk ta enjoy a fluff. It'd be a waste a pills. Thanks anyway."

"Know whut ya mean. Hadn't been this wrecked in'a long damn time. Ya workin' t'morrow?"

"Wouldn'a got this messed up if I was."

"How ya like havin' the office in town?"

"Rather be back out at the farm. We don't even take care'a the animals anymore. Hugo does all 'at now, but…it's his place. He thought movin' inta town'd be best f'r business."

Jerry slapped me on the back then meandered toward his back door.

I stumbled past the backside of the white shack Doug had attempted to dismantle at one time. The windows and doors were all boarded up now. I stopped at the foot of our stairs and looked up. The bedroom lights were out. The kitchen light was on. My head flopped forward, chin on my chest.

*Shit. Hope ta God she didn't wait up ta rip inta my ass.*

*My books! Fuck! Left 'em at the bar.*

*Oh, well. Jus' 'at much more ammunition for her.*

I crept up to the stoop, jiggled the door open a little at a time, and then peered in.

*Empty.*

It was going on 3:00. Bobbie rarely stayed up too much past 2:00 to yell at me.

*Maybe 'at's the trick. Stay out 'til 3:00.*

I turned out the kitchen light before easing quietly into one of the chairs at the table. I was spinning, my stomach churning. Head pounding.

*Too many cigarettes. Might'a caught a cold. How long were we in 'at fuckin' alley? Whose idea was 'at?*

I crossed my arms on the table and lay my head down. I began tumbling, head over heels over head over heels.

*Slowing down...slower...slower...stopped. Finally.*

*Damnation...*

taking a deep breath and rolling onto my back. The gentle rocking of the compartment and the quiet, rhythmic clacking of the wheels on the tracks made me feel like I was about to float away. The cabin, ornately appointed, was dimly lit. I looked over at the window. It was bordered by plush, red velvet curtains gathered in gold sashes.

*Night.*

Tiny bits of sleet ticked against the glass. The frozen dots, leaving wet, jerking trails, made their way across the window's surface to fix themselves to a growing mass of ice at its edge. Huge snowflakes blasted from the night, flashed through the windows glow, then disappeared back into the black. My eyes were burning. I rubbed them hard.

*Tired. So tired. Gotta start gettin' more sleep.*

I looked back at the window. I was startled by a grossly contorted face crushed against the wintry pane.

*A baby?*

Its eyes were wide and pleading. Tears, freezing in long, thin lines, streamed across the window. Ice and snow began to form in the baby's flowing, blond locks, trapping strands against the frigid surface of the glass. The face turned a pale blue. It was freezing to death.

*TRIPP!*

I threw myself at the window, frantically searching the perimeter for an emergency release.

I could hear him crying.

*Oh, my God! He's in so much pain! He's dyin'!*

I began beating on the window with my fists. His face was solidly frozen to the window now. He could hardly breathe. His eyes, fixed on mine, were crying out for help. He couldn't understand why I was letting this happen.

I kicked at the glass in a fury. I flung my body against it. Tripp was gasping. I could hear him gasping. Gasping and screaming. Screaming my name.

"GIL!"

I kept pounding on the window with all my might.

"GIL!"

Dark red splatters of blood with every blow.

"GIL! GIL! IT'S JERRY! GODDAMMIT, GIL! WAKE UP!"

A blurry, panic stricken Shauna was pushing me back and forth in the chair. Once my eyes were opened she grabbed my arm and started pulling, sobbing wildly and choking. I was stumbling all over myself, completely disorientated.

Bobbie tore through the hall curtain, demanding we shut up before we woke Tripp. She took one look at Shauna then scurried to her side, shoving me out of the way as she went. Joan arrived, Danny right behind her. I glanced at the clock. It was 6:30.

"IT'S JERRY!" Shauna screamed. "IN...IN...IN HIS... CHAIR!" between sobs.

I pushed past Shauna and Bobbie then half fell, half leaped down the stairs. I tumbled to the ground at the bottom of the steps, skidding several feet in the freezing mud. I struggled to my feet and ran, slipping and sliding through the drizzling rain to Jerry's back door. I charged into the living room and threw myself to the floor in front of a large, faded, overstuffed easy chair. I was panting heavily, dripping wet, muddy from head to toe. A portable, 45 rpm record player was quietly singing "Puff the Magic Dragon".

I sat back on my legs and looked up at Jerry. He was lounging quietly in the deep hollow of his favorite chair. His hands were in his lap, palms down, legs comfortably stretched out, ankles crossed. He'd kicked his boots off. His head rested in a timeworn depression at the top of the chair back. Lips slightly parted. Dull eyes staring blankly across the room.

I leaned forward and placed my fingers against his neck.

*Nothing.*

I grabbed his wrist.

*No pulse.*

I took an empty beer glass from the end table by the chair and held it close to his lips.

*Nothing.*

*He's...he's dead.*

"Puff" began again. I looked over at the player. Jerry'd lifted the top record arm up and moved it away from the 45 spool so the needle would return to the beginning of the song after every playing. A plastic, amber colored bottle of pills sat on the end table.

*Goddamn.*

*He fuckin' OD'd.*

*By accident.*

*He would'a taken 'em all if he was tryin' ta kill himself.*

*He just...fucked up an'...now he's dead.*

A single, heavy sob tore through my chest, leaving everything inside ripped to shreds.

*Jerry's...dead.*

\*\*\*

"Hand me one," as I pointed at a dozen or so restaurant cracker packs.

"Please," Homer.

"*Please*, hand me one," complying.

He slid several packets across the table to me. I opened a condiment pouch of mustard, squeezed its guts all over the cracker, and then shoved the cracker into my mouth.

"If *I* owned a fuckin' bar," I grumbled, "I'd stay open on Christmas Eve."

Homer could only nod, his mouthed stuffed with mustard-on-cracker hors d'oeuvres.

I was going to have to eat faster or go to bed hungry.

"There's pro'bly a ton'a people out there t'night with nothin' ta do," I frowned while preparing another one.

"Nope," burping. "We're the only ones."

Homer chased the crackers with a swallow of beer then wiped a bit of mustard from the bottle lip. He opened the last three packets.

"I'm not b'lievin' 'at," before I took a sip from the Old Charter bottle. "It wouldn't be fair ta be the only ones in Lubbock with nowhere ta go on Christmas Eve. There's gotta be some others, man."

"We had our chance," he grumbled. "If you would have cut

your hair, shaved, changed your whole damn attitude, and agreed to go to Christmas services, we could be sitting at your folk's house right now pigging out on tons of stuff and watching color TV."

"And if you'd'a changed y'ur name back ta Whiteman an' agreed ta marry 'at reservation honey y'ur aunt picked out for ya, we could be in Oklahoma sittin' at y'ur uncle's place gettin' trashed on 'at transmission fluid based moonshine'a his."

"And we could be sitting on the beach in Cancun if you were a more responsible money manager," filling his mouth with the last of the crackers.

"Ya don't manage an income like mine," I frowned. "Ya pitch it inta the street ever' payday an' watch ever'body an' his brother fight over what little there is of it."

Homer reached for the baggie and the Zig Zags then rolled a joint. He held the joint up for an opinion.

"Far cry from a Jerry roll," I said.

"He had the touch," lighting up.

We shared it, Homer putting the nub down with a shot of whiskey after what seemed like an unusually fast burn.

"In all 'at stuff you've been piecin' t'gether for the past coupl'a years...that Neti, Neti spiritual thing'a y'urs...is there an afterlife?" I asked seriously.

Homer, studying a refilled shot glass, thought for a while.

"I haven't written it down exactly like that," he finally answered. "I mean, I don't call it an afterlife."

"But ya think there might be somethin' out there after we die?"

"Maybe. I'd like to think so. It'd be nice to think something else happens," sipping his shot.

"What if there is an' it really sucks?"

"If it sucks, I guess it'll suck. Probably won't be much we can do about it. Unless Doug's idea about evolving is right."

"Why would *you* want there ta be an' afterlife?" I asked.

"There's a lot of people I'd like to see again. That's the only reason. If that's not a part of it, then I don't care about it one way or the other."

"I was thinkin' the same thing."

"It seems like such a waste to get so close to some people just to have them die and then that's the end of it. But, I'm afraid that's the way it's going to be. That's really fucked up."

"Absurd. 'at's what the existentialists call it."

Homer smiled.

"Absurd. Existentialist. Jerry's rolling over in his grave."

"No doubt."

Homer emptied his shot glass and refilled it.

"Know what some Muslims b'lieve about it?" I asked.

He grunted. I took that as a negative.

"Ray told me some Muslims b'lieve if they die defendin' Islam that, in Paradise, Allah rewards 'em with seventy 'r eighty virgins."

"No shit?" Homer, impressed.

"No shit."

"Is Paradise for eternity?" his brows furrowed.

"I guess."

"How could they stay virgins for eternity? Eventually, wouldn't they all be popped?"

"I don't know how 'at'd work," wiping a hand over my face. "Maybe their hymen keeps growin' back. Hell, if Allah can find eighty hot-ass virgins for every Muslim in history 'at's died in battle, then the hymen thing wouldn't be much of'a a problem for him. Don'ch ya think?"

"I suppose."

We were silent for a while then Homer leaned toward me.

"Can I ask you something?" resting his elbows on the table.

"Shoot."

"If you were a Muslim and died in battle, would you want

eighty virgins or would you ask Allah to bend the rules a little and let you spend eternity with only Bobbie?"

*Eternity? Shit...'at's a long damn time.*

I'd already hesitated too long. Homer, looking a bit disappointed, nodded.

"Bobbie," hoping to get in right under the wire.

"Okay," not at all convinced.

Homer fumbled through another joint rolling. We sat quietly while burning it up.


"Merry Christmas," Homer, offering me the butt when it had burned down.

"Merry Christmas," as I took it. "Ya know...I've got a Christmas story for the occasion."

"Let's hear it," filling both shot glasses to the top.

"Okay. Once upon a time, Christmas Eve, 1968, to be exact... overseas, I was on this patrol boat beached against the river bank along with three 'r four other PBRs. 'at's what these small boats were called."

"I know."

"Anyway, it was some little shithole creek off the Perfume River. The Perfume was a big-ass river."

"I know."

"We were all on the bank. Except the tub gunners. We were lookin' out over this field to where a trench full'a North Vietnamese Army regulars were. About fifty 'r so yards away. All of a sudden, right after midnight, I mean one *second* inta Christmas Day...we heard this beautiful tenor voice comin' from the enemy trench. He was singin' 'Oh, Come All Ye Faithful'. About six 'r so more joined in for the second verse. By the end'a that verse, some'a our guys had joined in. Includin' me. At the end'a the song, *ever'body*'d joined in. Then this guy in a standard issue, North Vietnamese Army pit helmet, walks inta the field carryin' a white flag. The chief put t'gether a white flag an' went out ta meet the guy. I'm not shittin' ya, Homer, within a few minutes, both sides had come t'gether in the middle'a 'at battlefield an' we were singin' 'Jingle Bells' at the top of our lungs.

"Nervous smiles turned ta warm laughter as raw fish an' half-cooked rice balls were exchanged f'r beef logs an' Santa Claus cookies. A make shift, six lane bowlin' alley was thrown together, the NVA providin' rocket propelled grenades f'r pins. Within minutes, mixed teams were goin' at it while an impromptu choir continued singin' carols in the background. Small knots'a men exchanged stories about past Christmas's back home. Then, as suddenly as it'd all begun, it came to an end with the first streaks'a dawn toppin' the tree line. Sad goodbyes were exchanged in hushed voices before we all slowly returned to our respective positions."

Homer lit a cigarette and leaned back in his chair.

"You know how I can tell your blowing smoke up my ass?"

"How?"

"Vietnamese hate to bowl."

"Volleyball," I shot back. "I meant...volleyball."

His face saddened. Homer fixed his gaze on the twisting column of smoke rising from his cigarette.

"Somethin' wrong?" I asked quietly.

"I've got a *real* overseas Christmas story," after a few long seconds.

"Let's hear it," easing back in my chair, taking the shot glass with me.

"It didn't happen exactly at Christmas," after a long pause. "It was a few weeks before Christmas day. For a month we'd been playin' fuck-fuck with each other."

"NVA?"

"Yeah. Nothin' real serious. Lot of pre-Christmas and pre-Tet truce fuck-fucking, but we were still taking some losses and shit. We got pulled out to go to a USO show about thirty minutes away by chopper. One of the smaller shows."

"I saw some'a those. The acts that weren't good enough ta tour with Bob Hope. But," quickly adding, "the smaller shows were a lot nastier. The girls..."

Homer appeared to be annoyed by the aside.

"I'm sorry," I apologized. "I'm drunk."

"Me, too," mumbling. "That's probably why I was thinking about it. I shouldn't be talking about it."

"No! Go ahead. I wan'a hear it. Serious."

"Nah. It'll just bum us out."

"Christ, Homer...look around ya," throwing my arms open and raising my eye brows.

"Yeah," he frowned. "I guess y're right."

Homer waited a while before picking up where he'd left off.

"The choppers came down in this field...rows and rows of choppers bringing guys in for the show. We moved through a line of trees and ended up in a clearing where a temporary stage had been set up. Big-ass speakers at each end of it and mics all over. This guy comes out and starts talking into the center mic, but you couldn't hear him very well because the choppers weren't allowed to shutdown. A bunch of half naked dancers, good looking ones, came out and started bouncing all over the stage. I fell asleep. My buddy woke me up near the end of the show. You know...the part when everybody in the show comes out and sings 'Silent Night' to signal the show is over?"

"Yeah."

"They sang two verses. The MC stepped to the mic, said 'Merry Christmas', and then everybody on stage started waving and smiling and throwing kisses. Way behind me a bunch of guys kept singing 'Silent Night'. A bunch more joined in. At the end of the verse, they started into another one. At the end of that verse the whole damn clearing was on its feet and singing. When that verse was done, we started in on another one. Then another. The people on the stage were crying. We must have sung ten or twelve versus when a big guy up front climbed onto the stage and walked over to the mic. He was battered. Really looked like hell. The song died away before the verse was finished. All we could hear was the choppers winding up. This grunt says 'It's time to go' into the mic then walks off the stage. That was it. We went back to the choppers. Went back to the...the bullshit."

Homer looked up at me.

"That's my Christmas story," got up, went to the sink, and then slugged down four or five shots of water.

There wasn't a thing I could think of to say. So, I didn't.

I stepped to the door and pulled it open. The blast of cold, fresh air was mind clearing. I walked out into the newly fallen snow. Homer came up behind me.

"Remember 'at Christmas when we went ta Midnight Mass a few years ago?" my breath clouding the air.

"Yeah. St. Elizabeth's."

"Wan'a go t'night?"

"What time is it?"

"Midnight. That's why it's called Midnight..."

"What time is it right now," shoving me.

I took my pocket watch out.

"11:38."

We coated up and walked down University toward Main. Homer pulled his bandanna from his back pocket and tied it in place.

I hung a quick left at Tenth.

Homer stopped.

"Where are you going?"

"This way'll get us there," continuing on.

I hurried up Tenth to the two-story we'd lived in for three and a half years. All the lights were out.

*The new renters must'a gone home for the holidays.*

This was the closest I'd been to it since October when everything had finally fallen apart between Bobbie and me. Jerry's OD was the last straw for her. She wouldn't take any more.

*Can't blame her.*

I headed toward Jerry's old place on the corner. Homer caught up with me in the alley and grabbed my arm.

"What the hell are you trying to do to yourself?" Homer, quietly.

I stared at the empty house. No curtains. No lights. No music.

*Looks cold. Haunted. Maybe that's why it still hadn't been rented... fuckin' haunted.*

"I don't know," I whispered. "I just wish that...that somehow...," but couldn't finish.

Homer let go of my arm.

"Let's go home," he said.

"Yeah," looking down. "Let's go home."

We walked down the alley to avoid passing the old place again.

# CHAPTER TEN
## January, 1975

I clipped along as fast as I could over the wind swept campus. *Gotta be aroun' zero with the fuckin' wind chill.*

By the time I got to the bar I was half frozen, eyes watering, nostrils frozen shut. I waved to Rupert at the pizza ovens. Annie, the new bartendress, was on her way to the bar. We exchanged smiles as she slipped ahead of me. She was a tight little package. Cute enough to overcome any hesitations most guys might have about her having two kids.

*Won't bother me one bit if I ever get the chance.*

I was surprised to find Hugo and Joan sitting at one of the tables. Hugo invited me to join them. Joan gave me a cordial nod.

"What's got you two in here on a weekday afternoon?" I asked.

"Startin' a week long cel'bration," Hugo drawled, slurring noticeably. "Annie! Double up 'at order."

*Sounds...drunk?*

"What's the occasion?" I asked.

*Oh, Shit! Hugo's proposed ta Joan!*

"My emancipation!" raising his voice a bit and toasting the ceiling.

*No proposal.*

"Last night, at exactly midnight, I became a free man," chuckling lightly, head bobbing.

Annie delivered two whiskey and waters to the table.

"Enjoy," as she slipped a sexy little wink in.

I winked back.

Hugo tapped his glass against mine.

"I am no longer tied to a business I once enjoyed immensely an' took a great deal'a pride in, but had grown ta despise f'r all its demands on my time. An' life."

"I...I don't understand," glancing at Joan.

"Hugo sold the business ta Roy," Joan.

"An' may God have mercy on his soul," Hugo muttered.

"What?" shocked. "But...when did ya..."

"Four months ago I decided enough was enough," Hugo. "Best kep' secret I ever had," toasting my glass again.

"Why? I mean..."

"Travel," and turned to Joan. "Travel an' enjoy life f'r a damn change."

Joan smiled as she reached over to pat his arm.

"An' Joan's graciously accepted my invitation ta accompany me once again. My travel companion," looking back at me

Joan looked into her lap and smiled.

*Gold diggin' little whore.*

The thought had pounced on me.

"Ya takin' off right away?" I asked.

"I'm throwin' a *big* get-together at the house next weekend. I'll make the official announcement then an' clear up all the questions. C'n ya make it?" then burst out laughing. "Course yew'll be there! Free booze!"

That stung.

"In June we leave for Europe," Joan, excitedly. "We'll end up in Spain an' stay there for a few months b'fore returnin'."

*When Hugo's money runs out.*

"Roy buyin' the ranch 'r just the business?" I asked Hugo.

"Only the business. Sold the land sep'rate."

*That's why he moved the shop inta town. He's been showin' the ranch ta buyers.*

"What about the animals? The buffalo?"

"Criswell an' Manson're goin' to a spread in south Texas. The rest'a that mangy herd 'r flock, 'r pack, 'r whatever the hell ya wan'a call 'em're stayin'. F'r now anyway. I'm glad ta be rid of 'em all."

That didn't sound right—the way he'd put it. It sounded a little mean, like he'd *never* given a shit about any of them.

"At least the toughest ta find a home for's been taken care of," looking down at his glass.

"Yeah," I nodded. "Not ever'body's got room for a coupl'a buffalo."

"Buffalo?" Hugo looked up at me. "I meant them pr'tty little fish."

*Slam!*

*Joan liked 'at.*

*Why's ever'body in my shit all of a sudden?*

"Excuse me," Hugo, touching the brim of his hat and standing up. "I need ta visit the facil'ties."

"Hugo's askin' Bobbie ta come to the party," Joan informed me as soon as he was out of ear shot.

She watched for a reaction at the mention of Bobbie's name—a remorseful gasp or an expression of agonizing grief.

"Good," trying not to pleasure her in the least.

"It'll be a nice break from her routine," glaring at me. "Her havin' ta work all the time."

*So that's what's goin' on. Bobbie's the good guy, I'm the bad guy an' ever'body's linin' up ta shit down my windpipe.*

"If she comes, she'll have ta bring little Tripp since she can't afford a baby-sitter."

*Fuckin' bitch is out f'r blood.*

"Good," beginning to strain. "Give me a chance ta even up with her on the child support. B'sides, I haven't seen Tripp in a week 'r so. That'll be nice."

"It's been over a month," she snapped. "Bobbie told me so."

*Fuck this!*

I stood up, walked over to the bar where I tipped a sweetly smiling, grateful Annie a crisp dollar bill.

"Tell Hugo I plan ta be at the party," as I passed Joan on my way out.

I circled around the building then took the alley to Homer's place. He was repairing a small church window.

"Hugo's sold his business," I practically shouted.

"Sold it?" and looked up.

"No shit."

"Still have a job?" going back to work.

"Yeah. I guess. Sold it ta Roy."

"I'll be damned," treating it a lot less like the earth shattering news I'd taken it to be. "How'd things go at the job center?"

"Waste'a time," I mumbled. "Not shit for a history major. Should'a picked up a teachin' certificate sometime durin' the past four years. Lots'a teachin' jobs posted. Engineerin' grads got it made too."

"Know what I've been thinking?" Homer as he continued to solder.

I lit a cigarette without answering.

"I've been thinking it's time to move on out to California," looking up. "Both of us. As soon as you graduate."

"Californya's y'ur plan, Homer. Not mine."

"We're wasting away here," and went back to soldering.

"What about Tripp?"

Homer placed the tip of the iron on a crushed beer can then strolled to the end of the table where I'd parked myself.

"In the long run," he said, "how much good are you doing him by staying in Lubbock? Y're going to have to go somewhere else to find a good job. Why not California?"

I looked out the front window and thought about it for a minute.

"Someday...yeah. I'll *have* ta leave, but not any time soon. I still need ta have Tripp close by right now."

"Well, think about it," returning to the repair. "We'd be going the day after we sober up from your graduation party. Wouldn't miss that party for anything."

"If ya wait ta leave 'til ya sober up after *that* party, you won't get out'a Lubbock 'til July."

"*We're* going to walk it."

"Hitchhike?"

"No. Walk. Petrified Forest, Grand Canyon, Yosemite. Whip up to Reno and spend a few days with Jonas and Holly then settle in San Francisco. "

"Y're leavin' out the part about New Mexico's badlands, a huge-ass mountain range, and crossin' Death Valley in June on foot."

"Left all that out on purpose," glancing up. "I didn't want to scare you into not going."

"Hey," trying to sound offended. "If I don't go it won't be b'cause I'm afraid to. Got that?"

Homer grinned and kept on working.

"You ever make it ta Fr'isco when ya were in?" I asked.

"Nah. How about you?"

"Yeah. Coupl'a times. I was in riverine training north'a there in Valejo b'fore goin' over. I'd be more than happy ta share some'a my Fr'isco pussy stories with ya if I thought for a second you'd b'lieve any of 'em."

"Thanks for sparing me. When were you there?"

"Summer, '68."

"Missed the summer of love. Too bad."

"Barely missed it. But it was still San Francisco. Flowers in y'ur hair. Free love, blah, blah, blah. We'd go inta the Haight wearin' our Navy issue, bellbottomed dungarees, buy a tie-dyed shirt an' some beads then walk around actin' stoned. Flashin' peace signs. Tellin' all the chicks ta make love not war an' shit. Anything ta nail some hippie ass."

"And it worked?" Homer, sounding doubtful.

"Almost. It was hard ta work around the short hair, the shaved faces, spit shined dress shoes an' this tattoo one'a my buddies had on his lower arm. It was a VC guy with a bloody bayonet in his head an' 'Kill' written in big letters under it."

"He could have worn a long sleeve shirt," Homer.

"It was a seventy-five dollar tattoo. He was proud of it."

"Seventy-five dollars?" Homer looked up. "You could have all gotten hippie whores for that kind of money."

"Now just how sportin' would that'a been?" I snorted.

"Uncle Lee used to tell me only well fed white men won't shoot a sleeping goose."

I looked at him curiously.

"Never mind. I guess it loses something going from Cherokee to English."

"Anyway, I really wanted ta see if hippie ass was ever'thing it was cracked up ta be. Oh, well."

"So you *were* going to lie to me about all the hippie pussy stories ya had?"

"Yeah."

"When'd you get back?" he asked.

"From over there?"

"Yeah."

"August, '69."

"Just in time for Woodstock."

"Couldn't make it. I was hooked up to a morphine drip in Naha for Woodstock."

"Bummer."

"Listen, if ya go ta Fr'isco, what's that gunna do ta y'ur search for that High Place y're always talkin' about? All the mountains an' deserts an' shit?"

"Fr'isco's part of the plan," unplugging the iron and placing it on the can holder.

Homer went to the desk in the back, returning with a road atlas. He opened it to northern California and plopped it down in front of me.

"Look at this," drawing an imaginary, elongated oval on the map with his index finger.

The oval extended from the Stanislaus National Forest at its southern end to the Plumas National Forest at its northern end and encompassed everything up to a hundred miles west of the Nevada-California border.

"We can temporarily work out of Fr'isco," he explained. "We should be able to get fairly good paying jobs there. We'll start scouting this whole area," redrawing the oval, "and find a place that fits the bill. And guess what?" drawing a second oval on the eastern side of the Nevada-California border with approximately the same northern and southern points as the first oval. "This whole area is called a *high* desert," brows raised. "High Place...high desert? Is that a sign or what?"

I tapped an area immediately southwest of Lake Tahoe called the Desolation Wilderness Area.

"Is *that* a sign 'r what?"

Homer pointed to Grass Valley.

I pointed to Donner Pass.

"Think about it," he said as he closed the atlas. "I'm going. No more excuses. I'm not letting anything get in the way this time."

"I'll give it some serious thought," and headed for the front door. "Gotta run. Oh, yeah," over my shoulder, "Hugo's throwin' a big bash ta celebrate sellin' the business. I'll tell ya more when I find out if he dudn't tell ya first," and stepped outside.

The cold wind lashed my face. The air ripped my lungs.

*Fr'isco'd be warmer if nothin' else.*

*Wonder if there's any hippie chicks still livin' there.*

\*\*\*

I jumped back into the house, slid the glass door shut, and then began blowing furiously on frozen hands. Danny was right inside by the door.

"My turn," pulling a pack of cigarettes from his coat pocket.

"Light up in here," I advised him. "It's blowin' like a bitch out there."

Danny lit up before slipping through the doorway into the storm.

Vann came over.

"Getting worse out?" he asked.

"Yeah. Goddamn pee froze b'fore it hit the ground," shivering violently.

"I think I'll catch a ride with the first person heading back to town," Vann. "I don't necessarily want to be stuck out here for the night. Too many people," looking around at the crowd.

"Then ya might be leavin' with me," glancing angrily across the room at Bobbie. "What time is it?"

"It's only eight," putting the watch to his ear to make sure it was still ticking.

*Shit. Some fuckin' party. Don't know half the people. Joan keeps flippin' me off with her eyes. Bobbie won't talk ta me.*

*Then April shows up half naked.*

*Fuck 'em all.*

Tomas and Ed joined us.

"You been outside, man?" Ed, concerned. "It's getting *baaad*, man. We're thinking about splitting."

"The tires on my car are bald," Tomas, obviously adding to their worries.

"Lemme find Homer," I said as I scanned the crowd, returning a wave to Stan and some of his cowboy buddies. "I thinks it's just about time ta get the fuck out'a Dodge," and began working my way through the mass to Roy.

"Ya seen Homer?" I asked him.

Roy put his hand on my shoulder, shut one eye, and then focused the other drunken eye on me.

"Y're gunna hate me f'r breakin' this to ya," he grinned broadly, "but...yeah. I seen him."

"Where?"

Roy motioned to the front door with his bottle hand.

"He walked out with April about ten 'r so minutes ago."

*That mother...*

"Her husband here?" I asked.

"Nope."

"Think they left the party?"

"Hell, I don't know. Homer may be plankin' her over in the office at this very moment. Right there on Hugo's bearskin rug."

"I doubt it. Not t'night, anyway. Homer's been drinkin', poppin' pills, an' smokin' grass since ten this mornin'. He fell asleep on the way out here."

"Then she'll be free f'r yew ta give her another shot'a clap," laughing and slapping my arm.

"April still drivin' a light blue pickup?" blowing it off.

"Yeah. B'lieve so," still laughing.


I went to the door, buttoned up, and then headed out into the storm. I checked the parking area then up and down the lane for a light blue pickup.

*Son of a BITCH! She's left with him.*

*Pro'bly took him ta the same goddamn motel we used ta go to. The same room. Just ta spite me.*

*Shit!*

I thrust my hand into my pocket.

*Good. I've got the truck key.*


I fought my way through the blizzard to Homer's truck and crawled into the cab. I started it up, cranked the heater to full blast, and then removed the ice scraper from the glove box. I climbed back into the storm and scrapped the windshield clean. Tossing the scraper into the bed of the truck, I hurried back inside the house.


Everyone gathered around the door stared at me like I'd just stepped out of a scene from Dr. Zhivago. Danny came over, immediately joined by Vann, Ed, and Tomas.

"I'm leavin'," I told them, shivering uncontrollably. "Homer took off with somebody already. Ya ready ta go, Vann?"

"Yes," zipping his coat up.

"Mind if we stop at the bar for a while," pulling my coat collar tight around my neck. "We can walk home from there if it gets any worse."

"No. Not at all. I'm still hungry. Finger sandwiches don't amount to much."

"How about you guys?" glancing at the others.

"Nope," Danny. "I'm sticking around."

"Guadalupe's too far of a walk from the bar in this kind of weather," Ed. "I think we'll go on home."

"See you guys later, then," shaking hands all around. "Drive careful," before making a dash to the truck.

The cab was as warm as toast. I had to rock the truck with the gears to break free of the ice and make it over the snow drift behind us. We crawled down the lane, then onto Ninety Eighth. It was slicker than snot and near white out conditions.

"Can you see to drive," Vann, nervously.

"Little late ta be askin' 'at," staring into a wall of swirling golf balls.

The truck slid into the parking space outside the bar and jumped the curb. I looked over at a visibly shaken Vann.

"Ya okay?" I asked.

"Of course. Enormously...exciting," dealing with it in typical Vann fashion. "Invigorating," studying his watch. "Nine thirty-seven," talking to himself. "A *very* invigorating fifty four minutes and twenty nine seconds."

"Sorry," I apologized. "At least I kept it on the road," as I threw the door open. "Let's get inside."

We ran for the restaurant entrance. The door flew open as we neared it. Vann and I slid and slipped through the opening.

"Saw y'all comin'," Rupert, drunk as usual, struggling against the wind to get the door shut again.

"Thanks," Vann.

Rupert motioned toward the bar.

"Go on back. Bars full. Nobody c'n make it to the strip on a night like this."

We made our way into the bar side.

Every seat was taken. It was standing room only. The old days, when the table by the bar was always held in reserve for the badass bikers, had long since passed. I recognized some of the faces, but not many. A few nods were exchanged as we headed back to the bar. All six stools were occupied by neatly bearded students sporting professionally done, male versions of a mini bouffant. Homer called it a white man's Afro. Charlie and Annie were busting ass trying to keep up with the drinks.

Annie was looking good. She winked.

*That'd be so sweet.*

I got behind the bar and helped out for a while, cutting a deal allowing Vann and I to drink for free all night.

I proceeded to get drunk. The drunker I got the friendlier I got with Annie. The friendlier I got, the more she let me know I could get even friendlier. I made a date with her. Pushing blunt-etiquette to its extreme, I promised her I was going to fuck her brains out. She informed me that she'd graduated from high school with straight A's.

Around 11:00 the bar began to clear. By midnight it was empty. After cleaning the place up we all sat around swapping stories, listening to some of Rupert's hillbilly tapes, and getting drunker. At two in the morning Vann, Charlie, and I agreed to leave. I tonsiled Annie and then followed Vann into the bitter cold morning. It had stopped snowing, but the wind was still brutal.

"Where's'a ice scraper," Vann, stumbling to the passenger side of the cab. "It's my turn to scrape. You scraped a' Hugo's," slurring terribly.

"Y'ur so drunk ya can't har'ly stan' up," slurring back. "I'll star' the car an' you min' the heater while I get the win'shield."

"Okay," and got into the cab.

I started to ask him to get the scrapper from the glove box then remembered I'd pitched it into the truck bed. I crawled into the bed of the truck, forgetting to turn the motor on. I started a painful search through the snow for the scraper, my bare hands turning numb.

*Fuckin' needle in'a hay stack...*

pulling an arm from the snow.

*What the fu...*

brushing more snow away and finding a shoulder. In a frenzy, I cleared away a face.

*Oh my fuckin' God!*

\*\*\*

"Mr. McNeil," a soft voice waking me.

My lids slowly parted. I recognized the nurse. I looked around the room for Vann and Danny.

*Must'a gone home.*

"Mr. McNeil...yew have'a phone call at the nurse's station."

"How's he doin'," hoarse, struggling into a standing position and rubbing my face.

"No change," she said. "That's a good sign at this stage."

I nodded and walked shakily to the nurse's station.

"Hello," coughing lightly.

*Need a cigarette.*

"Gil, this is Hugo," his voice low and gentle.

*Oh, God. Hugo. It's so damn good ta hear that voice.*

"Damn, Hugo," voice rasping. "Thanks for callin'. Thanks so much."

"I called the second I heard about it," drawling slowly. "We lost our phones in 'at storm last night. Now, ever'things gunna be okay. Hear me?"

"Yeah. Yeah, Hugo. I hear ya. Ever'things gunna be all right."

"How's he doin'?"

"Hugo, they won't tell me shit since I'm not kin."

"I'm surprised ya hadn't figured a way aroun' that 'un by now."

"I'm workin' on it."

"Have yew called his uncle?"

"Just a little while ago. I found his number in Homer's wallet."

"How'd it go?"

"Lee's leavin' Soper in the mornin'. He's plannin' on takin' Homer back ta Oklahoma when he's released an' take care of him up there."

"That's pro'bly best. Don't ya think?"

"Yeah. That'd be best," noticing how wrung out I was.

I could hear Hugo's slow, measured breathing over the phone.

"Gil?"

"Ye'sir."

"Yew gunna be okay?"

"I'll be okay."

"Ya know...we've had our differ'nces of late."

"I know. I hate it."

"We're puttin' at b'hind us."

I choked. I couldn't speak.

"When're ya gunna spell y'urself?" he asked.

"Soon as they tell me what the hell's goin' on."

"Good man. I'll be in there as soon as I c'n dig my way out'a here."

"Thanks, Hugo. Thanks for wantin' ta come in."

"Gil, I think the world'a that lad. Don't you think otherwise. Yew hang in there," and hung up.

"Mr. McNeil?" the nurse behind the counter.

I looked at her.

"Y'ur friends asked me ta tell ya they'd be back later," smiling warmly. "They didn't wan'a wake ya up."

"Thank you," nodding.

"There's a little chapel on the first floor. Y're welcome ta use it if ya don't wan'a go back ta the waitin' room. It'd be a lot more private."

"Thanks, ma'am. I'll keep 'at in mind."

A nurse approached the station. I didn't recognize her.

"How long have you been here?" smiling as warmly as the station nurse.

I looked at the clock in the station.

*Five in the afternoon.*

"About...fourteen hours," I told her.

"Have you eaten anything?"

"Yes, ma'am," I lied.

"Mr. McNeil," and stepped closer to me. "The doctor said you could look in on your friend, but only briefly. Just for a minute or two."

"Thanks. Thank him for me."

"Mr. McNeil...have you ever seen a...a severe case of frost bite before? It can be..."

"It won't bother me, ma'am," cutting her off. "I've seen arms an' legs blown off an' stomachs...,"

I thought she was going to cry.

"Come with me," turning and heading towards Homer's room.

I stepped inside as she held the door open for me. A small, dim night light on the wall above Homer's head shrouded the room in a ghostly pale. I'd spoken with some of the nurses off and on, so I'd expected the oxygen tent. The needles. All the wires, and tubes. I'd expected all the tiny dots of light covering the monitors by the bed—blue, red, green, white. Some blinking on and off. I'd expected the soft beeping noises coming from all the machines. Homer's irregular, labored breathing didn't throw me that much. What I wasn't ready for was this dark, swollen figure.

I think I made a noise of some kind. The nurse stepped to my side and placed her hand on my back.

*Oh, God. Oh, my God.*

I reached out to him.

The nurse stopped me. She eased me to the door and back into the hall.

"Is...is it normal ta...ta look like 'at?" I asked.

"It's a severe case of frost bite," dodging the question.

"How long before he can...before he wakes up?"

"The doctor will be in later this evening. He'll discuss all that with you," still dodging.

*It's bad.*

*Don't think that!*

*She's just a nurse. She pro'bly dudn't know shit. That's why she can't tell me anything.*

"I think I'll go find the chapel. Will ya get me when the doctor shows up 'r if Homer wakes up? I mean, even if he twitches a finger or blinks, will ya promise ta come get me?"

"I'll tell everyone in the wing where you can to be reached. Don't worry. We'll get you."

"One more thing...is Homer...how much pain is he in right now?"

"None at all," reaching out and touching my arm assuredly.

"Good. Good," looking down.

I popped my head up.

"Not that he couldn't handle it," I told her.

She smiled and started to turn away.

"One last thing," raising a finger in front of me, "Then, I swear, I'll leave ya alone."

She acted like she had all the time in the world.

"When Homer wakes up...I mean, the way he's layin' right

now is okay b'cause ya can't see it when he's on his back, but when he wakes up and sits up...could ya keep his bandanna handy? He has this bad scar on the back of his head an' he feels real uncomfortable about people seeing it. The bandanna's in his pant's pocket. That's where I put it. His clothes're in his room."

"Yes. In his locker. I'll make sure his head is covered before he sits up," she promised.

"Don't forget," reminding her, "I'll be in the chapel."

I made my way to the first floor and located the chapel. It was small, dimly lit, and quiet. Much better than the bright lights of the waiting room. Thick carpet that felt like walking on grass. Sweet, delicate aromas from all the flowers filling the little space. It was more like a garden than a church. I sank into the softness of a cushioned pew. I could feel myself melting into the restful warmth of the room's soothing promise of retreat. Peaceful isolation. I felt safe for the moment. Separated from everything making such a place so necessary at times. I could spend the rest of my life in this place, immersed in its deep velvet shadows. Swimming in its fragrance. Drifting in its quiet.

*I have ta share this with Homer. He needs ta know about this place. Right now.*

I slipped from the chapel and started down a narrow concrete corridor, skirting small puddles of water collecting at the end of thin rivulets trickling down the sides of the walls. The cold, damp corridor reeked of stale, confined cement. Bare bulbs in chipped, dirty porcelain sockets hung from the overhead at ineffective intervals, creating an alternating series of dull light and dark void.

The corridor made a sudden, ninety degree turn to the left. Several puddles later, a turn to the right.

Metal slamming against metal and laughter. Hearty, boisterous laughter.

I hurried on until I came to a door opening into a steamy locker room. I gazed inside. Dirty work clothes were piled all over wooden benches crowding the aisles between rows of dented, scratched, metal lockers. The floor was slick with a thin layer of water. Churning clouds of steam, mixed with the loud, splattering sound of wide open showers, boiled from a room to the right of the lockers.

The smell of sweat, soap, and aftershave.

Laughing. So much laughing as everyone in the room stripped down, cleaned up, and then hurried into liberty clothes, dress blues, and...

*Dress whites? Full dress whites? Medals. So many medals.*

*The chief!*

"Get your ass in gear, sailor!" the chief. "Formation's in twenty minutes, and do you call that a goddamned haircut?" turning sideways to get around me before charging up the corridor, jumping a few steps and shoulder slamming a heavy, metal door open. He disappeared into a burst of light before the door slammed shut.

*That's the fuckin' chief!*

"Liberty call, turd, so..."

*Jerry?*

"...step on it if ya wan'a ride inta town. I ain't waitin' aroun' all night f'r y'ur sorry ass."

A flood of familiar faces swirled by me on their way to the exit—Duval, Binneli, Shryer, Boats, Williams.

*Baha'u'llah? Jesus? Pastor McCombs?*

"Bes' git y'urself in there an' talk ta y'ur boy," JD growled as he squeezed by me.

I looked back into the steam choked locker room, straining to make out the features of a lone figure sitting, back towards me, at the far end of a bench. Long black hair framed a bald spot on the back of the man's head.

*I know that guy. Goddammit...what's his name?*

A woman sitting next to him glared at me.

"Whu'ch yew starin' at?" she snapped.

*I know that voice.*

"Get your butt out here, McNeil!" the chief yelled from the exit.

I moved toward the stairs.

*What the fuck is 'at guy's name?*

I moved down the passageway to the door and slowly eased it open. I stepped from the dank, dark corridor into a vast openness stretching unobstructed to a shimmering horizon.

I walked to the top of a small rise then turned to gaze back across the uncompromising emptiness, my footprints trapped in the dust—footprints leading from the base of a massive structure spanning the whole width of the vastness. I couldn't see its beginning and I couldn't make out its end. It was spectacular.

*We'd done a good job. Did it without a single blueprint. Made it up as we went, just knowing...it would look somethin' like...like this.*

A slender trail of dust was extending itself over the plain. It was coming straight at me and closing fast.

It was an old, rusting, faded green Nash.

*Dad's old car?*

It bounced up the hillside and slid to a stop. Dad, outfitted in his usual white tee shirt and khaki work pants, flung himself from behind the wheel and charged toward me—short, black, Brylcreamed hair sizzling in the heat of the sun, eyes flaring, jaws locked, rubber shower shoes slap, slap, slapping at a hundred miles an hour as he approached. He was in a rage. Dad came to a halt right in front of me. He thrust a finger into the air behind him and started yelling into my face.

"Is *this* what you've been working on for the past seventy-two years? A *dam* in the middle of a *desert?*"

"Turn around and look at it," I answered calmly. "It's...it's magnificent," looking over his shoulder at the marvel.

"It's made of cardboard and papier-mâché!" he screamed. "If a single drop of rain ever does fall inta this hellhole, it'll crumble! It's *useless!* What, in the name of God, were you thinking? Is that damn thing worth all the tears your mother's shed over you? The shame it's caused me? Was it worth your whole damn life? The life of your friends? It's not worth a goddamn thing!"

"What'a ya want from me, Dad? Huh? Can't ya see what we've done here? Ya won't even look at it! What'a ya want from me?"

"...what? What'a ya want?" jerking violently.

"Mr. McNeil? Wake up, Mr. McNeil," accompanied by a gentle shaking.

I was fighting to pull my head together. I was looking into the face of a male.

*Large glasses. Name tag on a white smock.*

*A doctor!*

I tensed and tried to sit up.

The doctor held me back.

"Relax. Sit back and relax."

"Homer. How's Homer," I mumbled hoarsely. "What time is it?"

"It's 10:30 in the evening."

"I wan'a see him if he's awake," and started to rise.

The doctor put his hand on the pew in front of us to block my exit.

We were staring at each other. He looked drained.

"Mr. McNeil," speaking slowly, "Homer never regained consciousness."

I could see the pain in his face. The doctor continued on in a soft, gentle voice that faded to nothing. Everything slowed. I watched his struggling, weighted gestures. His silent lips moving. His heavy, sluggish eyelids crawling open, creeping shut, crawling open.

Plodding minute after plodding minute after plodding minute until, finally, he patted me on the shoulder, stood up, and then drifted away.

I sat there.

And sat.

And sat, finally sliding from the pew to my knees.

I buried my face in the cushion.

*My God.*

*Oh, my fucking God.*

I wept.

***

I stood outside leaning against Homer's truck. Uncle Lee stepped through the double door entrance of the mortuary, clutching Homer's seabag in one hand. He stood by the doors and stared at me before making his way across the frozen lawn toward me. I put my cigarette out and straightened up.

"He don't want these things," dropping the seabag at my feet.

"I thought ya might wan'a put 'em in his...put 'em in with him. They meant a lot to him. He brought 'em back from y'ur dad's..."

"He don't want them," glaring at me.

"He would have wanted ta be buried with his grandfather's things," I insisted.

"He wanted to live!" pointing a quaking finger at me. "He *trusted* you. He thought you were his *friend*," lowering his finger. "And he froze to death in the back of a pickup truck while you drove all over town...getting drunk," tears running down his face. "How could you let this happen? *You* take those things," kicking the seabag. "He don't want them. And you can take his truck," kicking the door. "Anything that belongs to him in this town...you take it!" and headed back to the funeral home.

Before going inside Lee turned around.

"If you come to Soper for the funeral...I will shot you!" then reentered the building.

I grabbed the bag from the ground, tossed it into the cab, and then got behind the wheel, nerves shattered. I sped away, fishtailing in the melting ice and snow. My heart was racing, ears pounding.

*I know what I'm gunna do. I know exactly what I'm gunna fuckin' do.*

I drove to Hugo's old place. No one was there. I grabbed Homer's things and sloshed through the muddy field to the barn. The animals were acting like they'd missed a feeding or two—gathering around, squawking, honking. The stalls hadn't been cleaned out in days. I threw some alfalfa bales down from the loft and broke them up, scattering the sweet smelling slices inside the barn where it was dry. After tossing a couple of bales to the buffalo and livestock I scattered enough chicken feed to keep them happy for two days if they had the brains to ration it.

I found a pick, a shovel, grabbed the seabag, and then went to the north side of the barn. It was a sloppy mess. I began scrapping the surface looking for signs of previous digging. I ended up with a patch of disturbed ground somewhat larger than what I'd remembered the old grave to be. I turned over a few shovels full of mud before unearthing some mangled feathers that were much longer than a ducks feathers.

I bent over and took one of the feathers by the quill and pulled it from the goop.

*Peacock.*

I hadn't noticed either of the peacocks when I was in the barn.

*Goddammit. Those assholes came back an' shot the peacocks.*

*Not that long ago. At least since movin' the office inta town.*

I took my pocket knife and cut the top three inches of the feather off, carefully scraped as much of the mud from the blue-green iridescent eye as I could, and then eased it into my coat pocket.

I found a gas can in the garage. I carried a bale of straw from the barn, careful not to let it touch the mud. After dishing out a large, bowl shaped depression in the side of the bale, I placed it on the old burial site. I began removing each of the items in the bag and placing them in the depression—neatly folded furs, the ceremonial wing, powders, paint pots, small animal bones, candles, the leather drawing. There were a number of things that hadn't belonged to his grandfather—two wedding band style rings, JD's old straw hat, a small piece of carpet cut from the place on Tenth Street, military dog tags, and a dozen or so different buttons. I recognized one and picked it up.

*From my coat. I thought it'd just fallen off.*
I placed it back along side the others.

I fished nine small, shiny black stones from the bottom of the bag. They were almost identical to the one he'd given me. The one I always kept with me.

I pulled a faded blue bandanna from my pocket. It was worn to a thread in places, all four corners tattered. The nurse had sneaked it to me.

*I think this is the only one he ever owned. I'm sure it was.*
There were still a number of long, black strands of hair clinging to it. I placed it like a shroud over the pile then covered everything with his seabag.

I doused the bale with gas then lit it off. I periodically splashed the fire to keep it burning hot, each dousing sending the smoke circling and tumbling wildly above the flames before rising to the top of the barn where it was whisked away by the north wind.

I sat for an hour watching the pyre gradually reduce to smoldering ash strewn with what couldn't burn. The stones. The brass fittings on the seabag. Pieces of the little pots.

*What should I do with the stones?*
It was troubling. I wanted to do the right thing.
*Danny, Vann, Hugo...*
counting on my fingers...

*Eduardo, Tomas, Joan, Bobbie, Shauna...eight.*
*Hope. Nine.*
I carefully gathered the stones and put them in my pocket.

The breeze was beginning to carry puffs of ash away in light gusts.

Something didn't feel right. Something was being left undone.

I couldn't force myself to leave.

After a long while, I knelt down and leaned over the gray powder. I licked my finger tip, placed it on the center of the circle then brought the finger to my tongue.

I stood up, turned, and then walked away.

# CHAPTER ELEVEN
## May, 1975

Danny and I sat on the student workbench closest to the front of the shop, sucking on a beer while watching the blowing dust thicken outside. A street light came on.

*Two o'clock in the fuckin' afternoon an' the goddamn street lights come on.*

"So how's it feel ta be a college grad-e-ate?" Danny kidded.

"Feels good."

"Now what?"

"I'm leavin'. I've made up my mind."

"Again?"

"It's for sure this time. I'm all but there."

"Where's *there?*"

"As far as I can get from Lubbock."

Danny slipped from the table and came over to me.

"What about Tripp?"

"In the long run the best thing I can do for him is to get away from here. I'll stay in touch with him. I'm not gunna just disappear on him."

Danny nodded, lips pursed.

"I have ta get out'a Lubbock, though," I mumbled. "Somewhere nobody's ever heard of Gil McNeil."

"I hate to burst your bubble, but there's probably not that many people in Lubbock who've ever heard of Gil McNeil."

"One is one too many anymore," I snorted.

"What about Annie?"

"You can have her."

That pissed him off.

Danny strolled to the front window.

"So you think running away is the answer?"

"I'm not runnin' *away*. I'm runnin' *toward*. There's a big-ass diff'rence."

I hopped down and went to the back. I returned with a copy of the Stained Glass Quarterly. I opened it to a bent-cornered page and pointed to an advertisement circled in black ink. He took the magazine and began to read the ad to himself.

"You think you can pass yourself off as a," and began reading out loud from the ad, " '...fully trained, well-rounded, personable stained glass restoration expert'?"

"Sure."

" '...with *ten* years of experience', " continuing to read, " 'three of which must have been in supervision and project management.'?"

"Danny, I learned ta repair and restore windows from my father. I've been workin' with stained glass my whole damn life! An' when I got out'a the Navy in '70, I took the family business over an' I've been managin' it ever' since."

"Damn," Danny laughed. "You *are* qualified. And why are you walking away from a well established family business?"

"A tornado hit the shop, killed my father, an' we didn't have any insurance. Wiped me out. *Or,* how about this one...my father came down with cancer an' the medical bills forced us ta sell the business. Who gives a fuck what I tell 'em. The guy doin' the hirin' is desperate. This is the third time he's run the ad. All he's gunna care about is what I can do when I get there. I won't have any problems with it comin' down ta that."

"Well, if you can pull off moving from barback to bartender in one night, I guess you can pull this one off. Where's this job at?" looking back at the ad and continuing to read to himself.

I moved away.

"Columbus, Ohio!" waving the magazine at me. "Do you have *any* idea where Columbus, Ohio is? Do you have any idea how *cold* it gets up there? That shabby-ass coat of yours would feel like a tee shirt."

"I found it on the area code map in the front of the phone book," avoiding the coat issue.

"Have you ever been north of Oklahoma?"

"Vancouver, Canada."

"That's north*west*. The north*east* is a whole different galaxy than the northwest. This is...it's *nuts*!" exasperated.

"I'd never been ta Japan b'fore goin' there."

"Do you have the job? Have you talked to them?" closing the distance between us.

"Of course," stepping away.

" 'Of course' you have the job or 'Of course' you've only talked to them?" refusing to let up.

"I *have* the job."

*He knows I'm lyin'.*

Danny shook his head, tossed the magazine onto the table and walked back to the front window.

"So," looking outside, "y're going to leave a two bit, *hourly*, chaining job and move a hundred thousand miles away to take a two bit, *hourly* stained glass repair job?" turning to face me. "Why'd you even go to college?"

"So I can put the son of a bitchin' diploma on the wall an' tell ever'body that whatever it is I end up doin', I'm doin' it b'cause I *chose* ta do it," becoming irritated.

"It sounds like you've decided to be a ditch digger for the rest of your life and tell everybody you could have been the Dean of Harvard, but you didn't want to be. That all you ever really wanted to be was a fucking ditch digger!" raising his voice.

"I'm not talking about ditch digging! I'm talkin' about becomin' a professional, uh...a...a nationally known stained glass restorationist. Someday. I like, I *love* workin' with stained glass."

"You better. You move to Ohio and y're not gunna have much choice but to love it," turning back to the window. "Y're fucking up.

Big time. That's all I'm trying to get you to understand," sounding sincere in his concern for my well being. "You've got choices other than leaving, Gil. And you know it. Remember when you told me once you'd decided to come to Lubbock when you got out of the Navy because it was too hard to come up with an alternate plan. It was *easier* to simply come back here?"

"This hasn't been an easy choice. I'm goin' because it's best," firmly.

A long two minutes or so passed before Danny nodded.

"Fine. Go ahead. Leave."

*He dudn't think it's gunna happen.*

"You're not leaving before throwing an all night, drunken goodbye are you?" he grinned.

"No way."

"Promise?"

"Promise," and shook his hand.

He walked to the door and left.

*He thinks I'm gunna change my mind. I can just feel it.*

I called Roy at the office.

"Hugo's," in a gruff voice.

"Roy. This is Gil."

"I figur'd yew'd be callin' in an' whinin' ta git the next coupl'a days off so ya c'n celebrate graduatin'."

"I'm resigning Roy."

Silence. Stone silence.

"I'm leavin' town."

More silence.

"Well, dammit," Roy, sighing heavily. "I knew it was comin'. J'st didn't expect it right off like this."

"I got a job as the Director of Restoration and Repair at a big-ass stained glass studio in Columbus, Ohio," bracing myself for a load of crap about moving north.

Silence.

"It's salaried," I told him. "Pays thirty thou' a year ta start. Paid vacations, full insurance coverage, an' a retirement thing. The whole ball'a wax."

"Salaried. That's good. I guess 'at twelve years ya spent gittin' a degree in basket weavin' is actu'lly gunna pay off. Guess I was wrong about that 'un."

I could hear him spitting into a coffee can he kept by his desk.

"Yew ever been up north?" he asked.

He sounded concerned.

"Nope."

"Yew put a lot'a thought inta this thing?"

"Yeah."

"No talkin' ya out uv it?"

"Nope."

"When ya leavin'?" he asked, after a long pause.

"Uh, next week. Sometime next week."

"Good. We c'n throw ya a fittin' bon voyage an' graduation party."

"Yeah...you could do that. I guess," voice tapering.

"I'll be damned," hissing. "Goin' from a goddamn hippie ta bein' a goddamn yankee. Y're supposed ta git smarter with age, ya fuckin' idiot. What're ya doin' f'r money ta git up there an' settled in?"

"I've got plenty," trying to sound convincing. "Speakin' of money, though...I still owe Coleman around ten bucks f'r cigarettes an' beer an' I owe Gradel five bucks f'r losin' the bet on the Tech—A and M game last fall. Can ya..."

"I'll take care uv it. Yew c'n pay me back after Ohia runs y'ur ass back down here in a week 'r two. Stan's gunna be in tears. Bet yew ain't give one single thought ta how traumatized that poor..."

"Roy," quietly interrupting.

I took a deep breath and slowly exhaled.

"Roy...I'll be gettin' in touch as soon as I get a place and a phone number."

Another long pause.

"Won't be the same aroun' here without ya," he said slow and heavy.

"I'm gunna miss ya, Roy. I mean it. Listen, when ya finally hear from Hope, will ya lemme know right away?"

"Yew c'n count on it. All I need's a number."

"I'll get ya one first thing. Thanks f'r ever'thing, Roy."

"Hey!" raising his voice, then lowering it to a strong, steady warm, "Yew take care, Gil McNeil."

"I will."

"Hang on! Hugo jus' come in."

"Roy, I don't..."

Too late. I could hear Roy giving Hugo a quick briefing on my plans.

"Gil?"

"Yes, sir."

"This true? Ya leavin' us?"

"Yes, sir."

"This'll take some gettin' used to," he drawled.

"Hugo...I'm sorry f'r all the trouble..."

"You can knock 'at shit off right now, son. Nobody aroun' this place owes anybody an apology f'r anything, an' I want ya ta listen real close ta what I'm about ta say. Okay?"

"Yes, sir."

"I may not own this business anymore, but I'm gunna make sure Roy knows there's ta always be a job here for ya. Don't ever f'rget that, Gil. Hear me?"

" 'at means a lot, Hugo. Thanks. F'r ever'thing. I mean... ever'thing."

"You stay in touch," sternly.

"I promise," and slowly hung up.

I sat quietly for a while, waiting for the ache to find a tolerable place to settle.

## THE RAVING EUNUCH MONKS

I found a spray can of primer and went to the back door.

Danny,
It's time to go.
Gil, O5/28/75

## THE END
## BOOK ONE